DEBBIE MACOMBER

Navy Grooms

MIRA®

MIRA®

ISBN 0-7783-2253-X

NAVY GROOMS

Copyright © 2005 by MIRA Books.

NAVY WOMAN
Copyright © 1991 by Debbie Macomber.

NAVY BABY
Copyright © 1991 by Debbie Macomber.

NAVY HUSBAND
Copyright © 2005 by Debbie Macomber.

www.MIRABooks.com

Printed in U.S.A.

Dear Reader,

Here it is—the very last book of my Navy series, written in the summer of 2004. A lot has changed since I wrote those first five books in the late 1980s and early '90s. There have been huge technological advances that affect our everyday lives—and life in the navy, too.

Even after all these years, I'll never forget my first sight of an aircraft carrier when the *Nimitz* sailed into Sinclair Inlet that day in 1988. I still feel the excitement and joy experienced by the crowd of people waiting to see their loved ones. But I felt more than joy that day—I also felt pride and respect. All of those emotions led me to bring my hand to my heart and join in the singing of "God Bless America."

As you've probably figured out by now, I live in a navy town. The Bremerton shipyard is directly across Sinclair Inlet from Port Orchard. Many of my neighbors are active or retired military families, and a number of the women who attend my local autographings are navy wives. (I've even met a few navy husbands!) I'm proud to be part of this community, proud to support our military and their families. We are the land of the free because of the brave, and I don't ever want to forget that.

I hope you enjoy *Navy Husband*. In case you're interested, the navy tradition in my writing continues in the Cedar Cove series published by MIRA Books. (The next one, *50 Harbor Street*, is available in September.) This fictionalized town is based on Port Orchard and has lots of references to the navy and the shipyard.

Thank you for reading my books. Now sit back, put your feet up and enjoy *Navy Husband*.

Warmest regards,

Debbie Macomber

P.S. I love hearing from readers. You can reach me through my Web site, www.debbiemacomber.com (write your comments in the guest book) or write me at P.O. Box 1458, Port Orchard, WA 98366.

CONTENTS

NAVY WOMAN

Dedicated to
Betty Zimmerman
A remarkable woman and a very special aunt

Special thanks to
Cheryl K. Rife, LCDR, JAGC, USN

Chapter One

Rain. That's all it had done from the moment Lieutenant Commander Catherine Fredrickson, Judge Advocate General Corps—JA6C—arrived at the Naval Submarine Base Bangor in Silverdale, Washington. October in Hawaii meant balmy ocean breezes, *mai tais* by the pool and eighty-degree sunshine.

In other words she'd left paradise and had been transferred to purgatory.

If the weather wasn't enough to discourage her, the executive officer, Commander Royce Nyland was. Catherine had never met anyone who irritated her more. The legal staff stationed in Hawaii had shared a camaraderie that made working together a pleasant experience.

Bangor was a different story, but the contrast was most telling in the differences between Catherine's two superiors. She simply didn't like the man, and from all outward appearances the feeling was mutual.

From the first, Catherine knew something wasn't right. In no other station had she been required to stand duty so often. For four weeks straight she'd been assigned the twenty-four-hour watch on a Friday night. It was as if Commander Nyland had made it his personal goal to disrupt her entire life.

After a month, Catherine was getting downright testy about it.

"Fredrickson, do you have the files on the Miller case?"

"Yes, sir." She stood, reached for the requested file and handed it to the man who'd been dominating her thoughts for the majority of the day.

Commander Nyland opened the file and started reading as he walked away from her. Catherine's gaze followed him as she tried to analyze what it was about her he disliked so much. Perhaps he had something against brunettes. Although that sounded crazy, Catherine couldn't help wondering. Maybe it was because she was petite and small-boned. More than likely, she reminded him of someone he once knew and disliked intensely. Well that was just too damn bad. As far as Catherine could see, she'd done nothing to deserve his disdain, and frankly, she wasn't about to put up with any more of it.

Scuttlebutt had it that he was single. Catherine had no trouble believing it. If his behavior toward her was any indication of how he treated women, then this guy needed a major attitude adjustment.

His apparent dislike of her solved one problem. Catherine needn't worry about anything romantic developing between them. If she were looking for an effective way to end her Navy career, all she had to do was start fraternizing with a superior officer within the same command. It was the quickest way Catherine knew to be court-martialed. The Navy refused to tolerate such behavior.

Besides his rotten attitude, Commander Nyland wasn't her type. Catherine liked her men less rough around the edges and a whole lot more agreeable.

In eleven years of Navy life, Catherine had worked with her share of officers, but no one had ever struck such a strong, discordant note with her.

Nothing she did pleased him. Nothing. The closest she'd

ever gotten to praise from her XO had been a hard nod, as if that were sufficient compliment. A nod!

The crazy part of it was, Catherine had actually gotten excited over it. All day she'd gone around wearing a silly grin.

She needed to get back to Hawaii, and fast.

"Come into my office, Lieutenant Commander."

Catherine glanced up, startled to discover Commander Nyland standing directly in front of her desk.

"Yes, sir," she answered briskly. She stood and reached for a notepad before following him into his office.

Commander Nyland took his seat and motioned for Catherine to sit in the cushioned chair located on the opposite side of his desk.

Catherine glanced around and swallowed nervously. She didn't like the looks of this. The great and almighty commander was frowning. Not that it was the least bit unusual. To the best of her memory, she couldn't remember him ever smiling.

She quickly reviewed the cases she'd been working on for the past few days, and could think of nothing that would warrant a tongue-lashing. Not that he needed an excuse, of course.

The silence stretched to uncomfortable lengths as she waited for him to acknowledge her. It was on the tip of her tongue to remind him he was the one who'd called her into his office, but she'd be a fool to allow a hint of sarcasm into her voice.

"I've been following your progress for the past several weeks." His indifferent blue gaze raked her features. Catherine had never been more aware of her appearance. Her thick, dark hair was coiled in a businesslike knot at her nape, and her uniform jacket and skirt were crisp and freshly pressed. She had the impression if he found one crease, she'd be ordered to stand in front of a firing squad.

No man had ever made her feel more self-conscious. He continued to stare at her as if seeing her for the first time. There was no hint of appreciation for her good looks. Catherine wasn't conceited, but she was reasonably attractive, and the fact the man looked at her as if she were little more than a mannequin was vaguely insulting. Okay, she was being unreasonable, Catherine mused. If she had recognized a flicker of interest in those cobalt-blue eyes of his, that would have been worse.

"Yes, sir."

"As I was saying," he continued, "I've had my eye on your work."

She noted that he made a simple statement of fact without elaborating. If he'd been watching her, then she'd admit, not openly of course, that she'd been studying him, too. He may be disagreeable, and to her way of thinking, ill-tempered, but he was respected and generally well liked. Personally, Catherine found him to be a real pain, but her thinking was tainted by a four-week stint at standing duty on Friday nights.

Politics existed in every office, but there seemed to be more in Bangor than the other duty stations Catherine had been assigned. As the executive officer directly below Captain Stewart, Commander Royce Nyland was empowered to run her legal office. He did so with a detached, emotionless ability that Catherine had rarely seen. In many ways he was the best officer she'd ever worked with and, in others, the worst.

It was apparent the man was a born leader. His lean, muscular good looks commanded attention. His office demanded it.

Actually, now that she had an uninterrupted minute to analyze the commander, she was willing to admit he was fairly attractive. Not handsome in the classic sense. Appealing, she decided. Not ordinary.

His features weren't anything that would cause a woman to swoon. His hair was nearly black. Its darkness coupled with his deep blue eyes was a contrast not easily ignored. He was broad shouldered, and although she knew him to be of medium height, an inch or so under six feet, he gave the impression of power and strength in everything he did.

Her scrutiny didn't seem to bother him. He leaned back in his chair, expelled his breath and announced, "I'm pleased to tell you I've chosen you as a substitute coordinator of the physical fitness program for the base."

"Substitute coordinator," Catherine repeated slowly. Her heart beat dull and heavy before it dropped like a lead weight to her stomach. It took a second to right itself before she could respond. If there was one after-hours duty she would have done anything to avoid it was that of coordinator of the physical fitness program. It was by far one of the least envied jobs on base.

The Navy was serious about keeping men and women in top physical condition. Those who were overweight were placed on a strict dietary schedule and exercise regime. As coordinator, Catherine would be subjected to endless meetings to chart the individuals' progress. She'd also be expected to formulate an exercise program designed specifically to meet each person's needs. In addition, she would be given the painful task of having someone discharged from the Navy if they failed to meet the requirements in regard to weight and fitness.

"I believe you're qualified to handle this job effectively."

"Yes, sir," she said, biting her tongue to keep from saying more. Tackling this duty, even on a substitute basis, meant she wouldn't have time to breathe. It was a time-consuming, distasteful assignment. If the executive officer had been actively seeking to destroy any chance she had of developing a social life, he'd done so in one fell swoop.

"Lieutenant Osborne will meet with you and give you the necessary paperwork at 1500 hours. If you have any questions, you should gear them to him." Already he was looking away from her, dismissing her.

"Thank you, sir," she said, struggling with everything in her not to let her irritation show. She left his office and closed the door with a decided click, hoping he'd believe the wind had caught it. Hell, he was fortunate she didn't tear the damn thing right off its hinges.

With as dignified a walk as possible, she returned to her office. She set the pad down a little too hard, attracting the attention of Elaine Perkins, her secretary, who occupied the scarred desk outside Catherine's office.

"Problems?" she asked. As a Navy wife, Elaine was well acquainted with the difficulties of military life.

"Problems?" Catherine echoed sarcastically. "What could possibly be wrong? Listen, do I have something repugnantly wrong with me?"

"Not that I've noticed," Elaine was quick to tell her.

"I don't have bad breath?"

"No."

"Does my slip hang out from under my skirt?" She twisted around and tried to determine that much for herself.

"Not that I can see," Elaine assured her. "What makes you ask?"

"No reason." With that, Catherine stalked out of the office and down the hall to the drinking fountain. Her hand trembled slightly as she leaned forward and scooped up a generous mouthful, letting the cold water soothe her injured pride.

Catherine wished she could talk to Sally. The two were the only women officers in a command of several hundred men, but that wasn't possible now. Once she'd composed herself sufficiently to return, Catherine did so, forcing a smile.

"I'm *pleased* to inform you you've been chosen as the substitute coordinator of the physical fitness program," Catherine mumbled under her breath as she traipsed toward the running track several hours later. Dusk was settling over the compound, but there was enough time to get in a three-mile run before dark.

Pleased was right. Commander Nyland had looked downright gleeful to assign her the task. The more Catherine thought about it, the more furious she got.

Venting some of this discontent seemed like a good idea. Clouds threatened a downpour, but Catherine didn't care. She'd just received the worst collateral duty assignment of her career, and she needed to vent the frustration and confusion before she headed home to the apartment she rented in Silverdale. Taking giant strides, she crested the hill that led to the track, then stopped abruptly. Several runners circled the course, but one runner in particular stood out from the rest.

Commander Nyland.

For a long moment Catherine couldn't keep her eyes off him. There was a natural, fluid grace to his movements. His stride was long and even, and he ran as if the wind were beneath his feet. What struck her most was his quiet strength. She didn't want to acknowledge it. Nor did she wish to find a single positive attribute about this man.

If there was any justice in the world, lightning would strike him dead. Glancing to the sky, she was depressed to note a touch of blue in the far horizon. Typical. Just when she was looking for rain, the sun had decided to play a game of hide-and-seek with her. If lightning wasn't going to do the good commander in, then all she could hope for was a bad case of athlete's foot.

Once again she grumbled under her breath, seriously considering leaving the base without running. If she did go down to the track, it was likely she'd say or do something that would get her into trouble with the commander.

Evidently she'd done something horrible to warrant his dislike. After he'd ruined four weekends straight for her, he'd topped himself by giving her the least desirable assignment on base. What next? KP?

Catherine started to turn away, then abruptly changed her mind. She wasn't going to allow this man to dictate her entire life! She had as much right to run on this track as anyone. If he didn't like it, he could be the one to leave.

With that thought in mind, she stepped alongside the court and went through a series of warm-up exercises. Actually, the more she thought about it, she was downright eager to get onto the track. She was petite, but she was a fine runner. She'd been on the varsity cross-country teams in both high school and college and did a consistent seven-minute mile. If there was an area in which she excelled, it was running.

She did the first lap at a relaxed pace, easily lapping a couple of the overweight men. Commander Nyland didn't acknowledge her one way or the other, which was perfectly fine with Catherine. She'd hadn't come out here to exchange pleasantries with him.

The second and third laps, Catherine stepped up her pace. It normally took her a mile or so to fully warm up. As she increased her stride, she noticed that she was never quite able to catch her XO.

The one time she did manage to pass him, he scooted past her seconds later, leaving her to eat his dust. Frustrated, Catherine decided she might not be able to outrun him, but by heaven she'd outlast him. He was fast, but she'd easily outdistance him.

She continued her killing pace until she was sure she'd

gone six miles or farther. Her lungs ached, and her calf muscles strenuously protested the abuse. Yet she continued, more determined than ever not to surrender her pride to this disagreeable commander. If she was hurting, then so was he.

She would rather keel over from exhaustion than quit now! It was more than a matter of pride.

Soon fat raindrops fell from the darkening sky and splashed against the dry, gritty surface. Still Catherine and the commander ran. What few runners remained quickly dropped out until it was the two of them alone against the forces of nature. Against each other, in a silent battle of wills.

They didn't speak. Not once. Catherine ran until she thought she was going to be sick, yet she dared not stop. Night fell like a curtain of black satin around the grounds. Catherine barely managed to see her own feet, let alone the distant silhouette of the commander. Soon he disappeared from her range of view entirely. It wasn't until she heard his footsteps coming up behind her that she realized he'd been able to come all the way around to lap her. He slowed his pace until his steps matched her own without breaking his stride.

"How much longer are we going to keep this up, Fredrickson?" he demanded.

Damn, he didn't even sound out of breath, Catherine noted.

"I don't know," she returned, sounding very much as though she should have yielded several miles back.

"You're tiring."

How kind of him to tell her so. "You are, too," she insisted.

"I have to admit you're a hell of a runner."

"A compliment, Commander?"

She sensed his smile. It made absolutely no sense the way her heart reacted knowing that. It was as if she'd been blessed by an unexpected second wind. By some odd twist of fate, she'd actually managed to amuse ol' stone face.

"Don't let it go to your head."

"No chance of that," she quipped, wondering if she'd heard a hint of amusement in his tone. "I don't suppose you happened to notice it's raining." Although she attempted to make light of it, she was drenched to the bone.

"Is that what all this wet stuff is?"

"I'll tell you what," she said between breaths, "I'll stop running if you do. We'll call it a draw."

"Agreed." Royce slowed his pace to a trot, and Catherine reluctantly did the same, not sure even now that she could trust him. After several steps, she stopped and leaned over, bracing her hands on her knees while she struggled to capture her breath.

The rain continued to pound down with a vengeance. While they were jogging, it was a simple enough matter to ignore the downpour. Now it wasn't so easy. Her hair, which had once been neatly secured at her nape, was plastered to her cheeks like wet strings. A small river of rainwater was navigating over her neck and down to the small of her back.

"Go home, Fredrickson," Royce said after a moment.

Catherine bristled. "Is that an order?"

He paused. "No."

He started to walk away from her, then unexpectedly turned back. "Before you leave, satisfy a curiosity. You requested a transfer from San Diego several years back. Why?"

Catherine knew it was all part of her personnel file, but his question caught her off guard. Her response was quick, light-hearted, almost flippant. "Who wouldn't want to live in Hawaii?"

"That wasn't the reason you wanted out of San Diego." His voice was deceptively unconcerned, as if he knew far more than he was letting on. "You wanted that transfer and you didn't care if you got Hawaii or Iran."

"There were personal reasons," she admitted reluctantly. Catherine couldn't understand why he'd chosen to ask her these questions now. The man continued to baffle her.

"Tell me the truth."

Catherine tensed, disliking his casual tone. Nor was she pleased with the way he implied she was lying. By mentally counting to ten, she willed herself to remain calm.

"That is the truth. I've always wanted to live in Hawaii."

"My guess is that a man was involved."

Catherine's stomach knotted. She didn't often think about Aaron. For the past three years she'd done a superb job of pretending they'd never met. Leave it to Royce Nyland to harass her battered heart with memories of her former fiancé. All right, that was a bit strong. He wasn't exactly tormenting her, and her heart wasn't all that scarred.

"What makes you think my request had anything to do with a man?" she asked, making light of his comment. She increased her strides, wanting to get this interrogation over with as soon as possible.

"Because it generally is."

That wasn't the least bit true, but Catherine wasn't going to stand in the rain and argue with him.

"A change of scenery appealed to me at the time." She needed to get away from San Diego for fear she'd run into Aaron. She wouldn't have been able to bear seeing him again. At least that was what she told herself. Over time, she wasn't nearly convinced that was true. She'd fallen head over heels in love with him much too quickly. Then she'd flown out as a defense attorney for trials aboard the *Nimitz* and returned several weeks later to learn Aaron hadn't exactly been holding his breath waiting for her.

The first minute she was back, Catherine had rushed

to her fiancé's apartment to find him lying on the sofa with the young blond divorcée who lived next door. Aaron had scrambled off the davenport in a rush to explain while the red-faced divorcée hastily rebuttoned her blouse. It had all been innocent fun, Aaron claimed. Hell, how was he supposed to amuse himself while she was away for weeks on end? He advised Catherine to be a sport since he and the blonde had only indulged in a little entertainment.

In thinking back over the episode, Catherine was surprised by how completely emotionless she'd remained. The solitary diamond on her finger suddenly weighted down her hand. That much she remembered with ease. She'd stared down on it and then wordlessly slipped it from her finger and returned it to Aaron. For several moments he was paralyzed with shock. Then he'd followed her to the parking lot and pleaded with her to be more understanding. If it offended her so much, he'd make sure it didn't happen again. There was no need to overreact this way. None whatsoever.

In retrospect Catherine had come to realize that her pride had taken far more of a beating than her heart. She was almost relieved to have Aaron out of her life, only she hadn't realized that until much later.

"Catherine?"

Royce's deep, masculine voice pulled her back into the present. To the best of her knowledge it was the first time he'd ever used her name. Until then it had been Lieutenant Commander or Fredrickson, but never Catherine. This, too, had a curious effect upon her heart.

"There was a man involved," she announced stiffly, "but that was several years ago now. You needn't worry my former engagement will affect my work for you. Now or in the future."

"I'm pleased to hear it."

"Good night, Commander." They crested the hill where Catherine's bright red GEO Storm was waiting for her.

"Good night."

Trotting, Catherine was halfway down the hill when Royce stopped her.

"Catherine."

"Yes?" She turned around to face him, brushing the wet curls from her cheeks.

"Are you living with someone?"

The question took her by complete surprise. "That's none of your business."

Royce said nothing. He stood several feet away from her, his harsh features illuminated by the streetlight. His face was tight, as if he were holding himself in check. "Trust me, I have no interest in your love life. You can live with whomever you please or be engaged to five men at once for all I care. What does concern me is the legal department. The work is demanding and the schedule grueling. I like to know where I stand with my staff and try to avoid causing unnecessary complications in their lives."

Catherine didn't respond right away. "Since you find it so important, then I might as well confess I am shacked up with someone." From the distance Catherine couldn't tell if she got a reaction or not. Most likely he was telling the truth and he didn't care one way or the other. "Sambo."

"Sambo?" he repeated frowning.

"You heard me correctly, Commander. I live with a cat named Sambo." With that, she gave a cheerful laugh and was gone.

Royce found himself smiling in the dark, the rain pelting down around him in a great torrent. His amusement, however, vanished quickly. He didn't like Catherine Fredrickson.

"No," he muttered aloud, retracting the thought. That wasn't true. He did like her. There were any number of admirable traits about the Lieutenant Commander he couldn't help but respect.

She was dedicated and hardworking, and she'd fit in easily with the rest of his staff. She wasn't a complainer, either. Before he'd left the office that evening, he'd checked over the duty roster and was surprised to note that he'd assigned Catherine duty every Friday for four weeks running. He hadn't realized his mistake. Anyone else would have pointed it out to him, and rightly so. Her name had drifted easily into his mind when he learned Lieutenant Osborne was going on sea trials and a substitute coordinator was needed to take over the physical fitness program.

He knew Catherine wasn't overly pleased by the assignment. Her eyes had flashed briefly with rebellion, but that was the only outward sign she'd given that she wasn't thrilled with the added responsibility.

That woman had eyes that would mark a man's soul. Normally Royce didn't pay much attention to that sort of thing, but her eyes had garnered his attention from the first moment they'd met. They shimmered, and seemed to trap pieces of light. But more than that, they seemed warm and caring.

He liked her voice, too. It was rich and sweetly feminine. Female. Hell, Royce mused, he was beginning to sound like a romantic poet.

Now that thought was enough to produce a hearty laugh. There wasn't a romantic bone left in his body. His wife had squeezed every ounce of love and joy out of him long before she went to the grave.

Royce didn't want to think about Sandy. Abruptly he turned and walked toward his car, his strides hurried, as if he could outdistance the memory of his dead wife.

He climbed inside his Porsche and started the engine. His house was on the base, and he'd be home within five minutes.

Before long, however, it was Catherine who dominated

his thoughts again. He wasn't overly thrilled with the subject matter, but he was too damn tired to fight himself over it. When he arrived home, his ten-year-old daughter, Kelly, would keep him occupied. For once he was going to indulge himself and let his thoughts wander where they would. Besides, he was curious to analyze his complex reaction to Catherine Fredrickson.

Not that it was important. Not that he needed to know anything more about her than he already did. He was simply inquisitive. He supposed when it came right down to it, he didn't feel one way or the other about her.

No, that wasn't true, either. She intrigued him. He didn't like it. He didn't understand it. He wished he could put his finger on exactly what it was about her that fascinated him so much. Until that afternoon, he hadn't even been aware of it.

She wasn't that much different than the other Navy women he'd worked with over the years. Not true, he contradicted himself. She had a scrubbed-clean look about her, a gentleness, a gracefulness of heart and manner that piqued him.

Another thing he'd learned about her this evening. By heaven that woman was bullheaded. He'd never seen anyone run with cursed stubbornness the way she had. It wasn't until it had started to rain that Royce recognized the unspoken challenge she'd issued. Absorbed in his thoughts, he hadn't noticed she was on the track until she'd zoomed past him and then smugly tossed a look over her shoulder as if to announce she'd won. Hell, he hadn't even realized they were in a race.

As if that wasn't enough, she wouldn't stop. They both had reached their physical limits, and still that little spitfire continued and would have, Royce was convinced, until she dropped.

He pulled into the driveway and cut the engine. His

hands remained on the steering wheel as a slow smile spread across his features. *Woman,* he mused, *thy name is pride.*

The drape parted in the living room, Kelly's head peeked out. Just the way the drape was tossed back into place told him the ten-year-old was angry. Damn, Royce wondered, what the hell had he done this time?

Kelly usually ran outside to greet him. Not tonight. Whatever it was must have been a doozy. His daughter could be more stubborn than a Tennessee mule. This must be his day for clashing with obstinate women.

Chapter Two

Fresh from the shower, Catherine dressed in a warm robe, and wrapped her hair in a thick towel. She sat in the living room, her feet propped against the coffee table with Sambo nestled contentedly in her lap.

Sipping from a cup of herbal tea, Catherine mulled over the events of the day. A reluctant smile slowly eased its way across her face. Her dislike for Royce Nyland didn't go quite as deep as it had before their small confrontation on the racetrack. The man wasn't ever going to win any personality awards, that was for sure, but she felt a grudging respect for him.

Sambo purred and stretched his furry legs, his claws digging deep into the thick robe. Catherine stroked her pet, letting the long black tail slip through her fingers as she continued to mull over the time she and Royce had shared the track. The realization that she actually enjoyed their silent battle of wills warmed her from the inside out. For some unknown reason, she'd managed to amuse him. Because of the dark, Catherine hadn't been able to witness his stern features relax into a smile. She would have liked to have seen that, taken a picture to remind her that the man *could* smile.

Her stomach growled, and Catherine briefly wondered

what was stashed in her freezer. Hopefully something would magically appear that she could toss in the microwave. She definitely wasn't in the mood to cook.

On her way into the kitchen, she paused in front of the photograph that rested on the fireplace mantel. The man staring back at her had deep brown eyes that were alive with warmth, wit and character.

Catherine's eyes.

He was handsome, so handsome that she often stared at the picture, regretting the fact she had never been given the chance to know him. She'd been only three when her father had been shipped to Vietnam, five when he'd been listed as Missing in Action. Often she'd reached back as far as her memory would take her to snatch hold of something that would help her remember him, but each time she was left to deal with frustration and disappointment.

The man in the photo was young, far too young to have his life snuffed out. No one would ever know how he'd died or even when. All Catherine's family had been told was that his Navy jet had gone down over a Vietcong infested jungle. They never were to know if he survived the crash or had been taken prisoner. Those, like so many other details of his life and death, had been left to her imagination.

Catherine's mother, a corporate attorney, had never remarried. Marilyn Fredrickson wasn't bitter, nor was she angry. She was far too practical to allow such negative emotions to taint her life.

Like a true Navy wife, she'd silently endured the long years of the cruel unknowns, refusing to be defeated by the helplessness of frustration. When her husband's remains had been returned to the States, she'd stood proud and strong as he was laid to rest with full military honors.

The only time Catherine could ever remember her mother weeping had been the day her father's casket had arrived at the airport. With a gentleness and a sweetness that impressed Catherine still, her mother had walked over to the flag-draped casket, rested her gloved hand at the head and brokenly whispered, "Welcome home, my love." Then she'd slumped to her knees and sobbed until she'd released a ten-year reservoir of submerged emotions.

Catherine had cried with her mother that day. But in death, as he had been in life, Andrew Warren Fredrickson remained a stranger.

In choosing to become a Navy attorney, Catherine had followed both her parents' footsteps. Being a part of the military had brought her as close as she was likely to get to understanding the man who had given her life.

Lulled by her thoughts, Catherine ran the tip of her finger along the top of the gold frame. "I wonder if you ever had to work with someone like Royce Nyland," she said softly.

She did that sometimes. Talked to the photograph as though she honestly expected her father to answer. She didn't, of course, but carrying on a one-sided conversation with the man in the picture eased the ache in her heart at never having known him.

Sambo meowed loudly, announcing it was well past dinnertime, and Catherine had best do something quickly. The black feline waited impatiently in front of his bowl while Catherine brought out the pouch of soft cat food.

"Enjoy," she muttered, wincing as she bent over to fill the food dish. Holding her hand at the small of her back, Catherine cautiously straightened. Her pride had cost her more than she'd first realized.

"But, Dad, I've just got to have that jacket," Kelly announced as she carried her dinner plate over to the sink. She rinsed it off and set it in the dishwasher, a chore that went above and beyond her normal duties.

As far as Royce was concerned, she was going to have to do a whole lot more than stack a few dishes to change his mind.

"You have a very nice jacket now," he reminded her, standing to pour himself a cup of coffee. He supposed he should be grateful she'd chosen to overlook the fact he was forty minutes later than he'd told her he would be. After her initial protest she'd been suspiciously forgiving. Now he knew why.

"But my jacket's from last year and it's really old and the sleeve has a little tear in it and no one is wearing fluorescent green anymore. I'll be the laughing stock of the entire school if I wear that old thing."

"That 'old thing' as you put it, will do nicely. The subject is closed, Kelly Lynn." Royce was determined not to give in this time. He was walking a fine line with his daughter as it was, and loomed dangerously close to overindulging her. It was easy to do. She was a sweet child, unselfish and gentle. Actually it was something of a wonder that Kelly should turn out to be such a considerate child. The ten-year-old had been raised by a succession of baby-sitters. From the time she was only a few weeks old, Kelly had been lackadaisically palmed off on others.

Sandy had only agreed to have one child, and she'd done so reluctantly six years into their marriage. Her career as a fashion buyer had dominated her life, so much so that Royce doubted that his wife had possessed a single mothering instinct. When she'd been killed in a freak auto accident, Royce had grieved for her loss, but their relationship had been dead for several years.

If Kelly had been shortchanged in the mother department, Royce wasn't convinced she'd done much better with him as a father. Heaven knew Royce's reputation was that of a hard-nosed bastard. But he was fair and everyone knew it. He did the best he could, but often wondered if that was good enough. He loved Kelly and he wanted to do right by her.

"All the other girls in school have new jackets," she mumbled under her breath.

Royce ignored the comment and between sips of coffee placed the leftovers inside the refrigerator.

"I've already saved $6.53 from my allowance?" She made the statement into a question, seeking a response.

Royce returned the carton of milk to the shelf.

"Missy Gilbert said the jackets were going to be on sale at J. C. Penney and with next week's allowance I'd have almost one fourth of the total cost. I'm trying real hard on my arithmetic this year, you know."

"Good girl." The two of them had suffered through more than one go-round with fractions.

Kelly turned her big baby blues full force on him. "What about the jacket, Dad?"

Royce could feel himself giving in. This wasn't good. He should be a pillar of strength, a wall of granite. He'd already told her once the subject was closed. The jacket she had now was good enough. He remembered when they'd bought it last year. Royce had been appalled at the outrageous shade of putrid green, but Kelly had assured him it was perfect and she would wear it two or three years.

"Dad?" she asked ever so sweetly, the way she always did when she sensed he was weakening.

"I'll think about it."

"Thanks, Dad," she cried, rushing across the room and hugging his waist. "You're the greatest."

An odd sense of self-consciousness attacked Catherine when she went down to the track the following evening. As she suspected, Royce was there ahead of her, running laps, as were several other men.

Royce hadn't said more than a handful of words to her

all day, which wasn't unusual. He was as polite and as cool as always. When he came into the office that morning, he'd glanced her way, and Catherine could have sworn he was looking straight through her. His hard blue eyes had passed over her without so much as a flicker of friendliness. If she were to take the time to analyze his look, she suspected it had been one of cool indifference. It wasn't that Catherine expected him to throw his arms around her and greet her like a long lost friend. On second thought, maybe that was the problem.

They'd shared something on that running track, a camaraderie, an understanding and appreciation for each other. Catherine didn't expect warm embraces, but she hadn't expected him to regard her so impersonally. Apparently she'd read more into their talk than he intended.

That was her first mistake, and Catherine feared she was ready to commit mistake number two.

Squaring her shoulders, she traipsed down the hillside to the running track. She was later this evening than she had been the night before. No thanks to Commander Nyland. For the past two hours she'd been reviewing files and charting progress as the substitute coordinator for the physical fitness program. Her eyes hurt, her shoulders ached and she was in no mood to lock horns with the executive officer, unless, of course, he started something first.

Catherine completed her warming-up exercises and joined the others circling the quarter-mile track. She needed to unwind, vent the frustration she felt over being assigned this extra duty, which was an imposition she didn't need. It seemed that the commander had seen fit to delegate CDO duty that Friday night to someone else. Lucky for that someone.

Her first lap was relaxed. Catherine liked to ease herself into running, starting off slow and gradually gain her momentum, peaking at about the second mile and finishing off the third in a relaxed stride.

Royce passed her easily on the first go-round. Catherine fully expected that he would. Once again she was impressed with the power and strength she felt as he shot past her. His skin was tan and his muscles bronzed. It was as if he were a living, moving work of art, perfect, strong and male. Her heart raced much faster than it should. A rush of sensation so powerful it nearly knocked her off her feet took her by surprise. On the heels of that emotion came another, one more potent than the first. Anger. He zoomed past her again and it was all she could do to hold herself back from charging ahead.

On the third lap she couldn't help herself, and she let loose, running as though she were in the Olympic time trial and this was her one and only chance to make the team.

The sense of satisfaction she gained leaping past Royce was enough to make her forget how hard she was pushing herself to maintain this stride.

The feeling of triumph was short-lived, as she knew it would be. Royce stepped up his pace and quickly charged around her. Then he slowed down and waited for her steps to join his.

"Good evening, Lieutenant Commander," he greeted, cordially enough.

"Commander." She wasn't in any mood to wish him a pleasant anything. Once again he'd managed to irritate her. No man had evoked such heated feelings from her, whether they be reasonable or unreasonable. It was all because of Royce Nyland that she'd been the one poring over a carload of files late into the afternoon.

Royce increased his stride, and Catherine struggled to keep even with him. She had the feeling that he could have left her to eat his dust at any time, and was simply toying with her the way a cat enjoys playing with a cornered mouse. None of that seemed to matter as she pushed herself harder than ever.

After a couple of laps, Catherine sensed his amusement. No doubt she and her damnable pride were a keen source of entertainment to the obstinate executive officer.

Somehow Catherine managed to keep up with Royce for three complete laps, but she knew she couldn't continue the killing pace any longer. It was either drop out now or collapse. Catherine chose the former.

When she pulled back, slowed her pace to a fast walk, Royce raced ahead, then he surprised her by turning around and coming back. He kept his arms and feet in motion as he matched her speed.

"You all right?"

"Just ducky." She barely managed to breathe evenly, and prayed a sufficient amount of sarcasm leaked through to convey her mood.

A crooked smile slanted his mouth, his look cool and mocking. "Do you have a problem, Lieutenant Commander?"

"Off the record?" she asked, without hesitating. A month of frustration could no longer be contained, and she was bursting to let him know exactly what she thought of him.

"By all means."

Catherine might be digging herself in deeper than she dare, but her patience was shot. "Is there something about me that troubles you, Commander?" She didn't give him time to respond, but rushed ahead, "Because something's rotten in Denmark, and frankly, it isn't my problem…. It's yours."

"I don't treat you any differently than anyone else," Royce inserted smoothly.

"Like hell you don't," she shot back heatedly. Thankfully the others had left the track, which might or might not be a blessing.

"I don't see you assigning anyone else to stand duty four weeks straight. For some unknown reason you've chosen to destroy my weekends. I've spent eleven years in this man's Navy and I've never stood duty more than once a month. Until you were assigned my XO. Apparently you don't like me, Commander, and I demand to know why."

A nerve twitched in his lean, hard jaw. "On the contrary, I find your dedication to duty to be highly commendable."

Catherine didn't actually expect him to admit his dislike of her, but she wasn't willing to listen to his military rhetoric, either. "I suppose my dedication to duty is what made you decide to bless me with this plush job of coordinating the physical fitness program? Was that supposed to be a bonus for all the extra hours I put in on the Miller case? If so, find another way to thank me, would you?" She was trying to talk and draw in deep breaths at the same time and doubted that Royce could make out more than a few words.

Royce stiffened. "Is that all?"

"Not quite." She was only beginning to gain her momentum. "Off the record, Commander, I think you're a real jerk."

When she finished, Catherine was overwhelmed with a feeling of release. She started to tremble, but she wasn't sure if the shaking could be attributed to the fact she'd pushed herself physically to the point of collapse or that she'd stood on a military compound and shouted insults at her executive officer at the top of her lungs.

His look was impossible to read. The feeling in the pit of her stomach was decidedly uncomfortable.

"Is that a fact?" he demanded.

"Yes." Her voice wobbled with uncertainty, sounding as though it were coming from the bottom of a well. She drew in a deep breath, knowing she'd stepped over the boundaries of what should and shouldn't be said to a superior officer. The blood that seemed to have been pounding in her ears like ringing church bells suddenly went silent.

With her hands knotted into tight fists at her sides, she braced herself for the backlash. If she thought to clear the air, she was sadly mistaken. If she'd accomplished anything it was to sabotage her own career.

Royce didn't say anything for several moments, but the nerve in his jaw continued twitching. Then he nodded as though they'd casually been discussing the weather, turned and resumed running. Catherine was left standing alone to stare after him.

Catherine spent an uncomfortable night, tossing and turning and finally talking over her troubles with Sambo. To her way of thinking, Royce would either ignore her outburst or see to it that she was transferred to a Third World country. However he reacted, she would be getting exactly what she deserved. No one spoke to their XO the way she had. No one.

For hours she lay awake analyzing what had happened. After several soul-seeking sessions, she still didn't know what had caused her to get loose enough to say the things she did.

The following morning, Royce was already at his desk, behind closed doors when she arrived. She glanced cautiously toward his office. If there was a merciful God, then Commander Nyland would be willing to forget and forgive her outburst from the day before. She would apologize, grovel if need be, but leaving matters as they were was clearly unacceptable.

"Morning," she said gingerly to Elaine Perkins. "How's the great white hunter today?" she asked, hoping her secretary had had a chance to judge Royce's mood.

"Same as usual," Elaine told her, sipping coffee from a thick ceramic mug. Her voice drawled with a thick southern accent. "He asked me to send you into his office when you arrived."

Catherine felt the starch go out of her knees. "He asked to see me?"

"You heard me right. What are you looking so worried about? You haven't done anything, have you?"

"Nothing," Catherine whispered in reply. Nothing except stick her head in a noose and sling the other end of the rope over the highest branch in the tree.

Squaring her shoulders in her best military form, she walked across the office and knocked politely on the commander's door. When she was ordered to enter the room, she did so with her eyes focused straight ahead.

"Good morning, Lieutenant Commander."

"Sir."

"Relax, Catherine." He leaned back in his chair, his chin resting on folded hands as though he were still weighing his decision.

Relax, he'd told her to relax, only Catherine hadn't figured out how she was supposed to be at ease when her career was on the line. She hadn't joined the Navy like so many other women with her head in the clouds, seeking adventure, travel and a paid education. She knew from the beginning about the rigorous routine, the political infighting and the fact she'd be dealing with world-class chauvinists.

Nevertheless she loved being part of the Navy. She'd worked hard, and her efforts had been rewarded. Now this.

"Since our recent discussion I've been having second thoughts," Royce said flatly.

Catherine swallowed against the heaviness in her throat. She doubted if she could have spoken if she tried.

"From everything I've read about you, you have an excellent record." He leaned forward and closed her file. "Effective immediately, I'm removing you as the substitute coordinator of the physical fitness program, and assigning Lieutenant Johnson the duty."

Catherine was sure she hadn't heard him correctly. Her eyes, which had been trained on the opposite wall, skirted to his. A breathless moment passed before she could speak, "You're removing me from the physical fitness program?" She couldn't have been more surprised had he announced he was working for the KGB.

"That's what I just said."

Catherine blinked, not knowing what to say. "Thank you, sir," she finally managed.

"That will be all," he said, dismissing her.

She hesitated. She'd wanted to apologize for her outburst from the day before, but one look told her Royce wasn't interested in listening to her list her excuses.

As it was, her knees were knocking so badly that she walked over to her desk, slumped into the chair and held on to the edge as though it were a lifeline.

Catherine didn't see Royce for the remainder of the day, for which she was grateful. It gave her time to sort through her emotions, which were as confused and tangled as thin gold chains. She didn't know what to make of the executive commander. Every time she had him figured out, he'd do something more to confuse her. Complicating the matter even further were her muddled feelings toward him. He was by far the most virile man she'd ever met. She couldn't be in the same room with him and not experience that magnetism. Yet, she found herself intensely disliking him.

An early October drizzle moistened the air when Catherine walked out to the parking lot later that same afternoon. Rain, rain and more rain.

It was already dark, and her calf muscles were so sore she'd decided to skip running at the track. At least that was the excuse she'd given herself. How much truth there was to her rationale was something she'd prefer not to question.

Her GEO Storm was parked in the far end of the lot, and Catherine walked briskly toward it, hunching her shoulders against the chilly air. She opened her door, gratefully climbed inside and turned the ignition. Nothing. She tried again with the same results. The battery was completely dead.

With her hands braced against the steering wheel, Catherine groaned. She knew as much about the internal workings of a car as she did about performing brain surgery. Her automobile was only a few months old; surely there wasn't anything wrong with the engine.

Climbing out, she decided to check under the hood. How much good that would do was highly debatable, especially in the dark. It took her several minutes to find the clasp that would release the lock. In the dim light from the street lamp, she couldn't see much of anything.

The only thing she could think to do was call a towing service. She was walking back to her building when a low black sports car rolled past her, then circled around.

"Problems?" It was Royce Nyland.

Catherine froze, her first instinct was to claim she had everything under control and send him on his way. Lie, fib, anything that would postpone another encounter. She hadn't had the time to filter through her emotions from the one earlier in the day. Royce Nyland flustered her, and clouded her judgment. She wanted to dislike him, categorize him and wrap him up in one neat package. But every time she'd attempted to gain perspective, he did something to alter her opinion of him. He brought out the worst in her and yet she'd never worked harder to impress an officer. Then it came to her with driving force. She was sexually attracted to Royce Nyland.

Attracted in a way that spelled trouble for them both. As long as she was under his command, anything romantic between them was strictly prohibited. The Navy didn't pull any punches when it came to emotional involvement between men and women, one a supervisor to the other. Not even a hint of impropriety would be tolerated.

For her sake as well as his, she must ignore the fact her heart raced every time she saw him. She had to ignore the way her eyes sought him out whenever he walked into the room. When they were on the track together, she had to disregard the strength and power that radiated from him like warmth from a roaring fire. Royce Nyland was as off-limits to her as a married man.

"Is that your car?" he asked, obviously impatient with her lack of response.

"Yes…it won't start."

"I'll take a look at it for you."

Before she could tell him she was about to call for a tow truck, he switched gears and drove over to where her Storm was parked with its hood raised. By the time she walked back, he was sitting in the driver's seat.

"It looks like you left your lights on this morning. The battery's dead."

"Oh…I must have." She wasn't usually this slow-witted. Running around the track with Royce was one thing, but standing in the far end of the parking lot in the shadows was another. Instinctively she backed away.

"I have a battery cable in my car. I'll give you a start." It took only a matter of minutes for him to arrange the clamps linking the cables between the batteries of the two cars. They worked together and within a matter of minutes, her engine was purring contentedly.

She climbed out of the car while Royce disconnected the cable. Although it wasn't all that cold, she rubbed her hands together several times.

"Thank you."

He nodded, tossed the cable into the trunk of his car and was prepared to leave when she stopped him.

"Royce."

She hadn't meant to say his name, it had slipped out naturally. Apologizing had never come easy to her, but she owed him one—for the heat of her anger, the unreasonableness of her attack. "I shouldn't have said what I did the other night. If there's any excuse, it's that I was tired and short-tempered. It won't happen again."

"It was off the record, Fredrickson, don't worry about it." His mouth slowly curved into a smile. Their eyes met, solidly, hungrily and God help her, Catherine felt herself step toward him.

"I'm worried." But it wasn't what she'd said or done that she was talking about and she knew they both knew it. His eyes continued to detain hers. She'd never seen eyes so dark. They told her things she'd only suspected. Things she didn't want to know and had no business knowing.

He was lonely. So was she.

He was alone. So was she.

So alone she lay in bed at night and ached. The need to be touched and held and kissed sometimes filled her with desperation.

She sensed the same desperation in Royce. It was what had drawn them together; it was what was keeping them apart.

The seconds throbbed between them like a giant time clock. Neither moved. Catherine dared not breathe. She was one step from walking directly into his arms, one word from spilling out everything she was feeling. The tension between them was as threatening as a thundercloud in a sky of blue. As strong as a prize fighter.

It was Royce who moved first. Away from her. Catherine sighed, her relief was so great.

"There won't be any problems," he whispered, turned and walked away.

She knew he wasn't speaking about her car.

Catherine wished she could believe it, but something told her it was far from the truth.

Royce was shaking. His hands were actually trembling as he sat in his own driveway, composing himself before he walked inside the house. He'd come so close to kissing Catherine that even now the thought of her filling his arms was enough to produce an ache so powerful, so sharp, it took his breath away. Royce was a man who thrived on discipline. He prided himself on his self-control, and yet he'd come a hair's space from tossing away everything he knew was right. And for what reason? Catherine Fredrickson turned him on.

For three years, Royce had shut off the valve that controlled his carnal appetites. He didn't need love, didn't need tenderness or require a woman's touch. Those were base emotions, best ignored. And neglect them he had until he'd met Catherine.

From the moment she'd walked into his office, he'd been confronted with a surge of unexpected, and unwanted feelings. He hadn't recognized what he was dealing with in the beginning. Subconsciously he had, otherwise he would never have gone out of his way to ruin her weekends by assigning her duty four Friday nights running. It didn't take a psychiatrist's couch to figure that one. He'd been batting a thousand when her name was the first one that drifted into his mind when he learned a substitute coordinator was going to be needed for the physical fitness program.

In analyzing his deeds, Royce realized he was punishing Catherine. With just cause. The lieutenant commander was a constant thorn in his flesh, a reminder that he was a man with needs that refused to be denied any longer.

Unfortunately there was a good deal more at stake than satisfying a deep physical hunger. Catherine was under his command, which put pressure on them both. She was strictly off limits. Neither of them could afford to indulge in this attraction. It would only end up hurting them both. Their careers would suffer, and they'd both worked too damn hard to screw it up now over a few undisciplined hormones.

Dragging a fresh breath through his lungs, Royce closed his eyes and tried to push the picture of Catherine from his mind. He'd seen the emotions tearing at her in the parking lot, witnessed the pride-filled way in which she'd tilted her chin. Damn but the woman was proud. She apologized, accepting all the blame herself, although heaven knew everything she'd said was right. In that moment, he never respected a woman more. For her honesty, for her directness, for the fact she was willing to deal with whatever it was between them, lay it on the ground and call it what it was.

In those few words, heavy with meaning, Catherine had told him something he'd long suspected. Lieutenant Commander Catherine Fredrickson was a woman of substance. One so rare, one so beautiful, he didn't know what the hell he was going to do to get her out of his mind. All he knew was that he must succeed even if it meant requesting a transfer and uprooting Kelly from the only home she'd ever known.

Chapter Three

"Can we go to a movie, too?" Kelly asked, snapping her seat belt into place. They were on their way to the Kitsap Mall, where the all-important jacket was on sale. It was either buy his daughter the coat or ruin her life before the eyes of her peers. Royce couldn't remember clothes and shoes being so vital when he was in grade school, but the world was a hell of a lot different place when he was ten.

"Dad," Kelly pressed, "what about a movie?"

"Sure," he agreed easily enough. Why not? He'd been short-tempered all week, due mainly to the fact he was dealing with his feelings for Catherine. Kelly deserved a reward for putting up with his sour mood.

As for what was happening—or better said, what was *not* happening—between him and Catherine, Royce had rarely spent a more uncomfortable week. He couldn't walk into the office without being aware of her. Her presence was like a time bomb silently ticking in the corner of the room. Every now and again their eyes would meet and he'd be left to watch the emotions race across the landscape of her dark brown eyes. With everyone around them in the office, there hadn't been a problem. It was the evening run that tested his soul.

Every afternoon Royce told himself he wouldn't run.

Every afternoon, like precision clockwork, he was at the track, waiting for Catherine to arrive. They ran together, without speaking, without sharing, without looking at each other.

It was uncanny the comfort he found circling the track with the petite lieutenant commander at his side. The track was neutral ground, safe territory for them both. Those all-too-short minutes with Catherine were the reason he got out of bed in the morning, the reason he made it through the day.

When she smiled at him, Royce swore her eyes scored his heart. In the evenings when they'd finished jogging, Catherine would thank him for the workout and then silently return to her car. The moment she was out of sight, Royce was left feeling bereft. He hadn't realized what poor company a disciplined life-style could make, and what poorer company the long, lonely nights in an empty bed could be. The desolation was as powerful as a blow to his gut.

The evenings were another matter. He almost feared sleep because the moment he slipped into unconsciousness, Catherine filled his mind. She was soft and warm, and so real that all he had to do was reach out and draw her to his side. Royce would never have guessed his mind would play such cruel tricks on him. He was having trouble enough keeping Catherine at a distance, emotionally and physically. In sleep, his mind welcomed her, tormenting him with dreams he couldn't control. Dreams of Catherine running toward him on the beach, holding her arms out to him. Catherine feminine and soft in his embrace. Catherine laughing. Royce swore he never heard a sound more beautiful in all his life.

If there was anything to be grateful for, and it was damn little, it was the fact the dreams had never developed into anything even remotely physical between them.

In the mornings, Royce woke annoyed with himself, annoyed at Catherine for refusing to leave him alone and irritated with the world. With all the strength of his will, which was admittedly formidable, Royce pushed all thoughts of the lieutenant commander from his mind.

For as long as Catherine was under his command, all Royce could indulge himself in were involuntary dreams. He refused to allow himself the pleasure of recapturing the fantasy of him and Catherine alone together in quiet moments. Unhurried moments. With no demands. No deadlines. Moments when his heart and his soul were at rest.

Life could be a cruel hoax, Royce sharply reminded himself. He'd been taught that time and time again. He wasn't about to lose everything that was important to him over a woman, even if she did have eyes that looked straight through him.

The mall was crowded, but then it generally was on weekends, especially now that folks were gearing up for Christmas. Royce allowed Kelly to drag him into the J. C. Penney store. But that was only the beginning of the ordeal. The jacket she was so keen on had sold out in her size. The helpful salesclerk had phoned three other stores and there wasn't a single one available. Even the catalog had sold out.

"I'm sorry, sweetheart," Royce told her. She was bitterly disappointed and trying hard not to show it.

"Do you want to look around for a different coat?" Surely there was a father-of-the-year award for him in this offer. They'd spent nearly an hour on this wild-goose chase already, and Royce's patience had worn paper thin.

Kelly sat on the wooden bench outside the department store, her head bent low. Royce was about to repeat the question when she shrugged.

"How about something to drink?" Royce was half an hour overdue for a cup of coffee.

Kelly nodded eagerly. She stood and slipped her small hand into his. She didn't do that often, and Royce guessed she did so now needing his reassurance.

Royce bought her a Pepsi and himself a cup of fresh, hot coffee while Kelly scouted out a place for them to sit. Since it was close to noon, the tables were mostly occupied. They found one and sat down in the white wire chairs.

"Dad," Kelly whispered excitedly, "look at that pretty lady over there."

Hell, as far as Royce could see, the entire mall was filled with pretty ladies. "Where?"

"The one in the pink-and-green-and-blue jacket. Over there." Knowing it was impolite to point, Kelly wiggled her index finger back and forth in the general direction of where she wanted him to look. "Look, she's sorta walking toward us. Hurry and look before she turns away."

As he'd mused earlier, life could be filled with cruel hoaxes, and it was about to play another one on him now. Before he even realized what he was doing, Royce was on his feet. "Hello, Catherine."

"Royce." Her dark eyes were bright with surprise as well, and frankly, she didn't look any more pleased than he felt.

"How are you?" he heard himself ask stiffly.

"Fine."

"Dad." Impatiently, Kelly tugged on the hem of his leather jacket. "I like her coat…a whole lot."

Royce watched as Catherine's eyes momentarily left his and landed on Kelly. Once again surprise registered in the dark depths, but was quickly replaced by a gentleness and warmth that tightened strong cords around his heart. He'd never mentioned his daughter, and it was apparent she hadn't known he'd been married. Maybe she thought he was married still.

"This is my daughter, Kelly," Royce said, his voice low and throaty.

"Hello, Kelly. I'm Catherine." She dragged her eyes away from him and held out her hand to his daughter. "Your dad and I work together." She said this, Royce was convinced, as a reminder to them both. Hell, he didn't need it.

"Your jacket is real pretty," Kelly said quietly. She continued to tug on Royce's sleeve until he was convinced she'd pulled the armhole down to his elbow.

"What Kelly would like to know is where you bought it," Royce inserted dryly.

"And if they have kid sizes?" the ten-year-old asked excitedly.

"I got it right here in the mall, in Jacobson's."

"Dad," Kelly said, pushing aside her drink, "let's go look, okay?"

Royce glanced longingly at his coffee. He'd barely had time to take a single sip. Kelly was looking at him as if to say Jacobson's was sure to sell out in the next ten minutes if they didn't get there.

"I don't know if they have kid sizes," Kelly stated urgently, as though another five or ten minutes was sure to make the difference. "I know it's a ladies' store and everything, but you can wait outside if you want and I'll go in by myself."

"Why don't I take you down," Catherine suggested.

It took a fair amount of self-control not to leap up and kiss her. "You don't mind?" He had to ask. Pride demanded that much, at least.

"Not a bit. Go ahead and enjoy your coffee," Catherine suggested, her gaze returning to him. "We won't be more than a few minutes."

He should refuse. Royce knew it the minute she made the offer, but Kelly was looking up at him, her eyes alive with excitement, and before he could argue with himself, he nodded.

* * *

A daughter, Catherine mused. Royce had a daughter. Catherine had worked with him for five weeks, and no one had bothered to mention the fact he'd been married or that he was raising Kelly. The child was incredibly sweet, with long dark hair and eyes so blue they reminded Catherine of wild bluebonnets. Kelly was as gentle and cute as Royce was remote and indifferent.

Catherine had noted how closely Royce had watched her when he introduced Kelly. His eyes had darkened into a brittle defiance as though he expected her to do or say something about the fact she hadn't known about the child. She found herself staring at him and the proud lines of his chiseled features. Catherine's gaze had moved smoothly from father to daughter. There was no doubt in her mind the two were related. Kelly possessed the same beautiful blue eyes, and although her face was heart-shaped and feminine, she was clearly a Nyland.

Until she'd walked into the shopping complex, Catherine hadn't realized how hungry she was for the sight of Royce. From clear across the other side of the mall, she'd walked directly to his side, guided by instinct to the man who'd dominated her thoughts for days on end.

"We went to the J. C. Penney store," Kelly explained as they walked side by side down the wide concourse, "but all the jackets in my size were sold. We looked and looked and I was feeling really low so Dad bought me a Pepsi and then we saw you," Kelly explained in one giant breath. "Your jacket is just perfect."

Catherine had bought it a couple of weeks earlier. Being new to the Pacific Northwest, she needed something heavier than a raincoat. The jacket had caught her eye in a ski shop, and although Catherine didn't ski, she'd been attracted to the colors, just the way Kelly had.

"I like it, too. And as I recall, they did have children's sizes."

"Dad doesn't like to shop much," Kelly explained as they wove their way between the moving crowd. "He does it for me, but I know he'd rather be watching a silly football game. Men are like that, you know?"

"So I've heard." As far as understanding the male of the species, Royce's daughter knew a whole lot more than Catherine did. For as long as she could remember, it had always been her and her mother. In college she'd lived in a girls' dormitory.

"Dad tries real hard, but he doesn't understand a lot of things about girls."

Catherine couldn't help grinning at that. Evidently she wasn't the only one at a loss when it came to understanding the opposite sex. Apparently what she and Royce needed was a ten-year-old to straighten out their lives.

They found the store, and indeed there was a jacket almost identical to the one Catherine had that was in Kelly's size. After Royce's daughter tried it on and modeled it in front of a mirror, Catherine had the salesclerk put it on hold.

Kelly raced back to the large open eating area to tell Royce about the rare find. Catherine followed close behind.

"It's got pink and green and blue. Not the same shade of blue as Catherine's, but almost. I can have it, can't I?" She dug into her small pocket at the top of her jeans and dragged out the five single dollar bills one at a time and then several coins from a different pocket. "I'll pay for part of it."

Royce stood and tossed the empty coffee cup into the garbage. "All right, all right. I know when I'm defeated." He glanced over at Catherine and winked.

Catherine couldn't believe it. The iceman winked as if he were a regular human being. Royce Nyland was one man in the office, another on the running track and someone else entirely different when he was with his daughter.

"I...can see you've got everything under control here," Catherine said, thinking she should probably leave. She felt awkward with Royce.

"Don't go," Kelly cried, reaching for Catherine's hand with both of her own. "Dad said he'd buy me pizza for lunch, and I want you to come, too."

"I'm sure Catherine has other plans," Royce said matter-of-factly.

Catherine noted that he didn't repeat the invitation, which was just as well. Yet, she couldn't hold back the sense of disappointment. "Yes, I do have some things to do. I was just going into the pet store to buy my cat a new litter box."

"I love the pet store," Kelly piped in eagerly. "Once they even let me hold a new puppy. I wanted to buy it real bad, but Dad said we couldn't because there wouldn't be anyone home during the day to take care of him."

Catherine's heart melted as she gazed down on Royce's daughter. So young and tender. Catherine remembered herself at that age and how life had been such a wonderful adventure then.

"Oh, do come, Catherine. Please."

Catherine's gaze moved to Royce. She expected his eyes to be cool and unreadable as they were so much of the time. Instead she found them troubled and unsure, yet inviting. Catherine felt as if the air had been sucked from her lungs.

"I...are you sure I wouldn't be intruding?" By everything that was right, she knew she should refuse. They were standing so close to the fire, close enough to get burned, and yet they each seemed to be taking turns tossing kindling into the flames.

"I'm sure," Royce answered.

"Oh, good," Kelly cried, seemingly unaware of the tension between Catherine and her father. "I certainly hope you don't like anchovies. Dad gets them on his half whenever we order pizza. Those things are disgusting."

A half hour later, they were sitting in a pizza parlor. Catherine and Kelly shared an Italian sausage and olive pizza pie while Royce ate his own, covered with the tiny fish both women found so offensive.

Although it was comfortably warm inside the restaurant, Kelly insisted upon wearing her new coat.

"Are those fingernails actually yours?" Kelly asked halfway through the meal.

Catherine nodded, her mouth full of pizza.

"You mean you don't have a single acrylic tip?"

It was incredible to Catherine that a ten-year-old knew about such things. "Not even one," she assured the girl.

Kelly's eyes widened with renewed respect. She held up her hand for Catherine to examine, showing the short, stubby ends of her own nails. Catherine reached for her purse and brought out her fingernail kit for Kelly to examine, explaining each instrument.

"What are you two talking about?" Royce demanded in mock exasperation. "As near as I can figure, you women have your own language."

Kelly reverently closed the case and returned it to Catherine. Her eyes drifted from Royce to her and then back again. Catherine could almost see the tiny wheels churning in the little girl's head.

"Are you married, Catherine?" The girl asked innocently enough.

"Ah…no." Catherine's throat felt tight and dry all of a sudden.

"Neither is my dad," the ten-year-old added, her words fraught with meaning. "My mom died, you know?" Kelly said it with complete lack of emotion, as though losing a mother was simply part of growing up.

"No…I wasn't aware of that." Catherine avoided looking at Royce.

Kelly took another couple of moments to assess the situation. "So you and my dad work together?"

"Kelly Lynn." Royce used a tone Catherine had heard often in the office. It brought trained sailors to attention, and it worked just as well with his daughter.

"I was only asking."

"Then don't."

"All right, all right, but I didn't mean anything by it." Royce's daughter returned to her pizza, took a bite and chewed two or three times before adding. "Catherine's coming to the movie with us, isn't she?" The question was directed to Royce, who once more narrowed his eyes at his daughter.

"I'll let you choose the movie if you want," Kelly offered. Evidently the choice of which film they'd see was a long-standing battle between them, and that she'd offer to let him pick was a major concession.

Catherine didn't know what Royce was waiting for. He shouldn't even be entertaining his daughter's suggestion. The fact they were having lunch together was one thing, but sitting in a movie theater together would be…should be out of the question.

"Dad?" Kelly probed.

Royce looked to Catherine, and his hard blue eyes held hers for the long, drawn-out moment. Tension thickened the air until she was convinced neither of them was breathing.

"Catherine has other things to do," Royce informed his daughter.

Catherine was quick to reassure Kelly. "I really do, sweetheart. Perhaps we can all go another time."

Royce's young daughter accepted Catherine's decision with a quick nod, but it was apparent the girl was disappointed. She wasn't the only one. Catherine's heart felt as heavy as concrete. She'd never felt closer to Royce than this time with his daughter. He'd lowered his guard enough for her to glimpse the nurturing, caring man shielded behind the thick wall of pride and tradition.

After wiping her hands clean with a napkin, Catherine reached for her purse and slid from the booth. "Thank you both for lunch, but I really should be going."

Kelly slid out of the booth, too. "I wish you were going to the movie with us."

Her eyes found Royce's as she whispered, "So do I."

Catherine was halfway to the door when Royce stopped her. For a moment he didn't say anything, but stared down at her. His face revealed none of his thoughts, and briefly Catherine was aware of what a talent he possessed to hide his emotions so well.

His eyes continued to hold hers and seemed to scorch her with their intensity before he spoke, listing the movie and the time. "In case you change your mind," he said, before turning back to his daughter.

By the time Catherine was inside her car, she'd started to tremble. What was the matter with Royce? Had he gone mad? Had she?

Royce, her XO, knowing what they were both risking, seemed to be telling her he wanted her to come to the movie. But he was leaving the decision in her hands. God help them both, she wanted it, too.

A movie wasn't an affair, she reminded herself. If they both happened to show up at the same movie at the same time, no one would put the wrong connotation on that. The rule book didn't say they couldn't be friends. If friends just happened to meet at a movie, it wouldn't be unheard of for them to sit together. Would it?

Catherine didn't know what to do. Her head was telling her one thing, and her heart another. Both their careers could be jeopardized. It was far too much to risk for the pleasure of sitting next to each other in a matinee.

Yet when the time approached, Catherine was behind a line of preteens. Her heart was hammering so loudly, she was convinced everyone around her must be able to hear it, too. Once she glanced over her shoulder, thinking the shore patrol was on her tail. The thought was ludicrous, which only went to prove the state of her mind.

Royce was sitting in the last row, with Kelly in the seat next to him. The girl noticed Catherine immediately and leaped up from her chair as though she'd been sitting on a giant coiled spring. She hurriedly scooted down the aisle and enthusiastically hugged Catherine.

"I was hoping you'd come." She grabbed Catherine's hand and energetically led her to the seats.

Catherine didn't look at Royce. She feared what she'd read in his eyes.

"Missy's here," Kelly cried, and waved madly, as though the fate of the free world depended on how quickly her friend recognized her. "Can I go show her my new coat?"

Royce's hesitation was noticeable before he agreed, and Kelly raced away.

Catherine sat down, leaving an empty seat between them Royce continued to look straight ahead as though he'd never seen her in his life. "Are you crazy?" he hissed under his breath after an exaggerated moment. But it was the kind of anger that comes from caring too much, directed at himself as much as at her.

"Are you?" she came back just as heatedly. She was equally furious and for all the same reasons. She wasn't going to take the blame for this. She'd made her decision and her excuses at the restaurant. They both had. He was the one who'd dropped the anchor in her lap by making a point of letting her know which movie and what showing. He'd blatantly asked her to come, and now he seemed to regret she was there.

"Yes, I think I am crazy," Royce admitted reluctantly.

"I wasn't going to come," she told him softly. Even after he'd let it be known he wanted her with him and Kelly.

"Then why did you?"

Catherine didn't know. Maybe it was because she liked to live dangerously, walk as close to the edge of the cliff as possible without falling off. "I don't know. Why did you?"

Royce chuckled, but there was no amusement in his laugh. "Hell, I don't know. I guess I like tampering with the fates."

"Dad." Kelly was scooting down the narrow row sideways in a rush to return to her father. "Missy wants me to sit with her. You don't care, do you?"

Once again Royce hesitated before answering. "Go ahead."

"Thanks, Dad." Kelly scooted past Catherine, paused and winked. Winked! The same way Royce had winked at her earlier. Only she didn't know what Kelly meant any more than she'd understood the gesture from Royce.

Kelly left to join her friend, and the tension between her and Royce was so strong, Catherine didn't know if she could endure it any longer.

"I'll move." She started to stand, when he stopped her.

"No," Royce said automatically, his hand grasping her arm. "Stay." The word was soft and pleading.

Catherine couldn't refuse him, and when she sat down, he moved one seat over, sitting next to her. Almost immediately the theater darkened and music filled the room. Royce stretched out his long legs, and his thigh inadvertently brushed hers. Catherine's breath caught in her throat at the sudden rush of sensation that raced up and down her limb. Royce, too, gave a small gasp. The firm pressure of his leg felt muscular and hard. It was funny how easy it was for her to forget how good a man can feel. Catherine glanced up to find Royce openly studying her. His eyes were bright with a heat that warmed her from the top of her head to the soles of her feet. With a determined effort she dragged her gaze away from his.

Royce shifted his weight and with a good deal of reluctance moved his leg. They both breathed a little easier. This was difficult enough without adding more temptation, more fuel to the fire.

Catherine doubted that either one of them was able to follow the plot of the movie. If anyone had asked her, Catherine wouldn't have been able to discuss a single detail. Her concentration was centered on the man sitting next to her.

At some point, Royce thrust a bucket of popcorn between them. In an effort to fix her attention on the screen, Catherine reached for a handful of the kernels and ate them one by one. About the third or fourth dip into the bucket, Catherine's hand inadvertently bumped Royce's. She quickly withdrew her fingers, only Royce wouldn't allow it. He reached out and grasped her hand, then slowly, as if damning himself for his weakness, laced his fingers one by one with hers. His grip was tight, his nails cutting into her smooth flesh. It was as though he never intended on letting her go. The bucket of popcorn disappeared, and still Royce held her hand.

There was no way Catherine could explain the tumult of emotion that overtook her at the gesture. A host of unexplainable sensations assailed her, hidden, unrecognized emotions were so prominent that her head started to spin. If he was kissing her or touching her breasts or making love to her, Catherine could have understood, could have accepted her reaction.

But all he was dong was holding her hand.

She'd never felt more vulnerable or more exposed. She

was risking everything that was important to her. Royce was taking a chance with his career, and for what?

The question was a harsh one, and the answer…the answer was even harsher. She knew next to nothing about Royce. He'd been married, his wife had died and there was a child. He was Navy, a man born to lead others. He was respected. Admired. But they'd never sat down and talked about their lives, never shared anything beyond the basic everyday-working-together kind of conversation. That they should experience this powerful pull toward each other, this forceful attraction, was a quirk of nature. There was no rhyme. No reason. Yet it would have taken an act of congress to move Catherine out of that movie theater.

The film ended. Catherine was hardly aware of the fact until he released her hand. She wanted to protest, longing to maintain the contact, as innocent as it was, until the last possible moment.

"Catherine," he whispered, leaning close. "Go now."

"But…"

"For the love of God, don't argue with me. Just leave."

Something in his voice, a warning, a threat, Catherine didn't know which, prompted her to move quickly. "I'll see you Monday," she said, standing.

But she'd be thinking about him every minute in between.

"Is there something going on between you and Commander Nyland?" Elaine Perkins asked Monday morning when Catherine arrived for work.

Her heart sank to her knees before quickly rebounding. "What makes you ask that?" she asked, forcing her voice to remain light and breezy.

"He wants to see you first thing. Again."

"He wants to see me first thing?" Catherine was beginning to sound like an echo.

"And when the almighty commander speaks, we obey," Elaine said as a means of reminding them both. "All I want to know is what you've done this time?"

"What makes you think I did anything?" Catherine asked as she hung up her coat.

"Because he looks like he's in a mood to wrestle crocodiles. That man is as mean as a shark with a toothache, and if I were you, I wouldn't tangle with him."

"Don't worry." Squaring her shoulders, she approached Royce's office and knocked politely.

"Come in." His frown deepened when he saw her. Perkins was right; Royce didn't look any too cheerful. The iceman had returned. Gone was the indulgent father, replaced by the man so ingrained in military procedure Catherine was convinced she had been imagining someone else on Saturday.

"Sit down, Lieutenant Commander." She wasn't Catherine any longer, but a rank.

She did as he requested, not knowing what to expect.

Royce rolled a pencil between his palms. "I don't think it's a good idea for us to continue exercising together in the afternoons."

Catherine's eyes flew to his. It was the only thing they shared, that time together, and although it was entirely selfish of her, she didn't want to give it up.

"I realize you have as much right to use the track as I do, so I'd like to suggest a schedule. Unfortunately the afternoons are the only time I'm free…."

"My schedule if far less restrictive, *sir*," she said, bolting to her feet. "Don't worry. I'll make an effort to avoid any possibility of us meeting. Would you like me to stop frequenting the Kitsap Mall while I'm at it?"

The telltale muscle leaped in his jaw. Catherine didn't know why she was taking the offensive so strongly. He was only saying and doing what needed to be done, what should have been said long before now. But she felt as if the rug had been pulled from beneath her feet and she was teetering for her balance.

"You may shop wherever you choose."

"Thank you," she returned crisply. "Is that all?"

"Yes."

Catherine turned to leave.

"Catherine…" He stopped her as she reached his door. She turned back, but he shook his head. "Nothing, you may go."

Chapter Four

Catherine understood. Conclusively. Decisively.

Commander Royce Nyland, her executive officer, she reminded herself, was shutting her out. Apparently it was easy enough to do. He'd rerouted his emotions so often that barricading any and all feelings for her was a simple matter.

She, unfortunately, wasn't achieving the same level of success. Royce Nyland had invaded her life. As hard as she tried, her efforts to adjust her own attitude had done little, if any, good.

She didn't want to feel the things she did for him, and frankly she didn't know how to deal with them. This was a new experience for her. How was she supposed to block him from her mind when thoughts of him filled every minute of every day?

He'd ordered her to stop, she reminded herself. When a superior officer spoke, Catherine, ever loyal, ever Navy, obeyed. No one had told her it was going to be easy. But then again, no one had bothered to explain how damn difficult it would be, either.

Nothing like this had ever happened to Catherine before, and frankly… Frankly, she didn't want it happening to her now.

Royce didn't want to jeopardize his career. She didn't want to jeopardize hers, either. He had little use for love in his life; she'd lived without it so long she didn't know what she was missing. If he could ignore the empty hole that grew deeper and wider with each passing day, then, she determined, so could she.

Maintaining her daily exercise program became of primary importance to Catherine. Never having liked running in the streets, she ran on the base track at odd hours of the day. She was careful not to infringe on Royce's time, holding on to this small link with him because it was all she had.

Early Friday morning, two weeks after Royce had called her into his office for their latest discussion, Catherine parked her car close to the jogging track.

She'd just finished her second lap when another runner joined her, coming up from behind her, gaining on her easily.

"Good morning."

Catherine's throat constricted. She'd worked so hard not to intrude on his exercise time, running in the early morning hours in order to avoid the possibility of them stumbling into each other.

The immediate sense of unfairness and outrage was nearly overwhelming. Instantly she wanted to confront Royce, shout at him, demand that he leave her alone, but he spoke first. "You're angry."

"You're damn right I am. What are you doing here?" Her voice was low and accusing. Suddenly she felt tired. Tired of pretending. Tired of ignoring emotions so strong she was choking on them. Tired of hiding.

"I need to talk to you."

"So talk." Her nerves were raw, stretched to the breaking point. They had been for weeks.

They jogged half a lap before he spoke. For someone

who was so eager to communicate, for someone who'd broken the very rules he'd initiated, he seemed to be having a hard time getting started.

"I had to do it, Catherine," he said with enough force to shake the ground. The words weren't loud, but packed with emotion. "We've both been in the Navy too long, and love it too much to risk everything now."

"I know." Her anger vanished as quickly as it had risen and her voice trembled slightly despite her best efforts to keep it even and unaffected. She wasn't nearly as good as Royce when it came to disguising her emotions.

"What I didn't realize was how damn difficult it was going to be." He said this softly, as though admitting to a wrong-doing, as though it were important she know.

Catherine knotted her hands tightly at her sides. She never expected him to admit it, never dreamed he would. He'd given every indication that pushing her from his thoughts, from his heart, hadn't caused him a moment's concern. Surely he must have known how difficult it was for her. She'd buried herself in her work, repainted her entire apartment, stayed up late listening to Johnny Mathis records in a futile effort to forget Royce. But nothing worked. Nothing.

"Kelly asks about you every night," Royce confessed next.

"I'm sorry," she whispered, knowing that involving his daughter in this had made everything more difficult. "I didn't purposely run into you that day."

"I know. I'm not blaming you, I just wish to hell it hadn't happened. No," he altered quickly, regretfully, "that isn't true. I'm thankful Kelly met you."

"It would have been better for us both if it hadn't happened." Yet Catherine would always be grateful for that one day with Royce and his daughter. It gave her something to hold on to for all the long, lonely nights.

"There's a rumor going around," Royce said after a moment. Catherine's heart tripped. The fear must have shown in her eyes because Royce added, "It's not about us, don't worry."

The military abounded with rumors. That Royce thought it important enough to repeat one to her meant something was deeply troubling him.

"I heard by means of the grapevine that I may be sent over to Turkey to work at NATO."

His words fell like heavy stones upon Catherine's heart, each one inflicting a sharper, more profound pain. "Oh, Royce." Her tone was low and hesitant, filled with concern.

"If I am, I'll need someone to take Kelly for me."

Catherine would do it in a heartbeat, but surely there was someone else. A relative or a long-standing family friend. As a single parent, Royce must have completed a parenting plan so there would be someone to take Kelly with as little as twenty-four-hours' notice.

"I spoke to Kelly about the possibility of us being separated last night. I didn't want to alarm her, but at the same time I didn't think it was fair to hide it from her, either."

Catherine nodded, impressed with his wisdom in dealing honestly with his daughter.

"Kelly's lived in Bangor all her life, and I'd hate to uproot her."

"I understand." The ten-year-old had already lost her mother, and if her father were to be given shipping orders to the Middle East, everything that was familiar to Kelly would be stripped from her. The fact he'd been stationed at Bangor this long was something of an oddity.

"Sandy's family lives in the Midwest. She was never close to her mother and had lost contact with her father several years before. She has a couple of stepbrothers, but I've never bothered to keep in touch with them. To be honest, I haven't heard from her side of the family since the funeral."

"Kelly can stay with me," Catherine offered.

They had stopped running by this time and were walking the track, their pace invigorating. The air was cold and clean, and when Royce spoke, his breath created a thin fog in the autumn morning.

"If you can't, my parents will be happy to have her, but they're living in a retirement community in Arizona, and frankly, I hate to complicate their lives at this point."

"I mean it, Royce. I'd love to have Kelly stay with me."

"Thank you," he whispered. His voice was hoarse, and intuitively Catherine knew how difficult it was for Royce Nyland to admit he needed someone for something. Knowing he needed her, even if it was for his daughter's sake, did something to her heart. Her vulnerable heart. Susceptible only to him.

Royce picked up the pace, and they resumed jogging at a leisurely pace.

"How's Kelly taking the news?" Catherine asked, concerned about the grade schooler.

"Like a real trooper. I think she's more excited about the possibility of living with you, something she suggested by the way, than she's concerned about me leaving."

"Typical kid reaction."

"She really took to you."

Catherine smiled, her heart warming. "I took to her, too."

Royce laughed. It was the first time Catherine could remember ever hearing Royce amused.

"What's so funny?"

Royce sobered almost immediately. "Something Kelly said. Hell, I didn't even know she wanted a sister."

"A sister?"

Royce looked away abruptly. "Never mind," he said curtly.

They circled the track once more, their time slipping away like sand between splayed fingers. It felt so good to be with Royce, these moments together were like a rare, unexpected gift meant to be savored and enjoyed. Catherine had trouble keeping her eyes off him. He was tall and lean, his muscular shoulders broad. The sunlight was breaking over the hill, glinting on his thick, dark hair.

They parted at the last possible minute. Royce left first, heading toward the office. Catherine took a hurried shower. She stood under the spray, letting it pelt against her face and tried not to think of Royce being transferred all the way to Turkey.

It would solve one problem; she wouldn't be under Royce's command and if they chose to become romantically involved the Navy would not care. Of course they'd be separated by thousands of miles, but the Navy generally went out of its way to make falling in love difficult.

Catherine arrived at the office, feeling refreshed. She greeted her secretary, poured herself a cup of coffee and sat down at her desk. She didn't look for Royce, but lately she'd made a habit of not seeking him out, even if it was only with her eyes.

She was absorbed in her own work for an hour or more when Commander Parker strolled into her office. Catherine had briefly met Commander Parker when she was first assigned to the Bangor station. He was in his mid-thirties, single and something of a flirt. He'd asked Catherine out to dinner one of the Friday nights Royce had seen fit to assign her duty, and she'd been forced to refuse. Apparently he'd taken her rejection personally, and hadn't asked her out since.

"Have you seen Commander Nyland?" Elaine Perkins asked a minute or so later.

"He was on the track this morning," Catherine explained as nonchalantly as she could. "He left before I did and I haven't seen him since."

"Commander Parker's looking for him."

"I'm sorry, I can't help."

Perkins left and returned a few minutes later after a flurry of activity from several others. Apparently Royce wasn't anywhere to be found, which was highly uncommon. Catherine worked hard at disguising her growing concern.

The phone rang; Elaine Perkins answered, routing the call. Her hand was still on the receiver when she turned to Catherine. "I didn't know Commander Nyland had a daughter. Somehow I can't picture old stoneface as a parent."

Catherine grinned. Not long ago she would have thought the same thing herself. But she'd seen Royce interact with his daughter, seen the love and pride shining through his eyes as he looked down at her. "She's ten and an absolute delight," Catherine said before she could stop herself.

"So you've met her?"

"Ah…I ran into them at the mall a couple of weeks back," Catherine explained, returning her attention to the case she was reviewing.

"If you've met her," Elaine continued, emotion bleeding into her voice, "then you might be interested in knowing where Commander Nyland disappeared to. Apparently his daughter was hit by a car on her way to school. She's at the Navy Hospital."

Catherine swore her heart stopped in that moment. She went stiff with shock, then completely numb. Slowly she rose to her feet and blindly looked around her as if the air circulating the room would tell her it wasn't so.

Oh my God. Oh my God. Not Kelly. Please not Kelly, Catherine's mind chanted. The phrase kept repeating itself in her mind, a prayer, an entreaty to the heavenly powers to watch over the child Royce loved so dearly.

"Catherine?" She couldn't look at Elaine, fearing she

would read the stark terror in her eyes and know how much Royce and his daughter meant to her.

"Did…what's her condition?"

"I don't know. Are you all right?"

"I'm fine," she answered, reaching for her purse. "I'm…I'm taking my lunch hour."

"Sure thing," Elaine returned hesitantly. "I don't suppose you noticed it's only ten. It's a little early for lunch, don't you think?"

Catherine didn't bother to answer. She was already on her way out of the office. She rushed down the stairs and shot out of the building. It amazed her how calm she was. Outwardly, she was as cool and composed as an admiral. On the inside she was quaking with fear so stark and real the taste of it filled her mouth.

Please God, not Kelly. She must have repeated the phrase a hundred times as she raced across the asphalt parking lot to her car.

Catherine didn't remember any part of the fifteen-minute drive to the Navy Hospital in Bremerton. One moment she was at the Navy Base at Bangor, and the next thing she knew she was pulling into the hospital parking lot.

The emergency room receptionist must have recognized the urgency in Catherine's eyes, and after a few preliminary questions, directed her to the third floor.

She took the elevator up, repeating the room number over and over in her head as she raced down the wide polished corridor. The door was ajar when Catherine arrived.

Kelly, her face ashen against the sheets, was either asleep or unconscious, the metal railing around the bed raised. Catherine's heart, which had only recently righted itself, tripped into double time. Once more she prayed for the little girl who had come to mean so much to her in so short a time. Tears filled her eyes, and she bit into her lower lip in an effort to keep them at bay.

Royce was sitting in a chair next to the hospital bed, his face in his hands, oblivious to her presence.

"Royce."

He lifted his head, turned and fixed his eyes on her. He frowned as though he didn't believe it was her, as though he desperately needed an anchor. His face was ravaged with emotion, scored with myriad fears. Briefly he closed his eyes before he stood and walked over to her.

Thankfully Catherine had the presence of mind to close the door. No sooner had it swung shut when Royce hauled her to him, lifted her from the floor and locked his arms around her waist. A shudder ran down the length of him as he breathed in deeply and buried his face in the gentle slope of her shoulder.

Catherine felt the moisture slide down her cheeks, and she held on to Royce with equal ferocity, her arms looped around his neck.

"She's going to be all right," Royce assured her several moments later, his words more breath than sound. As if he feared he was hurting her, he relaxed his hold and slowly, hesitantly lowered her feet to the ground. "She's asleep now. The doctor wanted to keep her overnight for observation. Oh God, Catherine, it was so close, so very close. A few more feet and I might have lost her."

His eyes continued to hold hers. The barriers were down now, and she understood so many things he'd never allowed her to see before. Though he wished she'd never been transferred from Hawaii. Though he wished she was in anyone else's command but his. Though he wished to hell she'd stayed outside his life. He needed her. He needed her because he couldn't endure seeing his only child hurt and stand at her bedside alone. He needed her then. He needed her tomorrow. The need wasn't ever going to go away.

Without thinking, Catherine did what seemed natural.

She reached up and pressed her head to his chest, reassuring him the only way she knew how. His hands were trembling as his fingers tangled with her hair. Once again a tremor raced through his body.

"She's going to be all right," he said again.

"Thank God," Catherine whispered. She felt his heart pounding. Her breasts were flush against the hard wall of his chest, and it felt so incredibly good to be in his arms.

They might have remained like that forever if the sound from outside the room hadn't captured their attention. Even then neither one showed any inclination toward moving. Remembering all the unspoken promises they'd made to each other, Catherine gently broke away.

"Any broken bones?" was the only intelligent question she could think to ask. She ran her fingers down her cheeks, convinced her mascara was streaking her face. Using the back of her hand, she brushed the moisture aside.

"None," Royce said with a lopsided grin. "She was lucky that way. She has a bad concussion and plenty of scrapes and bruises."

"What happened?"

"One of the mothers was driving her kids to school when her brakes locked as she was coming to the school crossing. There wasn't anything she could do." Royce's eyes hardened as though he were picturing the frantic scene in his mind. The terror of the children helplessly scattering as the car slid toward them. The screams. The fear. The panic.

"Gratefully the car hit the curb before sliding into Kelly and Missy. From what I understand both were racing out of the way and were knocked hard to the ground."

"Was Kelly's friend hurt?"

"Cuts and bruises. The hospital released her to her mother."

Pressing her hands against the sides of Royce's clean-shaven jaw, Catherine closed her eyes, grateful that the accident hadn't been any worse than it was. Now that she was assured Kelly was going to be all right, she was more concerned about Royce. At one time she would have believed nothing could disconcert him, but Royce's Achilles' heel was his young daughter.

"Are you all right?"

He nodded, and offered her a weak smile. "Now that you're here, I am." He covered her hand with his own and roughly drew her palm to his mouth, tenderly kissing the inside. "Does anyone know where you are?"

Elaine Perkins had probably figured it out, but Catherine didn't want to worry Royce. "No."

"Good." His eyes were dark and intent. "Go back to the office."

"But…"

"And come back later this afternoon. Kelly will want to see you." His eyes revealed he'd want to see her again, too.

"All right," she said, reluctantly drawing away from him.

Royce reached for her hand, momentarily bringing her back to him, and pressed her fingertips to his mouth. "Thank you." He didn't need to tell her what for, it was there in his eyes for her to read. The eyes that had once seemed so hard and cold would never look the same again.

No man is an island. Royce had never completely understood those words until Kelly's accident. He'd been numb when security had come to tell him his daughter, his only child, had been taken by ambulance to the Navy Hospital. Numb with shock and disbelief. His heart had pounded so loud it sounded like a hand grenade exploding in his ears.

He hadn't said a word, but simply walked outside to his car, climbed inside and drove with a security escort to the hospital, praying, pleading with God for things to be different this time than they had been with Sandy's fatal accident.

Security Police had come to him then, too. All he'd known was that Sandy had been taken by ambulance to the Naval Hospital. The details with Kelly had been the same.

Only Sandy had been D.O.A.

Kelly had been spared.

Royce had loved his wife, at least in the beginning. He'd sensed from the first that she'd needed more love, more of him than he could ever supply. When they'd first married, the idea of being an officer's wife had excited her, but that novelty had quickly worn thin. She'd needed something more.

A career, she decided. One in which she would be appreciated and admired. One that would make her the envy of everyone she met.

Royce had encouraged her, which was his first mistake, but he hadn't expected her to become more involved with fashion than their lives together. After two years as a buyer for a major Seattle department store, she let it be known that if Royce were transferred, she'd stay behind.

In his ignorance, Royce had thought a child would help. Sandy had never been keen on raising a family. Insisting she bear him the child she'd promised was mistake number two.

After threats, tears and countless arguments, Sandy had agreed, but she'd never wanted Kelly. In some ways, Royce doubted that Sandy had ever loved their daughter.

Sandy worked up to a week before her delivery date and returned two weeks afterward. It was Royce who walked the floors when Kelly developed colic. It was Royce who dropped her off at the day-care center and returned to pick her up after work. It was Royce who changed her diapers and sat in the medical clinic when she developed repeated ear infections.

As Sandy claimed, if Royce was so keen on having a family, fine. She'd done her part.

By the time Sandy had been killed, their marriage, indeed every aspect of their relationship, had long since died a slow, painful death. They hadn't slept in the same room for three years and hadn't made love in over a year. Their lives were as separate as they could make them and still remain married.

Royce hadn't asked for a divorce. He didn't know why Sandy hadn't. They rarely spoke in those days. Rarely communicated.

Nevertheless, when she'd died, Royce had suffered. With guilt. With regret. With doubts. He should have tried harder. Done something more to make her happy. Appreciated her more. Something. Anything. Everything.

He hadn't shed a tear at her funeral. Any emotion he felt for Sandy had long since been spent. He felt guilty about that, guilty enough to promise himself he would never make the mistake of falling in love a second time.

Then he'd met Catherine.

He cursed the day she'd been assigned to his staff. In the same breath his heart swelled with gratitude.

Royce had come to believe he was a man who didn't need anyone. People needed him. Kelly needed him. The navy needed him. But he was an island, a man without needs.

He'd lived under that delusion until he'd seen Security approaching him that morning.

In that moment he'd needed Catherine. So badly that he shuddered at the memory of the way her name had raced into his mind. He'd sat in the emergency room, wanting her with him so much that he could feel himself start to unravel. A woman he felt closer to in little more than a month than he'd ever felt toward the wife he'd buried. He needed Catherine, the woman he'd never held. The woman he'd never kissed.

Royce had waited, for what seemed like hours, but in fact had only been a matter of minutes before he learned Kelly had suffered only minor injuries.

His relief had been so great that it demanded every ounce of strength he possessed not to reach for the phone and call Catherine then and there and assure her everything was all right. His hand shook as the realization washed over him like cold November rain.

Still he wanted Catherine with him. He needed her warmth, her generosity, her support. The man who needed no one, needed her.

She must have known, must have sensed his desperation because she'd come. From out of nowhere, she'd walked into Kelly's hospital room like an apparition. When he'd first looked up and seen her standing there, Royce was convinced she wasn't real. His anguish had been so overwhelming that his troubled mind had conjured up her form to satisfy the deep craving he had for her touch.

Then her eyes had slid so hungrily to his, and she'd bit into her bottom lip and battled back the tears. Ghosts didn't cry, did they?

This one did. Somehow Royce found himself on his feet walking toward her. He half expected her to vanish when he reached for her. Instead she was warm and solid and real. And his.

Royce had been so grateful, so engulfed with gratitude that he hadn't been able to speak. His heart, which he'd taken such measures to protect, had heated with a love so strong, his throat had grown thick with emotion.

He'd held Catherine for the longest time, soaking in her strength, her love, her concern.

When he had been able to speak, he didn't know if what he'd said was the least bit intelligible. Catherine had started asking questions; somehow he'd found the strength to answer, strength she'd lent him without even knowing it.

Then they'd heard a noise outside the room and realized their perilous position. He'd had to send her away. He'd had no choice.

"Daddy." The fragile child voice rose from the bed as delicately as mist on the moors.

"Hello, sweetheart."

"I fell asleep."

"I know." He lifted her small hand and clasped it in both of his. "You're going to be all right."

"What about Missy?"

"Her, too."

"Did I ruin my new jacket?"

How like a woman to be concerned about her clothes, Royce noted, amused. "If you did, I'll buy you another one."

Kelly brightened enough to offer him a weak smile. "I thought I heard Catherine. Did she come? I wanted to wake up and talk to her, but I couldn't. I guess I was too tired."

Royce nodded. "Don't worry, Catherine will be back later."

Kelly's soft blue eyes drifted shut, and she yawned. "Oh-h-h good, I like her so much."

"I like her, too."

Kelly's smile was lethargic. "I know you do, and she likes you a whole bunch...I can tell. Remember what I said, okay?"

"About what, sweetheart?"

"A baby sister," she reminded him, and winced. "Don't forget."

Royce hesitated. Now wasn't the time to lecture Kelly, but if she were to say anything to Catherine, it might prove extremely embarrassing. "Let me handle that part, all right?"

"All right."

Within a few minutes, Kelly was sound asleep once more.

* * *

As promised, Catherine arrived later that evening, her arms filled with a giant stuffed panda and a large vase of bright flowers.

"Catherine!" Kelly greeted. His child was sitting up in bed, looking very much like her normal self, Royce thought. The ten-year-old held out her arms as though she and the lieutenant commander were close friends.

If the truth be known, Royce was having something of a problem keeping from holding out his arms as well. Catherine looked beautiful, but then he couldn't remember a time that she'd been anything less.

Catherine set the vase of pink, red and white carnations next to the flower arrangement Royce had brought.

"Dad said you were here earlier, but I was asleep." She hugged the panda bear and Catherine in turn. "Thank you. I didn't expect everyone to buy me gifts just because Mrs. Thompson's brakes didn't work."

"We're all so pleased you weren't hurt worse."

"It was real scary," Kelly admitted, eating up all the attention she was receiving. "I tried not to cry, but it hurt too bad."

"I probably would have cried, too," Catherine confessed. She stood across the bed from Royce, who remembered the tears in her eyes as she'd rushed into the room earlier in the day.

"Wow, what happened to this place?" Catherine said with a grin, admiring the decorations. Her gaze briefly met with Royce's and seemed almost shy.

"My teacher brought me a poster," Kelly said, pointing proudly to the large sheet of brightly decorated butcher paper. "Everyone in the class wrote me a get-well message." The ten-year-old paused. "Everyone except Eddie Reynolds. He's never forgiven me for striking him out in baseball last year." She rolled her eyes as though to say men were all fools.

"Your friends did a beautiful job."

"Did you see the flowers Dad got me and the new cassette player?"

"Yes, they're very nice."

"I almost ruined my new jacket, but Dad says all we have to do is take it to the cleaners."

"Well, you're certainly looking chipper."

"I feel real good, but the doctor said I have to stay here overnight. Dad's going to come back early in the morning and bring me home. Then tomorrow night he's going to fix my favorite dinner. Will you come, too? Dad's a real good cook, and I have so much I want to show you."

Catherine's eyes shot to Royce's. It was clear she didn't know how to answer Kelly. It was also clear, at least to Royce, that she wanted to be there just as much as he and Kelly wanted her with them.

Chapter Five

"Okay, Dad, we're ready," Kelly called out excitedly from the family room.

Catherine shared a smile with the ten-year-old as Royce wiped his hands dry on a dish towel and wandered in from the kitchen. He was busy with the dinner preparations while Catherine was keeping Kelly entertained.

"See?" Kelly held out her arms, proudly displaying her fingernails. "Aren't they gorgeous?"

As a surprise for Kelly, Catherine had brought along press-on nails, and the two had spent an hour working the dragon-length fire-engine red nails onto the girl's fingers.

"How'd you do that?" Royce blinked and seemed genuinely amazed.

"We have our ways," Catherine said, smiling up at him.

"How long before dinner?" Kelly demanded. "I'm starved. Hospital food leaves a lot to be desired, you know." She was dressed in her pajamas and sitting on the L-shaped sectional with a thick feather pillow propped at one end. According to Royce, the doctor had given instructions to keep Kelly quiet for a day or two. A feat, Catherine was quickly learning, that was easier said than done.

"Hold your horses," Royce teased. "I'm putting the finishing touches on dinner now."

"Can I help?" Catherine offered.

"I want to help, too," Kelly chimed in, tossing aside the orange, yellow and brown hand-knit afghan.

"Stay put, the both of you," Royce insisted. "The table's set. All I need to do is dish up. It'll only take me a few more minutes."

The sight of Royce working in the kitchen had done funny things to Catherine's heart. If the wardroom could only see him now! A dish towel was tucked around his waist in apron fashion, yet it did nothing to disrupt the highly charged effectiveness of his masculine appeal. The sharp edges of his character were smoothly rounded when he was with his daughter, Catherine noted. Gone was the constrained, inflexible commander who ruled with a harsh, but fair hand. Royce Nyland was said to be a man with an iron will. Indeed, Catherine had bumped against it more than once herself. He was also said to be a man with an inner core of steel, but what few realized, what few saw, was that Royce Nyland also possessed a heart of gold. A man of iron. A man of gold.

Catherine had assumed she'd feel uncomfortable in Royce's home. She wasn't entirely sure that their being together like this didn't border on an impropriety, an indiscretion that could have serious consequences for them both. But Royce had been the one who'd seconded Kelly's invitation. They'd all wanted it so badly that Catherine had thrown caution to the wind.

"Dad makes marvelous spaghetti and meatballs," Kelly explained.

"Meat-a-balls," Royce corrected from inside the kitchen. "You can't eat Italian unless you speak it correctly. Try again."

"Meat-a-balls," Kelly returned enthusiastically. For someone who'd been hospitalized only a few hours earlier, the youngster revealed amazing vigor.

"Catherine." He pointed a sauce-coated wooden spoon in her direction.

"Meat-a-balls," she said, imitating his inflection perfectly.

"When are we going to stop talking about them and eat?" Kelly wanted to know. "I've been waiting all day for this."

"Now." Royce appeared and waved his arm toward the dining room. "Dinner is served."

The afghan on Kelly's legs went flying across the back of the sectional as she bounced to her feet. She sauntered into the dining room with her arms stretched out in front of her like a sleepwalker, her fingers splayed in an effort not to touch anything in case her nails weren't dry yet.

"Are you sure she can eat with those things?" Royce asked Catherine out of the corner of his mouth.

"I have a feeling she'll find a way."

Kelly had a problem eating at first, but once she got the hang of working her fork without her nails interfering, everything went smoothly. Although, Catherine had to admit, Kelly's first few attempts resembled something out of a Marx brothers movie.

After dinner, Catherine and Royce cleared the table and lingered over a cup of coffee in the family room.

"I can't remember when I've tasted better meat-a-balls," Catherine said, meaning it. "Kelly's right, you're an excellent cook."

Royce bowed his head, graciously accepting her compliment.

Sipping from her cup, Catherine's gaze drifted to the fireplace and the framed family photograph of Royce, Kelly and a dark-haired woman. It didn't take Catherine long to figure out the strong-featured female had been Royce's wife.

Royce's gaze followed hers. "That was taken a couple of years before the accident."

"She was beautiful."

Royce nodded, but it was clear to Catherine that the subject was a closed one. He didn't want to speak of his marriage any more than she wanted to summarize the details of her best-forgotten engagement to Aaron.

"There's a photograph on my fireplace mantel, too," she told him, struggling to keep the emotion out of her voice. She didn't often speak of her father, but she felt comfortable enough with Royce and Kelly to share this painful part of her life. When she'd finished, Catherine noted that Kelly was struggling to keep her eyes open.

"I think it's time I put her to bed," Royce whispered.

Catherine nodded, stood and took their empty coffee cups into the kitchen. Royce lifted a protesting Kelly into his arms.

"Good night, Catherine," Kelly said, covering her mouth as she yawned. When she finished, she held out her arms for a good-night hug.

Royce carried his daughter into the kitchen, and Catherine quickly gave Kelly a squeeze. Standing that close to Royce, however, feeling him tense as her breasts brushed against his forearm, did bizarre things to her equilibrium. She had barely touched him, in the most innocent of ways, and yet her body had sprung to life with yearning.

Danger. Imaginary red lights started flashing before her eyes, and Catherine knew if Royce and she were going to maintain their platonic relationship, she was going to have to find a way to get out of his home—and fast.

Royce disappeared, and not wanting to leave him with the dishes, she quickly rinsed and stacked them in the dishwasher. She was wiping down the countertop when he reappeared.

"Leave that," he said.

"I can't," she returned quickly, her eyes avoiding him. "My mother and I had this simple rule we followed for years, and now I'm a slave to tradition."

"What was this simple rule?"

Catherine continued wiping far more vigorously than was needed. "Those who cook shouldn't have to do the dishes."

"Catherine." His voice was low and seductive. "Come here."

She swore the tension in the air between them was so thick it could be sliced and buttered. "I think it would be best if I left now, don't you?" Slowly she raised her eyes to his, seeking confirmation.

"No, I don't." He said so much more in those few simple words. He told her he was weary of this constant tension between them. He was through waiting. His patience had reached its endurance level. So had hers, and he knew it. She wanted this, too. Sweet heaven how she wanted it.

Silence swelled between them, but for the first time in recent memory it was a comfortable silence unencumbered with misgivings and uncertainties. They both knew they were unwilling to wait any longer.

Royce took her by the hand and led her to the sectional sofa recently vacated by Kelly, pulling her down so they were side by side. They didn't speak, but there was no need for words, indeed words would have been a drawback.

Royce held her head between his hands and carefully studied her face. The look in his eyes, so earnest and intense, humbled her. They said she was the most beautiful woman in the world. His woman. Catherine wasn't going to argue with him, although she wasn't nearly as beautiful as he seemed to believe. His eyes smoldered with a blue light of yearning. Catherine was convinced his look was a reflection of her own. There was nothing between them. No pretense. No qualms. Only need. A need so honest, so comfortable, it seemed to flow between them like the peaceful waters of a rolling river.

Royce's mouth made a slow descent, and with a sigh,

Catherine closed her eyes and raised her chin to be rewarded with what she'd waited so long to receive.

Catherine thought she was prepared. How wrong she was. How ill equipped. The moment his mouth met hers, she was assaulted with a swarm of warm sensations that came at her with the force of a bulldozer. He was gentle, so gentle. She hadn't expected that. Not when the hunger was so wild. Not when she'd been smothered in sensation long before his mouth found hers.

Catherine was enveloped in tenderness. She'd known from the first that Royce's kiss would be special; she hadn't expected to feel sensations so unbelievably potent that tears crowded the edges of her eyes. Sensations so powerful it was as though she'd never felt anything before this moment.

Royce groaned and slipped his mouth from hers. Burying his face in her hair, he drew in a deep, shuddering breath. He was about to speak, but she intercepted his action by directing his lips back to hers. They both seemed ready this time, prepared to deal with the wealth of sensation, eager to accept it. His tongue sought hers; she met his eagerly with soft, welcoming touches.

They found a rhythm with each other. A cadence. It was as though they were familiar lovers, enjoying a long series of deep, lengthy kisses full of hunger and desperate need. Soon Catherine was clinging mindlessly to Royce. Prepared for anything, for everything.

"I knew it would be like this." He braced his forehead against hers as he drew in several deep, even breaths as though he were struggling to believe all that was between them.

Catherine hadn't known it would be anything close to this wonderful. She hadn't a clue. Nothing could have prepared her for the fierce onslaught of feelings. Her body pulsed with desire, a need so great that she hurt in strange places.

Royce's hands shook slightly as he unfastened the buttons of her gray silk blouse. He peeled it open and released the clasp of her bra, then caught her breasts in his open palms as they sprang free.

Catherine moaned at the fresh onslaught of warm sensations. Her nipples were hard long before Royce caressed them with the callused pads of his thumbs. She thought it impossible, but they tightened even more. The feelings were unfamiliar, this being so needy, so wanting.

Slowly he lowered his mouth to the summit of her breast, capturing the tender nipple between his lips, laving it with the rough edges of his tongue. When Catherine was convinced she could endure no more, he drew it into his mouth and sucked gently. Catherine moaned and buried her fingers in his short hair, needing to touch him. She felt so close to him, closer than she had to anyone. She loved him so much in that moment, it was all she could do not to weep. Royce loved her, too. Catherine was as confident of that as she was of his love for Kelly.

Royce transferred his attention to her other breast, and Catherine groaned once more. She recognized the sound. It was the type of whimpering noise a woman makes when she's ready to make love, ready to receive a man.

Royce apparently recognized it too, and slowly raised his head. His gaze melded with hers, seeking confirmation.

Catherine's heart was in her throat. She wanted him. He wanted her. Oh, sweet heaven, how she wanted him. Royce must have read the need in her eyes and, responding to it, reached for her once more, his hands cupping the undersides of her face.

His mouth found hers in a hot kiss of savage frenzy. He thrust his tongue forward and swept her mouth with a wild kiss that told her he was fast reaching the point of no return. Even as he kissed her, his hands dropped to work open the zipper in the jut of her hip.

Some shred of reasoning, some ray of sanity grasped hold of Catherine's mind before Royce managed to succeed in opening her slacks. Had they both gone crazy? With their very careers on the line, they'd walked into this with their eyes wide open. In one blindingly clear revelation, Catherine knew they had to stop. It wasn't what she wanted. It wasn't what Royce wanted, either. But it was necessary.

"Royce...no." She scrambled from the sectional, her chest heaving with the effort. She had to escape before it was too late, before he kissed her again.

"Catherine?" Her name became a mixture of shock and need. "What's wrong?"

"Nothing," she assured him, so close to tears her voice wobbled like a toy top. "Everything," she amended. She couldn't stand so close to him and not be affected. It was either move away or fall willingly back into his arms. She couldn't resist him; she couldn't think when he was looking at her with such tenderness and concern.

She moved across the room from him, and braced herself against the opposite wall, needing its support. Her heart was beating so hard, the sound ricocheted around the room, each beat stronger, each beat louder. Surely Royce could hear. Surely he knew.

"We can't do it...we can't," she whispered, fighting back the tears. "Don't you understand how foolish it would be for us both..."

Royce moved off the sofa and walked purposely toward her. "Why not? Kelly's upstairs asleep...."

"Please, oh, please, don't argue with me. This is hard enough...so hard." Explaining would have depleted her of the strength she needed to follow through with her resolve.

Capturing her hands in his own, Royce lifted them above her head, and then, leaning forward, boxed her in with his muscled arms. His body was so close, she could feel the heat radiating off him.

"Royce," she pleaded once again, rolling her head to one side.

His thighs, taut and hard, pressed against her. It wasn't the only part of his anatomy that was hard, and that was pressed against her as well. Catherine moaned as the excitement shuddered through her, and dropped her head, weakening. It would be so easy to swirl her hips, to move against him. She longed to savor his strength, his power. It would be so easy to surrender to the gnawing need.

"Royce, what?" His mouth was so close, so warm. He nudged his nose against her earlobe, then took it gently between his teeth and sucked. Once again wild excitement seized her, and it was all she could do to keep from buckling against him.

"Don't…oh, please, don't." But her pleas lacked conviction. If anything they sounded more like a siren's call, an inducement to continue doing the very things he was.

"You taste so sweet," he murmured, dragging his mouth down the slope of her neck, then taking nibbling kisses at the scented hollow of her throat. Catherine moaned and rotated her head, granting him access to his desires. And he did desire her. It was as if a giant storehouse of need had been building in both of them, and had burst open all at once.

His mouth found hers, his kisses hot, filled with an untamed urgency, his hunger as raw as her own. His tongue swept her mouth, and before she realized what she was doing, Catherine pulled her hands free from his and grabbed at his shirt, demanding more and more, holding on. Royce answered by ravishing her mouth in a kiss so blistering, so carnal that any and all resistance in Catherine melted.

Pinning her against the wall with his hips, Royce started to move against her. Their kisses were so fiery, the air sizzled. The night sizzled. They sizzled.

Abruptly Royce dragged his mouth from hers. "Tell me you want this as much as I do," he whispered. His voice was thick and hot. So hot against her skin his breath alone was enough to scorch her.

That Royce would need her assurance touched something deep within Catherine. "Oh, Royce, yes…only…"

"What?"

"Only I won't be able to hide the way I feel if we make love. Not from anyone." Monday morning Elaine Perkins would guess what had happened between her and Royce. Catherine didn't doubt it for a moment. "I'm not nearly as good at disguising my feelings as you. It's hard enough now, but if we make love…if we do this… Everyone will know."

Royce went still for several heart-stopping moments before making a low, guttural sound of frustration and defeat. His shoulders heaved once as he rolled away from her and pressed his own back against the wall. "You're right."

"If I'm so right, then why is it so damned hard?"

"I don't know." He spoke through gritted teeth as he reined in his desire.

Catherine felt like weeping. "What are we going to do?"

Royce expelled his breath forcefully. "The hell if I know. I just hope to God the Navy appreciates this." Straightening, he heaved in one giant breath, squared his shoulders and with some effort managed to snap her bra closed. Then with deliberate businesslike movements he fastened her blouse, kissed her one last time sweetly, gently and whispered, "Now go, before I change my mind."

"Morning, Dad," Kelly said as she walked into the kitchen, dressed in her housecoat and slippers. She pulled out the chair and reached for a section of the Sunday paper. "What time did Catherine go home last night?"

"Early." Too damn early, Royce mused. Unfortunately

it hadn't been soon enough. Royce couldn't believe how far matters had developed the night before. How far he'd *let* them develop. He'd never been closer to defying Navy regulations. If the commanding officer were to learn he was having an affair with Catherine Fredrickson, their lives would be ruined. Royce had seen it once before. An acquaintance had fallen in love with a woman in his command. They'd been discreet, or so they believed. Eventually it was discovered and they were investigated. No allowances had been made. No leeway given. Both parties involved had been immediately court-martialed.

Royce didn't know what the hell he'd been thinking. That was just it. He *wasn't* thinking. Thank God Catherine had the presence of mind to call an end to matters when she had. She was right. If they made love, neither one of them would have been able to continue with the pretense. True, Catherine was far more readable than he was, but Royce knew himself well enough to recognize there would be problems with him, too. Major problems.

"Can I call Catherine?" Kelly asked, reaching across the table for the comics.

"I don't think that would be a good idea."

"Why not?"

Royce wasn't in any mood to argue with his daughter, and his voice was sharp when he spoke. "Because I said you couldn't. I don't want any arguments about this, Kelly. Catherine is off limits." To them both, unfortunately.

Kelly gave him an indignant look, scooted out of her chair and stalked out of the kitchen. Just before she reached the doorway, she bolted around and glared at him. "Sometimes you're an unreasonable grouch."

If Kelly thought he was bad now, give him another six months of working side by side with Catherine, knowing he'd never be able to hold her or kiss her again.

* * *

"What's with Commander Nyland?" Elaine Perkins questioned when Catherine returned from a session in court early Friday afternoon. Catherine had been in and out of the office all week acting as prosecutor on a series of criminal trials. If Royce's mood had been anything other than normal, she hadn't noticed.

"What's wrong?" she asked, setting a load of files down on her desk.

"If I knew that I wouldn't be asking you. He's been in a bad mood all week, making unreasonable demands on himself and everyone else. You would think once he found out his daughter wasn't badly hurt he'd be in a good mood. If anything it's gotten worse."

"If Commander Nyland has a problem, trust me, he isn't going to share it with me." Catherine did her best to maintain the pretense that she and Royce did nothing more than work together. She hadn't talked to him outside the office all week. The fact didn't trouble her; they both needed distance to put order to their thoughts.

Now that she thought about it, Catherine was willing to admit that Elaine did have a point. Royce seemed to be putting in plenty of hours, making too many demands on himself and consequently everyone else. He'd never gone out for any personality awards, nor was he in a popularity contest. If that were the case he'd lose hands down.

A couple of the other clerks rolled back their chairs. "Ever read much about arctic seals, Lieutenant Commander?" Elaine Perkins asked as the others slowly gathered around the secretary's desk.

"No." Catherine wondered what the men were up to.

"Apparently when danger is near they gather on a floating iceberg. The problem is they don't know when the danger has passed and so a sacrificial seal is thrown into the water. If he survives the others know it's safe to leave the iceberg."

Catherine stared at the small party of men gathered around Elaine's desk. A couple had leaned forward, pressing their hands to her desktop. "So?" Catherine demanded, not liking the sounds of this.

"We just voted you to be our sacrificial seal."

"What?" If she hadn't been so amused, she might have been concerned. Apparently she hadn't done as good a job as she'd hoped, hiding her feelings for Royce. The staff seemed to think she had some influence with their XO. A dangerous sign.

"It makes sense for you to be the one to approach him," Elaine explained before Catherine could ask why they'd bestowed the dubious honor upon her. "Commander Nyland may have all the sensitivity of seaweed, but he's still a man, and as such he's as susceptible as the rest of us to a pretty face."

"And what exactly am I supposed to say to him?"

"I don't have a clue. You're supposed to figure that out yourself. Just do whatever it is you do to put a man into a better mood."

"Please do it soon," Seaman Webster added. "I've had to type the same paper five times. He wants it perfect. The last time I had a comma out of place, and you would have thought the free world was in jeopardy."

"Sorry, fellows," Catherine said, walking back into her office, ignoring them as much as possible. She was staying away from this situation with Royce with a ten-foot pole. "You picked the wrong lady to do your dirty work for you. If Commander Nyland's in a foul mood, you'll ride it out together the way you always have. Furthermore I find your attitude highly chauvinistic."

"Oh, I agree," Elaine Perkins commented. "But we're desperate."

"I said no," she returned crisply. "And I mean it."

There was a fair amount of grumbling, but the staff gradually returned to their desks. Elaine Perkins, however, continued to study Catherine. "I thought you and the commander were friends."

"We are," Catherine said, doing her best to keep her tone light and unaffected.

"I understood that the two of you jogged together most afternoons."

Catherine wondered when she'd heard that and from whom. "Not anymore. I usually run in the mornings."

"Damn. I was hoping you might be able to talk to him casually some afternoon, find out what's bugging him. There isn't any need to make the rest of us suffer just because he's unhappy about something."

"Are you suffering, Mrs. Perkins?" Royce demanded from behind Catherine's secretary in a voice so cold, the words froze in midair.

Elaine went pale. "No, sir," she answered briskly.

"I'm glad to hear it." He hesitated long enough to look toward Catherine. "I'd like the Ellison report on my desk before you leave tonight."

"Yes, sir," Catherine returned just as crisply. She was hours from being anywhere close to finishing the report. Royce must have known it. Apparently she, too, was to receive the brunt of his foul mood, but then why should she be different from anyone else?

With that, Royce returned to his office and closed the door.

Elaine slumped back into her chair and released her breath in a slow exercise. "He wants you to have that report done by tonight?" she moaned.

"Don't worry, it won't take me long." Longer than she would have liked, but that couldn't be helped.

"Do you want me to stay and type it up for you?"

Catherine appreciated the offer, but it wasn't necessary. "No, thanks, it won't take me long."

"Aren't you furious with him?" Elaine asked under her breath, her gaze leveled on the closed door that led to Royce's office.

"No." Maybe she should be, but Catherine had learned long before that Royce's bark was far worse than his bite. She said as much to Elaine.

"Right, but you don't seem to be the one he's biting all the time."

The humor drained out of Catherine. The more she thought about Elaine's comment, the more concerned she became. Was it true? Had Royce given her more slack than the other members of his staff? Apparently they'd all felt the brunt of his bad mood in the past several days. But if what Elaine Perkins said was true, something had to be done, and quickly.

Catherine waited until later that same afternoon when Royce went down to the track. She gave him enough time to run several laps before she joined him. He looked over at her and frowned, his look so dark and uninviting that a shiver of apprehension moved over her. "The Ellison report is on your desk."

"Is there a problem?" He hadn't decreased his speed any, and she was having a problem maintaining his pace.

"Ah...ever hear of a sacrificial seal?"

"I beg your pardon?"

"Nothing...forget I said that."

They ran half a lap, then he turned to stare at her again. His eyes were cold, his look detached. That should have pleased her, should have assured her Elaine was imagining things, but it didn't. "We might have a problem."

"Is that a fact, Lieutenant Commander? Thank you so much for taking it upon yourself to inform me of this."

"More than...the usual problem."

"And what, tell me, is the *usual* problem?"

"There isn't any need to be so damned sarcastic," she said, affronted by his attitude.

"Isn't there?" he returned. "What do I have to do, order you off this track? I thought I'd made myself clear about the subject of us jogging together."

"You did, but…"

"Then kindly respect my wishes."

The wall was back in place, so firmly erected that Catherine was left to wonder if everything that had blossomed between them was a figment of her imagination. Royce was so cold. So caustic.

"What about my wishes?" she asked softly.

Royce came to an abrupt halt. His blue eyes had never been more piercing. "Listen, Lieutenant Commander, you have no wishes. If you didn't learn that early in your Navy career then we have a real problem. I'm your executive officer. You will do what I say, when I say it, without question. Is that understood?"

Catherine swallowed back a cry of protest. She blinked and nodded. "Yes, sir."

"Good. Now stay off this track from five o'clock on." He made it sound like a direct order, when in fact he had no right to tell her when she could or couldn't be on the track.

"Is that clear?" he demanded.

"Very clear, sir." The "sir" was shouted.

"Good." There was no regret in his voice. No emotion. Only a wall so high and so thick, Catherine doubted she'd ever be able to scale its heights again.

Chapter Six

The phone was ringing when Catherine let herself into her apartment Saturday afternoon. Setting the bag of groceries on the kitchen counter and ignoring Sambo's protest over being ignored, she lurched for the receiver.

"Hello," she said, fighting breathlessness.

"Hi." It was Kelly, that much Catherine could tell, but it sounded like Royce's daughter was talking with her head inside a bucket.

"Kelly?"

"Yeah, it's me."

"What's wrong?"

"Nothing. It's just that I'm not supposed to be calling you, and if Dad finds out I'm in big trouble. I've got the phone cord stretched into the closet and I'm whispering as loud as I can. Can you hear me all right?"

"Just barely. Now tell me what's up." Catherine did her best to ignore the pain of Royce's most recent order.

"You still like me and my Dad, don't you?"

"Oh, yes, sweetheart, of course I do." But it was more complicated than that, and Catherine couldn't allow the youngster to go on thinking matters could continue the way they had. "There are problems, though."

"I know, Dad explained everything to me." Kelly

paused, and Catherine could hear the frustration and disappointment hum over the telephone wire with every word the youngster spoke. "Sometimes I hate the Navy."

"Don't," Catherine pleaded softly. "Those rules were made for a very good reason."

"But Dad said we couldn't have you over to the house anymore and that we couldn't go to the movies or go out to dinner or things like that. He said it would be best if I forgot all about you because that was what he was going to do."

Kelly's words went through Catherine like a steel point. The pain was so sharp and so real that she swallowed hard and bit her lower lip.

"I don't want to forget about you," the ten-year-old whispered, her voice trembling as if she were close to tears, "I kept thinking that Dad and you…that you might be my mom someday. I asked God to send me a mom, especially one with pretty fingernails, and then Dad met you and he was listening to me when I asked him about getting me a baby sister and then all of a sudden…"

"And now everything looks so bad. I won't forget you, sweetheart, and the Navy doesn't have anything to say about the two of us being special friends."

"It doesn't?"

"Not in the least. We'll give your dad and me time to work matters out at the office, and once everything is settled there, I'll invite you over for the night and we can order pizza and rent a movie and we'll do our fingernails."

"Oh, Catherine, could we really? I'd like that so much."

"I'd like that, too."

There was a bit of commotion behind Kelly that sounded like a door being jerked opened. "I've got to go now, *Missy*," Kelly said deliberately loud, placing heavy emphasis on her friend's name.

"I take it your dad just opened the closet door?" Catherine asked, unable to contain a smile.

"Right."

"All right, sweetheart. Now listen, it probably would be best if you didn't phone me again for a while. But I promise I'll talk to your dad…"

"Only do it soon, okay?" she pleaded.

"I will, I promise," Catherine pledged, feeling more depressed than ever.

The despair had grown heavier and more oppressive a week later. Royce hadn't spoken one unnecessary word to her in all that time. It was as though she were invisible. A necessary body that filled a space. Necessary to the legal department, but not necessary for him. If Royce did happen to glance in her direction it was by accident, and it seemed he looked straight through her.

The weekend hadn't been much better. Catherine couldn't remember a Saturday and Sunday that felt more empty. On Saturday she'd done busywork around her apartment and answered mail. At least her good friend Brand Davis from Hawaii was happy, she mulled, reading over the wedding invitation. Then on Sunday, after church services, she'd attended a matinee and cooked a meal she didn't feel like eating, and ended up giving the leftovers to Sambo, who apparently wasn't interested, either.

Outwardly everything was as it always had been, but inside Catherine felt empty. As empty as a black hole. How stark her life felt, how barren. Until she'd met Royce, she'd been blissfully unaware of the lonely nothingness of her life. Royce had stirred her soul to life, and now she hungered for someone to share the everyday routine, someone to give meaning to her bleak existence.

The single red rose in a crystal stem vase was sitting on her desk waiting for her when she walked into the office Monday morning. Her heart quickened at the beauty of the delicate flower, but she knew immediately it couldn't, wouldn't be from Royce. He wasn't a man who would allow a rose to do his speaking for him. He wasn't a man to indulge in such romantic extravagances.

A card was pinned to the shiny red ribbon attached to the narrow vase. Catherine stared at the envelope for several moments, calculating in her mind who would have given her a rose.

"Aren't you going to read who it's from?" Elaine asked, much too casually to fool Catherine.

"In time." She unpinned the card and slipped it free of the small envelope. The name was scrawled across the face of the card in bold, even strokes. She grinned, somewhat amused. It was exactly who she thought it would be. Knowing Elaine was watching her, she replaced the card in the envelope, then set the rose on the edge of her desk.

"Well?" Elaine demanded impatiently. "Who sent it?"

"My, my, aren't you the nosy one?"

"If you must know, it's a little more than idle curiosity."

Catherine pulled out her chair and sat down. "I suppose you've got money riding on this."

"Ten bucks." Then without hesitation, she asked, "Commander Parker, right?"

Catherine grinned and nodded.

"I knew it all along," Elaine said, grinning broadly.

Catherine was pleased her secretary took such delight in the fact Commander Dan Parker had seen fit to flatter her with a red rose, but frankly, her secretary was more thrilled about it than she was.

Her lack of appreciation, Catherine realized, could be attributed to the fact she realized what was sure to follow. An invitation she didn't want to accept. It happened just as she suspected, just when she was preparing to leave the office that same afternoon. Commander Parker strolled into the room, grinning boyishly.

"Good afternoon, Catherine," he greeted, and struck a

casual pose. He was tall and reasonably good-looking, his features well defined. From the scuttlebutt Catherine had picked up around the base, Dan Parker had the reputation of being a playboy.

"Good afternoon, Commander," she responded formally, wanting to keep it impersonal.

His gaze drifted over to her desk, where she'd left the rose. "I see you found my little surprise."

"It was very thoughtful of you," she said, eyeing the door, anxious to get away. The office was deserted, and she didn't want to get stuck in a long, boring conversation with a man she had no interest in cultivating a relationship with.

"I'm pleased you enjoyed it so much."

"It's lovely." She reached for her coat and slipped into it, doing her best to give the appearance that she was about to leave. Anything that would cut short this game of cat and mouse.

Commander Parker would ask her out, and she'd decline. Then he'd give her his well-practiced hurt-little-boy look, and she'd be required to spend the next ten minutes making up some excuse why she wouldn't go out with him. Something that would soothe the ruffled feathers of his substantial male ego.

"I don't suppose you have plans Friday night?" he asked right on cue.

"Sorry, I'm busy." Which was true. She planned on changing Sambo's litter box. Not exactly an exciting prospect, but it gave credence to her words. She looped the strap of her purse over her shoulder, determined not to play the game.

"I was hoping you'd let me take you to dinner."

"Another time perhaps," she suggested, heading toward the door.

"What about the Birthday Ball?" Every October the

Navy celebrated its birthday with an elaborate ball. The celebration was coming later this year because the admiral had been gone. "It's two weeks away, and I was hoping you'd accompany me."

Catherine didn't have a single excuse. Her presence would be expected, but she hadn't given the matter of a date more than a fleeting thought.

The idea of spending the evening with anyone other than Royce didn't interest her. Her attitude was excessively stupid. They'd be able to dance once, maybe twice without raising suspicions. Risking anything more than that would be foolish in the extreme. The way matters were between them presently, it was doubtful Royce would go anywhere near her.

"Catherine," Dan prodded. "The Birthday Ball?"

She forced herself to smile as though it was a difficult decision. "I appreciate the invitation, in fact I'm flattered, but no thanks. I'm…I've decided to go stag this year. It's nothing personal, Dan."

Commander Parker's smile didn't waver, neither did the light in his dark eyes dim, if anything it brightened. Slowly, without hesitation, he raised his hand and ran one finger down the side of her cheek. "I think I know why."

Catherine's heart thundered against her chest with alarm. She stared up at him and blinked, certain he could read everything she felt for Royce like a notice on a bulletin board.

"Don't worry," he whispered sympathetically, "your secret is safe with me."

Squaring her shoulders, Catherine's only choice was to pretend he couldn't be more wrong. "I don't know what you're talking about. I prefer to attend the Birthday Ball alone this year, and whatever connotation you put on that decision is of your own making."

Dan chuckled. "You're right, of course. Absolutely

right." He straightened and was about to leave when he turned back, his friendly eyes suddenly somber and dark. "Good luck, Catherine, but be careful. Understand?"

Before she could continue with the pretense, Catherine nodded. "I will."

Royce was in a foul mood, but that wasn't anything new. He'd been in a dangerous one for nearly two weeks, and frankly he couldn't see it lessening anytime soon. The fact he'd recently spoken to Dan Parker hadn't improved his disposition any. Of all the foolish, mule-headed deeds Catherine had committed since he'd met her, rejecting Dan's invitation to the Birthday Ball took the cake. He'd like to wring her skinny neck.

"Ha," he said aloud, discrediting his thoughts. The last thing he wanted was to see Catherine suffer. Anytime he was within ten feet of her it was all he could do not to haul her into his arms and breathe in the fresh, womanly scent that was hers alone. He wanted to drink in her softness, savor her warmth and her love. He needed her so damn much, he was about to go out of his mind.

Royce didn't know what the hell he was going to do. One thing for sure, they couldn't continue like this much longer.

Royce had done everything he could think to do to forget her. He was working himself into an early grave, spending all kinds of extra hours at the office. Kelly was barely speaking to him, and he'd lost just about every friend he'd made in seventeen years of military service.

Something had to be done, and fast, before he ended up destroying himself and in the process, Catherine, too. He just didn't know what the hell the solution was.

A polite knock on his door interrupted his thoughts. Whoever it was possessed the courage of David facing Goliath to confront Royce in his current mood.

"Come in," he barked.

When Catherine opened the door, Royce's heart dropped to his knees. What now? He couldn't be any less encouraging than the last time they spoke. He couldn't have been any more sarcastic. No matter what he said, no matter what he did, she just kept coming back. By heaven, that woman was stubborn.

"Yes?" he demanded, giving the illusion of being busy, too busy to be intruded upon.

"I need to talk to you."

How sweet her voice sounded, how soft and feminine. Royce had lain awake nights tormented by the memory of her making delicate, whimpering love sounds. How close he'd come to breaking the very code of honor he'd sworn to uphold.

"There's nothing more to say," he said, forcefully pushing all thoughts of her and that night from his mind. "I thought I made that fact perfectly clear." His voice was as brittle and hard as he could make it.

"It's about Kelly."

"My daughter is none of your business, Lieutenant Commander." Royce felt as though he'd been kicked in the stomach. Catherine had no way of knowing that Kelly continued to bring up her name night and day until he'd absolutely forbidden his own daughter to speak of her.

"If you have no objection, I'd like Kelly to spend the weekend with me and…"

"No." The word was edged with steel.

"Wanting to spend time with Kelly has nothing to do with you and me," Catherine insisted softly. "But everything to do with Kelly. She needs…"

"I'll be the one to determine my daughter's needs."

The silence between them stretched to ear-splitting proportions. Royce half expected the window glass to shatter under the pressure. Neither spoke. Neither daring. Neither willing to give an inch.

Royce feared an inch would soon lead to two and three, and before he could stop himself, he and Catherine would become lovers. The very word brought a tight hardening to his loins. It didn't take much for his tormented mind to envision her soft and willing beneath him, opening her life and her heart to him. The ache grew worse, but he wasn't sure which hurt worse: the pain in his loins, or the one in his heart.

"I understand you turned down Commander Parker's invitation to the Birthday Ball," he said when it became apparent she was going to continue with the same argument. His best tactic, he decided, was to change the subject.

"How'd you know that?" she asked, her beautiful dark eyes narrowing.

"Dan told me."

"Like hell, he did," she flared. "Commander Parker is a typical man. He isn't likely to tell anyone I refused his offer unless he was asked and…" She paused, and a deep shade of red seeped steadily up her neck and invaded her cheeks. "You…you asked him to invite me, didn't you?" She made it sound as though he'd attempted to involve her in treason. "You went to Dan and encouraged him to take me to…to the Birthday Ball." She closed her eyes momentarily, as though mortified to the very marrow of her bones.

"Listen, Catherine…"

Leaning forward, she pressed her hands against the side of his desk. "How dare you."

"You're out of order here, Lieutenant Commander." Royce could see he was digging himself in deeper than he intended. The most expedient way of extracting himself was to pull rank. Not the wisest means, but the most practical.

She ignored him as she straightened, then started pacing the length of his office, her steps clipped and angry. "You have one hell of a nerve, Royce. What makes you think you can rule my life?"

"Our discussion is over." He reached for his pen and commenced writing. He didn't know if a single word was legible, but that wasn't the point. Catherine, her eyes bright with unshed tears, stared at him with her heart on her sleeve. He had to get her out of his office before he did something foolish. Before he succumbed to what would, in the end, destroy them both.

"Why?" she asked. The lone word was saturated with emotion.

"You know the answer to that," he informed her stiffly, fighting back the urge to shout at her. She wasn't stupid; surely she could figure out his motives on her own.

"You honestly think it would help if I were to become involved with Dan?" Her words were low and disbelieving. When he didn't answer right away, she raised her voice. "Do you?"

"This discussion would be better left for another time," Royce informed her in his best military voice. "You may leave now." This was the tone he used often, expecting immediate and unquestioned compliance to his words.

"No way," she said, then stalked across the room and slammed closed the door, although they both knew they were alone. "We won't discuss this another time, because we're going to have this out here and now."

Royce bolted to his feet, as angry now as she. "If you value your commission, Lieutenant Commander, then I suggest you do as I ask."

She didn't so much as blink. "What exactly have you *asked?* That I date Commander Parker?"

"It certainly wouldn't hurt matters any," he said pointedly. She knotted her fist at her side, and Royce had the impression she did so in an effort to hold on to her anger, and it required both hands.

"It may come as something of a surprise to you, Commander Nyland, but it's none of the Navy's business whom I date. It most certainly isn't any of yours!"

"In this case it is." Royce amazed himself by remaining calm, at least on the outside. Inside, he was a mess, something he wasn't willing to admit often, but Catherine had driven him to the outer edges of sanity.

"What makes you think dating Dan would help either of us? Answer me! I'm downright curious."

"Just do it, Catherine, for both our sakes."

"No," she cried, "if you want me out of your life, that's your business, but I refuse to make it easy for you."

A tear rolled down the side of her face, her precious sweet face, and it was all Royce could do not to reach out and comfort her. He slumped back in his chair and rammed all ten fingers through his hair in an urgent effort to regain control of himself. Shouting at each other wasn't going to accomplish anything. Neither was pretending.

"Sit down, Catherine," he instructed, motioning toward the chair.

"I prefer to stand." She was as stiff as plastic, eyes focused straight ahead. The evidence of that lone tear or any others had long since vanished.

"Fine. Have it your way." The fight was out of him, and he leaned back in his chair and braced his index fingers beneath his chin the way he did when he needed to think. "You were right," he stated after a while.

She blinked as though she wasn't sure she'd heard him correctly. "About what?"

"About what would happen if we'd made love that night."

Catherine's eyes briefly found his. "Even if everyone in the entire office hadn't guessed afterward, it would have been wrong."

"Only because the rule book claims it is," she argued. Her look told him the love between them was right, and always would be, no matter what the Navy decreed.

"No," he argued, gaining conviction. "Don't you understand? Can't you see? That night would have only been the beginning. Once we crossed the physical boundaries, there'd be no going back for either of us."

"I agree, but that doesn't make it wrong."

"We'd live in constant fear of being discovered, of someone, anyone finding out the truth," he continued with conviction. "We'd both make an effort, but it wouldn't be long before we'd be so desperate for each other that we'd be meeting in out-of-the-way spots—"

"We wouldn't," she cried, shaking her head in denial.

"Renting cheap hotel rooms," he added, and cringed inwardly at the thought. Catherine was too much a lady for clandestine meetings in dirty rooms. An affair would destroy the warm, generous woman he'd come to love. An affair would destroy them both. What had started out so pure and good would become tarnished and ugly. In the end it would devastate them both. He loved her too much to put her through that kind of heartache.

"No," she cried a second time, "we wouldn't let it go that far."

"Do you honestly think we'd be able to stop? Do you?" he demanded.

Catherine had gone terribly pale, so pale that Royce was tempted to take her by the hand and lead her to a chair before she collapsed. He was grateful when she chose to sit of her own accord.

"What about your transfer?" she asked, lifting her eyes to his.

Her gentle pleading was back, and it cut deep at his heart to deny her anything. If he had received the NATO assignment, although it meant they'd be separated by thousands of miles, the Navy restrictions would no longer apply.

"What I heard was a rumor," he reminded her, "nothing more. It's not going to happen." Kelly would be able to remain with him, but the blessings were mixed ones. His life with his daughter would go on without disruption, but he was going to be forced to drive the woman he loved out of his life.

"I see," she murmured, her words layered with defeat.

"What happened that Saturday night was entirely my fault." Royce felt he should admit that much. "I was so sure I was going to receive that transfer that I let matters go too far. Way too far. Monday morning I learned Commander Wayne Nelson out of San Diego had been given the assignment."

"It isn't necessary to assign blame."

In theory Royce agreed with her, but he wanted to accept the responsibility. He'd felt so close to Catherine that evening. Closer than he had to anyone ever. They'd kissed, and the sensation had struck him as powerfully as a bolt of lightning. It seemed melodramatic to compare her touch with the forces of nature, but Royce could think of no other way to describe it. His skin had felt branded by her gentleness, and his heart…his heart had swollen with a love so strong it left him weak and trembling. He'd never desired a woman more than he had Catherine that night.

It wasn't until later, after Royce learned that the NATO assignment had gone to an acquaintance of his, that he realized his mistake. He'd lowered his guard, allowed to happen what he'd promised himself never would. As a result, he was faced with an even more difficult problem than before.

"What about Kelly?" Catherine asked, her voice so thin he could barely hear her. Slowly she raised those same pleading eyes to his. She seemed to be saying how unfair it was to punish the little girl for something that was beyond Kelly's control.

Royce had learned early in life that the book on fair had yet to be written. He wanted to do what was right for his daughter, but he couldn't do or say anything that would mislead the ten-year-old into thinking there could be a relationship between him and Catherine.

"It's a delicate situation, and best left alone," he said reluctantly.

"No," Catherine argued with surprising strength. "I won't let you do it. I won't use Kelly…you have my word on that—but she needs a woman just now, and I…I seem to be the one she's reaching out to. Please, Royce…"

He hesitated. Saying no to Catherine was as difficult as refusing his own flesh and blood. "All right," he agreed, praying he was doing the right thing.

"We sat up all night and talked and talked and talked, and Catherine painted my toenails and she even let me paint hers."

"So you had a good time?"

"The best." Kelly squeezed him tight around the stomach. Friday night and all day Saturday the house had been as quiet as a tomb. Royce had aimlessly walked around feeling lost and alone. Kelly had spent the night with friends before, and he'd never felt as he had this time. This particular aloneness. Perhaps it was because he'd wanted to be with Catherine so much himself.

By noon, he found himself glancing at the clock every five minutes. When Catherine dropped Kelly off around three, it was all he could do not to run outside and greet her. Only it wasn't Kelly he was so eager to see.

It was Catherine.

Hell, he'd been a fool to think this was going to work.

"…I don't think she's feeling very well, though."

Royce heard the tail end of his daughter's comment as she blurted out the details of each and every minute she and Catherine had been together.

"What makes you say that?" Royce asked, trying to hide his concern behind a casual facade.

"We went shopping, and then…oh," Kelly cried excitedly, "I nearly forgot to show you, Catherine bought me a surprise. Just a minute and I'll go get it." Before he could divert Kelly back to his original question, she was racing up the stairs. Two minutes later, she returned wearing a pair of hot pink earmuffs. She put them on her head, then twirled around to show him the full effect.

"Aren't they cute?"

"Beautiful. Now what makes you think Catherine isn't feeling well?" Gone was the carefully concealed apprehension.

"Oh." Kelly frowned and removed the earmuffs. "After lunch we went out for Mexican food and Catherine ordered a chili something…"

"That explains it," Royce teased.

"No. She wasn't feeling bad until she got her mail. I think it had something to do with that. She opened a letter, and the next thing I knew she was staring out the window, looking real spacey. I think she might have been crying, but when I asked her, she said she had something in her eye."

The gutsy woman Royce knew wouldn't easily give in to tears unless something was drastically wrong.

Kelly hesitated. "I think she was crying, though…I don't know. Catherine's not the type to let on about that sort of thing."

"What happened next?" he pressed, losing patience.

"Well, she made herself a cup of tea and said it was time to run me home. I didn't want to come back so soon, but I didn't say so because I knew she wanted to be alone."

"How did things go on the ride home?" Royce was beginning to feel like a detective, ferreting out each bit of information he could.

"She was real quiet. That's why I think she's not feeling very good."

Catherine was on Royce's mind for the remainder of the day. Hell, what was so unusual about that, he asked himself as he turned out the lights before heading up to bed. The beautiful Lieutenant Commander was in his mind about ninety-nine percent of the time, despite his best efforts to forget about her. Having Kelly chatter about her for hours on end certainly didn't help matters any.

Royce swore the kid had talked nonstop from the moment Catherine had let her off at the door. She'd repeated everything two and three times, so excited about every detail of their time together. Royce hadn't realized how much Kelly needed a mother's influence.

As was his habit, Royce read each night. It helped relax him. He expected to have a difficult time falling asleep, but as soon as he turned out the light, he felt himself effortlessly drifting off.

A phone call, especially one in the middle of the night, was never good news. It rang, waking Royce from a deep sleep. He groaned and groped for the receiver, dragging it across the empty pillow at his side.

"Yes?" he demanded.

Silence.

Royce scrambled into a sitting position. Something told him it was Catherine on the other end of the line. Some inner instinct.

"Catherine?" he asked, his heart racing. "Answer me. What's wrong?"

Chapter Seven

Catherine felt like an idiot, phoning Royce in the middle of the night. She didn't know what had prompted her to do anything so foolish, nor did she know what she intended to say once he picked up the receiver. As soon as he answered, she realized her folly and was about to disconnect the line when he called her name.

"H-how'd you know it was me?" She pushed the hair off her forehead and drew in soft, catching gasps in an effort to stop the flow of tears that refused to cease.

"It was a good guess," Royce admitted gently. "Now tell me what's wrong."

If only he'd been outraged, instead of caring. She might have been able to avoid telling him, but she needed him so desperately—as desperately as she'd ever needed anyone. "I'm fine, really I am," she lied. "It's just that I'm a little out of sorts and…" She couldn't admit to him she hadn't wept, really down-and-out wept in years, and once the tears had started, it was like a dam bursting over a restraining wall. Nothing she tried to do helped.

"Catherine, love, it's two-thirty in the morning. You wouldn't have phoned if everything was peachy keen."

She swallowed a sob and knew the noise she made

sounded as though she were drowning, going underwater for the third and last time. "Thank you."

"For what?"

She gnawed on the corner of her lip and ran a tissue under her nose. "For calling me your love. I…need that right now." She was convinced he had no idea he'd used the affectionate term.

He hesitated, then gently pried again. "Are you going to tell me what's wrong?"

Catherine sat curled up on her sofa, her feet tucked beneath her. The pages of her mother's letter were scattered across the top of her coffee table. She'd moved the picture of her father down from the mantel and set it in front of her as well. For part of the night she'd held it to her breast and rocked to and fro in a frantic effort to hold on to him. The area around her was strewn with used tissues.

"Catherine," Royce repeated. "What's wrong?"

"I…I shouldn't have phoned. I'm sorry…I was going to hang up, but then you said my name."

"I'll be right over."

"Royce, no…please don't." She couldn't deal with him, not now. In addition, her apartment complex was full of Navy personnel. If anyone were to see Royce coming in or out of her apartment in the early hours of the morning, it could be disastrous.

"Then tell me what's troubling you."

Catherine reached for another tissue. "I got a letter from my mother…" she sobbed. A fresh batch of hot tears coursed down her face, streaking it with glistening trails of pain. Even now, hours after reading the letter, her mother's news had the power to wrench her heart. "You're going to think I'm so stupid to be this upset."

"I won't think anything of the sort."

"She's getting married. I don't expect you to understand…how can you when I don't understand myself…but it's like she's turning her back on my father after all these years. She loved him so much. She deserves to be happy but I can't help thinking… there'll be no one to remember…my dad."

"Just because your mother's marrying doesn't mean she's forgetting your father."

"I've been telling myself that all night, but it just doesn't seem to sink into my heart. I'm happy…for h-her." Catherine sobbed so hard her shoulders shook. "I'm really p-pleased. She's been dating Norman for ten years. It isn't that this is any surprise…I don't even know why I'm crying, but now I can't seem to stop. I feel like such a fool…I'm sorry I woke you. Please go back to sleep and forget I—"

"No," he whispered softly. "There's an old road off Byron Way. Just head north and you can't miss it. I'll meet you there in thirty minutes."

"Royce…" She meant to tell him to forget everything, that she was overreacting, behaving like an insecure child. Instead she found herself asking, "What about Kelly?"

"I'll have a friend come over. If he can't, I'll bring her along. Don't worry." The buzzing noise told her he'd hung up the receiver.

She shouldn't meet him. Catherine told herself that at least a dozen times as she drove down Byron Way. It wasn't fair to Royce to drag him out of bed in the middle of the night to an obscure road just because she couldn't deal with the fact her mother was marrying Norman. Dear, sweet Norman, who'd loved her mother for years and years, who'd patiently waited for her to love him enough to let go of the past.

Catherine managed to hold back the emotion while she struggled to find the road Royce had mentioned, but she felt as unstable as a hundred-year-old prairie farmhouse in a tornado. The first gust of wind and she'd collapse.

Royce was standing outside his car, waiting for her. The moonlight reflected off the hood, illuminating his face, which was creased with anxiety.

Catherine pulled off to the side of the road and turned off her engine. She didn't need a mirror to tell her she looked like hell warmed over, as her mother so often teased. Her eyes were red and swollen, and heaven only knew which direction her hair was pointing.

None of that seemed to matter when Royce walked over to her. He stared down on her as if she were a beauty queen, as if she were the most attractive woman in the world. His world. His eyes wandered over her face, and he raised his hand and caressed her cheek with his fingers.

If he hadn't been so gentle she might have been able to pull it off. She might have been able to convince him she was fine, thank him for his concern and then blithely drive away, no worse for wear. Royce destroyed her plans with his tenderness. He demolished her thin facade with a single look. Tears welled in her eyes, and she placed the tips of her fingers over her mouth in an effort to hold back the wails of grief and anguish that she had yet to fathom.

Royce reached for her then, pulling her into his arms. She went sobbing, banding her arms around his waist. She buried her face in his chest, not wanting him to know how hard she was weeping.

He led her to his Porsche and helped her inside, then joined her, taking her once more into the sanctuary of his arms. Again and again, he stroked the back of her head, again and again he whispered soothing words she couldn't hear over the sound of her own weeping. Again and again, he brushed his chin over the top of her head.

"It's all right," he whispered. "Go ahead and cry."

"I…can't seem to stop. Oh, Royce, I don't understand why I feel like this. I'm…I'm so afraid everyone is going to forget him. And it would be so unfair."

"You aren't going to forget."

"Don't you see?" she sobbed even harder. *"I don't remember anything about him."* Her throat was so thick she couldn't speak for several moments. "I was so young when he went away. Mom tried to help me remember. She told me story after story about all the things we used to do together and how much he loved us. As hard as I try I can't remember a single detail. Nothing."

"But he's alive here," Royce said gently, pressing a hand over her heart, "and that's all that matters."

Catherine wished it were that easy. But her emotions were far more complicated, as complicated as her love for Royce. Being in his arms, drinking in his strength and his comfort, helped to abate the tears.

"Kiss me," she pleaded, craving the healing balm of his love. "Just once and then…I promise I won't bother you again. I'll leave, and you can go back home."

He didn't hesitate. His hands were in her hair, his splayed fingers buried deep, angling her head so that his mouth could sweep down to capture hers the way a circling hawk comes after its prey.

Catherine sighed in appreciation, opening to him. Royce groaned, thrusting his tongue deep into the moist warmth of her mouth. She sighed anew and welcomed the spirals of heat that coiled in her stomach. Her hands gripped his shirt, holding on to him, needing the anchor of his love now more than ever before. The emotion that had been playing havoc with her senses all evening burst wide open and spilled over her like warm, melting honey.

Catherine whimpered.

Royce moaned softly, seeming to experience the same wonder. His hands roved over her back, dragging her forward until their hearts were pressed against each other's, each pounding out a chaotic rhythm of love and need.

When her breasts made contact with his chest, Catherine experienced a sensual hunger she had never known, a need that went beyond the physical. It was as if she were emotionally starved, as if the bleakness of her existence had been laid bare.

Royce's lips claimed hers a second time with an urgency that took her by surprise, his kiss of fierce possession, a deepening urgency, a ferocious hunger neither would be able to tolerate for long.

Royce must have sensed it, too, because he abruptly broke away, his chest heaving with the effort. Catherine longed to protest, but he raised his hand to her face and gently pressed his palm against her heated cheek. Her fingers covered his, and she closed her eyes, savoring this closeness.

When she looked up at him, she found him staring at her. Her eyes didn't waver from his. With unhurried ease, he bent forward and kissed her again, only this time his kiss was slow and tender, as slow and tender as the one before had been untamed and harsh.

"I want to taste you." The heat in his eyes and in his words caused her to shiver. His hands expertly parted her blouse, and when he discovered she wasn't wearing a bra, his eyes narrowed into blue slits. His hands cupped her breasts and lifted them until they'd formed perfect rounds in his palms. Her nipples had tightened even before he began stroking them with his thumbs. Catherine went still, afraid even to breathe, her eyes half-closed as she dealt with the intense pleasure his hands brought her. His mouth followed, and she rolled her head back and moaned even before his mouth closed over her nipple. With her eyes slammed shut, she arched her back. The impact was so keen, so intense, she longed to cry out.

All too soon his mouth returned to hers and she opened to him, greedily accepting what he was offering. Her hands slid along the curve of his back and up to the thickness of his mussed hair.

Royce's kisses were sweet and warm. Sweet and gentle; too gentle. He broke away completely and rubbed his face against the side of her jaw with a moist foray of nibbling kisses, working his way down her neckline.

"I want to make love to you," he whispered, then quickly amended. "I *need* to make love to you, but damn it all, Catherine, I refuse to do it in the front seat of a car."

With eyes still closed and her heart thundering like a Nebraska storm, she grinned. "Any bed will do."

"You're making this difficult."

"Has it ever been easy for us?"

"No," he growled, his hands continuing to caress her breasts. "You make me feel seventeen all over again."

"It's the car, trust me."

"Maybe." He shifted his weight and groaned, the sound rich and masculine. "I just hope the seamstress who sewed these pants took her job seriously."

Involuntarily, Catherine's gaze dropped to the bulge in his loins. Against her better judgment she trailed her knuckles over it, feeling the heat even through the thickness of his jeans.

The temptation was so powerful that she had to force herself to look away. She sighed, her shoulders lifted several inches with the effort.

Wrapping his arms around her, Royce pulled her toward him, until her back was cushioned by his chest. He leaned forward and slowly rotated his cheek over hers, nuzzling her ear with his nose. "Tell me about your mother."

Catherine grinned, content for the first time since the mail had arrived. "You'd like her. She's wonderfully witty and intelligent. To look at her, you'd never guess she's in her early fifties, almost everyone assumes she's at least ten years younger. The best part is that she's strikingly attractive and doesn't realize it. For the past fifteen years she's lived in San Francisco, and works at the corporate headquarters for this huge importing business. That's where she met Norman. He's a widower, and I swear he fell in love with Mom the minute they met. He's waited ten years for this day, and as much as I love my father, I can't begrudge Mom and Norman any happiness."

"It sounds like mother and daughter are a good deal alike." Royce murmured.

Catherine had to think on that a moment. "Yes, I suppose that's true...I just never thought much about it." Catherine hesitated, then added, "She loved my father."

"Loves," he corrected gently.

"Loves," Catherine agreed softly.

"You're close?"

"Always. She's incredible. If you meet her and still think we're alike, then it would be the greatest compliment anyone could ever give me."

"I think you're incredible," he whispered, playfully nuzzling her neck. His arms were tightly wrapped around her middle, and she felt as though she were in the most secure place in all the world—in Royce's loving arms.

Content, Catherine smiled, folded her arms over his and closed her eyes. "What are we going to do, Royce?"

She felt the harsh sigh work its way across his chest. It was a question she was sure he'd asked himself a hundred times. One that had hounded them both for weeks, and they were no closer now to a solution than they had been before.

"I wish I knew." It went without saying that if they continued in this vein they were both going to be booted out of the Navy. "I never thought I'd be jealous of my own daughter."

"Of Kelly?" Catherine didn't understand.

"Yes, of Kelly." His grip around her middle tightened. "She, at least, can spend the night with you."

Catherine grinned and nestled back in his arms.

"How do you think I felt learning that you sleep in a little slip of lace that's all see-through on top?"

"She told you that?" Catherine asked, twisting around.

"Yes! Is it true?"

"Yes."

Royce groaned. "You could have lied…I wish you had lied."

"Did she also tell you I sleep on ivory-colored satin sheets?"

"No, she was merciful enough to skip over that part," he growled in her ear. "Oh, sweet heaven, it feels so good to hold you in my arms. I could get drunk on you."

Catherine was equally content, although she was likely to suffer in the morning. The console was digging into her hip, but it was a small price to pay for the pleasure of being in Royce's arms.

"You're going to be all right now?"

She nodded. "I don't know what came over me. Obviously I have a lot of unresolved feelings for my father."

"Don't get so philosophical. Your mother is letting go of an important part of your lives together. It's only natural for you to feel a certain amount of regret."

There was a lot more than regret in that raging storm of tears that overtook her, but Royce didn't know that. Catherine had yet to fully comprehend the blitz of feelings herself. Her emotions were hopelessly tangled. But it didn't matter, she could face anything or anyone as long as Royce was by her side, as long as the man she loved would hold her tight.

The orders Royce received to conduct an under way inspection aboard the USS *Venture,* a small service craft used by the base, seemed like a godsend. Royce needed time away from Bangor, and from Catherine. The time away was essential to his peace of mind. Three days aboard the

Venture would help him gain some perspective on what was happening between them.

A hundred times he'd told himself to stay away from her. They were playing with a lit stick of dynamite. The fact they were both doing it with their eyes wide open frustrated him even more.

Royce had done everything he knew to get her out of his mind. He'd ignored her, pretended she didn't exist. When it came to dealing with her at the office, he made her a faceless name and tried to react to her that way. He'd had women under his command before without there ever being so much as a hint of a problem.

The difficulty was it didn't work. Royce couldn't ignore Catherine any more than he could jump over the moon. It was a physical impossibility. He couldn't look at her, even in the most impersonal way, and not hunger for the taste of her. It went without saying that a single taste would never satisfy him, and he knew it. He had to feel her, had to run his hands down the soft curving slopes of her body and experience for himself her ready response to his touch.

Some mornings he walked into the office and with one glance at her he'd been forced to knot his hands at his sides just to keep from reaching for her. The ache would start then and last all day and sometimes long into the night. Was it any wonder his men had come up with a few choice names for him while he was in his present state of mind?

The physical frustration was killing him, and as far as Royce could tell it was going to get a hell of a lot worse before it got better.

Just when Royce was foolish enough to believe he had everything under control, she'd called him, weeping in the middle of the night. If he hadn't been so starved for her, he might have been able to handle the situation differently. But the moment he'd heard her weep, the urge to take her in his arms and comfort her had been overwhelming. Already it was happening. What he swore never would. He arranged for them to meet in some out-of-the-way place where no one was likely to see them.

Royce justified the meeting, remembering how she'd been there for him when Kelly was in the hospital. Helping her deal with the fact her mother was going to remarry was returning the kindness, nothing more.

To further vindicate his actions, he'd convinced himself that he'd have done the same thing for anyone under his command. That might be true, but he doubted that he'd meet them at the end of a long dirt road. Nor would he hold and kiss them the way he did Catherine.

From that night forward, matters had only gotten worse. Royce could feel his control slipping even more than before. Twice he found himself looking for excuses to call her into his office just so he could hear the sound of her voice. It was coming to the point that she was able to maintain protocol much better than he was. A bad sign. A very bad sign.

Kelly wasn't helping matters any. If having to deal with Catherine at the office wasn't bad enough, Kelly talked about her constantly. The kid was crazy about Catherine and had been from the moment they'd met. At first Royce was convinced it was the fingernails, but gradually, in a slow and painful process, he'd come to realize how badly Kelly needed a mother figure. Why she chose Catherine and not Missy's mom or any of the mothers of her friends, Royce had yet to understand. Instead she'd chosen the one woman who was driving Royce slowly out of his mind.

This assignment aboard the *Venture* was exactly what he needed. Time away.

Royce was packing his bag when Kelly wandered into the bedroom. She plopped herself down on the edge of the mattress and sighed as though she were being abandoned.

"How long are you going to be gone?"

Royce had told her no less than four times, but she continued to ask anyway. "Three days."

Kelly had wanted to spend the time with Catherine, but it made more sense for her to stay with Missy's family since the two girls were in the same class at school. Kelly hadn't been overly thrilled, but she hadn't argued. At least not any more than she usually did.

"When you get back, can we go for pizza?"

"Sure," Royce agreed, glancing up long enough to smile at her. He didn't know why she asked, they always went out to eat when he arrived home from an assignment. It had become tradition.

The phone rang, and Kelly leaped off the bed as though she'd received an electric shock. Even though Royce was less than three feet away, she screamed at the top of her voice, "I'll get it."

Inserting his little finger in his ear, Royce cleared the passageway and resumed packing.

Kelly appeared a minute or so later. "It's for you," she said, sounding disappointed. "It sounds like Captain Garland."

Royce nodded. "Tell him I'll be right there."

Royce finished tucking his socks into the corner of the bag and then went down the hallway. Kelly handed him the phone and leaned against the wall and waited until he'd finished.

The conversation with his commanding officer didn't last more than a couple of minutes. But each one of those minutes might as well have been a lifetime as far as Royce was concerned. What was it that was said about the best laid plans? He didn't know. Hell he didn't know much of anything anymore.

"What's wrong?" Kelly asked once he'd replaced the receiver.

"How do you know that anything's wrong?"

"Because you've got that look again."

Royce didn't know what she was talking about, and frankly he wasn't sure he cared to.

His daughter, however, was bent on telling him. "It's hard to explain," Kelly added on a thoughtful note. "It's a look you get when you're mad and trying not to show it. Your ears get red on the top and your mouth goes like this." She scrunched up her lips like an old prune.

"I never look like that," Royce told her with more than a suggestion of impatience.

"If you say so."

At least she was smart enough to know when not to argue with him, look or not. For that, Royce could be grateful.

He was halfway back to his room when he decided he might as well let Kelly know. "Catherine's coming along with me."

"She is?" Kelly sounded downright thrilled. "How come?"

"There's been a complaint of sexual harassment on board the *Venture* that she's going to investigate. Captain Garland felt it made sense to send us both up at the same time."

"He is the captain," the ten-year-old said with an air of great wisdom.

If Kelly thought to comfort him, she'd failed. Miserably.

It wasn't until they were both aboard the plane that Royce spoke to Catherine. She was sitting in the seat next to him, but he'd done his damnedest to ignore her. Not that it had done any good. Not that it ever did, but he liked to pretend otherwise.

"How'd you arrange this?" he demanded, his voice dripping with sarcasm.

"I didn't," she said, without looking up from the report she was reviewing. "I was ordered to accompany you." She made it sound as though she'd rather be anyplace else than sitting next to him.

Royce looked out the window, unexpectedly amused by her tart reply. Apparently she wasn't any more pleased about this than he was. Well that was par for the course as far as their relationship went.

"If it's any comfort to you I'll be away soon enough." There was a militant strain in her voice that challenged him.

Catherine was going away? It wasn't any comfort, in fact it was cause for alarm. "What do you mean?"

"I'll be attending my mother's wedding."

"I see." Royce hadn't seen the request yet, but he knew there wouldn't be any problem in granting her leave.

"Unfortunately that isn't going to help," he growled. The need to touch her, even in the smallest way, was so strong Royce couldn't fight it anymore. He moved his leg just enough so his calf could brush against hers. He nearly sighed in relief. Her skin felt silky and smooth, so smooth.

The movement, almost invisible to anyone else quickly captured Catherine's attention. She jerked her head up and frowned at him.

"Royce," she breathed, "what are you doing?"

"Looking for a way to get booted out of the Navy it seems."

She yanked her leg away, expelled a shuddering sigh and returned to the report she was reading. But Royce noticed that her hands were trembling.

Who was he kidding? If anyone was shaking it was he. It started that first afternoon on the track when Catherine had refused to stop running, and it hadn't lessened since.

Royce laid back his head and closed his eyes. He needed to think. He'd come a hair's space from making love to her in the front seat of a car. He was meeting her on dirt roads. Now he was reduced to trying to feel her up while on a military transport.

He was in bad shape. Worse than he thought. Only a desperate man would have pulled that trick. Which said a lot about his mental condition. This assignment was going to be a hell of a lot more difficult than he'd imagined.

That thought proved to be more prophetic than Royce ever dreamed. The first day into the inspection he was so angry he walked around in a red haze. He wasn't civil to be around. It was so bad, he didn't even like himself. And for what reason? Because Lieutenant Commander Masterson had taken an instant liking to Catherine. The man had made his interest in her known from the moment they'd stepped on board the *Venture*.

Royce was making notes when he inadvertently happened upon Masterson talking to Catherine in the narrow hallway. He didn't like the familiar way in which the young lieutenant commander was leaning toward her. Nor did he appreciate the way the other man was looking at her as though he couldn't wait to get her into his bed.

"Are you finished with your report?" he demanded of Catherine.

"Not yet." She looked surprised that he'd even ask since the account of the complaint wasn't due for several days after their return.

"Then I suggest you start work on it."

"Yes, sir." She started to walk past him when Royce turned on Masterson, his eyes narrowed into dark slits. He couldn't remember a time he'd wanted to take a man down more.

"Problems?" Masterson asked innocently enough.

"This isn't the Love Boat, Lieutenant Commander," Royce said as scathingly as he could. "Captain Garland didn't ask Lieutenant Commander Fredrickson to accompany me for your entertainment."

The other man's eyes widened at the verbal attack.

"I suggest you keep your hands to yourself."

"But he didn't…" Catherine intervened, until Royce

turned on her, making sure his eyes were hard enough to effectively silence her. She had no business speaking to him. No business defending Masterson, and that infuriated him even more.

"You're both dismissed," he said harshly, and waited until they'd retreated in opposite directions.

In the next twenty-four hours, Royce didn't say more than a handful of words to Catherine. In fact he was avoiding her. She was avoiding him, too. Like the plague. But then so was everyone else—not that he blamed them.

Royce was tired. Mentally and physically. But keyed up at the same time. Before heading off to bed, he decided to stop off in the galley for a cup of coffee. Caffeine sometimes helped to relax him.

He apparently wasn't the only one who needed something that night. Catherine sat at the table and glanced up when he appeared. She looked startled, as though she'd been caught doing something illegal.

"I'll leave," she said, slowly coming to her feet.

"No, stay," he returned crisply, walking over to the coffeepot.

"Is that an order?"

He had to think about it a moment. "Yes."

Her hands cupped the mug. Her gaze was centered on the steaming liquid as though something were about to leap out.

Royce poured himself a cup and sat down across from her. He didn't say anything for several moments, then decided now was as good a time as any to speak his mind. As bad a time as any for that matter. At least they were alone.

"I don't like the way Masterson's been looking at you," he admitted, frowning as he did so.

Catherine's head flew up so fast it was a wonder she didn't injure her neck.

"Lieutenant Commander Masterson?"

"Yes," he said roughly. He knew he sounded possessive, but he couldn't help himself. It had been eating at him from the moment they'd arrived. Mark Masterson had made a fool of himself over Catherine. Everyone had noticed. Certainly Catherine must have. Royce had even heard a couple of the men talking about the way Masterson had an eye for the ladies.

"You mean to say you've been acting like a…a…" Apparently she couldn't think of anything bad enough. "Like a moron because you're… jealous?" Her words were issued vehemently in a whisper.

"I have not been acting like a moron," he denied hotly, in the same low tones she used. "I have eyes."

"And what would you like me to do about it?"

Her words took Royce by surprise. He expected her to deny it, claim it was all in his head. He even thought she'd call him a fool for saying it. Okay, she'd called him a moron. That was close. What he hadn't anticipated was her acceptance of the problem.

"Well?" she demanded.

"What do I expect you to do about it?" he repeated. The answer came to him then, as profoundly as anything he'd ever felt. It was all so simple. It was all so complicated.

"Marrying me would settle it."

Chapter Eight

"You don't mean that," Catherine whispered, confident Royce's proposal had been prompted by a fit of jealous rage. She would never have guessed that Royce would be so insecure.

Sadly, Catherine couldn't deny that the lieutenant commander had gone out of his way to let her know he was interested. In what, she wasn't entirely sure. Mark Masterson had been more than attentive from the moment she and Royce had landed aboard the *Venture*. He hadn't done anything offensive, and under other circumstances Catherine might have been flattered. Certainly she'd done nothing to encourage his attention.

"The hell I don't mean it," Royce countered sharply, impatiently. His face was scowled in an intimidating frown that pleated his brow in thick folds.

"You don't need to shout at me."

Royce lowered his voice several decibels. "I am not yelling. Will you or won't you marry me?"

"I can't," she felt obliged to remind him. She was under his command, which was something he'd conveniently forgotten. Any relationship, other than one that involved Navy business, was strictly prohibited. He knew it. She knew it. But for pride's sake Royce had chosen to over-look the fact.

Slowly Royce stiffened, as though anticipating a body blow, as if he were unsure of her and her love. "Would you marry me if it were possible?"

"Probably."

"Probably," he repeated, his eyes rounding. It was as though she'd issued him the greatest insult of his life.

"Yes, probably," she returned just as heatedly. "If the pro-posal weren't issued on the tail end of a fit of jealousy and…and if I were convinced to the soles of my feet that you loved me."

"I love you." This, too, was discharged as if he were tal-lying points in a heated debate. "So what's your answer? Yes or no?"

"Just like that?"

"Just like that." He made it sound as if there shouldn't be anything to consider, as if he were asking her out to din-ner, instead of a complicated relationship that would in-volve disrupting both their lives, and Kelly's, not to mention their careers.

"Why?" she charged, "so I can inform Masterson I'm an engaged woman?"

"Yes," Royce confirmed without pause. His hands were cupped around his coffee with enough force to shatter the ceramic mug.

"Then thanks, but no thanks." Battling righteousness, Catherine stood abruptly, prepared to leave the room. How dare Royce offer her marriage in an effort to salvage his precious male pride. The only reason he'd even sug-gested it was out of concern she might be attracted to Mark Masterson. The ironic part of all this was that Royce had only recently tried to arrange a date for her with Dan Parker. In the space of a few short weeks, he'd gone from one extreme to another. Catherine didn't know what to expect next.

"What do you mean *no thanks?*" Royce demanded, leaping to his feet with enough force to topple his chair. Somehow he managed to catch it before it crashed to the floor.

"I don't know how much plainer I can make it, Commander. The answer is *no.*"

He looked positively stunned, as if she'd stepped forward and thrust a sword between his ribs. He'd been so sure of himself, so damned arrogant, as if it were a foregone conclusion she'd accept his offer of marriage without even needing to think it over. It hurt her pride that he'd proposed in such a callous manner with a complete lack of tenderness or romance.

"If and when I marry," she felt obliged to explain, "it will be to a man who doesn't behave like a jealous idiot. Someone who demonstrates his love with a tad more finesse than to shout out a proposal in a ship's galley because he's afraid someone else might do it before he gets the chance. Now, if you'll excuse me, I'm going to my stateroom." With that she stalked away.

To her dismay, Royce followed her down the long, narrow passageway. He was so close behind her, Catherine feared he was about to step on her heels. She hadn't a clue what he intended to say or how far he planned on following her. Outside her quarters, she vaulted around and confronted him.

"You wanted to say something?" she demanded.

"You're damn right I do."

In all the time Catherine had worked with Royce, she'd never seen him like this, as though he'd been driven to the very limit of his endurance.

"Might I suggest we discuss this at a more appropriate time, Commander," she said, her voice bordering on impertinence. She'd gone about as far as she dared with

Royce, but she couldn't, wouldn't allow him to pull rank on her with an issue that was strictly personal.

"No, you may not." After looking both ways, he opened the door to her quarters and gently pushed her inside.

"What the hell do you think you're doing?" she insisted.

Royce didn't answer her. Instead he backed her against the bulkhead. His large, muscular hands settled over her shoulders, dragging her against him. Her struggles were of little good against his superior strength. Arching her back was a mistake as well. It only served to bring the lower half of her body in intimate contact with his. She was about to cry out in protest when his mouth smothered hers, his lips ruthlessly grinding over hers. Immediately his tongue was there, flickering softly over her lips, coaxing them open. Catherine fought him, fought herself for as long as she could hold out, which was a humiliatingly short time. With tears crowding her eyes, she parted her lips, welcoming the intrusion of his tongue, meeting it with her own. Royce groaned when she opened to him, and her moans of outrage and anger quickly became soft cries of bliss.

"Royce!" she cried, jerking her head to one side. Her shoulders heaved with the effort. "Are you crazy?"

"Yes." He didn't bother to deny it. Gradually he released her and took a moment to compose himself. "I have no excuse for this. Forgive me, Catherine." No sooner had the words been spoken when he was gone, leaving her to wonder if anyone had witnessed him coming out of her quarters.

Marilyn Fredrickson moved around the kitchen, her silk robe knotted at her trim waist. As Catherine watched her mother, she was struck anew by what an attractive woman Marilyn was. Petite, beautiful and intuitive, far more intuitive than Catherine remembered.

Marilyn brought the coffeepot around the kitchen counter where Catherine was sitting on a high stool. She, too, was dressed in her housecoat, her hair mussed. Catherine loved her mother's kitchen more every time she came to visit. It was painted a light shade of cheery yellow, with bright sunlight spilling in from the three skylights overhead. The counters were white with a huge wicker basket of dried flowers decorating the corner.

"So are you going to tell me about him?" Marilyn asked, slipping onto the stool next to Catherine.

She hadn't mentioned a word about Royce. Her flight from Seattle had landed late the night before. Her mother and Norman had picked her up at the airport, and they'd driven directly to the condo in San Francisco's refurbished Marina District. Catherine and her mother had stayed up half the night, but all the talk had evolved around her mother and Norman. Not once had Catherine mentioned Royce.

"About who?" she asked innocently, not sure even now she could talk about him.

Her mother's smile was chiding. She raised the coffee cup to her lips and took a sip, then sighed. "I remember the day Norman asked me to marry him. It wasn't the first time, mind you, but he hadn't pressed me in more than a year. I asked for more time, the way I always do. Ever the gentleman, Norman accepted that, but then he said something he never had before. He said he loved me, and always would, but he explained that a man only has so much patience. He was tired of living his life alone, tired of dreaming of having me for his wife one day. Then he asked me if I truly loved him."

"You do." Catherine already knew the answer to that.

"Of course I do, I have for years." Marilyn paused once more for another drink of her coffee, which gave her time to compose her thoughts, it seemed. "That night as I was getting ready for bed, I stood in front of the bathroom mirror to remove my makeup. As I stared at my reflection I realized there was a certain look about me, a certain…I hesitate to use this word, readiness."

"Readiness," Catherine repeated.

"Yes. Right then and there I realized what a fool I'd been to wait so many years to marry Norman. The time was right to accept his proposal, it had been right for a good long while, only I hadn't realized it. I couldn't even wait until morning, I phoned him right then." Her lips quivered gently with a smile. "I took one look at you this morning, Catherine, and there's a certain look about you not unlike the one I saw in myself."

"Readiness?" Catherine joked.

"No, not that. You have the look of a woman in love, but one who doesn't know what she's going to do. Do you want to talk about it?"

"I…don't know." Catherine had left for California shortly after her return to Bangor from the *Venture*. She hadn't seen Royce in three days prior to her departure, nor had she spoken to him since that one horrible night aboard the Navy vessel. Every time she thought about Royce's marriage proposal, she was forced to wade through a mine field of negative emotions, each one threatening to explode in her face.

Her mother was watching her closely, and Catherine realized she owed her some explanation. "There are difficulties."

"Is he married?"

Her startled gaze flew to Marilyn's. "Nothing that drastic."

"I take it he's in the Navy?"

Catherine nodded. "That's the problem. He's the executive officer, my boss."

Her mother knew what that meant without Catherine needing to explain it. The dark brown eyes narrowed slightly. "Oh, Catherine, sweetie, you do like to live dangerously, don't you?"

"It wasn't like I planned to fall in love with him," she cried, defending herself. No one in their right mind would purposely put themselves through this torment.

"Does he return your feelings?"

"I think so." After the night he'd met her on the dirt road, Catherine was convinced she'd never question the way he felt about her. Then he'd pulled that stunt aboard the *Venture* and she was left sinking with doubts.

"You think so?" Marilyn repeated slowly, thoughtfully. It seemed her mother was incredulous that Catherine wouldn't know something this important.

"He loves me," she amended.

"He just has a difficult time showing it?"

"Exactly." Catherine replayed the latest incident and how he'd followed her into her cabin. It had been a foolish risk that might have cost them both dearly.

"I take it you rejected his marriage proposal?"

"Of course I did. He asked for all the wrong reasons."

"But if he asked for all the right ones, what would you have said?"

"Honest to God truth?" Catherine asked.

"Honest to God truth."

"Yes. In a heartbeat. Oh, Mom, I'm so crazy about this guy—I don't know what's right anymore. I never dreamed I'd defy Navy regulations. It's simply not done. Yet here we are so crazy in love we're acting like complete idiots, risking our careers and our reputations and everything else I always thought was so important...I still think is important.

"I know Royce was upset that I'd been assigned to accompany him on the *Venture*. He'd wanted this time apart to gain some perspective about us and our relationship. At least I assume that was what he intended. Then I was ordered to accompany him, and it made everything much worse. Everything seems to be working against us."

"What's going to happen when you return?"

Catherine sighed and slowly shook her head. "I wish I knew."

"Royce…that's his name?" At Catherine's nod, Marilyn continued. "He'll have the time you seem to think he needs."

"But, Mom," Catherine said, feeling more miserable than ever, "if he does decide it would be best for us to marry, it won't help matters any. We'd both continue to paddle in the same leaky boat as before."

"But if you marry Royce, won't you give up the Navy?"

"No," she cried vehemently. "Why should I? I love the military. I'm not about to relinquish an eleven-year investment just because I happen to fall in love. And getting out of the Navy isn't all that easy, either. It takes up to a year, unless I were to find myself pregnant."

Marilyn's eyebrows shot toward her hairline.

"Oh, Mother, honestly. There's no possibility."

"I'm sorry, sweetie, it's just that I'd love to have grandchildren someday."

"I'll do my best—someday."

Marilyn rested her elbows on the counter and released an elongated sigh. "I hadn't realized getting out of the Navy would be such a hassle."

"I'm not leaving the Navy," Catherine reinforced.

"So what's going to happen?"

Her mother asked the question as though Catherine kept a crystal ball in her pocket and consulted it regularly. "The only thing either one of us can do is put in a request for a transfer."

"But you just moved to Bangor from Hawaii."

"I know. It isn't likely the Navy will look favorably upon shipping me elsewhere anytime soon."

"What about Royce? Can he put in a request?"

Catherine bit into her lower lip. It was a thought she'd entertained often, although she'd never spoken to Royce about it. "Yes, but I don't know that he will. He's been stationed at Bangor for several years now, and he'd hate to uproot Kelly. It's the only home she's ever known. Of course there's always the chance he'd be reassigned to one of the other commands in the Puget Sound area. We can hope, of course."

"Kelly? Who's Kelly?"

Catherine doubted that her mother had heard anything beyond the point that she'd mentioned Royce's daughter's name. "His daughter. She's ten and oh, Mom, she is such a delight. We get along so well. She's just at the age where she's discovering what it means to be a girl. It all started with me painting her fingernails when she was hurt in an accident. We've gotten so close. The last time we met, Kelly wanted her hair cut, so I took her to a salon and stood over the hairdresser like an old mother hen. When she'd finished, Kelly looked so cute."

"You're spending a lot of time with her, I take it?"

"As much as I can," Catherine said, and hesitated. "You're wearing that worried look again."

"I can't help it," Marilyn murmured. "I don't want to see you get hurt."

"I won't," Catherine assured her with more confidence than she was feeling. "Now quit being such a worrywart. This is your wedding day, and I certainly don't want you looking all serious and somber fretting about me." Catherine took a sip of her coffee and glanced at her watch. "Oh, my goodness," she said, sliding off the stool. "Look at the time! We've got to get ready, or you'll be late for your own wedding. Norman will never forgive me."

The wedding was lovely. Her mother made a radiant bride, Catherine mused during the plane trip on the way back to Seattle. Norman had never looked more distinguished or handsome. The two, backed with long years of steady friendship, were the ideal couple. Catherine had heard several people say as much as she wandered through the reception, making sure everyone had what they needed. Norman had insisted the affair be catered, but Catherine had made busywork in an effort to keep herself absorbed. If she'd sat back and relaxed, there might have been time to think about the young, handsome man in the photograph that rested on her fireplace mantel. The father she'd never known.

It was ironic that Catherine would be better acquainted with her new stepfather than the man who'd given her life.

When it came time for her mother and Norman to exchange their vows, Catherine had felt a sudden rush of emotion crowd her eyes. A tear or two did manage to slip down her cheek as she stood beside her mother, clenching a floral bouquet. If anyone noticed, and Catherine prayed they didn't, she sincerely hoped they assumed it was a tear of shared happiness.

Catherine *was* happy for her mother and Norman. Even more so now that she'd experienced these few days with them. It was almost comical watching the two. They were like young lovers, so involved with each other the rest of the world didn't seem to exist.

In many ways Catherine was envious. Her love for Royce was so much more complicated.

As the Boeing 737 cut a wide path through the thick layer of clouds, Catherine couldn't help wondering what kind of reception Royce would have for her upon her return. Would he be pleased she was back? Would his eyes search hers out so she'd know how much he'd missed her? Would he find an excuse to be alone with her? Or would the brick facade he so often carried be tightly locked in place? So secure he'd look right through her and reveal little of what he was thinking and none of what he was feeling.

Catherine was exhausted when the plane landed at Sea-Tac. When she walked off the jetway into the airport terminal, she found her gaze scanning the crowds, hoping that Royce would be there waiting for her.

He wasn't.

It was ridiculous to expect him. As far as she knew, he wasn't even aware of her flight schedule. Then why, she asked herself, did she experience this heavy letdown?

"You're an idiot," she whispered as she walked down the concourse to the baggage claim area.

Again she reminded herself what a fool she was when she unlocked her apartment door over an hour later, after she'd picked Sambo up from the neighbor's. To her disappointment, there wasn't anything on her answering machine from Royce, either. Kelly had left two messages. The first call was to tell Catherine that her story about the Princess and the Dragon had been chosen by her teachers for the Young Authors Program. Kelly was so excited and had been talking so fast it was difficult to understand her. The second message had been made that afternoon, Catherine decided, and the purpose was to tell her Kelly missed her and wished she'd hurry back soon.

Catherine toyed with the idea of phoning the ten-year-old, then noted the time and realized Royce's daughter was probably already asleep for the night. It was unlikely that he'd appreciate the intrusion.

Nevertheless, she couldn't give up the idea. Five minutes later, against her better judgment, she found herself reaching for the phone.

It was Royce who answered. His voice was as rich and masculine as ever, and just hearing it sent goose bumps up her spine.

"It's Catherine," she said, managing to keep any emotion out of her voice, "I'm calling for Kelly."

He hesitated, as though she'd caught him off guard. "She went to bed about half an hour ago."

The tension crackled over the telephone wire like static electricity. "Will you tell her I phoned?"

"Of course."

Catherine closed her eyes against the lack of sentiment in his voice. It was as if he were speaking to a casual acquaintance and not the woman he'd once claimed he loved. Once, only once, and then it had come as part of a jealous rage.

"I…I won't keep you then," she announced stiffly.

"You aren't keeping me from anything more than television." His control had slipped just a little, as if he were reluctant to disconnect the line. For that, at least, Catherine could be grateful.

"How was the wedding?" he asked, as though looking for ways to make polite conversation.

"Beautiful," she told him, meaning it.

"How were you?"

He didn't need to explain the question. He was asking how she'd dealt with the emotions she'd had so much trouble accepting when she'd first learned her mother intended to marry Norman.

Involuntarily, Catherine's gaze drifted to her fireplace mantel. "Fine," she whispered. She'd dealt with it splendidly, far better than she'd expected. "Mom made a beautiful bride." Once more there was a noticeable silence. He'd done his part, now it was her turn. "How did everything go at the office?"

"There weren't any problems."

"Good," she whispered. "I'll be back in the morning."

"So I understand."

Say something, Catherine pleaded silently. *Let me know*

what you're feeling. Tell me you missed me as dreadfully as I missed you. Tell me you regret that we parted without settling our differences.

Nothing. The line went so quiet that for a moment all Catherine could hear was the sound of her own breathing.

"I'll see you in the morning," she said, when it became apparent Royce had no intention of continuing the stilted conversation.

"Right…in the morning." How clipped he sounded, how eager to be rid of her, but all changed abruptly when he said, "Good night, Catherine."

There was such hunger in those few words, such longing. "Good night," she responded softly.

She pressed the receiver more closely to her ear when she heard him call her name.

"Yes," she said, trying hard to disguise the eagerness in her voice. She sounded like a silly schoolgirl and couldn't have cared less.

"About Mark Masterson."

"Yes?" Her eyes drifted closed, ready to savor his words of apology, ready to apologize herself, anything that would dislodge this ten-foot wall between them. This wall of pride and pain.

"He phoned for you while you were away." Royce's voice hardened until each word fell like a chip of concrete against a hammer.

"Lieutenant Commander Masterson?" Catherine had trouble believing it. She'd done everything possible to discourage the *Venture*'s officer. Catherine couldn't understand why Mark, who had recently gone through a divorce, would turn to her.

"He left a number where you can get in touch with him."

"I have no intention of contacting him," she confirmed, in case Royce suspected she was even remotely interested in the other man.

"What you do or don't do is none of my concern." The hard note in his voice progressed to a savage undertone. "You're free to do as you wish."

"Do you honestly want me to date him?" she challenged, losing patience with Royce.

"What I want isn't a concern here. Masterson left a message for you. Why he chose to contact me to give it to you is anyone's guess. Apparently he's going to be in Bangor sometime soon. Heaven only knows how he arranged that, but he did, and he told me to let you know he'll be looking for you."

"What's that supposed to mean?" Catherine demanded.

"You can put your own connotation on it because I assure you I don't have a clue."

"I'll bet you don't," Catherine muttered.

"I beg your pardon."

"You heard me, Royce Nyland." The tension between them was stretched beyond the breaking point.

"Listen, Catherine, if you're waiting for me to tell you you're free to date Masterson, then you've got it. Feel free. There's nothing between us."

Catherine was so hurt and angry, she started to shake. "Is that a fact? Well, I must admit I find that interesting. One minute you're demanding I marry you, and in the next you're practically ordering me to date another man." She was so upset, she could feel her anger overwhelming her good sense. Sucking in a giant breath, she forced herself to stop before she said something she'd regret. "The dirt road off Byron Way," she said, as calmly as she could manage. "Meet me there in half an hour."

She didn't wait for him to confirm or deny his being there, but replaced the receiver.

She was walking toward the door when the phone started to ring. Ignoring it, she reached for her coat and purse and walked out of her apartment.

Forty minutes later, Catherine was standing outside her car, her hands stuffed in the pockets of her jacket, searching the night for Royce's headlights. She'd just about given up hope when she saw his car come barreling down the road. At least she assumed it was Royce.

He turned off the engine and leaped out of the car and stood there. For all his rush, he didn't seem to have a thing to say.

For that matter, Catherine didn't, either. They stood staring at each other, the moonlight cascading over them like a golden waterfall, splashing light on either side of them.

He looked dreadful, as though he hadn't slept in days. His face was stern and harsh, as austere as she'd ever seen it. Her gaze slid to his. It seemed for a moment that he wanted to avoid looking at her, but apparently something compelled him to meet her gaze, but he did so reluctantly. Catherine gasped softly at the way his deep, cobalt-blue eyes plunged into hers as though he would have drowned just looking at her.

"Oh, Royce," she whispered, stepping toward him, stretching out her arms. Her heart was so full of love she would cry if he didn't hold her soon.

He met her halfway, wrapping his arms around her waist and lifting her off the ground. With a growl, his mouth met hers in a frenzy of need and desire. They were so starved for each other that an eternity passed before either of them stopped to breathe.

Royce buried his face in the curve of her neck. "I'm sorry, so sorry," he chanted. "I've never been so insanely jealous in my life. I don't know how to deal with it. I've behaved like a fool."

Catherine's hands framed his face. "Just be quiet and kiss me," she ordered ruggedly against his lips. She slipped her tongue forward to meet his, not giving him the opportunity to argue if that had ever been his intention.

If Royce was holding back anything in reserve, he gave it to her then. With a deep-throated moan, he tightened his arms around her, flattening her breasts to his chest. Catherine could feel every part of him, every fiber of his military issue coat, every button, every crease. The kiss was the most primitive they'd shared. The most punishing. Catherine opened to him, and his tongue met hers.

She coiled her arms around his neck and slid down his front. Apparently she became too heavy for him because he lowered her feet to the frozen ground. His hand ran down the length of her spine and then intimately over the curve of her hip. He continued to slide his hands up and down her sides as though he couldn't get enough of her, as though he couldn't believe even now that she was his.

Catherine felt as though the whole world was spinning. It didn't matter. Nothing did as long as she was in his arms.

In the middle of the sweetest, hottest, most intimate kiss of her life, Royce reluctantly tore his mouth away from her. She was gratified to note that his breathing was as labored as her own.

"This doesn't settle anything," he whispered, his breath mingling with hers. His eyes remained closed as though he didn't possess the strength to refuse her anything.

"You're right," she whispered, "but it sure as hell helps." With that she directed his mouth back to her own.

Chapter Nine

"I need to get back. I left Kelly at the neighbor's," Royce whispered close to Catherine's ear. They were snuggled up in the front seat of Royce's car, her back against his chest with Royce's arms draped around her. They'd spent the last hour just this way, savoring these stolen moments, not wanting to part for fear of how long it would be before they'd have the chance to hold each other again.

"I need to get back, too," Catherine admitted reluctantly, but neither of them seemed in any hurry to leave.

"One last kiss?" Royce suggested, while spreading nibbling kisses down the side of her ivory neck, pausing now and again to swirl the moist tip of his tongue around her earlobe.

"You wanted a single kiss a half hour ago," she reminded him in a low whisper, "and the next thing I know my bra is missing and you're cursing because you can't find the zipper in my pants."

"That was your fault."

"Mine?" Catherine was indignant. He'd been all over her. They'd been all over each other, so hungry with need it was a gnawing ache in the pit of her stomach still. If it hadn't been for the gearshift, Catherine was convinced they'd have made love several times over by now.

"Yes, your fault," Royce repeated huskily. "If you didn't have such beautiful, tempting breasts." His hands slid up from her midriff to rest against the undersides of her fullness. His hands were close enough to reignite the achy, hollow feeling within her. Her breath escaped in a trickle as his thumbs lazily grazed her throbbing nipples.

"All right," she agreed softly. "Just one kiss." She arched her back and strained upward until her mouth unerringly found his.

Royce claimed her lips roughly, reeling her senses into oblivion. As his mouth worked over hers, his hands roved under her sweater after what seemed like an excruciating delay. Catherine moaned at the sheer wonder of his touch. Royce's tongue breached the barrier of her lips, probing, promising, as his hands caressed the weighted fullness of her breasts, kneading the heated flesh.

Soon Catherine was panting with primitive needs that curled deep inside her. "We're steaming up the windows again," she told him, knowing full well it was their moans and sighs as much as their breaths that were misting the car windows. It was becoming increasingly difficult to rein in their desires, and each time they were together, it became more of a strain, more of a struggle. Catherine had never felt more wanton. Never more wanting.

"The windows are the least of our problems," Royce said in a husky murmur.

She threaded her fingers through his hair and arched upwards, loving him so much she felt drunk with the emotion.

Royce lifted his weight, but his knee slammed hard against the gearshift. He cursed under his breath and rubbed the injured part of his leg. "I'm getting too old for this," he complained.

"We're both too old for this."

"I'm pleased you agree." His hands were at the band of

her wool slacks. His touch was warm, and his lips, against the underside of her chin, were decidedly hot. A fluttery sensation rippled over her skin as he slipped the button at the side of her hip free and eased the zipper downward. The sound buzzed in the close confines of the car like a roaring chain saw. Catherine's heart was pounding just as loudly.

Royce was convinced there was a limit to how much sexual frustration one man could endure. He'd reached it the night before with Catherine in the front seat of his car. *The front seat of his car*. The thought was a sobering one. A man who'd reached the age of thirty-seven shouldn't be attempting to make love in a car seat. There was something ideologically wrong with that.

Only the physical restrictions had prevented him from taking Catherine. If he'd possessed any talent as a contortionist he might have been able to manage it, but he was long past the age of attempting acrobatics.

Royce, however, promised himself he'd never buy a two-seater vehicle again. Never. No matter how sporty looking it was.

That thought was sobering as well. Everything he'd predicted about his and Catherine's relationship was coming to pass. Everything he'd feared. They were already meeting in out-of-the-way places. The sad fact was, Royce knew he wouldn't be able to handle any more sessions like the one they'd recently shared.

The next step was the hotel room. He'd been ready for one the night before. He'd been so incredibly hot for Catherine, he hadn't given a thought to propriety. If the circumstances had been somewhat different he would have driven Catherine to the nearest hotel and damned the consequences. He'd needed her, had wanted her that desperately.

He hadn't, of course, and consequently he'd been try-ing to forget about his unspent passion for the past twelve hours, with little success.

Once they'd gotten past the physical aspect of their need, or as near to satisfying it as was possible, they'd held each other for another hour and talked.

Royce was amazed that they could find so much to talk about and not mention the one thing that was on both their minds.

What the hell were they going to do?

Royce didn't know. Catherine apparently didn't, either.

Sitting back from his desk, Royce rolled a pen between his palms as he pondered the situation between him and Catherine for the hundredth time that day.

The office was unusually quiet. Everyone had gone home for the day, which was just as well. Catherine was due back from a court session anytime. Royce had left word for her to come directly to his office.

He was anxious to see her. When the hell wasn't he anx-ious to see her, he asked himself caustically.

It was her eyes, he decided. She had the darkest, most expressive eyes of any woman he'd ever met. They were wistful eyes, that clearly spelled out her thoughts.

And, if he could read her thoughts, then surely every-one else could, too.

How were they supposed to combat that? Royce knot-ted his hands into tight fists of frustration. He wasn't any closer to finding a solution now than he had been weeks earlier when the problem first presented itself.

Catherine's eyes were also the most provocative ones he'd ever encountered. She'd look up and smile at him, that secret, sexy smile, and then her eyes would meet his, and Royce swore she told him everything she hungered for in a single look. Apparently she found her own thoughts embarrassing because she'd start to blush and her eyelashes would flutter and she'd quickly glance away. It was all Royce could do not to make love to her then and there.

If there was anything to be grateful for, Royce realized, it was that she'd yet to give him that look while in the office.

The polite knock at his door cut into Royce's thoughts. He recognized the short, abrupt rap as Catherine's.

"Come in," he called out.

She stepped inside the room and automatically closed the door. "You wanted to see me?"

He noted that her gaze just missed meeting his. Royce didn't know whether to be grateful or not. Matters being as they were, he probably should be.

"Sit down, Lieutenant Commander."

Her gaze briefly skidded to his, and he knew she was attempting to read his mood. Generally he didn't refer to her by her rank unless he was attempting to put some distance between them.

Catherine pulled out the chair and sat down.

Royce had spent a good portion of the day struggling with the problems between them, trying to formulate a solution. He wasn't any closer now than the time he first accepted his feelings for Catherine weren't going to go away. It was either deal with them now or later. And later could prove risky to their careers.

"How are you?" he asked, not knowing exactly where to start. Asking about her health was a stall tactic and not one he employed often.

"Fine. And you?"

"Well." As well as could be expected under the circumstances, he amended mentally.

Her fingers were clenched tightly in her lap, and she flexed and unflexed them a couple of times in nervous anticipation. Royce wondered briefly why she should be so ill at ease. Then he realized that the only times he'd ever called her into his office it had been to reprimand her for one thing or another.

"Relax, Catherine," he said, lowering his own guard. "We need to talk, and this seemed to be the safest place." And the most dangerous, but Royce felt it essential to clear the air between them. To do it without the physical temptations clouding their judgments as had so often happened in the past. The only other place he could think to speak to her was the jogging track, and he couldn't be assured of privacy there.

"I was thinking we needed to talk, too," she said, her voice little more than a faint murmur.

"Then it looks like we've come to similar conclusions."

Her beautiful, expressive eyes shot to his, and he could read her alarm as clearly as if she'd spelled it out.

"W-what have you decided?" she asked outright.

If only Royce could reach a conclusion. "I haven't," he admitted with heavy reluctance. "I thought I'd have a chance to sort everything out while I was aboard the *Venture*. When that didn't pan out, I was hoping to have some time to think while you were with your mother." He'd soon discovered, however, that he missed her too much to be objective.

"I thought I might be able to do some thinking myself," Catherine interjected softly.

"And did you come to any decisions?"

She hesitated, as though she wasn't sure she should voice them. "Only that the…way I feel toward you isn't going to change."

There was a grim sort of satisfaction knowing that. It didn't solve anything, but it soothed his battered ego to hear her admit this wasn't just a sexual thing between them, founded on good old-fashioned lust. He'd considered that aspect himself. He'd been without a woman since Sandy's death, and perhaps his body was starting to play cruel tricks on him. It had been a cause for concern, but one quickly dismissed.

"I want a month," he stated decisively.

"I beg your pardon?" She blinked and scooted to the edge of her seat as though she wasn't sure she'd heard him correctly and was straining to understand.

"I need a month. Right now our feelings for each other are running high." That was putting it mildly. A blacksmith's poker was less hot than they were for each other.

"H-how do you mean?"

"No contact except what's absolutely necessary here at the office. Nothing more. Not even a phone call. I want us to remain as separate as we can and still work in the same command."

Catherine considered the suggestion for a moment, then nodded. "That sounds fair."

"I realize it's going to be difficult for us both."

"But necessary," she added, sounding as reluctant as he felt.

"Unfortunately, it is necessary," Royce agreed. "We can't go on the way we have."

"Something's got to be done."

At least on that they were of one accord.

"What about Kelly?" Catherine asked, her beautiful eyes bright with concern.

"Kelly," Royce repeated in a slow exercise. His daughter was a problem. He'd never seen her take to anyone the way she had Catherine. If he was going to force Kelly not to see Catherine for an entire month, he was likely to have a revolt on his hands. Yet he didn't know how he could maintain his distance from Catherine with Kelly spending time with her. He considered the situation a moment longer, then decided. "As you were quick to remind me not so long ago, it wouldn't be fair to punish her for a problem between us."

Catherine lowered her eyes, and her shoulders sagged as though she were greatly relieved. "Thank you."

"We can set up a time now to talk in exactly one month." He leaned forward and flipped forward the pages of his calendar, finding the date and marking it.

She stood, her eyes somber and determined. "One month," she repeated on her way out the door.

Catherine had known from the moment Royce asked for a month's separation that it wasn't going to be easy. What she hadn't understood was exactly how difficult it would be.

She found herself watching him far more than she ever had before, hungry for contact with him. Each time they were in the same room together, her heart was bathed in a strange blend of emotions. On one hand he was her executive officer, the man she'd been trained to obey without question, without hesitation. On the other hand, he was the man she loved. Mere words were an injustice to describe the strength of what she felt for Royce. She ached for him emotionally and physically. Some nights she'd walk into her apartment so mentally exhausted from this silent battle of longing between them that it was all she could do to feed Sambo.

If this time apart was trying for her, and God knew it was, then it was equally difficult for Royce. They never spoke, not unless it was absolutely necessary. Yet they couldn't be anywhere close to each other without that throbbing awareness breaking out between them. They could be standing in a room filled with other people, yet the intimacy between them was as strong as anything Catherine had ever known. The air was thick and the sensations undeniable.

The first test of their self-imposed restriction came within the first week. Commander Dan Parker stopped

Catherine outside the building one chilly afternoon. She'd stayed late working on a complicated case, knowing it was safe to do so since Royce had already left the office. Catherine assumed he'd gone down to the jogging track, as was his habit.

"Hello, Catherine," Dan greeted, strolling purposely toward her.

Catherine envied his carefree smile, and despite everything, found herself responding to it. He must have found encouragement in it, because he paused and asked, "Since you've already rejected my offer to the Birthday Ball, how about soothing my battered ego by agreeing to have dinner with me?"

To be honest, Catherine hadn't given the gala event more than a passing thought since the first time he'd mentioned it. She should give some thought to the ball, but her thoughts were far from festive. "Dinner…when?"

"What's wrong with tonight?"

"I can't," she answered automatically. Dan seemed to be waiting for an excuse, but she had none to offer. "I'm busy," she answered finally. Busy missing Royce. Busy being miserable. Busy pretending how busy I am.

"It is short notice," Dan admitted. "How about tomorrow night then, after work? We'll unwind over drinks."

Catherine had no reason to refuse. She was convinced Dan had guessed her and Royce's feelings for each other, and although it would be out of the question to discuss the situation, Dan might be able to give her some insight into Royce's personality.

"All right," she agreed, but there wasn't a lot of enthusiasm in her voice.

"Five o'clock at the Yachting Club?"

"Sure, that sounds great."

"Come on, I'll walk you to your car," Dan offered, pressing his hand at her elbow. The comfort Catherine felt at his touch, however impersonal, was enough to bring a rush of surprising tears to her eyes. She managed to blink them away, embarrassed at the unexpected show of emotion.

They were walking toward the asphalt lot, when Royce appeared from out of nowhere. He rounded the corner in a dead run and nearly collided with them. He stopped abruptly, his breath coming in deep gasps.

"Sorry," he said, leaned forward and balanced his hands on his knees. "I didn't think there was anyone left around here."

"No problem," Dan assured him.

Slowly Royce straightened. His eyes avoided looking at Catherine. "What are you doing here so late?"

Dan chuckled and possessively moved his hand up Catherine's back to cup her shoulder. "Talking Catherine into having dinner with me, what else?" Dan joked. "You don't honestly believe I'd stick around this late for Navy business, do you?"

Although everything seemed perfectly normal on the surface, Catherine was well aware of the way Royce's body tensed. The undercurrent between them was so strong she was about to drown in it.

"I see," Royce said, his smile decidedly forced. "I take it our very capable attorney has agreed."

"Not without my having to twist her arm, but once again the Parker charm has won out."

Royce raised his hand in a friendly gesture. "Then don't let me delay you any longer," he said cheerfully. "Have a good time."

"We're going to have a great time," Dan returned, squeezing Catherine's shoulder.

"Good night," Royce said, looking away, but before his eyes left them, Catherine noted that he dragged his gaze across her lips.

"'Night," Dan murmured. The minute Royce was out

of view, he demurely dropped his arm. "I'll meet you tomorrow," he said, grinning, and left.

Catherine stood exactly where she was for several seconds. She didn't know what game Dan Parker was playing, let alone the rules. All she did know was that she had to speak to Royce. Had to explain why she'd agreed to spend time with Dan Parker.

Royce had gone into the building, and not standing around to debate the wisdom of her actions, she followed him inside.

She found him sitting at his desk, his back to her as he stared off into the distance.

"Royce," she said softly, wondering if it would have been better to greet him formally.

He didn't answer her. The silence seemed to stretch for a hundred miles.

"Royce?" she tried again. "Could we talk for just a minute? I know we agreed not to, but I feel...I wanted you to know why I..."

"I already know why," he said in a loud voice, then lowered his voice and swiveled his chair around. "There's no need to explain."

"But..." To her he looked so pale, beaten. Vulnerable.

"We agreed on one month," he reminded her, but the words didn't come easily from his lips.

"Yes, I know." Still she couldn't make herself leave. It felt so good to be in the same room with him, to talk even if it was only for a few moments on a subject that was painful to them both.

Blue eyes sparred with deep, dark ones in a silent, loving battle of wills.

"Catherine, for the love of God, just leave," he begged in a whisper.

"I can't...."

"As your XO I demand that you go."

The silence returned, this time punctuated with pain. Knowing she was defeated, Catherine crisply saluted, turned and abruptly left.

Catherine didn't see Royce for the next three days. Her appointment with Dan, she hesitated to call it a date, was much ado about nothing. He was charming, undemanding and a perfect gentleman the entire time. Not once did he raise the subject of Royce, and for that, Catherine was grateful enough to agree to see him again sometime soon. They left the date open, another fact for which Catherine was thankful.

Time had never passed so slowly. Catherine had come to her decision the first week. She loved Royce, and wanted to be his wife. What they'd need to do to arrange their marriage, if indeed that was what Royce chose, was another matter entirely. She loved him, she loved Kelly, but she loved the Navy, too.

As did Royce.

Being a part of the military was more than their career choice, it was a way of life each had freely embraced. Her commission was just as important to her as Royce's was to him. Both their careers were bright, with room for advancement. Several years down the road, Catherine could easily envision Royce progressing through the ranks. For her part, Catherine hoped to become a judge. Falling in love, marrying and having a family shouldn't mean they had to jeopardize their careers.

It did mean changes would have to be made, however. Complex changes, as complicated as their love for each other.

Catherine's thoughts were interrupted by the phone. Sambo wove his furry, overfed body between her feet as she stood in the kitchen in front of the can opener. While still holding the can of moist cat food, she reached for the phone. Her intention was to continue feeding Sambo, who could be downright insistent, and talk at the same time.

"Hello."

"Catherine?"

She immediately recognized the small, trembling voice as belonging to Kelly.

"What's the matter?" she asked immediately.

"I'm not afraid."

"Of course you're not," Catherine said, abandoning the cat food entirely. "Tell me what's wrong."

"Dad's not here."

"Yes, I know." Royce was away at scheduled meetings for most of the week. "Isn't Cindy or one of the other neighbor girls with you?" Whenever Royce was going to be away, he paid one of the high-school girls in the neighborhood to come and stay with Kelly.

"Cindy's supposed to be."

"But she's not?" Catherine pried gently.

"Her mom's sick and needs her there. Cindy called and wanted me to go over to her house, but I didn't want to do that because I don't want the flu. I hate throwing up."

Catherine grinned, empathizing with that. "I don't blame you, but there really should be someone with you."

"I'm ten years old!" Kelly declared forcefully. "I'm not a baby anymore."

"I know, sweetheart, but there's no telling how long your father's going to be and it's much more fun to have someone stay with you than to be alone."

"Are you alone?"

That was a trick question if Catherine ever heard one. "Sambo's with me."

"A-are you afraid in the dark?" The question was made in the same trembling voice Kelly had used earlier.

"Sometimes," Catherine admitted. "Why?"

"B-because all the lights went out."

Catherine's heart tripped with concern. "You mean to tell me you're all alone in the dark?" Somehow she managed to curtail her anxiety.

"Yes." Once again Kelly's voice was small and weak. "I'm sure the electricity will come back soon, it's just that it's so-o dark."

"Your dad will be there anytime." Catherine hoped some confidence leaked into her voice. The thought of Kelly pretending to be brave brought out a strong motherly instinct in Catherine.

"Dad's probably on his way now," Kelly said, but she didn't sound any too sure of it. "But in case he isn't…do you think you could come over and stay with me until he gets here? I'm not afraid, really I'm not…I'm just a little bit lonely." She paused and sucked in a deep breath. "It wouldn't be too much trouble for you to come, would it?"

Catherine didn't so much as hesitate. "I'll be there in ten minutes." She hung up the receiver and had already reached for her coat when Sambo reminded her he had yet to be fed. Hurrying across the kitchen, Catherine placed the can of food directly on the floor. Sambo was appeased, but he let it be known he didn't appreciate her haphazard methods of serving him his evening meal.

When Catherine arrived, her headlights silhouetted Kelly, standing in the window with the drapes pulled back, waiting. The minute Catherine turned off the engine, the drape swished back into place. Kelly was standing at the front door waiting for her.

"Hello, sweetheart," Catherine greeted.

Kelly's small arms circled her waist and hung on tightly. "I'm glad you're here. I'm not scared or anything."

"Yes, I know," Catherine said, a smile curving the corners of her mouth. The house was pitch-black. "When did the electricity go off?"

"Just a little before I called you." Kelly aimed the flashlight across the living room. "Dad keeps this one handy in the top kitchen drawer, and I found it right away."

"You were a clever girl."

"You really think so?" Kelly sounded proud of herself.

With her hand on Royce's daughter's shoulder, they advanced into the family room and sat down on the sectional together. Kelly chatted easily, as though it had been ages and ages since they'd last talked, which in fact had been several days.

There was a peacefulness that settled over the area, and the dark, which had once seemed so intimidating and uninviting, began to feel like a welcome friend.

Kelly must have sensed it, too. She placed the back of her hand against her mouth and yawned loudly.

"Are you tired?"

"Not really," Kelly answered just before she yawned a second time, but she snuggled closer to Catherine, propping her head in Catherine's lap. Within minutes the measured, even sounds of Kelly's breathing convinced her the girl was sound asleep.

Catherine must have drifted off herself, because the next thing she knew the lights were on. Straightening, she rubbed the sleep from her face just as Royce walked in from the kitchen.

He stopped abruptly and frowned. "What are you doing here?"

Chapter Ten

"**K**elly was alone," Catherine explained in a husky whisper. "The lights went out and she was afraid." Royce looked shocked, as though he were viewing a ghost. She was certainly the last person he expected to stumble upon in his own home.

Carefully, so as not to waken the slumbering youngster, Catherine gingerly moved from the sectional. She reached for her coat and purse. "Now that you're here, I'll go." She removed the afghan from the back of the sectional and spread it across Kelly, who was dozing peacefully.

"What happened to Cindy?" Royce wanted to know before she left. His mouth had twisted into a tight line of impatience, and Catherine didn't doubt that the teenager was out of a job.

"Her mother came down with a bad case of the flu and she needed her there. She did phone and ask Kelly to walk over to her house."

"It's six blocks. I don't want my daughter traipsing around in the dark." Once more his mouth tightened.

"Kelly didn't go because she hates throwing up."

Royce frowned.

"She didn't want to catch the flu," Catherine explained. The tight features relaxed, and the two shared a warm smile that seemed to arch between them like two ends of a magical rainbow. It had been so long since they'd shared something so intimate. So long since they'd lowered their guards to allow themselves the simple pleasure. Their eyes met and held for the longest moment. Their breaths seemed to echo each other's. Half a room separated them, and yet it was as though they were standing close enough to touch. A thought Catherine found infinitely appealing. There was security in Royce's arms. Security and love.

It was Royce who dragged his eyes away. His hands were buried deep within his pockets. Catherine would have liked to believe he'd placed them there to keep from reaching for her.

"It was good of you to come by," Royce said evenly.

"It wasn't any problem." The only problem was loving him so much and having to pretend otherwise, even when they were alone together. Such pretense went against the very core of her nature.

Royce followed her into the entryway, stepped ahead, then paused, his hand on the doorknob. His back was to her when he hesitated. "How was your dinner with Dan?"

The question caught her by surprise. Idle curiosity was the last thing she expected from Royce. In addition, she'd nearly forgotten that she'd ever gone out with the commander.

"Forget I asked that," Royce stated gruffly, and jerked open the door.

"Dinner was very good. The company, however, was charming, but decidedly uninteresting."

Royce raked his fingers through his hair and kept his gaze lowered. "Are you going out with him again?"

"No."

Royce's eyes, round and dubious, flew up to meet hers. "Why not?"

Catherine felt as though the weight of the entire world

DEBBIE MACOMBER

were pressing down upon her shoulders. Royce honestly seemed to need to know why she had no interest in dating another man. Had she been so lacking in communicating her love? Had she failed in letting him know that he was the very reason she lived and breathed? Didn't he understand that she was prepared to risk everything that was important to her for him?

"You want to know why I'm not dating Dan?" she asked, having trouble hiding how incredible she found the question. "Because, you idiot," she said, battling the urge to sock him, "I'm in love with you."

Royce stood directly in front of her, blocking the door. His eyes, his beautiful blue eyes, drank thirstily from hers, as if it had been years instead of hours since he'd last seen her.

"I shouldn't have asked that." His words were low and dark, laced with a thread of anger, as though he was furious with himself for his lack of control.

"It doesn't matter, really it doesn't," she countered softly, her voice as thin and delicate as the fluttering of her heart.

"Your love matters to me." His eyes lowered to linger on her mouth.

Catherine thought she'd go crazy if he didn't soon kiss her. She wanted him so much that she could taste the desire building within her. It circled her like a binding rope, imprisoning her.

Royce lifted his hand, and his movements were so slow and deliberate. He touched her face, his fingers gently caressing her cheek as if he were blind and was acquainting himself with her. His touch, so light and tender, seemed to reach all the way to her soul. Nothing could have prepared her for the utter beauty of it, the sheer magnitude of these precious, silent moments.

Royce must have felt it, too, the intensity of it. The beauty of it. He was breathing hard when he pulled his hand away, much too hard for such a nondemanding task.

"Thank you for coming," he said, jerking the door open.

"Royce." She wouldn't let him send her away, not again. Not when she needed him so desperately.

"Please…just go." The words were wrenched from him. Sagging with defeat, Catherine did as he requested.

Catherine had dreaded the Birthday Ball all week. She wasn't in any mood to celebrate. Nor was she in the frame of mind to socialize and stand idly by while Royce waltzed around the room with one woman after another. Not when she so longed to be the one in his arms.

She hadn't talked to him since the night she'd gone to be with Kelly. These days were by far the most miserably long ones of her life. It was as if their brief moments together had been ripped out of time. Royce hadn't spoken to her, hadn't looked at her, hadn't acknowledged her.

Catherine had talked to Kelly only once on the phone, hungering all the while for some word from Royce. Something. Anything.

The situation didn't seem to be going any better for him. In the past few days he'd been in one bear of a mood. Half the time it seemed as if he was looking for an excuse to slam his fist through a wall. He wore his bad-boy image as tightly as a glove. It fit him well.

It had taken Catherine only one week of this trial time to make several valid perceptions. She now accepted the fact she was in love with Royce Nyland. But she'd known that before this self-imposed restriction.

She'd also realized that if he asked her to marry him, even if the proposal came on the tail end of a bout of jealousy, or a bout of anything, she'd accept.

What she hadn't anticipated was this heart-wrenching loneliness. The silence that had once fit so comfortably in her life, she now found deafening and painfully disturbing. The pleasure of her own company was sadly lacking.

A hundred times, in a hundred different ways she found herself missing Royce even more than she had in the beginning. Since the night with Kelly, she missed the looks they'd often shared, the strong communication between them that made words superfluous. The throaty sound of his laughter. Oh, how she loved hearing him laugh.

She saw him every day, walked past him, spoke to him as if he meant nothing to her, as if they were little more than casual acquaintances. If she found it hard to continue the sham before, it was doubly so now. Painfully so.

Following through with this charade was difficult enough during the day, but to purposely expose herself to it for this Birthday Ball was a challenge she dreaded.

Catherine was forced to admit, however, how beautiful everything was. The orchestra was playing on the opposite end of the room while a mirrored ball hung overhead, casting reflections of warm light about the room. Romance, music, muted light surrounded the couples that circled the polished dance floor. From a distance they resembled graceful swans coasting on a mirrored lake. It was all so beautiful. So splendid.

Catherine stood on the outer edges of the crowd and looked on, admiring the handsome men dressed in either their dress uniforms or tuxedos. The women wore a variety of gowns. Catherine had chosen to wear the formal evening dress uniform with a long straight skirt of navy blue, with matching jacket.

It wasn't until she'd arrived that she understood her choice of outfit for the evening. She needed to remember she was in the Navy. All too often of late, she'd wanted to disregard the pledges she'd made when she accepted her commission. Love seemed far more important than the rules and regulations, which only went to prove how dangerously shaky her thinking was becoming. Royce was right. They needed this time apart, and since he seemed determined to use every one of these thirty days, she had no recourse but to stand by patiently until he'd come to a decision.

Catherine arrived. Royce noticed her the moment she walked in the door. It was as if everything came to a sudden, grinding halt. The music faded, the dancers went still, even the lights seemed to have dimmed. Royce stood, frozen. An air-raid alarm wouldn't have budged him. He simply stood and watched her, soaking in every delicate nuance of her. She was lovely, so breathtakingly lovely that she quite literally held him spellbound. He'd missed her. Dear Lord, how he'd missed her. He felt as though it had been a thousand years since he'd held her in his arms, a thousand years since he'd tasted her lips. Royce was so damned hungry for her that he would have gratefully accepted a few stolen moments alone even if it meant sitting in the front seat of his Porsche on a lonely deserted road.

"Evening, Nyland."

Royce turned to find himself face-to-face with Admiral Duffy. "Good evening, sir," he said, having trouble even then pulling his eyes away from Catherine.

Catherine found herself scanning the dancers, watching, searching. She wasn't fooling herself, she knew who she was looking to find. She didn't see Royce, at least not at first. It wasn't until later, after she'd gotten herself a cup of punch and was wandering around chatting with casual acquaintances that she found him.

He was across the room from her, involved in a conversation with two other men. The first was the admiral, she could tell that much. The second man was turned at an angle so Catherine couldn't identify him, not that it mattered. Royce captured her full attention.

She knew she was cheating on their promise to each other to be watching him the way she was. But the pleasure she found compensated by far for any feelings of guilt.

Royce was different from when she'd first met him, she mused, extraordinarily pleased by the realization. The changes had been subtle over the weeks, but nevertheless they were there. His features remained harsh, though they relaxed more often into a smile than they used to. He would always possess the same rugged appeal, that wasn't likely to ever change. But there was now a serenity about him, she noted, that had been missing when they'd first met, a tranquillity.

Again Catherine experienced a greedy sense of pride, knowing her love was what had made the difference.

"Lieutenant Commander."

The voice behind her was friendly and familiar. "Good evening, Elaine."

Her secretary was dressed in a red velvet gown and stood next to a tall middle-aged lieutenant, who Catherine recognized immediately as Elaine's husband. "This is my husband, Ralph Perkins."

"How do you do?" Catherine said, extending a hand to the man who played such a large role in her secretary's life. "Your wife is as valuable as my right hand."

"Oh, I know," Ralph said in a smooth southern drawl that caused Catherine to think of antebellum homes with wide sweeping lawns and warm pecan pie fresh from the oven. "I couldn't get along without her, myself."

The three chatted a few minutes longer, before Elaine and her husband headed for the dance floor. For a few moments, Catherine watched them, envious of their freedom to express their love and enjoyment of each other. As she continued to hold on to her punch glass, Catherine's gaze drifted to the floor while she gathered her strength. She was going to need it if she were to make it through this night. When she felt strong enough, she looked over to where she'd last seen Royce.

He was gone. Experiencing a momentary sense of anxiety, she glanced around the room. She couldn't find him anywhere. She searched once again, scanning the crowded ballroom, her gaze moving from one area to another until she happened to catch a glimmer of dark hair and blue eyes when he swirled past her.

Royce was dancing, Catherine realized. Dancing. And it wasn't likely that it was the admiral in his arms.

Catherine had to stop and carefully analyze her feelings. Envy. She would have dearly loved to be the woman in Royce's arms. But she doubted that they would have been able to pull it off. Not tonight, not here with the admirals and captains and all the big mucky-mucks looking on. She was envious, yes, but not jealous.

Royce circled past her a second time, the music crescendoing to a loud climax. Immediately Catherine recognized the white-haired woman in his arms as Admiral Duffy's wife. She felt a little better, knowing the woman was happily married and had been for thirty years. It was little comfort, damn little, but it helped.

Her eyes were on Royce when she felt someone move next to her. "Hello, Catherine."

"Good evening, Dan," she greeted, doing her best to sound friendly. Despite the fact Dan enjoyed playing the role of devil's advocate, Catherine couldn't help liking him. He knew how she felt about Royce and was probably equally knowledgeable of Royce's feelings toward her. But the three of them chose to pretend otherwise. It was amazing when she stopped to think about it.

"Have you saved a dance for me?"

"I...I..."

"More excuses?" he asked with a knowing smile.

"If you don't mind, I'd rather sit this one out."

"My heart is mortally wounded, but I'm becoming accustomed to you knocking my ego around like a tennis ball."

Catherine grinned at the image that sprang readily to her mind. If anyone's heart had been abused, it was her own. And Royce's. Involuntarily, her gaze moved back to him. He really did look...

...she looked distressed. It was ridiculous to waltz around the dance floor with the admiral's wife in his arms and calculate every step so he could watch Dan Parker make a move on Catherine. Ridiculous or not, that was exactly what Royce was doing.

At one time, he'd actually encouraged Dan to ask Catherine out. It had been a futile attempt to stop what was happening between him and Catherine. He couldn't believe he'd done anything so stupid. It wouldn't have worked. There'd never been the slightest possibility of that, but at the time he'd been desperate. He could still remember how angry Catherine had been at him, how she'd walked into his office, her eyes sparking with outrage and fury.

A good deal of water had passed under the bridge since then. The waters of discernment, the waters of perception. What he felt for Catherine was real. Strong. Heady. He hadn't meant to fall in love. He'd avoided love for years. Struggled with it, contested the fact it was possible for a man and woman to truly love each other. His first taste of it had left a bitter aftertaste, and he wasn't eager to experience it again.

"You needn't have turned Dan down, you know."

Breathless emotion clenched Catherine's heart when she realized it was Royce who was speaking to her. She whirled around to discover him standing only a few feet away.

"It wouldn't have mattered," he assured her.

Her heart beat mercilessly against her ribs. She blinked

as though she wasn't sure she should trust herself not to have conjured him up. Her emotions were exhausted. Her nerves shot. This charade was killing her in inches.

"Shall we?" Royce held out his arms to her.

Catherine didn't question the right or wrong of them holding each other on the dance floor. Nor did she object when he slipped his arms around her waist. It was as though they'd been partnering each other for years. Their bodies were in perfect sync, they moved in flawless harmony, swaying naturally, rhythmically to the music.

Catherine's eyes held his, so greedy for the opportunity to study him that she didn't care what he could read in her eyes or who saw them. Nothing mattered but Royce. Her life had been a confused jumble from the time she'd first met Royce Nyland. Why should anything be different now?

"Why do you have to be the most beautiful woman here tonight?" Royce whispered the question close to her ear.

"It's in the genes, what can I tell you?" Catherine teased, and was rewarded by the feel of his mouth smiling against her hair. She knew he was holding her closer than he should, but she couldn't bring herself to ease away.

"I'd give everything I possess to be able to kiss you right now."

Catherine's response was half moan, half sigh. Unfortunately, she was feeling much the same thing herself. She dared to look into his eyes and was rewarded with the promise of sensual delights. For sanity's sake she quickly looked away, but it didn't prevent a hot flush to her cheeks.

"I don't think it's a good idea for you to say things like that…at least not here."

"Oh, and why's that?"

"Royce," she groaned, "you know why. Oh, stop, please stop…someone might notice." His hands were on her waist, and he was dragging her even closer, to a more solid intimacy. Her body was aligned with his in such a way, she could feel every subtle, and not so subtle, part of him.

"Let them look," Royce challenged, his words a low growl in her ear.

"But…"

His lips brushed her cheek. "Do you think I care?"

"Yes," she cried. "We both care."

"Not anymore." Once again his lips bounced lightly against her forehead.

"What…do you mean?"

"I mean there're reasons for us to do this sort of thing without worry, without fearing the consequences."

Catherine's heart clashed like two giant cymbals beating together. Holding her breath, she eased her head back so she could examine his face. His eyes readily met hers, and Catherine gasped softly at what she saw. Love. A love so strong and so determined that it would survive whatever they had yet to face. Royce loved her, with a love that defied logic, defied description. A love that was destined to be the moving force behind what remained of their lives. Neither one of them would ever be the same. Neither one of them would want to be the same.

"I love you so damn much."

Catherine closed her eyes to battle back a flood of feelings so strong they threatened to overwhelm her.

"We're getting married," he announced next.

The very eyes that had drifted shut only a moment earlier, shot open. "When? How?"

Royce laughed, that same throaty, hoarse laugh that had haunted her sleep for nearly two weeks. "I haven't got that part figured out yet, but I'm working on it. It seems, my dear, sensible wife-to-be that I'm about to be transferred."

"When? Where?"

"That's something else that has yet to be decided, but it's in the works."

He was so close, too close, but she needed that, needed the reality of him holding her in his arms even if they were supposed to be dancing. The fact their feet were barely moving didn't seem to concern either of them.

"When did you find out?"

"Tonight," he told her. "Shortly after you arrived. I was watching you, wanting you so much my heart was about to burst wide open when Admiral Duffy decided now was as good a time to tell me my request had been granted. He'd apparently been in contact with the detailers in Washington, D.C."

"You asked for a transfer…you never said—"

"I couldn't go on the way we were."

"Oh, Royce." She'd been watching him this evening, too. She longed to tell him how she'd looked for him the moment she arrived, hungry for the sight of him. But her throat was too thick. She'd tell him later when she could speak without the threat of tears.

"I want you, Catherine, by my side for the next fifty years. I want to make love to you so often they'll need another category in *The Guinness Book of Records*. When I wake up in the mornings, I want you sleeping at my side."

"Oh, Royce."

"Right now I want to kiss you so damn much that I'd be willing to risk shocking every man and woman in this room." His voice had grown reedy with impatience. "Let's get out of here before I do forget where we are and do exactly as my instincts demand."

"Oh, Royce."

"Frankly," he teased, his mouth tantalizingly close to her ear, "I don't remember you having such a limited vocabulary." The music stopped, but he didn't release her. If anything his hold grew more possessive.

"Royce," she hissed, "be good." She feared anyone even remotely glancing at them would immediately know what they felt for each other.

"I want to be bad," he whispered seductively. "Do you want to be bad with me?"

"Oh, yes…"

"Good, then we agree. Now let's leave before someone arrests me for thinking what I'm thinking."

Slowly, with enough reluctance to make her heart long to sing, Royce lowered his arms and released her. "Get your coat and meet me in the parking lot." A lazy grin slashed his mouth. "By now I'm sure you know which car is mine."

"Royce, I…do you honestly think…" Catherine pulled herself up short. "Just exactly how bad do you want to be?"

He chuckled. "I love it when you blush. I don't think I've ever found a woman more appealing than you are right this moment."

"I think you're crazy."

"We both are."

He left her then, hurrying across the room to make his excuses and gather his own coat. Catherine didn't linger. Within a few moments she was outside, searching through a sea of parked cars for Royce's. Before she could spot his black Porsche, he pulled to a fast stop directly in front of her.

The passenger door opened, and Catherine slipped inside. She had barely had time to sit down when Royce reached for her chin, directing her mouth to his for a surprisingly brief, but thorough kiss.

"Royce," she cried, alarmed. "What are you doing?"

"Kissing you." He took advantage of her open mouth by giving her a fleeting taste of his tongue. Despite the fact there could be several important people watching them who wouldn't take kindly to this public display of affection between two officers, one subordinate to the other, Catherine found herself drifting toward him.

"Hold on," he said, shifting gears so hard and fast they ground angrily. The car shot forward. Royce didn't take her far. Just to the other end of the parking lot where it was dark and private. "There's no need to be so impatient," he said, reaching for her even as he spoke. "You're going to have the opportunity to make love to me every night for the rest of our lives."

Chapter Eleven

"Have you gone out of your mind?" Catherine demanded with a free-flowing happiness that refused to be contained.

Royce eased to a stop at the red light, leaned over and kissed her soundly. Once more he used his tongue to tantalize and tease. His eyes were closed when he pulled away. "I am crazy," he murmured, unwilling to deny it, "crazy in love with you."

Catherine felt as though she were in a haze. "I can't believe this is happening."

"Believe it."

The light changed, but Catherine was convinced that, had it stayed red much longer, Royce would have reached for her a second time.

"Just where are you taking me?" The joy seemed to bubble out of her like fizz from an expensive bottle of champagne. If Royce had claimed he was headed for the moon, she would have held on for the ride.

"My house," he told her without hesitating.

"Your house," she repeated slowly.

"Kelly's going to want to be in on this. If we wait until morning to tell her, she'll be furious." Royce's gaze momentarily drifted away from the road, and his rugged features relaxed into a coaxing smile. "I'm convinced Kelly knew there was going to be something between us even before we did."

Catherine sighed and rested her head against the hard cushion of Royce's shoulder. It felt so incredibly good to be with him, so incredibly wonderful. There was nothing in this world to describe it.

A couple of minutes later, Royce eased his Porsche to a stop in his driveway. He turned off the engine and in one smooth movement reached for her. He kissed her hard and fast, and Catherine kissed him back with every ounce of her being.

Royce moaned as he deepened the contact. His tongue dipped to hungrily drink from her love. His hands were in her hair, and when he drew himself away, it was as though he were forcing himself to walk away from the gates of paradise.

"Let's go inside," he suggested, as though they'd best do it soon or else pay the piper.

Catherine nodded. At the moment, formulating words was beyond her passion-drugged brain.

The baby-sitter, a neighborhood teenager, was slouched across the sectional in the family room, watching television and drinking Pepsi. She looked mildly surprised to see Royce home so early. Her gaze left Royce and rested with candid curiosity on Catherine.

"Kelly's asleep," the teenager explained, her gaze drifting away from Catherine long enough to speak to Royce.

"Fine, thanks for coming, Cindy," Royce said, pulling out the money to pay her. He walked her to the door, opening it for her. "Goodbye, now."

"Bye." Cindy peeked around the door at Catherine one last time. She raised her hand. "Bye," she said, directing the comment to her.

"Bye," Catherine said, raising her fingertips.

Royce eased the door closed and locked it after the teenager. When he turned back, his smile was gone. He murmured something Catherine couldn't understand. "I apologize for not introducing you, but there's a very good reason I don't want Cindy to know who you are." He rammed all ten fingers through his hair in an exercise of ill-gained patience. "Although heaven knows she's probably already guessed."

"Don't worry about it." Catherine stepped forward and pressed the tips of her fingers over his mouth. It didn't take much for her to figure out that Cindy was the daughter of someone who could make trouble for them. "I'm not going to let anything or anyone ruin this night."

Gripping her by the shoulders, Royce braced his forehead against hers. "Have I told you how much I love you?"

"Yes, but I'd be willing to listen to it again if you're inclined to tell me."

"I'm inclined," he murmured, his mouth brushing hers. "Get ready because it's going to take me a lifetime to say it properly."

They kissed again. The moment was gentle and sweet, so sweet that Catherine had trouble believing everything that was happening between them was real.

"I better get Kelly," Royce said, unwillingly easing himself from her. "While I still have the strength to pull away from you."

Catherine didn't know who found it more difficult, Royce or her.

"Wait here," Royce said, positioning her at the bottom of the carpeted stairs. "I'll be back in just a moment." He kissed her once more and raced up the stairs, taking them two and three at a time. Catherine could hear Royce talking to Kelly, but as far as she could tell the conversation was strictly one-sided.

Royce appeared at the top of the stairs a few moments

later, a sleeping Kelly draped over his shoulder. The young-ster had on her robe, one patterned with the faces of her favorite rock group, and her feet were dangling with hast-ily donned fuzzy slippers.

"Kelly?" Catherine coaxed softly. "Your father and I have something important to tell you."

Yawning, the sleepy-eyed girl slowly lifted her head from her father's shoulder. "Catherine?"

"I told you she was here," Royce reminded his daughter.

Rubbing her eyes with small fists, Kelly straightened. "But you said Catherine couldn't come over anymore. I'm not supposed to phone her or even say her name unless you tell me it's all right first."

Royce looked downright chagrined. He cast an apolo-getic glance to Catherine, cleared his throat and explained, "Your name came up far too often."

"No, it didn't," Kelly denied, placing her head back down on Royce's shoulder as he carried her down the stairs.

"That's all going to change," Catherine told the young-ster. "Real soon."

"I asked Catherine if she'd marry me, and she's agreed," Royce said. A brilliant smile sat contentedly at the edges of his mouth.

Kelly's head came off Royce's shoulder so fast it was downright comical. "You're going to marry Catherine?" she cried, then squeezed her dad around the neck. Royce's shining eyes met Catherine's, and he stuck out his tongue as though he were in danger of being strangled.

"Oh, Catherine, I'm so happy." Kelly broke away from her father, twisted around and reached for Cather-ine, squeezing her equally hard. "I can't believe it! This is the happiest day of my whole, entire life. I'm not dreaming, am I?"

"No, sweetheart," Royce said, sharing an intimate look

with Catherine, "this is very real." He set a squirming Kelly down on the carpet.

"This is great. This is *really* great." Kelly slapped her hands hard against the sides of her legs. "What I want to know is what took you guys so long?"

"Ah…" Catherine hesitated.

"I realize there were a few minor problems, but as far as I could see you both stretched everything way out of proportion. Heaven knows how long it would have taken you to come to your senses if it hadn't been for me."

"That's true," Royce agreed, looking to Catherine and poignantly rolling his eyes. He moved to her side and slipped his arm around her shoulder with a casual easiness that suggested he'd been doing so for a good long while. "The thing is, sweetheart," Royce said, his eyes dark and serious, "we're going to have to keep this a secret. Understand?" The entire wedding would need to be handled discreetly.

Kelly nodded, then pretended to zip her lip closed.

"When?" Kelly demanded.

Royce's gaze caught Catherine's. "Soon, I hope."

"Great. Now, listen, we don't have a whole lot of time to waste with this." The ten-year-old stalked into the living room, sat down and crossed her legs. "Well, come here," she said, gesturing for them to follow her.

Catherine and Royce stared blankly at each other.

"Come here," Kelly repeated when they hesitated. "We don't have all night, you know."

"Exactly what is it you want to talk to us about?" Royce demanded.

"What else is there to discuss?" Kelly cried. "My baby sister!"

"Ah…" Catherine's gaze darted to Royce, who did a good job of looking as stumped as she. Children. Kelly wanted to discuss enlarging their family when they hadn't decided on a wedding date. Good heavens, Catherine had yet to figure out how they were going to pull this whole shenanigan off without anyone from the base finding out, and Kelly wanted to discuss a baby sister.

Royce's arm circled Catherine's waist as they moved into the formal living room. "What's the matter, darling, has the cat got your tongue?"

"A baby sister," Catherine repeated slowly, thoughtfully. She didn't want to burst Kelly's bubble, but at the same time the ten-year-old needed to be aware that there were several things to consider before they discussed a pregnancy.

Catherine sat down on the bronze velvet sofa. Royce sat slightly behind her, his arms circling her waist. "I was hoping we could talk about other matters," Catherine suggested, thinking of a tactful way of changing the subject.

"We could." Kelly was willing to concede that much. "I can be the flower girl, can't I?"

"Anything you want." Catherine hadn't gotten around to thinking that far ahead, but she certainly didn't have any objections if that was what Kelly wanted.

"I was thinking pink."

"Pink?" Royce repeated as though he'd never heard the word before. "Pink what?"

"For the wedding colors, of course." Kelly tossed him a look that suggested his presence wasn't at all necessary, at least not right then. "You look real pretty in pink, Catherine, and it's a nice omen."

"Omen?" This time it was Catherine who couldn't find her way around Royce's fast-talking daughter.

"For my baby sister."

"Of course, how silly of me." Catherine was beginning to feel that Kelly wasn't so much interested in gaining a mother as she was looking for a vehicle to deliver her long-awaited sibling.

"What if we have a son first?" Catherine wanted to know. She should find out these things just in case Kelly intended to boot her out of the family for having delivered something other than the specified request.

Kelly wrinkled her nose as if she found the mere suggestion distasteful. "I suppose a boy would be all right. I've heard lots of talk from the girls at school about how dads really like having sons. Personally, I'd much prefer a sister, but I guess this is just one of those things that we'll leave up to God."

"I have no idea where she comes up with this stuff," Royce whispered for Catherine's benefit.

"Does this mean we're moving?" Kelly wanted to know next, her look pensive.

Royce went tense behind Catherine. She realized this was the part Royce dreaded most. Bangor was the only Navy base Kelly had ever known, although Royce had been stationed in other Puget Sound bases. Uprooting his daughter had been Royce's primary concern about the two of them marrying. "More than likely we'll be moving."

After having a good deal to say about everything else, Kelly simply nodded.

"Does that bother you?" Catherine asked.

"Not really. Lots of other kids in my school have lived all over the world. Everyone says that if you join the Navy you get shipped everywhere. I think it's our turn. Actually, when you think about it, it's time we left Bangor."

"I don't know where we're going yet."

"But where do you think?" Kelly pressed.

"I'm hoping to be assigned to the Navy station in Bremerton, but we can't count on that."

"Really!" Kelly jumped off the couch and clapped her hands. "That'd be great. We could move to Catherine's apartment and Sambo could sleep with me and it'd hardly be moving at all."

"But we can't count on that. Admiral Duffy's promised to see what he can do."

"Where else?"

"There's always a chance I'll go to Pensacola, Florida."

Once again Kelly was on her feet clapping wildly. "All right, Disney World here I come."

"Sweetheart," Royce said, looking more than a little surprised by his daughter's reaction to the possibility of moving across the country. "Just remember, I haven't a clue where we're headed. So we should be prepared for anything."

"Does it matter where we move?" Kelly asked with a sanguine smile. "Catherine will be with us."

"Maybe," Royce corrected.

Kelly's bright blue eyes narrowed suspiciously. She set her fists against her hip bones and glared across the room. "Exactly what do you mean by that?"

"First we have to find out where your father's going to be stationed," Catherine explained, loving the expressive way Kelly had of letting her feelings be known. "Then I need to request a transfer there myself, or at least to a base close to where your dad's stationed. We still won't be able to be in the same command, but—"

"What happens if the Navy decides to send Dad one place and you another?"

It was a distinct possibility, and one Catherine prayed they'd never have to consider.

"We'll cross that bridge when we come to it," Royce assured the three of them.

Kelly's nod was profound. "Good thinking." She crossed her arms and leaned back against the sofa. "Now that we've got that out of the way, there are a couple of other things we need to discuss."

"Is that a fact?" Royce said, but the look he shared with Catherine suggested that he was as much at a loss as she.

Kelly cleared her throat, and her face grew dark and serious. "No hanky-panky."

"I beg your pardon." Royce was indignant.

"You heard me." Kelly's index finger shot out in a way that would have made teachers across America proud. "Not until you're married at least. I'm not a little kid anymore," Kelly informed them with a righteous tilt to her chin. "I know what kind of stuff goes on between men and women. I watch MTV."

"I don't believe this is any of your concern, young lady." Royce was frowning, but Catherine wasn't entirely sure what was bothering him; the fact Kelly watched racy music videos, or that she was insisting on curtailing their romantic involvement.

"You wouldn't want to taint my young mind, would you?"

"If I'm going to taint anything, it'll be your backside," Royce announced loudly.

The threat was real enough for Kelly to sit on her hands to protect her posterior.

"This is the same kid who was afraid in a power outage," Catherine whispered to Royce.

"That was a trick."

"She turned off all the lights herself?"

"No," Royce said, and shook his head for emphasis. "She called you over knowing I'd be back any minute, thereby forcing the two of us to deal with each other."

"You always told me it's impolite to whisper," Kelly said indignantly from across the room. She stood, yawned once and headed for the stairs. "I'll be back in just a moment."

"You'll be back?" Royce repeated.

"Of course. I'll need to go with you when you take Catherine home. You don't honestly expect me to stay here alone, do you?"

"Ah…"

"What's the matter, love?" Catherine murmured, flexing her long nails against Royce's arms, which were wrapped securely around her waist. "Has the cat got your tongue?"

"I'll only be a minute," Kelly said, rushing up the stairs.

"Which means…" Royce said, drawing Catherine back on to the thick sofa cushions. He felt solid and strong, and just the feel of him was enough to ease the terrible loneliness that had haunted her for nights on end.

Catherine raised her arms to link them around his neck. His eyes were on her. "So much for us being bad." He lowered his mouth and feasted.

"Ho hum." Kelly coughed loudly, disrupting them a few minutes later. "Not a good idea," she announced. "There's plenty of time for that sort of thing later. Right now we've got a wedding to think about."

"A flower girl," Royce murmured, slowly untangling his arms from around Catherine. "I have a feeling that by the time this wedding takes place, Kelly may be in a boarding school in Switzerland."

The following week was impossible. That was the only way Catherine could think to define it. Knowing Royce was being transferred, but not knowing where made any planning impossible. They couldn't arrange for a wedding until several factors were figured into the equation. First and foremost they needed to know when Royce would be dispatched. The news of his new duty assignment could come at any moment, and Royce could be ordered to ship out with as little as twenty-four-hours notice and as much as six months.

The restrictions upon them were just as stringent as before. As Kelly had so eloquently put it, *no hanky-panky.* Catherine would have paid anything just for the opportunity to "be bad" with Royce, but that, too, was prohibited. They'd come too far to risk everything now.

Catherine was sitting at her desk when Royce strolled into the office. "Lieutenant Commander, could I see you in my office, right away?"

"Yes, sir."

Elaine Perkins scooted back to her chair as Catherine left her office, her secretary's gaze following Royce. "Ol' stoneface seems to be in a pleasant enough mood lately, don't you think?"

"I wouldn't know," Catherine said before she let something slip that she'd soon regret. She'd long suspected that her observant secretary was aware of her feelings for Royce, but it was a subject neither dared broach.

"How can you not have noticed?" Elaine demanded. "I actually saw Commander Nyland smiling the other day. Smiling. Not that I could see there was anything to smile about, but that's not my concern. Up until recently I assumed it would take an act of Congress to get that man to so much as grin. Lately that's all changed."

Catherine didn't comment. "Do you want me to ask him what he found so amusing? I'll tell him you're curious to find out."

"Funny, Catherine, very funny."

Amused herself, Catherine walked into Royce's office and closed the door. "You wanted to see me?"

"How do you feel about living in Virginia?" he asked without warning. "I've been assigned to Submarine Force, Atlantic Fleet at Norfolk."

"Virginia," she repeated slowly. Her heart was pounding hard. "I'd love Antarctica if I could be there with you."

Royce grinned, and their eyes held each other. "I feel the same way."

"How much time do I have?" She arched her brows expectantly, waiting for him to respond.

"Two weeks."

"Two weeks." Catherine's heart sank as she lowered

herself into a chair and closed her eyes. Her mind started buzzing. It wasn't possible. It simply wasn't possible.

But it had to be! She'd do whatever she must to arrange it so they could be married before he was deployed.

"Catherine?"

She was on her feet again and not quite sure how she got there. She blinked once, then smiled over to Royce, confident her smile covered her entire face. "Two weeks," she repeated, and nodded once, willing to accept the challenge. "I've got a whole lot of planning to do."

Royce looked concerned. "I don't want to postpone the wedding." It went without saying that the ceremony would have to be discreet. For the two of them to marry so quickly after Royce was detached from the command would be a problem. They'd discussed it at length and had agreed to fly to San Francisco for the ceremony.

Catherine cast him a look that assured him otherwise. "I don't want to wait, either." They were both well aware that it would be better for them to let several months pass. But neither found that acceptable. "I'll contact my mother right away. She'll help with the arrangements. Personally, I doubt that I'd be able to pull this off without her."

"You can contact the whole state of California if that's what you want. Just as long as you're at the church on time."

"I'll be there, don't you worry."

"Mom, it's Catherine."

"Sweetheart." Her mother's voice was elevated with pleasure. "It's so good to hear from you."

"How's work…I mean, you're not into anything heavy, are you?"

"No more than usual."

"Good." Catherine hesitated. She really would be asking a good deal of her mother, who was a newlywed herself, but there was no help for it.

"Good? Why's that?" Once again her mother's voice was raised with curiosity.

"Because I need you to do something for me…"

"Of course, whatever you need."

"I need your expertise—" She wasn't allowed to finish.

"Catherine, you're a fine lawyer, I'm sure you don't need my opinion, and furthermore I don't think the Navy would take kindly to my interfering in something that has to do with the military."

"Not in the courts, Mom." Catherine couldn't keep from grinning. The happiness was oozing out of her. "Royce asked me to marry him."

"I thought he'd already done that."

"He wasn't serious then, only jealous."

"I take it he's serious this time?"

"Very serious. He arranged for a transfer before he proposed. He's been assigned to the submarine base in Virginia. I've put in for a transfer there myself."

"And?" The question came after a noticeable pause.

"And I haven't heard yet. But we want to be married as soon as possible. We can't let anyone know, at least not right away. The whole thing has to be handled delicately."

"Of course. But once you're married, the Navy wouldn't separate a husband and wife, will it?"

"You're joking, Mom?" Catherine asked with a light laugh. "I thought you knew the military better than that. The Navy does what's most convenient for the Navy. Royce and I have no right falling in love in the first place."

"But he'll be in Virginia, and you might well end up stationed in Washington."

"We don't know that yet. Royce is pulling every string he can to make sure that doesn't happen. Even if worse comes to worse and I do have to stay here, it won't be forever. Eventually we'll be together."

"I don't like the sound of this, Catherine," her mother said in low, concerned tones.

"Trust me, it's essential for right now."

"Not necessarily. Sweetheart, don't you think you should consider resigning from the Navy?"

It was an argument Catherine had been having with herself for several days. She'd talked it over with Royce, and they'd batted the idea back and forth several times, but she'd been adamant and he hadn't pressured her. "I'm not leaving the Navy," she argued forcibly with her mother. "I'm not giving up my career just because I happened to fall in love."

"You'll always be an attorney, and frankly, I've never understood why you don't simply join a law firm, you'd do much better financially."

"That's an old argument and not one I'm going to get involved with now. I've come too far to resign now. Besides, of all the people in the world, I would have thought you'd understand my feelings about the Navy. Resigning isn't even up for consideration. Royce knows that and accepts it."

"But, Catherine, sweetheart, be reasonable, what man wants to be separated from his wife by thousands of miles?"

"You're making it sound like a foregone conclusion that I won't be transferred with him. In every likelihood I will, so quit worrying about it," Catherine stated heatedly. She immediately felt contrite. Her mother wasn't telling her something she hadn't already debated long and hard. The Navy was important to both her and Royce. Catherine noted, however, that no one suggested he resign his commission and become a civilian because he wanted to marry her.

"What about children?"

"Mom, I don't think we're gong to accomplish anything

productive going over this now. I've got less than two weeks to make all the necessary arrangements. Royce is detaching from his command here, which helps. Can you send us whatever it is we need to file for a wedding license in California?"

"Of course."

"Good." But her mother was right. What about children? Catherine didn't know if she was being greedy to want it all. A career, a family and the Navy. That was a question she had yet to face.

The next few days passed in a whirlwind of frantic activity. Catherine barely saw Royce, barely talked to him. Late in the week he and Kelly flew to Virginia to make the necessary arrangements for housing.

Friday after work, Catherine returned to her apartment in a haze of concern. Over the next two days she spent hours on the phone with her mother, arranging for the florists, photographers and trying on every wedding dress within two counties.

Royce called her late Sunday evening. "Hello, beautiful," he greeted in a soft, sexy voice that curled her toes.

She was exhausted physically and mentally. "Hello yourself," she answered, fighting back a powerful need to have his arms around her. Instead she forced herself to ask all the right questions. "Did you and Kelly find a house?"

"Within the first day. It's perfect. Three bedrooms, nice family room, a large kitchen and all for a reasonable rent." Royce hadn't been able to obtain housing on the base, which made the move just a little more difficult. Kelly had considered it important to accompany him on this trip so she could scout out the schools and choose the right kind of neighborhood, which meant one with lots of girls her age.

"What did Kelly think of Virginia?"

"It was radical this and radical that. At least that's what

I seem to remember her saying. Right now everything's new and fun. I don't think she's going to have any problems making the adjustment."

Catherine snuggled up on the sofa, the phone cord stretched as far as it would go from the kitchen wall. Her gaze rested on the photograph of her father, lingering there for several moments. "Kelly's going to be making a whole lot of adjustments in the next few weeks." It worried Catherine that Royce's daughter was suffering the brunt of the sacrifices they each were forced into making for this marriage.

"Kelly's resilient. Trust me, she would have willingly moved to the jungles of darkest Africa if it meant you were going to be part of our family."

"I love you." Catherine felt the need to say it. It suddenly seemed important for her to voice her feelings.

"I love you, too." After the hectic craziness that had surrounded them for what seemed like months on end, it was good to sit in the solitude of her home and cherish the words she'd longed to hear for so many weeks.

"I didn't want to love you, at least not at first," Royce admitted roughly. "God knows I tried to stay away from you."

"I tried, too."

"I'd give anything to have you in my arms right now."

"That's all going to change soon, and I'll be in your arms for the rest of our lives." She said it as a reminder to herself, wiping the moisture from her cheek. She should be the happiest woman in the world. Within a matter of days she and Royce would be man and wife. Yet the envelope sitting on the corner of her desk was a constant reminder of how quickly that happiness could be tarnished.

Royce paused, and although he must be exhausted, Catherine realized he'd picked up on the fact she was miserably unhappy. She tried so hard to hide it behind busy questions and a cheerful facade.

"Are you going to tell me?" he demanded softly.

"There's no need to spoil everything now. You'll find out soon enough…. You're back safe and sound, and that's what matters. Mission accomplished. Kelly's happy. What more could you possibly want?"

"You."

"Oh, my darling, you have me. You've held on to my heart for weeks on end, don't you know that?"

"I already know, Catherine," he told her softly. "You don't need to hide it from me."

She sucked in her breath. "When did you find out?"

"Friday before I left."

Her request for transfer had been denied. The worst scenario. Her worst nightmare. She was going to be stationed in Bangor while Royce and Kelly were on the other side of the country.

"Oh, Royce," she asked softly, "what are we going to do?"

"Exactly what we're planning. I'm marrying you, Catherine, come hell or high water."

Chapter Twelve

The wedding ceremony took place Friday evening in a small San Francisco chapel with the pastor from Marilyn Fredrickson-Morgan's church. The altar was decorated with brilliant red poinsettias, and although Royce wasn't much into flowers, he was impressed with the traditional Christmas flower that crowded every square inch of floor space around the altar. Catherine and her mother had done a beautiful job. Even Kelly who'd first suggested a pink color scheme approved of the festive red bows and other complements.

As for the ceremony itself, Royce remembered little of what progressed. The moment he'd stepped over to join the reverend and viewed Catherine slowly marching down the aisle toward him, he'd been so lost in her loveliness that everything else around him had faded.

Even the small reception afterward with both families and a few close friends remained hazy in his mind. Catherine fed him a piece of heart-shaped cake bordered with red roses and sipped champagne. They even danced a couple of times.

There had been gifts, too. Royce couldn't get over how many when there were less than fifty people at the entire wedding.

Kelly had been in her element. Royce's parents had flown in from Arizona, along with a couple of his aunts and uncles. Even his younger brother and his family had managed to make it up from the southern part of the state. Kelly had basked in all the attention. She'd taken to Marilyn and Norman almost as quickly as she'd taken to Catherine herself.

His daughter delighted in announcing to any and everyone who would listen that he and Catherine owed everything to her. She'd also sounded like something of a parole officer when she admitted to Catherine's mother that she'd personally seen to it that no hanky-panky had been allowed before the wedding ceremony.

At the moment Catherine was changing clothes, something she'd done once or twice already since the wedding. He couldn't understand why she insisted on dressing when he fully intended on undressing her the minute they arrived at the hotel room he'd booked.

Royce would much rather have chosen someplace romantic for their honeymoon. Unfortunately they weren't going to have a whole lot of time together before he assumed his duties in Virginia. With a limited time schedule, Royce quickly decided he'd rather spend it in bed with Catherine than on the road seeking out the perfect romantic hideaway.

A private room on one of the beaches might have worked out nicely, but the San Francisco hotel offered one advantage the others didn't. Room service.

Royce had two short days with Catherine, and he sure as hell didn't plan on spending any of it sightseeing.

It seemed to take the taxi forever to reach the hotel. They chatted about the wedding, teased and even managed to kiss a couple of times. It wasn't until they'd registered and were on their way up to the honeymoon suite that it hit Royce.

He was nervous.

Royce Nyland jittery! It was almost enough to make him laugh. Marriage wasn't a new experience to him. He'd been through it all before. If anything was different it was the fact he and Catherine had yet to make love.

Sandy had been sleeping with him for months before they'd seriously discussed getting married. Royce wished to hell he'd made love to Catherine before now. It might have eased the knot twisting his gut.

No it wouldn't, he amended promptly. When it came right down to it, he was glad they'd waited. It hadn't been easy, even with Kelly wagging her finger under their noses at every opportunity.

He didn't need his daughter reminding him to be good, or anyone else for that matter. The Navy had seen to it all on its own. He'd followed the law book, with only a few minor infractions. He'd made the best of a sticky situation. But, by heaven, Catherine was his wife now, and he was ready to attempt a new world's record for lovemaking!

A warm sensation softened his heart. He was doing everything right this time. Right by Catherine. Right by himself. Right by the Navy. There was a gratifying sort of comfort knowing that.

"Are you hungry?" he asked.

"A little." Royce swore she sounded as on edge as he did, which pleased him. At least he wasn't the only one experiencing qualms.

"Do you want to order something from room service?" He found a menu by the phone and scanned the list of entrées. Nothing sounded particularly appetizing, but if Catherine was interested, he'd order something for her.

"I'd be willing to eat something," she said lightly, but Royce wasn't fooled. Dinner was a delay tactic for them both.

They ordered a fancy meal, but Royce noted that neither of them seemed to have much of an appetite once the food arrived. So his gutsy Catherine was nervous, too. Royce found that endearing, and he was charmed by her all the more.

What they really needed to get things rolling, Royce decided when he set the food tray outside their door, was the front seat of a car. The thought produced a wide grin, one he suspected would have made a Cheshire cat proud.

"You're smiling," Catherine said when he returned. "What's so amusing?"

"Us. Come here, woman, I'm tired of pussyfooting around this. I want to make love to you, and I'm not waiting any longer." He held his arms open to her, and she walked toward him, slipping tidily into his embrace. They fit together perfectly. Royce believed they had been created for each other. For a cure for all the lonely, barren years he'd spent alone. Years she'd spent alone.

He kissed her once gently and felt her breath, hot and fiery, against his throat. One kiss and Royce was suddenly as weak as a newborn kitten. It didn't help matters any to have her snuggle against him, her skin silky and warm.

Royce's hands were trembling as he reached for the zipper at the back of her dress. Catherine straightened and raised her arms so he could lift the silky garment over her head. It slipped right off, and she rewarded him for his efforts by trailing her lips over the corded muscles of his neck and shoulders, her tongue slipping over the hollow of his throat.

Royce closed his eyes to the deluge of feelings. His heart started to pound, but that wasn't his only reaction. His whole body had started throbbing. He couldn't remove his clothes fast enough. Once his shirt was free of his waistband, Catherine took over for him, slowly, too slowly to suit him, unfastening the buttons one by one. She sighed softly and fanned her hands across his chest, her nails innocently tugging against the hairs of his chest like a kitten yearning for attention.

"Oh, Royce... Kiss me, please kiss me."

He caught his breath and then did as she asked, spreading hot kisses across her delicate shoulders, then up the side of her exquisite neck until their mouths met in a burst of spontaneous combustion that was so fierce it threatened to consume them both.

Her tongue shyly met his, and he groaned, the sound rough and masculine to his own ears. Catherine moaned, too, and it was the most sensual, erotic whimper Royce had ever heard. He had to touch her, had to feel for himself her excitement, had to taste it and know she wanted him as desperately as he hungered for her.

His hands massaged her back, and he was gratified to realize she'd removed her bra. She leaned into him, absorbing what little strength he possessed, and looped her arms around his neck. Royce's hands cupped her breasts. They were soft and full, so marvelously lush and round. The nipples instantly pearled, and the feel of them puckering, hardening, then scraping against his palms as she moved against him sent a wave of molten sensation over him.

Royce raised his head and judged the distance to the bed. Lifting her into his arms, Royce stalked across the carpet like a warrior hauling his conquest into the middle of camp.

He pressed Catherine onto the mattress and then joined her, being sure he didn't suffocate her with his weight.

He kissed her again and again, so many times he lost count, so many times that she melted against him, her eyes pleading with him for the completion they both sought.

Royce couldn't wait another moment, another second. His hands caught the sides of her lace panties and dragged them down her silken legs. He rolled aside long enough to glide open the zipper of his slacks and ease them over his own hips.

Once they were both free of restrictive clothing, he knelt over her. Her eyes were golden, hot with need. Royce nearly groaned just looking at her, just feeling the heat radiating from her smooth ivory skin.

She raised her hand to his face, her fingertips grazing his cheekbone. "Love me," she whispered. "Just love me."

Her words, her touch were all the inducement Royce needed. He positioned himself over her, using his thighs to part hers. She opened to him without reserve, without restraint.

By all that was holy, Royce didn't know where he found the strength to go slowly, to linger, prolonging the moment. Her eyes held his as he pushed forward, gliding the throbbing, aching staff of his manhood into her.

If he were ever going to die from pleasure, it would have been at that moment. Catherine was ready for him, waiting for him, so sweet and hot and moist, Royce knew in a heartbeat that he dare not move.

His eyes returned to hers, which were half-closed as she, too, drank in the exquisite tumult. After giving her a moment to adjust to him, Royce continued easing himself into her until she had taken in all of him.

Breathing hard, Catherine raised her knees and bucked beneath him. Royce groaned aloud as a flash of white-hot pleasure shot through him. Unable to endure much more, he pushed forward and was nearly consumed with the second wave of moist, hot bliss. When his eyes connected with Catherine, he noted that she was biting hard into her lower lip.

"I'm hurting you?" He didn't know if her reaction was one of pleasure or pain.

"No…oh, no," she whispered. "I never knew anything could feel this good."

"This is only the beginning," he promised. He closed his

eyes in order to savor every sensation, drink in every fiery aspect of their lovemaking.

He honestly meant to go slow. He had to, he felt, in order to fully appreciate the magic between them. But once he started to rotate his hips, he was lost. Lost in pleasure. Lost in the storm, but he wasn't alone. Catherine clung to him, answering each bold thrust with one of her own.

It was a storm. One of need. One of fury and frenzy. It came on quickly, with such intensity that Royce was pitched from one world to another until he realized there was no slowing down, no going back. No stopping. Not for heaven, not for hell. For pain or for pleasure.

His climax came as a searing completion, far too quickly to suit Royce. He didn't want it to end, not now. Not so soon.

Catherine's labored breathing matched his own, and the sound of it was the only thing that shattered the silence as they both burned in the wake of the sweetest tempest Royce had ever known.

Royce woke around three to the sounds of Catherine singing. She was taking a shower. In the middle of the night no less.

Grinning, he rolled onto his back and raised his arms, cupped his head beneath his hands. They'd made love twice and then fallen into an exhausted sleep. The last thing Royce remembered was Catherine snuggling close to him, berating the fact she had yet to put on the special lace nightie she'd bought for their wedding night.

She came out of the bathroom and was bent over, briskly rubbing a towel over her wet hair. When she raised her head, she noted that Royce was lying in bed, watching her. Something he was sure she'd enjoy doing for many more years yet to come.

"I didn't wake you, did I?"

"As a matter of fact, you did." She had on the skimpiest nightie he'd ever seen. Although he was exhausted and physically drained, seeing her in that slip of black lace seriously threatened his composure.

"I apologize. I guess I shouldn't have started singing, but I just couldn't help myself…I don't know when I've been so happy. I don't think I ever want to leave this room."

Royce was thinking much along those same lines himself. He held out his arms. "Come here, woman."

Surprised, she glanced toward the bathroom. "I was going to blow-dry my hair."

"Later. You woke me, and there's a penance to be paid."

"But, Royce, it's the middle of the night. We've already…you know…several times."

"Come here." He grew impatient waiting for her. He rolled off the bed, walked over to where she was standing and removed the towel from her head, letting it fall to the carpet. He threaded her wet hair through his splayed fingers, cherishing the feel of her, so warm and moist. That caused him to think of other places on her delectable body that were warm and moist, too.

"What are you doing?"

"What am I doing now or what do I intend to do later?" he asked, wiggling his eyebrows provocatively.

"We've already done everything there is to do," she announced primly.

"Is that a fact." He kissed her, sweeping his mouth across hers and giving her a taste of his tongue.

"Well, maybe not everything," she amended. He nibbled his way across her jaw to her earlobe and whispered seductive promises to her. He smiled, loving it when she responded with a sharp gasp.

"Royce… Why that's indecent."

"Oh, really." He kissed her a second time, sliding his tongue across the parted seam of her lips. Once more he captured the lobe of her ear between his teeth and sucked lightly. Then he whispered what he intended to do to her in a very short while.

"Royce!" Her eyes went wide. He loved watching her cheeks turn a fetching shade of pink.

Royce couldn't help it, he laughed. "And not just once, either. I have a lot of time to make up for, and you, my dear, sweet wife, have fallen right into my hands."

"But I...oh, Royce," she moaned as he traced a row of moist kisses across her face until he found her lips. The kiss was wet and wild. Wild and sweet.

His hands were busy trying to figure out how to take off the flimsy black nightie she wore. He eased the satin straps down her shoulders. She worked her arms free for him until he could remove the top completely, liberating her luscious breasts. He slid his palms over their fullness. Up and down, savoring her softness. Her femininity.

Unable to wait a moment longer, he lifted her into his arms and carried her to the bed, pressing her into the mattress. His body followed, covering hers. Instinctively she opened to him, and he entered her in one swift movement.

Catherine moaned.

Royce sighed.

Then the storm took over and they moved as one to hold back the torrent, or perhaps to bring it on—Royce didn't know which. The world went spinning out of control, a hurricane of wild need that consumed them both.

Catherine woke slowly. A serene smile lifted the corners of her mouth, and she rolled onto her back and raised her arms high above her head, as content as Sambo stretching after taking a long nap in the sunlight. Instinctively she rolled onto her side, seeking the warmth and comfort of Royce's body.

The space beside her was empty, however. And cold.

Her eyes opened, and sadness settled over her, blocking out the early-morning sunlight.

They'd spent less than five nights together. Five nights out of a lifetime, and she continued to search for him. At night she tossed restlessly in her sleep, seeking his warmth, seeking his strength. No one had warned her how dangerously addictive it was to sleep with a husband.

Royce and Kelly were in Norfolk and had been for two weeks. They communicated often. Letters arrived nearly every day, and their phone bill rivaled the defense budget. Yet Catherine found the grating loneliness inescapable.

She didn't know which was worse. Loving Royce and being forced to hide the way she felt behind a deluge of Navy regulations or being married to him and separated by two thousand endless miles.

It wouldn't be any worse if Royce were stationed aboard one of the submarines, at least that was what she told herself. They'd be apart for months on end. Just the way they were now.

Before he and Kelly had left for Norfolk, they'd made plans for Catherine to join them over the Christmas holidays. That wasn't so long to wait.

A few days. Surely she could hold on to her peace of mind for a few more days, especially when they were said to be the shortest days of the year.

Catherine did manage to survive, but just barely. Royce and Kelly were waiting for her at the airport when her plane touched down. The minute Kelly saw her, she flew into Catherine's arms, hugging her as though it had been years since they'd last seen each other.

"Oh, Catherine, I'm so glad you're here."

Catherine was glad, too. She raised her head, and her eyes connected with Royce's. His were warm and welcoming. She stepped into his embrace and squeezed tight.

"We've got everything ready for you," Kelly told her excitedly. "Dad and I worked real hard putting up the Christmas tree and wrapping presents. I even helped him clean the kitchen and everything."

"Thank you sweetheart. I appreciate it so much." She gave the ten-year-old a second bear hug. She'd missed Royce's daughter, too, more than she'd thought possible.

"Can we do my nails again?" Kelly asked, holding out her hands for a visual inspection. "They look just wretched, don't they?"

"Of course we'll both work on our nails."

"Shopping, too. Dad's simply impossible, but then he always was."

Royce collected her luggage and led the way through the terminal to the parking garage. The ride into Norfolk took only a few minutes. The weather had cooperated beautifully, and the sky was crisp and clear with a sprinkling of stars scattered boldly across the horizon of black velvet.

The colonial house was exactly as Royce had described. Catherine liked it immediately and felt its welcome the minute she walked through the wreath-covered door.

"Did you miss me?" Kelly asked, clinging to Catherine's arm. "Because I sure missed you," Kelly said, and then her voice lowered. "Dad missed you, too."

"Oh, sweetheart, I missed you both so much."

"What about…" Kelly paused and darted a look toward her father. Once more she lowered her voice several decibels. "You know."

Catherine didn't know. "What?"

Losing patience, Kelly clenched her fists against her hipbones. "A baby. Are you pregnant yet, or not?"

"Not," Royce informed his daughter crisply.

"Not," Catherine echoed in a far more gentle tone. Unfortunately. Catherine had given a good deal of thought to the idea of them adding to their family. True, Kelly want-

ing, or rather demanding a baby sister, had been the cat-
alyst, but when Catherine analyzed it, she had to admit
the ten-year-old had a valid point. Royce was already in
his late thirties, and she was at the age when all the internal female workings were at their peak.

Catherine wasn't keen about going through a pregnancy
without Royce being close to love and pamper her during
the discomforts she was likely to encounter. Yet Navy officers through the ages had suffered no less. She wasn't an
exception.

Beyond all the other token reasons, Catherine longed
for Royce's child. The matter had been on her mind every
minute that she'd been separated from Royce these past
two weeks. She might be rushing matters, but the idea
strongly appealed to her. She planned to approach her
husband about the subject during this brief visit. If everything went according to schedule, this might well be a
bonus Christmas.

Kelly chatted for the next hour, telling Catherine all
about her school and her new friends. Catherine had heard
it all before, but gave her rapt attention to Kelly while
Royce brewed hot-buttered rums.

"All I get is hot butter," Kelly said with a grimace when
Royce delivered the steaming drinks.

"The only reason you get that is so you'll go up to bed
the way you promised."

"Dad!" Kelly exclaimed. "It's Christmas Eve's eve. You
don't honestly expect me to go to bed at the regular time,
do you?"

"It's two hours past your bedtime already," he reminded
her. "Now drink up and hit the sack."

"You just want time alone with Catherine," the young-
ster accused as she sipped from the edge of her mug. "But,"
she added with an expressive sigh, "I can understand. People in love need that."

"Thank you, Dear Abby," Royce teased. "Now scoot."

Kelly took one last sip of her drink, then set it on the counter. She gave both Royce and Catherine hugs, then dutifully marched up the stairs.

Now that Catherine was alone with her husband, she watched as he stood and turned out the lamps until the only light illuminating the room came from the ones blinking on the Christmas tree. Although dim, the beautifully decorated tree gave off a soft glare, enough for her to realize Royce was studying her. His cobalt-blue eyes said all sorts of things that words could never express. They told her how much he'd missed her and how he woke each morning searching for her. He'd been left to confront a cold empty space just the way she had. His eyes also told her how much he needed her. Physically. Emotionally. Mentally. Every which way there was to need a woman, he needed her.

Slowly, never taking his eyes from her, he removed the steaming mug from her hands, setting it aside. He reached for her then, gently taking her into his arms and kissing her with a hunger that told her his nights had been as achingly lonesome as her own. While his mouth was hotly claiming hers, he was working at opening her blouse and bra. He was so eager to love her, his hands shook.

"Royce," she pleaded, "the bedroom's upstairs."

"We can't, at least not yet," he argued. "Kelly won't be asleep."

"But she might come down here."

"She won't. I promise." His voice was a low growl, heavy with impatience.

"Don't you think we should wait?"

"I can't. Not a second longer. Feel me." He grabbed hold of her wrist and boldly pressed it to him. "I need you," he said, his voice strained as she took the initiative and moved her open palm back and forth.

"I need you, too," she returned in a husky murmur, closing her eyes to the loving way in which he sought her breasts, lifting them, scoring the undersides with his thumbs. If she hadn't been so fascinated with touching him, with receiving his touch, she would have been rushing to remove her clothes.

"I've thought of nothing else but this from the moment we parted."

"Oh…yes."

"I want you so damn much I can't think straight."

"Me, too."

"I want you more than I ever believed it was possible to want another human being."

"You know what I want?" She didn't wait for him to answer. "I want you to stop talking about wanting me, and hurry up and carry me to bed so we can make love."

He laughed, and Catherine swore it was the most wonderful, melodious sound in the world. He reached her hand and hurried her up the stairs. They tiptoed past Kelly's bedroom with Catherine clenching her blouse closed.

The instant they were alone, his mouth sought hers in a fierce kiss that sent her senses reeling.

The winds of their passion were building, gaining momentum. Royce scooped her into the shelter of his arms and pressed her against the mattress. Then, without hesitation, he removed her clothes with a few agile movements.

Catherine raised her arms, waiting to curl them around his neck as he quickly removed his own clothing.

"Come here, husband," she whispered wantonly. "Let me show you exactly how much I missed you…."

Catherine woke several hours later. She was in bed with Royce cuddling her spoon fashion as though they'd been sleeping together for years. He really was a romantic creature, but it would have embarrassed him had she told him so.

The flight across the country had exhausted her. A smile scooted across her lips. Perhaps it had, but not nearly as much as the session with her husband.

Royce rolled onto his back, giving her the opportunity to study him in the dim moonlight. His features were relaxed in slumber, and the musky scent of their lovemaking lingered. Her heart felt full, open wide to receive all the love he had to give her. It was a good feeling.

"Catherine?"

"Did I wake you?"

"Yes," he said, yawning, "and you know the penalty."

"Oh, Royce," she whispered, grinning, then gave an exaggerated sigh. "Not again."

"Oh, yes…'again' as you so eloquently put it."

Elevating her head, she leaned over and kissed him gently. "Can we have a talk first?"

"Must we?"

"Yes." Her lips briefly touched his. "Please."

"This sounds serious."

She kissed him again, cherishing the taste of him.

His hands held her face away from his. "Either we talk or we kiss. We can't do both."

"All right. One kiss and then we talk. Seriously." His hands were in her hair, unerringly directing her mouth to his for an intimate kiss that was slow and familiar.

"Enough," he whispered, dragging his mouth from her. "Now talk."

"Royce," she said, drawing in a deep breath. "What would you think if I were to become pregnant?"

The air went cold and still. "Are you?"

"No, but I'd like to be."

His eyes closed briefly as though he were greatly relieved. "Not a good idea."

"Why not?" His attitude stung more than she ever thought it would. She expected some hesitation on his part, but nothing like this.

"As long as you're in the Navy there won't be any children for us. I thought you understood that."

Chapter Thirteen

"What do you mean?" Catherine demanded, sitting up in the bed and grabbing the sheet by her fists to cover her bare breasts.

"Exactly what I said." Royce was frowning heavily. "There won't be any children for us as long as you're in the Navy. I thought you understood that."

"I want to know when the hell I agreed to that." She was angry, but damn it all, she couldn't help it. How arrogant. How high-handed of him. She was the one who was willing to go through with the pregnancy. The one who'd offered to balance both her career and a family. It was what she wanted, what she'd planned all along. She'd swallow a gallon of seawater before she'd ever agree to no children.

"We talked about it before we were married," Royce announced coolly.

"The hell we did."

"Catherine, think about it. We had several serious discussions about what we would do if you weren't transferred to Norfolk with me. Remember?" His patience was as grating as his words.

Various conversations they'd had about her transferring did come to mind, and she reluctantly nodded. "Yes, but I certainly don't remember us saying anything about children."

"Trust me, we did."

"Wrong," she returned heatedly. "You're making the whole thing up...I would never have agreed to it. I want a baby, I've always wanted a baby. Two babies." That should really outrage him. Imagine her being greedy enough to want more than one!

An ironic grin quirked the edges of his mouth. "Fine, if that's what you want, we'll have three or four children. More if you want."

"Good." Apparently he wasn't going to make as much of a fuss over this as she'd originally thought. The outrage slowly drained out of her.

"We'll work hard on getting you pregnant," Royce added purposefully, "just as soon as you resign your commission."

"What?" Catherine was on her knees, the protective shield covering her nakedness long forgotten. She was so furious, she leaped to her feet and started traipsing across the mattress in giant steps. Leaping onto the carpet, she searched for something to cover herself with and grabbed a shirt of Royce's that was hanging in the closet. She jerked it so hard the hanger clattered to the floor.

It didn't help matters to have Royce casually sitting up in bed, propped against two fat pillows. "Is there a problem with that?"

"You're damn right there is."

"Then why don't we sit down like two civilized people and discuss this rationally."

"Because," she cried, hands braced on her hips, "I'm too damn mad. I never dreamed...not once that you'd do something like this."

"Catherine, if you'd cool off for a moment we could talk this over rationally."

"I'm cool," she shouted, holding back her hair with both hands. "Answer me one thing."

"All right."

"Do you want a baby?" The whole world seemed to stop. It was as though their marriage, indeed their relationship, hung on a delicate balance, weighed by his answer.

"Yes," he whispered with enough feeling to convince her it was true. "I've tried to tell myself it didn't matter. That I'd leave everything up to you, but damn it, yes, I would like another child." He said it almost as if he were admitting to a weakness.

Catherine was so grateful, her knees weakened. "Oh, Royce, I do, too, so much."

"Apparently the communication between us isn't as good as I'd thought."

"Why are we arguing?" she asked softly.

He grinned. "I don't know. Damn it, Catherine, I love you too much to fight with you."

"I'm glad to hear that." The long-sleeved shirt she'd so hastily donned silently slipped to the floor. With an unhurried ease, she walked over to the side of the bed, her head held high and proud. "As far as I'm concerned the sooner we make a baby the better, don't you think?"

"Catherine?" Royce sounded unsure, which wasn't like him.

"I want to make love." She sat on the edge of the mattress and sought his mouth, kissing him so lightly that their lips barely touched.

Royce groaned, grabbed her by the hair and plunged his tongue deeply into the moist hollow of her mouth. The kiss was so hot it threatened to blister them both.

"We need to finish our talk first," he murmured breathlessly, but even while he was speaking, he was kissing her. He groaned and shook his head. "Catherine...we can't do this."

"Later… We'll talk later."

"I don't think that would be a good idea." He firmly grabbed hold of both her wrists in an attempt to push her back, but the maneuver didn't work. Instead of fighting, she leaned into him, taking full advantage of the fact his hands were occupied. Murmuring words of love and sexual need, she seduced him. Whispering to him between kisses, she told him all the things she planned to do for him. All the things they'd do for each other.

"Catherine…" He didn't sound nearly so insistent as before. "I don't…we need to talk before we do anything… first."

"If that's what you really want," she whispered, taking his earlobe between her teeth and biting lightly. "Touch me," she pleaded softly. "Oh, Royce…I need you so much."

His hold on her wrist slackened. "Catherine, I don't think it would be a good idea—"

"I do…" She was kneeling over him, her thighs spread wide, anticipating the contact, knowing it would play havoc with them both. This was what she wanted, what she needed.

Royce hesitated; his face was hard, his eyes closed, blocking her out, because that was the only way he had of resisting her. The power she felt was strong enough to intoxicate her.

Neither moved. Neither breathed. The pleasure was too intense for either. There was no beginning. No end. The pleasure, once it started, only grew better. The joy burst forth in Catherine's heart until it filled every ounce, every pore of her being.

Joy. Pleasure. The tenderness so sweet it was violent. The beauty of their lovemaking transcending anything she had ever experienced.

When they'd finished, Royce cradled her in his arms. Neither spoke. After what seemed like forever, Royce reached for the blankets, covering them both. His arms held her close, nestling her head against his hard chest. He kissed the crown of her head, and whispered that they would talk in the morning.

Morning. Catherine's eyes slowly drifted open, and she snuggled against Royce's cozy warmth. He must have sensed that she was awake, because he ran his hand over the top of her head, smoothing her hair.

"Are you going to argue with me again?" he whispered.

"That depends on how unreasonable you intend on being," she said, rolling onto her back and arching her body, yawning. "I'm…sorry about last night." She was embarrassed now at the brazen way in which she'd come at him. Using their physical need for each other as a weapon to twist his will was not a tactic she'd ever intended to employ. But he'd made her so furious, she hadn't been thinking properly.

"I want a child, Royce," she told him, her voice low and determined.

"It's not a problem," he assured her, "as long as you're out of the Navy."

His stubbornness stunned her. "Why should I be the one to give up my commission?" she asked, in what she hoped was a reasonable tone. Her emotions were pitching around like a small rowboat upon a stormy ocean. The waves of righteousness slapped roughly against the sides. It was all so unfair. She had to make Royce understand that.

"How about if you give up your commission first?" she offered, hoping he'd see the foolishness of his logic.

He didn't answer her right away. "You agreed before we were married. We discussed it and—"

"We didn't," she denied vehemently.

"…and you chose to stay in the Navy," Royce finished

as though she'd never spoken. "Obviously it wasn't as clear as I'd thought it was, and that's unfortunate, but the fact remains…"

"I'm going to have a child, Royce, and I'm going to be the best mother you ever saw. I'm going to prove to you that I can also be a damn good lieutenant commander as well—"

"No." His voice was gruff and angry.

"Why do I have to be the one to resign?" She wasn't being flippant this time, but she honestly wanted to know.

"Because a child deserves a mother."

"What about a father?"

"One of us has to accept the majority of the responsibility."

"We can't share the duty?"

"No," he argued, more heatedly this time.

"Why are you being so stubborn about this?" she demanded. Royce might be a lot of things, but she'd always found him to be fair.

"Because Sandy—"

"Now just a minute," Catherine said, struggling into a sitting position. She narrowed her eyes as she stared down on him. "Get this straight right now, Royce Nyland. I refuse to be compared with your first wife. I'm not Sandy, and I won't have you holding me up to her." She climbed off the bed and stalked across the room, heading for the bathroom to take a long hot shower and cool off her indignation. She paused, her hand on the doorknob. "There's something you should know." She didn't dare look at him. "I woke up…in the middle of the night last night…" She wasn't proud of this and refused to turn around and look at him as she admitted what she'd done.

"And what?" Royce demanded.

"I…I flushed my birth control pills down the toilet."

She heard his muffled curse as she stepped inside the bathroom.

The shower was running, and Catherine was standing under the stinging spray when the door was thrust open and Royce stepped inside.

"What the hell did you do that for?" He didn't need to explain what he was asking about.

"Because." Catherine was well aware her answer didn't make sense.

"It won't make a whole lot of difference. All I have to do is make a trip to the drugstore."

"Fine. Do it." She reached for the bar of soap and lathered the washcloth. "I'm tired of having everything rest on my shoulders. It's time for someone else to take responsibility."

Royce frowned at that. The water pelted down around him, splashing against the sides of the cubicle. "I'm not going to argue with you. These days are too precious to spend fighting. Even if we were to agree about you getting pregnant, it's too soon. Let's wait a year and talk about it then. A lot could change in that time. There's no need for either of us to get caught up in our disagreements when there's so much we do agree on."

He shouldn't make this much sense. It should be black-and-white. Cut-and-dried.

His hand was under her chin. "I love you, Catherine, I'd much rather be making love to you than standing here debating a subject I assumed was closed." He leaned forward and gently brushed moist lips over hers.

Heaven help her, but she couldn't resist him. Not like this. She stood on her tiptoes and looped her arms around his neck, easing her softness against his hard, lean strength. Steam fogged the windows and mirrors, but Catherine was convinced it had nothing to do with the hot spray of water and everything to do with the way Royce was kissing her.

As it happened, the water turned cold a whole lot sooner than either of them did.

* * *

Catherine was frying bacon for Kelly's breakfast when Royce came bolting down the stairs. He grabbed his jacket and was heading toward the front door when Kelly stopped him.

"Where're you going, Dad?"

He hesitated and cast a dark frown in Catherine's direction. "Shopping."

"It's too early in the morning for anything to be open," Kelly informed him with perfect logic.

"A drugstore will be," he muttered, and moved out the front door, slamming it behind him.

Smiling contentedly to herself, Catherine continued to fry the bacon.

It wasn't supposed to happen like this, Catherine told herself a month later. A woman didn't flush her birth control pills down the toilet one minute and, bingo, turn up pregnant the next. This was one for the record books. Something like this was supposed to take weeks. Months.

Not seconds.

As far as Catherine could figure it out, she was more fertile than the Napa Valley.

She didn't know what she was going to tell Royce. Or when. Not soon, she decided. This pregnancy was something that would demand diplomacy and tact. Good grief, only a handful of people in Bangor even knew she was married.

If only she weren't so thrilled about it. So excited. Of course being separated the way they were, she might even be able to have the baby without Royce knowing.

But that was ridiculous. He was the father. He deserved to know. Kelly deserved to know.

She waited all day for his phone call, deciding to play it

by ear. At precisely six, her time, just after she'd poured herself a cup of coffee, the phone rang.

She grabbed it off the hook, holding the receiver tight against her ear. She reminded herself that she was an accomplished attorney who knew her way around the courtroom. She could argue with the best of them. Her arguments had swayed more than one judge. All she needed to do was remain collected and poised. This child, although unexpected, was a welcome gift. Once Royce saw things from her point of view, he'd change his mind. He didn't have any choice. The deed was done.

"Catherine?"

"Hi," she answered cheerfully. "How are you? How's Kelly? Not much happening around here except that the strip turned blue." Catherine couldn't believe she'd blurted it out like that, although it was unlikely that Royce knew she was referring to the home pregnancy kit she'd picked up at the pharmacy.

"What are you talking about?"

"Oh, nothing. Just a bit of local humor. Are you missing me?"

"You know I am." His words were low and seductive.

They talked for a half hour, the longest thirty minutes of Catherine's life. The minute they were finished, she rushed into the bathroom and hung her head over the toilet. She was never going to be able to pull this off. Royce would guess by the end of the week. She didn't know what would infuriate him more, the fact she hadn't told him right away or that she was pregnant in the first place.

Catherine gained two important lessons from her thirty-minute conversation with Royce. First, that she would need to confide in someone, and second, she wasn't going to be able to drink coffee for the next nine months.

* * *

"Hi, Mom," Catherine greeted.

"Sweetheart, what's wrong?"

"How did you know anything was?"

"You mean other than the fact you're phoning and it's past midnight? Don't worry, I wasn't asleep. Norman went to bed hours ago, but I'm up reading one of Mary Higgins Clark's mysteries."

"Midnight. I didn't realize it was that late."

"You always call late when you're upset."

Catherine didn't realize that, either. "Say, Mom, what would you say if I told you the strip turned blue?"

The pause was only slight. "Is this a trick question?"

"No…I'm dead serious."

"A strip turned blue. I don't know, sweetheart, probably that you should see a doctor."

"Right answer," she said on the tail of a breathy sigh. "Now comes the difficult part. Can you guess why I need a doctor?"

Again there was a semi-lengthy pause. "I'd say it was because you were pregnant, but I know that's not the case."

"Wrong answer."

"You mean…Catherine, do you honestly mean to tell me you and Royce are… But you've only been married a short while, and he's in Virginia and you're in Washington state. Honey, how did it happen?"

"You want me to explain it to you?" Catherine asked incredulously.

"You know what I mean." Catherine could almost see her mother blushing.

"Christmas," Catherine whispered.

"You don't sound like you're sure you're pleased about this."

"I'm thrilled, Mom, honest I am."

"Are you going to leave the Navy?"

"No!"

"But, Catherine, can't you see how impossible it will be? You and Royce live two thousand miles apart. A child deserves to know his father."

"Royce will see the baby."

Her mother must have sensed the argument brewing just below the surface of Catherine's stubborn pride, because she diplomatically changed the subject.

"I'm going to tell you something I never have before," Marilyn said softly, gently. "You, my darling daughter, were a surprise."

"I was?"

"Actually, you were more of a shock."

Catherine grinned. Her sense of timing never had gotten straightened out, it seemed.

"Your father and I were in college. Young. Idealistic. Foolish."

"Do you mean to tell me you and Dad *had* to get married?"

"No, but as best as I can figure you were born nine months and one day after our wedding. I didn't know how I was going to tell your father. As it turned out, he was delighted. I was crying—the hormones really did a trick on me. I'll never forget how gentle he was, how pleased. It was as though I were the only woman in the world who'd ever endured a pregnancy." Her mother paused, and Catherine could hear the slight quaver in her voice.

"In those days the father wasn't often allowed in the delivery room. But Andy refused to leave me. For a minute there I thought he and the doctor were going to come to blows."

Catherine enjoyed hearing these loving details about her father. Her gaze rested tenderly on the fading color photograph that rested atop her mantel.

"When you were born, I was afraid he would be disappointed with a daughter. But not Andy. The delivery room nurse placed you in his arms, and he sat beside me and wept for joy.

"After they wheeled me into the recovery room, I was exhausted and fell asleep. But Andy was too excited to stand still. The nurses told me he dragged everyone from the janitor to the hospital administrator up to the nursery to take a look at you. Not once did he regret that I'd become pregnant so soon." Her mother paused, and Catherine could hear her voice tremble with soft emotion.

"I love hearing stories about him," Catherine admitted, discovering she was close to tears herself, which probably meant this pregnancy was going to play havoc with her emotions.

"Royce doesn't know yet, does he?" her mother pried softly.

"No."

"When exactly do you plan to tell him?"

"Next year when it's time to figure our income taxes?"

Her mother's laughter echoed softly over the long-distance line. "Oh, Catherine, you remind me so much of myself, and so much of your father. Royce is a good man, I don't think you have a thing to worry about."

They spoke for a few minutes more, and then Catherine hung up. Slowly, thoughtfully, she walked over to the fireplace and gently ran her finger along the top of her father's picture. It was something she did often when she needed to feel close to him. She prayed her mother was right and that Royce would be thrilled. Her gaze rested on her father's handsome features. A lone tear streaked her face as she regretted once again her inability to remember him.

Royce was weary as he drove down the maple-lined street and pulled into his driveway. He missed Catherine.

It had been nearly three months since he'd last seen her, and it could well be another three before he did again. He tried not to think about it.

They were close, as close as any two married people could be that were separated by the width of an entire country. If anything troubled him it was the fact she was so content with their arrangement. They talked two times a week and wrote nearly every day. Only on rare occasions did Catherine reveal any regrets on their being so far removed from each other.

Not so with Royce. He wanted his wife with him. If he was being selfish, inconsiderate, then so be it. The nights were lonely. Friday nights were always the worst. Kelly usually spent it with a friend, which left him to fend for himself. He was pleased his daughter had such an active social life; his, however, was wrapped around a woman two thousand miles away.

He really knew how to pick them, he mused darkly. Career women. First Sandy and now Catherine, both so eager to make a place in their chosen profession…. No, he wasn't going to dwell on it. He'd done that too much lately. He'd gone into this marriage with his eyes wide open. From the first he'd known how important the Navy was to Catherine. He'd married her still, loving her enough to place a distant second in her life if that was all she was willing to give him.

His life was good. He had only a few complaints. He liked Virginia much better than he ever expected he would. He enjoyed his job, and over the past few months had developed several interests. He wasn't much into hobbies—at least he hadn't been until he married Catherine. Now he had to find something to fill the time or go crazy thinking about how much he missed her.

He just wished there was some way he could get her transferred out to the East Coast. Even if she were stationed in Florida, it would be a whole lot closer than Washington state.

The lights were on in the house, and Royce was trying to remember if Kelly was going to be home or not. Home, he guessed.

He opened the front door and removed his jacket and hung it in the hall closet. Someone was cooking in the kitchen. Whatever it was it smelled like heaven. Royce was going to have to say something to Kelly about fixing dinner. She was too young to be attempting it without adult supervision.

"Kelly?" He paused to sort through the mail.

"I'm in the kitchen, Dad." She sounded downright pleased about something. Probably that she'd managed to cook his dinner without burning down the house.

"What smells so good?"

"Yankee pot roast, mashed potatoes, steamed baby carrots and fresh-baked apple pie."

The mail dropped out of Royce's hands as he slowly turned around. He was dreaming. He had to be, because it was Catherine's honey-sweet voice that was talking to him and not Kelly's. She stood in the kitchen doorway, a towel tucked into the waistband of her jeans, holding a wooden spoon in one hand.

"Catherine?" He was almost afraid to reach for her for fear she'd vanish into thin air. Either real or imaginary, he had to hold her. Two steps later, and she was in his arms.

He closed his eyes and breathed in the warm, familiar fragrance of her, intoxicated within seconds. His arms were wrapped around her so tightly that he'd lifted her half off the floor without even realizing it.

"Are you surprised?" Kelly asked.

"You knew?" He couldn't believe that she'd managed to keep it a secret from him.

"Only since yesterday."

He kissed Catherine with a hunger that quickly stirred awake dormant fires. "How long can you stay?" Mentally he was tabulating how many times they could make love in three days.

"How long do you want me for?"

A lifetime! Fifty years or whichever came first. "How long have you got?" No use aiming for the stars. He'd take what he could get and be damned grateful.

"A while." She kissed him, tantalizing him with the tip of her tongue, and then casually sauntered back to the stove.

"A while," Royce repeated, not understanding.

"Now?" Kelly demanded, looking up at Catherine.

Catherine nodded mysteriously. Royce's daughter held up her two hands. "Ten minutes," she said. "That's all the time I'm giving you."

"It shouldn't even take that long," Catherine assured her.

Kelly was gone in a flash, racing up the stairs.

"Ten minutes," Royce repeated once Kelly was out of the room. "Honey, I don't know what you've got in mind, but I'd appreciate a bit more leeway than ten minutes."

"I want you to read something." She walked over to the table and handed him an official-looking envelope.

Royce stared at it for several moments, not knowing what to think.

"And while I've got your attention, I think you should know we killed a rabbit."

"What?" The woman had become a loony tune. A three-month separation had driven her over the edge. He knew it had him, so it shouldn't come as any big surprise.

"Actually I don't think it's officially a rabbit these days."

"Woman, what are you talking about?"

"You mean you honestly don't know?" He clearly seemed to not know.

He wouldn't be standing there with his mouth open,

looking like a fish out of water if he did. "I don't have a clue," he admitted reluctantly.

"We're pregnant."

Royce shook his head, convinced she was playing a practical joke on him.

"It's true, Royce." Her eyes met his, shyly, as though she were honestly afraid of his reaction. She was studying him closely, judging his response, watching him for any signs of emotion.

Royce felt the sudden need to sit down. "When?"

"As-s best I can figure, sometime over Christmas. My guess was that morning…in the shower."

He nodded. He felt too numb to do much of anything else. He started figuring dates. It had happened at Christmas, and they were already into the second week of March.

"But that was…"

"A few months ago now," she finished for him.

"You're three months pregnant?" She'd kept it a secret for all those months.

She nodded. "Aren't you going to say anything? Oh, Royce, please don't keep me in suspense any longer. Are you happy?"

He struggled for words, but the emotions had jammed in his throat. He swallowed and slowed his breath before nodding. "Yes." He reached for her, taking her by the hips and drawing her to him. He flattened his hand over her stomach and closed his eyes. It was impossible for him to speak.

"Read the letter," she whispered, and tears slipped from the corners of her eyes and ran unrestrained down her cheeks. She brushed them aside. "Don't worry, I'm terribly emotional these days. I start weeping at the drop of a hat, but the doctor said it wasn't anything to be concerned about."

Royce withdrew the paper from inside the envelope.

He scanned the contents twice, certain there was some misunderstanding.

"You're leaving the Navy?" he asked, his voice incredulous.

"Yes, but I'm still in the Reserves."

"Why?" After all her arguments about keeping her commission, he couldn't believe that she'd voluntarily give it up.

Catherine's arms circled his neck, and she lowered herself onto his lap. "Because I finally figured out why the Navy was so important for me."

Royce stared up at her, not understanding.

"I was searching to know my father, looking to find him in Navy life... I know it all sounds crazy, but having no memory of him has troubled me for years. Hanging on to the Navy, especially now, was like grasping at straws, because I wanted to find something about him to hang on to."

"But what changed your mind?"

"Our baby. I realized I could do it. Raise our child and everything else when we were so far apart. Then it dawned on me how silly I was being, grasping to find my own father and denying my own child the privilege."

Royce kissed her, worshipping her with his mouth, loving her until they were both trembling.

"Have you told him yet?" Kelly demanded from the top of the stairs.

"She told me," Royce answered.

Kelly raced down. "What do you think, Dad?"

He grinned and held out his hand to his daughter, bringing her into the circle of their love. It was more than he ever dreamed, more than he deserved. Taking Catherine's hand, he pressed her fingertips to his lips. Their eyes held, and in hers Royce saw the warm promise of tomorrow.

Epilogue

Royce was whistling a catchy tune when he pulled into the driveway and turned off the engine. The station wagon was parked alongside of his black Porsche, a baby seat strapped in the rear seat.

Andy was fast outgrowing the padded chair, which worked out well since Jenny would soon be needing it. His three-month-old daughter was growing like a weed.

Pushing a tricycle out of the way, Royce opened the front door and hung his hat and jacket on the brass coatrack. "I'm home."

Four-year-old Andy let out a cry of glee and came tearing around the corner at top speed. Royce swept his son high above his head and hugged him close.

"How's Daddy's little man? Did you help your mother today by being a good boy?"

"Aye, aye, sir." Andrew Royce Nyland saluted sharply, then squirmed, wanting back down. The minute his feet hit the floor, Andy was back to whatever it was that had captured his attention in the first place.

"Royce," Catherine greeted, coming into the entryway, holding their daughter. A smile came automatically to his lips. It never ceased to amaze him, after all these years, all this time, how his heart quickened at the sight of her. She was in a blue business suit with a fancy silk blouse, and Royce vaguely remembered her telling him she'd had to go into the office later than usual. He was proud of the way Catherine had found a position in a prestigious law firm. Proud of her for showing him it was possible to mix a career with a family. She worked three days a week now, but when the time was right, she would eventually take on a forty-hour week. Frankly, Royce felt his wife had something of an advantage over other attorneys. She was so damn beautiful and intelligent he couldn't see a jury in the land disagreeing with her.

"Oh, Royce, I'm glad you're home." Catherine paused to give him a quick but satisfying kiss, handing him Jenny. No sooner was his daughter in his arms, when Catherine was reaching for her coat.

"Where are you headed?"

She turned around and chastised him with a smile. "I told you about the Navy wives meeting this evening, don't you remember?"

"Oh, right." Royce recalled nothing of the sort. He had trouble keeping track of his own schedule, let alone everyone else's.

"Kelly will be home within a half hour," Catherine informed him. "And she's bringing a young man home with her."

"A boy?"

"Royce, she's almost sixteen. This is important to her, so don't make a fuss. All she asks is that you give her a little privacy."

"Hey," he grumbled, reaching for his wife. "How does she rate? If anyone deserves a little privacy, it's us." He kissed her along the side of the neck, savoring her special fragrance. "What time are you going to be home?"

"Not late," she promised, rubbing her mouth over his lips in a slow, erotic exercise. "I promise."

Royce reluctantly released her. "Good, because I've got plans for tonight."

"You've got plans for every night," she teased, "which is a good thing because if you didn't, I would have." She grabbed her purse, started for the front door and turned back around.

"Forget something?"

"Yes." She patted Jenny's sleeping brow and then raised her mouth to his. The kiss was one for the record books. Teasing. Coaxing.

Royce felt his knees grow weak, and if it hadn't been for Jenny, he would have wrapped his arms around Catherine and hauled her up the stairs right then and there.

Catherine sighed and hesitantly broke away from him.

"What was that for?" he asked breathlessly.

"Just so you'd know how much I love you. How grateful I am that you were patient enough to allow me to come to my own decisions. About the Navy. About my joining the law firm. About having Jenny."

"I sincerely hope you intend on thanking me again later."

"You know I do." She grinned and started for the door. Royce turned toward the kitchen, whistling contentedly.

To my uncle, A. D. Adler.
How special you are to me.
I love you!

Chapter One

On her knees on the bathroom floor, Hannah Raymond viewed parts of the toilet that were never meant to be seen at such short range. Her stomach rolled and heaved like a tiny canoe being swept down a raging river. The tile felt icy against her knees, yet beads of perspiration moistened her brow. Closing her eyes in an effort to hold back the waves of nausea, Hannah drew in several deep, even breaths. That seemed to help a little, but not enough.

"Oh, God," she prayed silently, "please, oh, please, don't let me be pregnant." No sooner had the words crossed her lips when she lost what little breakfast she'd managed to down that morning.

Her monthly period was late. Over two months late. But that could be attributed to the stress she'd been under these past several weeks. The stress and the grief. It had been nearly four months since Jerry's death. She ached to the bottom of her soul for him, and would, she was convinced, until the end of her life. She'd loved Jerry for six years, had planned her entire life around him. They were to have married soon after the first of the year.

Now there would be no wedding because there was no Jerry. Grief caught her once more in a stranglehold of pain and she squeezed her eyes closed, battling the tears, as well as the nausea. Adding to her torment was the knowledge that if she was pregnant, the child she carried wouldn't be Jerry's.

The face of the sailor had imprinted itself onto her mind, bold as could be. He was tall, powerfully built and strong featured. With a sense of dismay she pushed his image away, refusing to think about that July night or dwell on her folly.

Once again her stomach heaved, and Hannah brushed the thick folds of shiny brown hair away from her face and leaned over the porcelain toilet.

"Hannah?" Her father knocked politely against the bathroom door. "Honey, you'd best hurry or you'll be late for Sunday school."

"I…I'm not feeling very well this morning, Dad." Her words were immediately followed by another bout of vomiting.

"It sounds like you've got the flu."

Bless his heart for offering her an excuse. "Yes, I think I must." She prayed with everything in her being that this was some intestinal virus. If living a good life, following the Golden Rule and being the best preacher's kid she knew how to be were ever to work on her behalf, the time was now.

"Go back to bed and if you feel up to it later, come over for the service. I'm preaching from the Epistle to the Romans this morning and I'd like your opinion."

"Sure, Dad." But from the way she was feeling now, she wouldn't be out of bed any time within the next week.

"You'll be all right here by yourself?" Her father's voice echoed with concern.

"I'll be fine. Don't worry." Once again she felt her stomach pitch. She gripped the sides of the toilet and her head fell forward, the effort of holding it up too much for her.

Her father hesitated. "You're sure?"

"I'll be all right in a little bit," she managed in a reed-thin voice.

"If you need me," George Raymond insisted, "just call the church."

"Dad, please, don't worry about me. I'll be much better soon. I'm sure of it."

Her father's retreating footsteps echoed in the hallway, and Hannah sighed with relief. She didn't know what she was going to do if she was pregnant. Briefly she toyed with the idea of disappearing until after the baby was born. Going into hiding was preferable to facing her father with the truth.

George Raymond had dedicated his life to serving God and others, and having to confess what she'd done didn't bear contemplating. Hannah loved her father deeply, and the thought of disgracing him, the thought of hurting him, brought a pain so strong and so sharp that tears instantly pooled in her eyes.

"Please God," she prayed once more, "don't let me be pregnant." Slowly rising from the floor, she swayed and placed her hand against the wall as an attack of dizziness sent the room spinning.

She staggered into her bedroom and fell on top of the mattress. Kicking off her shoes, she sat up long enough to reach for the afghan neatly folded at the foot of the bed. Spreading it over her shivering shoulders, she gratefully closed her eyes.

Sleep came over her in swells as though the ocean tide had shifted, lapping warm, assuring waves over her distraught soul. She welcomed each one, eager for something, anything that would help her escape the reality of her situation.

It had happened in mid-July, only three short weeks after the tragic accident that had claimed her fiancé's life. Her father had been out of town, officiating at a wedding in Yakima. He was staying over and wasn't scheduled to arrive back in Seattle until late Saturday afternoon. Hannah had been invited, too, but she couldn't have borne sitting through the happy event when her own life was filled with such anguish. How grateful she'd been that her father hadn't asked her to travel with him, although she knew he would have welcomed her company.

Before he left, George Raymond had asked if she'd take a load of boxes to the Mission House in downtown Seattle. He'd done it, Hannah knew, in an effort to draw her out of the lethargy that had claimed her in the weeks following Jerry's funeral.

She waited until late in the afternoon, putting off the errand as long as she could, then loaded up the back of her father's old Ford station wagon without much enthusiasm.

Hannah had driven into the city, surprised by the heavy flow of traffic. It wasn't until she'd found a parking spot in the alley in back of the Mission House that she remembered that Seafair, the Seattle summertime festival celebrating ethnic heritages and community, was being held that weekend. The whole town was festive. Enthusiasm and good cheer rang through the streets like bells from a church steeple. Several Navy ships were docked in Elliott Bay and the famed torchlight parade was scheduled for that evening. The city sidewalks and streets were crammed.

None of the excitement rubbed off on Hannah, however. The sooner she delivered the goods, the faster she could return to the safe haven of home. She'd been on her way out the door when she was waylaid by the mission director. Reverend Parker seemed genuinely concerned about how she was doing and insisted she sit and have a cup of coffee with him. Hannah had chatted politely, trying not to be impatient, and when he pressed her, she adamantly claimed she was doing well. It was a lie, but a small one. She didn't want to talk about how angry she was. How bitterly disillusioned. Others had borne even greater losses. In time she'd heal. In time she'd forget. But not for a while; the pain was too fresh, too sharp.

Hannah knew her friends were worried about her, but she'd managed to put on a facade that fooled most everyone. Everyone, that was, except her father, who knew her so well.

"God works in mysterious ways," Reverend Parker had told her on her way out the door. He'd paused and gently patted her back in a gesture of love.

Until Jerry's death, Hannah had never questioned her role in life. When others grieved, she'd sat at their sides, comforted them with the knowledge that whatever had befallen them was part of God's will. The words came back to haunt her now, slapping a cold hand of reality across her face. Several had issued the trite platitude to her, and Hannah had quickly grown to hate such meaningless clichés.

God's will. Hannah had given up believing all the religious jargon she'd been raised to embrace. If God was so loving and so good, then why had He allowed Jerry to die? It made no sense to her. Jerry was a rare man, good and godly. They'd been so much in love and even though they were engaged to marry, they'd never gone beyond kissing and a little petting. They'd hungered for each other the way all couples deeply in love do, and yet Jerry had always managed to keep them from succumbing to temptation. Now, with everything in her, Hannah wished that once, just once, she could have lain in his arms. She'd give everything she would ever have in this life to have known his touch, to have surrendered her virginity to him.

But it was never meant to be.

Stirring, Hannah woke, rolled over and stared blankly at the wall. Her hands rested on her stomach, which seemed to have quieted. A glance at her watch told her that even if she rushed and dressed she'd still be late for the church service. She didn't feel like listening to her father's sermon. It wouldn't do her any good now. Huge tears brimmed in her eyes and slipped unheeded down her cheeks, soaking into her pillow.

Sleep beckoned her once more, and she closed her eyes. Once again the sailor's face returned, his dark eyes glaring down on her as they had the night he'd taken her to the hotel room. She'd never forget his shocked, distressed look when he'd realized she was a virgin. The torment she'd read in his gaze would haunt her all the way to the grave. His eyes had rounded with incredulity and disbelief. For one wild second Hannah had feared he would push himself away from her, but she'd reached up and brushed his mouth with her own and then…

She groaned and with a determined effort banished him from her mind once more. She didn't want to think about Riley Murdock. Didn't want to remember anything about him. Certainly not the gentle way he'd comforted her afterward or the stark questions in his eyes as he'd pulled her close and held her until she'd slept.

Go away, she cried silently. *Leave me in peace.* Her strength was depleted, and without effort she drifted into a restless slumber.

Riley was there waiting for her.

Following her conversation with Reverend Parker, Hannah had gone out to the alley where she'd parked the station wagon. To her dismay she discovered that while she'd been inside the Mission House, several cars had blocked her way out of the alley. By all rights, she should have contacted the police and had the vehicles towed away at the owners' expense, but it would have been uncharacteristically mean.

Since the parade was scheduled to begin within the next hour, Hannah decided to stay in the downtown area and view it herself. There wasn't any reason to hurry home.

The waterfront was teeming with tourists. Sailors were everywhere, their white uniforms standing out in the crowd, their bucket hats bobbing up and down in the multitude.

Sea gulls lazily circled overhead, casting giant shadows along the piers. The fresh scent of the sea, carried on the warm wind off Elliott Bay, mingled with the aroma of fried fish and simmering pots of clam chowder. The smell of food reminded Hannah that she hadn't eaten since early that morning. Buying a cup of chowder was tempting, but the lines were long and it was simply too much bother.

Life was too much of a bother. How different all this would be if only Jerry were at her side. She recalled the many good times they'd spent with each other. A year earlier, Jerry had run in the Seafair race and they'd stayed for the parade, laughing and joking, their arms wrapped around each other. What a difference a year could make.

The climb up the steep flight of steps that led from the waterfront to the Pike Place Market exhausted Hannah. Soon, however, she found herself standing along the parade route, where people were crowded against the curbs. Several had brought lawn chairs and blankets, and it looked as if they'd been camped there a good long while.

Vendors strolled the street, selling their wares to children who danced in and out of the waiting crowd like court jesters.

Hannah was amused by their antics when little managed to cheer her those days. She was so caught up in the activities going on around her that she wasn't watching where she was walking. Before she realized what she was doing, she stumbled headlong into a solid male chest. For an instant she assumed she'd blundered into a brick wall. The pair of strong hands that caught her shoulders convinced her otherwise. His grip tightened to keep her from stumbling backward.

"I'm sorry," she mumbled, once she'd found her voice. He was a sailor. One tall and muscular sailor. As nonsensical as it seemed, he had the look of a pirate about him—bold and daring. His hair was as dark as his eyes. He wasn't strikingly handsome; his features were too sharp, too craggy for that. Then his finely shaped mouth curved into a faint smile, flashing white, even teeth.

"I'm…sorry," she stammered again, staring up at him, embarrassed at the way she'd been openly appraising him. She couldn't help being curious. He seemed so aloof, so withdrawn that she felt forced to embellish. "I wasn't watching where I was going." She offered him a feeble smile, and when he dropped his hands, she blushed and looked away.

"You weren't hurt?"

"No…no, I'm fine. What about you?"

"No problem." His gaze swept over her, and he moved on without saying another word.

Following the brief encounter, Hannah decided it would be best if she stood in one place. She selected a vantage point that offered her a good view of the parade, which was just beginning.

With mild interest she viewed the mayor and several other public officials as they rode by, sitting atop polished convertibles. She lost count of the number of bands and performing drill teams that passed. A fire-flashing baton twirler was followed by a variety of enchanting floats.

Enthralled almost against her will, Hannah stayed until the very end, when it was well past dark. The crowds had started to disperse, and hoping the station wagon was no longer blocked, she headed down the steep hills toward the Mission House. Since there were still people about, she didn't think there'd be a problem of being alone in a bad section of town. But as she neared the Mission House, she discovered there were only a few cars left parked in the area. Soon there was no one else in sight.

When she first noticed the twin shadows following her she was pleased, naively thinking there was safety in numbers. But when she turned and noted the way the two were closing in on her, with menacing looks and walks, she knew she was in trouble.

As she approached the street on which the Mission House was located, she noted that the pair was still advancing. Quickening her pace, she clenched her purse to her side. An eerie sensation ran up and down her spine, and the taste of dread mingled with a growing sense of alarm filled her mouth.

Although she was moving as fast as she could without breaking into a run, the pair was gaining. She'd been a fool to separate herself from the crowds. She hadn't been thinking right. Again and again her father had warned her about such foolishness. Maybe she had a death wish. But if that were the case, then why was she so terribly afraid? She trembled, her heart was pounding like a storm trooper's.

The instant she saw the lights of a waterfront bar, Hannah breathed a little easier. She rushed forward and slipped inside grimacing as she walked straight into a thick wall of cigarette smoke.

Men lined the bar, and it seemed that every one of them had turned to stare at her. Beer bottles were clenched in their hands, some raised halfway to their mouths, frozen in motion. A pool table at the back of the room captured her attention, as did the handful of men dressed in black leather who stood around it holding on to cue sticks. One glance told Hannah they were probably members of a motorcycle gang.

Wonderful. She'd leaped out of the frying pan directly into the roaring flames. Hannah sucked in her breath and tried to behave naturally, as though she often wandered into waterfront bars. It seemed, however, that she'd become the center of attention.

It was then that she saw him—the sailor she'd bumped into earlier that evening. He was sitting at a table, nursing a drink, his gaze centered on the glass. He seemed to be the only one in the room unaware of her.

Where she found the courage to approach him, Hannah never questioned. Squaring her shoulders, she moved across the room and placed her hand on the chair opposite him. "Is this seat taken?"

He looked up, and his eyes lit with surprise before a frown darkened his piratical features. The only thing that made him less threatening than the others in the room was the fact he wore a sailor's uniform.

Not waiting for his reply, Hannah pulled out the chair and promptly sat down. Her knees were shaking so badly she didn't know if she could stand upright much longer.

"Two men were following me," she explained. Her hands continued to tremble, and she pushed the hair away from her face. "I don't mean to be rude, but it made sense to scoot in here." She hesitated and looked around her, noting once again the menacing-looking men at the bar. "At least it did at the time."

"Why'd you choose to sit with me?" He seemed to find the fact somewhat amusing. The corner of his mouth lifted in a half smile, but she wasn't sure it was one of welcome.

Why had she chosen him? "You were the only one not wearing leather and spikes," she said, but in retrospect she'd wondered what it was that had caused her to approach him. The fact she recognized him from earlier in the evening was part of the answer, she was convinced of that. Yet there was something more. He was so intense, so compelling, and she'd sensed integrity in him.

A half grin had widened into a full one at her comment about him being the only one there not wearing leather and chains.

He raised his hand, and the waitress appeared. "Two of the same."

"I don't know if that would be a good idea," Hannah

said. She intended to stay only long enough to discourage the pair waiting for her outside.

"You're shaking like a leaf."

Hannah didn't argue with him. It would do little good, and he was right. She continued to tremble, but she wasn't completely convinced fear was the reason. Even then, something deep inside her had known. Not consciously, of course. It was as though some deep inner part of herself had reached out to this stranger. Intuitively she'd known he would never harm her. The waitress delivered two amber-colored drinks. Hannah didn't have a clue what she was tasting. All she did know was that a small sip of it was potent enough to burn all the way down her throat and settle in her stomach like a ball of fire. The taste wasn't unpleasant, just potent.

"Do you have a name?" the sailor asked her.

"Hannah. What about you?"

"Riley Murdock."

She grinned, intrigued by the name. "Riley Murdock," she repeated slowly. She watched as he raised the glass to his lips and was struck by how sensuous his mouth was. With some folks, Hannah had noted over the years, the eyes were the most expressive feature. One look at her father's eyes and she could easily read his mood. Riley was different. His eyes were blank. Impersonal. But his mouth competently telegraphed his thoughts. He was intrigued with her, amused. The way the corners turned up just slightly told her as much.

"Are you here for Seafair?" she asked, making polite conversation. A second sip burned a path down the back of her throat.

He nodded. "We're only in port for the next few days."

"So, how do you like Seattle?" She was beginning to grow warm. It was a good feeling that radiated out from the pit of her stomach, and it had the most peculiar effect on her. It relaxed Hannah. The tension eased from between her shoulder blades and the stiffness left her arms. She was a little dizzy, but that wasn't entirely unpleasant, either.

"Seattle's all right." Murdock sounded like a man who'd been in too many ports to appreciate one over another. He finished the last of his drink and, not wanting him to think she was unappreciative, Hannah sipped from her own. Actually, once she grew accustomed to the flavor, the taste was mellow and smooth. It still burned, but the fire was warm and gentle. Welcome.

"Finish your drink and I'll walk you to your car," Murdock offered.

Hannah was grateful. It took her several minutes to down the potent liquor, but he was patient. He didn't seem to be the talkative sort and that suited her. She wasn't interested in conversation any more than he was.

If the two men who'd followed her were waiting for her outside, Hannah didn't see them. She was glad. A confrontation was something she wanted to avoid, although she was surprised by how formidable Riley Murdock looked when he stood. He was easily six feet if not an inch or two taller. And rock solid. His arms weren't bulging with muscles, but there was a strength in him that Hannah had sensed from the moment she'd first seen him. A physical strength, yes, but a substantial emotional fortitude, as well. Although she wasn't good at judging ages, she guessed him to be somewhere in his early thirties. Light-years beyond her twenty-three.

Moonlight cascaded over the street as they started walking. The sky was filled with stars as though someone had scattered diamond dust across endless yards of black satin. Riley rested his hand on her shoulder in a protective, possessive gesture that Hannah found comforting. If she were to shut her eyes, she could almost pretend it was Jerry at her side and not some sailor she barely knew. He was so near, so strong, and being with him, standing this close,

blocked out the sharp edges of the pain that had dominated her life these past few weeks.

For the first time since her father had come to break the
news to her about Jerry, the dull ache was gone. It felt so
good not to hurt, so pleasant that she didn't want this time
to end. Not so soon. Not yet.

An unexplainable comfort radiated from her shoulder
where Riley had placed his hand. His touch was light, gentle, nonthreatening. Hannah had to force herself to lean
into him and absorb his strength. It felt so good to have
him at her side, so strong and reassuring.

They paused at a street corner and Hannah glanced up
at him; her gaze slid warmly into his. She smiled briefly,
feeling a little shy and awkward, yet at the same time more
bold than she could ever remember being. It was the
drink, she told herself, that had lent her the courage to behave the way she had.

From the corner of her eye she noticed the light change,
but neither moved. He was openly studying her, reading
her. Hannah boldly met his gaze. Gently his hand slid up
the side of her neck. She closed her eyes and slowly, seductively, rubbed her chin across the tops of his fingers in
a catlike motion. Warm sensations enveloped her and she
smiled contentedly. This was what she'd had before and
lost. Heaven help her, she needed something to hold on
to through the years, something that could never be taken
away from her the way Jerry had been. If she were to be
damned for seizing the moment, then so be it. Without
thinking, without calculating her actions, she turned and
placed her arms around Riley's neck, stood on the tips of
her toes and kissed him. She knew from his reaction that
she'd taken him by surprise. Hannah had never done anything more brazen in her life. She guessed there were sub-
tler ways of letting him know what she wanted, but she
was a novice at this and was reacting to impulse and not
reason.

Kissing a stranger was completely out of character for Hannah. Everything had taken on an unreal quality. At least when she was in Riley's arms she was feeling again. And it was so good to experience something other than pain, something more than the agony that stampeded her heart and soul.

Riley slipped his hands over her hips and held on to her waist as if he weren't sure what he wanted. His gaze pierced hers, and Hannah smiled shyly back. He plunged his fingers through her hair and stared down on her for several breath-stopping moments before he kissed her. Sighing, Hannah leaned toward him. Together they made warm, moist kisses, each one increasing in intensity. His tongue edged apart the seam of her lips and then traced the roundness of her mouth.

When they reluctantly parted, neither spoke. Hannah could feel him assessing her, but what conclusions he drew, she could only speculate. She didn't want him to ponder her boldness too much, because then she'd be forced into thinking herself, and that was the last thing she wanted to do. Leaning her weight against him, she stroked her long fingers against his nape, sliding them into his hair. Soon she was directing his mouth back to hers.

If there had been a sensible thought left in her head, Hannah banished it as she sought his kiss. He didn't disappoint her, displaying an eagerness, a willingness that made her stomach warm. Gradually the sensation plummeted to the lower half of her body. The delicious, delightful excitement seemed to increase with each sweet foray of his tongue and mouth. Wanting to squeeze out every inch of feeling, she started to rotate her hips, pressing against him where she ached the most.

He caught her by the waist, forcing her to still.

"Hannah—" he breathed her name in a soft sexy way that sent chills scooting down her spine "—do you know what you're asking for?"

She bit into her lower lip and nodded.

"Then let's get a hotel room. A decent one."

She should have stopped him, called a halt at that very moment. She might have if he hadn't kissed her again. It should be Jerry she was loving; but he was gone and Riley was very much alive, and she needed him. The havoc his touch created within her was too powerful to resist. It was as if she were wading in floodwaters, struggling to remain upright against a raging storm of need. Sensation abounded, so full, so abundant, her inhibitions toppled over one another like tumbling dominos.

Hannah remembered little of anything else until they were inside the rented room. She recalled that Riley had stopped every now and again on the moonlit sidewalk to kiss her as if he feared she might change her mind.

The fact they didn't have any luggage wasn't a concern to the clerk who handed them the key and pointed the way toward the elevator. The minute they were inside the antique contraption, Riley pulled her back into his arms.

Hannah was convinced that if the room had been on the tenth floor instead of the third, he would have made love to her then and there.

He unlocked the door but didn't bother to turn on the light switch. The drapes were open, and the moonlight spilled softly across the bed. With his arm around her waist, he guided her inside and closed the door, leaning her against it.

His hands, pressed on either side of her face, imprisoned her against the hard door. His eyes found hers, as if he needed some form of reassurance.

Hannah smiled and, raising her fingertips to his mouth, unhurriedly traced his lower lip. His mouth was warm and moist, soft to the touch. Enticing. Leaning forward, she kissed him, shyly using her tongue as he'd done with her.

Riley moaned, and catching the back of her head, deepened the kiss until they were both breathless with need.

Even in the dark, Hannah could see how intense his eyes were, filled with a desire so powerful that just looking at him caused her skin to tingle.

Then slowly, purposefully, he unfastened the buttons of her blouse—one by one, starting at the bottom and working his way up. It was as though he expected her to stop him, and he seemed mildly surprised when she didn't. He removed her shirt and then her bra, dropping both to the floor. Once she was bare, he seemed to let an inordinate amount of time pass before he removed his own shirt.

Gently, as though he sensed he was frightening her, he caught the lush fullness of her breasts in his palms, lifting them. "You're very beautiful."

She blinked, not knowing what to say. "So-o are you."

He smiled as if she'd amused him and, leaning down, caught her nipple in his mouth, closing over the fullness of her soft, feminine mound before lavishing it with greedy attention. His tongue laved the tightening hardness and then he sucked fiercely. Hannah whimpered at the startling wave of pleasure it gave her. Gradually she grew accustomed to his attentions and relaxed, closing her eyes as she delved her fingers into his hair. He repeated the process with her other breast, and Hannah felt a stirring sense of wonder at each powerful tug of his mouth. The warm, heavy feeling she'd experienced earlier in the lower half of her body returned a hundredfold, and she moved instinctively against the hard bulge in his loins.

"That's right, baby," he murmured as his hand found the snap on her jeans.

Once they were both free of their clothes, Riley picked her up in his arms and effortlessly carried her to the bed.

He was eager then; too eager to go slowly. He mounted her, settling himself between her open thighs. Not sure how much pain to expect, Hannah tensed, gritted her teeth and turned her head to the side. He caught her by the chin, however, and kissed her deeply, causing the heat to rise to the exploding point. Not knowing how else to ask for him to make love to her, Hannah raised her hips.

It seemed to be what he was waiting for as he settled between her legs, his heated shaft nudging apart the creamy folds of her womanhood. Once again Hannah tightened her jaw as he relentlessly entered her, pausing only when he met the restrictive barrier of her virginity.

He stopped then, frozen. Hannah's gaze found his, and she read his confusion. He pulled back his head, gritting his teeth, his look tense and confused.

"It's all right," she whispered softly. Fearing he might leave her, she looped her arms around his neck and drew his mouth to her own. The kiss was wild, tempestuous, a battle of wills.

Hannah wasn't sure who won. In the end it didn't matter. Slowly, determined to bring her whatever pleasure he could, Riley continued forward, tiny increment by tiny increment until he was buried so deep inside her, she was convinced he could go no deeper.

She was panting with pain, panting with pleasure. He gave her a moment to adjust to him, to allow her senses to recover. She felt his heat, his strength, his hardness envelop her, and she felt as though her heart reached out to him, bonding them in ways she never expected. Twinges of pleasure gradually overcame those that had brought her pain.

Slowly he began to move within her, in long easy strokes that lingered and then opulently replenished the pleasure.

Heat encompassed her, and when it became too much, she moaned and bit into her lip, breathlessly searching, striving for what she didn't know. In the end, release came, making her senses explode in shattering waves so strong they lifted the upper portion of her body off the bed.

He held her for a long time afterward; he kissed the crown of her head gently, then rolled onto his side, taking her with him. His arms continued to hold her as he brushed the hair from her face with gentle fingers and wiped the moisture from her eyes. He was full of questions—Hannah sensed them as profoundly as if they were spoken—yet he left them unasked. For a long time he did nothing but hold her, and for then it was more than enough.

She fell asleep, and woke chilled. Riley was awake still, and when he saw her tremble, he pulled up the covers, then gathered her close into his arms once again.

"Why?" he asked her, his voice deep and impatient.

Hannah could think of no way to explain. At least not with words. Tilting back her head, she brushed her lips over his, loving the velvet feel of his mouth and tongue.

"That doesn't explain a whole lot."

"I know." She had no answers for him. The emptiness was back—reality so harsh and brutal that she couldn't bear it a moment longer. Not knowing any other way to ease it, she raised her arms and brought his mouth down to hers and kissed him once more. He wanted answers, not kisses, but soon his physical need overpowered everything else and he made love to her a second time.

Hannah woke at dawn, sick with guilt and self-recrimination, and quietly slipped from the room. It was the last time she'd seen Riley Murdock.

She lay in bed, eyes open wide as she stared at the ceiling. The time had come for her to quit fooling herself. The week before, she'd bought a home pregnancy test at the local drugstore, hiding it under a magazine until she'd reached the checkout stand. It was in her underwear drawer now.

Reading the instructions carefully, she did as they said and waited the longest fifteen minutes of her life for the results.

Positive.

She was pregnant. By her best calculations, almost three

months. Dear God, what was she going to do? Hannah had no answers. None. If her mother had been alive she might have been able to confide in her, seek her advice. But her mother had died when she was thirteen.

By rote Hannah set a roast in the oven and waited for her father to return from the church service. At twelve-thirty he walked in the back door, and his gentle eyes brightened when he saw her sitting at the kitchen table.

"So you're feeling better?"

She offered him a feeble smile and clenched her hands together in her lap. "Daddy," she whispered, her eyes avoiding his, "I…I have something to tell you."

Chapter Two

Riley Murdock had been in one bitch of a mood for nearly three months. He'd done everything within his power to locate the mysterious Hannah and cursed himself a hundred times over that he hadn't thought to ask for her surname.

Once he found her, he didn't know what the hell he intended to do. Strangling her seemed like a damn good idea. The woman had driven him crazy from the moment she first stumbled into him on the festive Seattle sidewalk.

When he'd woken to find her gone that morning, he'd been devastated with self-recrimination. Then he'd grown furious. In the weeks since, his wrath hadn't diminished. He didn't know what game she was playing, but by heaven he intended to find out.

If there was anyone to blame in this fiasco, Riley noted, it was himself. He'd known from the first that she wasn't like the other women who frequented waterfront bars. The story she'd told him about a couple of men following her was true. She'd been genuinely frightened, trembling with anxiety. The look in her eyes—damn, but she had beautiful gray eyes—couldn't easily be fabricated. Why she had opted to approach him, he didn't know. The woman was full of surprises.

If he was astonished by the fact she'd chosen to sit at

his table, then he should have been a candidate for a heart transplant when he discovered she was a virgin. As many times as Riley had analyzed what happened between them, nothing added up right.

She'd approached him. She'd been the one to kiss him. Hell, she'd practically seduced him. Seduced by a virgin. No wonder the tally kept coming up inaccurate. He should have realized, should have figured it out. Instead, he'd been left to deal with this incredible sense of guilt. If only she hadn't disappeared without explaining. Anger tightened his stomach every time he thought about waking up that morning and finding her gone. He'd damn near torn apart the desk manager trying to find out about her. But apparently no one had seen her go.

Riley blamed himself still. He feared he'd frightened her so badly that she'd fled in horror. Had he hurt her? She'd been so tight and so small. It was all he could do not to slam his fist into the wall every time he thought about their brief encounter, which was damn near every minute of every day. What had happened to her since? Was she sick? Alone? Frightened? Pregnant?

He'd been in control of their encounter until she'd kissed him. Now it was weeks later and he still reeled at the memory of the gentle, shy way in which she'd pressed her lips to his. He cursed how he could close his eyes and continue to taste her. How sweet she'd been. How warm and delicate. Her lips had molded to his, and her flavor reminded him of cotton candy. That alone was enough to torment him, but it wasn't all. Her fragrance continued to obsess him. It wasn't a commercial one he could name. The only way he could think to describe it was to imagine walking waist-deep in a field of wildflowers.

The woman had somersaulted into his life, sent his senses cartwheeling, and then, without a thought, without a care, had vanished, leaving him bitter and confused.

The hell with her, Riley decided rashly. He'd wasted

enough time, energy and expense trying to find her. He'd return to his well-ordered life and forget her. Which was obviously what she intended to do with him.

If only he could forget her.

"Dad," Hannah pleaded softly, fighting to hold back a sob, "say something."

The truth was out, and Hannah hung her head waiting for the backlash of anger and disappointment. It was what she deserved and what she expected.

To her surprise, her father said nothing. He sat in the chair and stared into space, his face devoid of expression. Then he stood, laboriously, as if he were feeling old and beaten. Without a word he walked out the back door.

Tears filled Hannah's eyes as her gaze followed him. He stood on the porch for several moments, his hand wrapped around the support beam, and stared into a cloudless October sky. Then, stepping off the porch, once again with slow and strained movements, he crossed the parsonage lawn and entered the old white church. Hannah sat at the kitchen table and gave him fifteen minutes before she followed him.

She found her father kneeling at the front of the church, before the altar, his head and shoulders slumped forward. Her heart constricted painfully at the sight of him there on his knees.

"Daddy," she whispered, speaking to him as she'd done as a frightened child. She *was* frightened. Not of what he'd say or of what he'd do, but because the circumstances surrounding this pregnancy were so complex.

George Raymond opened his eyes and straightened. Placing his hand on his knee, he rose awkwardly to his feet. His gaze rested on her, and she watched as his Adam's apple moved up and down his throat while he struggled to restrain the emotion. He tried to smile, a weak attempt to comfort her, then took her hand and together they sat in the front pew.

Hot tears brimmed in Hannah's eyes, threatening to spill over. The lump in her throat felt as large as a basketball, making swallowing nearly impossible. Her father had every right to be angry with her, to rage at her for her stupidity. What she'd done had been the height of irresponsibility. In her anguish she'd rebelled against everything she'd been raised to believe—an incredible departure from anything she'd ever done.

If she could offer any excuse, it was that she hadn't been herself. The hours she'd spent with Riley had been the first in days, in weeks, in which she wasn't suffocating in her grief. She'd reached out to him, a stranger, needing his touch, needing to be held and loved and protected. Needing a reprieve from her pain to ease the frustration of having been cheated from this experience with Jerry, the only man she'd ever truly loved. She'd been despondent, and in her anguish she'd sought the comfort of a stranger. It had been sheer stupidity on her part. And now she was faced with the knowledge that the one major indiscretion of her life was about to bear fruit.

Even if she hadn't gotten pregnant, even if she'd been able to bury the events of that night for what remained of her life, she had changed. Not only in the physical sense. It had taken her several weeks to realize the physical aspects of her experience were only a minor portion of their lovemaking. Her emotions had become involved. She didn't know how to explain it or what to make of it. She'd assumed that once she left the hotel room, she'd never think of Riley again. But she did, almost constantly, against every dictate of her will.

"I'm sorry, Dad," she whispered brokenly. "So sorry."

Her father wrapped her gently in his arms. "I know, Hannah, I know."

"I was wrong…. I was so angry at God for taking Jerry. I loved him so much."

With a tenderness that pitched knives at her heart, her father brushed the hair from her face. "I needed a few moments alone to think through this situation. I've been reminded that God doesn't make mistakes. This child growing under your heart was planted there for a reason. I don't know why any more than I understand the reason God took Jerry home. Nevertheless you are going to have a baby, and the only thing we can do is make the best of the situation."

Hannah nodded, not knowing what to say. She didn't deserve so wonderful a father.

"I love you, Hannah. Yes, I'm hurt. Yes, I'm disappointed in your lack of judgment. But there is nothing you could ever do that would change my love for you or the fact you're my daughter."

Hannah closed her eyes and breathed deeply, clinging to her father's strength and his love.

"Now, tell me his name," he said, breaking away from her.

Keeping her gaze lowered, she whispered, "Riley Murdock... We met only once—the night of the torchlight parade. He's in the Navy, but I don't have a clue where he's stationed." Finding him now would be impossible, which was just as well. Hannah didn't want to think about what Riley would say or do once he found out she was carrying his child. Frankly, she wondered if he'd even remember her.

Her father gripped her hand in both his own, and once again Hannah noted how frail he looked. The lines around his eyes and mouth had formed into deep grooves and there was more gray than reddish brown in his thick thatch of hair. Funny how she hadn't noticed that earlier. The changes had come since Jerry's death, but she'd been so consumed by pain and uncertainty that she hadn't noticed he'd been dealing with his own grief.

"The first thing we have to do," he said gently, "is make

a doctor's appointment for you. I'm sure Doc Hanson will be able to see you first thing Monday morning. I'll give him a call myself."

Hannah nodded. Unwilling to face the truth, she'd delayed contacting a physician longer than she should have. Doc Hanson was a friend of the family and could be trusted to be discreet.

"Then," Hannah told him, drawing in a deep sigh, "we'll need to decide where I should go."

"Go?" Her father's dear face darkened, the age lines becoming even more pronounced.

"I won't be able to continue living here," she said, her tone weary. She wasn't thinking of herself, but of her father and of Jerry's memory.

"But why, Hannah?"

She inhaled deeply. "Everyone will assume the child is Jerry's." With everything in her heart she wished her fiancé had fathered her child, but she had to deal with the cold, harsh facts. Riley Murdock—a stranger from the Seattle waterfront—was the father. Although it was tempting, very tempting, to allow her church family and friends to believe she carried Jerry's child, she couldn't have lived with the lie. Not when he'd always been so morally upright.

"We'll simply explain to everyone that the child isn't Jerry's," her father stated with one hard nod of his head, as if that alone would set everything right.

"Do you honestly think the congregation will believe me?" she asked him, the words tight in her throat. "I have to leave, Dad," she said firmly, unwilling to compromise.

For her father's sake she must leave Seattle. He'd been such a loving and kind parent, and there were sure to be those in the church who would malign him for her wrongdoings. There would be an equal number who would stand beside them both with loving support, but Hannah couldn't bear to see her father suffer because of her mistakes.

"I'll go live with Aunt Helen until after the baby's born...."

"And then what?" her father demanded, sounding uncharacteristically alarmed.

"I...don't know. I'll cross that bridge when I reach it." So many questions and concerns were coming at her, like a spray of rocks from a speeding car. Hannah didn't feel capable of fending off a single one, at least not now.

"We don't need to decide anything yet," he assured her after a moment. But he wore a thoughtful frown as they walked back to the house, where Hannah had left dinner simmering.

The frown didn't seem to leave her father's features from that moment forward. Hannah had been in to see Doc Hanson, who confirmed what she already knew. He ran a series of tests and prescribed iron tablets and vitamins because she was anemic. He'd been gentle and kind and didn't ply her with questions, for which she was grateful.

It was Friday afternoon nearly two weeks after Hannah had first told her father about the pregnancy. Exhausted from her day's work as an underwriting assistant for a major insurance company, she walked into the house and discovered her father waiting for her in the living room. He sat in his favorite chair, his hands curved around the faded upholstered arms, his gaze fixed straight ahead. Hannah called it his "thinking chair." To discover him resting in the middle of the afternoon was highly unusual.

"Good afternoon, Dad," she greeted with a smile, and walked across the worn beige carpet to kiss his weathered cheek. "Is everything all right?"

"It's just fine," he said, returning her smile with an absent one of his own. "Keep your coat on. We're going out."

"We are?" Offhand, Hannah couldn't think of any appointment she'd made. Only infrequently did she accompany her father on house calls, and those were generally scheduled for Tuesday and Thursday evenings. George Raymond made it a point to visit every family in his congregation at least once a year.

His hand protectively cupped her elbow as he led her out the front door and down the steps. The station wagon was parked in the driveway.

"Where are we going?" Hannah questioned. Rarely had she seen her father look more resolute. It was as if he were marching with Joshua, preparing to face the walls of Jericho.

When he didn't answer, she assumed he hadn't heard her and she repeated the question. That, too, was ignored.

He drove silently for several minutes before he reached the freeway, and then he headed south toward Tacoma. The car was warm, and although she was curious as to what was happening, Hannah soon found her eyes drifting closed. Her head bobbed a couple of times as she struggled to remain awake. If only she'd get over this depressing need for extra sleep. It seemed she couldn't last through the day without napping. Lately she'd taken to heading for bed nearly as soon as she'd finished the dinner dishes. She shifted positions and opened her eyes when they crossed the Narrows Bridge and headed toward the Kitsap Peninsula.

She woke when her father made a sharp turn and eased to a stop in front of a guard house. He rolled down the window, and a blast of cold air alerted Hannah to the fact they'd arrived at their destination. She straightened and looked around. Although she'd never been on one before, she recognized immediately that they were entering a military compound.

"Dad?" she quizzed. "Where are we?"

"Bangor," he announced a little too loudly. "We're meeting Riley Murdock."

In Chaplain Stewart's office Riley sat, ramrod straight, across the room from Hannah Raymond and her stern-faced father. Riley's gaze narrowed as he fired a look in her direction. Not once did she deign to glance his way. She sat, her back as rigid as his own, but although she held her head high, her gaze refused to meet his. Perhaps it was just as well.

First thing the previous morning, Riley had been called before his commanding officer. When he arrived, he'd discovered Chaplain Stewart and Lieutenant Commander Steven Kyle.

"Do you know a woman by the name of Hannah Raymond?" the chaplain had asked him.

Riley had reacted with surprise. For three months he'd been frantically searching for her, spending every available weekend combing the Seattle waterfront, asking if anyone had seen a woman of her description. He'd followed the leads, but each one had led to a frustrating dead end. He'd gone so far as to contact a detective agency, but they'd offered him little hope. All Riley knew about her was her first name and the fact she had shiny brown hair and dove-gray eyes. There simply hadn't been enough information, and the agency had been discouraging.

"I know her," Riley admitted.

"How well?"

Riley had stiffened. "Well enough."

"Then you may be interested to learn she's pregnant," Chaplain Stewart stated abruptly, looking at Riley as though he were the spawn of the devil.

Riley felt as if someone had knocked his feet out from under him, and then, when he was laid low, viciously kicked him.

"Pregnant," he repeated, stunned, as though he'd never heard the word before.

"She claims the child is yours," his CO explained. "She maintains it happened during Seafair, which means she'd be about three months along. Does that time frame gel with you?"

Fury and outrage twisted inside Riley until he couldn't speak. All he could manage was a sharp nod. He clenched his powerful fists at his sides until he was sure he'd cut off the blood supply to his fingers.

"At Seafair?" the commanding officer pressed.

Again Riley nodded. "That would be about right." The woman had put him through three months of living hell, and he wouldn't soon forget or forgive that. "When did she contact you?" he asked his CO.

It was Chaplain Stewart who answered. "She didn't."

"Then who did?" he demanded.

"George Raymond, Hannah's father. He's had an extensive investigation done on you, as well."

Great. Wonderful. Now Riley was going to be left to deal with an irate father. That was exactly what he needed to start his day off on the wrong foot.

"George and I attended seminary together," the chaplain had continued, and it was clear from the way he spoke that the two men had been good friends. "When Hannah confessed that the father of her unborn child was in the Navy, George contacted me, hoping I'd be able to help him locate you."

Riley couldn't believe this was happening. The desire to wring Hannah's scrawny neck increased by the minute.

Hannah was pregnant! If he had any luck, Riley swore, it was all bad. Okay, so he was being mildly unreasonable. But she was the one who'd come on to him. He'd assumed, at least in the beginning, that she must be using protection. If he'd believed otherwise he would have taken care of the matter himself. It wasn't until after he'd discovered she was a virgin that he had briefly wondered. And worried. He'd admit now that the deed was staring him in the face.

"What does she want?" Riley demanded. Support, medical bills, maybe even an allotment to cover her expenses while she was unable to work. Riley had no intention of sloughing off his duty. He was the one responsible and he'd own up to it.

Chaplain Stewart stood and walked across the room. He paused and then rubbed his hand along the back of his neck, as if he needed extra time to shepherd his thoughts.

"As I told you earlier, George Raymond is a minister. In his mind there's only one thing to be done."

"And that is?" Riley demanded, remembering he'd left his checkbook at his apartment.

"He wants you to marry his daughter."

"What?" Riley was so shocked he nearly laughed out loud. "Marry her? Hell, I don't even know her."

"You know her well enough," the chaplain reminded him, throwing Riley's own words back in his face. "Listen, son," he continued thoughtfully, "no one's going to force you to marry the girl."

"You're damn right about that," Riley returned heatedly, slightly amused that he'd gone from Satan's spawn to "son" in a matter of a few minutes.

"Hannah's not like other women."

Riley didn't need to be reminded of that, either. No one else he'd ever kissed tasted half as good as she had, or smelled so fresh and lovely. No other woman had loved him nearly as well, Riley reminded himself regretfully; her untutored responses haunted him still. He'd felt engulfed by her tenderness, awed by her beauty and jolted by her hungry need. She'd been so tight and so hot that even now, he couldn't think about their night together without wanting her again.

"You have to understand," Chaplain Stewart went on to say, "Hannah's been raised in the church. Her mother died when she was in her early teens, and she took over the family responsibilities then. Her older brother's in the mission field in India. This young woman comes from as traditional a background as you can imagine."

That was all fine and wonderful. She'd cared for her family, and he didn't doubt she possessed more than one admirable trait, but Riley wasn't convinced marriage would be the best solution to the problem. Not only weren't they acquainted, Hannah's life couldn't have been less like his own had they sat down and drawn up a composite of opposite family types.

"Wanting to protect those she loves, not wanting to shame her family, Hannah's apparently opted to move away."

"Where?" Riley demanded, instantly alarmed. He had the feeling he was going to end up following this woman halfway across the country before this was over.

"I'm hoping her leaving the area won't be necessary," Chaplain Stewart said pointedly.

"What the chaplain is saying," Lieutenant Commander Kyle stressed, "is that if you married the young lady it would solve several problems. But I want it understood, that decision is yours."

Riley stiffened. No one was going to force him into marrying against his will. He'd rot in jail before he'd be pressured into wedding a woman he didn't want. At his silence, Riley's CO leafed through his file, which was spread open across the top of his desk. Riley would be up for Senior Chief within the next couple of years, and the promotion was important to him. Damn important.

"Think about what Chaplain Stewart has said," Lieutenant Commander Kyle urged. "The Navy can't and won't force you to marry the woman."

"That's true enough," the chaplain added. "But from everything I've seen and heard, I believe it's the only decent thing you can do."

Both men were looking at him as if he'd enticed Hannah Raymond into his bed. They weren't likely to believe she'd been the one who'd seduced him!

Riley had brooded over the meeting with Lieutenant Commander Kyle and Chaplain Stewart all night. Hannah was pregnant with his child and the chaplain was breathing down his back like monster dragons exhaling fire. Although his CO hadn't said it, Riley had the impression his promotion might well hang in the balance. Everyone else seemed to know what he should do about it. Everyone, that is, except him.

Now that he saw Hannah again, Riley was even more uncertain. He remembered her as being a lovely creature, but not nearly so delicate and ethereal. She was thin—thinner than when he'd met her that July night—and so pale he wondered about her health.

Riley feared the pregnancy had already taken its toll on her, and he couldn't help being concerned about her wellbeing. The urge to protect and care for her was strong, but Riley pushed it aside in favor of the anger that had been building within him for the past several months.

He had damn good reason for being furious with her.

"Are you convinced the child is yours?" Chaplain Stewart directed the question to Riley.

The room went still, as though everyone were on tenterhooks anticipating his reply. "The baby's mine," he answered firmly.

Hannah's soft gray gaze slid to his as if she longed to thank him for telling the truth. He wanted to leap to his feet and remind her that she'd been the one to run out on him. It hadn't happened the other way around. If anyone's integrity was to be questioned, then it should be hers.

"Are you prepared to marry my daughter?" demanded the thin, graying man Riley could only assume was Hannah's father.

"Dad?" Hannah gasped, pleading with her father. "Don't do this, please." Her voice was soft and honest, and Riley doubted that many men could refuse her.

Reverend Raymond looked at Riley as if he fully expected him to sprout horns and drag out a pitchfork. If that were the case, it was ironic that the minister was demanding that Riley marry his daughter.

"As your father, I insist this young man do right by you."

"Chaplain Stewart," Hannah said, coming to her feet, ignoring her father. "Could Riley and I talk for a few minutes…alone?" The last word was added pointedly.

The two older men seemed to reach a tacit agreement. "All right, Hannah" the Navy chaplain agreed, coming to his feet. "Perhaps that would be for the best. Come on, George. I'll pour us a cup of coffee and we'll leave these two to sort out their problems in their own way. I have faith young Murdock means well."

Riley waited until the door had closed before he leaped to his feet. He glared across the room at Hannah, not knowing what to do first—shake her until her teeth rattled or gently take her in his arms and demand to know why she was so deathly pale. Before he had the opportunity to speak, she did.

"I'm terribly sorry about all this," she murmured. "I had no idea my father had contacted you."

"Why'd you leave?" he bit out the question between clenched teeth, still undecided about how he was going to deal with her.

She frowned as if she didn't understand his question. Her brow creased until she understood, and then it creased even more. "I suppose I owe you an apology for that, as well."

"You're damn right you do."

"I didn't mean for any of this to happen."

"Obviously," he retorted, trapped in his anger. "No one in their right mind would do this to themselves. The question is, what the hell are we going to do about it now?"

"Oh, don't worry. It isn't necessary for you to marry me. I don't know what ever made Dad suggest that."

She seemed so damn smug about it, and that riled him all the more.

"Apparently your father feels differently. He seems to think my marrying you would salvage your honor."

She nodded. Her hair was tied at her nape, giving Riley a clear view of the delicate lines of her face. As pale as she was, she resembled a porcelain doll, fragile and easily breakable. She looked dangerously close to that point right then.

"My father is an old-fashioned man with traditional values. Marriage is what he would expect."

"What do *you* expect?" His tone was less harsh, his concern for her outweighing his irritation.

Hannah placed her hand on her smooth stomach as though she longed to protect the child. Riley's gaze dropped there, and he waited a moment, trying to analyze his own feelings. A child grew there. *His* child. Try as he might, he felt nothing except regret mingled with a healthy dose of concern.

"I…I'm not sure what I want from you," Hannah answered. "As I tried to tell you before, I feel terrible about dragging you into this mess."

"It takes two. You didn't create that child on your own."

Her smile was shy. "Yes, I know. It's just that I never meant to involve you…afterward."

That didn't set any better with Riley than the implied threat from his commanding officer. "So you intended to run off and have my child without telling me?"

"I…didn't have a clue as to how to find you," she argued.

"Your father didn't seem to have much of a problem."

She looked away as though she wanted to avoid an argument. "I didn't know if you wanted me to contact you."

She sure the hell had a low opinion of him. It rankled Riley that Miss High-and-Mighty would make those kinds of assumptions about him.

"Next time don't assume anything," he barked. "Ask!"

"I apologize—"

"That's another thing. Quit apologizing." He held both hands to his head, hoping the applied pressure to his scalp would help him think.

"Are you always this difficult to talk to?" she asked. He was pleased to hear a little mettle in her voice. It told him he hadn't been wrong about her. This woman had plenty of spirit. It also assured him her health wasn't as bad as he suspected.

"I am when I've been backed into a corner," Riley stormed.

She stood and reached for her coat. "Then let me assure you I'm not the one forcing you into a marriage you obviously don't want."

"You're right. It isn't you. It's the United States Navy."

"The Navy? I…don't understand."

"I don't expect you to," Riley barked. "It's either do right by you or kiss a promotion I've been working toward for the last several years goodbye." Lieutenant Commander Kyle had implied as much in a few short words.

"Oh, dear. I had no idea."

"Obviously not." He rammed all ten fingers through his hair, then dropped his hands to his sides. "My career could be on the line with this one, sweetheart." That was an exaggeration, but in some ways Riley felt it could be true.

Hannah grimaced at the derogatory way in which he'd used the term of affection. "But surely if I spoke to them…if I were to explain…"

Riley laughed shortly. "Not a chance. Your father made sure of that."

"I didn't know."

"The way I see it," he said with thick agitation, "I don't have a hell of a lot of choice but to go ahead and marry you."

Hannah's head snapped up at that. "You…can't seriously be considering going through with a wedding."

"I've never been more serious in my life."

Chapter Three

In a matter of hours, Hannah was scheduled to become Mrs. Riley Murdock. She sat on the end of her bed, wrestling imaginary crocodiles of doubt and indecision. They might as well be real, she mused, clenching and unclenching her hands. She felt as though there were powerful jaws snapping at her, jagged teeth tearing at her confidence and determination.

It was Jerry she loved, not Riley. Nothing would ever make the hard-edged sailor into another seminary student. Hannah wasn't foolish enough to believe the Torpedoman Chief was likely to change. One look at his cold, dark features the afternoon of the meeting at Bangor reminded her what a rugged life he led. There was nothing soft in this man. Nothing.

The day of the meeting, he'd been both angry and restless, stalking the room, thundering at her every time she attempted to apologize. In some ways she was convinced he hated her.

Yet it was his child growing within her womb. Hannah flattened her hand across her abdomen and briefly closed her eyes. Despite the complications this pregnancy had brought into her life, Hannah loved and wanted this baby.

Hannah knew that Riley wasn't marrying because of the pregnancy. By his own admission, he was doing so for political reasons. Both her father and Chaplain Stewart had seemed relieved when Riley had announced they had agreed to go through with the wedding.

Hannah had agreed to no such thing. She'd been trapped into it, the same way Riley had. She wasn't sure even now, sitting in her room, dressed for her wedding ceremony, that she was making the right decision.

They were so different. She didn't love him. He didn't love her. They'd barely spoken to each other—and it was because they had nothing in common except the child she carried. How a marriage such as theirs could ever survive more than a few weeks, Hannah didn't know.

"Hannah," her father called after politely knocking on her bedroom door, "it's time we left."

"I'm ready," she said, standing. She reached for the two suitcases and dragged them across the top of her bed. This was all she would bring into their marriage. The pot-and-pan set, the dishes, silverware and other household items she'd collected over the years were gone. She'd donated them to the Mission House the evening she'd met Riley. The irony hadn't been lost on her. Nor had she forgotten how Reverend Parker had announced that God works in mysterious ways. Her entire life felt like an unsolved mystery, and she'd long since given up on deciphering the meaning.

She opened the bedroom door and found her father standing on the other side, waiting for her. He smiled softly and nodded his approval. "You look beautiful."

She blushed and thanked him. She didn't feel beautiful in her plain, floor-length antique-white dress, but having her father smile and tell her so lent her some badly needed confidence. The fact he seemed so sure that marrying Riley was the right thing helped a great deal. She'd always trusted her father and had never doubted his wisdom.

George Raymond took the suitcases from her hands and led the way down the stairs. As he loaded the luggage into the back of the station wagon, Hannah stood on the porch and glanced around her one last time. Bright orange, gold and brown leaves blanketed the sloping lawn, and the skeletal limbs of the two chestnut trees that ruled the front yard rose toward the deep blue sky. She would miss all this, Hannah realized, wondering how long it would be before she returned.

The ride to Bangor took almost two hours. Her father did most of the talking. He seemed to sense how nervous Hannah was and sought to reassure her.

Chaplain Stewart, Riley, and a man and woman Hannah didn't recognize were waiting for them in the vestibule of the base chapel. The chaplain and her father broke into immediate conversation. From the other side of the room, Riley's eyes found hers. His facial expression didn't alter, and he nodded once.

He looked tall and distinguished in his white dress uniform, and although it was little comfort, Hannah realized, that she was marrying a handsome man. In the days since their last meeting, she'd had repeated nightmares about him. In her dream he came at her like a huge monster, eager to devour her. Seeing him now produced a shiver of apprehension.

"If you'll excuse us," Hannah said, her voice barely audible, "I'd like a few minutes alone with Riley."

The conversation came to an abrupt halt as Chaplain Stewart cast an accusing glare in Riley's direction. If the other man's censure disturbed him, he gave no indication. Silently he led the way to the opposite end of the room.

"You've changed your mind?" His tight features told her nothing of his thoughts. Perhaps that was what he was hoping she'd do.

"Have you?"

The corner of his mouth lifted slightly. "I asked first."

"I'm...willing to go through with the wedding, if you are."

"I'm here, aren't I?"

He didn't look any too pleased about it, and she decided against saying so.

"You wanted to talk to me?" he demanded gruffly.

"Yes. I thought we should reach an understanding regarding…the sleeping arrangements before we…you know…before we…"

"No, I don't know," he returned impatiently. His gaze narrowed sufficiently. "Listen, if you're saying what I think you're saying, then the deal's off. If I'm going through the hassle of marrying you, then I want a *wife,* not a sister. Do I make myself understood?"

Hannah lowered her gaze, clenching her hands tightly together in front of her. "Do I have to be your…wife right away?" Her voice was soft and low.

He was silent for so long that she wasn't sure he'd heard her. "I don't suppose it would hurt any if we took some time to get to know one another better first."

"That's what I thought." She raised her head and looked up at him, relieved that he was willing to give her the time she needed to adjust to their marriage.

"How long?" he demanded.

She blinked at the sharpness of the question. "Ah…I'm not sure. A few weeks at any rate. Possibly a couple of months."

"A couple of months!"

Hannah was convinced the entire chapel heard him roar and would immediately guess the gist of their conversation. Her face filled with boiling color. "Couldn't we just…well, let it happen naturally?"

His face had tightened into a brooding frown. He wasn't pleased and didn't bother to pretend otherwise. "I suppose."

"Of course, we'll be sleeping in separate bedrooms until such time that we're both comfortable with that aspect of…our marriage."

"Right," he returned caustically before turning away from her. "Separate bedrooms."

Separate bedrooms! The words repeated themselves in Riley's mind throughout the brief wedding ceremony Hannah's father officiated. The fact that he didn't give Riley the chance to kiss the bride wasn't lost on him. What he hadn't figured out was why the old man had demanded Riley marry his daughter in the first place. His father-in-law was as straitlaced as they come. It remained a mystery why George Raymond had insisted Riley marry Hannah. Hell, if it came down to it, Riley wasn't entirely sure what had prompted him to go with the wedding himself. What his CO claimed had carried some weight, that was true enough, but Riley knew himself well. No one could have forced him into marrying Hannah if he'd been completely opposed to the idea. Which obviously meant, he reasoned, he wanted her as his wife.

Glancing at her now, sitting by his side as they drove to his apartment in nearby Port Orchard, gave him further cause to wonder. She hadn't said more than a handful of words since the ceremony. He hadn't a clue what she was thinking, but he figured she was looking for some way to get out of this.

"It was very nice of Chaplain Stewart and Lieutenant Commander Kyle to arrange housing on the base for us, wasn't it?" she asked softly.

"Very nice," he repeated. He wondered how many strings his CO had had to pull to come up with that. The news had come as a surprise to Riley, who'd lived in a small apartment complex for the past two years.

"When will we be moving?"

"Soon."

"How soon?"

Hell, first he couldn't get her to talk, now he couldn't shut her up. "Next weekend."

"Good. Packing will give me something to do while you're gone during the day. Once we've moved, I'll look for a job."

"I don't want you doing any lifting, you hear?" She flinched at his harsh tones, and he regretted speaking so forcefully. He'd recently bought a book on pregnancy and birth, and it had stated that lifting anything heavy should be avoided. Riley was surprised at the overwhelming urge he felt to protect Hannah and the baby.

"But I want to help."

"We'll do the packing together." He left no room for argument.

"But what will I do every day?"

"What you normally do."

"I've always worked."

He was silent at that, not knowing what to tell her. He didn't want her out looking for a job. It was plain the pregnancy had already taken a toll on her health. "Relax for a while," he suggested after a moment. "There isn't any need for you to rush out and find a job now."

She sighed and closed her eyes, leaning her head against the back of the cushion. "I think I could sleep for a week."

She looked as if she'd do exactly that, but not in his bed, Riley noted bitterly. Not in his bed.

Riley's apartment was on the second floor of a complex overlooking Sinclair Inlet. The *Nimitz,* an aircraft carrier, and several other large Navy vessels were moored along the piers of the Puget Sound Naval Shipyard. Standing on the balcony, Riley pointed out each ship for her, telling her its classification and type. Most of the information went over Hannah's head, but she found the aircraft carrier easy to distinguish from the others.

The apartment itself was compact. It was clear he'd made an effort to clean up the place a bit. The fact pleased her. The living room had been straightened and newspapers neatly stacked in the corner. The carpet was olive green and blended well with his furniture, which consisted of a black recliner and a three-quarter-length sofa.

"You thirsty?" he asked, taking a beer out of the refrigerator.

Hannah's gaze fell on the alcoholic beverage as she shook her head. She had the feeling he'd offered it to her for shock value. "No, thank you."

Riley shrugged, twisted off the cap and guzzled down half the contents in a series of deep swallows. His Adam's apple bobbed with the action. Hannah turned away from him, and looked back at the narrow waterway.

"We have a minor problem," he said, joining her at the wrought-iron railing.

"Oh?" It was barely four, and already the sky was darkening.

"The apartment only has one bedroom."

Hannah's heart sank. "I see."

"Lieutenant Commander Kyle assured me the place on the base would have two, but for now we're here. What do you want to do about the sleeping arrangements?"

Hannah didn't know. At least not right then. "I could rest on the sofa, I guess."

Riley snickered at that and turned away from her, pausing at the sliding-glass door. "You'd better come in before you catch a chill."

That wasn't likely with her wearing her full-length wool coat, but she didn't want to argue with him. He closed the door behind her, finished the beer and tossed the brown bottle into the garbage. It made a clanking sound as it hit against a glass object, probably another beer bottle. Hannah had never been around a man who regularly indulged in alcoholic beverages and she wondered if this would become a problem between her and her husband.

"You don't approve of drinking, do you?"

That he could read her thoughts so clearly came as a shock. "Would it matter if I did?"

"No."

"That's what I thought." She hesitated, then couldn't resist asking, "Do you do it often?"

"Often enough" was his cryptic reply. He moved past her to lift her two suitcases, which he'd set down just inside the front door, and carry them into the lone bedroom.

Curious to see the rest of the apartment, Hannah followed him down the narrow hallway. The bedroom was the only room on the left. The drapes were closed and the double bed was poorly made. Hannah guessed that he didn't often bother to make it in the mornings.

He placed her suitcases on top of the bed, then sat on the end of the mattress. "You won't get much sleep on that sofa. It's old and lumpy. In case you didn't notice, it's also short."

"I'll manage."

"I'm not a monster, you know."

She blushed, remembering the dreams she'd had the past week about him springing horns and giant teeth. "I know."

"You don't sound all that convinced." He flattened his hands and leaned back, striking a relaxed pose. "If you recall the night we met, you were the one who—"

"Please, I'd rather not talk about that night." She abruptly left the room, walking into the kitchen. He followed her just the way she knew he would.

"In case you've conveniently forgotten, you were the one who seduced me."

"I…prefer to think we seduced each other," she returned boldly.

"Naturally, that's what you'd choose to think."

Her face felt fire-engine red. "Do you mind if we change the subject?"

"Not in the least. Answer me one thing, though. What

do you expect will happen if we share the same bed? You don't want me to touch you, then fine, I wouldn't dream of it. You have my word of honor."

Hannah ignored the question and the man. Opening the refrigerator, she removed a head of lettuce and a package of half-frozen hamburger. "How does taco salad sound for dinner?"

"Fine, for tomorrow night."

Her gaze flew to his, not understanding him.

"We'll be dining out this evening."

"We are?"

"Right," he said, grinning at her, his look almost boyish. He seemed to enjoy teasing her, bringing up details that would embarrass her, possibly because he fancied seeing her blush. "Far be it for you to tell Junior how you were forced to cook on our wedding day."

"Junior?" Funny, but she'd never given the sex of their baby any thought. The fact that he had, warmed her heart.

"We'll call him that for now, unless you'd rather not."

Her eyes met his, and for the first time that day she felt like smiling. "I don't mind, although I think you should be prepared for a juniorette."

"Boy or girl, it doesn't matter to me. A baby is a baby."

His matter-of-fact attitude stole a little of her good cheer, but she didn't let it show.

"It's ladies' choice tonight. What's your pleasure?"

Hannah hesitated. She'd been craving seafood for weeks, but it was expensive and she didn't want him to think she was extravagant. "Any place would be fine."

"Not with me. It isn't every day a man gets married. How would you feel about a seafood buffet? It's a bit of a drive, but there's a wonderful restaurant on Hood Canal that serves fabulous lobster."

"Lobster?" Hannah's eyes rounded with pleasure.

"And shrimp. And oysters and scallops."

"Oh, stop," she said with a laugh. "It sounds too good

to be true." This man had the most incredible knack of reading her mind.

He reached for her hand, and grinning, he led her out the front door and down the stairs to where his red CRX was parked. The drive took the better part of an hour, but once they arrived and were seated, Hannah realized it had been well worth the effort. The smells were incredible. The scent of warm bread mingled with garlic and freshly fried oysters.

Hannah piled her plate high with steamed clams and hot bread. As soon as she was finished, she returned for a slice of grilled salmon and barbecued shrimp, balancing a cup of thick clam chowder on the edge of her plate. The waitress came by with a glass of milk, which Riley had apparently ordered for her. She was pleased to note that he chose coffee for himself.

"This is wonderful," she exclaimed, after returning to the buffet table for the third time. She took a sampling of finger lobster and some oysters.

Riley was openly staring at her.

"Is something wrong?" she questioned, after adjusting the napkin on her lap.

"I would never have guessed one person could eat so much."

Hannah gazed at her plate. "I've made a glutton of myself, haven't I?" She rebounded quickly and smiled up at him. "You have to remember, I'm eating for two."

"You're eating as if you're expecting triplets," he teased, but the way his mouth lifted up at the corners told her he was pleased.

Breaking off a piece of bread, Hannah reached for the butter. "Is there anyone you want to tell about the wedding?" she asked conversationally.

"Who do you mean?" Her question appeared to displease him.

"Family," she said, not understanding his mood.

"I don't have any family."

"None?" It seemed incomprehensible to Hannah, who was so close to her own.

"My father ran off when I was eight, and my mother… Well, let's put it this way: she wasn't much interested in being a mother. I haven't had any contact with her in years."

Hannah set the bread aside. "I'm sorry, Riley. I had no idea… I didn't mean to bring up unhappy memories."

"You didn't. It's in the past and best forgotten."

"How'd you end up in the Navy?"

He seemed to find her query amusing. "How else? I enlisted."

"I see." It had been a stupid question, and she grew silent afterward.

They left the restaurant a few minutes later. A full stomach and the warm blast of air from the heater lulled her into a light sleep. She was only mildly aware of Riley turning on the car radio, switching stations until he found one that specialized in Easy Listening.

Hannah woke when he stopped the engine. It took her a second to realize her head was resting against his shoulder. She straightened abruptly as though she'd been caught doing something wrong. "I'm sorry, I didn't realize—"

"Don't be," he said brusquely, as though she'd displeased him far more by offering an apology than using his shoulder as a support.

He came around and helped her out of the car and cupped his hand under her elbow as they walked up the flight of concrete steps to his apartment.

Once they reached the top, Riley unlocked the door. Shoving it open, he turned to Hannah and without a word calmly lifted her into his arms.

Taken by surprise, she let out a small cry of alarm. "Riley," she pleaded, "put me down. I'm too heavy."

"Let me assure you, Hannah Murdock, you weigh next to nothing." With that he ceremoniously carried her over the threshold, gently depositing her in the leather recliner.

Hannah smiled at him, a little breathlessly, although he'd been the one to do all the work. This man was full of surprises. All week she'd been convinced she was marrying a monster, but Riley had gone out of his way to prove otherwise. Perhaps this marriage had a chance to survive, after all.

Riley turned on the television and reached for the evening paper and, after a few minutes, Hannah excused herself and began unpacking a few of her things. Since they would be moving within a matter of days, she only removed items she'd be needing.

Since Riley seemed wrapped up in something on television, she decided to bathe. The water was warm and soothing, and as she rested her head against the back of the tub, she traced her index finger over her stomach. There was no evidence her body was nurturing a child— at least not yet—but she hadn't reached the fourth month of her pregnancy. The doctor had told her to expect to feel movement at any time, and the prospect thrilled her.

When she'd finished, she dressed in a thick flannel gown and brushed her hair away from her face. Riley was still in the living room, sitting on the edge of his cushion, punching his arms back and forth. She noticed he was watching a boxing match, and she cringed inwardly.

He must have noticed her, because he reached for the television control and turned down the volume. His eyes widened as he assessed her.

"Is something wrong?" she asked, glancing down at herself.

"You normally wear *that* to bed?"

"Yes." He made it sound as if she'd donned sackcloth and ashes.

He nodded and punched the control, turning up the volume. "Then my guess is Junior will be an only child."

Hannah bristled; then, not knowing what else to do, sat down and tucked her feet under her. The fight taking place on the television screen was violent, with two boxers slugging it out as though they had every intention of badly maiming each other. Hannah winced and closed her eyes several times.

"Why would anyone fight like that?" she asked during a commercial break.

"Ten million might have something to do with it."

"Ten million dollars?" Hannah was incredulous. Standing, she looked around for something else to do. She walked into the kitchen and poured herself a glass of water. The evening paper was on the floor next to Riley's chair. She picked it up and read through it.

"Would you like to go to church with me tomorrow?" she invited.

"No." His eyes didn't stray from the screen.

She set the paper aside and yawned.

"Go ahead and go to bed. I'll wake you when I come in."

Hannah was skeptical, but the fight was only in the sixth round and it looked as if it could continue for a good long while. "You don't mind?"

"Not in the least," he answered, and waved her toward the bedroom.

Hannah found an extra blanket in the hall closet and wrapped that around herself as she lay on top of Riley's bed. It would have been presumptuous of her to crawl beneath the covers when she fully intended to sleep in the living room after Riley had finished with his program.

Although she was exhausted, Hannah had a difficult time falling asleep. What an unusual day she'd had. She'd married a man who was little more than a stranger to her, and discovered in the short time they'd spent alone that he was easy enough to like. She sincerely doubted that she'd ever grow to love him the way she had Jerry, but then Jerry had been a special man. It wasn't likely that she'd ever find anyone like him.

Riley was rough around the edges; she couldn't deny that. He drank beer as though it were soda and enjoyed disgusting displays of violence. Yet he'd gone out of his way to see to it that she had a wonderful wedding dinner. He appeared to be trying.

She smiled at the memory of how he'd hauled her into his arms and carried her over the threshold, then immediately frowned when she recalled the way he'd looked at her in her nightgown and announced that Junior would be an only child.

With a determined effort, Hannah closed her eyes. She knew she wouldn't sleep, but lying in bed was a hundred times more appealing than being subjected to the boxing match.

Hannah stirred, feeling warm and comfortable. Her arm was wrapped around a pillow, although now that she thought about it, this particular pillow was anything but soft. Her eyes fluttered open, and she found a pair of intense eyes staring back at her. She blinked, certain she was seeing things.

"What are you doing here?" she asked.

"The question, my dear wife, is what are you doing clinging to me as if you never intend on letting me go?"

Hannah immediately removed her arm and bolted upright. To her surprise, she was beneath the covers. "How'd you do that?" she asked, noticing at the same moment that he wasn't.

"Do what?" Riley asked with a yawn. He sat up and stretched his hands high above his head and growled as though he were an injured bear stalking the woods. The sound was so fierce it was all Hannah could do not to cover her ears.

"You said you'd wake me," she reminded him, not the least pleased with this turn of events.

"I tried."

"Obviously you didn't try hard enough." Primly, she tossed aside the covers and leaped out of bed. "You had no right… We agreed—"

"Hold on a minute, sweetheart, if you're—"

"Don't call me sweetheart. Ever." She hated the way he said it. Jerry had always spoken it with such tenderness and love, and she wouldn't have this man who was her husband desecrate the few precious memories she had of her fiancé.

"All right," Riley said, holding up his palms. "There's no reason to get bent out of shape. For your information, I did try to wake you, but it was obvious you were in a deep sleep. It was either haul you into the living room or leave you be. I chose the latter."

Hannah glared at him. She'd risen quickly and neither the baby nor her stomach appreciated the abrupt change of position.

"Hannah, you're looking pale. Are you all right?"

"I'm perfectly fine," she lied. The all-too-familiar sensation was taking root in the pit of her stomach. Her brow broke out in a cold sweat and her knees grew weak.

"There's no reason to be so upset," Riley continued, undaunted. "I did the gentlemanly thing and slept on top of the covers. Our skin never touched, I promise you." He paused. "Hannah…"

She didn't hear whatever he intended to say. With her hand over her mouth, she rushed down the hallway, making it to the toilet just in time to empty her stomach.

Riley helped her to her feet when she'd finished, and gently wiped her face with a damp cloth. "I didn't mean to upset you. Damn, if I'd known you were going to get sick, I'd have slept on the sofa myself. I'll tell you what—you can take the bed and I'll camp out there until we move."

He was so gentle, so concerned. Hannah raised her fingertips to his cheek and offered him a feeble smile. "My being sick didn't have anything to do with being upset. It's the baby."

He was silent for a moment. "How often does this happen?"

"It's better now than the first few months."

"How often?" he repeated firmly.

"Every morning in the beginning, but only once or twice a week now."

"I see." He released his hold on her and handed her the washcloth. "In that case, forget what I just said. If you want to sleep on the sofa, be my guest."

Chapter Four

"Hannah!" Riley bellowed as he walked inside the apartment. He startled her so much she nearly dropped the box she was carting. "How many times do I have to tell you, you aren't to lift anything?"

"But, Riley," she protested lamely, "this one isn't the least bit heavy."

"I don't care. Your job is to stay out of the way. Once we're into the other house you can start unpacking. If I see you touch a single one of those boxes again, I'm going to lock you out on the balcony. Is that understood?"

It was understood three apartments over, Hannah was sure. Riley had been surly all morning. He'd left before dawn to pick up the rental truck and returned in time to find her hauling boxes from the kitchen into the living room. She was only trying to help, and he'd made it sound as if she should be arrested.

They'd been married a week now, and if these past seven days were any indication of how their lives would blend together, Hannah wasn't sure they'd last the month. Riley seemed to be under the impression that she was one of his men—someone he could order about at will.

With so much to be done before the move, it was ridiculous that he expected her to do nothing.

The afternoon he'd returned to find a neatly organized

row of packed boxes stacked in the corner had resulted in a tirade that had left Hannah shaken and pale. No one had ever stormed at her the way Riley did. He seemed to think she should laze around sampling bonbons while watching daytime television.

He regretted his outburst later and offered an abrupt apology, but by then it had been too late; Hannah could barely tolerate looking at him. She escaped into the bedroom and closed the door.

If only he wasn't so unreasonable. He didn't want her cleaning for fear the solvents would harm her or the baby. Nor did he want her painting, although he was often up till the early hours of the morning. In the evenings when he returned from the base, he wouldn't even take time to eat the meals Hannah had so carefully prepared. Generally he grabbed a few bites on the run while she sat at the table, napkin in her lap, determined to ignore him as he shouted warnings at her about doing this or that.

The doorbell chimed, and Riley took the box from her arms, set it aside and answered the front door. Three men of varying sizes and shapes casually strolled inside. The first was dressed in jeans and a sweatshirt, the two others in football jerseys and sweatpants. The trio paused just inside the door when they noticed Hannah.

Riley stepped over to her and looped his arm around her shoulders, drawing her close to his side. "Hannah, this is Steve, Don and Burt," he said, nodding toward each one. "They're my friends. Guys, this is my wife, Hannah."

"Your wife?" the tallest of the three echoed, obviously stunned.

"My wife," Riley repeated brusquely. "Do you have a problem with that, Steve?"

"None." Riley's friend glanced apologetically toward Hannah. "It's just that good friends are generally invited to the wedding, if you know what I mean."

The one in the University of Miami sweatshirt rubbed

the side of his jaw as he blatantly stared at Hannah. "Is this the gal you spent all that time—"

"Are you going to stand around here all morning gawking, or are you going to help us move?" Riley demanded, lifting a box and shoving it into Don's arms.

Don let out a loud grunt as the box was shoved against his chest, then cast the others a rueful grin before carrying it out the front door to the waiting van.

The four soon formed a small caravan, carting furniture and boxes. Within less than a half hour, everything in the kitchen and living room was neatly tucked inside the moving van.

In the bustle of activity, Hannah was left to her own devices. Before she misplaced her purse, she carried that down the stairs along with a bag of cleaning supplies and set them on the floor of the truck, locking the door. As she stepped away, she heard Burt murmur something to Riley about a woman named Judy. The short, stocky man who wore a Seahawk football jersey number twelve seemed concerned and abruptly stopped speaking when he noticed Hannah.

Riley turned and frowned, as though anxious she might have heard something he'd prefer she didn't.

"You weren't carrying anything, were you?" he demanded when the silence seemed as loud as thunder.

"My purse," she returned softly, and hurried up the stairs, pressing herself against the railing halfway up when Don and Steve walked past her, each holding one end of the mattress. As soon as they were safely past, she rushed up the steps, pondering what she'd overheard.

Judy.

From the way Burt and Riley behaved, it was apparent they hadn't wanted her to hear. Their reaction led her to only one conclusion: Riley had been involved with the mystery woman. The fact he was married had certainly come as a surprise to the very men he'd labeled his friends.

So Riley had a woman friend; it shouldn't come as any surprise. He was a virile man, and not once had she believed he'd lived the life of a hermit.

A weary feeling came over her when Hannah entered the apartment. Naturally Riley wouldn't tell his friends about their marriage. No man would want to admit, even to the best of friends, that he'd been forced into marriage. Hannah swallowed at the growing lump in her throat. She'd been a fool not to realize Riley would be involved with someone else. Not only had her night of folly wreaked havoc in her own life, it had disrupted several others as well. Recriminations pounded at her like tiny hammers, and she sucked in a giant breath as she battled with her renewed sense of guilt.

Brushing the hair away from her face, Hannah walked over to the sliding-glass door that led to the balcony. Several long-legged cranes walked along the pebbled beach, their thin necks bobbing as they sauntered along the edge of the shallow water. Hannah folded her arms around her middle as she stiffened her spine. It had been Riley's choice to marry her, she recalled. He'd insisted. She might have been able to dissuade her father from this marriage, but when Riley concurred, Hannah had agreed, too weak to battle the pair of them. Riley had chosen to marry her of his own free will, whatever his reasons, and despite the fact that he was currently involved with someone else.

Judy. Hannah was shocked by the hard fist of resentment that struck her as she mentally repeated the other woman's name. Recognizing she was being utterly unreasonable didn't help. It wasn't as though her marriage was a great love match. Riley had never led her to believe it would be. No doubt he'd been with any number of women over the years.

The four men walked into the apartment, diverting her attention for the moment. Riley paused when he found her in the kitchen. His blue eyes searched her as if to read her thoughts, and when she offered him a weak smile, he seemed genuinely relieved.

Doing her best to stay out of the men's way, Hannah did what she could to help the loading go as smoothly as possible. Generally, this consisted of directing traffic and answering minor questions.

It amazed her how smoothly everything was going. She'd assumed it would take most of the day to move, but the four men worked well as a team and handled the burdensome task with an economy of effort.

When the apartment was nearly empty, Hannah moved into the bedroom to push some boxes into the center of the room. She wanted to do something, anything other than stand idle. Never in her life had she stood by, wasting time while watching others work. It went against the very grain of her personality, and she deeply resented it now.

"Hannah!"

"I'm only trying to help," she cried. "You're treating me like an old woman."

"I'm treating you like a *pregnant* woman," he countered sharply, gripping her by the shoulders. Despite the anger in his voice, his touch was light. Hannah raised her gaze to his, and when their eyes met, something warm and delicate passed between them. The silence swelled, filling the room. It was a comfortable silence that chased away the doubts she'd experienced earlier.

Whatever his reasoning, whatever hers, they were married now; and each in their own way seemed determined to make the best of the situation. If Riley had lost his love, then it was behind him now. She, too, had loved another.

Riley's hands inched their way from her shoulder, caressing the sides of her neck. His eyes continued to hold hers, then with excruciating slowness, he lowered his gaze to her mouth. Hannah felt her stomach tighten. The soft throaty sound that slipped from between her lips came as a surprise to her. Her face was flooded with color as she realized she'd practically begged Riley to kiss her again. The very thought mortified her. After all, she'd been the one to lay the ground rules in this relationship, and that had included no touching, at least not for a while. To his credit, Riley had respected her wishes all week. They'd lived as brother and sister—or, more appropriately, as drill sergeant and draftee.

A smile captured his eyes as he lazily rubbed his moist lips over hers. His kiss was gentle and undemanding. Their lips clung as his mouth worked against hers, deepening the pressure and the intensity. Hannah found herself opening up to him. Her hands slid up the hard wall of his chest as she leaned into his strength, absorbing it. Fire danced in her veins as a welcome, foreign excitement filled her.

Riley ended the kiss abruptly, dragging his mouth reluctantly from her. "I don't want you helping anymore. Understand?"

"But, Riley…"

"That's my baby you're carrying."

No sooner were the words out when Steve walked into the room. The other man's gaze shot from Hannah to Riley and then back to her again, as though he weren't sure he'd heard correctly. He didn't comment, but it was apparent the information came as a shock, for his gaze grew deep and troubled.

"I can't stand around doing nothing," Hannah protested heatedly, biting into her lip. Riley might have announced her condition with a bit more diplomacy, instead of dropping it like a hot coal in his friend's lap a few minutes after introducing her as his wife.

A flustered Steve grabbed a box and left the room. Tears of embarrassment filled Hannah's eyes as she abruptly moved away from her husband. Silly tears, she realized. There was no need to hide the fact she was pregnant; it would become obvious to all soon enough, and everyone would know the real reason Riley had married her.

"Hannah?" Riley's tone was gentle, concerned. "I'm sorry. I didn't mean to be so tactless."

Assuming he'd left with his friend, Hannah stiffened and kept her back to him as she smeared the moisture across her cheek. "I overreacted…. I guess I'm just a little tired is all."

"You're doing too much."

Hannah couldn't help smiling at that. She'd barely lifted a finger all morning. Once again his hands rested on her shoulders; and he gently turned her into his arms. As before, his touch was tender. His breath mussed the soft brown curls that had escaped the scarf that held the hair away from her face. Closing her eyes, she soaked in the comfort she felt in his arms, which seemed to outweigh the revelations of that morning.

"Steve and the others would have figured it out sooner or later."

Unable to resist, she flattened her hands against his hard chest and rested her head there for several seconds. "You're right. It's probably best this way. It's just that—"

"You'd have preferred for my friends to digest one piece of information at a time. You needn't worry that they'll judge us, you know. Friends wouldn't." He smiled down on her and then leaned over to brush his mouth against hers once again.

Hannah blinked as he moved away from her, lifted a heavy box upon his shoulders and seemingly without effort carted it out the door.

She stood for a moment and pressed her fingertips to her mouth. These few brief kisses were the first they'd exchanged since that fateful night. It had been incredibly good. Incredibly wonderful.

Once the truck was loaded, Riley came for Hannah, escorting her down the stairs and unlocking the van door before helping her inside the cab. Coming around the front, he hopped into the driver's seat, started the engine and then grinned over at her. "You ready, Mrs. Murdock?"

His smile and mood were infectious, and she nodded and grinned herself. "Ready."

Switching gears, he gripped the steering wheel and started whistling a catchy tune. It was the first time in a week or so, it seemed, that they hadn't been at odds with each other; the first time that Hannah felt that her husband wasn't going to storm at her for some imagined wrongdoing. Thus far into their relationship, he seemed more like a caretaker than a husband.

He continued whistling, smiling over at her every now and again. His hand reached for hers, and he linked their fingers together. He stopped whistling long enough to raise her hand to his mouth and kiss her knuckles.

"Who's Judy?" The question was out even before Hannah realized she was going to ask it. Her timing might be lacking, but she was relieved to have the subject out in the open.

Riley stopped whistling; his happy sound was cut off abruptly as a weary silence filled the cab.

"What makes you ask?" He merged with the flow of traffic as they followed the highway that curved around Sinclair Inlet, his gaze not wavering from the roadway.

"I'm not stupid, you know," she returned, resenting his attitude. "I heard you and Burt talking. If you were involved with someone else, the least you could do is give me fair warning."

Riley's frown deepened. "Judy and I are not involved— at least not the way you're implying."

"I wasn't implying anything," she answered primly. "I was just trying to save myself from future embarrassment."

"Future embarrassment?"

"Yes. It's obvious your friends know nothing about me,

and others might share the same concern as Burt had about…Judy. I don't mean to make a federal case out of it." Indeed she deeply regretted bringing up the subject. "All I want to know is if someone is going to give me weird looks and then inconspicuously inquire about Judy when you introduce me."

"All Burt did was ask a simple question. One, by the way, that was none of your business," Riley returned shortly. His hands tightened around the steering wheel.

"None of my business," she repeated calmly. Obviously she was traipsing across ground he had no intention of mapping. "I see."

"It's obvious you don't. Damnation, woman, you're making a mountain out of a molehill."

"I most certainly am not," she replied, doing her best to hold back the flash flood of anger that threatened to drown her. "If anyone is being unreasonable, it's you. Apparently the subject is a touchy one and best dropped. I'm sorry I said anything."

"So am I."

It seemed that Riley wasn't watching the road as well as he should have been, because a car shot past them and the driver hammered on the horn as he sped by. Her husband muttered something under his breath that Hannah pretended not to hear.

"Are there others?"

"Other what?" Riley shouted. His frustration with her was clearly getting the best of him.

"Women," Hannah explained serenely. "I should know about them, don't you think? It might save us both a good deal of embarrassment."

"Are you asking for a list of every woman I've ever made love to? Is that what you want? Are you sure that'll be enough to satisfy you? I married you, didn't I? What the hell more do you want? Blood?"

The knot that formed in Hannah's throat was so large

it made swallowing difficult and conversation impossible. So he and this Judy had been lovers. He'd implied as much by suggesting he list his affairs for her. Tilting her chin at a regal angle, she stared out the side window and dropped the subject entirely. He seemed relieved at the silence, although it grated sharply on Hannah's nerves.

Once they had passed through the gates at Bangor, Hannah watched with interest as they wove their way through a maze of streets toward the assigned housing. The long rows of homes were identical, painted gray and adorned with white shutters.

Riley pulled the van into the driveway of a corner lot and leaped out. He came around and helped Hannah down, then sorted through his keys until he found the one he was looking for.

"The house is quite a bit larger than the apartment," he said as he unlocked the front door, his eyes avoiding hers. He paused, then added, "The second bedroom is considerably smaller than the other." He seemed to be waiting for her to comment.

"I don't mind taking the smaller one."

Her answer didn't appear to please him, and after the door was opened, he stalked back to the truck and lowered the tailgate so the others could start to unload.

Left to her own devices, Hannah walked inside alone. It was a pleasant home, clean and well maintained. The living room was spacious, and had a brick fireplace and thick beige carpet. The kitchen was more than adequate with a raised counter for stools. The bedrooms were as Riley had explained—one larger than the other.

As she'd agreed, Hannah chose the smaller one for herself, leaving the door open. When Burt appeared carrying her two suitcases, she directed him into the room.

"I thought these were your things?" he said, and from the confused look he wore, he was sure he'd misunderstood her.

"Yes, please. The bedroom set I ordered will be delivered sometime this morning."

Burt looked over his shoulder, as if he fully expected Riley to appear and jerk the suitcases out of his hands and deposit them in the master bedroom.

"You're sure about this?"

"Positive," she answered with a gentle smile.

Riley happened upon them just then. He hesitated when Burt scratched the top of his head, set down Hannah's luggage and walked out of the smaller bedroom.

"Did you have to make such an issue of the fact we're not sleeping together?" he asked between clenched teeth.

"I wasn't making an issue of it," she returned sweetly. "Truly, Riley, I wasn't."

Grumbling, he stalked out of the house.

Riley returned to the van where his friend Steve was standing on the back lifting out the cardboard boxes for the others to haul inside.

"So you and Hannah aren't sharing a bedroom," he teased, taking delight in doing so. "I never thought Riley Murdock would allow any woman to lead him around by the nose."

Riley didn't deign to comment. He'd wanted to tell his three best friends about the marriage. The slight hadn't been intentional. There'd been enough to do in the past week, getting ready for the move, without worrying who knew about his marriage and who didn't. It wasn't as though he were trying to keep it a secret, and he regretted his lack of foresight now.

Matters weren't going well between him and Hannah. The woman was more stubborn than anyone he'd ever known. He'd insisted she not lift anything, concerned for her health and that of the baby. Every day, it seemed, she took delight in defying him. Invariably he lost his patience with her. She never argued with him, not once, but his tirades left her pale and withdrawn. Afterward, Riley felt like a heel. On more than one occasion he hadn't been able to live with himself and he'd gone to her and apologized, feeling like a brute for having chastised her. Just when things seemed to be working out between them, Burt had mentioned Judy Pierce. His friend certainly hadn't helped his cause any.

Judy was a friend—nothing more. But Riley sincerely doubted that he'd ever convince Hannah of that. The two had dated a few times over the past several years, but nothing had developed from it. His friends might have drawn a few conclusions about the relationship, conclusions that Judy herself might have implied. It didn't matter what Judy had told the others; she meant nothing to him and never would.

There hadn't been another woman in Riley's thoughts, night or day, from the moment he'd met Hannah. She'd had him twisted up in knots for months. Riley had never experienced frustration the way he had since meeting her. Attempting to locate her after she'd run out on him had demanded time, effort and money. When everything he knew how to do had failed, he'd resigned himself to never seeing her again, only to have her thrust back into his life like a sharp knife. A double-edged one, at that. She was his wife now, but he might as well have entered a seminary, for all the good it did him to have spoken marriage vows.

Frankly, Riley didn't know how much longer he was going to last under this insane arrangement. If anyone had told him he would go more than a week after his wedding without making love to his wife, he would have sworn they were crazy. He'd agreed to Hannah's terms for one reason only. Perhaps it was a bit conceited of him, but he'd firmly believed he'd have her in his bed within a matter of days. After that first night, when he'd upset her so badly by sleeping at her side, he hadn't even tried. Hannah cer-

tainly hadn't gone out of her way to encourage his attentions. The kiss they'd shared in the apartment had been
his first sign of hope in days. Once they got moved in and
settled down a little, he'd work on getting her into his bed.
If everything went right, it shouldn't take long.

The furniture and boxes were nearly unloaded when
the truck from the furniture store arrived. The two men
delivered the oak frame, mattress and nightstand and
within a matter of minutes were promptly on their way.

Riley had hoped their timing would have been a little
more to his advantage, but since Hannah had already let
the others know they weren't sharing a bedroom, it didn't
much matter.

The last of the furniture was in place and Riley was unloading what remained of the boxes when Don approached him, looking apologetic.

"What's wrong?" Riley asked. "Did you break something?"

"Not quite." The electrician pushed up the sleeves of his
shirt, glanced up at Riley and shrugged. "I'm sorry, man,
I didn't mean anything."

"What the hell did you do?" Don wasn't exactly known
for his tact.

"I called Hannah…Judy. I swear it was a mistake…. I
just wasn't thinking."

Riley groaned. "What did she do?"

"Nothing. That's just it. She corrected me and then
went about organizing the kitchen. It was the way she
looked—so, hell I don't know, fragile, I guess, like she
didn't have a friend left in the world. It got to me, man. It
really got to me. I tried to apologize, but everything I said
only made it worse."

Riley knew from experience the look Don was talking about. He'd been the recipient of "the look" several
times himself this week. Riley wondered if his wife realized she possessed this amazing talent for inflicting guilt.

It wasn't anything she said, or even did, but when she lowered her eyes and her bottom lip jerked, it was all he could do not to fall to his knees and beg her forgiveness. To his credit, he hadn't given in to the impulse. At least not yet.

"I think you ought to go talk to her. Clear the air about Judy before someone else makes the same mistake."

Riley nodded.

"We'll wait out here," Steve suggested. Since he was the only one of the four who was married, Riley readily agreed. Women were known to be unreasonable about the silliest things. He should have explained about Judy when Hannah had asked, but something inside him had hoped she might be a little jealous. Keeping her in the dark about an old girlfriend could help his cause. Apparently he was wrong again. Damn, but he wished he'd paid closer attention to women's feelings when he was young.

He found her in the kitchen, unpacking dishes. She glanced up at him, and her gaze narrowed into cold slits. Riley paused. He'd never seen her wear that particular look before, and instinct cautioned him.

"Hannah." He said her name gently.

She slammed a pan on the stove and winced at the crashing sound it made. For an instant he thought she was going to apologize, she looked so shocked. She surprised him once more by straightening out her arm and pointing at him as though he were in a police lineup and she was identifying him for the authorities. Her mouth opened and closed twice before she spoke.

"We might not be sleeping together, but there's something you'd best understand right now, Riley Murdock."

She braced her hands against her hips, digging her fists into her waist. Her slate-gray eyes flashed like nothing he'd ever seen. Her hair had pulled free of its tie and soft brown waves spilled haphazardly over her shoulders. Riley had seen Hannah frightened, humbled, browbeaten and mussed from lovemaking, but he'd never seen her like this. She was so damned beautiful, she took his breath away.

"Is something wrong?" he asked innocently, almost enjoying her outrage.

"Yes, something's very wrong. I want one thing understood: I will not tolerate infidelity. If you're in love with this Judy, then I'm sorry, but it's me you're married to and I fully expect…no, I *demand* that you respect our wedding vows."

To the best of his knowledge, Riley had never given her cause to believe he intended to do otherwise. He wasn't sure what Don or one of the others had implied, but he'd best clear up the misconception now, before matters got out of hand.

"I'll honor my vows."

She hesitated as if she weren't entirely sure she should trust him. After a long moment, she nodded once and mumbled something he couldn't hear.

"Tell me," he said, walking toward her, fully intending to take her in his arms; a couple of kisses might reassure her even more. "You wouldn't happen to be jealous now, would you?"

"Jealous?" She threw the word back in his face as though he'd issued the greatest insult of her life. "If you can honestly mistake integrity and principles for jealousy, then I truly wonder what kind of man I've married."

With that she turned and walked into her bedroom and closed the door. Hannah had probably never slammed a door in her life, he realized.

Air seeped between Riley's clenched teeth. He'd done it again. Just when he was beginning to make headway with her, he got cocky and said something stupid. It was becoming a bad habit.

He let a few moments pass, then decided to try once again. He knocked on her bedroom door, but didn't wait for her to answer before turning the knob and walking in.

A husband should be allowed certain rights. Hannah turned and glared at him accusingly.

"I didn't mean what I said."

She held a blouse to her front and stared stonily back at him. "I see. So you fully intend to cheat on me."

"No, dammit." He jerked his fingers through his hair. "You're purposely misconstruing everything I say." His patience was wearing paper-thin. "I shouldn't have said anything about you being jealous. Judy doesn't mean anything to me. I haven't seen her in weeks. We may have talked twice in the last three months. I've been trying to cool the relationship. She resented that."

Hannah deposited the blouse in the closet with the others. "I see."

"I don't wish to argue with you, Hannah. Can we drop the subject of Judy now?"

She lowered her gaze and nodded. "I…I didn't mean to shout earlier. I don't generally get angry like that…. It must be the pregnancy."

"I understand what you're saying."

"You do?" Her beautiful gray eyes leveled with his.

He nodded. "You see, I've had this problem for several months now," Riley admitted, stepping across the room. "There's been this woman on my mind."

Her eyes were unbelievably round, and she was staring up at him. Her moist lips immobilized him, and in that moment he knew he had to taste her again. His need was beyond reason, beyond his control. He reached for her, barely giving her time to adjust to his embrace before his mouth smothered hers. He caught her unaware and used it to his advantage to slip his tongue into her mouth. He expected her to protest the unfamiliar invasion, but she surprised him once more by giving him her own. Their mouths played with each other, danced, sang, rejoiced in the intimacy they shared.

Sliding his hands down the length of her spine, he drew

her to him, pulling her into the heat of him. For an instant she resisted, and Riley feared he had gone too far, frightening her when that was the last thing he wished. He wanted to make love to her, the way he'd been dreaming about doing for nearly four months. Every minute she made him wait seemed like an eternity.

Hannah wasn't like any other woman he'd known. She was delicate and sweet and deliciously provocative, innocently provocative. He couldn't hold her without experiencing the sensation of walking through a field of blooming wildflowers. With his hands at her hips, he dragged her closer, letting her feel the heat rise in him. He edged his way toward the bed, thinking if he were able to get her on top of the mattress, he might be able to remove her blouse. The thought of tasting her breasts, of holding them in his hands once more, was so powerful he lost his balance. He caught himself and her, before they went crashing to the floor. It was then that he noticed the framed picture lying on top of an unpacked box.

He stopped abruptly as a cold chill raced over him. His eyes narrowed as he looked down on her. "Who's that?" he demanded.

Chapter Five

"Who is he?" Riley demanded a second time. Instinct told him the photo wasn't one of a relative. He knew he was right when Hannah's gaze shot toward the box in question. The look that came over her features was incredible, a mixture of pain and of love so strongly mingled that it was as if she were no longer aware of who or where she was.

"Jerry Sanders," she answered in a voice so low Riley had to strain to hear. "We were engaged."

"Engaged?" Riley repeated the word, not because the news shocked him or because he didn't believe her, but because…if she'd been engaged to Jerry Sanders, then why the hell had she been a virgin? Furthermore, why had she gone to bed with him? Questions came at him like exploding rockets.

"He…died a…few months back…in a car accident." It was apparent that even speaking of her former fiancé was painful for Hannah.

Suddenly everything clicked into place for Riley. The way she'd stared at him that night on the waterfront. The ethereal look about her, the pain and uncertainty he'd read in her eyes. No wonder he'd felt this overwhelming urge to take her in his arms, hold her, protect her, love her. She had been walking around emotionally wounded, absorbed in her grief.

"When?"

She understood his question without him having to elaborate. Tears crowded her eyes, and when she spoke it was with difficulty. "July second."

A sick, sinking sensation landed with a hard thud in the pit of his stomach. Three weeks. Seafair, when he'd met Hannah, had been a scant three weeks following Jerry's death. No wonder she'd come warm and willing to his bed. She'd been in such grief she hadn't a clue what she was doing. This also explained why she'd run from him early the following morning.

Closing his eyes, Riley roughly plowed his fingers through his hair. When he opened his eyes, he found Hannah staring at him. "Do you love him?" he asked, his heart pounding like a giant hammer inside his chest. It wasn't in Hannah to lie. Of that, Riley was certain.

She looked away and nodded.

Riley didn't know why he felt compelled to ask. Seeing the reverent way in which she'd gazed at the other man's picture had told him everything he needed to know. The fact she was married to him was damn little comfort.

"You've got your nerve talking about fidelity to me," he said forcefully, battling the dual demons of anger and pride. Their entire marriage was a farce, only he hadn't been smart enough to figure it out. How incredibly stupid he'd been. Exhaling sharply, Riley felt like the world's biggest fool. For months, she'd had him dangling by a thread, toying with his mind; had him worrying about her, frightened about what had become of her. Their time together, those brief hours he'd treasured beyond all others, had meant nothing to her. Not one damn thing. She'd been looking for him to give her what her fiancé never had; perhaps pretending he was another man the entire time they'd been making love.

She'd used him.

The sickening feeling in his stomach intensified.

"Keep the damn thing out of sight!" he shouted. "You're married to me now, and I won't tolerate having another man's picture in my home. Is that understood?"

Hannah stared at him blankly, her features so pale and drawn he couldn't look at her.

"Throw it away." If she didn't do it, by God, he would. Riley would be damned before he'd allow another man to haunt his marriage. When she didn't immediately comply, he stalked across the room and reached for the photograph.

Hannah let out a small cry, scrambled across the bed and jerked the frame from his reach. From the way she reacted, he might as well have been coming toward her with a chain saw.

"No!" she cried, holding the photograph against her breasts as if it were her most valuable possession. "I'll keep it out of sight…I promise."

He stared at her, wanting with everything in him to smash the photograph to the ground, and with it destroy the memory of the man she loved. He would have done it, but one look told him Hannah would fight him like a wildcat to see that nothing happened to her precious photograph.

He scowled, then turned sharply and walked out of the bedroom and the house, not stopping until he was outside where his three friends were waiting. He forced himself to smile and loop his arms over the shoulders of Burt and Don. There had never been a time in his life when he felt more like getting fall-down-on-his-face drunk.

Hannah raced to the window in time to see Riley pull away. Tears streaked her face and she brushed them aside with the heel of her hand, feeling wretched. From the first, she'd meant to tell her husband about Jerry, but never like this. Never like this.

He'd made her so angry suggesting she was jealous over Judy. The very idea was ludicrous. Good heavens, she'd never even met the woman. Riley had infuriated her and she'd reacted in spite, knowing he'd eventually notice Jerry's picture. Once he did, she'd reasoned, then he would realize she couldn't possibly care one way or the other about his former lady friends.

What was important to her was the sanctity of their marriage. They'd spoken vows before God and man, and the promises they'd made to each other were meant to be taken seriously. The circumstances surrounding their wedding weren't ideal—Hannah would be the first one to admit as much—but they'd agreed to make an effort to do whatever they could to ensure this marriage worked. If they were to have any chance of that, a fundamental trust had to be implanted early in their relationship. It was for that reason alone that Hannah had brought up the subject of fidelity. Certainly not because she cared one whit about Riley's on-again/off-again relationship with the mysterious Judy.

A deep, painful breath tore through her chest. The stone-cold way in which Riley had glared at her stabbed at her heart. She knew her confession had wounded him deeply.

Her husband wasn't a man who often betrayed his feelings. A hundred times in the past week she'd attempted to read him, tried again and again to understand this man with whom she'd vowed to spend the rest of her life. She'd found the task nearly impossible. He was often quiet, more often withdrawn. Other than to order her about, he'd rarely spoken to her.

Every once in a while she'd find him studying her, but when their eyes would meet, gauging his thoughts had been impossible. That wasn't the case when he'd found Jerry's picture, however. Riley had been murderous. His eyes, his features, everything about him had spelled out his fury. And his pain. Hannah would give anything she owned to have kept Jerry's picture safely tucked away in a drawer.

The sardonic way in which Riley had glared at her clawed at her tender heart. Hannah wanted Riley to know about Jerry, but it had never been her intention to hurt him.

Then again, maybe it had.

He was so unreasonable. So demanding. First he'd taunted her about another woman and then he'd infuriated her. In her anger she'd struck back at him, but she hadn't meant to hurt him. Never that.

She reached behind her and tugged free the scarf that tied the hair away from her face. Regret ebbed over her. As soon as Riley returned, she'd apologize. She owed him that much.

When he hadn't come home several hours later, Hannah became concerned. She'd unpacked and systematically arranged the kitchen to her liking. That took what remained of the morning. Once she was finished, she made herself lunch, then wandered into the living room, holding the sandwich in her hand. Pausing at the window, she looked out, hoping, praying she'd find some sign of Riley. Her pulse accelerated when she noted his car was parked at the curb, but then she remembered he'd returned the truck to the rental agency and was apparently with one of his friends.

Discouraged, she went back to the kitchen and finished her glass of milk. The sandwich had lost its appeal, and she dumped it in the garbage. Looking around her, she went into the bedrooms, making up the beds.

It was well past dark when Hannah finished straightening up their little house. She surveyed her efforts, standing in the middle of the living room, hands on her hips. The transformation was a little short of amazing. What had seemed like a barren shell of walls and empty space now resembled a home.

Her brother's photograph rested on the fireplace mantel along with one she found of Riley. She guessed that it

had been taken several years earlier, soon after he'd enlisted in the Navy. She'd stumbled upon it while unpacking a box of books and spent several moments studying
the intense young face staring back at her. She hoped to
gain an insight into her husband, but she'd found the photograph as difficult to read as the man.

It had taken a good deal of effort to arrange the furniture the way she wanted, and she was likely to incur her
husband's displeasure for having worked so hard, but that
wasn't anything new. What did he expect her to do while
he was away hours on end? Twiddle her thumbs?

After stacking the empty boxes in the patio off the
kitchen, Hannah fixed herself a bowl of clam chowder for
dinner. She soaked in a hot bath once she finished the dishes.

Riley's disappearance was beginning to irk her. The
least he could do was phone—only they didn't have one,
not yet. She was concerned, but hadn't wanted to admit
as much. The urge to contact her father was compelling.
Not because she was willing to admit she'd made a mistake—which she was strongly beginning to believe—but so
that she could hear the sound of his voice. In his own quiet
manner, George Raymond would lend her encouragement, which she needed so badly just then. But again they
had no phone. Hannah had rarely felt more cut off from
those she loved, or more alone.

By ten, she made her way into her bedroom, weary to
the bone, both mentally and physically. The urge to weep
was nearly overwhelming. Her marriage couldn't be going
any worse.

Hannah stirred at the sound of Riley crashing around
the house. Checking her clock radio, she noted that it was
nearly three in the morning. Tossing aside her blankets,
she leaped out of bed and rushed down the hallway to discover Riley awkwardly straightening a kitchen chair he'd
knocked to the floor. He seemed to be having trouble
keeping his balance.

"Riley." She was so pleased to see him, so excited, she ran directly into his arms. "Thank God you're home…" She hugged his middle, pressing her flushed face to his chest and squeezing tightly. The hours he'd been away had seemed like an eternity.

Although she'd labored most of the day, setting their house to order in an effort to put him out of her mind, it hadn't worked. She'd been worried. All evening her mind had played tricks on her, listing the places he might have gone, the people he could be with, until everything had crashed together in regret and confusion.

Apparently she'd caught Riley by surprise, and he stumbled backward until he collided with the kitchen counter. His arms supported Hannah, and when she looked up at him, fearing he might be hurt, he caught her chin with his hand. His eyes clouded for an instant as if he were surprised to find her in his home, then without warning, without giving her any indication of what he intended, his mouth came crashing down on hers.

The kiss was hard, almost brutal as he lifted her from the floor. The hand at the back of her head held her prisoner, although she didn't struggle. He'd taken her so completely by surprise that for a moment she was numb with shock. This was a Riley she didn't know. One that frightened her with his fierce, hungry demand.

"Riley," she said, pulling her mouth free. "No…"

He answered her by kissing her again, dragging his mouth back to hers. Gone was the gentleness she'd always found in him, the tender concern. Instead she was met with desperate need. He tasted of restless passion. Against her will, against her pride, Hannah felt herself responding. Her hands clawed at his shirt as she clung tightly to him.

Riley moved his hands to her face, covering her ears as he worked his mouth from one side of her lips to the other. She wanted to protest, but the instant she opened her mouth, his tongue was there, boldly claiming the right to taste, to possess any part of her that he wished. The few times Riley had kissed her in this manner, he'd gently stroked the inside of her mouth. Now he used his tongue ruthlessly, sweeping it in and out from between her lips, plunging, probing, swirling it over her own, over and over until she was so weak she would have slumped to the floor without his support.

"No more," she said forcefully, pushing against him, needing to be free. Free of the warm, delicious sensations he was capable of making her feel. Free of the endless hours of worry and regret. Free of the past that clung like tentacles around her heart.

Riley's breathing was labored as he buried his face in the curve of her neck, kissing her there while his hands roved at will down her back and over her buttocks.

Again, Hannah made the effort to free herself. "You're drunk!"

She felt his smile against the hollow of her throat. "You mean it took you this long to figure it out?" he asked with a weary laugh. "You really are an innocent, aren't you?"

"May I remind you I was an innocent until I met you!" she cried, backing away from him. In his present mood, he might drag her into his bed and have his way with her and not even realize what he was doing.

"Don't look so worried," he said with a slurred laugh, reaching for her. "You're safe. Even if I wanted to make love to you, I'm so drunk, I doubt I could do anything about it." He laughed once more, but there was no humor in the sound. No humor and no amusement.

With some effort she managed to untangle his arms from her. In her eagerness to right the wrong she'd committed against him, she hadn't even noticed his condition.

"I'm not your precious Jerry," he said with a sneer. "But you can pretend. That's what you did that night in Seattle, isn't it? Pretend I was him." He waved his index finger back and forth in front of her face. "You didn't think I'd figure it out, did you?"

"Stop it," she cried, tears blurring her eyes.

"Well, go ahead and pretend all you want, my sweet. I don't mind playing a few pretending games myself. But ask yourself this, who shall I pretend you are? Judy, perhaps?"

Hannah felt sick to her stomach, nauseous and dizzy both at once. Unable to listen to another word, she turned and rushed into the bedroom, slamming the door. Not sure if she could trust him to leave her alone, she shoved the chair across the carpet and propped it under the handle.

He must have heard her efforts because he paused outside her door and gave a slurred, sick-sounding laugh. "Don't worry, my sweet. You're safe for tonight."

Riley woke the following morning with a compound headache. His temple throbbed like a giant piston firing inside his head. The pain was complicated by the sounds of Hannah in the kitchen. From all the racket she was making, it sounded like ten women instead of one.

Holding his head between his hands, he staggered out of his bedroom. "What the hell are you doing?" he demanded, grimacing at the sound of his own voice.

Hannah turned around and glared at him as though he were the devil incarnate. When she did deign to answer, she did so with a lofty tilt of her chin, as though speaking to him were beneath her. "I'm cooking breakfast."

"At this ungodly hour?"

"It's after nine." She set the cast-iron skillet down on the burner with enough force to break it in two. "But for those who choose to…to carouse to the wee hours of the morning, nine must indeed be an ungodly hour."

"Indeed," he echoed. If his head wasn't hurting so damn much, Riley might have been able to enjoy her tirade. Unable to understand why she was so angry, he watched as she slapped a piece of bacon in the pan, then jabbed it with a fork as though it needed to be killed before frying.

"Did you want something?" she demanded, when he continued to stand in his underwear in the middle of the kitchen.

"Peace and quiet," he suggested hopefully. "I don't suppose that would be so much to ask, would it?"

"Not in the least." With a flair for the dramatic, she turned off the stove, removed the pan and tossed the fork into the sink. Jerking the apron free from her waist, she hurled that at him, hitting him full in the face. By the time he'd managed to remove it, Hannah had walked out the front door, slamming it with enough force to shake the windows.

"Hannah!" he shouted, storming after her. He stopped abruptly when he reached the porch, realizing he couldn't very well traipse after her in his skivvies. "Get back here right this minute," he ordered, pointing his finger at the ground.

She tossed him a defiant, mocking look and continued down the sidewalk. A suffragette couldn't have stepped with any more conviction than his wife, Riley noted wryly.

His first instinct was to let her go. If she was going to behave like a shrew, then to hell with her. His head was spinning, his ears rang and frankly he wasn't in any mood to deal with her temper tantrums.

As he was walking back to his bedroom, intent on ignoring Hannah and her outburst, it struck him how unusual it was for the sweet, gentle-natured Hannah to rage at him or anyone.

Holding his hands to his head, he tried to remember what he'd said to her to get her so irritated. Briefly he remembered their encounter from the night before. She'd shocked him by the eager way in which she'd raced into his arms and hugged him. They'd kissed, and the need he felt for her had all but consumed him. Then she'd pulled away from him just as she had every time he'd touched her since that night in Seattle, and he'd gotten angry with her. What had he said? Riley couldn't remember, not for the life of him.

He released a swearword and reached for his pants, urgently jerking them up his long legs. He couldn't let her traipse down the street alone. Hell, she hadn't even taken a sweater with her. In her condition, she might harm herself and the baby if she were to catch a chill.

Riley grabbed a jacket on his way out the door, jogging after her, furious with her and outraged at himself for letting her leave the house.

It amazed him how far she'd gotten by the time he reached her. She didn't slow her pace until his steps matched hers, and even then she continued walking, ignoring him.

"Hannah?" He spoke her name softly when he noticed the moist trail of tears that streaked her face. "Would it help any if I told you I was sorry?" He didn't know what he was apologizing for, but it was apparent he'd hurt her, and knowing that didn't sit right.

She stopped and looked up at him through narrowed, suspicious eyes.

"Whatever I said, I didn't mean it," he tried once more.

"You don't remember?" She sounded incredulous.

"No," he admitted, reaching for her hand. "Come back to the house and we'll talk about it. All right?"

She seemed to be trapped with indecision. He raised his hands to her face and gently rubbed the tears from her cheeks. Each one was an accusation against him. His heart constricted at how pale her features were, how fragile she looked. It demanded every ounce of control he possessed not to take her in his arms and beg her forgiveness. He was a reckless bastard to inflict his drunkenness on so delicate a soul, and he silently vowed never to do it again.

"Come on," he urged, wrapping his arm around her

shoulders and steering her back toward the house. She resisted momentarily.

"You aren't wearing socks," she apparently felt obliged to point out.

"I didn't have time to slip them on. My wife took off on me," he said as a means of making a small joke. "I had no idea where she was headed."

"Church," she admitted in a tight whisper.

"Church," he repeated wryly as the fear evaporated within him. From the determined way in which she was running away from him, Riley had been convinced she was walking out of his life. He'd rushed after her, nearly paralyzed with the fear that she was going to disappear again. He couldn't allow that—not if it was within his power to stop her.

"Come back with me?" he asked, looking down the street to their house.

"I'll...I suppose I could attend the second service," she answered softly.

He kept his arm around her as they strolled back to the house, savoring those few moments that he could hold her in his embrace. There were so few opportunities to feel close to her. It wasn't a comfortable feeling, needing Hannah, wanting her. She'd have done them both a favor if she'd chosen someone else that night; but despite everything, he was pleased she hadn't.

"How's Junior this morning?" he asked, wanting to make light conversation.

"Fine."

"And Junior's mommy? How's she feeling?"

"About as good as Junior's daddy."

Riley grinned and rubbed his chin across the top of her head. "That bad?"

"I...I didn't sleep much last night."

"We'll both take a nap this afternoon," he promised, and

in his mind he was thinking how good it would be if he could convince her to lie down with him.

The first week after they'd settled into their new home was a busy one for Hannah. She scheduled her first appointment with the Navy physician and went looking for a part-time job.

It was a rainy, cold morning on Thursday, and Hannah had just put some kidney beans on the stove to soak, thinking she'd make a batch of chili for dinner, when there was a knock at the front door.

She opened it to find a tall, slender woman with bright brown eyes standing on the other side. "Hello," she said, grinning broadly. "I know I'm supposed to wait for our husbands to introduce us, but I couldn't stay away a minute longer. I'm Cheryl Morgan, Steve's wife." She extended her hand to Hannah.

They exchanged a brief handshake while Hannah led the way into the kitchen. "Steve," she repeated, then remembered. "He helped us move."

"Right," Cheryl said with quick nod. "I would have come along, too, but I was working." Hannah noted they were around the same age and knew immediately that she was going to like Cheryl Morgan.

"When Steve came home and told me Riley was married, I couldn't wait to meet you. I hope you don't mind me stopping in unannounced this way."

"Of course not. I've been bored to tears all morning." Hannah put the teapot on to boil and brought down two cups and saucers. "I suppose…Riley's marriage must have come as a shock."

"I'll say," Cheryl agreed, reaching for one of the sugar cookies Hannah had set on the table and crossing her long legs. "I plied Steve with questions, but he seemed rather close-mouthed about the whole thing."

Not wanting to explain their marriage and the pregnancy both at once, Hannah busied herself readying the tea, attempting to disguise her uneasiness. "It happened quickly."

"A whirlwind courtship. How romantic."

Hannah wasn't sure how to respond to that. A whirlwind was right, but it hadn't been much of a courtship. Not with her father and Chaplain Stewart running the show.

Once the water was boiling, Hannah added it to the teapot, leaving it to steep a few moments before pouring. "I'm so pleased you stopped by. I was beginning to wonder if I was going to meet anyone on the base."

"I'm glad I stopped by, too." Cheryl paused and slowly shook her head. "That Riley is a sly dog. He had me worried sick he was going to marry—"

"Judy," Hannah supplied for Cheryl when she stopped abruptly. For a moment her newfound friend looked as though she wanted to stand up and grab back the words.

"Then you know about her?"

Hannah nodded without elaborating. She knew her name and that Riley claimed she didn't mean a thing to him, but beyond that she was in the dark.

Cheryl slapped her hand over her chest. "You'll have to forgive me. I have this terrible habit of saying whatever's on my mind. I can't seem to stop myself."

"Don't worry. You haven't offended me." Hannah smiled as she added sugar to her tea and stirred lightly. "I'll admit I don't know a lot. Riley hasn't said much. But from what I gathered, they'd been seeing each other regularly."

"They were pretty thick in the beginning of the summer," Cheryl explained, sipping from her cup. "Then the relationship cooled. Judy is…nice, don't get me wrong. But she's accustomed to getting what she wants, and she'd set her sights on Riley. I don't think she took kindly to his sudden loss of interest."

Hannah wasn't sure how to comment, so she simply nodded, hoping that would suffice.

"I know why Riley married you," Cheryl said, not unkindly.

Hannah dropped her gaze as color crept up her neck. Naturally Steve would have told his wife about the pregnancy; that only made sense. Cheryl was probably also aware Hannah and Riley weren't sharing a bedroom, too.

"You're perfect for someone like Riley."

"I…am?" It came out in the form of a question rather than the positive statement she'd intended.

"Absolutely perfect. He's this rough-and-tough macho guy. The strong, silent type who's too stubborn for his own good. I'm sure you know what I mean."

Hannah was quick to agree with a nod.

"For a long time after I first met Riley, he made me uncomfortable," Cheryl admitted, glancing anxiously toward Hannah. "He isn't an easy man to know. It's impossible to figure out what he's thinking. He keeps everything to himself. Even though Steve's probably his best friend, he didn't know about you."

No one knew about her, but Hannah understood what Cheryl was saying. Riley kept most of his thoughts to himself. It was what had made these past few weeks so difficult. They'd sit down across the dinner table from each other and he'd ask her a few questions about her day and share nothing of his own. Her few attempts at drawing him into conversation had been met with silence. Yet he was genuinely concerned about her. Solicitous. Hannah knew he was trying as hard as he knew how to make everything right for her.

Sunday morning had been a turning point. They'd both seemed to regret the events of the day before and worked hard at overcoming the hurt they'd inflicted on each other. Riley had driven her to church and then returned later to pick her up. They'd talked more that day than the entire previous week. When she'd set dinner on the table, he had raved about her efforts and then insisted upon doing the dishes himself.

"It took me a year or more to feel at ease with Riley," Cheryl continued.

A year! Hannah groaned inwardly. They maintained a fragile peace even now. He was concerned about her health and that of their baby. He was the one who insisted she make a doctor's appointment and that she schedule it at a time when he could go in with her. He hadn't argued with her about finding a job, but she knew from his lack of enthusiasm that he'd prefer it if she remained home. But he hadn't insisted she not look for employment.

Thus far, her efforts had been restricted to part-time office positions at the base. Several were available, and she'd gone in to fill out the paperwork and was told she'd be contacted for an interview sometime soon. For now, all she could do was be patient.

"As I said earlier, you're a perfect complement to Riley," Cheryl remarked, munching on her second cookie. "You're gentle and sweet. What I want to know is how that crusty hardheaded sailor ever met someone like you."

Chapter Six

"How we met?" Hannah repeated slowly. Rather than confess the truth, she glanced shyly in Cheryl's direction and said, "That's rather an involved story, and if you don't mind, I'd prefer to leave it for another time."

"Of course," Cheryl returned, easily appeased. She glanced anxiously at her watch. "I've got to be at the hospital in an hour. If I'm not careful, the time will slip away from me."

"You work at the hospital?"

Cheryl nodded. "In Labor and Delivery."

Hannah brightened. "Really? That must be interesting work."

"Believe me, it is. I find it incredible how many babies decide to be born while Daddy's out to sea. Speaking of which," she said, waving her hand as she hurriedly finished a sip of tea, "isn't it the pits Riley and Steve are leaving for that training session? I hate it when the Navy does this, but then I should be accustomed to the way the military works by now. Steve isn't any more thrilled about this than I am, and I bet Riley feels the same way."

Hannah hadn't a clue what Cheryl was talking about, but she didn't want the other woman to know it. If Riley was going on deployment, he hadn't shared the news with her. Hannah felt lost in the dark, groping around, searching for meaning. She forced a smile when she noticed Steve's wife anxiously studying her. "The pits is right."

"So soon after you two are married."

"Do they know exactly when they'll be going?" Hannah hoped she effectively disguised the eagerness in her voice. She felt hollow inside, as if a giant void had opened up and exposed what a farce her marriage really was. It hurt more than she thought possible for Riley to have hidden this from her.

"It looks like they're scheduled to head out Monday morning, but I doubt it'll be a full cruise. At least, that's what the scuttlebutt claims. They should be home before Christmas, at any rate, although I fully expect them to be gone the entire seventy days this spring."

Seventy days. Hannah's mind went blank. Spring was when their baby was due. Alarm gripped her chest, and she struggled to conceal the apprehension. It was bad enough being cut off from her father and friends and from all that was familiar to her, but knowing she'd be facing the birth of her baby without Riley terrified Hannah. She pushed her fear aside, determined to deal with it later.

"I wish I could be here Friday night," Cheryl added, downing the last of her tea. "I would have been content to meet you then, but I'm scheduled to work. The next time the guys get together for poker, the two of us will have our own night out."

Hannah managed a smile and nod. "That sounds like fun."

They spoke a few minutes more, then Cheryl had to leave for the hospital. Hannah saw her to the door and impulsively hugged her, grateful Steve's wife had taken the time to stop by and introduce herself. Their conversation had been a fruitful one.

For hours afterward Hannah felt numb. A disquieting, uncomfortable knot lodged itself in her stomach. In three short days Riley would be leaving for a lengthy patrol, and he had yet to say a word to her about it. Nor had he mentioned it was likely he'd be at sea during the birth of their child. Surely a wife should be entitled to such information. Hannah felt she had a right to know. Every right.

She was frying up hamburger for chili when Riley walked into the house two hours ahead of schedule. He hesitated when he saw her. "You're not ready," he said, his tone lightly accusing.

"For what?" She had a difficult time burying her sarcasm. Perhaps there was something else he'd purposely forgotten to mention. He seemed to think she was a mind reader.

"The doctor's appointment."

"Oh…dear." After her conversation with Cheryl, her appointment with the Navy physician had completely slipped her mind.

Flustered, she headed toward the bathroom. "I'll only be a minute." She ran a brush through her hair, applied a fresh coat of lip gloss and changed her top all within five minutes. When she returned to the kitchen, she found Riley adding the cooked meat to the simmering kidney beans. He replaced the lid on the Crockpot.

As they drove to the clinic, Hannah glanced over at her husband several times, amused by how well his personality was portrayed in his facial features. His chin was nothing short of arrogant. His jaw was as sharply chiseled as his pride. His eyes and nose and mouth—every part of him gave the overall impression of strength and power. Yet he was a stranger to her, sharing little of his thoughts and even less of himself. She felt like an intruder into his life, extra baggage he was forced to drag around with him.

Riley must have felt her scrutiny, and when he returned her look, she blushed and dropped her gaze to her lap, then waited a moment before nonchalantly glancing at him again.

She felt dangerously close to repeating everything she'd

learned that morning from Cheryl Morgan. She would have if she hadn't been anxious to learn how long it would take Riley to tell her of his plans. She was his wife, although she was more certain than ever that he didn't want her in his life and only tolerated her presence. No, Hannah decided, she'd say nothing. She would play his waiting game.

Riley was anxious about Hannah's health. He'd never known anyone could be so pale. Her coloring had something to do with it; but it was more than that, far more, and he was concerned. He intended on talking to the doctor, to reassure himself she'd be all right while he was out to sea.

The fact he'd be gone for a few weeks didn't sit well with him, either. He hadn't broken the news to her yet, delaying the inevitable as long as possible for fear of upsetting her. There'd been enough upheaval in their lives in the past few weeks without this. When it came right down to it, Riley realized he'd rather not leave Hannah, but the training schedule wasn't optional. Damn little in the Navy was.

Riley loved the sea, loved life aboard the nuclear-powered submarine, the USS *Atlantis*. But he didn't want to leave Hannah. Not so soon. Not yet.

He'd had several days to assimilate what he'd learned about her and her former fiancé. It didn't sit well with him that Hannah loved another man. He tried not to think about it, to push the other man to the far reaches of his mind and pretend Jerry had never existed. It was the only way Riley could deal with knowing Hannah might be married to him, but she would never truly belong to him.

Hannah made Riley feel vulnerable. He didn't understand what it was about her that touched him in ways no other woman ever had. One hurt look from her had the most curious effect upon him. It was as though someone had viciously kicked him in the solar plexus. The irony of it all was that the person Riley sought to protect her from most was himself. His insensitivity. His pride. His anger.

If what he felt for Hannah was love, Riley couldn't say. His brushes with the emotion were best described as brief. He cared about her in ways that had never concerned him with others. That was understandable, though; no other woman had ever carried his child. He was anxious about her health; she was a fragile thing, delicate and rare. It seemed all he could do was make her as comfortable as possible, and that felt like damn little.

Other than a few slips, Riley was working hard at gaining her trust. Convincing her to share his bed was motivation enough. He longed to have her by his side, to rest his head upon her stomach and feel for himself the new life her body nurtured. Every once in a while he'd lie awake and grow wistful, dreaming of the time she would willingly turn into his arms and snuggle her lush womanly body next to his own. Marriage had made him fanciful, Riley decided. He'd enjoyed the physical delights a woman's body could give him from the time he was in his teens, but he seldom spent the night with a woman. Hannah had been an exception from the first. He'd wanted her the night he met her in Seattle, and nothing had changed. The fact she was in love with another man didn't seem to matter.

The time Dr. Underwood, the obstetrician, spent with Hannah added to Riley's concern about his wife's pregnancy. The doctor took several minutes to talk to them both, and ordered blood tests for Hannah.

Riley's concern must have registered because Dr. Underwood took a few extra minutes to explain the reasons for the additional tests. He strongly suspected Hannah was still anemic, and as soon as the results were available he would write a prescription for a higher dosage of iron tablets. There were several questions Riley had, as well, although it was apparent Hannah felt it irrelevant to have Riley bring up her sleeping habits and the fact she still suffered from occasional bouts of morning sickness.

Riley was silent on the short drive back to the base. His mind was digesting the answers the doctor had given him. If the truth be known, he was worried. Damn worried.

"You're being awfully quiet," she said as they exited the freeway. "Is something troubling you?" Casting anxious glances his way, she seemed to be waiting for him to make some declaration. Riley hadn't a clue what she wanted him to say.

"I'm fine," he answered shortly.

She gazed out the window then, turning her head away from him. Feeling bad for the brusqueness with which he'd responded to her, he reached for her hand, lacing her fingers with his own. "I'm concerned you're not eating the way you should be," he said as an explanation.

"I'm very conscious of everything that goes into my mouth."

"You pick at your food. I swear you don't eat enough to keep a bird alive."

"That's ridiculous."

Riley swallowed a tart reply. The last thing he wanted to do was argue with her, although she seemed to be looking for an excuse herself. They'd done too much of that in the past few days. He didn't want to leave for the training exercises with matters strained between them—at least not any more strained than they already were.

"I've gained two pounds since I was in to see my family doctor," she said, apparently unwilling to let the matter rest.

He didn't respond, knowing it wouldn't help to chastise her further. "You promise to take the iron tablets?"

"Of course," she returned, then hesitated before adding, "Junior is my baby, too, you know."

Junior. Riley cracked a smile. He'd nearly forgotten

there was a baby involved in all this. His primary concern had been for Hannah, so much so that he'd forgotten the very reason she was sitting at his side.

When they got back to the house, there was a message on the answering machine informing Hannah of a job interview scheduled for the following afternoon. If she couldn't make the appointment, she was to contact the personnel office first thing in the morning.

Hannah's eyes brightened as she listened to the message, and she smiled over at Riley.

"The job's right here on the base," she said, sounding pleased.

"Doing what?" In an effort to disguise his uneasiness about the whole issue of her working, Riley opened the refrigerator and brought out a chicken leg, munching on it although he wasn't the least bit hungry.

"Secretarial work. I…was employed at an insurance agency before…before we were married."

Riley nodded. "Is the position you applied for full-time?"

"I…I think so. It must be."

"I see."

Hannah glared at him as though he'd attacked her family's heritage. "Why'd you say it like that?"

"Like what?" He pretended not to understand, although he had a fair idea what she was talking about. He wasn't keen on her taking on a forty-hour workweek—not when her health was so delicate. Riley swore he never knew anyone who required nine hours of rest a night the way she did, although Dr. Underwood claimed this need for extra sleep would soon pass.

"Like…like you don't approve of my working."

"I don't." There, he'd said it, bold as could be. "I don't happen to think it's a good idea."

"Why not?" Hannah demanded. "Because of the baby?"

"Yes. And other factors."

"What other factors?"

Riley sighed. Already their voices were raised, and he could see he wasn't going to be able to extract himself from this easily. He tossed the chicken leg into the garbage and washed his hands, carefully considering his words. Hannah was staring at him, impatiently waiting. "You claimed you needed some time to adjust to our marriage."

"What's that got to do with anything?"

"I feel you should put your efforts into our relationship."

She took her own sweet time to digest his words, but when he looked in her direction, he noticed she didn't seem pleased with his straightforward answer.

"In other words, if I agree to sleep with you, you'd approve of my working."

That wasn't what he'd meant in the least. Yes, he'd been honest enough to admit he wanted to make love to her. He'd made that fact abundantly clear on their wedding day. A brother-and-sister relationship didn't interest him then, and it appealed to him even less now.

"Well?" she asked, demanding a response from him.

"I don't want to quarrel over this, Hannah." He was smart enough to recognize a loaded question when he heard one. Smart enough to extract himself as best he could, too. "All I'm saying is that I'd prefer it if you invested as much time in our relationship as you would in a job. There are only so many hours in a day. You can't do everything, you know."

"In other words you wouldn't be willing to help with the cooking or the housework?"

Riley was quickly losing his grip on his patience, which had always been in short supply. Hannah seemed to be looking for an excuse to pick a fight with him by tying him up in verbal knots. She had been from the moment he'd arrived home. Hell if he knew what he'd done that was so terrible now.

"I'd be willing to help with the cooking and house-work." He fully expected his answer would take the starch out of her arguments. How willing he actually would be to help around the house was another question entirely. Having her there when he walked in the door after a long day with dinner prepared and waiting was a luxury he could easily become accustomed to enjoying.

"What about the times you're out at sea?"

"What about them?" Frankly he couldn't understand why that would make any difference. If anything, it was a strong argument to keep her home. With him away, no one would be around to make sure she wasn't overworking herself.

"I'll...be bored without a job."

"What makes you say that? The other wives seem to have plenty to do to occupy their time. You will, too."

Once again she seemed to need time to assimilate his words. For several minutes she said nothing. Then, as if by rote, she stepped over to the cupboard and brought down dishes and began to set the table.

"Do you want any help?" He felt downright noble asking. It seemed like a husbandly thing to do.

"No," she said softly, shaking her head. "Dinner will be ready in a few minutes."

Apparently this was the end of their discussion. "What about the job interview?" he asked, trying not to let his feelings on the issue leak into the question. True, he'd rather she didn't work, but he wouldn't stop her if that was what she truly wanted. Once again he felt the fleeting twinge of being truly virtuous.

"I...I'm not sure what I intend to do about the job yet."

Riley felt encouraged by that. At least she wasn't going to openly defy him, and was willing to take his concerns into consideration. Other than a few rocky places, their marriage was coming along nicely. They were learning the give-and-take necessary to make any relationship work, and Riley couldn't help feeling good about that.

Dinner was ready twenty minutes later. There was a batch of steaming corn-bread fresh from the oven, and the tureen of hot chile con carne. All homemade. All delicious. Riley eyed the table with appreciation, complimenting her.

They ate in silence, and once again Riley noted how she continued to glance his way several times, as though expecting something. What, he wasn't sure. He complimented her once more on the excellent dinner and made some fleeting remark about never having eaten better, which was true. Before he'd married Hannah, dinners had consisted of microwave specials or something he could grab on the run. Nothing like the home cooking he'd enjoyed since their marriage.

When they'd finished, he helped clear the table. He rinsed the dishes and set them in the dishwasher. With only the two of them, the task was complete in a matter of minutes.

Hannah stored the leftovers in the refrigerator and wiped down the counters. The evening news was on, and Hannah sat on the chair across from Riley's recliner and picked up her knitting. The sight of her needles working the soft pastel yarn into a blanket for their child had a curious effect upon his heart. It warmed him in ways he was only beginning to understand. It dawned on him suddenly that she loved and wanted this baby.

Glancing up, Hannah found his eyes on hers. She openly glared at him before looking away, as though she deeply resented it was him sitting across from her and not Jerry, the real love of her life. The good feelings he'd experienced a few moments earlier drowned in a sea of resentment.

A heavy dose of anger simmered in him for several minutes before he stood and made himself a cup of instant coffee. Reaching for the evening paper, he worked the crossword puzzle.

"I'd like to visit my father over Christmas," Hannah said, working the knitting needles with a vengeance. She jerked hard on the ball of yarn, then looked up at him as if she fully expected an argument.

"Fine." He rarely made plans for the holidays. Frankly, they didn't mean that much to him. "Am I included, or would you rather I stayed away?"

Once again she glanced upward, obviously surprised by his question. "Included, of course. We are married."

Riley didn't know what to read into that comment, if anything.

Following the brief snatch of conversation, the only sound in the entire house was the gentle hum of the dishwasher and the noise coming from the television. Riley thought of several topics he wanted to discuss, but dismissed them all. It was apparent Hannah wasn't in any mood to chat.

Looking away from her, Riley realized that despite everything, he wanted this marriage to work. For their child's sake, for Hannah's sake, for his own peace of mind, Riley was determined to do everything he could to ensure its survival.

He'd taken the biggest gamble of his life by agreeing to marry Hannah. He'd done it without realizing he was playing with a loaded deck, but he was coming to grips with her love for Jerry. The stakes were too high to back down now. Something told him, something deep and primal, that Hannah and their child represented his one chance for finding happiness, and he was taking hold of this opportunity with both hands and holding on tight.

By eight-thirty, right on schedule, she was yawning. Although he pretended an interest in a television program, Riley was aware of Hannah with every fiber of his being. He'd hoped by this time to be able to kiss and hold her whenever the mood struck him, which he knew would be often. Looking at her now, busy tearing out several rows of stitches, her back ramrod straight, Riley marveled that in two weeks of marriage that he'd been allowed to kiss her as often as he had. She'd never looked more untouchable than she did at this moment.

"A penny for your thoughts." Riley couldn't believe he'd said that. He hated the ineptitude he experienced, attempting to deal with his wife. He felt like a bungling youth when it came to understanding her moods.

"You don't honestly want to know what I'm thinking," she replied stuffing her knitting into the wicker basket resting on the carpet next to her chair.

"I would," he countered sharply.

She stared at him, and Riley was shocked to read the stark emotion marred by a glistening veneer of tears. Although she battled to conceal the stubborn pride, it burned from her eyes. With some difficulty, she managed to keep the tears at bay. "I...I was just thinking I'd adjust to our marriage a whole lot easier if you behaved more like a husband."

Riley didn't have time to react before she stood and hurried to her bedroom, closing the door. He intended to follow her when he heard the lock slip noisily into place. Sharply expelling his breath, he stood alone in the living room, wondering what the hell she'd meant by that. Maybe, he mused, he would start acting more like a husband when she started behaving like a wife.

The interview went poorly. As childish as it seemed, Hannah would have liked to blame Riley for that. She'd slept fitfully all night and felt nauseous the moment she lifted her head from the pillow. The bouts of morning sickness had all but disappeared of late, and she delayed getting out of bed as long as she could. By sheer determination she managed to hold down her breakfast until Riley left for work. The last thing she needed or wanted was him fussing over her.

Hannah wasn't proud of the way she'd acted the night before. She'd been cranky and unreasonable and on the verge of weeping. Her emotions were playing havoc with her, and she hated being so thin-skinned. Riley had hurt her. He didn't know or understand that, which only complicated matters. If only he'd tell her he was leaving. She'd done everything she knew to prompt the information out of him. It hadn't worked, and she battled a deep sense of betrayal and regret.

Although she felt physically wretched, she dressed carefully for the interview and went into the office with high expectations. Her credentials were excellent, as were her skills, but as soon as the interviewer learned she was pregnant, everything had taken a turn for the worse. It seemed the office was interested in someone older. In other words, a secretary beyond her childbearing years.

Riley was home by the time she returned. He stood when she walked in the door, glancing anxiously in her direction.

"I didn't get the job," she announced on her way through the living room. Her voice shook slightly, and she did her level best to ignore him. Dealing with one disappointment at a time was her limit.

He followed her into the kitchen. "What happened?"

"It seems they aren't interested in a secretary after all. They want a…a grandma."

"A what?"

"Someone who isn't pregnant," she explained tersely. "Only they dressed it in more delicate terms. I could sue them."

"There'll be other job interviews."

Hannah had fully expected Riley to gloat when he learned she hadn't gotten the job. He didn't want her working, and had said as much. Having him gently reassure her only served to confuse her. Her throat thickened—something she'd always hated because it was a sure sign she was close to tears. Hannah hated to cry. Some women had perfected the art of weeping with a natural feminine grace. That wasn't the case with Hannah. Her skin got blotchy, her nose ran, and if she tried to speak, her words sounded as though they were coming out of a pepper grinder.

"I'll never get a job," she said, hating it when her voice cracked.

"Sure, you will."

Hannah glared at Riley. She was depressed and miserable. The last thing she wanted was for her pragmatic husband to pretend to be Mary Sunshine, especially when she was fully aware of the fact he didn't want her to take the job in the first place.

"I...I find your optimism to be downright hypocritical." She tossed the words at him with a vengeance.

"Hannah, whether you decide to take on an outside job is entirely up to you. I voiced my concerns and left the matter in your hands. Better than anyone, you know how much you can or cannot do."

"You're singing a different tune than you were yesterday."

He nodded. "I talked it over with a friend."

"Steve, I suppose. After all, Cheryl's employed full-time, isn't she?"

His eyes flew to hers. "How'd you know...?"

"She stopped in the other morning to introduce herself." Hannah refused to look away, hoping he could see the pain that was in her heart. She was doing everything she knew to be the best wife she could to Riley Murdock. More than anything, she longed for this marriage to work, but they didn't stand a chance if her husband insisted upon keeping her emotionally at arm's length. He should have told her he'd be leaving for six weeks the minute he'd learned that he'd been assigned sea duty. It cut deep slices against the grain of her pride whenever she realized how short a time they had left to be together. In a matter of hours he was scheduled to leave for heaven only knew how long—weeks, possibly months—and he hadn't seen fit to so much as tell her. But then she was holding him at arm's length herself, refusing to make love with him.

"I'm pleased you had a chance to meet Cheryl. I'm hoping the two of you will be friends."

"I'm sure we will be."

Riley glanced anxiously at his watch. "Listen, Steve reminded me of something this afternoon. I apologize that I didn't have time to talk it over with you, but apparently it's my turn to host the poker game."

"The poker game," she echoed, playing innocent.

"Yeah. Four of us from the *Atlantis* get together every other week or so and play low-stakes poker. With the wedding and the move, the game completely slipped my mind. Steve mentioned it this afternoon. I couldn't very well cancel it on such short notice."

"In other words, you'd like for me to disappear for the next several hours?"

"Not at all. You can stay, if that's what you want." But his words didn't sound the least bit sincere. "Only…"

"Yes?" she prompted.

"The guys aren't used to having a woman around. Steve's the only one who's married, so there might be some objectionable language. I'll do my best to be sure the guys tone it down."

"I see." Hannah could picture it already. She'd be as out of place at her husband's poker party as she was the night she rushed into the waterfront tavern. No doubt if she stayed she'd be wheezing cigarette smoke and picking up countless empty beer bottles.

"We generally drink a few beers, too, but not enough to get drunk," he added, confirming her suspicions.

"I get the point, Riley," she said, reaching for her coat and purse. "How long should I be gone?"

Her husband wasn't a man to hesitate. He didn't do it often but he did so now. He exhaled sharply and jerked his fingers through his hair. "I wish you wouldn't look at me like that. I feel like enough of a heel as it is."

"One movie? Or should I plan on taking in a double feature?" she asked stoically.

"I forgot about the stupid game, all right? There've been other things on my mind lately. If you want to crucify me for that, then go ahead."

She took her own sweet time buttoning her coat. "Do you need me to fix you something for dinner before I leave?"

Riley shook his head. "No, thanks."

"All right then, I'll go now. I assume you have no objections to my taking the car?"

"Of course not."

"Fine. Then I'll plan on being back as late as I can."

He closed his eyes tightly. "Why do I feel so damn guilty?" he shouted. "I forget about a stupid poker game and—"

"Perhaps it's the other thing you're forgetting that's troubling you," she announced calmly. Her heart was pounding at double time, but for all outward appearances she was the picture of serenity. A deep blue mountain lake couldn't compare with the tranquillity she faultlessly portrayed.

"The other thing?" he yelled. "Damn it all to hell. There's nothing I hate more than a woman who refuses to talk straight. If you have a problem, I suggest you spell it out right now, because I refuse to play guessing games with you."

"Guessing games?" she returned flippantly. "I don't like playing them myself." With a scornful tilt of her head she tapped her finger against her lips. Until she'd married Riley, Hannah hadn't known it was in her to be so sarcastic. "Now let me see, when will Riley be shipping out next? I do wonder."

His mouth tightened. "Cheryl told you."

"No," Hannah cried, battling fury and pain. "She assumed I knew…assumed any husband would tell his wife. Only I'm not any wife, am I? You want me about as much as you want this marriage. You couldn't have spelled it out any plainer than this. Well, I don't want this marriage, either."

The crescent-shaped lines around Riley's mouth went white. His eyes, sharp, clear, intense, cut into her as effectively as a hunting knife. It was all too apparent he was having difficulty holding on to his composure. "We'll discuss this later."

"There's nothing more to discuss," she retorted. "You've already told me everything I need to know. I'm an encumbrance in your life. You don't want to be married to me. Trust me, it doesn't come as any shock. I didn't want this marriage, either—you were the one who insisted. I don't understand why. I never intended to drag you into this. I never even intended for you to know about the baby. You were the one… Why, Riley, why did you insist upon marrying me? I have a right to know that much."

Her demand was met with stark, naked silence. She rubbed the heel of her hand down her face, wiping away evidence of her tears. She stared at him, damning him for being there that fateful night. How much simpler her life would have been if she'd called a cab. She'd been such a fool, and her stupidity was ruining three lives.

"Why did I insist upon marrying you?" he repeated hoarsely. "Because I didn't want my son to grow up a bastard the way I did."

Chapter Seven

A hard knot tightened Riley's stomach as the color drained from Hannah's pale features. He felt raw and angry; the pain of years past clawed at his nerves. "I was two years old before my mother got around to marrying Bill. He didn't last long, though. None of my mother's men friends ever did."

Hannah's gaze met his. Damn, but he wished she'd say something. Anything. Until she'd demanded to know why he'd insisted on marrying her, Riley hadn't given the matter much thought. The answer was complicated by a multitude of other factors. Rather than stick his reasons under a microscope, Riley preferred not to think about them. Marriage was the best solution, or so it had seemed at the time. Riley wasn't sure of that any longer.

Unshed tears glistened in Hannah's dove-gray eyes. She'd never looked more frail, as though it was all she could do to remain upright. He noted how ragged her breathing was as she edged her way past him. Riley reached out to her, wanting with everything in him to ease her mind in some small way, but she flinched and snatched her arm from him before he could touch her.

He stood numb and empty. The power of her silence wounded him deeply. He was aware, too, of her pain; and knowing he was the one responsible cut unmercifully at his heart.

Riley watched her move down the hallway, her steps like those of a sleepwalker. As she opened the door to her room and walked inside, he experienced a weighty sadness. He was standing there trying to decide what to do, if anything, when the muted sounds of her sobs reached him. Riley wasn't sure who she wept for—him or for herself. Perhaps her sorrow was for their unborn child.

Unable to listen to her anguish and do nothing, Riley reacted to his instincts. God as his witness, he'd never meant to hurt Hannah. Her door wasn't locked, and for that much he was grateful. She was curled up in a tight ball on top of her bed, her soft dark hair cascading over her face and neck. Her shoulders were racked with sobs.

Led by impulse, Riley moved to her side and sat on the edge of the mattress. With gentle fingers, he brushed the hair from her face, fearing she'd pull away from him again. He couldn't have borne it if she had. As strange as it seemed, he needed her at that moment as much as she needed him, although he was certain neither would be willing to admit as much.

Not knowing how to relieve her anxiety, or his own, he lay down beside her, resting his head on the same pillow as hers. For long moments he simply watched her, hoping his being there would lend her comfort. After a while her tears abated and she opened her eyes. They were round and weary, as if mirroring her soul. Her innocence and her beauty stirred him, and without examining the sudden, fierce need that flamed to life within him, he kissed her.

Riley intended for the kiss to be uncomplicated, a gesture of apology, a form of absolution for the hurt they'd inflicted upon each other. But once his mouth met hers, all was lost. Moaning, Hannah opened to him. He reached for her, entwining his fingers in her hair, dragging her closer to him. Deepening the kiss, he sought her tongue with his own.

When she shyly moved her tongue against his, Riley felt

as though the bed had fallen out from under him. They kissed again, and it was slow and gentle, so damned gentle that it produced an overpowering ache. Not a physical ache, as Riley would have expected, but an emotional one, buried so deep that at first he couldn't identify it. He felt close to Hannah, closer than he had in all the time they'd been married. The walls of misunderstanding and pride were down, broken, shattered by a newfound willingness to help each other.

His hands caressed her cheeks and tenderly brushed aside the stray tendrils of hair from her sweet face. Their gazes met in a rush of need and longing. The questions were there, as bold as ever, but they didn't bother with words, didn't bother with explanations.

Riley had never known a silence so blissful. A contented silence. The sweetest silence he'd ever known. Precious moments of tenderness unlike anything he'd ever experienced.

Shyly, Hannah leaned forward and kissed him, curling her tongue around his. Heat against heat. Hand against hand, fingers entwined. Their mouths dueled in a love-starved battle as though they had an eternity to do nothing but savor one another. Wherever his life would lead him, whatever happened between him and Hannah, Riley realized he would always treasure these few, precious moments with her.

Ending the kiss slowly, Riley buried his face in her shoulder and dragged several deep breaths through his chest. He dared not look at her when he spoke, afraid of what he would read in her eyes.

"Can you feel Junior move yet?"

"I...don't know," she whispered back, her smile evident. "Sometimes I'm sure I do, but then I convince myself it's all part of my imagination. The doctor said I should feel him kick any time now."

"Can I feel?"

She smiled and nodded. Taking his hand, she pressed it against her stomach, holding it there. Her hand over his. His hand over her abdomen. Riley lifted his gaze until it met hers, waited for movement, then sadly shook his head. He was barely able to distinguish the slight thickening at her waist, and only then because she was so thin.

"There…are other changes," she whispered.

Once more he raised questioning eyes to hers, not sure he understood.

"My breasts are fuller."

Risking all, Riley gently cupped his hands over her glorious breasts, lifting them, allow them to fill his palms. Touching her so intimately had an immediate effect upon him. The hardness eloquently portrayed his plight. He wanted her. He needed her. It would be weeks before he'd be able to hold her and touch her again, and knowing that lent an urgency to his desire. For two weeks he'd been patient, doing nothing to pressure her, but he needed her now as he never had before. So much so that he was willing to broach the forbidden subject.

"I want to make love to you." Riley had always been direct. He might have dressed up his desire with a bunch of fancy words, or drugged her with kisses until she willingly submitted. But he wasn't willing to do either. When Hannah came to his bed, he wanted her to be fully aware of what she was doing and with whom.

A long moment passed, and he was encouraged by the indecision he felt in her. At least she was considering it, which was a giant step from the sharp rejection she'd given him the day of their wedding.

"Why?"

If she needed a little inducement, Riley was more than willing to supply it. "I'm going to be away six weeks. That's a hell of a long time for a husband to be without his wife…."

"No," she said flatly, and pushed herself free from his

grasp. Sitting up on the edge of the bed, she brushed the hair away from her face, using both hands. He was surprised to realize she was trembling.

"Hannah, for the love of heaven, we're married!"

"Six weeks without making love must be some sort of record for you. Your pressure tactics aren't going to work with me."

"Pressure tactics!" Riley exploded. He could have had her, could skillfully have brought her to the point of desperate physical need. Instead he'd taken a more direct route and in the process robbed himself of the very love he craved. "Before you start accusing me of anything, you'd best examine yourself."

She blushed and looked away. "I don't know what you're talking about."

"My breasts are fuller," he mimicked in a high falsetto voice. "Sweetheart, you were asking for it."

Hannah's face went fire-engine red. "That's ridiculous!"

Riley gave a short, disbelieving laugh. "What's so wrong about us making love? I don't know of any place where it's a crime to sleep with one's wife."

Her gaze narrowed. "If I'm your wife why didn't you tell me you were leaving? A...a stranger comes to my door and tells me my own husband will be gone for several weeks—a *stranger*, for the love of heaven."

"I thought I was doing you a favor."

"Spare me any more of your favors."

Riley swore he'd never known a more unreasonable woman. What had he done that was so unforgivable? His crime had been to delay letting her know about the training cruise so she wouldn't fret about him going. He was being kind. Thoughtful. Just as a husband should be. Instead, the whole thing had blown up in his face.

Riley was prepared to argue with her when the doorbell rang. For a split second he couldn't decide if he should answer it or not. In the end he decided it wouldn't do any good to talk sense to Hannah. She was bent on thinking ill of him, and he wasn't likely to say or do anything that could change her mind.

The weekend passed in a haze for Hannah. Riley barely spoke to her, which was just as well since she worked equally hard to avoid any contact with him. The tension in the house was as thick as a London fog; thick enough to slice up and serve for dinner, although it would have made bitter fare.

Hannah spoke only when asked a direct question. Riley was constrained and silent. No unnecessary words passed between them. Nor looks, and certainly no touching. He camped in one area of the house and she in the other, and they both went overboard to be certain their paths didn't cross.

Monday morning Hannah heard her husband rummaging through the house several hours earlier than normal. Realizing he was probably preparing to leave for the *Atlantis,* she lay in bed, trying to decide if she should make the effort to see him off properly.

Her preference was to leave matters as they were, but soon the decision was taken from her. Riley politely rapped against her bedroom door just loud enough to wake her if she were sleeping, but not enough to frighten her. She sat up, holding the blankets protectively against her breasts, although it was unnecessary since she wore a thick flannel nightgown and the possibility of him viewing any part of her anatomy was highly unlikely.

"Yes?" she called out, working hard to put a frosty tone in her voice.

He opened the door, and his six-foot frame was stiffly silhouetted against the light that spilled into the hallway from the kitchen. He didn't move into the bedroom and continued to hold on to the door handle. "I'll be leaving soon."

She nodded, confident there was nothing she could add to the announcement.

"I left two phone numbers on the kitchen table for you. If a problem arises and you need anything, call either one of those numbers." His words were heavily starched and devoid of emotion. He might have been discussing the weather, for all the feeling he displayed.

"All right."

He dropped his hand away from the door and hesitated for a moment. "Goodbye."

"Goodbye," she returned just as tautly.

He closed the door, and with willful determination, she laid her head back down on the pillow. Closing her eyes, Hannah stubbornly decided to go back to sleep and ignore her husband the way he'd ignored her. She supposed she should consider herself lucky he'd taken the trouble to bid her farewell.

An achy heaviness weighed down her chest, and Hannah realized she was on the verge of tears. She hated the wetness that rolled down the sides of her face, dampening the pillow. She hated Riley for making her feel so loathsome, as though she'd done something very wrong. It felt wrong to have him leave for six weeks of sea duty when so much remained unsaid between them.

Rolling onto her side, she was determined to ignore her husband, the Navy and her conscience. Closing her eyes, she waited for the void of sleep to willingly claim her once again. If there was ever a time in her life when she was looking for the escape of slumber, it was now. Instead, the painful weight pressing against her breast threatened to suffocate her with every breath she drew.

Tossing aside her covers, she sat on the edge of the bed, her pride battling her conscience. If she rushed out to him, what could she possibly say? Hannah didn't know. That she was sorry? The words would have lacked conviction, and Riley would know immediately and would use it against her. She didn't want him to leave like this, but she knew of no way to end the tension and keep her pride intact.

It was while she was debating with herself that she heard the front door close. Hurriedly shoving her feet into her slippers, Hannah rushed into the living room. She reached the front window and parted the drapes in time to watch Riley climb into his friend Burt's battered blue pickup. Burt must have said something to Riley about seeing her at the window, because Riley's gaze reluctantly returned to the house.

Her heart demanded that she do something. Raise her hand in a gesture of farewell. Press her fingers to her lips in an effort to let him know he'd be missed. Something.

Hannah, however, did none of those things. Unshed tears burned her eyes, and still she stood there, wanting to blame him, blame herself for ever having agreed to this farce of a marriage. No more than a few seconds passed before the pickup pulled away and the opportunity was lost.

Two weeks into the training cruise, Riley was convinced he was the biggest heel who'd ever walked the face of the earth. If he'd plotted the ruin of his marriage, he couldn't have done it with any more expediency.

He'd wanted to talk over their problems with her before he shipped out, but a man has his pride. Everything he'd done or tried to do, she mistrusted. Okay, so he'd made a mistake by not telling her he had orders for the training cruise. Surely a man was allowed one small error in judgment. The least she could do was cut him some slack; he was new to this husband thing.

Not Hannah. Not his dear, sweet wife. She'd settle for nothing less than blood.

He'd made the mistake of viewing her as a timid soul. His wife, he soon learned, had more fight in her than some tigers. Misjudging her wasn't a mistake he planned on making again.

Personally, he didn't think withholding information from one's spouse was grounds for placing him in front of a firing squad. Hell, Hannah might as well shoot him for all the good he was doing the Navy. Riley had never felt emotionally lower in his life. It showed in his attitude and in everything he did. If this was the way matters went, he didn't know how the hell he was ever going to last....

Six weeks had never seemed so long to Hannah. Two of those weeks had slipped by with sluggish disregard for her remorse. Not an hour passed when she wasn't thinking about Riley, regretting the way they'd spent their last few days together. They'd wasted those precious hours when so much could have been resolved. Instead she was left to wait day after day, week after week, for his return just so she could tell him how terribly sorry she was.

They were both so damned proud, so damned stubborn. Neither one of them had been willing to give an inch. Their stubborn pride was like a cancer that had eaten away at their better judgment. Both were at fault. Above everything else what was troubling her was the knowledge that if they continued to feed the mistrust and the doubts, in time it would destroy them. There was too much at stake to play such cruel games with each other: their child's future, their future.

When two people are married, Hannah reasoned, no matter what the circumstances, they must learn to make concessions. She'd been so willing to find fault with Riley, so willing to place the blame on...

Her. Riley openly acknowledged as much after a month of missing Hannah. Never again would he leave her behind with unsettled business between them. This time apart was pure torture because he'd been too damned stubborn to talk out his feelings. She accused him of not being a husband, and he'd found her lacking as a wife.

Four long weeks had softened the tough hide of his arrogance, and he willingly admitted his mistake. He'd never been strong on relationships, preferring to live his life independent of others. Caring for another, putting her needs before his own was new to him, and he'd committed several blunders.

His damn pride was the crux of the problem. Hannah was carrying his child, and if she was a bit sensitive over some matters, the least he could do was to be a little more understanding.

His inexperience in dealing with the opposite sex posed other problems. Riley had never lived with a woman. He didn't know what to expect or how to act toward her. They both needed time to adjust to each other, make allowances. This infernal need to look for the bad instead of the good in their marriage was destined to doom them.

They'd made mistakes aplenty, but that was to be expected. They were both new to this marriage business. For years Hannah had assumed she'd be marrying Jerry Sanders, a seminary student. It was little wonder she was having a difficult time adjusting to life with a beer-drinking, poker-playing sailor.

Despite all that, they were physically attracted to each other. The child Hannah carried was testimony of that. The desire he felt for Hannah hadn't changed. Riley dreamed of the day she would willingly share his bed. Closing his eyes, he could almost smell the sweet scent of wildflowers that was hers alone. Dear sweet heaven, he missed her—more than he'd ever dreamed it was possible to miss anyone. He'd gotten impatient, wanting to make…

Love. Riley hadn't been unreasonable that night. What he'd said about a husband and wife sharing a bed had struck a raw nerve with her. Waiting to make love until she was more comfortable with their relationship had seemed like a good idea to Hannah when she had first mentioned it. She'd since altered her opinion. Mingled with the other regrets she was suffering since his deployment was the fact she had never spent the night in his bed. Riley wasn't a brute. He would never have forced her. His kisses were gentle and thorough, speaking more of commitment than passion. His touch, so warm and special, conveyed all the wonderful things a man and woman, a husband and wife, could expect in a loving, long-lasting relationship. He'd never pressured her or rushed her, and had been willing to grant her all the time she required. Her anger and pride had pushed him away, leaving her to brood six torturous weeks over what might have happened.

Never again, Hannah promised herself, would she send Riley off to sea the way she had this last time. When the USS *Atlantis* docked, he'd know how sorry…

He was. Riley was determined to make up for this rocky start with Hannah. Never again would he give her reason to doubt him. He was committed to her, committed to their marriage, committed to their child; and God willing, he fully intended to prove it.

"You're sure I don't look too fat?" Hannah asked, carefully watching Cheryl's reaction to the maternity top. There was no disguising the soft swell of her abdomen any longer. She'd changed in other ways, as well. Her thick brown hair fell past her shoulders, the ends curving under naturally. She'd pulled the thick waves away from her face, locking them into place with two gold barrettes.

"Oh, Hannah," Cheryl whispered, her voice lowering slightly, "you look so…beautiful."

Drawing in a deep breath, Hannah sincerely hoped her friend was right. The USS *Atlantis* was due to dock that afternoon, and she'd spent a good portion of the morning preparing herself and the house for this homecoming celebration with Riley.

Everything was ready, right down to the last-minute details. Thick steaks were marinating in the refrigerator; a homemade apple pie, Riley's favorite, was cooling on the kitchen countertop. A single bottle of beer was resting in a bucket of ice along with a soda for her. The table was set with a lace tablecloth and dishes. The centerpiece of carnations and candles was ready to be lit. The only thing needed to make the celebration complete was her husband.

Although she'd had six long weeks to work out what she planned to say to him, Hannah could think of no words that could adequately voice what was in her heart. She was anxious about this meeting, concerned, longing for everything to be as perfect as she could make it. She had missed him dreadfully and sought to prove how much by planning every aspect of his homecoming.

"I doubt that Riley will be able to keep his eyes off you," Cheryl told her. In the weeks that their husbands had been out to sea, the two women had become good friends. "His hands, either," Cheryl added. "Trust me, I know what I'm talking about. When Steve comes off a cruise, he can't leave me alone for two or three days straight. Not that I'm complaining, mind you."

Hannah found speaking so frankly about one's love life slightly embarrassing. Especially when her and Riley's marriage had yet to be consummated. Looking away from her friend, Hannah smoothed the maternity top over her hips in an effort to disguise her uneasiness.

"I'm showing now.... I wasn't when he left.... Do you think he'll notice?"

"No," Cheryl admitted, laughing. "He won't be able to take his eyes off those beautiful eyes of yours long enough to realize you're into maternity clothes now. Besides, Riley isn't going to be looking at your stomach."

"He'll notice." Of that Hannah was sure. "I can barely button my coat." She wasn't even six months pregnant, and already she felt like a blimp. The baby was so active now, no longer leaving her guessing when he chose to thrash about. The love she experienced for her unborn child overwhelmed her. Often when she sat, she flattened her hand over her abdomen, reaching out to her child, reassuring him. At night in bed, she spoke to him, telling him about his father and all that she was doing to prepare for his arrival. When she'd first suspected she might be pregnant, Hannah had tried to ignore the pregnancy, push it from her mind, unable to cope with the fruit of her night spent with Riley. Now, the baby dominated every thought and action.

The day was bright and cold, Hannah noted as they rode down to the waterfront. The nuclear-powered submarine was docked at Delta Pier, the largest of the three wharves at Bangor.

Other family members of the *Atlantis* crew were crowding the waiting area by the time Cheryl and Hannah arrived, although they were several minutes early. The air was thick with excitement and anticipation as wives and children anxiously looked for signs of their loved ones.

The early-December wind cut through the front of Hannah's coat, but she was too nervous to think about being cold. She stuffed her hands in her pockets and turned her back to the intermittent gusts.

As the men started down the gangplank, Hannah bit into her lower lip as the waiting crowd hurried forward to greet their husbands and fathers. A small pain gripped her stomach, but she ignored it, certain it must be nerves; certain everything would be all right the instant she caught sight of Riley.

"There's Steve!" Cheryl exclaimed, pointing out her tall, lanky husband, then waving the small bouquet of flowers she'd brought as a welcome-home gift. "Oh, damn, I'm going to cry," Cheryl added, smearing the moisture across her cheeks. "I hate it when I do this. His first look at me in weeks and I'll have mascara streaks running down my face. I'll look like a zebra."

Hannah smiled at her friend's joke, impatiently watching as the men of the *Atlantis* disembarked, eagerly searching through a sea of unfamiliar faces, hoping to find the one that was.

"Riley's three men behind Steve," Cheryl said, pointing him out to Hannah. It took her a moment to locate him, but when she did, her mind spun at a feverish pace, attempting to make sense of all that was happening to her. Her heart thudded. After all these weeks of torturous waiting, she was about to come face-to-face with the man who'd overshadowed every waking moment of her thoughts. All that she'd done, everything she'd bought, every place she'd gone, every person she'd talked with receded into the background as she focused her attention on Riley.

He paused at the top of the gangplank and seemed to be searching through the crowd. He didn't see her, Hannah knew, just by the way he squared his shoulders and shoved his duffel bag over his shoulder. There wasn't any reason he should expect her. The only means of communication between the submarine crew and family members during deployment was family grams, and Hannah hadn't known what those were until it was too late to send one. Even if she had known, she wasn't certain what she could have said in a few short lines.

As Riley stepped onto the pier, Hannah hurried forward, scooting around several other women and children. Riley seemed oblivious to the heartwarming scenes going on around him, determined to make it off the wharf as quickly as possible. She thought to call out to him, but her throat was so tight she would have choked on his name.

Riley stopped midstep when he saw her, his brow pleating into a look of surprise and wonder. The duffel bag slipped from his fingers seemingly without notice.

Hannah smiled and ran into his arms, closing her eyes as she savored the feel of his powerful arms when they surrounded her. He was warm, and even through several layers of clothing she could feel his heart pound against her own until it seemed that the two had merged and beat as one.

His hands were in her hair and his lips were searching out hers. His mouth was rough and urgent as he claimed her lips with a tender violence.

"Hannah… Oh, God. I'd hoped you'd come," he whispered between kisses. "But I didn't expect it."

"I'm sorry, so sorry for everything," she sobbed.

His mouth covered hers, halting her words. "Shh," he pleaded, kissing her face, her neck, bouncing his lips off hers as though he weren't certain even now that she was there with him and that she was actually in his arms.

Hannah had to pinch herself to know it was real. Nothing could have prepared her for the kaleidoscope of wild emotions that burst to life within her. It was as if she'd lain dormant the entire time Riley had been to sea. Only upon his return could she feel again, and feel she did: warm and loved and needed. Tears splashed down the side of her face.

"We'll talk later," Riley promised. "But for now let me kiss you."

"Yes," she cried, "yes." She slipped her arms around his neck, standing on her tiptoes as she nestled her face in the curve of his neck. For now there was no mired past, only the present, which felt incredibly right, incredibly good.

Several minutes sped past. It might have been hours, for all Hannah knew. Riley gently eased her away from him as he carefully studied her. His eyes widened when he noticed how nicely round her stomach had become. Silence stretched into silence.

Hannah pushed the knotted emotion from her throat enough to be able to speak normally. "As you can see, I've been eating well."

His gaze rested on the strained buttons of her coat, and a gloating, happy smile curved up the corners of his mouth. "How are you feeling?"

She grinned. "Never better."

"And Junior?"

"He's growing like a weed. I...I think we might have a soccer champion on our hands."

Riley laughed outright. "So he's doing his share of kicking these days?"

Hannah nodded. "You'll be able to feel him now."

"Good. I'll look forward to doing exactly that." He reached for his duffel bag, tossing it over his shoulder with familiar ease. "Shall we go home, my love?" he asked, draping his free arm over her shoulders.

Hannah agreed with a quick nod of her head. Home. Their home. It was where she belonged. Where Riley belonged. The two of them together.

Chapter Eight

In all his years of military life, Riley had never experienced a homecoming more profound. There'd never been anyone waiting at the wharf to greet him before. No wife to rush forward and run into his waiting arms. No one to shout with joy and excitement when he stepped down the gangplank.

Until this day, Riley never realized how much he'd missed. His heart felt full, brimming over with a happiness, a contentment that radiated from deep within his soul.

He couldn't stop staring at Hannah as they drove back to the house. She'd changed, and the transformation left him dumbfounded. Her hair was different—longer, thicker, shinier. She wore it pinned up, away from her face, exposing high, prominent cheekbones and gray eyes so beautiful it was like staring into a darkening winter sky. Her color was back, her cheeks rosy and her eyes clear and bright.

The beauty he saw in her was enough to steal his breath. He struggled for words, wanting her to know what was in his heart; but a hard lump had formed in his throat and it was impossible to speak. He slowed his breathing and swallowed, hoping to ease the pressure so he could say the things he wanted, but for then it was impossible. There was so much he longed to tell her, so much he wanted to explain. He would in time, when he could say it without trembling like a schoolboy.

He'd been starved for the sight of her, rushing through the crowds along the wharf in his eagerness to hurry home, praying she'd still be there, praying she could find it in her heart to forgive him, praying she'd be willing to put the ugly past behind them and start anew. He hadn't dared to hope she'd be at Delta Pier waiting for him with the other wives and families.

Riley parked in front of the house and felt its welcome penetrate him like a hot bath on the coldest day of the year; warmth, love and acceptance awaited him inside. He climbed out of the car, went around to the passenger side and opened the door for Hannah. Together they walked into their home, shutting out the winter.

Riley was struck almost immediately by the changes that greeted him. The house had been living quarters before he was deployed; he returned to a home. It took him a few minutes to ascertain the differences. First he noticed a bright orange, gold and bronze afghan draped over the back of the sofa, with matching pillows tucked at the corners. A large oak rocking chair rested between his recliner and the end table. This, too, was new. But by far the most prominent addition was a large oil painting hanging on the wall above the fireplace. His gaze had been drawn to it almost immediately.

"I wondered if you'd notice that," Hannah said shyly.

"It's beautiful." Rolling hills of blooming blue and gold wildflowers waving in the wind beneath a blue summer sky. Fluffy clouds skirted the horizon. It must have cost a fortune, but Riley didn't care how much she'd spent on it. Wildflowers were damn special to him.

"I'm so pleased you think so," Hannah responded happily, looping her arm around his and pressing her head to his shoulder.

"Where'd you ever find it?"

She paused. "I didn't exactly find it."

"Oh?" He dropped his duffel bag and was removing his coat.

"I painted it myself."

Riley went still, stunned by the richness of her talent. "I didn't realize you painted."

"I didn't, either," she returned with a light, slightly embarrassed laugh. "It was something I'd always longed to do, but had never had the time. I signed up for classes while you were away. Come," she said, her voice bubbling with excitement, "there's something I want to show you." She took him by the hand and led him through the kitchen and down the hallway to the bedrooms.

She opened her door, stepped briefly inside to turn on the light, then stood back proudly for him to see.

Riley glanced inside and turned to his wife, awestruck. "You painted this?" She'd turned one entire wall into a mural for the baby. A long-necked giraffe nibbled foliage from a bright green apple tree heavy with luscious fruit. In the background two lambs frolicked along a hillside, chasing butterflies.

She nodded, smiling broadly. "Do you think Junior will like it?"

"He'll love it."

"Cheryl and I found this in a garage sale last weekend," she went on, excitement creeping into her voice as she moved across the room to the closet, opening the door and retrieving a bassinet. She looked up at him expectantly.

The white wicker bed seemed more suited to a little girl's dolls than an infant. "Junior will fit in there?"

"For about three months. Then we'll need a crib. I've been pricing them," she said as her eyes rose steadily to his. "Be prepared. I was shocked by how expensive they are, but," she added quickly, "we might be able to find a used one that's far more reasonable."

Riley nodded, barely hearing her. His attention was

caught by the stack of tiny clothes and blankets Hannah had put inside the bassinet. He held up one impossibly small T-shirt, amazed that any human could ever be so tiny.

"I've been picking up a few things for the baby every paycheck," Hannah explained, running her palm across the top of the freshly folded cotton diapers.

Riley couldn't understand the hesitation in her voice, as though she feared he'd disapprove of her spending his money. He lifted his gaze to connect with hers.

"I...took a part-time job as a legal assistant. I work fewer than twenty hours a week," she ventured haltingly. "I hope you don't mind."

"Of course not. I shouldn't have been so dictatorial before. You know far better than I how much you can and can't do."

She seemed relieved at that, as though she'd been dreading telling him about her part-time employment.

"We'll buy a new crib," Riley stated decisively and, unable to resist, he threaded his fingers through the hair at her temple and gently kissed her there.

She smiled, her eyes as warm as fresh honey. "I was thinking we should...since we'll probably be using it again a few years down the road."

For Riley, the implication was like a silken caress. In time there would be other children.

"Oh," she said excitedly, rushing toward her dresser drawer, "I nearly forgot." She opened the top drawer and pulled out a piece of paper and handed it to Riley, enchanting him with her smile. He had trouble dragging his gaze away from her. He swore he'd never seen anyone so beautiful.

When he could, he looked at the slip of paper for several moments, puzzled by the series of dark circular lines that followed no pattern that he could discern. To him it resembled a sonar reading. "What is it?"

Hannah's sweet, delicate laugh filled the room. "Not what! He…or she. That's Junior."

"Junior?" Riley was amazed.

"It's an ultrasound. The doctor took it on my last visit. See," she told him, pointing out the vague outline of the baby's head and spine. "Oftentimes they can determine the sex of the baby by these pictures."

"And?" He didn't bother to disguise his curiosity.

"Junior was sleeping with his back to us so we can't be sure. Dr. Underwood will probably do another one in a few months."

"We might well be having a daughter, you know," he said, returning to the bassinet and holding up a pale blue sleeper. Nearly everything Hannah had purchased was geared for a boy. For some odd reason, the realization pleased him immensely. Repeatedly he'd told himself the sex of their child didn't matter; but deep down, he longed for a son, although he hadn't admitted it even to himself.

"I'm prepared for that." Her face lit up with pleasure as she dug through the small pile of clothes until she found a frilly pink dress with lace trim. "I couldn't resist this. Isn't it adorable?"

Riley nodded, thinking he'd never seen anyone more adorable than Hannah. Her eyes widened and her gaze shot to Riley. "He's kicking now. Do you want to feel?"

His nod was eager. Sitting down on the edge of the mattress, he flattened both hands against the soft swell of her stomach.

"You might not be able to feel him through all these clothes," she said, pushing aside her pretty green top. Her skin was warm and as smooth as silk as she gripped him by the wrist and pressed his palm just below the elastic waistband of her wool slacks. "Here," she whispered as though she feared she'd disturb their child, sliding Riley's hand to the right. "He's kicking now. Can you feel?"

Riley closed his eyes, concentrating, then with a shrug of disappointment, shook his head. "Not yet."

"You will soon."

He nodded, brushed his lips over the distended round-ness at her waistline and then reluctantly righted her clothes. Hannah sighed softly and wrapped her arms around his head, gently laying her cheek over his crown. "Junior and I have missed you so much."

"I missed you, too," he murmured, wrapping his arms around her waist and hugging her close. He shut his eyes, savoring her softness, drinking it in the way a man dying of thirst swallows down a glass of cool, clear water.

They held each other for several moments, swaddled in tenderness and appreciation for what they'd found, for what they'd both come so close to destroying. For the love he'd feared would forever escape him.

Yes, love, Riley realized. He hadn't wanted to admit it until now, but he did love Hannah. He knew so little of the emotion, his acquaintance with it was so brief, that he hadn't recognized what should have been obvious. Some part of him had known it the night they'd met. It should have been obvious later when he spent so much frustrated effort on locating her again, tearing up the city in a futile attempt to find her.

Her hands were in his hair, gently fingering his nape. "Are you hungry?" she asked after a while.

Riley tried to speak, but the words didn't come. His heart, his throat, were too full, so he simply nodded and with a good deal of reluctance released her.

"I've got dinner all planned," she announced happily. "Steak, twice-baked potatoes, fresh green beans with al-mond bits, and salad."

"It sounds delicious."

"I wanted to bake homemade rolls, but I ran out of time. I did get an apple pie made."

He felt like laughing for no reason and knew she was

watching him, hoping he wasn't disappointed. "Apple pie is my favorite."

"I thought it might be."

Hand in hand, they strolled into the kitchen. They'd moved through it earlier, but Riley hadn't had time to notice everything Hannah had done to prepare for this homecoming. His heart swelled with appreciation as he saw the table and centerpiece.

"Can I do anything to help?"

Hannah shook her head and reached for an oven mitt. "No, thanks, I've got everything under control. It'll only take me a few minutes to cook the steaks."

"What about the mail?"

"I...opened some of it—what looked like bills—and paid those when your check arrived. The rest I set on top of your dresser."

He nodded, kissed her cheek and headed for his bedroom.

As she'd promised, dinner was ready in only a few minutes. Riley couldn't remember a meal he enjoyed more. The steak, juicy and succulent, was cooked to perfection. The salad, crammed full of sliced fresh vegetables was a small work of art. The piecrust seemed to melt in his mouth. He complimented her again and again. Hannah blushed with pleasure each time.

Sweet promise filled Riley's heart. Later, perhaps this very night, he told himself, he'd approach her about sleeping in his room. He wouldn't pressure her into anything physical, he promised himself. He'd go out of his way to be sure she understood that he'd be content to hold her in his arms. When she was ready for lovemaking, she should let him know. They'd go slow and easy, and she could write her own ticket as far as the physical part of their marriage went. It sounded reasonable, and he felt good about it, waiting for just the right moment to make the suggestion.

The right moment never came.

About halfway through their dinner something changed. For the life of him, Riley didn't know what. Hannah grew quiet. One moment she was chattering like a magpie and the next she went still and silent. Not understanding what was happening, Riley made up for the lack of conversation, conscious of the abrupt change in her mood the entire time he was speaking. In an effort to cover the uncomfortable silence he told the details of what he was allowed to relate about the cruise and his job, filling in the everyday particulars of his life aboard the nuclear-powered submarine. She seemed genuinely interested in what he described, and asked questions, but he couldn't shake the feeling he'd said or done something terribly wrong.

After dinner she quickly washed up the dishes, refusing his help. "I'm going to bed now," she announced stiffly, then disappeared into her bedroom, closing the door.

Riley was left standing in the kitchen, stunned. Mentally he retraced everything that had passed between them for something, anything that might offend her. He could think of nothing. Not one damn thing. An altar boy couldn't have faulted his behavior. Hell, he was so much in love with her he would have cut out his tongue rather than hurt her.

Walking into the living room, Riley sat in his chair and reached for the evening paper. He scanned the headlines three times without comprehending a word of what he was reading.

Ten minutes, he decided. He'd give her ten minutes to come to her senses, and if she didn't, then he was going in after her. He'd demand to know what the hell he'd done that was so terrible, if it came to that.

The frustration ate at him like acid. Usually, when he arrived home from any length of time at sea, he stopped in at the apartment just long enough to drop off his duffel bag and change clothes. Then he'd meet up with his friends and they'd hit the streets and celebrate. This time, not once, from the moment he'd stepped off the *Atlantis,* had he considered leaving Hannah.

His own ten-minute deadline passed. Tossing aside the evening paper, Riley braced his elbows on his knees and rubbed his hands over his face. So this was what it meant to be married, Riley mused, sighing heavily. To hand a woman his heart and his soul and then have her trample upon it for some imagined wrong.

He knew what she wanted. He hadn't been fooled by her sweet, docile ways. Everything she'd said and done had been computed to convince him of his wrongs. Now she was looking for him to meekly follow her into the bedroom and beg her forgiveness.

Like hell. If he'd committed some terrible crime, then she'd have to tell him face-to-face instead of hiding herself away in her bedroom, waiting for him to come and grovel at her feet. He'd gladly suffer her indignation before he'd lower himself to that.

Riley's heart beat high in his throat as he soared to his feet. It would serve her right if he were to disappear, leave her to wonder and fret while he stayed out half the night, carousing with his friends.

He toyed with the idea, fueling it with angry frustration, when his gaze happened upon the oil painting above the fireplace. His breath came in jagged bursts as he recalled the pride and eagerness that had flashed from her eyes as she'd studied his reaction, so eager for his approval.

Had everything she'd said and done been calculated to bring him to his knees? Riley found it hard to believe. Difficult to fathom. Hannah knew little of subterfuge.

He stepped over to the sofa, his steps slow and measured. Picking up the crocheted pillow, he ran his hands over the surface, admiring Hannah's work. His thoughts were in turmoil, torn between what his heart was saying and what his head was shouting.

Hannah could never love anyone like him. He was too crude, too coarse for someone as gentle and sweet as a preacher's daughter.

Anger and bitterness swelled up inside him, nearly choking off his breath. Venting his frustration, he bunched up the soft pillow in his hands and tossed it back down to the sofa with a fiery vengeance.

So that was love! he decided, feeling neglected and abused, irritated with himself for peeling open the gates of his heart. The emptiness inside him had never seemed more hollow. He was left vulnerable and alone, and his pride gave him damn little solace.

He'd go to her, he determined, if that was what it took. Have this out, once and for all.

Two steps into the kitchen, he found Hannah. Her hands were gripping her stomach, and when she glanced up at him he found tears in her eyes. He'd never viewed such stark terror in anyone.

"Riley," she moaned, reaching out to him, "something's wrong. I'm losing the baby!"

Chapter Nine

Riley's heart dropped to his knees. Without a word he moved forward and swung Hannah into his arms. Not stopping for his coat or anything else he rushed out the front door, slamming it closed with his foot.

Panic clawed at him like a shark's jaws, but for Hannah's sake, he dared not reveal his fear. One look at her ashen features told him she was frightened half out of her mind and a hairbreadth from hysteria.

Once she was safely deposited in the front seat, he raced around the car, jumped inside and started the engine. The tires squealed as he roared down the street, leaving a cloud of black smoke in his wake.

"We're about ten minutes away from the hospital," he said, praying he was able to keep the fear and trembling out of his voice.

"Hurry, please hurry," she begged.

Hannah bit into her lower lip and turned her head away from him, pressing her hands against her stomach, determined to hold on tightly enough to save their child.

"I don't want to lose my baby," she sobbed. "Oh, Riley, I love him so much." She was in terrible pain, he realized. Her breath came in quick rushes, each accompanied by a small animallike cry. His fears became rampant as he worried that she might hyperventilate.

Riley pulled into the emergency entrance at the hospital in record time and slammed on the brakes. Leaping out of the car, he didn't even bother to close his door as he sprinted around to Hannah's side. Scooping her up in his arms, he ran toward the double glass doors that automatically flew open for him.

"My wife!" he shouted when a physician approached. "She's having a miscarriage." An orderly rushed forward with a gurney, and Riley laid Hannah on it, gripping her hand as they raced down the wide corridor.

Once they were inside a cubicle, the emergency-room staff pulled closed the curtain surrounding the bed. The physician, calm and professional, patted Riley on the shoulder. "It'd be best, son, if you waited outside."

Riley looked to Hannah for confirmation, but her eyes were tightly closed and her lips were moving and he knew she was lost in a world of pain and prayer.

"The baby?" Riley pleaded.

"I'll do everything I can," the stocky man vowed. "I promise you." His hands gently pushed Riley from the room.

Feeling helpless and full of despair, Riley staggered down the hall, his heart pounding so loudly it stormed in his ears. He was trembling so badly he had to sit down. The waiting room was deserted, and he mechanically lowered himself into a molded plastic chair.

Over the years, Riley had routinely faced danger. Twice he'd stared death in the face and hadn't flinched. Death had no grip on him, nothing to blackmail him into submission. Whether he lived or died was in the hands of the fates, and he hadn't particularly cared one way or the other.

Now the bitter taste of fear filled his mouth, swamping his senses with dread that went soul-deep. His breathing turned shallow and he balled his fists, clenching and unclenching them as his heart roared louder than a jet engine.

Riley wanted this child more than he'd ever realized. He hadn't given much thought to Hannah's pregnancy while he'd been at sea. He'd been too concerned about his relationship with his wife to think much about their child. Although Hannah's pregnancy had greatly impacted on his life, Riley had experienced no deep emotion concerning their baby. "Junior" hadn't seemed real to him.

It wasn't that way any longer. Riley had touched the bed where his son or daughter would sleep, had held the T-shirt that would warm his or her body. He'd viewed a scrambled photograph, a progress report of his baby's physical development, and had seen for himself the perfection of this young life. His own hand had pressed against Hannah's womb, communicating his love to his unborn infant.

Love Junior he did, with a weight that crushed him. A weight so crippling that tremors of fear pulsed through his body as he waited in agony. Waited for some word, some sign of what was happening behind closed doors. Of what was happening to Hannah, happening to Junior, happening to himself.

Whom did one plead with in instances such as this? Fate? Riley didn't know. Fate had always been a joker to him, playing cruel pranks on him from the time he was born. He wasn't about to plea-bargain with lady luck.

The stark terror he'd read in Hannah's eyes returned to haunt him. He felt so damn helpless. Her desperation was as keen as his own. Her fear and pain had been alive in her eyes. And there hadn't been a damn thing he could do. The last he'd seen before he was forced out of the emergency room was her lips moving in silent, desperate prayer.

God, Riley decided. One spoke with God when there was nowhere else to turn. He wasn't a man accustomed to religion. There'd never been anything or anyone that he'd needed or wanted badly enough to risk going before the Almighty.

Until now.

He rose awkwardly to his feet, standing as he would before a superior officer. His shoulders were back, his eyes straight ahead, his hands dangling loosely at his sides.

A thick tightness gripped his throat as words escaped him. It didn't seem right, somehow, to make so important a request without offering something in return. His thoughts stampeded ahead to what he might possibly have to bargain with, but there was nothing. Nothing.

Unable to hold still, Riley started pacing, his mind and his heart confused. "I don't know why you sent Hannah into my life," he whispered. "But thank you."

He felt a little less inept once he started talking. "I promise you I'll be a good husband to her…. I'm probably going to need some help with that." His intentions had always been good, but he didn't know much about the way women thought, so if God was willing to give him a few pointers along the way, then Riley would be more than happy to receive them.

Now that he'd breached the barrier of his own self-consciousness, Riley found it wasn't so difficult to speak his mind.

"I'm not the kind of man who finds it easy to ask for something," he began again. "It seems wrong to come to You with a request and not be able to give something back in return. It's about Hannah, God, and Junior. I can't do a thing for either of them. It's out of my hands entirely. If you'll take care of them both, I'll tell you what—I'll start attending church services with Hannah." It was the best he could do. Heaven knew that would be sacrifice enough for someone who'd only darkened a church door for weddings and funerals. Twice now, she'd invited him to come with her. That sort of thing seemed important to his wife. But then Riley should have expected that; after all, she was a preacher's daughter.

"If you can think of anything better, let me know," he ended, then in afterthought added, "Amen."

Riley felt a little better after that. He sat back down, analyzing the events of the afternoon. It didn't take long for him to realize Hannah must have started feeling bad sometime during their dinner. She hadn't said anything to him. Nothing. He continued to sort through his thoughts, adding up the obvious, when the physician approached.

Riley rose slowly to his feet, his heart beating so hard his rib cage ached. "How is she?"

The physician smiled. "Fine. The baby, too."

The wild sense of relief Riley experienced was beyond words. He went weak with it.

"You can go see her now, if you like."

"Thank you, sir," he said, reaching for the man's hand and pumping it several times. He started toward the cubicle when the corpsman stopped him.

"Hey, is that car yours? You're going to have to move it."

He nodded, ignored him and raced back to the small examining room where they'd taken Hannah.

Hannah felt like such a fool. She'd been convinced she was losing the baby, and the fear had struck terror in her heart. In fact, she'd been suffering from a bad case of indigestion.

For days she'd been anxiously waiting for Riley's return. They'd parted in anger, and she had no way of knowing what his mood would be once he returned. After the horrible way they'd treated each other, he might wish to end their marriage. The pains had started early that afternoon, long before she'd had anything to eat—small, barely distinguishable cramps that she'd dismissed as nerves, which in fact they were.

It was later, during dinner, that the sharp, hard, contractionlike spasms had started. Not knowing what they were, she'd tried to ignore them, hide them from Riley, hoping they'd go away. Instead they'd grown more intense while she was doing the dishes. Not wanting to alarm her husband, she'd excused herself as soon as she could and gone into her bedroom. If she lay down and rested, she'd reasoned, it might help to ease the pain.

Instead the cramps had grown steadily worse, so piercing and constant that she'd convinced herself she was suffering a miscarriage. Her fear and panic had added to her physical distress—at least that was the doctor's explanation. Nevertheless she felt like such an idiot, frightening Riley the way she had. He'd driven like a madman in his rush to get her to the hospital, and it had been for naught.

"Hannah?" Riley pulled back the white curtain and stepped inside. How pale he looked, colorless and stricken as if he'd aged ten years in the last thirty minutes.

She held her arms out to him, and he hastened to her side, gathering her in his embrace and holding her so tightly against him that he nearly stole her breath.

"You're all right?" he asked, brushing the hair away from her face, examining her as though he could read in her eyes everything he needed to know.

She blushed and nodded. "The baby, too."

He grinned at that. "I heard." He pulled a chair to her bedside and sat down. He took hold of her hand, gripped it in both his own and pressed it to his cheek. "Tell me what happened."

"I…I'm not exactly sure. I started feeling pains earlier this afternoon."

"Why didn't you say something? I'm your husband—you should have told me." He sounded so angry, and with good reason, she supposed; but that didn't restrain the tears from flooding her eyes, brimming and spilling down her face.

"I'm sorry," he added quickly, once he viewed her distress. "I didn't mean to shout. It's just that…"

"I'm the one who's sorry," she said between sniffles. "I

feel just dreadful putting everyone through this trouble for…for a case of nerves."

"Nerves," Riley bellowed loud enough to shake the windows. He slumped back down into the chair and rubbed his hand down his face. "Nerves," he repeated, as if he hadn't heard her correctly the first time.

"Hey, buddy," the corpsman said, walking abruptly into the room, "I told you before, you're going to have to move your car. You're blocking the roadway."

Riley looked at him as though seeing a ghost, then turned back to Hannah. "Are they going to let you come home?"

She nodded eagerly. "The doctor gave me something to settle my stomach, but he wants to check me in another ten minutes and see how I'm feeling."

"You gonna move that car? Or are you going to force us to tow it away?"

"I'll move it," Riley answered without looking at the impatient corpsman. Riley paused long enough to kiss Hannah, shook his head and then turned and walked away.

She might have imagined it—in fact Hannah was sure she had—but as her husband started out the door, she thought she'd heard him mumble something about indigestion and God not playing fair.

Sunday morning the alarm woke Hannah. She reached out, turned off the buzzer and pulled the blankets over her shoulders, wrapping them around her.

Three days had passed since her episode at the hospital, and she still hadn't forgiven herself for creating such a terrible fuss and alarming Riley the way she had. He'd taken it all in good humor, teasing her about it, but always in fun, being careful not to embarrass her.

They were much more at ease with each other now. The terrible tension that had existed between them the first awkward weeks of their marriage had disappeared.

As she lay in bed, savoring the warmth, she mulled

over the strange events of the past few days. Riley had been so gentle with her, solicitous, making few demands on her.

Too few.

She'd hoped once he'd returned from sea duty that he'd say something or make some token gesture toward inviting her into his bed.

Thus far it hadn't happened. If Hannah were more worldly or a bit more sophisticated, she would have approached him herself. But she'd hoped her husband would make it apparent that he wanted the two of them sharing a bed. Perhaps she'd ruined everything early on when he'd asked her to make love and she'd callously rejected him. A hundred times since, Hannah had regretted it. She'd been so foolish. Her pride was hurting them both.

Perhaps Riley, disgusted by her attitude, didn't intend to ask her again. Perhaps he was waiting for her to voluntarily come to him. She mulled over the thought several moments, wondering how she'd go about it. Should she broach the subject herself? Hannah didn't know how she'd do it without becoming flustered and red-faced.

While he'd been at sea, she'd often gone shopping with Cheryl. One Saturday, a week before the men were due home, the two had gone into a lingerie shop at the Kitsap Mall. Cheryl had bought a skimpy black nightie with a fur hem. She'd joked that the hem was there to keep her neck warm.

While they'd been in the shop, a lovely peach-colored silk gown had caught Hannah's eye. Cheryl had convinced Hannah it was perfect with her coloring, and with a little encouragement from the saleslady, Hannah had purchased the gown.

The night before, she'd trifled with the idea of putting it on for Riley. She hadn't, caving in to her insecurities instead, convinced her pregnancy was too advanced to be sexy.

Sexy. She smiled to herself. Women who were nearly six months pregnant weren't seductive looking no matter what they wore to entice their husbands. No, the peach gown wouldn't work at this late date. She needed something else—something that would convince her husband she wanted him. Only she wasn't sure what.

"Hannah?" Riley knocked politely at her door. "Are you up?"

"Not yet," she answered, surprised that he was.

"You'd best hurry or you'll be late for church."

He was right, although she hated to crawl out of a toasty bed. She didn't have time to dally this Sunday. After Riley had gone to sea, she'd joined the church choir and had been asked to sing a solo for the first service.

With a limited wardrobe to choose from, Hannah shed her nightclothes and slipped the olive-green street-length dress over her head and adjusted the waistband. In another couple of weeks, she wouldn't be able to wear this one, either. Sighing, she ambled out to the kitchen, pleasantly surprised to find the coffee brewed and waiting for her.

"You're up bright and early," she said to her husband, bringing down a mug.

He nodded, more interested in reading the Sunday paper than conversing with her. Hannah watered down her coffee with a generous portion of milk, then carried it into the bathroom with her while she worked her hair into a French plait.

When she'd finished, she went back into her bedroom for her coat. Normally she fixed herself something small to eat—a piece of toast with a piece of fruit—but she didn't want anything to coat her vocal cords before she sang.

Buttoning up her coat, she reached for her purse, prepared to leave the house. As she walked through the living room, Riley set aside the morning paper and stood. He was dressed in slacks and a sweater.

"You ready?" he asked.

"Yes." Hannah wasn't sure she understood. It wasn't until they were in the car that it dawned on her that Riley meant to attend the church service with her.

His wife continued to amaze Riley. He'd been taken by surprise when she had stood in the middle of the church service, following the communion meditation, and approached the piano. She slipped onto the mahogany bench and skillfully ran her fingertips over the keyboard. Riley hadn't had a clue she could sing, any more than he'd been aware that she possessed such extraordinary talent at the piano. As he'd sat back and listened to her hauntingly beautiful voice, his heart had filled with a renewed sense of appreciation for the incredibly gifted woman he'd married. The poignant words of the song had touched him in ways that were completely foreign, and he'd sat for several moments afterward, pondering their meaning.

Following the worship service, he'd suggested they go out to breakfast.

"Why didn't you tell me you could sing like that?"

Hannah finished spreading jelly on her toast before she answered. "You never asked."

He frowned and reached for the syrup. "How long have you been playing the piano?"

She shrugged. "I started lessons when I was about six, maybe seven. I don't remember. My mother was the pianist for the church until she died, and I took over for her."

"I had no idea you were so gifted."

"Oh, Riley. Honestly, you make it sound like I'm another Chopin or something."

"You're damn good. Have you ever thought of doing anything with your music?"

She smiled sweetly up at him and shook her head. "Heavens no. I played the piano because, well, because it was expected of me. Don't misunderstand me. I love it— in fact I miss it quite a lot. But music isn't my life."

Riley thought about this and nodded when the waitress came by with the coffeepot to refill his cup. "Are there any other talents you possess that I don't know about?"

Hannah mulled that over and shrugged once more. "I'm quite a good seamstress."

"Where's your sewing machine?"

"I left it at my father's house when we…married. I was hoping to pick it up over Christmas. You might have noticed the stack of material I've been buying lately. It's on the floor in the bedroom. I've got to do something about clothes."

"Buy yourself anything you want," he offered, not understanding why she hadn't before now. It was apparent she was growing out of almost everything she owned.

"It's much cheaper to make them, and I enjoy it."

"Will you have the time?"

"Yes, Mr. Worrywart."

She grinned, and Riley swore he could drown in her eyes. She'd smile, and his heart would melt. She had the uncanny talent for making him feel like a schoolboy—flustered and inexperienced. There wasn't anything he wouldn't do for her. He'd practically given up drinking, and he hadn't even noticed. With the exception of Steve, he was losing touch with his friends. There wasn't anyone he'd rather spend time with than Hannah.

There were problems, however. He wasn't keen on them maintaining separate bedrooms. He wanted her sleeping by his side. Damn it all to hell, that was where she belonged. He just hadn't figured out how he was going to get her there. The first night he'd been home, she'd been rummy with the medication the doctor had given her and had fallen asleep on the return trip from the hospital. The following afternoon he'd been assigned duty and she was in bed asleep by the time he arrived home. Asleep in her own bed.

"If it's all right with you, I thought we'd leave for Seattle about two o'clock Christmas Eve," she said, interrupting his thoughts.

"Sure," Riley answered, cutting a fat link sausage with the side of his fork. "That'll be fine."

"Dad's anxious to see us both. I've missed him."

Riley nodded, preoccupied. "It might be a good idea if we go shopping soon for a crib and whatever else we're going to need."

"Already?"

"I'd like to have everything set up for the baby before the middle of January."

"Why?" She stopped eating, setting her fork down as she studied him.

The apprehension in her eyes ate at him like battery acid. "I'll be away again. This time until April."

She swallowed tightly. "The baby's due the middle of March."

"I know. I won't be here, Hannah. I'd give anything to be with you, but I can't."

"I...know," she admitted reluctantly. "But don't worry, I'll be fine. Cheryl volunteered to be my birthing partner...but I wish it could be you."

"I wish it could be, too." More than she'd ever know, but it wouldn't do any good to stew about it. Several of his peers had become first-time fathers while out at sea. He'd do it, too, although it didn't sit right with him to have Hannah go through the delivery and birth without him there.

"Would you like to do some Christmas shopping this afternoon?" Riley asked, hoping to lighten the mood.

Her nod was eager. "I love Christmas. I guess I'm just a little kid at heart."

"We all are when it comes to receiving presents," Riley murmured. Until recently he hadn't a clue what he should buy for Hannah, but he'd inadvertently stumbled upon the perfect gift for his wife. Now, all he had to do was keep it a secret for the next three weeks.

* * *

"Dad!" Hannah called out as she stepped into her child-hood home, feeling engulfed in its warmth and welcome. "We're here."

George Raymond stepped out from the den, a pair of wire-rimmed glasses perched on the end of his nose. He wore slacks, a shirt and the old gray wool sweater she'd knitted for him several years back. His smile was broad and automatic as he spied Hannah and Riley just inside the front door.

"Welcome, welcome," he greeted, holding open his arms. He gave Hannah an enthusiastic hug and exchanged hearty handshakes with Riley.

"Let me get a good look at you," her father said excitedly, stepping back to examine her.

Hannah couldn't help but blush. She removed her coat and hung it in the hall closet, self-conscious the whole time of how prominent her pregnancy was becoming. A little nervous, as well, knowing she'd be confronting members of her father's congregation. It wouldn't take long for any-one to realize she'd been several months pregnant when she married Riley.

"I'm getting so fat," she murmured, resting her hands on her bulging stomach.

"I don't believe I've ever seen you more beautiful," he told her thoughtfully. "My goodness, girl! You look more like your mother every day."

"Where would you like me to put these things?" Riley asked. He'd returned to the car and had carted back an armload of goods Hannah had insisted they bring.

"Oh, my goodness, I forgot about the pies. In here," she said, directing Riley toward the kitchen.

He followed her into the country-style kitchen and set the flat boxes that contained the pumpkin and apple pies on the countertop. "I swear you packed enough food to feed an army," he chastised. But she noted he wasn't complaining too loudly since she'd baked the apple pie especially for him.

"Dad wouldn't have known what to have ready," she explained for the sixth time. She'd gone grocery shopping the day before, picking up everything they'd need for Christmas dinner. Her father had relied on her to cook the main meal at Christmas for so many years, she doubted that he knew what to have on hand. Rather than leave it to chance, she'd brought everything with her, much to Riley's chagrin.

As Riley and her father carried everything inside, she sorted through the grocery sacks, tucking several items inside the cupboards.

It felt good to be home again, Hannah mused. She felt keenly the warmth of her father's welcome, although she'd had mixed feelings about this visit for several weeks.

Oh, she was pleased to see her father again. They'd spoken regularly on the phone, taking turns contacting each other, and he'd been the one to suggest she and Riley make the two-hour trip to Seattle for the Christmas holiday.

Hannah had agreed without giving the invitation a second thought. It wasn't until much later that she realized it would be difficult to hide her pregnancy. Although most everyone in her father's congregation was kind and loving, there were sure to be some who'd feel it was their God-given duty to point out that she'd married much too quickly and quietly after losing Jerry; and when they noticed her stomach, they'd know why.

Jerry.

Funny, she hadn't thought about her late fiancé in weeks. Although he was never far from her mind, the love she felt for him seemed far removed from the life she shared with Riley now. Jerry would always be someone special in her life and in her heart, but he was gone. Without her ever realizing it, the emptiness she'd experienced in the grief-filled weeks following his death had come to be filled with the love that had flourished for Riley and their child.

Even so, someone was bound to mention Jerry during her visit, and she wasn't sure how Riley would react when it happened.

The weeks since his return from the training cruise had been idyllic—so perfect that she didn't want to risk ruining the fragile peace between them.

"Hannah, my goodness!" her father called out from the living room. "So many gifts."

She left the kitchen to find Riley bent under the Christmas tree, unloading two shopping bags filled with brightly wrapped gifts.

"Ho, ho, ho," he teased, grinning up at her.

"What's that?" she asked, noticing a large square box she hadn't seen before.

Riley tucked it at the back of the tree, out of her reach. "Never you mind."

"The candlelight service is at seven," her father reminded them.

Hannah glanced at her watch. "I'd better change my clothes now," she said, heading toward the stairway.

"I put your suitcases in your old room," her father called out after her. Hannah stopped midstep and glanced back at her husband, her eyes wide with apprehension.

Riley read her look and followed her up the stairs. "What's wrong?" he asked, once they were out of earshot of the living room.

"Dad doesn't know," she whispered, hating the way color crept into her cheeks.

"Know what?"

Rather than go into a long explanation, she climbed to the top of the stairs and opened her bedroom door for him to see for himself. Inside sat two suitcases: one belonging to her and the other to Riley.

"Dad assumes we're sleeping together," she said. "If we don't…he might think something is wrong. Would you mind very much, Riley, just for tonight?"

He paused just inside the room, and his eyes slowly found hers. "No, Hannah," he told her after a while. "I don't mind at all."

Chapter Ten

Riley couldn't be more pleased at this turn of events. His own father-in-law had inadvertently laid the groundwork Riley had been impatiently waiting weeks to arrange. Hannah and he would be sharing a bed for the first time since their marriage nearly three months past. It was all Riley could do not to wear a silly grin.

"Will you be joining us for the candlelight service?" George Raymond asked Riley once he was back downstairs.

Personally, Riley hadn't given the matter much thought. He'd been attending services with Hannah for the past few Sundays and was surprised to find church wasn't nearly as bad as he'd assumed. The sermons had practical applications to everyday life. He listened carefully, hoping to gain insight into Hannah's personality. And into his own.

"Hannah told me you'd been going to church with her lately," George added, wearing a proud look, as though he'd always known his daughter would turn Riley's life around. "I'm pleased to hear it."

Riley nodded, swallowing down a sarcastic reply; but one good turn deserved another, and his father-in-law had gotten Hannah into his bed—a feat Riley had been attempting for weeks. Christmas Eve candlelight service, however, seemed above and beyond the call of duty.

It wasn't until they walked the short distance from the parsonage to the white steepled church that Riley understood why George had made an issue of inviting him to the service. It would be the first time Hannah had been home since their wedding. With them married short of three months and her pregnancy apparent, there was sure to be stares and a few harsh questions.

Riley's arm tightened around Hannah's shoulders; he wanted to shield her from gossip and candid looks. He was grateful when they sat toward the front of the church, away from discerning eyes.

Once they were situated in the polished wooden pew, Riley's gaze found the manger scene. The baby nestled in the straw captured his attention, and he couldn't help wondering how Joseph must have felt the night Mary had been in labor. At least he hadn't been out to sea, worrying about his wife, wishing he could be with her. The scene hit too close to home, and drawing a heavy breath, he looked away.

The service started shortly after they arrived. One thing Riley appreciated about church was the music. When they stood and sang Christmas carols, his loud baritone voice boomed through the building, bringing several stares and a few appreciative nods.

Hannah glanced up at him and smiled so sweetly that for a few measures, Riley had trouble singing. Love did funny things to a man, he realized meaningfully. Last Christmas Eve he'd been sitting in a bar, hitting on the waitress. Twelve months later, he was standing in a church singing "Silent Night" at the top of his lungs.

George Raymond moved toward the altar and lit a candle, using it to ignite others. Two men stepped forward and accepted the lighted candles. Protecting the flame by cupping their hands behind the wick, they moved down the center aisle, lighting the candle of the parishoner sitting at the end of the pew. That person shared the flame with the one sitting next to him, who turned to share it with the next person, until the light had been passed all the way down the row. Soon every candle in the church was burning.

There were a few more rousing Christmas carols. George might not have intended them to be sung boisterously, but Riley was in a spirited mood and it felt good to sing loud and strong as if he'd been doing it every Christmas of his life. At least he knew the tunes of these hymns. Some of the others he'd heard in church the past few weeks sounded as though they'd come straight out of the Middle Ages.

The sermon was short and sweet, just the way Riley liked them. He'd wondered what kind of preacher his father-in-law would be, suspecting George Raymond would be the fire-and-brimstone type, but Riley was pleasantly surprised.

There was another carol, and Riley was thinking the service would soon be over. He was mentally calculating how early he could pretend to be tired and urge Hannah to go up to bed. Since it was barely eight, he figured it would take another hour or so.

"This has been a painful year for our church family," George announced, stepping close to the podium microphone. "A year of change and transition. A year of pain and renewal. There seems no better time than Christmas to honor Jerry Sanders."

Hannah went still beside Riley. Still and rigid. She reached for his hand, squeezing it tightly, but Riley had the impression she would have held on to anyone's hand. Her breathing went shallow, and he was left to wonder at her strange behavior. It took a few moments to understand what was happening, to realize the man his father-in-law had chosen to honor was the Jerry Hannah had been engaged to marry.

Once he'd figured it out, it was all Riley could do to re-

main in the pew. To be forced to sit and listen to the trib-
ute to Hannah's former fiancé was like holding Riley's face
underwater and asking him to try to breathe.

"Are you all right?" he whispered to Hannah, wishing
there was something he could do to spare her this. To spare
himself this.

"Are you?" Her gaze—ripe with meaning, ripe with
memories—slid to his.

He nodded, taken aback by her question. No man enjoys being trapped into listening to the limitless virtues of
the man his wife loved…loved still; but the choice had
been taken away from Riley. He tried to relax and let his
mind wander.

"I doubt there is a life in this church that Jerry Sanders
didn't touch," George continued, his low voice vibrating
with grief. "From the time he was in his teens, Jerry felt
God's call to the ministry, but he wasn't pious or overly
devout. He was a man who loved others and reached out
when he saw a need. Once, when Jerry was twelve, he
brought a young mother to the church door, explaining
that he'd met her outside a gas station. Her husband had
abandoned her with a three-month-old child and she had
nowhere to turn. Jerry couldn't leave her and do nothing,
so he did the only thing he knew how. He brought her to
his church."

Hannah's fingers tightened around Riley's. Her features had gone pale, and Riley hedged, debating how
much attention they'd garner if he picked her up and carried her out of the church. Too damn much, he decided
reluctantly.

"It wasn't only strangers Jerry helped—he touched all
our lives," George continued, and stepped away from the
podium. One by one, three men and one woman moved
forward, sharing incidents that involved Jerry Sanders.

Riley didn't want to listen, didn't want to hear any of
this, but he had no choice. Each story revealed the other

man's generosity and love in a new light. As the tales were recounted, Riley realized he'd never known anyone as generous or as kindhearted as Jerry Sanders. What George had said earlier about Jerry not being a goody-two-shoes was right. He'd been real, reacting with indignation to the wrongs committed around him, reaching out to help others even when he faced impossible odds. He was the type of man Riley would have liked to count as a friend.

The realization struck a sharp cord within him. It wasn't an easy thing to admit, even to himself.

No wonder Hannah had loved him, and grieved still. Jerry's death had dealt her a crippling blow. How unfair it must have seemed to her. How wrong that Jerry should be taken from her. He glanced over at her and noticed the tears streaking her face. She struggled to hide them, but it did little good.

Leaning forward, Riley reached into his back pocket and handed her a handkerchief. Slowly, as though she feared what she'd find, her gaze sought his.

Riley hurt. What man wouldn't? But his concern at the moment was more for Hannah. For the loss she'd suffered, for the pain she experienced being forced to rip open the half-healed wounds of her grief.

By the time the testimonials were finished and the plaque unveiled in Jerry's honor, Riley was ready to weep himself. Weep with frustration and anger. Weep because the comparison of his life and Jerry's was so striking. It was all he could do not to haul Hannah out of the church. And escape himself.

He wanted to make a quick getaway, but as soon as the service was over, several friendly folks crowded around them, looking for an introduction. Their eyes were curious as they noticed Hannah's stomach, but no one said anything.

Hannah amazed him with the warm way in which she handled the potentially disastrous situation. She looped her arm around Riley's, smiled adoringly up at him and introduced him with such pride and devotion that she fooled even him. Anyone listening would have thought their marriage was the love match of the century. It was left to him to complete the picture, and for her sake, he did the best he could.

How well he succeeded remained to be seen.

It seemed to take forever before they could escape. Riley turned his back on his father-in-law who stood in the vestibule, bidding the last well-wishers a joyous Christmas.

"I'm going to kill him," Riley muttered under his breath as they walked out the side door of the church. "How could he do that to you?" The tracks of her tears had left glistening streaks down her cheek.

"I'm sorry, Riley. So sorry."

"What have you got to apologize for?" he demanded brusquely.

"For Dad. He'd never do anything to intentionally hurt one of us. He simply wasn't thinking. I'm married to you now, and he doesn't realize you even know about Jerry. Dad loved and misses him still. Jerry was as much a son to him as my brother, and he's still grieving."

"He might have warned you."

"Yes. I'm sure he intended to, then simply forgot."

Hannah could offer a hundred excuses, but it did damn little good. Riley claimed a few minutes to himself, making the excuse that he wanted to check the car. He did that, then walked around the block until the sharp tip of his anger had worn off. Then and only then, did he return to the house.

George Raymond, his look apologetic, was waiting for him when Riley stepped in the front door. "Hannah's upstairs."

Riley didn't trust himself to say one word. He bounded up the stairs, taking them two at a time. Tapping lightly against the bedroom door, he waited until Hannah answered before letting himself in.

She was sitting on top of the bed, in a sexless flannel nightgown, brushing her hair. She cast her gaze self-consciously downward as he walked into the room and started unbuttoning his shirt after pulling it free from his waist.

He wished she'd say something. She didn't.

Riley sat on the side of the mattress, his back to his wife, and removed his shoes and socks. When he stood to unbuckle his pants, Hannah peeled back the bedspread.

"I...generally read for a while before I turn out the light," she said softly. "You don't mind, do you?"

"No."

With a maddening lack of haste, she walked around the end of the bed and rooted through the suitcase for her book. Bending over the way she did offered Riley a tantalizing view of her long, slim legs. It wasn't more than a fleeting glimpse, but then it didn't take much to get his juices flowing. Riley wondered how the hell he was going to lie next to her all night and not touch her.

Hannah was worried about Riley. In her heart, she knew her father hadn't meant to hurt her. Or Riley. Even now, George Raymond seemed oblivious to what he'd done. Rather than cause a strain in their close relationship, she'd silently gone up the stairs following the candlelight service to wait for Riley. He seemed to take forever to join her. Not everything her father did was thoughtless or illadvised; by chance he'd managed to get her and Riley into bed together, which was a feat she'd been working toward for weeks.

Had she realized they'd be sharing a bed when she packed, Hannah realized sadly, she would have brought her silky peach gown. Pregnancy or no pregnancy, she wanted to view Riley's reaction when she wore it.

Riley was under the covers, lying back, his hands tucked behind his head, staring at the ceiling when she returned with the book she intended to read. He was so far over on his side of the bed it was a wonder he didn't slide onto the floor. He continued to stare straight ahead at the light fixture while she hurried under the blankets, shivering with the cold. Still he remained where he was.

Hannah read for no more than fifteen minutes, then hurried out of bed, turned off the light and rushed back. She rolled onto her side, tucking her knees under her breasts in order to get warm again.

"You all right?" Riley asked in the darkness.

"Yes…I'm just a little cold." She hoped he'd snuggle up against her and share his body's heat, but he didn't. The silence was strained, but she didn't know what to say to make it better. Feeling helpless and inadequate, and like the world's worst wife, she buried her face in the pillow to hide the ever-ready flow of tears.

"Hannah?"

"Yes."

"Are you crying?"

"No."

He gave an abrupt, hollow laugh. "You never could lie worth a damn. What's wrong?"

If he wouldn't come to her, then she'd go to him. Once the decision was made, she rolled onto her other side and aligned her body with Riley's, pressing her head to his shoulder. He felt hard and muscular, warm and whole.

Slowly, as though he were going against his better judgment, he brought his arm out from beneath his head and wrapped it around her shoulder. It felt so good to have him hold her, to have him touch her, that she closed her eyes on a deep sigh.

"You have nothing to fear from him, you know," she whispered, once her throat was clear enough to talk evenly, unemotionally. The love she felt for Jerry was far removed from the life she had now.

"You love him."

Hannah couldn't deny it. "A small part of me always will. He was a special man."

Riley grew silent, but she could tell from the even rise and fall of his chest and the steady beat of his heart that he hadn't taken offense, but was mulling over her words.

"When I was little, I can remember my father telling me that when God closes a door he always opens a window. This time he opened two. I don't regret being married to you, Riley. I feel honored to be your wife."

His hand gently stroked her shoulder. The day had been long and emotion packed. Hannah yawned and, nestling her face near Riley's neck, closed her eyes.

A smile curved her lips as she felt his mouth brush a soft kiss at her temple. Within minutes she could feel herself drifting off to sleep.

Until he'd met Hannah, Riley hadn't realized how full of irony everyday life could be. He'd dreamed, plotted, schemed to get her into his bed, and once she was there, he found he was afraid to touch her. Afraid and unworthy. He, Riley Murdock, actually feared her moving close to him, tempting him beyond endurance, snuggling her lush breasts against him. He trembled at the thought of his body, so hard and powerful, filling Hannah's delicate softness. The problem, he recognized, was one of his own making. Knowing that didn't alter the situation, however.

Hannah openly admitted her love for her dead fiancé, and after learning what he had that evening, Riley didn't blame her. Jerry Sanders had been one hell of a man.

A far better man than he'd ever be. Riley had been born on the wrong side of the blanket. By the time he was in junior high, he'd been labeled a troublemaker and a rabble-rouser. His headstrong, rebellious ways had repeatedly gotten him into trouble throughout high school. He was lucky to have escaped reform school, not to mention prison. Actually, he had the Navy to thank for rescuing him from a life of crime.

He'd enlisted the day after he graduated from high school, at the bottom of his class. His cocky attitude hadn't lasted long; by the end of boot camp he'd realized the Navy could well be his one chance to turn himself around. It was up to him to decide.

It had taken him fifteen years to make the transformation from a street-smart, foulmouthed kid with a chip on his shoulder the size of a California redwood to a responsible Navy chief. A few of the rough edges of his personality had been rounded off over the years, but he'd never be the educated, cultured husband Jerry Sanders would have been to Hannah.

Riley would like to hate Hannah's fiancé, challenge him face-to-face for her heart. But everything he'd heard that night in church convinced Riley that, had he known Jerry, he would have liked him. Jerry Sanders had been the kind of man everyone looked up to and admired. A natural leader, a lover and defender of justice. Hell, the man had been near perfect. There wasn't anything to fault him with. He'd been a saint. He must have been, to be engaged to a woman as beautiful as Hannah and restrain from making love to her.

Hannah, who'd been sheltered and protected all her life, was the perfect match for such a man as Jerry. She was generous and sweet, a delicate rose; and by God, she deserved a better husband, someone far more decent than he'd ever be.

The problem was, what would Riley do about it now? Even if he found the courage to leave her for her own good, he couldn't turn away from her now. Not with her six months pregnant with his child.

What was a man to do in such a situation? The hell if Riley knew. He wasn't even close to being good enough to deserve Hannah. She'd crashed into his life when he least expected to meet a woman like her. One night with her had left him frantic with worry, furious and baffled. He hadn't known who she was or where she'd come from; all he had known was that he had to find her again.

He was getting too old, Riley decided. Too tired. Too weary. He was losing his cutting edge. His emotional resilience was gone. He'd like to blame Hannah for that, as well, but he couldn't. The problem was his own. The stark truth of the matter was he'd never been in love before and he'd lost his heart to her that night in Seattle.

His heart and his mind.

All his life he'd been waiting to meet someone like her. He just never expected it to happen in a waterfront bar. He'd seen her and wanted her immediately, not recognizing himself what it was he found so damned appealing about her. After three months of marriage, he knew. He'd been attracted to her innocence, her generosity of spirit and her awesome ability to love. For once in his life, Riley needed a woman to love him. Someone who belonged to him. Someone not bound to a memory.

He couldn't, he wouldn't share her.

But he did already.

As he lay next to Hannah, her measured, even breathing echoing in his ear, the implications of his situation pounded at his temples with the sharpness of a hangover.

He could fight her love for Jerry, do everything he could to wipe out the other man's memory. In essence Riley could shadow-box with a dead man. Or he could accept her love for the seminary student and go on, doing his utmost to be the best husband he knew how to be—always knowing, always conscious that he was a damn poor second choice.

The choice, however, had already been made. The gold wedding band on his finger was reminder enough of that. The child growing in Hannah's womb convinced him there could be no turning back now. That being the situation, the best Riley could hope for was that, in time, she'd be able to look past the hard outer crust he wore like battle armor and come to love him, too.

Love.

No one had told him it was such a painful emotion. Powerful enough to break a man, topple him from his prideful perch and leave him shaken and unsure. Riley loved Hannah and their unborn child beyond reason. Enough to cast all pride aside.

She stirred and rolled closer to him, draping her arm across his stomach. Her bare legs scooted next to his as she drew in a deep, even breath. Lying as she was, her stomach nestled against his side, reminded him how grateful he was that she hadn't lost Junior. He'd never experienced such panic as he had the night he'd driven her to the hospital.

It happened then, and Riley's eyes flew open. The baby kicked, and he'd felt it as strongly as if Hannah herself had poked him. An involuntary grin grew and grew.

"Riley," she whispered, "did you feel him?"

"Yes."

"I told you he was going to be a soccer player."

"He's so strong."

Her smile was evident even in the dark. "Tell me about it." She yawned, holding her hand in front of her mouth. "What time is it?"

Riley read the illuminated dial of his wristwatch. "A little after two."

"Did Junior wake you?"

"No. I was lying here thinking."

"About what?" she quizzed.

She sounded worried, and he sought to reassure her. "About what we should name Junior. I was thinking…that if you wanted, we could name him after Jerry."

Her silence confused him. He turned his head toward her, hoping there'd be enough moonlight in the bedroom to judge her expression.

"That's the most beautiful thing you've ever said to me," she murmured, her voice breaking with emotion. She pressed her hand on his shoulder and kissed his cheek. "Actually, I've been giving some thought to a name myself."

"And?" he pressed.

She hesitated, as though she expected him to disapprove of her choice. "There's a Hannah in the Bible. I didn't know if you were aware of that or not."

Riley wasn't, but that shouldn't come as any shock. Now that he thought it over, it made sense that a godly man like George Raymond would give his only daughter a scriptural name.

"She was married and desperately wanted children. She tried for years and years to become pregnant, but was barren."

"So far I don't see any similarities between the two of you," he teased, and was rewarded with an elbow in his ribs.

"Might I continue?"

"By all means."

"Hannah went to the temple to pray, asking God for a child, and soon afterward she found herself pregnant. When her son was born, she named him Samuel."

"Samuel," Riley repeated slowly, testing the name. It had a nice solid sound to it. Samuel Murdock. "I like it, but aren't you taking a lot for granted? We could very well be having a daughter."

"Samantha, then."

"All right," Riley said, gathering her close in his arms, pressing his chin against the crown of her head. "Samuel or Samantha it is."

"Samuel Riley Murdock."

Riley felt his throat thicken. "Or Samantha Hannah Murdock."

"But Riley, that's too awkward a name for a little girl. Samantha Lynn or Samantha Anne would be better."

"It's Samantha Hannah, so don't argue with me."

"In that case I certainly hope we have a son," she muttered under her breath, just loud enough for him to hear. She tugged the blankets more securely around her shoulders and continued to use his chest for a pillow. It wasn't the most comfortable position, with her breasts brushing against him and her thighs rubbing his own, but Riley hadn't the strength to ask her to move.

"Good night, Hannah," he said, closing his eyes, content for the first time in hours. "Good night, Sam," he added, and nearly laughed out loud when a tiny foot or arm jabbed him in the side.

"Oh, Riley!" Hannah cried as she pried open the lid to the large rectangular box he'd squirreled away beneath the tree. "Oh, Riley," she repeated, tears brimming in her eyes as her gaze shot over to him. With infinite care, she removed a soft pink maternity dress from the tissue wrapping and held it against her waist. "How'd you know?"

"You mean other than the fact you went back to the clothes rack four times to look at it?"

"But it's much too expensive…. I could probably sew one like it for half the price. But I'm so pleased I don't have to! I've only got a couple of things I can wear to work as it is. Oh, Riley, I love it so much. Thank you." She rushed to his side, threw her arms around his neck and hugged him hard.

"Tears, Hannah," her father teased.

"Don't worry, I get emotional so easily now. Dr. Underwood said it was to be expected."

"Your mother was the same way. She'd start to weep over television commercials when she was carrying your brother and you." His eyes grew warm at the memory as he leaned back in his chair and smiled down on his daughter.

"Riley, open my gift next," she said, breaking away long enough to pull a purple and blue gift-wrapped box from beneath the tree. "I made it myself while you were away."

Riley examined the box, shaking it.

"Careful, it might break." The blue wool sweater, complete with matching hat and scarf would do no such thing, but she enjoyed baiting him.

Riley took his time unwrapping the gift, and it was all Hannah could do not to rush to his side and help him tear away the paper. She watched closely as he lifted the lid. No emotion registered in his eyes as he carefully unfolded the garments one by one and brought them out of the box.

"I hope it fits," Hannah said in a rush, her words blending together.

Riley stood and tried on the sweater, slipping his long arms into the sleeves and then tugging them up past his elbow. He glanced over to her, and appreciation gleamed from his deep blue eyes. "I've never owned anything finer." With a flair that delighted Hannah, he wrapped the scarf several times around his neck and set the hat upon his head. His eyes met hers, and a surge of warm emotion filled her heart. His look penetrated the very core of her being and communicated to her a feeling of love so strong, she wondered why she'd never noticed it before.

Riley did love her, and yet…and yet, he'd barely touched her all night. It seemed he went out of his way to avoid doing so. Hannah strongly suspected he would have stayed on his side of the bed the entire night and made no contact whatsoever if she hadn't moved over to him.

Perhaps having her father so near had intimidated him and he hadn't wanted to consummate their marriage while in his father-in-law's home. But her father's bedroom was downstairs and he slept like a brick. She'd made a point of telling Riley so, although she'd wondered at the time if he was listening.

"Do I get a turn here?" her father asked, effectively cutting off Hannah's train of thought.

"Of course," she answered, pleased he'd chosen the gift she'd made for him. It was a small painting, one of a small loaf of french bread and a chalice of wine set on a rough-hewn wooden table. Although the entire focus of the painting was the bread and wine, she'd worked hard to depict the symbolic nature of the simple elements that had been part of the Last Supper.

"Hannah," her father said, awed as he held up the painting, "this is fabulous. Where did you ever find it?"

She beamed with pride and joy as she told him.

Hannah couldn't remember a Christmas she'd enjoyed more. The meal was excellent, and they ate early in the afternoon. She sat at the old upright piano and played Christmas music for her father and Riley, who seemed to thoroughly enjoy singing the timeless carols. Afterward she took a nap and woke to discover that Riley and her father had done the dishes. While she'd been resting, Riley had loaded the car and seemed anxious to return to the base.

They bade their farewells while it was still light outside. Riley was quiet during the long ride home, but when she asked if there was anything bothering him, he smiled, assuring her there wasn't.

As they approached the base, she realized he was speeding. Riley was a responsible driver, and she couldn't understand why he seemed in such a hurry.

Once they pulled up in front of the house, her husband made an excuse about unloading the trunk and insisted she go inside ahead of him. She offered to help him carry something, but he wouldn't let her.

Not knowing his thoughts, she did as he said, pondering his strange mood. She inserted the key into the front door and pushed it open. Turning on the light switch, she was halfway through the living room before she saw it.

There, against the wall, was a beautiful mahogany piano decorated with a huge red bow.

Chapter Eleven

Hannah stood frozen, unable to speak or move. A piano! A beautiful new piano that Riley had bought just for her. When she could move, she walked across the room and ran her fingers over the polished ivory keyboard. The joyous sound of her music filled the room. She continued playing while she scooted out the bench with her foot and sat down.

She proceeded with every Christmas song she could recall from memory, filling the house with music the way it did her heart and mind. When she finished, she laid her hands in her lap and exhaled a deep sigh.

Turning around, she found Riley leaning his shoulder against the wall, his powerful arms crossed over his chest, studying her.

"How…when?" She couldn't seem to ask a coherent question.

"I take it you're asking about the piano?"

She nodded, knowing she'd only make a mess of it if she were to try to explain. Her heart was full, bubbling over with love and excitement. Not once had she suspected. He'd been so closemouthed about it.

"After hearing you sing and play in church, I decided we needed a piano," Riley explained in that relaxed way of his, as if they were discussing a minor purchase.

"But…"

"There are no buts about it. You're too talented not to have one. You enjoy it. The way I figure, you can sing Sam to sleep."

"Oh, Riley, I can't believe you." She could think of no way to thank him. Nothing she could do or say would ever be enough. She walked over to him and kissed him the way that had been their habit of late, brushing her lips over his. Lightly. Briefly. First on his cheek, then his lips. But the all-too-hasty contact left her feeling empty and wanting. Standing on the tips of her toes, she leaned into him and wrapped her arms around his neck. Kissing him long and hard on the lips, she opened to him, introducing her tongue into his mouth until she created a warm, wet, gentle demand.

Riley held himself stiff against her, then groaned from deep within his throat. He sounded like a man absorbed in pain, and Hannah wondered if she'd done anything to hurt him.

With another groan he wrapped his arms around her waist, lifting her effortlessly from the floor so that her face was level with his own. Their gazes met for an instant before he directed her mouth to his. She'd been the aggressor, but that changed abruptly as he took control.

His tongue circled hers as his lips nibbled at her own. Riley was experienced in the ways of love; Hannah had known that from the first night they'd met. She'd responded to that experience, helpless to refuse him anything. To refuse herself. He seemed to need some kind of response from her, something more, she realized; otherwise he wouldn't be holding himself in check the way he was.

Stroking her fingers through his thick, dark hair, her lips fluttered open, granting him everything she had to give: her mind, her heart, her soul.

Riley's kiss was hungry and demanding, until slowly it

began to happen. Her sensations were drowning in warm feelings—feelings she'd experienced so rarely in her life and only with this man. She ached in places she'd never thought to ache. Her breasts throbbed, and she recalled with vivid detail the night on the Seattle waterfront when Riley had taken her nipples in his mouth; and she wanted that again. Anything to ease the heavy swollen feeling that controlled her. The sensation didn't stop there, but sank lower—much lower—to the juncture of her thighs. She felt hot and quivery, hot and excited; needy in ways she barely understood. Suddenly Hannah knew what she wanted. What she needed.

Her husband.

An electric shudder passed through her. Riley must have felt it because he abruptly broke off the kiss.

Hannah sighed. Riley's lungs emptied of air as he slowly released his hold on her waist. His hands reached for hers, which were gripping his neck, and he gently pulled them free.

"I'd better finish unloading the trunk," he said, his voice so low it was a gentle whisper. Following that, he walked away.

Hannah was stunned. He'd wanted her as much as she'd wanted him, and yet he'd pushed her aside and given some flimsy excuse to leave her. She didn't know what was happening, didn't understand the significance of it. What she did feel was alone and lacking. And more needy than she'd ever felt in her life.

Riley stood by the car, letting the cold December wind slam against him. He drew in several breaths, sucking the air deep into his lungs. His head was swimming with the reality of how close he'd come to breaking his self-proclaimed code of honor and making love to Hannah. He opened the car trunk, and his hands shook. Not only his hands, but every part of him—his legs, his belly, his head.

It was the kind of shallow-breathing, head-pounding shaking that comes when one realizes what a close brush one has had.

They couldn't have gotten any closer. Another minute, and Riley would have hauled her into the bedroom and damned the consequences. If he were to make love to her now, needing her so desperately, he'd frighten her half to death. Hell, he needed her so damn much it frightened *him.* He was concerned, too, about hurting the baby.

He'd made a promise to himself, one he fully intended to keep. He'd woo Hannah, love her the way a husband loves a wife, but only after she'd delivered the baby. Riley had lain awake most of the night before, sorting through his feelings for Hannah and, more important, what he'd learned about Jerry. He'd never be the husband her fiancé would have been. The way Riley figured it, Jerry, having been the noble man he was, wouldn't have pressured her to make love while she was pregnant, so Riley wouldn't, either.

"Admit it," Riley said aloud. He clenched his hands into tight fists at his sides, resisting slamming them against the trunk lid. It was more than the pregnancy issue. "You're afraid."

The psychologists probably had a fancy name for it. The irrational, inane fear of making love to one's wife. It would take time for him to analyze what was going on inside his head. He didn't doubt his love. Riley was crazy about her, and committed to her, their child and their marriage.

In some ways, as weird as it sounded, Riley felt that he had a responsibility to Jerry Sanders. It fell heavily upon his shoulders. The *Atlantis* would be leaving again in the middle of January, a short three weeks away. All he had to do was keep his pants zipped until then. If he avoided situations such as the one he'd just encountered, everything would work out fine. Once he was back, Sam would be born and he'd face the issue then. But for now, he'd be content to let matters rest as they were.

Hannah didn't know what was different about Riley, but a subtle change had taken place in her husband since Christmas. He was attentive, generous, solicitous. Nevertheless Hannah couldn't shake the feeling he was avoiding her physically. If she had to come up with a word for it she'd say he'd become stingy with his kisses. *What* kisses? she mused, feeling both abused and melancholy.

She was baking cookies, remembering a piece of sage advice from years past. It was said the way to a man's heart passed directly through his stomach. Hannah swore that if chocolate-chip with walnuts didn't do the trick, she was going to do something desperate… like seduce him.

The thought was almost comical. What did she know of seduction? Well, she determined valiantly, she could learn.

Riley walked into the house sometime after five. Hannah had planned it carefully, so the aroma of melting chocolate would have its greatest impact right around then.

"What's cooking?" he asked, eagerly strolling into the kitchen. Absently he gave her a peck on the cheek and reached for a still-warm cookie.

Hannah had left her hair down, brushing it until it shone. She'd once read that men preferred it when women wore their hair loose. She'd dressed in her best pair of navy blue slacks and a pretty lavender top. There was no hiding her pregnancy, and she didn't even try.

"How'd your day go?" he asked conversationally while sorting through the mail, keeping his back to her. He gave no outward indication that he noticed she'd taken extra care with her appearance. Hannah swallowed a sigh of disappointment. Apparently it was going to take more than freshly baked cookies and a different hairstyle. She wasn't worried, however; there was always Plan B.

"My day went great. I got a call from the department

store." She paused for effect and lifted the last of the cookies off the baking sheet. "The crib and dresser we ordered are in." She glanced at him out of the corner of her eye. "The man said he could have them delivered tomorrow." She told him the last part, making sure her voice dipped significantly.

"Are you going to be around?"

Hannah nodded. "That isn't the problem."

"Then, what is?"

"Well…it's just that the baby's bedroom is going to be terribly crowded." She raised her eyes meaningfully to Riley, her look heavy with implication. Riley was an intelligent man. It wouldn't take him long to make the obvious connection and suggest she move her things out of her bedroom and into his. The chocolate-chip cookie he was eating stopped halfway to his lips. The bite that was in his mouth seemed to go down his throat whole—a lump moving in such tiny increments that she was certain he would choke on it.

"I was thinking," she continued, "I'd move my things into your room." If he wouldn't suggest it, then she would. "You don't mind, do you?" She smiled over at him, as sweetly as she knew how, and realized he'd gone pale.

"That shouldn't be any problem," he said after a long moment. "I'll move everything for you after dinner."

"Good." Hannah couldn't keep the excitement out of her voice.

Riley mumbled something under his breath, but Hannah didn't hear what it was. She would have asked him to repeat it, but she didn't think what he said was meant for her ears.

Riley walked over to the stove and picked up the lid of the small pot of stroganoff that was simmering on the back burner. He stared into the pot an extra-long time before replacing the top, then turned and walked toward the living room.

"Oh, before I forget, Cheryl phoned," Hannah added. "She invited us over to play cards next Saturday night. Do you have anything planned?"

"No." The word came out sounding far huskier than normal.

"I'll call her tomorrow then and tell her we'll be there. I told her I didn't know how to play pinochle, but she said it was easy to learn and that I'd pick it up in no time."

He nodded, but Hannah had the impression his mind wasn't on Cheryl's invitation or playing pinochle. "Isn't this Friday your poker night?"

He didn't answer her and seemed to be lost in a fog. "Riley?"

His gaze turned upward, meeting hers. The air in the room seemed to go still. Even the radio, which was playing in the corner, seemed to fade. Their gazes locked. Riley's expression was so tender, as though he derived a good deal of joy just looking at her. This night—either by hook or by crook, Hannah decided—she was going to make love with her husband.

From out of nowhere came the memory of the first night they'd slept together. She remembered the way he'd shaped his body around hers, holding her against him cocoon style, his long legs entwined with hers. She recalled, too, how she'd been forced to carefully lift his arm from her waist in order to escape his hold and steal away the following morning. A king-size lump formed in her throat, and it was all she could do not to promise him she'd never run away again.

"Poker?" he repeated after what seemed like a millennium. "I...don't remember. Why?"

"No reason. I was just wondering."

He walked out of the kitchen as though he weren't sure where he was headed. He stood in front of the picture window in the living room for several moments, although there was nothing going on outside that she could tell.

Hannah had the oddest feeling that if she were to speak to him, he wouldn't hear her. It was at times like these that she felt at such a loss.

True to his word, Riley helped transfer her personal items from one bedroom into the next while she washed the dinner dishes. He cleared a space for her in his closet and then carted her clothes across the hallway several hangers at a time. The chest of drawers took far more time and effort.

They played a game of Scrabble, which she won handily, and watched a little television. By nine-thirty Hannah was ready for bed.

Not so, Riley. He made an excuse of needing to gas up the car. He rejected her offer to go with him and suggested instead that she go to bed without him. He promised to join her later. Hannah could only agree, but she was determined to stay awake. He wouldn't thwart her that easily.

Riley sat in his car in the dark of the night, trying to come up with a logical excuse to find somewhere else to sleep for the next ten nights. It was only ten lousy nights before the *Atlantis* was scheduled to be deployed. Thus far he'd managed to keep his hands off Hannah, but he swore the woman was enough to tempt the saints.

Riley Murdock was no saint.

He didn't even make the pretense of being one. Hannah was home sleeping in his bed, and short of spending the night sitting in the cold, he'd soon be joining her there.

Hannah, all soft and warm with sleep, waiting for him to join her. In their bed. The very thought was enough to drive Riley to his knees.

He hadn't slept worth a damn since Christmas night, when she'd rushed into his arms and they'd come so close to making love. He'd seen the look in her eyes then: bold as could be.

Passion. A desire so strong that it awed him, and had haunted him every night since.

Riley didn't know how he was going to be able to resist her.

He knew his actions since Christmas had confused and flustered Hannah. Hell, he was baffled himself. Questions paraded through his mind each and every night. Plenty of questions and not a single answer.

He was a crazy man not to make love to Hannah when she'd given every indication that she'd welcome his attentions. He was certifiable. A candidate for intensive counseling.

The frightening part of all this was how much he wanted to make love with her. He thought about it constantly, but he couldn't make himself breach the barrier of his fears.

He'd hurt her again. He might injure the baby. He'd been too large for her that first night. She'd been so damned tight and hot.

Quickly Riley banished the memory from his mind, knowing if he didn't find something else to think about, he'd soon fall victim to his own needs.

Slowly, with a good deal of reluctance, he drove back to the house, noting when he walked inside that it was only a little after eleven. Hannah would be asleep by now. At least he wouldn't be left to contend with any of her questions. He wouldn't have any answers for her, either.

He undressed in the dark, showered and as silently as humanly possible, he slipped between the sheets, staying as far away from her as he could. It surprised him how easily he drifted off.

Riley woke sometime in the middle of the night to find Hannah lying facing him. He opened his eyes and breathed in the fresh, clean scent of her. Wildflowers. In full bloom.

A thick strand of hair had fallen across her face, and

although he feared he might wake her, he chanced lifting the shiny brown curl from her cheek and gently brushed it aside.

She was wearing the flannel nightgown. Riley never thought he'd appreciate the sexless thing, but he was wrong. He was eternally grateful she hadn't donned one of those sheer nighties. Or something made of silk. Silk was his downfall. The mental image of Hannah wearing a silk gown blossomed in his mind, and he banished the thought before it could take root. He had enough of a problem dealing with the reality of her in his bed without complicating his life by introducing fantasy.

Releasing a deep rush of air, Hannah scooted closer. So close he could almost hear her heart beating.

Closing his eyes, Riley tried to force himself to go back to sleep. Damn, but he could hear her heart beat. It was pulsing like crazy. No, he decided a second later; that was his own heart.

Slowly, against his better judgment, he brought his hand up to the front of her gown—just to determine if it was her pulse that was pounding so violently, he assured himself. If it was, then perhaps there was something medically wrong with her, or with the baby.

His hand slipped past the small pearl buttons, past the lace trim and edging of pink embroidery.

Past the point of no return.

A thin layer of perspiration broke out across Riley's upper lip as he pressed his palm to her chest.

The tips of his fingers felt for her pulse, but the heel of his hand rested against the bulging fullness of her lush breast. Riley's heart seemed to be working just fine, but his breathing came to an abrupt halt. An ache, low in his belly, began to pound like a giant fist.

Only it wasn't his stomach that was throbbing.

A better man than he might be able to resist Hannah. Jerry could resist her, but not Riley. Not for a second longer. His hands shook like a schoolboy's as he captured her breast in his palm. He lifted it, savored its weight and pear shape. She was right; they were fuller, sweetly fuller than he remembered.

Dear God, she felt good. He'd thought to relieve one ache and in the process created another—one that was ten times worse than the first.

He had to touch her, he realized; really touch her, or go mad. The pearl buttons slipped free of the restraining material with little more than a flick of his fingers, her gown spilling open wider and wider, granting him ample room to slip his hand inside.

He sighed out loud as her breast fell into his palm. Her nipple formed a hard bead against him, and unable to restrain himself, he groaned at the small intimacy.

Oh, God, what was he doing? Riley was nearly frantic with the knowledge of how far he'd allowed this little experiment to take him. His breathing was labored and deep. His heart beat high in his throat.

He was about to pull free, thinking he had never sunk lower than he had at that moment, when he noticed Hannah's beautiful gray eyes watching him in the dark.

Then she smiled—the sweetest, most dazzling smile he'd ever seen in his life. It seemed to light up the entire room.

"I remember how you sucked on them," she whispered into the stillness. He remembered, too, and against every dictate of his will he grazed the hard rosy tip with his thumb. He marveled at her quick, ready response.

"Do it again, Riley," she pleaded softly. "Like you did that night."

Riley didn't take the time to think; he couldn't. Instead, he crushed her mouth with his, frightening himself with the powerful need she created in him.

Their kiss was wet and wild. As their mouths ground against each other, Riley cupped her breasts, marveling once more at how incredibly soft her skin felt; softer than anything he'd ever touched. Softer than velvet. Softer than fur or silk.

Consumed in a fire of his own making, Riley slipped his mouth down the ivory perfection of her shoulders and finally to the swell of her breasts. His lips sought the nipple, drawing it forward, feasting on her, suckling until she moaned and arched her hips, seeking the pleasure she'd experienced all too briefly, all those months ago.

Riley longed to show her all the delightfully scandalous things they could do to please each other. But he dared not…not with Hannah. He would shock her, repulse her.

He used his tongue to create a wet, slick trail between her breasts, moistening, laving, sucking. He altered between gentle and not-so-gentle until Hannah raised the entire upper half of her body off the mattress in silent entreaty.

All ten of her fingers dug into his scalp. "Riley," she pleaded, "I need…"

Riley needed her, too. Needed to be released from the desire that was so strong it pained him. So wild it frightened him. So deep it humbled him.

He lifted his head and kissed her, keeping his hands busy molding, kneading, shaping her breasts. God help him, but he couldn't get enough of the feel of her.

Where he found the strength, Riley never knew. Slowly, he drew her head down to his chest and closed his eyes to the agony of physical frustration.

"Riley?"

"Shh… Sleep." He gently stroked her hair, praying, pleading, doing everything he could to force his mind from the beautiful soft woman in his arms.

"Sleep?"

"Sleep," he repeated. "We've both got to work tomorrow."

She was frustrated, too. Unsure. But he wouldn't answer her questions. It took some time before the smooth, even flow of her breathing convinced him she'd drifted off. At least one of them would get some rest that night, but it wouldn't be him.

Hannah chose the soft pink dress Riley had given her for Christmas to wear to Cheryl and Steve's for cards a week later. With a patience she hadn't expected, Riley had spent the better part of two evenings going over the fundamentals of pinochle with her. She'd never played cards much, but she was willing to learn, and Riley was tolerant with her lack of skill.

"You look...beautiful," he said, coming out of the bedroom. He stopped as though he couldn't take his eyes off her; but if that was the case, then he shouldn't be able to keep his hands off her, either. That certainly didn't seem to be a problem of late. They might as well not be married for all the good it did them. Riley was scheduled to ship out sometime early the following week, and they'd yet to make love.

Not from lack of trying, at least on Hannah's part.

Sometimes Hannah suspected he was playing a cruel game with her, but if that was the case, he was the one who was suffering.

Not once in the week since she'd moved into his bedroom had they managed to go to bed at the same time. Inevitably Riley came up with some nonsensical excuse to linger several minutes, and oftentimes hours after she was already in bed. Although she tried to wait up for him, she almost always fell asleep.

She found it uncanny that he would know just when she would be sleeping before he'd join her. Only once had he woken her, but when she'd tried to talk to him, he'd pretended to be exhausted, had rolled away from her and gone directly to sleep.

Pretended. Hannah was sure he was as wide-awake as she was.

In every other way, other than the physical aspect of their

marriage, he was a model husband. With the exception of the first night she'd moved into his bedroom, they hadn't so much as cuddled, at least not that Hannah was aware.

"I'm going out to start the car," Riley said, turning away from her. He'd taken to doing that lately—making sure it was warm and cozy inside before he came for her, not wanting to chance her catching a chill.

Hannah had been looking forward to this evening with Cheryl and Steve, even if it did involve playing cards. She was grateful for the friendship of the other Navy wives she'd met through Steve's wife.

Riley's hand was on her shoulder as they stood at the front door and rang the Morgans' doorbell.

"They must be making this a round-robin," he murmured.

"Round robin?" Hannah asked.

"That's Lenny's car across the street. And I noticed Floyd's one block over."

The door opened just then and Cheryl stepped forward, grinning from ear to ear. Standing between them, she took Riley's arm and then Hannah's, leading them into the living room.

Pink and blue strands of crepe paper were draped across the ceiling and the table was set with a large lace tablecloth and a pretty bouquet of pink and blue carnations.

"Surprise!" Cheryl cried, laughing and throwing her arms into the air.

Immediately people started popping out from every corner. Four jumped up from behind the davenport. Three came from the kitchen and as many more from the coat closet.

"What's going on here?" Riley asked, clearly perplexed.

"Don't you recognize a baby shower when you see one?" Cheryl chided.

"A baby what?" Riley asked again, scratching his head. He looked to Hannah for an explanation.

"It's a party for the baby," Hannah told him, smiling. She recognized several of the wives and a couple of the husbands.

"Here, 'ol buddy," Steve said, handing Riley a cold can of soda. "Sit down and we'll explain everything." Riley cast a dumbfounded look over his shoulder as Steve led him toward the front of the room and sat him down. Next, Riley's friend escorted Hannah to the second chair and then placed a paper crown from a fast-food restaurant on top of each of their heads.

"I thought only women had parties for babies," Riley muttered under his breath.

"I did, too," she whispered back.

Cheryl dragged out a card table stacked high with gifts.

Hannah couldn't remember a time when she'd had more fun. Jenny Blackwell, Floyd's wife, had baked a cake in the shape of a stork delivering the baby and had done an incredible job. It was almost too beautiful to eat. Riley, however, had no such qualms. He sliced off huge pieces and passed them around to his friends, then wolfed down two slices himself.

When it came time to open the gifts, everyone gathered around. Hannah was self-conscious about being the center of attention as she carefully pried away the paper. Each gift touched her heart. There were so many things, big and small, they needed yet for the baby, and it meant so much to her that Riley's friends would do this for them.

"Is this the gal?" Floyd Blackwell asked, claiming the empty chair beside Riley while the others chatted around them. He had a kind, round face, and a bald spot was beginning to form on the crown of his head.

"Yes," Riley replied stiffly, glancing anxiously toward Hannah.

"I thought it must be." He laughed and took a generous bite of the cake his wife had baked. "I'll tell you right now," he said to Hannah, "you certainly sent Riley on a merry goose chase. He spent the entire month of August looking for you." He turned to Riley, disregarding the deep scowl. "Did that private detective ever turn up anything?"

"Floyd," Riley prompted meaningfully between clenched teeth, "don't I hear Jenny calling you?"

"Jenny. Naw, she's across the room talking to Cheryl. Oh… Oh, right. Yes, well, it was nice meeting you, Hannah," he finished, rushing to his feet.

"What was Floyd talking about?" Hannah asked her husband a few minutes later.

"Nothing. He was just blowing some hot air."

Hannah didn't believe that for a moment, and was left to ponder Floyd's words. Had Riley tried to find her after that night? It certainly sounded like it. The knowledge did funny things to her heart. He had cared even then.

It was after eleven by the time they arrived back home. Riley unloaded the gifts from the car while Hannah carried in leftover cake. The night had been such fun, and Hannah had enjoyed every minute of it. Even Riley seemed to be in an extra-good mood.

To Hannah's way of thinking, the time to strike was while the iron was hot, an old cliché she'd often heard her father use.

While she was in changing for bed, Riley sat out in the living room, reading the newspaper.

He didn't look up when she entered the room, and she noticed that he'd brewed himself a cup of coffee as though he intended to stay up a while longer. His hand held a pen as if he planned on working through the crossword puzzle.

She was determined to see that that didn't happen.

"Riley, come to bed."

"I will in a few minutes," he replied, studying the paper, still not glancing toward her.

"Not tonight."

"I beg your pardon." He looked up, and Hannah could have kissed him for the reaction he gave. She'd combed her hair, spreading it across her shoulders like a giant fan. The peach silk gown clung to her, and she reached for its satin tie, releasing the front.

"It's time to come to bed. Now," she said, holding her hand out to him.

Chapter Twelve

Riley's heart sank all the way to the soles of his feet. Never in all his life had he seen a woman more beautiful than Hannah in this silky peach gown, her thick shiny hair as rich looking as velvet.

His heart rebounded just enough for him to breathe. Just enough for the overwhelming physical attraction to bombard his stomach. Nothing seemed real anymore. He felt as though he were sitting in a thick fog, a haze of remorse. Riley had the feeling that if he were to find the strength to stand, he'd crumple to the carpet like a rag doll.

"Hannah," he managed to say, although his voice was little more than a hoarse whisper, "what is this?"

"You mean you don't know?"

The hell if Riley knew how someone so innocent in the ways of seduction could be so damned provocative. She sashayed toward him, swaying her hips with the right amount of allure. A stripteaser couldn't have walked as enticingly; Riley was convinced of that. He couldn't take his eyes off her, feasting on the outline of her swollen breasts and the way the silk seemed to wrap its way around her thighs. His thoughts were in a muddle as he scrambled for some excuse, something to say or do that would help him to gently turn her away.

"It's time for bed," she announced, her smile so sweet

it was all he could do not to go into a deep trance just looking at her.

He sat numb, unable to move or think. "I…ah…I'm not quite ready yet. You go on ahead without me."

"Not tonight, Riley." She continued smiling down on him as she removed the pen from his lifeless fingers and tugged the newspaper free from his grasp. Like a man lost in a stupor, he allowed her to do both without offering the least bit of resistance.

She hesitated when he didn't rise from the recliner and mindlessly follow her into the bedroom. It seemed to take her a few seconds to regroup, but she did so with amazing dexterity. She smiled once again and nestled herself into his lap with a childlike eagerness. Only there wasn't anything childish about the look in her eyes, or the captivating way the corners of her mouth tilted upward.

Her gaze continued to hold his as her fingers expertly unfastened the buttons of his shirt. She wasn't satisfied until she had peeled it open and could press her hands fully against his heaving chest. At the feel of her fingers against him, Riley's breath escaped on a ragged sigh. Encouraged by her success, she sighed, too, and her smile deepened.

"Hannah…I don't think…" He didn't finish. His wife bent forward and pressed her soft, sweet mouth against the side of his neck. Her touch—velvet gentle, satin smooth—went through him like a hunting knife. Her breath was as hot as fire. Hotter than a raging inferno. Using the moist tip of her tongue, she seared a trail of moist kisses against his throat.

Riley's head fell back and he closed his eyes.

Despite his pleading, Hannah continued to work her mouth across his face. She paused at his earlobe, taking it into her mouth and sucking lightly, flickering her tongue around the outer edges and gently probing inside. Riley moaned, willing his hands not to touch her, clenching them into tight fists at his sides. The minute he experienced for himself her incredible softness, he'd be lost, and he knew it.

Her splayed fingers slid upward until they'd linked at his nape. Slowly she released his ear, continuing her journey downward, sliding her tongue over the muscular cords of his neck, pausing at the hollow of his throat. Unexpectedly she paused, altering the course of her lips, moving upward, along the underside of his chin and the sharp angles of his jaw, journeying toward his mouth.

"Hannah…oh, God…no." His hands locked around her wrists, his grip viselike. He pushed her away from him and held her there. His eyes burned into hers while his chest heaved with the overwhelming effort of resisting her.

"Yes," she countered softly, apparently not understanding. She was soft and warm and so beautiful. Every part of him throbbed with the need to give her what she was asking for. Come morning, however, he would regret it. Riley knew it as surely as he knew he loved her. He was protecting her, protecting their child.

Turning her away was far more painful for him than it was for her. In time she'd understand he was doing the admirable thing. In time she'd appreciate the sacrifice he was making.

"Not now," he said again, more forcefully this time.

She blinked, stunned. "When?"

"Later," he answered with confidence. "After the baby's born."

Hannah jerked her head back and went pale as if he'd slapped her hard. She was in such a rush to leave him, she nearly fell onto the carpet in the process of climbing off his lap. Her breath came in staggered gasps as she backed away from him, her hands at her throat. Huge, glistening tears brimmed and then spilled like pearl-shaped drops of dew from her eyes. She had the stricken look of someone in great pain.

"Hannah…" Riley thought he'd feel noble and generous, doing the right thing. Instead, he felt like a louse. "I…want you. It's just that—"

"Not now, you don't!" she raged, tears streaming down her face in a flood of emotion. "Not when I'm fat and ugly with your child!" She stumbled as she turned to run from him, nearly colliding with the end of the sofa. She caught herself, then raced toward their bedroom, slamming the door. The sound echoed in the room like a pistol shot.

Hannah's sobs tore into Riley's heart like the edge of a dull, rusty knife. He'd never meant to hurt Hannah. He was only trying to do what was right.

Suddenly he felt weary, more tired than he'd ever been in his life. Tired of being virtuous. Sick and tired of living up to the standards of a dead man. He'd leave nobility for men like Jerry Sanders, who'd been born for such things.

Abruptly he stood, and never feeling more at a loss in dealing with his gently reared wife, he headed for the bedroom. His hand was on the knob when he paused. Sure as hell, he'd hate himself in the morning if he made love to her. The regret would eat at him like battery acid, the way it had the night of Seafair. The guilt of breaking the promise he'd made to himself would consume him, come dawn. It would follow him out to sea and haunt him the long months they'd be apart. If there were any complications when the baby was born, Riley knew he would blame himself for these moments of weakness.

Regrets were a funny thing, Riley mused darkly. He'd lived with them most his life in one form or another. One important rule about remorse, something profound he'd garnered over the years: if he was going to suffer regret, then he made damn sure it was worthwhile.

With that thought in mind, he pushed open the door and walked inside their bedroom.

Hannah was sprawled on top of the mattress, sobbing as though her heart were shattered. Knowing he was the cause of those tears ate at him like the teeth of a piranha. Not knowing exactly what to do to comfort her, he hesitantly walked across the room and sat on the edge of the bed. Poising his hand above her, he hesitated still, then gently began to pat her shoulder.

The instant she felt his touch, Hannah jerked away as though she found him repulsive.

"Leave me alone," she wailed.

"Can we talk?".

"No." She scooted out of his reach, so far away it was a wonder she didn't topple onto the carpet on the other side of the bed.

"I don't find you ugly," Riley said, rushing to ease her mind. "You're so beautiful, I can't keep my eyes off you."

She raised her head and glared at him, her look hot enough to blister paint. It was more than apparent she didn't believe him.

"Come here, Hannah."

"No… If you so much as touch me, I swear…I'll phone the police."

"You'd better start dialing now," he muttered. Standing, he shucked his shirt, balled it up in his hands and tossed it on the floor. His slacks came off next.

"Wh-what are you doing?" she demanded, her voice trembling. She crowded into the corner of the bed, drawing her feet under her, her hands clenched over her breasts.

"What does it look like?" he answered calmly. "I'm getting ready to make love to my wife."

Royalty couldn't have tilted a chin with more finesse. "Don't do me any favors, Riley Murdock."

"The only favors we'll be giving will be to each other," he assured her, pulling back the sheets and climbing inside the bed. She continued to stare at him as though he were a stranger. In many ways he was, even to himself. "I'm going to need some help," he told her, unaccustomed to dealing with the intensity of the feelings she aroused in him. Even though she was on the other side of the bed, her effect upon him was total. His need for her clawed at him. "I don't want this to be like the first time. I don't want to hurt you."

"You didn't," she whispered in a soft, meek voice. "It... was just that I wasn't expecting...you know."

"Yes, I do know. I'm sorry." He held out his arms to her. "We'll start by kissing and go slow and easy. Just promise to tell me if I'm hurting you."

She hesitated as if she weren't sure she could believe him, as though she were frightened even now that he'd reject her.

"Promise me," he repeated, holding his arms out to her.

"I promise." She made the short journey across the bed to his side, slipping her arms around him and pressing her head to his chest. Every place she touched him branded Riley. Closing his eyes, he willed himself to remain cool-headed and in control. They'd go about this slow and easy. With that thought in mind, he directed his mouth to hers.

His intentions were lost, cast into a never-never world where all good intentions eventually landed, the instant their lips touched.

Riley was desperate for Hannah. Desperate and greedy. And she for him. Their kisses were primitive and wild, a raging storm of need, too long repressed.

The desire to woo Hannah, to seduce her gently, to cast aside all fear and pain, was lost; vanished on a tide of need so overwhelming there was no turning back, no time for second thoughts, no time except to feel.

Hannah moaned in welcome, opening her mouth to him. Riley plunged his tongue forward, probing deeply, to mate with hers in a frenzied erotic game. He lowered his head and dragged a gulp of air into his lungs as he blazed fire-hot, love-hot kisses down her throat and neck. Her hands clawed at him, wanting more, demanding more. He tangled his fingers in her hair and rushed his mouth back to hers. Her lips were wet and warm and welcome, so damned welcome.

The sound of her whimper was the purest form of ecstasy he'd ever known. His groan echoed hers as he dragged his hands, almost against his will, down the silky-smooth front of her gown. He was rewarded as the fullness of her breasts filled his palms. Her nipples hardened instantly, and it was all Riley could do not to cry out. Hannah whimpered anew and arched toward him.

Riley's hands continued their downward progression, resting on the swell of her abdomen that was their growing child, reminding him of the rich fruit their lovemaking had planted.

"I'm so big," she moaned between kisses.

"So damned beautiful."

His hands roved around the thickness of her waist and over the sculpted contours of her hips to the perfect roundness of her buttocks. He dragged her closer to him, savoring the feel of her against the heat of his groin. Inch by sweet inch, Riley's fingers worked the silk gown upward until his hands met her bare thighs. Fire, the hottest he'd ever known, singed his fingers as he stroked the warm silk on the insides of her smooth legs.

"Hannah…" He felt he had to warn her of the coming invasion. "I'm going to touch you."

"Yes, oh…please." She parted for him, her eyes bright with passion, locking with his in the muted moonlight. She bit into her lower lip as his finger slipped steadily upward. She groaned softly as he deftly parted the folds of her womanhood. Riley stilled, his heart racing, afraid he was doing something to pain her.

"Don't stop," she pleaded, her long fingers digging into his shoulders. Her hips swayed, urging him to continue. Riley didn't need any encouragement. He wanted this as much as she did. He was ready to explode, had been from their first kiss and he wasn't even inside her yet.

His finger continued its silken journey until he'd sunk as far as he dared go. The heat of her, the moist honey of her readiness produced a groan of heady excitement from Riley.

"Are you ready?" Her body was prepared, but he found it equally important that she be mentally primed for the physical realities of their lovemaking.

His hands trembled as he tugged the gown over her head and discarded it. He longed to talk to her, to ease her fears and any discomfort she might experience when he entered her. But he found himself incapable of muttering a single sound. His fears were rampant. He was afraid he'd be too heavy for her. That he was too large for her. He feared his weight might somehow injure the child.

Hannah must have read the uncertainty in his eyes. "It's all right," she whispered, linking her arms around his neck, bringing him down to her. She kissed him as though that would convince him all was well.

"The baby?"

"Will be fine…. I'm not so sure about me, though, if you keep me waiting much longer."

Riley loved her in that moment, more deeply than he thought it was possible to love another. Taking infinite care, he moved over her, lowering himself between her legs, which she'd willingly parted for him. His gaze burned into hers. Going as slowly as his body would allow, he positioned himself and entered her unhurriedly, watching her closely for any sign of pain or discomfort, giving her ample time to adjust to him, to his body invading hers.

Hannah closed her eyes and dragged in a deep breath.

"I'm hurting you?"

"No…not in the least. I…don't remember it feeling this good." Her hands tightened around his neck, and she hooked her feet around the backs of his knees and shifted upward, as though taking in every part of him were of the utmost importance.

When he was as deep as he dared sink, he shuddered, surrounded as he was by the most intense pleasure. Surrounded by joy. And love. He stared down on her, his heart full, and she looked up at him, her gaze as warm as liquid honey.

"You're sure?" He had to ask, had to know.

"Yes…oh, please."

A frenzy of long-denied need overtook him then as his hips pumped against hers. Rhythm was lost to him. So was the proper pacing. He took her swiftly. Then slowly. Then fiercely. Then gently. Their mating was wild and raw and hot. So unbelievably hot that Riley felt consumed by the fire of his need. Of her need. Of them together.

Riley's completion came in minutes, with a flash of pleasure so keen it bordered on pain. It was over. Far too quickly. Much too soon.

He hadn't finished making love to Hannah and already he was worrying about how long it would be before he could have her again.

Holding her against him, his hands in her hair, he savored the closeness they shared. Wrapping his legs around hers, Riley rolled onto his side, taking her with him, maintaining the intimate link between them.

Their eyes met and Hannah released a soft, feminine sigh, then smiled. Tears streaked her face, and Riley reached out and, frowning, brushed them aside. He'd hurt her, only she'd never admit it. His stomach tightened.

Hannah must have read his fears. She captured his hand and brought it to her mouth, kissing his palm. "No…you don't understand. It was so…beautiful. What took you so long, my love? What took you so long?" She draped her arms around his neck and snuggled against him, engulfing him in tenderness and warmth. Her warmth. Her love.

Within minutes she was sound asleep.

Not so, Riley. He lay there, soaking in her nearness, savoring these few precious hours. Drinking in her gentle ways, her generosity and her love. He'd never thought to experience this time with a woman.

If it hadn't been for Hannah, he probably would never have married. He'd rejected the idea years before, not wanting a woman complicating his life. Instead he had brief affairs, so that he could walk away with callous indifference whenever he chose. He preferred it that way, he'd assured himself. He wasn't interested in commitment; he didn't want demanding relationships.

He'd never realized, he'd never known all that he'd been missing until Hannah came into his life. Hunger claimed him—not a physical craving, but an emotional one—for what he'd learned, for what he'd discovered because of the woman asleep in his arms.

Resting his hand on the rounded curve of her stomach, Riley closed his eyes to the wealth of love and emotion he experienced for their child. With everything in him, he regretted he'd be gone when his son or daughter was born. The thought of Hannah in pain, struggling to give life to his child, sent cold chills down his spine.

He knew little of the ways of a woman's body and even less about babies. He had heard the birthing process was often difficult and always painful. It wasn't unheard of for a woman to die while in labor. The mere thought of losing Hannah sent his heart into a panic. From the first visit, Dr. Underwood had assured Riley that Hannah's pregnancy was progressing normally; as far as he could judge. And he'd delivered hundreds of babies. Hannah's delivery would be routine.

Riley fretted about her being alone, but he'd spoken to Cheryl Morgan, who'd faithfully promised him she'd keep in close contact with Hannah.

From a few subtle questions she'd asked and the odd look she'd given him, Riley knew his friend's wife was openly curious about how someone like him had married a sweet innocent like Hannah. It remained a mystery to nearly everyone. Only a handful of people was aware of the story—his commanding officer, the chaplain and a couple of others. For Hannah's sake, Riley strove to keep it that way. The less anyone knew, the better. Not that he felt the need to protect Hannah's reputation. Hannah had more admirers than she knew. His single friends would have welcomed the opportunity to defend her honor, especially Don and Burt.

Riley got a kick out of the way they acted around her. Both were foulmouthed, hard-drinking cusses who welcomed an excuse to fight. Riley found it downright comical the way they stumbled over one another looking for a reason to do things for her.

The baby shower was a prime example. Riley knew Cheryl Morgan had organized it, but he'd never thought he'd see the day Don and Burt would sit around making small talk and eating cake with a bunch of Navy wives. Hell, he'd never thought he'd see the day himself. Nor would he ever believe he'd hold up tiny little sleepers and ooh and ahh over them like a softhearted woman. But he had, and his burly friends with him.

Riley could feel welcome sleep coaxing him into a soothing void. Sam would be born with or without him sometime within the next two months; and God willing, all would go well.

"Riley," Hannah whispered in the early-morning light. He slept soundly at her side; the even rise and fall of his chest had mesmerized her for the past several minutes. She scooted closer and pressed her head against his chest.

"Hmm."

"I love you." She had to say it, had to let him know what had been in her heart all these weeks. Tell him or burst with emotion. "I'm so proud to be your wife."

"After the incredible sex we just shared, I'm proud, too."

His arms cradled her against him, and he wore a silly, lazy grin. "What time is it?"

"Four."

"What are you doing awake at this hour?" His eyes were closed, and he seemed far more interested in sleeping than carrying on a conversation with her.

"Watching you. I have a…question." She was pleased it was still dark, otherwise he'd know she was blushing.

"Hmm?"

"That night…in Seattle?"

"Yes?" Slowly, reluctantly, he opened his eyes and looked at her.

"We…you know…made love twice?"

Riley frowned, as though he weren't sure he understood what she was asking. "Yes."

"Do…men and women often do it twice in one night?" Her finger made lazy circles on his chest, curling the short, kinky hairs around her index finger. Her eyes purposely avoided his.

"Sometimes."

"Oh." She released a long, meaningful sigh.

"Why do you ask?"

"I was curious."

"I'm curious, too," he whispered hoarsely, and tunneling his fingers through her hair, he brought her mouth to his, slipping his tongue inside. While their mouths were joined, he rolled onto his back, taking her with him so that her legs were straddling his torso.

She raised questioning eyes to his, slowly, meaningfully. "There are other ways?"

He grinned, his look almost youthful as he nodded. "Plenty. With you like this there's less likelihood we'll injure the baby."

It was in her mind to assure him they hadn't earlier, but the need for assurances was taken from her as Riley directed her mouth down to his. The only words either murmured after that were sighs, and moans, and whimpers of pleasure and love.

"You've got the doctor's phone number by the bed stand?"

"You know I do," Hannah answered. He'd asked the same question no less than three times in the last ten minutes. She sat on the edge of the mattress, leaning back on her hands, while he finished packing his duffel bag.

"Your bag is packed?"

"Riley," she said with an exasperated sigh, "the baby isn't due for another eight and a half weeks. Worry about your own packing. I'll be doing mine soon enough."

He stalked to the far side of their bedroom and stuffed what remained of this gear into the thick canvas bag with enough force to punch out the bottom. "I don't want you lifting anything heavier than three pounds, understand?"

"Aye, aye, sir." She gave him a mocking salute behind his back.

"Your job?"

"We agreed when I was hired it would only be for a few months. I won't work past February. I promise." Once again she smiled.

"Dammit, Hannah, this isn't a laughing matter."

"I'm not laughing," she assured him, giving her voice just the right amount of contriteness to convince him she was sincere.

"Then why do I have the feeling you find this all a big joke?" He straightened and plowed his fingers through his hair. It was so rare to see Riley ruffled that Hannah honestly enjoyed it. Now that he was only a few hours from deployment, the realization he'd be leaving seemed to have hit him like a sledgehammer.

"Honest to God, Hannah," he whispered, "I've never been more terrified in my life and you're handling the whole thing like some…"

"Joke," she finished for him. "The baby and I are going to be just fine. There's nothing to indicate we won't be, so stop worrying."

"I know. But things could go wrong."

"They won't."

"I wish I could be here."

"I do, too. I'm sorry you can't, sorrier than you know. But it isn't the end of the world." She did her best to give the appearance of being cool and collected. No one knew better than she how overwrought her husband had become in the last few days before deployment.

"You'll keep in touch?"

Like everything else, he'd explained how the family grams worked a dozen or more times. Half the instructions he'd given her had been repeated so often that Hannah could recite them in her sleep. "I'll send one every available opportunity."

He sighed once more. "You realize the chaplain's office might not be able to contact me right away."

"Yes," she said patiently. "You already explained that, too. If the *Atlantis* is in an 'alert' status, then it could be some time before you're notified of Sam's birth."

"I won't be able to contact you even when I am told."

"I realize that, too," she assured him softly. The teasing banter she'd hidden behind earlier vanished as the reality hit her. She wasn't frightened—not of the actual birth—but everything within her longed for Riley to be able to share the experience with her.

"I couldn't bear it if anything happened to you," he whispered hoarsely.

"Nothing will. I promise." She bravely attempted to console him with a smile.

"Take care of yourself?" His gaze had never been more tender.

"Every minute of every day."

He moved across the bedroom and sank to his knees in

front of her. He gripped both her hands and pressed his lips against the tips of her fingers. His shoulders heaved as he exhaled a sharp, anxious sigh. Gently, lovingly, he moved his hands over her abdomen and leaned forward to gently, sweetly kiss her stomach.

"Chinese, again?" Cheryl asked.

Hannah giggled. "I have this incredible urge for pork-fried rice, and before you ask, I wouldn't even think of using soy sauce."

The two were spending a lazy Saturday afternoon in the Kitsap Mall, window-shopping. Hannah's due date was a week away, and she'd never felt more hearty. In the last week she'd accomplished more than in the past several that Riley had been out to sea.

The days had sped past on winged feet, one often blending into the next. She was so busy that despite dreadfully missing Riley, the days piled on top of one another like professional football players.

Her visits to Dr. Underwood were weekly now. Hannah had felt huge at seven months. Months eight and nine were like nature's cruel joke. No longer could she stand upright and view her feet. She'd given up wearing shoes that entailed tying; it would be simpler to wrestle a crocodile. If there was anything to be grateful for, it was that Riley wasn't there to fuss over her. If he'd been solicitous at seven months, she hated to think how he'd behave now.

She was miserable, true; but not overly so. If she had anyone to complain about it was Cheryl, who'd become as much a mother hen as Riley had been. Hannah honestly thought Cheryl had taken lessons from Riley.

Hannah swore her friend would follow her into the bathroom, if she would let her. The only thing she could figure was that Riley had gotten hold of the nurse and made her promise on her mother's grave to take care of Hannah.

For a nurse who dealt daily with the birthing process, Cheryl behaved as though Hannah were the first woman alive to become pregnant.

"Isn't that blue dress a knockout?" Cheryl asked, pausing in front of MaryLou's Dress Shop. "I should try it on, just for the fun of it. Something like that would drive Steve wild. Not that he needs much." She laughed at her own joke. "Hannah?"

"Oh, it's cute, real cute." The dress was that and more, although Hannah had given it only a fleeting glance.

"Something's wrong?"

"No…" Hannah wasn't sure.

Cheryl gripped her arm, dragging her to the thick polished bench in the middle of the mall floor. "Let's sit down."

"I'm all right," Hannah protested. "I'm just feeling a little…strange."

"Strange as in how?"

"Strange as in…oh…oh." Her eyes rounded as she shot her gaze up to her friend. "If I'm not mistaken, that was a…labor pain."

Chapter Thirteen

Riley had been on edge all day. As Hannah's due date approached, the weight of their separation pressed on him unlike anything he'd ever experienced. To love a woman, to care so deeply about her well-being was foreign to him. He was at a loss to know how to deal with his worries.

Others around him slept without a qualm. But the escape of slumber evaded Riley. Rather than fight it, he'd lain back in his berth and stared into the dark. His thoughts were heavy, his anxiety high.

In the last two family grams he'd received, Hannah had claimed all was well with her and Sam. But no matter how many times he'd read the words, analyzed the few sentences she was allowed to transmit, Riley was left with the feeling something wasn't right. His fears were widespread, and once again he silently cursed the necessity of being at sea during these last worrisome months of her pregnancy.

His friends were little help. Steve wasn't a father yet, so he knew little of the…

A father. Riley hesitated as the word passed through his mind with the speed of a laser beam. He was about to become a father. Funny, from the time he'd learned of Hannah's pregnancy, he'd never thought of himself in those terms.

A father.

He knew little of such matters, he acknowledged, frowning. He'd never had the opportunity to know the man who'd sired him. From what Riley understood, his own father had been unaware of his birth. The man, who would forever remain a mystery to him, had contributed little to his emotional and physical well-being. The only male influence Riley had received had come from his stepfather, an abusive alcoholic who'd paid him little attention.

Riley experienced an overwhelming surge of gratitude that he'd learned of Hannah's pregnancy. In different circumstances he might never have known of it. He would have gone about his life blithely unaware of Sam's existence, and would have missed so much more than he'd ever thought to experience.

Considering the responsibility that awaited him with his child's birth overwhelmed Riley. He knew so little of the ways of a father, and even less of love. But Hannah had taught him the very meaning of the word, and he was confident Sam would give him all the instruction he'd need to be a father.

A daddy, he amended, grinning.

A sigh quivered through his lungs, and he closed his eyes, content for the first time that day. He could sleep now, entrusting the well-being of his wife and child to a far greater power than his own.

"Lieutenant Commander Kyle would like a word with you."

Riley's heart skipped a beat, then raced with such velocity he went dizzy and weak. There was only one reason the executive officer would want to speak to Riley.

Hannah.

The rush with which he moved through the tight quarters of the nuclear submarine caused more than a few stares. His eyes connected with the other man's, and the lieutenant commander grinned broadly.

"You wanted to see me, sir?"

Lieutenant Commander Kyle was the best kind of officer. Riley had known him several years and liked him immensely. There wasn't a man aboard the *Atlantis* who didn't. Word had it the executive officer had been divorced for nearly two years and then had reunited with his wife. He'd been to hell and back, according to those who knew him best. Whatever the cause of his problems, he'd solved them and took an interest in his men and their lives.

The CO's grin broadened as he held his hand out to Riley. "Congratulations are in order. We received word a few minutes ago that your wife has given birth to a healthy eight-pound three-ounce boy. Mother and son are doing well."

"A...son." The words barely worked their way past a lump in his throat that was so large it made it painful to breathe.

"Hannah?"

"According to the wire, she's fine."

Riley nodded. He'd heard the CO say it once, but he needed to be sure, to calm the doubts and the fears that crowded his heart and mind.

"Eight pounds?"

"Big and healthy." The lieutenant commander slapped him across the back. "You look like you need to sit down, Murdock."

"I feel like I need to."

The commanding officer chuckled. "I understand that well. My second child, Patrick, was born while I was at sea. I wasn't a damn bit of good to the Navy until I knew Carol had had a safe delivery."

A numbness had claimed hold of Riley, starting in his chest and radiating outward, paralyzing his lungs.

"A son," he repeated when he could.

"I take it you wanted a boy."

Riley didn't answer right away. "I suppose I did, but I wouldn't have been disappointed with a daughter."

The other man nodded. "Our first was a girl, and I couldn't have been more pleased, although I'd convinced myself I wanted a son. Somehow, once they arrive, all pink and soft, it doesn't seem to matter."

They spoke for a few minutes more, then Riley returned to the torpedo room. He felt fiercely proud, an emotion so profound it was all he could do not to throw his arms in the air and shout for the sheer joy of it. The crazy part was, the desire to fall to his knees and weep was just as compelling.

He had a son. Samuel Riley Murdock. Moisture blurred his vision, and Riley realized it was tears of jubilation; his heart felt so full of love he couldn't contain it any longer.

He had a son.

Hannah studied the clock on the wall of her hospital room, which was partially obliterated by two bright-blue helium balloons that were tied to the foot of her bed. Cheryl Morgan was scheduled to go on duty in fifteen minutes and had promised to stop in for a short visit beforehand.

Hannah had been waiting to talk to Cheryl all afternoon. Her mind was on her son, who was sleeping serenely at her side. She'd been overwhelmed by the outpouring of love and attention she'd received after Samuel's birth. She hadn't lacked for visitors. Cards lined her nightstand, and her small locker was filled with gifts.

"So how's it going, little mother?" Cheryl asked, stepping into the room. She was dressed in her uniform and a soft blue sweater.

The minute Hannah saw her, she couldn't help herself— she burst into tears. "I'm fine," she wailed, and reached for a tissue, blowing her nose.

"New-mother blues?" Cheryl asked sympathetically, handing Hannah the entire box of tissues. "Don't worry, it's to be expected. With so many hormones swimming around, your emotions are bound to be in upheaval."

"It's not that," Hannah sobbed, pointing toward the window ledge where a beautiful bouquet of a dozen red and white roses was perched. "Riley had one of his friends on the base send them to me… The card…"

"The card was sweet and sentimental?" Cheryl coaxed.

"No," she wailed. "The next time I see that man I'm going…to…slap him silly. I'm…so angry I could just spit."

"Angry?"

"Read it for yourself. Then you'll know." Hannah picked up the small envelope and handed it to her friend.

Cheryl's gaze narrowed as she slipped out the card and read the few scribbled words. Slowly she raised her gaze to Hannah, her look wide and questioning. "It says, 'I love you.' It's signed, 'Riley.'"

Hannah sobbed once more and in a fit of righteousness tossed the damp tissue to the foot of her bed. "See what I mean?"

"Those are certainly fighting words if I ever heard them," came the sarcastic comment. "Are you going to torture him with the silent treatment once he arrives home?"

"I should." Using the heels of her hands, Hannah rubbed the moisture from her burning cheeks, irked all the more. "He hasn't even got the common decency to tell me to my face," she announced, and swallowed a hiccup.

"Let me see if I understand this," Cheryl said, pulling up a chair and sitting down. "The card claims he loves you, and that makes you angry?"

"Yes," Hannah snapped.

"He's not supposed to love you?"

"Well, of course he is."

"I see," Cheryl replied, frowning.

It was apparent her friend didn't understand anything

of what had happened. "You don't see," Hannah argued. "Otherwise you'd be as outraged as I am."

"Maybe you'd better explain it to me." Cheryl crossed her legs and leaned back as though convinced it would take considerable time to explain why Hannah had taken such offense at Riley's card.

Actually, Hannah wasn't eager to rationalize her outrage, but there didn't seem to be any help for it. "It's Riley."

"That much I gathered."

"He…had his friend send the flowers with the card."

"I'm with you so far," Cheryl prompted with one solid nod of her head.

"It's what he said on the card—that he loves me."

"I understand that part, too, only I seem to be missing some key link."

Hannah's eyes filled with fresh tears. "I love him so much and…and he's never told me he loves me. Not even once—and then he has to do it in a stupid card when I can't be there to look in his eyes."

"Ah," Cheryl murmured after a significant pause. "So you doubt he truly loves you?"

"Not really. It's just that he's been too stubborn to realize it. I knew he would in time…. It's just that I wanted to be there when he finally got around to admitting it."

"Ah." The light was dawning in Cheryl's expressive eyes.

"You know what he is? A coward," Hannah answered her own question, without giving Cheryl the opportunity. "Riley Murdock is a living, breathing coward. If word got out what a…"

"Coward," Cheryl supplied.

"Right. If the Navy knew what I do about him, they'd ask for his resignation." She looked to Steve's wife for confirmation and was disappointed.

"I don't agree."

"Come on, Cheryl. You can't join my pity party if you're going to be obstinate about everything."

Her friend's face broke into a wide smile. "Anyone with one good eye would know how Riley feels about you. The man's so bewitched it isn't even funny."

Hannah felt herself go all soft. "Do you really think so?"

"Hannah," Cheryl said, her eyes brightening as she spoke. "If I hadn't seen it for myself, I would never have believed it. The man's crazy about you. He loves you so much it's eating him alive."

"But he's never said so."

"I doubt that he knows how."

"Really?" To Hannah's way of thinking, it would have been a simple matter for him to tell her. She'd told him often enough during the last days before he left for sea duty. Oftentimes she'd been left to wonder. The only time they'd made love was the night of the baby shower. It had been so beautiful, so perfect. Just thinking about the tender way in which her husband had made love to her filled Hannah's eyes with fresh tears.

Her disappointment had been keen when he didn't make love to her again before his departure. She knew he was worried about leaving her, worried about the baby being born while he was at sea. Hannah doubted he'd slept two winks that last night. He'd held on to her tightly until dawn. She'd woken once to find his hand softly rubbing her stomach. Hannah had wanted to assure him that she and Sam would be fine, but in the end he was the one offering promises before coaxing her back to sleep.

"Give Riley time," Cheryl advised softly. "I've seen so many changes in him since you've come into his life, and I'm beginning to think we've only viewed the tip of the iceberg."

Gradually, after listening to her friend, Hannah agreed. Her marriage was in its infancy; the best was yet to come.

"It won't be long now," Hannah whispered to the sleeping infant tucked securely in her arms. Her gaze rested lovingly on her five-week-old son as she held him tightly against her, blocking out the April wind. Within a few minutes, her husband would view his son and see for himself the thick thatch of brown hair and high, smooth brow that was all Riley. The dimple on Samuel's chin wasn't as pronounced now as it had been the first couple of weeks following his birth. Their son was perfect, beautiful. If some doubted Riley was Samuel's father, all they'd need do was to look into her son's deep blue eyes and note the strong, dominant chin to be reassured.

As before, the wharf was crowded with the wives and children of the members of the *Atlantis* crew. Hannah had heard plenty of grumbling among the wives. Cheryl and Hannah had muttered their own fair share. The nuclear submarine was docking nearly two weeks later than the wives had been told to anticipate.

The last sixty minutes felt like sixty years to Hannah. And the days before had merged together—day into day, lonely night into lonely night. If Samuel hadn't demanded nearly every minute of every day, and half of the nights, Hannah swore she would have gone crazy with anticipation.

As before, she'd helped to pass the interminable waiting by preparing every detail of Riley's return—from the candlelight dinner of Riley's favorite meal, chicken enchiladas, to the new pale pink silk gown she intended on wearing to bed that very night. Only this time she didn't need any encouragement from Cheryl to purchase the frothy bit of lingerie. She'd gone down to the Kitsap Mall and bought it all on her own. She might have a long way to go before she could ever be termed a seductress, but Hannah was determined to learn.

The first men disembarked the *Atlantis,* and Hannah heaved a grateful sigh of thanksgiving. "It won't be long now," she whispered into her son's ear. "Daddy's coming."

Cheryl was standing on the tips of her toes. "I see Steve."

"Is Riley close?" Hannah asked, hating the fact she wasn't five inches taller and able to see for herself.

"Not yet… Oh, wait, he's in front of Steve, scooting past everyone, making a nuisance of himself. My goodness, that man is determined to create enemies."

"Cheryl, please, don't tease."

"Who's teasing? One would think he was in a hurry to see his wife and son."

Hannah saw Riley just then, and it was as if the earth came to a sudden, abrupt standstill. The entire world seemed to tip on its axis as though awaiting the outcome of their reunion.

"Riley!" she shouted, raising her hand and waving like a crazy woman. She wasn't the only woman behaving out of character. There was something about these reunions that did that to a Navy wife.

She edged her way past a couple of women and met Riley halfway. He stopped brusquely in front of her, his eyes drinking in the sight of her as his duffel bag slipped from his hands and fell to the pier.

She smiled up at him, but her vision blurred when her eyes filled with tears of profound happiness. After all the trouble she'd gone through with her makeup, she struggled to keep them at bay, not wanting to ruin the effect.

His hand found her face, gently cupping her cheek. His touch rippled through her like an electric shock as his thumb caught the single tear.

"You're more beautiful than I remember."

"Oh, Riley."

Being careful of the baby, Riley wrapped her in his arms and buried his face in the curve of her neck, breathing in deeply as if the scent of her were the only thing in the world that would revive him.

He kissed her then, his mouth desperate but tender. Their lips clung as the tears spilled down Hannah's wind-chapped cheeks.

"Oh, Lord, Hannah," he growled, his arms circling her and dragging her as close as they could with the slumbering child between them. "I love you so damned much. I love you." He chanted the words as if they'd been burning on his lips, in his heart and mind, ready to be shared for far too long.

He searched for her mouth and worshiped her in a kiss that left Hannah trembling and shaken. His tongue sought hers, firing to life a need so strong it burst like fire inside her. "Riley...you make me forget the baby."

He raised his eyes to her as though he'd forgotten for the moment that their son was between them. Slowly he lowered his gaze to Samuel.

All her life Hannah would cherish the look of wonder and love that came into her husband's eyes.

"Riley," she said softly, "meet your son. Samuel, this is your daddy."

Chapter Fourteen

"Hannah?" Riley called to his wife, certain the infant in his arms was about to wake and cry. His heart thundered with dread at the possibility.

"Yes?" She stuck her head out from the kitchen. He didn't know what she was cooking, but he hadn't smelled anything so delicious in months. She'd banished him to the living room, claiming dinner was a surprise. Everything about Hannah was incredible. He'd been struck by her beauty many times, but never more profoundly than now. It took him several minutes to realize the marked difference. In the process of having Sam, she'd made the passage into womanhood. There was a maturity in her beauty, a radiance and freshness that awed him.

She was reed slim, her waist as narrow and trim as the night they'd met. And her hair was longer now, reaching halfway down her back. Watching her as she walked caused his fingers to ache with the need of her. It was too soon after the baby's birth, he realized, to consider making love. Riley was almost relieved. He released a jagged sigh. Many a lonely night, he'd fallen asleep remembering how remarkably good the loving had been between them. A hundred or more times he'd cursed himself for wasting the last precious days they'd spent together. He'd wanted her with a desperation that was with him still. Yet he held back, convinced he was doing the right thing.

"Sam's awake," Riley murmured. After all the torturous days of waiting for this moment to hold his son in his arms, Riley felt terrified. Eight pounds had sounded large for a baby, but the tiny being in his arms seemed incredibly… tiny. Riley was almost afraid to breathe for fear of disrupting him.

"He won't break," Hannah explained softly, walking into the living room, "I promise you. Relax. You're as stiff as cardboard."

A second sigh quivered through Riley's chest. Samuel stared up at him and cooed softly, seeming to enjoy his father's discomfort.

"He's not nearly as frightening as he looks," Hannah teased on her way back into the kitchen.

Riley didn't know how she could be so calm about it. To the best of his knowledge he'd never held a baby in his life. It seemed to him that one should ease into this heavy responsibility. Riley, however, had been given little option. The minute they arrived home, Hannah had donned an apron and thrust Samuel into his arms and suggested the two become acquainted while she put the finishing touches on dinner.

Samuel stirred, wide-awake now. He gazed up at Riley with huge, quizzical eyes that were the precise color of his own, Riley realized, feeling inordinately proud. A warmth took root in his heart unlike anything he'd ever experienced. His heart full, Riley bent down and gently kissed Samuel's brow.

Doing his best to relax, Riley eased his back against the recliner. Only a few months before, he'd lived his life independent of others, free to do as he wished. If he wanted to party away the night and stagger home drunker than a skunk, he'd done so without a qualm. He'd answered only to himself. His life had been his own, free of entanglements.

All that had changed from the minute he'd met Hannah. He'd married her for reasons he had yet to grasp fully. Because of the sins of the past. Because it had been the right thing to do. For her. For his future with the Navy. For his son.

He'd said his vows before the chaplain, never realizing he was bound by far more than a few spoken words. Hannah, and now Samuel, had sunk tender hooks into his heart, and he would never be the same man again.

Gently lifting Samuel in his arms, Riley awkwardly placed his son over his shoulder and patted the impossibly small back.

This was his son. The fruit of his desire for a beautiful woman who had come to him in grief and pain—only Riley had been so absorbed by her beauty and her purity that he hadn't noticed. It came to him that he should plead for Hannah's forgiveness for his lack of insight. By all that was right, he should set her free to marry the kind of man she deserved—someone like Jerry Sanders. While Hannah fussed in the kitchen, Riley tried to imagine what his life would be like without her now. His thoughts grew heavy and dark as his mind froze with dread and fear of an empty life without his wife and son.

He'd found contentment with Hannah. And love. God help him from being weak and greedy, but he needed her.

Hannah returned to the room, paused and smiled lovingly when she viewed them. "Much better. You look almost comfortable."

Riley frowned. "Why do I get the impression you're enjoying this?"

Her smile deepened. "Because I am. Did you count his fingers and toes?"

"No. Should I?" It hadn't entered Riley's mind that there might be an abnormality.

"No." She laughed at his distress. "Honestly, I had no

idea you'd be such a fretful father. When they brought Sam to me the first time, I held him in my arms and peeled open the blanket just to be sure. I thought you might feel the same compulsion to check everything about him."

Riley shook his head. "I haven't gotten over the fear of holding him yet. Next time around, I'll think about peeking under the blanket."

"Dinner's almost ready," she told him, taking Samuel out of his arms. She disappeared for a moment and returned with a fresh diaper. Placing Samuel inside the bassinet, she laid open his blanket. The ease with which she changed the infant's diaper astonished Riley. He supposed that in time, he'd work his way up to that, as well.

"I'll feed Sam first," Hannah explained, gently lifting him into her arms, "then put him down to sleep. Hopefully we can have an uninterrupted meal."

She settled in the rocking chair and, mesmerized, Riley watched as she pulled up her blouse, released her bra and pressed her extended nipple into his son's mouth. With an eagerness Riley could appreciate, Sam latched on to the nipple and sucked greedily. Tiny white bubbles appeared at the corners of his mouth.

"Does it hurt…you know?" Riley asked self-consciously. "Nursing?"

Hannah tottered gently in the padded rocker. "It felt strange at first, a little uncomfortable. But gradually we learned to work together. We've gotten to be real handy at this, haven't we, Sam?" Using her index finger, she brushed a wisp of dark hair from their son's brow.

"What about labor?" It was a question that had stayed fixed in his mind for over a month. The thought of Hannah in pain did funny things to Riley's heart. He'd hated not being with her and had often dwelled on what it had cost her to bring Sam into the world. Each time he contemplated her labor, he suffered a multitude of worries. A part of him—a damn small part of him—was grateful he hadn't been with her, fearing he would have been more of a hindrance than a help.

"Labor was the most difficult thing I've ever done," she answered after a few silent moments. "It wouldn't be fair to play it down. I honestly thought I was prepared. Cheryl and I attended every birthing class. I had the breathing down to an art form and faithfully exercised every day, but when the time came it seemed impossible to focus my attention on anything but the pain."

Riley noted that her eyes dulled at the memory; then she looked up and it vanished under the radiance of her smile. Riley wasn't sure he'd ever seen anything like what he saw in Hannah. It was as though the curtain to her soul had been drawn open and he'd been granted a rare privilege. In those few fleeting moments, Riley caught a glimpse of the core of goodness and gentleness of this woman who had so thoroughly captured his heart.

"Then Samuel was born, and Riley…I can't even begin to explain how beautiful the experience was. He was squalling like an angry calf. Then Cheryl started crying and so did I, but not from pain. I felt so incredibly happy. I just couldn't hold it inside me any longer. It was a contest to see which one of us could cry the loudest. I can just imagine what Dr. Underwood thought."

"I wish I'd been with you." It hurt to know his best friend's wife had shared these moments with Hannah instead of him.

The sweetest smile touched her eyes. "I know. Next time we'll try to plan the pregnancy so you can be with me."

Next time. Riley's heart came to a sudden standstill. He stood and walked over to the window, staring blindly at the street in front of their home. That Hannah would be willing to bear him another child, after everything she'd endured, wreaked havoc with his mind and his senses.

Considering her health, considering the pain she'd suffered delivering Sam, Riley found it incredible she'd even consider the possibility. As far as he was concerned, one pregnancy was enough. He didn't know if his heart could withstand another.

Dinner was as delicious as the spicy aroma coming from the kitchen had promised. Riley enjoyed these uninter-rupted moments with his wife, answering her questions, asking his own. It would forever remain one of the great mysteries of his life that someone like Hannah could be married to him, Riley mused as he stood an hour later, wanting to help her with the dishes.

He couldn't stop studying Hannah, noting once more the subtle changes he found in her—the fullness of her beauty, the radiance of her goodness, the love for their son that shone so brilliantly in her dove-gray eyes each time she mentioned him.

As hard as he tried to turn his mind to other matters, it was difficult to forget the kisses they'd shared on Delta Pier. Her lips had been soft and sweet and so damn tempt-ing. Even now, hours later, he had to regulate his breath-ing in order to restrain the mounting desire building within him. He felt the raw, hungry need eating away at him, and repeatedly cursed himself for his weakness.

Hannah set the last of their dishes in the dishwasher, then turned her back to the kitchen counter, her hands braced against the edge. Her elbows weren't the only part of her anatomy that was extended. Riley's stomach pitched unevenly at the way her pear-shaped breasts captured his attention. It was improbable, unlikely, but they seemed to be pouting, demanding his attention. It was all he could do to look elsewhere. Yet again and again, he found his eyes drawn back to her front.

"Did you really miss me?" she asked him softly.

"You know I did," he answered gruffly, reaching for the dishrag so he could wipe off the stove. That was his first mistake in a series he was doomed to commit if he didn't do something quick. As he extended his arm, his forearm inadvertently brushed against a hardening nipple. His breath caught in his throat. Riley felt as though he'd scorched his arm. He froze, his mission forgotten.

"You haven't kissed me since we arrived home," she whispered.

"I haven't?" Riley was more aware of it than she knew.

"No. Don't you think we should make up for lost time?"

"Ah…sure."

He kissed her, licking his tongue across the seam of her lips, delving into the corners of her sweet mouth. He trembled then, trembled with a need so powerful his knees went weak; trembled with the shock of how painfully good she felt in his arms—in his life.

Hannah wrapped her arms around his neck and moaned in wanton welcome, opening to him. A better man might have been able to resist her, but not Riley. Not now. Not when he was starving for her touch.

"Oh…Riley, I've missed you so much," Hannah moaned as if she were feeling everything he was. And more.

They kissed again, too hungry for each other to attempt restraint. Riley felt Hannah's need. It shuddered through her, reaching him, touching him, continuing to transmit into his own body with devastating results.

He twisted his mouth away from hers, inhaled sharply and buried his face in her neck, praying to God for the strength to stop before he went too far. Before he'd reached the point of no return. Before the hungry ache of his need consumed what remained of his will.

"I think we should stop." From where he found the strength to speak would forever remain an enigma to Riley.

"Stop?"

"It's too soon," he argued. He stepped away from her, his chest heaving with the effort. Every part of his body protested the action.

"Riley, love, don't worry. I...talked to the doctor." She blushed as she said it, and lowered her gaze. "It's not too soon, I promise you."

"I'd be more comfortable if we waited."

"Waited? Really?" She sounded bitterly disappointed.

Hell, she didn't know the half of it. "Just for a little while," he promised, but he didn't know whom he was speaking to—Hannah or himself.

"If you insist." She bore the disappointment well, Riley decided. In fact she seemed downright cheerful about it, he reflected later that evening.

Humming softly, she gave Sam a bath, dressed him in his sleeper and nursed him once more. The need to be close to her was overpowering. Riley followed her around like a lost lamb, satisfied with tidbits of her attention.

"I think I'll take a bath," she announced a little while later, when she was assured Sam was sleeping peacefully.

Riley nodded, deciding to read the evening paper. He could hear the bathwater running and didn't think much of it until the delicate scent of spring lavender wafted toward him. Lavender and wildflowers.

The fragrance swirled toward him with the seductive appeal of a snake charmer's music. Hannah and wildflowers. The two were inseparable in his mind. During the endless, frustrating nights aboard the *Atlantis,* Riley had often dreamed of Hannah traipsing toward him in a field of blooming flowers, a wicker basket handle draped over her arm. It didn't take much imagination to envision her in the picture she'd painted that hung above the fireplace.

"I'm tired. Let's go to bed," Hannah suggested softly. Riley looked up to discover her standing in the doorway to the kitchen, one arm raised above her head, leaning against the frame in a seductive pose. She wore a pale pink gown that clung to her breasts and hips like a second skin. Gone was Sam's mother and in her stead was Riley's wife: the most beautiful woman he'd ever known.

He swallowed tightly. She didn't help his breathing any when she stepped over to the recliner and took his hand. The power to resist her escaped him, and Riley obediently rose out of the chair and followed her into the bedroom.

"I'm...not quite ready for bed yet." He managed somehow to dredge up a token resistance.

"Yes, you are," she returned without a pause. "We both are—if those kisses in the kitchen were any indication."

"Ah...that was a mistake." Riley had rarely felt more tongue-tied in his life.

Hannah's sweet face clouded. "A mistake?"

"It's too soon.... I think we should wait a few more months until you're completely healed." That sounded logical. Sensible, even. The type of thing any loving husband would say to his wife after the birth of a child.

"A few months?" Hannah repeated incredulously.

"At least that long."

The air went still, so still it felt like the distinct calm before the storm. It was. Hannah bolted off the bed as though she'd been burned. Stalking past him with a righteous flair of her hips, she stopped just the other side of the door, then slammed it hard enough to break the living-room windows.

He heard another door slam and then another, flinching with each discordant sound.

Riley closed his eyes, then buried his hands in his hair, uncertain what he should do. He could follow her and try to explain, but he didn't know what he would say. He wasn't rejecting her; he was protecting her.

Hannah was too angry, too hurt to stand by and do nothing. Slamming doors wasn't helping, and if she didn't stop soon, she'd wake Sam.

Riley was impossible. Just when she was convinced he truly loved her, he pulled this stunt. One rejection was bad enough. Twice was unforgivable. She'd leave him; that was what she'd do. But she had nowhere to go. Nowhere she *wanted* to go, she amended reluctantly.

She didn't doubt Riley's love. She'd seen the emotion in his eyes when he'd looked down on Sam for the first time. Surely she hadn't misread him, and he held some tender spot in his heart for her, as well.

Quite simply, she decided, he just didn't find her physically attractive. She might as well own up to the fact and learn to live with it. This was the second and last time she'd play the part of a fool. He'd trampled across her heart and her pride for the last time.

Dragging the bucket from the storage closet, she sniffled and reached for the mop. It was either vent this incredible frustration one way or cave into the deep, dry well of self-pity.

She mopped the kitchen floor with a vengeance, rubbing the mop over the already spotless floor as though it were caked with a thick layer of mud.

"Hannah."

She jerked upright and swung the mop around with her. She held it out in front of her like a knight's swift sword, intending to defend her honor. "Stay away from me, Riley Murdock."

"I think we should talk."

She brandished the mop beneath his nose in a warning gesture. Water drenched the front of his shirt, and a shocked look came into his eyes. "You can forget that. I'm through with...talking." She hated the way her voice cracked. Riley seemed to find it a sign of weakness and advanced toward her. Once again Hannah swung the mop around, determined to deter him. "You've already said everything I care to hear," she informed him primly. "I got your message loud and clear. First thing in the morning, I'll move my things into Sam's bedroom."

"Why would you do that?" he demanded, his temper

rising. He attempted to grab hold of the mop, but she experienced a small sense of triumph by eluding his grasp.

"Why?" she repeated with a harsh laugh. "I refuse to sleep with a man who finds me so unattractive." Just admitting as much hurt almost more than she could bear. Tears filled her vision until Riley's image blurred and swam before her.

"It's not you who's lacking," Riley explained. "It's me."

"I don't believe that for a moment," she countered sharply, struggling to hold back the emotion. "I don't 'turn you on.' Isn't that what people say nowadays?"

"Don't turn me on? Are you nuts?"

"Apparently so." She jabbed the mop into the bucket with enough force to slosh the water over the sides. Without bothering to drain off the excess liquid, she slopped it onto the floor. "You must find my attempts to lure you into bed downright hilarious." She gave a short laugh, as if she, too, found them amusing.

"Hannah, for the love of heaven, will you listen to me?"

"No…just leave me alone." She raised the mop threateningly in an effort to persuade him she meant business.

"Put that thing down before you hurt yourself," he demanded with a growl.

"Make me." Hannah couldn't believe she'd said anything so childish. Riley had driven her lower than she'd ever thought she would sink.

Riley shook his head as if he, too, couldn't believe she'd challenge him in such a juvenile manner. When she least expected it, his hand shot out and he jerked the mop free of her grasp and hurled it to the floor.

Hannah was too stunned to react. She backed against the kitchen counter, feeling very much like a small, cornered animal, left defenseless and alone. She'd never felt more isolated in her life. Not even when she'd first realized she was pregnant with Riley's child.

"I'm not good enough for you," he admitted in an emotion-riddled breath. "Don't you understand?"

"No, I don't," she cried.

"Loving you isn't right."

Hannah glared at him with all the frustration pent up in her heart and then hurled the wet dishrag at him, hitting him in the shoulder. The damp cloth stuck there as if glued into place.

"It's a fine time to tell me that!" she shouted. "What am I supposed to tell Sam? That he was a terrible mistake and you rue the day you ever met his mother?"

"Of course not. Hannah, please, try to understand. By everything that's right, you should be married to Jerry Sanders."

"Is that a fact? What would you like me to do about it? Tell God He made a mistake so He can send Jerry back for a wedding?"

"Don't be ridiculous."

"Me?" she countered with a short hysterical laugh. "You're so eager to be rid of me, you're willing to pawn me off on a dead man."

Riley closed his eyes. "I've never known you to be so unreasonable. Think about it for a minute, would you?"

"Think about what? That you don't want me? How will that help matters any? Answer me one thing," she demanded between tears of rage and tears of pain. "Do you regret being married to me?"

An eternity passed before he answered. When he did, she had to strain to hear him. "Yes, but not for the reasons you think."

It would have pained her less had he stabbed her through with a knife. The fight drained out of her, and she dropped her hands lifelessly to her sides. All the weeks and months she'd loved him, cherished each precious moment they were together, treasured the tenderness and the caring. All along, it had been a lie. "I see."

"I'm a bastard!" Riley shouted. "I grew up on the wrong side of the tracks. If I'd looked at a girl like you when I was in high school, I would have been arrested. The fact we're married is a crime. You could have had any man you wanted, and frankly, sweetheart, you could do a hell of a lot better than me." He paused and seemed to wait for his words to sink in. "There are others out there like Jerry. Good, honest men. You should be married to one of them. Not me."

"You seem to be forgetting one minor detail," she said in a voice that was little more than a whisper. "I'm already married to you."

The tortured look Riley wore suggested he didn't need to be reminded. "If I didn't love you so damn much, I would have released you from our vows."

"You want to prove your love for me by abandoning me?" The very idea was too ludicrous to consider.

"Our marriage can't be annulled any longer," he admitted with a pained look. "I ruined any chance of that the night we made love."

"Ruined it… You mean you were honestly considering doing such a thing?" Hannah was too furious to think. She glanced around, ready to hurl the first available object she could find directly at her husband. His thinking was so twisted. He left her defenseless and more outraged than she could ever remember being in her life.

Moving quickly, Riley stepped forward and caught her in his arms. The tears he saw in her eyes appeared to distress him, and frowning, he brushed them aside. Closing her eyes, Hannah jerked her face away. She struggled, but Riley wouldn't release her and she soon gave up the effort.

"I love you so damn much," he confessed.

Hannah was about to argue with him when he pulled her mouth to his and kissed her, not bothering to hide the desperation and the pain of his confession.

For the first time, Hannah was able to put aside the rejection of the pain and understand everything Riley had been saying to her. He did love her—more than she dared credit, more than she dared to dream, enough to do what he felt was right and good where she and Sam were concerned.

Her hands found his face, and she slanted her mouth over his, opening to him. Again and again Riley kissed her, and she kissed him until she felt feverish with need.

"Oh, God, Hannah," he whispered, pressing his forehead against hers. "You make me crazy."

"I know," she murmured, raining nibbled kisses along the underside of his jaw. "I've been listening to crazy talk from you for the last several minutes, and I refuse to hear any more."

"Hannah, for the love of God…"

She silenced him the most effective way she knew how. "My turn," she said, holding him against her, wondering if any man could ever make her want him as much as she did him.

She led him into the living room and lowered him into the recliner. Once he was seated, she settled on his lap, to be sure she could intercept his arguments before they had time to form.

"You're right. Jerry Sanders was a special man. I loved him—he'll always hold a special place in my heart. But that in no way discounts my love for you."

Riley's eyes widened, and it looked as though he intended to argue with her, but she pressed her mouth on his, teased apart his lips with her tongue and then made a lightning-quick strike before abruptly ending the kiss. Riley was left panting and helpless, just the way Hannah meant to keep him until he listened to reason.

"You're my husband. The love I feel for you and Sam is so powerful it sometimes overwhelms me. I never knew a person could hold so much love inside. It overflows sometimes, and all I can do is sit and weep and thank God for sending you into my life."

"Hannah–"

"Let me finish," she interrupted, pressing her finger to his lips. "The night…we met, Reverend Parker at the Mission House and I had a talk. I remember it as clearly as if it were this afternoon. He reminded me that God works in mysterious ways. I didn't believe him at the time–I was hurting too much. Now I understand. God took Jerry from me and then He sent you and Sam into my life. If you want to question God's wisdom that's certainly your right, but I don't. There's a balance to nature. Out of my grief were born the greatest joys of my life– you and Samuel."

"But–"

"I'm not done yet," she chastised gently. "You can go ahead and try to get rid of me if that's what you really want, but I'm telling you right now, it won't work. I plan on sticking around for a good long time. Ninety years or more."

Riley went quiet and still. He closed his eyes, blocking her out. He seemed to be battling within himself, fighting her love and everything she was offering him. She knew she'd won when he opened his eyes and studied her, his eyes intensely blue. "You're sure about this?"

"Very sure. Do you think I might be able to convince you to tag along for the ride?"

The slightest hint of a smile touched Riley's bottomless eyes. "Are you going to attempt to unman me with any more mops? Or hurl more cold dishrags at me?"

"That depends on whether you refuse to make love to me again," she informed him with a prim lift to her voice.

"I don't think that's going to be much of a problem in the future."

Hannah grinned and relaxed. "I'm glad to hear it."

"In fact, I'm thinking we should follow your earlier suggestion and make up for lost time." His hands were at her waist, stroking her hips in a seductive, caressing motion.

"There's lots of time to make up for," she reminded him, linking her arms around his neck.

"It could take all night," he told her, looking so eager it was all Hannah could do not to laugh outright. In one swift motion he rose to his feet, scooping Hannah into his arms as he did so. He carried her through the house toward their bedroom.

"All night?"

"Perhaps days," he said, his eyes shining into hers.

"Days?"

"As long as a month."

Hannah sighed and pressed her mouth against his neck, loving the salty, manly taste of him. "A month?"

"Possibly years."

"Years?" she echoed incredulously.

"What was it you suggested? Ninety years?"

"At the very least," she whispered in reply. "Ninety years and at least three children."

"Three!" Apparently her husband hadn't learned his lesson. He fully intended to argue with her, but Hannah knew the most effective way of all to end contention between them.

NAVY HUSBAND

To Geri Krotow, navy wife,
with appreciation for all her assistance.
Dream big dreams, my friend.

Chapter One

"This is a joke—right?" Shana Berrie said uncertainly as she talked to her older sister, Ali, on the phone. Ali was the sensible one in the family. She—unlike Shana—wouldn't have dreamed of packing up her entire life, buying a pizza and ice-cream parlor and starting over in a new city. Oh, no, only someone completely and utterly in need of a change—correction, a *drastic* change—would do something like that.

"I'm sorry, Shana, but you did agree to this parenting plan."

Her sister was a Navy nurse stationed in San Diego, and several years ago, when she'd asked Shana to look after her niece if necessary, Shana had immediately said yes. It had seemed an unlikely prospect at the time, but that was before her sister became a widow.

"I did, didn't I?" she muttered lamely as she stepped around a cardboard box. Her rental house was cluttered with the makings of her new life and the remnants of her old.

"It isn't like I have any choice in the matter," Ali pointed out.

"I know." Pushing her thick, chestnut-colored hair away from her forehead, Shana leaned against the kitchen wall and slowly expelled her breath, hoping that would calm her pounding heart. "I said yes back then because you asked me to, but I don't know anything about kids."

"Jazmine's great," Ali assured her.

"I know, but—but…" she stammered. Shana wasn't sure how to explain. "The thing is, I'm at a turning point in my own life and I'm probably not the best person for Jazmine." Surely there was a relative on her brother-in-law's side. Someone else, *anyone* else would be better than Shana, who was starting a new career after suffering a major romantic breakup. At the moment, her life still felt disorganized. Chaotic. Add a recently bereaved nine-year-old to the mix, and she didn't know what might happen.

"This isn't a choose-your-time type of situation," Ali said. "I'm counting on you, and so is Jazmine."

Shana nibbled on her lower lip, trapped between her doubts and her obligation to her widowed sister. "I'll do it, of course, but I was just wondering if there was someone else…."

"There isn't," Ali said abruptly.

"Then it's me." Shana spoke with as much enthusiasm as she could muster, although she suspected it must sound pretty hollow. Shana hadn't had much experience as an aunt, but she was going to get her chance to learn. She was about to become her niece's primary caregiver while her sister went out to sea on an aircraft carrier for a six-month deployment.

Shana truly hadn't expected this. When Ali filled out the "worldwide availability" form—with Shana's name—she'd explained it was so the Navy had documentation proving Jazmine would have someone to take care of her at all times, ensuring that Ali was combat-ready. It had seemed quite routine, more of a formality than a possibility—and of course, Peter was alive then.

Ali had been in the Navy for twelve years and had never pulled sea duty before now. She'd traveled around the world with her husband, a Navy pilot, and their daughter. Then, two years ago, Peter had been killed in a training accident and everything changed.

Things had changed in Shana's life, too, although not in the same unalterable and tragic way. Brad—Shana purposely put a halt to her thoughts. Brad was in the past. They were finished. Done. Kaput. She'd told her friends that she was so over him she had to force herself to remember his name. Who was he, again? *That* was how over him she was. Over. Over and out.

"I don't have much time," Ali was saying. "The *Woodrow Wilson*'s scheduled to leave soon. I'll fly Jazmine up this weekend but I won't be able to stay more than overnight."

Shana swallowed a protest. For reasons of national security, Shana realized her sister couldn't say any more about her schedule. But this weekend? She still had to finish unpacking. Furthermore, she'd only just started training with the former owners of her restaurant. Then it occurred to Shana that she might not be the only one upset about Ali's sudden deployment. She could only guess at her niece's reaction. "What does Jazmine have to say about all this?"

Ali's hesitation told Shana everything she needed to know. "Oh, great," she muttered under her breath. She remembered her own childhood and what her mother had termed her "attitude problem." Shana had plenty of that, all right, and most of it was bad. Dealing with Jazmine's moods would be payback, she supposed, for everything her poor mother had endured.

"To be honest, Jazmine isn't too excited about the move."

Who could blame her? The little girl barely knew Shana. The kid, a true child of the military, had lived on Whidbey Island in Washington State, then Italy and, following the accident that claimed her father's life, had been shuffled to San Diego, California. They'd just settled into their Navy housing, and now they were about to leave that. In her nine years Jazmine had been moved from country to country, lost her father, and now her mother was shipping out for six long months. If that wasn't enough, the poor kid was being foisted on Shana. No wonder she wasn't thrilled.

"We'll be fine," Shana murmured, doing her best to sound positive. She didn't know who she was kidding. Certainly not her sister—and not herself, either. This was going to be another in a long line of recent disasters, or life-changing events, as she preferred to call them.

"So it's true you and Brad split up?" Ali asked with a degree of delicacy. She'd obviously been warned against bringing up his name.

"Brad?" Shana repeated as if she had no idea who her sister was talking about. "Oh, you mean Brad Moore. Yes, it's over. We were finished quite a while ago, but either he forgot to tell me or I just wasn't paying attention."

"I'm so sorry," Ali said.

The last thing Shana wanted was Ali's sympathy. "Don't worry, I've rebounded. Everything's great. My life is fabulous, or it will be in short order. I've got everything under control." Shana said all of this without taking a breath. If she said it often enough, she might actually start to believe it.

"When Mom told me that you'd decided to leave Portland and move to Seattle, I thought it was job related at first. You never said a word." She paused. "Did you move all those plants, too? You must have about a thousand."

Shana laughed. "Hardly. But yes, I did. Moving was…a spontaneous decision." That was putting it mildly. One weekend Shana had driven to Seattle to get away and to consider her relationship with Brad. She'd finally realized that it wasn't going anywhere. For five years they'd been talking marriage. Wrong. *She'd* been talking marriage. Brad had managed to string her along with just enough interest to placate her. And she'd let him until…

Unexpectedly, Shana had stumbled on Brad having lunch with a business associate. This so-called associate just happened to be a willowy blonde with a figure that would stop a freight train. It was a business lunch, he'd claimed later, when Shana confronted him.

Yeah, sure—monkey business. Shana could be dense at times but she wasn't blind, and she recognized this so-called associate as someone Brad had once introduced as Sylvia, an old flame. Apparently those embers were still very much alive and growing hotter by the minute, because as Shana watched, they'd exchanged a lengthy kiss in the parking lot and drove off together. She was embarrassed to admit she'd followed them. It didn't take her long to see where they were headed. Brad's town house— and she didn't think they were there to discuss contracts or fire codes.

Even when confronted, Brad insisted his lunch date was a client. Any resemblance his associate had to Sylvia was purely coincidental. The more he defended himself, the more defensive he got, complaining that Shana was acting like a jealous shrew. He'd been outraged that she'd question his faithfulness when *she* was the one so often away, working as a sales rep for a large pharmaceutical company. He'd been so convincing that—just for a moment— she'd wondered if she might've been wrong. Only when she mentioned that she'd followed them to his town house did Brad show any hint of guilt or regret.

He'd glanced away then, and the righteous indignation had been replaced by a look of such sadness she had to resist the urge to comfort him. He was sorry, he'd said, so sorry. It had been a fling; it meant nothing. He couldn't lose her. Shana was his life, the woman he intended to marry, the mother of his unborn children.

For a few days, he'd actually swayed her. Needing to sort out her feelings, Shana had driven to Seattle the next weekend. After five years with Brad she felt she knew him, but it now seemed quite clear that she didn't. He wanted her back, he told her over and over. He was willing to do whatever it took to reconcile, to make this up to her. He suggested counseling, agreed to therapy, anything but losing her.

That weekend, Shana had engaged in some painful self-examination. She desperately wanted to believe the afternoon rendezvous with Sylvia was a onetime thing, but her head told her it wasn't and that they'd been involved for months—or more.

It was while she sat in Lincoln Park in West Seattle, analyzing the last five years, that she concluded there was no going back. Her trust had been destroyed. She couldn't build a life with Brad after this. In truth, their relationship had dead-ended three years ago. Maybe sooner; she could no longer tell. What Shana did recognize was that she'd been so caught up in loving Brad that she'd refused to see the signs.

"I was feeling pretty miserable," Shana admitted to her sister. Wretched was a more accurate description, but she didn't want to sound melodramatic. "I sat in that park in West Seattle, thinking."

"In West Seattle? How'd you get there?"

Shana sighed loudly. "I took a wrong turn when I was trying to find the freeway."

Ali laughed. "I should have guessed."

"I ended up on this bridge and there wasn't anyplace to turn around, so I followed the road, which led to a wonderful waterfront park."

"The ice-cream parlor's in the park?"

"No, it's across the street. You know me and maple-nut ice cream. It's the ultimate comfort food." She tried to make a joke of it, but at the time she'd felt there wasn't enough maple-nut ice cream in the world to see her through this misery.

"Brad drove you to maple nut?"

Shana snickered at Ali's exaggerated horror. After her decision to break off the relationship, she'd grown angry. Okay, furious. She wanted out of this relationship, completely out, and living in the same city made that difficult.

"Actually, West Seattle is a charming little community. The ice-cream parlor had a For Sale sign in the window and I got to talking to the owners. They're an older couple, sweet as can be and planning to retire. As I sat there, I thought it must be a nice place to work. How could anyone be unhappy surrounded by ice cream and pizza?"

"So you *bought* it? Shana, for heaven's sake, what do you know about running any kind of restaurant?"

"Not much," she said, "but I've worked in sales and with people all these years. I was ready for a break, and this seemed practically fated."

"But how could you afford to buy an established business?"

Shana had an answer for that, too. "I had a chunk of cash in savings." The money had originally been set aside for her wedding. Saving a hundred dollars a month and investing it carefully, she'd managed to double her money. Just then, she couldn't think of a better way to spend it. Buying this business was impulsive and irrational but despite everything, it felt…right.

That Sunday in the park she'd admitted there would be no wedding, no honeymoon with Brad. Shana drew in her breath. She refused to think about it anymore. She'd entered a new phase of her life.

"It's a cute place. You'll like it," she murmured. She had lots of ideas for fixing it up, making it *hers*. The Olsens had promised to help transfer ownership as seamlessly as possible.

"You rented a house?"

"That very same Sunday." Once she'd made her decision, Shana had been on a mission and there was no stopping her. As luck would have it, there was a house two streets over that had just been vacated. The owner had recently painted it and installed new carpeting. Shana had taken one look around the 1950s-style bungalow with its small front porch and brick fireplace and declared it perfect. She'd given the rental agent a check immediately. Then she drove home, wrote a letter resigning her job—and phoned Brad. That conversation had been short, sweet and utterly satisfying.

"Making a move like this couldn't have been easy," Ali commiserated.

"You wouldn't believe how easy it was," Shana said gleefully. "I suppose you're curious about what Brad had to say." She was dying to tell her.

"Well…"

"I called him," Shana said without waiting for Ali to respond, "and naturally he wanted to know where I'd been all weekend."

"You told him?"

Shana grinned. "I couldn't get a word in edgewise. He was pretty upset. He told me how worried he was, and how he'd spent the entire weekend calling me. He was afraid of what I might've done. As if I'd do something lethal over *him*," she scoffed. Shana suspected that his concern was all for show, but none of that mattered now. "When he cooled down, I calmly explained that I'd gone for a drive."

"A three-day drive," Ali inserted.

"Right. Well, he got huffy, saying the least I could've done was let him know I'd made plans." What came next was the best part. "So I told him I'd made plans for the rest of my life and they didn't include him."

Ali giggled and it sounded exactly the way it had when they were girls, sharing a bedroom. "What did he say then?"

"I don't know. I hung up and started packing stuff in my apartment."

"Didn't he try to phone you back?"

"Not for the first couple of days. He e-mailed me on the third day and I immediately put a block on his name." That must have infuriated him—not that Shana cared. Well, she did, a little. Okay, more than a little. Unfortunately she didn't have the satisfaction of knowing what his reaction had been. In the past, she'd always been the one who patched any rift. That was her problem; she couldn't stand conflict, so she'd done all the compromising and conciliating. Over the course of their relationship, Brad had come to expect her to make the first move. Well, no longer. She was finished. Brad Moore was history.

Instead of kicking herself for taking so long to see the light, she was moving ahead, starting over…and, to be on the safe side, giving up on men and relationships. At twenty-eight, she'd had her fill. Men weren't worth the effort and the grief.

"I never was that fond of Brad," Ali confessed.

"You might've said something." Shana realized her tone was a little annoyed. In the five years she'd dated Brad, there'd certainly been opportunities for Ali to share her opinion.

"How could I? We just met once, and you seemed so keen on him."

"If you'd stayed in one place longer, we might've gotten together more often."

Ali's sigh drifted over the phone. "That's what happens when you're in the Navy. They own your life. Now honestly, are you all right?"

Shana paused to consider the question. A second later, she gave Ali her answer. "Honestly? I feel great, and that's the truth. Yes, this breakup hurt, but mostly I was angry with myself for not waking up sooner. I feel *fabulous*. It's as if I've been released from a spell. I've got a whole new attitude toward men."

Her sister didn't say anything for a moment. "You might *think* you're fine, but there's a chance you're not totally over Brad."

"What do you mean?"

Again her sister hesitated. "I remember what it was like after Peter died. The shock and grief were overwhelming at first. I walked around in a fog for weeks."

"This is different," Shana insisted. "It's less…important."

"It is and it isn't," Ali fired right back.

"But you feel better now, don't you?"

"Yes. One day, out of the blue, I discovered I could smile again. I could function. I had to. My daughter needed me. My patients needed me. I'll always love Peter, though." Her voice wavered but eventually regained strength.

"I'll always love Peter, too," Shana said, swallowing hard. "He was one of a kind." Her brother-in-law had been a loving husband and father, and her heart ached for her sister even now. The situation with Brad didn't compare.

"I'll give you my flight information for this weekend," Ali said, changing the subject.

Shana had nearly forgotten that she was about to become a substitute mother. "Oh, yeah. Let me find a pen." Scrabbling through her purse, she dug one up and found a crumpled receipt she'd stuffed in there. Good—she could write on the back.

She was looking forward to some time with her sister. They saw each other so rarely, thanks to Ali's career. This upcoming visit would be a brief one, but Shana hadn't seen Ali—and Jazmine—since the funeral.

"You and Jazmine will do just fine," Ali said warmly.

"Jazmine's a great kid, but be warned. She's nine going on sixteen."

"In what way?"

"Because she's an only child, she's rather…precocious. For instance, she's reading at ninth-grade level. And the music she likes is sort of—well, you'll see."

"Thanks for warning me."

"I'm sure this'll be easy for you."

Shana had her doubts. "If I remember correctly, that was what you told me when I asked if I could fly off the top bunk."

"What did I know? I was only six," Ali reminded her. "You've never forgiven me for that, have you?"

"I still remember how much it hurt to have the wind knocked out of me." It felt the same way now. Despite the assurances she so freely handed out, Shana was still struggling to recover her equilibrium—to reinvent her life on new terms. No Brad, no steady paycheck, no familiar Portland neighborhood. Now, her niece was about to complicate the situation. The next six months should be very interesting, she thought. Very interesting indeed.

She vaguely recalled an old Chinese saying, something about living in interesting times. Unfortunately, she also recalled that it was intended as a curse, not a blessing.

Chapter Two

Alison Karas couldn't help being concerned about leaving her nine-year-old daughter with her sister, Shana. This wasn't a good time in Jazmine's life, nor was it particularly opportune for Shana. Her sister *sounded* strong and confident, but Ali suspected otherwise. Despite Shana's reassurances, she'd been badly shaken by her breakup with Brad, even though she'd initiated it. Jazmine hadn't taken the news of this deployment well, and was reluctant to leave her newfound friends behind and move to Seattle.

But Ali really had no other option. Ideally, Jazmine would go to either set of grandparents, but in this case that wouldn't work. After the sudden loss of her father ten years earlier, her mother hadn't done well. She'd never recovered emotionally and was incapable of dealing with the demands of a young girl. Peter had been an only child and his parents had divorced when he was young. Both had gone on to other marriages and other children. Neither set of paternal grandparents had shown any great interest in Jazmine.

Jazmine wandered into Ali's room just then and flopped down on the bed with all the enthusiasm of a slug.

"Are you packed?" Ali asked, her own suitcase open on the opposite end of the bed.

"No," her daughter muttered. "This whole move is crap."

"Jazmine, watch your mouth!" Ali refused to get into an argument with a nine-year-old. The truth was, she'd rather not ship out, either, but for Jazmine's sake she put on a good front. This was the most difficult aspect of her life in the Navy. She was a widow and a mother, but she was also a Navy nurse, and her responsibilities in that regard were unavoidable. That was made abundantly clear the day she accepted her commission. When the Navy called, she answered. In fact, she wouldn't have minded six months at sea except for her daughter.

"Uncle Adam lives in the Seattle area," Ali reminded her. She'd been saving that tidbit, hoping the news would make her daughter feel more positive about this most recent upheaval in their lives.

"He's in Everett," Jazmine said, her voice apathetic.

"I understand that's only thirty or forty minutes from Seattle."

"It is?"

Her daughter revealed her first spark of interest since they'd learned of the transfer. "Does he know we're coming?" She sat upright, eager now.

"Not yet." Busy as she'd been, Ali hadn't told Adam Kennedy—her husband's best friend and Jazz's godfather— that Jazmine would soon be living in Seattle.

"Then we *have* to tell him!"

"We will, all in due course," Ali assured her.

"Do it now." Her daughter leaped off the bed, sprinted into the living room and came back with the portable phone.

"I don't have his number." Ali hadn't been thinking clearly; their phone directory had already been packed away and she simply didn't have time to search for it.

"I do." Once more her daughter made a mad dash out

of the bedroom, returning a moment later. Breathless, Jazmine handed Ali a tidy slip of paper.

Ali unfolded it curiously and saw a phone number written by an adult hand.

"Uncle Adam sent it to me," Jazmine explained. "He told me I could call him whenever I needed to talk. He said it didn't matter what time of day or night I phoned, so call him, Mom. This is *important*."

Ali resisted the urge to find out if her daughter had taken advantage of Adam's offer before now and decided she probably had. For Jazmine, it was as if the sun rose and set on Peter's friend. Lieutenant Commander Adam Kennedy had been a support to both of them since the accident that had abruptly taken Peter out of their lives.

It sounded so cut and dried to say a computer had malfunctioned aboard Peter's F/A-18. He hadn't had a chance to recover before the jet slammed into the ground. He'd died instantly, his life snuffed out in mere seconds. That was two years ago now, two very long years, and every day since, Peter had been with her. Her first thought was always of him and his image was the last one her mind released before she went to sleep at night. He was part of her. She saw him in Jazmine's smile, in the three little lines that formed between the girl's eyebrows when she frowned. Peter had done that, too. And their eyes were the exact same shade of brownish green.

As an SMO, or senior medical officer, Ali was familiar with death. What she didn't know was how to deal with the aftermath of it. She still struggled and, as a result, she understood her sister's pain. Yes, Shana's breakup with Brad was different, and of a lesser magnitude, but it was a loss. In ending her relationship with him, Shana was also giving up a dream, one she'd held and cherished for five years. She was adjusting to a new version of her life and her future. Shana had flippantly dismissed any doubts or regrets about the breakup. Those would come later, like a sneak attack—probably when Shana least expected it. They had with Ali.

"Mom," Jazmine cried, exasperated. "Dial!"

"Oh, sorry," Ali murmured, punching out the number. An answering machine came on almost immediately.

"He isn't there?" Jazmine asked, studying her. She didn't hide her disappointment. It was doom and gloom all over again as she threw herself backward onto the bed, arms spread-eagled.

Ali left a message and asked him to get in touch.

"When do you think he'll call?" Jazmine demanded impatiently.

"I don't know, but I'll make sure we get a chance to see him if it's possible."

"Of *course* it's possible," Jazmine argued. "He'll want to see me. And you, too."

Ali shrugged. "He might not be back by the time I need to fly out, but you'll see him, don't worry."

Jazmine wouldn't look at her. Instead she stared morosely at the ceiling, as if she didn't have a friend in the world. The kid had moved any number of times and had always been a good sport about it, until now. Ali didn't blame her for being upset, but there wasn't anything she could do to change her orders.

"You'll love living with your aunt Shana," Alison said, trying a new tactic. "Did I tell you she has an ice-cream parlor? How much fun is that?"

Jazmine wasn't impressed. "I don't really know her."

"This will be your opportunity to bond."

Jazmine sighed. "I don't want to bond with her."

"You will eventually," Ali said with forced brightness. Jazmine wasn't fooled.

"I'm not glue, you know."

Alison held back a smile. "We both need to make the best of this, Jazz. I don't want to leave you any more than you want me to go."

Her daughter scrambled to a sitting position. As her shoulders slumped, she nodded. "I know."

"Your aunt Shana loves you."

"Yippee, skippy."

Alison tried again. "The ice-cream parlor is directly across the street from the park."

"Yippee."

"Jazmine!"

"I know, I know."

Ali wrapped one arm around the girl's shoulders. "The months will fly by. You'll see."

Jazmine shook her head. "No, they won't," she said adamantly, "and I have to change schools again. I hate that."

Changing schools, especially this late in the year, would be difficult. In a few weeks, depending on the Seattle schedule, classes would be dismissed for the summer. Ali kissed the top of Jazmine's head and closed her eyes. She had the distinct feeling her daughter was right. The next six months wouldn't fly, they'd crawl. For all three of them…

Shana wanted children, someday, when the time was right. But she'd assumed she'd take on the role of motherhood the way everyone else did. She'd start with an infant and sort of grow into it—ease into being a parent gradually, learning as she went. Instead, she was about to get a crash course. She wondered if there were manuals to help with this kind of situation.

Pacing her living room, she paused long enough to check out the spare bedroom one last time. She'd added some welcoming touches for Jazmine's benefit and hoped the stuffed teddy bear would appeal to her niece. Girls of any age liked stuffed animals, didn't they? The bedspread, a fetching shade of pink with big white daisies, was new, as was the matching pink throw rug. She just hoped Jazmine would recognize that she was trying to make this work.

She wanted Jazmine to know she was willing to make an effort if the girl would meet her halfway. Still, Shana didn't have a good feeling about it.

Her suspicions proved correct. When Ali arrived, it was immediately apparent that Jazmine wanted nothing to do with her aunt Shana. The nine-year-old was dressed in faded green fatigues and a camouflage army-green T-shirt. She sat on the sofa with a sullen look that discouraged conversation. Her long dark hair fell across her face. When she wasn't glaring at Shana, she stared at the carpet as if inspecting it for loose fibers.

"I can't tell you how good it is to see you," Ali told Shana, turning to her daughter, obviously expecting Jazmine to echo the sentiment. The girl didn't.

Shana moved into the kitchen, hoping for a private word with her sister. They hadn't always been close. All through high school, they'd competed with each other. Ali had been the more academic of the two, while Shana had excelled in sports. From their father, a family physician, they'd both inherited a love of science and medicine. He'd died suddenly of a heart attack when Shana was twenty.

Within months, their lives were turned upside down. Their mother fell to pieces but by that time, Ali was in the Navy. Luckily, Shana was able to stay close to home and look after their mom, handle the legal paperwork and deal with the insurance, retirement funds and other responsibilities. Shana had attended college classes part-time and kept the household going. At twenty-two, she was hired by one of the up-and-coming pharmaceutical companies as a sales rep. The job suited her. Having spent a good part of her life around medical professionals, she was comfortable in that atmosphere. She was friendly and personable, well-liked by clients and colleagues. Within a few years, she'd risen to top sales representative in her division. The company had been sorry to see her go and had offered an impressive bonus to persuade her to stay. But Shana was ready for a change, in more ways than one.

The last time the sisters had been together was at Peter's funeral. Shortly afterward, Ali had returned to Italy. Although she could have taken an assignment back in the States, Ali chose to finish her tour in Europe. As much as possible, she'd told Shana, she wanted Jazmine to remain in a familiar environment. A few months ago, she'd been transferred to San Diego, but no one had expected her to be stationed aboard the *Woodrow Wilson,* the newest and largest of the Navy's aircraft carriers. According to her sister, this was a once-in-a-career assignment. Maybe, but in Shana's opinion, the Navy had a lousy sense of timing.

"Jazmine doesn't seem happy about being here," Shana commented when they were out of earshot. She understood how the girl felt. The poor kid had enough turmoil in her life without having her mother disappear for six months.

"She'll be fine." Ali cast an anxious glance toward the living room as Shana took three sodas from the refrigerator.

"Sure she will," Shana agreed, "but will I?"

Ali bit her lower lip and looked guilty. "There isn't anyone else."

"I know. These next six months will give Jazmine and me a chance to know each other," Shana announced, stepping into the living room and offering Jazmine a soda. "Isn't that right?"

The girl stared at the can as if it held nerve gas. "I don't want to live with you."

Well, surprise, surprise. Shana would never have guessed that.

"Jazmine!"

"No," Shana said, stopping her sister from chastising the girl. "We should be honest with one another." She put down Jazmine's drink and sat on the opposite end of the sofa, dangling her own pop can in both hands. "This is going to be an experience for me, too. I haven't been around kids your age all that much."

"I can tell." Jazmine frowned at the open door to her bedroom. "I hate pink."

Shana had been afraid of that. "We can take it back and exchange it for something you like."

"Where'd you get it? Barbies R Us?"

Shana laughed; the kid was witty. "Close, but we can check out the Army surplus store if you prefer."

This comment warranted a half smile from Jazmine.

"We'll manage," Shana said with what she hoped sounded like confidence. "I realize I've got a lot to learn."

"No kidding."

"Jazmine," Ali snapped in frustration, "the least you can do is try. Give your aunt credit for making an effort. You can do the same."

"I am trying," the girl snapped in return. "A pink bedroom and a teddy bear? Oh, puleeeze! She's treating me like I'm in kindergarten instead of fourth grade."

Shana had barely started this new venture and already she'd failed miserably. "We can exchange the bear, too," she suggested. "Army surplus again?"

Her second attempt at being accommodating was less appreciated than the first. This time Jazmine didn't even crack a smile.

Ali sat in the space between Shana and Jazmine and threw her arms over their shoulders. "If I've learned anything in the last few years, it's that women have to stick together. I can't be with you, Jazz. That's all there is to it. I'm sorry, I wish things were different, but they aren't. If you want, at the end of this deployment, I'll resign my commission."

Jazmine's head rose abruptly. "You'd leave the Navy?"

Ali nodded. This was as much a surprise to Shana as it was to her niece. From all indications, Ali loved military life and had fit into it with comfort and ease.

"Now that your dad's gone, my life isn't the same anymore," Ali continued. "I'm your mother and you're far more important to me than any career, Navy or not. I won't leave you again, Jazmine, and that's a promise."

At those words the girl burst into tears. Embarrassed, she hid her face in both hands, her shoulders shaking as Ali hugged her.

Ali seemed to be trying not to weep, but Shana had no such compunction. Tears slipped down her cheeks.

It would be so good to have her sister back again. If she had any say in the matter, Ali would move to Seattle so the two of them could be closer.

"If you get out of the Navy, does that mean you'll marry Uncle Adam?" Jazmine asked with the excitement of a kid who's just learned she's about to receive the best gift of her life.

"Who's Uncle Adam?" Did this mean her sister had managed to find *two* husbands while Shana had yet to find one? Ah, the old competitive urge was back in full swing.

"He was one of my dad's best friends," Jazmine supplied with more enthusiasm than she'd shown since she'd arrived. "He's cute and funny and I think Mom should marry him."

Raising one brow, Shana turned to her sister for an explanation. Ali had never mentioned anyone named Adam.

"Uncle Adam is stationed in Everett. That's close to here, right?" Jazmine demanded, looking to Shana for the answer.

"It's a bit of a drive." She wasn't entirely sure, never having made the trip north of Seattle herself. "Less than an hour, I'd guess."

"Uncle Adam will want to visit once he learns I'm here."

"I'm sure he will," Ali murmured, pressing her daughter's head against her shoulder.

"You like this guy?" Shana asked her. Ali was decidedly closemouthed about him, which implied that she had some feelings for this friend of Peter's.

"Of course Mom likes him," Jazmine said when her mother didn't respond. "So do I. He's totally *fabulous*."

Ali met Shana's gaze and shrugged.

"Another pilot?" Shana murmured.

She shook her head. "He's a Supply Officer. You'll like him," her sister was quick to say, as if this man might interest her romantically. No way. Shana had sworn off men and she was serious about that.

"He said I can talk to him anytime I want," Jazmine went on. "I can phone him, can't I?"

"Of course you can." Shana was more curious than ever about this man her sister didn't want to discuss.

Shana turned to gaze at Ali, silently pleading for more information. Her sister ignored her, which was infuriating. Clearly, Adam had already won over her niece; he must be the kind of guy who shopped at the army surplus store.

Chapter Three

First thing Monday morning, Shana drove Jazmine to Lewis and Clark Elementary School to enroll her. Shana had to admit her stomach was in knots. The school yard was jammed with kids, and a string of vehicles queued in front, taking turns dropping off students. Big yellow school buses belched out diesel fumes as they lumbered toward the parking lot behind the building.

Shana was fortunate to find an empty parking space. She accompanied Jazmine into the building, although the girl walked ahead of her—just far enough to suggest the two of them weren't together.

The noise level inside the school reminded her of a rock concert and Shana felt the beginnings of a headache. Or maybe it was caused by all those students gathered in one place, staring at Jazmine and her.

The school bell rang and like magic, the halls emptied. Within seconds everyone disappeared behind various doors and silence descended. Ah, the power of a bell. It was as if she were Moses, and the Red Sea had parted so she could find her way to the Promised Land, or in this case, The Office.

Wordlessly Shana and Jazmine followed the signs to the

principal's domain. Jazmine was outwardly calm. She gave no sign of being ill at ease. Unlike Shana, who was on the verge of chewing off every fingernail she owned.

"This is no big deal," Jazmine assured her, shifting the backpack she carried. It was the size one might take on a trek through the Himalayas. "I've done this plenty of times."

"I don't feel good just leaving you here." They'd had all of one day together and while it was uncomfortable for them both, it hadn't been nearly as bad as Shana had feared. It hadn't been good, either.

When they took Ali to the airport, Shana had been the one in tears. Mother and daughter had hugged for an extra-long moment and then Ali was gone. It was Shana who did all the talking on the drive home. As soon as they were back at the rental house, Jazmine disappeared inside her bedroom and didn't open the door for hours.

Dinner had been a series of attempts on Shana's part to start a conversation, but her questions were met with either a grunt or a one-word reply. Shana got the message. After the first ten minutes, she said nothing. And *nothing* was what Jazmine seemed to appreciate most. They maintained an awkward silence and at the end of the meal, Jazmine delivered her plate to the kitchen, rinsed it off, stuck it in the dishwasher and returned to her room. The door closed and Shana hadn't seen her again until this morning. Apparently kids this age trea-sured their privacy. Point taken. Lesson learned.

"This must be it," Shana said, pointing at the door marked *Office*.

Jazmine murmured something unintelligible, shrugging off the backpack and letting the straps slip down her arms. Shana couldn't imagine what she had in that monstrosity, but apparently it was as valuable to the child as Shana's purse was to her.

"I was thinking you might want to wait a bit, you know," Shana suggested, stammering, unable to identify her misgivings. "Not do this right away, I mean." The students she saw in the hallway didn't look particularly friendly. Jazmine was only nine, for heaven's sake, and her mother was headed out to sea for half a year. Maybe she should home-school her. Shana considered that option for all of half a second. First, it wouldn't be home school; it would be ice-cream parlor school. The authorities would love that. And second, Shana was completely unqualified to teach her anything.

"I'll be all right," Jazmine said just loudly enough for Shana to hear.

Maybe so, but Shana wasn't completely convinced *she* would be. This guardianship thing was even harder than it sounded. The thought of leaving her niece here actually made her feel ill.

Jazmine's eyes narrowed accusingly. "I'm not a kid, you know."

So nine-year-olds weren't kids anymore? Could've fooled Shana, but rather than argue, she let the comment slide.

Enrolling Jazmine turned out to be surprisingly easy. After Shana completed a couple of forms and handed over a copy of her guardianship papers, it was done. Jazmine was led out of the office and into a classroom. Shana watched her go, forcing herself not to follow like a much-loved golden retriever.

"It's your first time as a guardian?" the school secretary asked.

Shana nodded. "Jazmine's been through a lot." She resisted the urge to mention Peter's death and the fact that Ali was out at sea. Instinctively she realized that the less anyone knew about these things, the better for Jazmine.

"She'll fit right in," the secretary assured her.

"I hope so." But Shana wasn't sure that was true. There were only a few weeks left of the school year. Just when

Jazmine had managed to adjust, it would be time for summer break. And what would Shana do with her then? It was a question she couldn't answer. Not yet, anyway.

With reluctance she walked back to her parked car and drove to Olsen's Ice Cream and Pizza Parlor. She'd thought about changing the name, but the restaurant had been called this for the last thirty years. A new name might actually be a disadvantage, so she'd decided to keep everything the same for now.

Shana's day went smoothly after her visit to the school. She was on her own now, her training with the Olsens finished. They insisted the secret to their pizza was the tomato sauce, made from their special recipe. That recipe had been kept secret for over thirty years. Only when the final papers had been signed was Shana allowed to have the recipe, which to her untrained eye looked fairly unspectacular. She was almost sure her mother used to make something similar for spaghetti and had gotten the recipe out of a "Dear Abby" column years ago.

There was a huge mixing machine and, following the Olsens' example, she went into the shop each morning to mix up a batch of dough and let it rise. Once the dough had risen, it was put in the refrigerator, awaiting the day's pizza orders. The restaurant opened at eleven and did a brisk lunch trade. How much or how little dough to make was complete guesswork. Shana's biggest fear was that she'd run short. As a consequence she usually mixed too much. But she was learning.

At three o'clock, Shana found herself watching for the school bus. Jazmine was to be dropped off in front of the ice-cream parlor. From noon on, she'd constantly checked the time, wondering and worrying about her niece. The elementary students she'd seen looked like a rough crowd—okay, maybe not the first- and second-graders, but the ones in the fifth and sixth grades, who were giants compared to Jazmine. Shana just hoped the girl could hold her own.

Business was constant—people waiting to catch ferries, high-school students, retired folk, tourists. Shana planned to hire a part-time employee soon. Another idea she had was to introduce soup to the menu. She'd already experimented with a number of mixes, both liquid and dry, and hadn't found anything that impressed her. Shana was leaning toward making her own from scratch but her experience in cooking large batches was limited.

A bus rolled into view and Shana instantly went on alert. Sure enough, Jazmine stepped off, wearing a frown, and marched inside. Without a word to Shana, she slid into a booth.

"Well," Shana said, unable to disguise her anxiety, "how was it?"

Jazmine shrugged.

"Oh." Her niece wasn't exactly forthcoming with details. Thinking fast, Shana asked the questions her mother had bombarded her with every day after school. "What did you learn? Anything interesting?"

Jazmine shook her head.

"Did you make any new friends?"

Jazmine scowled up at her. "No."

That was said emphatically enough for Shana to surmise that things hadn't gone well. "I see." Glancing over her shoulder, Shana sighed. "Are you hungry? I could make you a pizza."

"No, thanks."

The bell above the door rang and a customer entered, moving directly to the ice-cream case. Shana slipped behind the counter and waited patiently until the woman had made her selection. As she scooped chocolate chip–mint ice cream into a waffle cone, she realized something was different about Jazmine. Not until her customer left did she figure out what it was.

"Jazz," she said, startled, "where's your backpack?"

Her niece didn't answer.

"Did you forget it at school? We could run by to pick it up if you want." Not until the parlor closed at six, but she didn't mention that. During the summer it wouldn't be until eight o'clock; she didn't mention that, either.

Jazmine scowled even more ferociously.

Shana hadn't known how much fury a nine-year-old girl's eyes could convey. Her niece's anger seemed to be focused solely on Shana. The unfairness of it struck her, but any attempt at conversation was instantly blocked.

It was obvious that someone had taken the backpack from Jazmine. No wonder the girl wasn't in a happy frame of mind.

Feeling wretched and helpless, Shana slid into the booth across from her niece. She didn't say anything for several minutes, then gently squeezed Jazmine's hand. "I am so sorry."

Jazmine shrugged as if it was no big thing, but it was and Shana felt at a loss. Without her niece's knowing, she'd speak to the principal in the morning and see what could be done. She guessed it'd happened on the bus or off school grounds.

"Can I use your phone?" Jazmine asked.

"Of course."

Jazmine's eyes fleetingly met hers as she pulled a piece of paper from her hip pocket. "It's long distance."

"You're not calling Paris, are you?"

The question evoked an almost-smile. "No."

"Sure, go ahead." Shana gestured toward the phone on the back wall in the kitchen.

Jazmine thanked her with a faint smile. This counted as profuse appreciation and Shana was nearly overwhelmed by gratitude. Despite their shaky beginning she was starting to reach this kid.

"I'm phoning my uncle Adam," Jazmine announced. "He'll know what to do."

This uncle Adam seemed to have all the answers. She hadn't even met him and already she didn't like him. No one could be that perfect.

On Monday afternoon, Adam Kennedy opened the door to his apartment near Everett Naval Station, glad to be home. He'd just been released from the naval hospital, where he'd recently undergone rotator cuff surgery. His shoulder throbbed and he felt so light-headed he had to brace his hand against the wall in order to steady himself. He'd be fine in a couple of days, but at the moment he was still shaky.

The apartment was dark with the drapes pulled, but he didn't have the energy to walk across the room and open them.

It wouldn't be like this if he had a wife, who'd be able to look after him while he felt so weak. This wasn't the first time that thought had occurred to Adam. He'd never intended to be a thirty-two-year-old bachelor.

Adam sank into his favorite chair and winced at the pain that shot down his arm. Leaning his head back against the cushion, he closed his eyes and envisioned what his life would be like if he was married. A wife would be fussing over him now, acting concerned and looking for ways to make him comfortable. Granted, if comfort was all he wanted, he could pay for it. A wife—well, having a wife meant companionship and sharing things. Like a bed… It also involved that frightening word, *love*.

If he was married now, she'd be asking how he felt and bringing him tea and *caring* about him. The fantasy filled his mind and he found himself smiling. What he needed was the *right* woman. His track record in that department left a great deal to be desired.

He'd started out fine. When he graduated from college he'd been engaged, but while he was in Officer Candidate School, Melanie had a sudden change of heart. Actually, she still wanted to get married, just not to him. The tearful scene in which she confessed that she'd fallen in love with someone else wasn't a memory he wanted to reminisce over, especially now. Suffice it to say, his ego had taken a major beating. In the long run, though, Melanie wasn't that great a loss. If she had a roving eye this early in their relationship, it didn't bode well for the lengthy separations a Navy career would demand of their marriage.

The thing was, Adam wanted children. One of his proudest moments was when Peter had asked him to be Jazmine's godfather. He took his duties seriously and loved that little girl, and he'd felt especially protective of her since his friend's death. He hadn't heard from her in a while and wondered how she was doing after the recent move to San Diego. He'd have to get in touch with her soon.

Adam had envied Peter his marriage. He'd never seen two people more in love with each other or better suited. They were about as perfect a match as possible. Adam suspected that fact had been a detriment to him in his own quest for a relationship. He kept looking for a woman as well suited to him as Ali had been to his friend. If such a woman existed, Adam hadn't found her, and he'd about given up. It wasn't Ali he wanted, but a woman who was his equal in all the ways Ali had been Peter's. A woman with brains and courage and heart. At this stage he'd take two out of three. Ali had brought out the best in Peter; she'd made a good man better.

A sense of sadness came over him as he thought about Peter. Adam had a couple of younger brothers, Sam and Doug, and the three of them were close, but Peter and

Adam had been even closer. They'd met in OCS, Officer Candidate School, kept in contact afterward and later were stationed together in Italy. During weekend holidays, Peter and Ali had him over for countless dinners. The three of them had sat on their balcony in the Italian countryside drinking wine and talking well into the night. Those were some of the happiest memories of his life.

Then Peter had been killed. Adam had been a witness to the accident that claimed his best friend's life. He still had nightmares about it and experienced the same rush of horror, anger, frustration he'd felt at the time. He'd gone with the Casualty Assistance Counseling Officer to tell Ali that her husband was dead. In his heart, he'd promised Peter that he'd look out for both Ali and Jazz but the Navy hadn't made it easy.

Ali was currently stationed at the hospital in San Diego and he was in Everett. He phoned at least once a month to check up on them and Jazmine called him every now and then when she needed to talk. He always enjoyed their conversations. Peter would be proud of both the women in his life, he mused. Jazmine was a great kid and Ali was a wonderful mother.

Adam noticed the blinking light on his answering machine. He knew there were more messages than he had the patience or endurance to deal with just yet. He'd leave it until morning when he had a fresh supply of energy.

He sighed. He wasn't used to feeling like this—despondent and weary. Coming home to an empty apartment underlined a truth he didn't want to acknowledge. Lieutenant Commander Adam Kennedy was lonely.

He stared blankly across the room, half toying with the notion of a romantic relationship with Ali. It didn't take him more than a second to realize it wouldn't work. He loved Ali—like a sister. Try as he might, he couldn't seem to view her as a marriage prospect. She was his best friend's widow, a woman he admired, a woman he thought of as family.

Yet…he wanted what she'd had, what she and Peter had shared, and the deep contentment their marriage had brought them.

By morning, he would've forgotten all these yearnings, he told himself. He'd lived alone so long now that he should certainly be accustomed to his own company. When he was at sea, it was a different story, since he was constantly surrounded by others. As a Supply Officer he was normally stationed aboard the *Benjamin Franklin*. Unfortunately the *Franklin* was currently headed toward the Persian Gulf. Until his shoulder healed, he'd be twiddling his thumbs behind some desk and hating it.

After a while Adam felt better. His head had stopped spinning and the ache in his shoulder wasn't quite as intense. It would be easy to close his eyes and sleep but if he slept now, he'd spend the whole night staring at the ceiling.

A wife.

It was something to consider. Maybe he should resume his efforts to meet someone, with marriage in mind. The time was right. His parents wanted more grandchildren and he was certainly willing to do his part. According to Ali, he was an excellent candidate for a husband and father. She'd tried any number of times to fix him up, but nothing had ever come of her matchmaking efforts.

A wife.

He relaxed and smiled. He was ready. All he needed now was the woman.

Chapter Four

Lieutenant Commander Alison Karas had been assigned as senior medical officer aboard the *USS Woodrow Wilson*. As much as she wanted to be with Jazmine and as difficult as it had been to leave her daughter with Shana, Ali was determined to fulfill her duty to the Navy. During her twelve-year career, she'd never been stationed aboard a ship. Before Jazmine was born, she'd done everything in her limited power to get such an assignment, but it hadn't happened.

So far, she'd served in a number of military hospitals. And now, when she least wanted sea duty, that was exactly what she got. Still, she loved the Navy with the same intensity her husband had.

Her quarters were shared with another woman officer. There hadn't been time to exchange more than a brief greeting before they'd each begun their respective assignments. The crew was preparing to set out to sea. Within a couple of days, the jets would fly in from Naval air stations all over the country. It was standard procedure for the F-14s to link up with the aircraft carrier.

Unlikely though it was, she hoped for an opportunity to watch, since the pilots' precision and skill were so impressive. Pilots were a special breed, as she well knew.

Peter had wanted to fly jets from the time he was in grade school, according to his mother.

She smiled sadly at the thought of her husband. The pain of his loss remained sharp and—as always—Ali hoped he hadn't suffered. There must have been a moment of sheer terror when he realized he wouldn't be able to recover. She tried not to think of that.

Trite as it sounded, she'd learned that life does go on. It hadn't seemed possible in the beginning, when she'd been blinded by her grief. She was surprised to discover that everything continued as it had before. Classes were held in Jazmine's school; the radio still played silly love songs. People drove their cars and ate meals and bickered with each other. Ali hadn't been able to understand how life as she'd once known it could go on as though nothing had changed.

Jazmine was in good hands. Shana would look after her well. Ali needed to reassure herself of that several times a day. Leaving her daughter had been traumatic, but for Jazmine's sake, Ali had tried not to let her emotions show. Before she returned to San Diego, they'd talked, and Ali had a heart-to-heart with Shana, too.

She was still a little worried about Shana, but once they'd had a chance to really discuss the situation, Ali accepted that this impulsive change in her sister's life was probably the best thing she'd done in years. Shana needed a fresh start. The ice-cream parlor was charming and would undoubtedly be a big success. Jazmine had a bit of an attitude, but that wouldn't last long. And it helped that Adam was close by. The biggest disappointment of her stay was that they hadn't been able to reach him. Once he checked his messages, she knew he'd get in touch with Jazmine.

Ali found her daughter's suggestion that she marry Adam downright amusing. Ali thought the world of her husband's best friend, but there was no romantic spark on either side. What was particularly interesting was the fact that Jazmine seemed ready to discuss bringing another man into their lives.

Despite that, Ali had no intention of remarrying. She hadn't mentioned that to either her sister or Jazmine because it sounded too melodramatic. And both of them would argue with her. But a man like Peter only came around once in a lifetime, and she wasn't pressing her luck. If, by chance, she were to consider remarrying, she was determined not to fall in love with a Navy man. She'd already had one Navy husband and she wasn't going to try for two.

Ali had never removed her wedding band. After all these years, that ring represented perhaps the most significant part of her life. And although shipboard romances were strictly prohibited, it was a form of emotional protection, too. As far as her shipmates knew, she was married and that was the impression she wanted to give.

After spending her shift in the sick bay checking supplies, Ali went to the wardroom, where the offi-cers dined. Two other women officers were in the room but their table was full and they seemed engrossed in conversation. Sitting alone at a corner table, she felt self-conscious, although she rather enjoyed watching the men and women as they chatted. In a few weeks, she'd probably be sitting with one of those groups. Life aboard a carrier was new to her, but eventually it would become familiar and even comfortable.

Just as she was finishing her dinner, the group that included the other women was joined by Commander Dillon. Ali read his name tag as he walked past her table. He acknowledged her with a stiff nod, which she returned. From the reception he received, it was clear that he was well-liked and respected by his fellow officers. She had no idea what his duty assignment might be.

Without being obvious—at least she hoped she wasn't—she studied Dillon. He was tall and lean with dark hair graying at the temples, which led her to believe he must be in his early to midforties. His most striking feature was his intense blue eyes. To her chagrin, she found herself looking at his ring finger and noticed it was bare. Not that it meant anything. Wedding rings were dangerous aboard ship, although she chose to wear hers. More than once Ali had seen fingers severed as a result of a wedding band caught in machinery.

As soon as she'd finished her coffee, Ali went back to her work space at the clinic and logged on to the Internet to write Shana and Jazmine a short note. Her sister and daughter would be anxious to hear from her after her first full day at sea.

Sent: May 19
From: Alison.Karas@woodrowwilson.navy.mil
To: Shana@mindsprung.com
Subject: Hello!

Dear Shana and Jazmine,

Just checking in to see how things are going with you two. It's a little crazy around here and I'm still finding my sea legs. Not to worry, though.

Hey, Jazz, I was thinking you should help your aunt come up with ideas for ice-cream sundaes. Remember how we invented our own versions last summer? Hot fudge, marshmallow topping and crushed graham crackers? You called it the Give Me More Sundae. Not bad.

Shana, be sure to look over Jazz's homework, especially the math. Okay, okay, I'll stop worrying. Send me an e-mail now and then, okay? I'm waiting with bated breath to hear how you two are surviving.

Love ya.
Ali (That's Mom to you, Jazz!)

It wasn't much of a message, but Ali was tired and ready to turn in for the night. As she started back to her quarters, she met Commander Dillon in the long narrow passageway. She nodded and stepped aside in order to allow him to pass.

He paused as he read her badge. "Karas?"

"Yes, sir."

"At ease." He glanced down at her left hand. "Your husband is Navy?"

"Yes, sir." She looked self-consciously at her wedding ring. "He—" She'd begun to explain that she was a widow, then stopped abruptly. Rather than make eye contact, she stared into the bulkhead.

"This is your first time aboard the *Woodrow Wilson?*" The question was casual, conversational in tone.

She nodded again. "This is my first time on any ship. I'm wondering how long it's going to take before I get used to it." She laughed as she said this, because being on an aircraft carrier was so much like being in a building. Every now and then, Ali had to remind herself that she was actually aboard a ship.

Commander Dillon's eyes narrowed slightly as he smiled. "You'll be fine."

"I know I will. Thank you, sir."

That very moment, an alarm rang for a fire drill. All sailors were to report immediately to their assigned stations.

A sailor rushed past Ali and jolted her. In an effort to get out of his way, she tripped and fell hard against Commander Dillon, startling them both. The commander stumbled backward but caught himself. Instinctively he reached out and grabbed her shoulders, catching her before she lost her balance and toppled sideways. Stunned, they immediately grew still.

"I'm sorry," she mumbled, shocked at the instant physical reaction she'd experienced at his touch. It had been an innocent enough situation and meant nothing. Yet it told Ali a truth she'd forgotten. She was a woman. And, almost against her will, was attracted to a man other than Peter.

He muttered something under his breath, but she didn't hear what he said and frankly she was grateful. Without another word, they hurried in opposite directions.

Ali's face burned with mortification, but not because she'd nearly fallen into Commander Dillon. When her breasts grazed him and he'd reached out to catch her, he could have pulled her to him and kissed her and she wouldn't have made a single protest. Her face burned, and she knew she was in serious trouble. No, it was just the close proximity to all these men. At least that was what Ali told herself. It wasn't the commander; it could've been any man, but even as that thought went through her mind, she knew it was a lie. She worried that the commander might somehow know what she'd been feeling. That mortified her even more.

The scene replayed itself in her head during the fire drill and afterward, when she retired to her quarters. Once she was alone, Ali found a pen and paper. It was one thing to send Jazmine an e-mail but a letter was a tangible object that her daughter could touch and hold and keep. She knew Jazmine would find comfort in reading a note Ali had actually written.

When Ali had first started dating Peter, they'd exchanged long letters during each separation. She treasured those letters and savored them all, even more so now that he was gone.

On the night of their wedding anniversary last year, while Jazmine was at a slumber party, Ali had unearthed a stack and reread each one. She quickly surrendered to self-pity, but she had every reason in the world to feel sorry for herself, she decided, and didn't hold back. That night, spent alone in her bedroom, grieving, weeping and angry, had been an epiphany for her. It was as if something inside her—a wall of pretense and stoicism—had broken wide-open, and her pain had gushed forth. She believed it was at that point that she'd begun to heal.

Oh, she'd cried before then, but this time, on the day that would have been her twelfth wedding anniversary, she'd wept as if it was the end of the world.

By midnight she'd fallen asleep on top of the bed with Peter's letters surrounding her. Thankfully Jazmine hadn't been witness to this emotional breakdown. Her daughter had known the significance of the date, however, and had given her mother a handmade anniversary card the following afternoon. Ali would always love that sweet card. After she'd read it, they'd hugged each other for a long time. Jazmine had revealed sensitivity and compassion, and Ali realized she'd done her daughter a grave disservice.

All those months after Peter's death, Ali had tried to shield Jazmine from her own pain. She'd encouraged the child to grieve, helped her deal with the loss of her father as much as possible. Yet in protecting Jazmine, Ali hadn't allowed her daughter to see that she was suffering. She hadn't allowed Jazmine to comfort her, which would have brought comfort to Jazmine, too.

Later that same day, after dinner, Ali had shared a few of Peter's letters with Jazmine. It was the first time they'd really talked about him since his death. Before then, each seemed afraid to say more than a few words for fear of upsetting the other, Ali learned how much Jazmine needed to talk about Peter. The girl delighted in each tidbit, each detail her mother supplied. Ali answered countless questions about their first meeting, their courtship and their wedding day. Jazmine must've heard the story of their first date a dozen times and never seemed to tire of it.

Once Ali's reserve was down, not a night passed without Jazmine's asking about Peter. As a young child, her daughter had loved bedtime stories and listening to Ali read. At nine she suddenly wanted her mother to put her to bed again. It was so out of character for her gutsy, sassy daughter that it'd taken Ali a couple of nights to figure out what Jazmine really wanted, and that was to talk about her father.

In retrospect Ali recognized that those months of closeness had helped prepare Jazmine for this long separation. Ali didn't think she could have left her with Shana otherwise.

Shana. An involuntary smile flashed across her face as she leaned back in the desk chair. These next six months would either make or break her strong-willed younger sister. She'd taken on a lot all at once. Buying this restaurant on impulse was so unlike her. Shana preferred to have things planned out, down to the smallest detail. Not only that, this new venture was a real switch for her after her sales position.

If there was anything to be grateful for in Shana's sudden move to Seattle, it was the fact that Brad Moore was out of her life. Ali had only met him once, during a brief visit home, but he'd struck her as sleazy, and she hadn't been surprised to hear about his duplicity. Ali wondered how he'd managed to deceive her sister all this time, but whatever charms he possessed had worked about four and a half years longer than they should have. She supposed that, like most people, Shana had only seen what she'd wanted to see.

Before she returned to San Diego, Ali and Shana were able to spend a few hours together. Jazmine was asleep and the two sisters sat on the bed in Shana's room talking.

She'd seen how hurt Shana was by Brad's unfaithfulness. In an effort to comfort her sister, Ali had suggested Shana try to meet someone else as quickly as possible.

Her sister hadn't taken kindly to the suggestion. In fact, she hadn't been shy about sharing her feelings with regard to the male of the species. Shana claimed she was finished with men.

"You're overreacting," Ali had told her.

"And you're being ridiculous." Sitting with her knees drawn, Shana shook her head. "The absolute last thing I want to do now is get involved again. I was 'involved' for the last five years and all I got out of that relationship, besides a lot of pain, is two crystal champagne glasses Brad bought me. He said we'd use them at our wedding." Not that he'd actually given her an engagement ring or set the date. "Those glasses are still in the box. If he'd thought of it, he probably would've asked for them back."

"You feel that way about men now, but you won't always."

Shana frowned. "You're one to talk. I don't see you looking for a new relationship."

"Okay, fine, neither of us is interested in men."

"Permanently," Shana insisted.

Ali had laughed then and said, "Speak for yourself."

Funny, as she reviewed that conversation, Commander Dillon came to mind. It was unlikely that she'd see him on a regular basis; with a crew of five thousand on this ship, their paths wouldn't cross often. Ali wasn't entirely sure why, but she felt that was probably a good thing.

Chapter Five

The next few days were intense for Shana. She insisted on driving Jazmine to school, and every morning she joined the long line of parents dropping off their kids at the grade school. If Jazmine appreciated her efforts to build a rapport between them, she gave no indication of it. The most animation she'd witnessed in the girl had been after Monday's lengthy telephone conversation with her uncle Adam.

Shana, her aunt, a blood relative, was simply Shana, but Adam Kennedy, family friend, was *Uncle* Adam. The *uncle* part was uttered with near-reverence.

Okay, so she was jealous. Shana admitted it. While she struggled to gain ground with her niece, Jazmine droned on about this interloper.

Tuesday afternoon, the school bus again let Jazmine off in front of the ice-cream parlor. Her niece had dragged herself into the shop, as though it demanded all her energy just to open the door. Then she'd slipped onto one of the barstools and lain her head on her folded arms.

Wednesday afternoon, Shana watched the school bus approach and the doors glide open. Sure enough, Jazmine was there, but this time she leaped off the bus and hurried toward the restaurant.

Shana stopped and stared. No, it couldn't be. But it was.

Jazmine had her backpack. From the size and apparent weight of it, nothing seemed to be missing, either.

The instant Jazmine stepped inside, Shana blurted out, "You've got your backpack." It probably would've been better to keep her mouth shut and let Jazmine tell her, but she'd been too shocked.

"I know." Jazmine dumped her backpack on the floor and hopped onto the barstool with a Bugs Bunny bounce, planting her elbows on the counter. "Can I have some ice cream?"

Taken aback, Shana blinked. "Who are you and what have you done with my niece?"

"Very funny."

Shana laughed and reached for the ice-cream scoop. "Cone or dish?"

"Dish. Make it two scoops. Bubblegum and strawberry." She paused, her face momentarily serious. "Oh– and thank you."

"You're welcome." Bending over the freezer, Shana rolled the hard ice cream into a generous ball. "Well," she said when she couldn't stand it any longer. "The least you can do is tell me what happened."

"With what?" Jazmine asked, then giggled like the nine-year-old she was. "I don't know if you noticed or not, but I was pretty upset Monday afternoon."

"Really," Shana said, playing dumb.

"Two girls cornered me in the playground. One of them distracted me, and the other ran off with my backpack."

Shana clenched her jaw, trying to hide her anger. As Jazmine's legal guardian, she wanted these girls' names and addresses. She'd personally see to it that they were marched into the principal's office and reprimanded. On second thought, their parents should be summoned to the school for a confrontation with the authorities. Perhaps it would be best to bring in the police, as well.

"How'd you get it back?" Shana had given up scooping ice cream.

Looking more than a little pleased with herself, Jazmine straightened her shoulders and grinned. "Uncle Adam told me I should talk to them."

Wasn't *that* brilliant. Had she been asked, Shana would've told Jazmine the same thing.

"He said I should tell them it was really unfortunate, but it didn't seem like we could be friends and I was hoping to get to know them." This was uttered in the softest, sweetest tones Shana had ever heard from the girl.

"They fell for it?"

Jazmine's eyes widened. "I meant it. At first I thought they were losers but they're actually pretty cool. I think they just wanted to see what I carried around with me."

Frankly Shana was curious herself.

"Once they looked inside, they were willing to give it back."

"You're not missing anything?"

Jazmine shook her head.

"Great." Muttering under her breath, Shana dipped the scoop into the blue bubblegum-flavored ice cream. The bell above the door rang, but intent on her task, Shana didn't raise her head.

"I'll have some of that myself," a male voice said.

"Uncle Adam!" Jazmine shrieked. Her niece whirled around so fast she nearly fell off the stool.

Hearing his name was all the incentive Shana needed to glance up. She did just in time to watch Jazmine throw her arms around a man dressed casually in slacks and a shirt. From the top of his military haircut to the bottom of his feet, this man was Navy, with or without his uniform. His arm was in a sling and he grimaced when Jazmine grabbed hold of him but didn't discourage her hug. From the near-hysterical happiness the girl displayed, a passing stranger might think Shana had been holding Jazmine hostage.

"You must be Ali's sister," he said, smiling broadly at Shana.

She forced a smile in return. She'd been prepared to dislike him on sight. In fact, she'd never even met him and was already jealous of the relationship he had with Jazmine. Now he was standing right in front of her—and she found her tongue stuck to the roof of her mouth. He seemed to be waiting for her to reply.

"Yes, hi," she said and dropped the metal scoop into the water container, sloshing liquid over the edges. Wiping her wet hand on her white apron, she managed another slight smile. "Yes, I'm Ali's sister."

On closer inspection, she saw that he was tall and apparently very fit. Some might find his looks appealing, but Shana decided she didn't. Brad was just as tall and equally fit—from spending hours in a gym every week, no doubt admiring himself in all the mirrors. Adam's hair was a deep chestnut shade, similar to her own. No. Not chestnut, she decided next, nothing that distinguished. His was plain brown. He might've been considered handsome if not for those small, beady eyes. Well, they weren't exactly *small,* more average, she supposed, trying to be as objective as she could. He hugged Jazmine and looked at Shana and—no.

But he did. He looked at Shana and *winked.* The man had the audacity to flirt with her. It was outrageous. This was the very man Jazmine wanted her mother to marry. The man whose praises she'd sung for two full days until Shana thought she'd scream if she heard his name one more time.

"I'm Adam Kennedy." He extended his free right hand.

She offered her left hand because it was dry and nodded politely. "You mean *Uncle* Adam." She hoped he caught the sarcastic inflection in her voice.

He grinned as if he knew how much that irritated her. Okay, now she had to admit it. When he smiled he wasn't ordinary-looking at all. In fact, some women—not her, but others who were less jaded—might even be attracted to him. That she could even entertain the remote possibility of finding a man attractive was upsetting. Wasn't it only a few days ago that she'd declared to her sister that she was completely and utterly off men? And now here she was, feeling all shaky inside and acting like a girl closer to Jazmine's age than her own. This was pathetic.

In an attempt to cover her reaction, Shana handed Jazmine the bowl of ice cream with its two heaping scoops.

"Uncle Adam wants one, too," Jazmine said excitedly, and then turned to him. "What happened to your arm?" she asked, her eyes wide with concern. "Did you break it?"

"Nothing as dramatic as that," he said, elevating the arm, which was tucked protectively in a sling. "I had a problem with my shoulder, but that's been taken care of now."

Jazmine didn't seem convinced. "You're going to be all right, aren't you?"

"I'll be fine before you know it."

"Good," Jazmine said; she seemed reassured now. Taking Adam by the hand, she led him across the restaurant to a booth.

Shana could hear Jazmine whispering up a storm, but hard as she strained, she couldn't hear what was being said. Working as fast as her arm muscles would allow, she hurriedly dished up a second bowl of ice cream. When she'd bought this business, no one had mentioned how hard ice cream could be. She was developing some impressive biceps.

She smiled as she carried the second dish over to their booth and hoped he enjoyed the bright teal-blue bubble-gum ice cream. After she'd set it down in front of him, she waited. She wasn't sure why she was lingering.

Jazmine beamed with joy. Seeing her niece this happy about anything made Shana feel a pang of regret. Doing her best to swallow her pride, she continued to stand there, unable to think of a thing to say.

Her niece glanced up as if noticing her for the first time. "I was telling Uncle Adam about my backpack. He's the one who said those other girls just wanted to be friends. I didn't believe him, but he was right."

"Yes, he was." Shana might have been able to fade into the background then if Adam hadn't chosen that moment to turn and smile at her. Ignoring him would be easy if only he'd stop smiling, dammit.

"The girls gave it back?" Adam's gaze returned to Jazmine.

Her niece nodded. "Madison asked me to sit next to her at lunch today and I did."

Adam reached across the table and the two exchanged a high five. "That's great!"

"Can I get you anything else?" Shana asked, feeling like a third wheel. These two apparently had a lot to discuss, and no one needed to tell her she was in the way. Besides, she had a business to run. Several customers had come in; at the moment they were studying the list of ice-cream flavors but she'd have to attend to them soon.

"Nothing, thanks." He dipped his plastic spoon into the ice cream. Then, without giving her any warning, he looked at Shana again and their eyes met. Shana felt the breath freeze in her lungs. He seemed to really *see* her, and something about her seemed to catch him unawares. His brow wrinkled as though he was sure he knew her from somewhere else, but couldn't place her.

"How long can you stay?" her niece asked.

Adam turned his attention back to Jazmine.

Shana waited, curious to know the answer herself.

"Just a couple of hours."

"Two hours!" Jazmine didn't bother to hide her disappointment.

"I've got to get back to base for a meeting."

"Right," Shana said, diving into the conversation. "He has to go back to Everett. We wouldn't want to detain him, now would we?" She didn't mean to sound so pleased about sending him on his way, but she wanted him out of there. Shana disliked how he made her feel—as if…as if she was on the brink of some important personal discovery. Like she'd told her sister, she was off men. For good. Okay, for a year. It would take that long to get Brad out of her system, she figured. Now, all of a sudden, there was this man, this uncle Adam, whose smiles made her feel hot, then cold. That wasn't a good sensation for her to be having. It contradicted everything she'd been saying—and it made her uncomfortable.

"I'll stop by again soon," Adam promised, looking directly at her as he said it.

"I want to know what happened to your arm," Jazmine insisted.

"Surgery."

"Does Mom know?"

Adam shook his head. "She's got enough on her plate without worrying about me."

"You've talked to her?" Shana demanded. She forgot that she was pretending not to listen to their conversation. Catherine, the woman who worked part-time, arrived then and immediately began taking orders while Shana handled the cash register.

Adam shifted toward her. "She e-mailed me."

"Oh." Embarrassed, Shana glanced away. "Of course."

"I wish the base were closer," Jazmine muttered.

"Everett isn't that far and with light duty, I'll have more time to spend with you."

"Exactly how soon do you have to leave this afternoon?" Jazmine pressed. "Couldn't you please, please have your meeting tomorrow?"

This kid wasn't easily put off, Shana thought. While she was more than ready to usher Adam Kennedy out the door, her niece was practically begging him to stay.

"It's not really up to me. I've got to go soon, but I'll visit as often as I can."

"He's busy, I'm sure," Shana said before his words sank into her consciousness. *He'd be back...often.* In other words, she'd better get used to having him around, and judging by that smirk, he intended to smile at her some more. Oh, great.

"As often as you can?" Jazz repeated. "What does that mean?"

"I'll make sure I'm here at least once a week to check up on my favorite girl."

Instead of shouting with happiness, Jazmine hung her head. "*Only* once a week?"

Once a week? That often? Shana's reaction was just the opposite. As far as she was concerned, weekly visits were far too frequent.

Ali's little sister seemed oversensitive, Adam observed with some amusement as Shana returned to the ice-cream counter. That wasn't the only thing he'd noticed, either. She was beautiful with classic features, dark hair and eyes and a face he found utterly appealing. Ali was a beautiful woman, too, but in a completely different way. Although both had dark brown hair and eyes, the resemblance stopped there. Shana was the taller of the two and model-thin, whereas Ali had more flesh on her. If he were ever to say that out loud, she'd no doubt be insulted, but it was the truth. Ali wasn't overweight by any means, just rounded in all the right places. In his opinion, the little sister could stand to gain a few pounds.

He wasn't sure why he was concentrating on the physical, because his reaction to Shana was much more complex than that. He was attracted to her. Period. He liked what he saw and he liked what he didn't see—what he sensed about her. Attraction was indefinable, more about the sum of a person than his or her parts. People called it chemistry, sparks, magic, all sorts of vague things. But whatever you called it, the attraction was obviously there.

Something else was obvious. *She* felt it, too. And she didn't want to. In fact, she seemed determined to make sure he knew that. He didn't go around ravishing young women, willing or unwilling, but he definitely got a kick out of her reaction to him. He couldn't keep from grinning as he headed into the heavy freeway traffic on I-5 North.

On second thought, *he* might be overreacting. Perhaps it was all those musings about his lack of female companionship following his release from the hospital. Pain could do that to a man. Maybe he was wrong about Shana's interest in him; maybe he'd simply been projecting his own attraction and— Damn, this was getting much too complicated.

That same evening, when Adam logged on to the Internet, he discovered two messages from Ali. In the first, she was eager to know if he'd made contact with Jazmine; in the other, she asked if he'd be able to give her sister a break now and then. He immediately e-mailed back that he'd seen Jazz and everything seemed to be fine with her and Shana. He also said he'd visit as often as he could. Several questions regarding Shana went through his mind, but he didn't ask them, not wanting Ali to get the wrong impression. He also feared she'd relay his interest to her sister— and he just wasn't ready for that.

An hour later, his phone rang. It was Jazmine, who spoke in a whisper.

"Where are you?" he asked.

"In the closet." She was still whispering.

"What's the problem?" So Jazmine wanted to talk to him without her aunt listening in. Interesting.

"I hate it here and—oh, Uncle Adam, it's just so good to see someone I know."

Adam wished he could be there to wrap his arm around the girl's thin shoulders. "It'll get better." He didn't mean to sound trite, but he couldn't come up with anything else to say. "Didn't you tell me you'd made friends with those two girls who took your backpack?"

"Yeah, I guess, but it isn't like California. Seattle isn't like anyplace I've been. I miss my mom and…I just don't like it here."

"I feel that way whenever I've got a new duty assignment," he said, wanting to comfort her and not knowing how. "I'm in a new work environment myself and to be honest I'd much rather be in Hawaii. It's the perfect duty station. But you do get used to wherever you are, Jazz…."

"I just want to be with my mom," Jazmine said, sounding small and sad. "I wouldn't care where it was."

"Are you getting along with your aunt?"

Jazmine hesitated. "She tries, and I appreciate everything she does, I really do, but she doesn't know that much about kids." As if she felt bad about criticizing her aunt, the girl added, "It's not as bad as it was on Monday, but…"

Adam wanted to continue asking questions about Shana, but he preferred not to be obvious about it. "She seems nice."

"She is, but she's got issues, you know."

It was difficult for Adam not to laugh outright at Jazmine's solemn tone. "What kind of issues?" he asked gravely.

Jazmine snickered. "Where would you like me to start? She has this old boyfriend that she dumped or he dumped her—I don't know which—but she won't even say his name. I heard her talking to Mom, and every time she got close to mentioning his name, she called him that-man-I-used-to-date. Is that ridiculous or what?"

Adam murmured a noncommittal reply.

"That's not all. Shana used to have a regular job, a really good one for a drug company. Mom said she made fabulous money, but she quit after she broke up with this guy. Then she bought the ice-cream parlor. She doesn't know a thing about ice cream or pizza or anything else."

Still, Adam had to admire her entrepreneurial spirit. "She seems to be doing all right."

"That's only because she phones the former owners ten times a day, and I'm not exaggerating. She finally figured out she can't do everything on her own and she hired a lady to come in during the afternoons to help her. I'm only nine-going-on-ten, and *I* figured that out before she did." Jazmine stopped abruptly, as if something had just occurred to her. "You're not *attracted* to her or anything, are you?"

Adam relaxed in his chair and crossed his ankles. "Well…I think she's kinda cute."

"No, no, no!" Jazmine said, more loudly this time. "I was afraid this would happen. This is terrible!"

Adam loved the theatrics. "What is?"

"Shana," Jazmine cried as if it should all be perfectly logical. "What about *Mom?* If you're going to fall in love with anyone, make it my mom. She needs you, and you'd be a great stepdad."

"Jazmine," he said, the amusement suddenly gone. "I think the world of your mother. She's a wonderful woman, and I love her dearly, but—"

He had no idea how to put this without upsetting her. "Your mother and I, well…"

"You love her like a sister," Jazmine finished for him. She sounded resigned and not particularly surprised.

Adam almost wished he *could* fall in love with Ali. Perhaps if he'd met her before Peter did, things would've been different. But he hadn't, and now it was impossible to think of Ali in any other way.

"That's pretty astute of you," he said.

"What's astute?"

"Smart."

Jazmine sighed heavily. "Not really. I said something about you to Mom, and what she said is she loves you like a brother."

So it was a mutual feeling, which was a relief. "Did your mother tell you she was ready for another relationship?" he asked.

"I think she is," Jazmine replied after a thoughtful moment. "But I don't know if *she* knows it." She hesitated, and he could almost see her frown of concentration. "Mom's been different the last few months." She seemed to be analyzing the situation as she spoke. "She's less sad," Jazmine went on. "We talk about Dad a lot, and Mom laughs now and she's willing to do things and go places again. I guess someone mentioned that to the Navy, because they decided to give her sea duty."

"I'm grateful your mother's feeling better about life. When the time's right, she'll meet someone special enough to be your stepdad."

"But it won't be you."

Adam heard the sadness in her voice and regretted it. "It won't be me," he said quietly.

"You *are* attracted to Shana though, right?"

"Maybe." That was all he'd admit. He found himself wondering about the man Shana had recently dumped or been dumped by.

"So this guy she used to go out with—"

"They were *engaged,* I think, but she won't talk about it." There was a pause. "She didn't get a ring, though."

Engaged? Even an unofficial engagement suggested this had been a serious and probably long-term relationship. Which could explain why Shana had seemed so skittish.

"Are you gonna ask her out, Uncle Adam?"

Adam wasn't prepared to make that much of a commitment, not yet, anyway. "Uh, we'll see."

"I think she'd say yes," Jazmine said brightly. "Don't you?"

"I don't know. Some women seem to need a man in their lives, but…" His voice trailed off; he wasn't sure how to complete that thought.

Jazmine muttered a comment he couldn't hear.

"Pardon?" he said.

"Just remember, she's got issues—lots and lots of issues."

Adam managed to stifle a chuckle. "I'll do my best to keep that in mind. Listen, Jazz, do you feel okay now?"

"Yeah… I guess I should come out before Shana finds me in here. Oh!"

That small cry was followed by some muffled words, but he caught the drift of what was happening. Shana had just discovered where Jazmine had taken the phone.

Chapter Six

"You don't like him, do you?" Jazmine asked the next day as they drove home from the restaurant. She sat next to Shana with her arms defiantly crossed.

Shana knew better than to pretend she didn't understand that her niece was referring to Lieutenant Commander Adam Kennedy. "I think your uncle Adam is... nice." The word was lame and the hesitation was long, which gave Jazmine cause to look at Shana intently. But really, what else could she say? Her unexpected attraction to this man had completely overwhelmed her. She could only hope it passed quickly. How could she be devastated by her breakup with Brad and at the same time, experience all the symptoms of extreme attraction toward another man? A man she'd met for about five minutes and been determined to dislike on sight.

"He's really cute, too." Jazmine seemed to feel obliged to remind her of this.

As if Shana needed a reminder.

"He is, isn't he?" Jazmine challenged.

"All right, he's cute." The words nearly stuck in her throat, but with no small effort, Shana managed to get them out. She didn't know why Jazmine was so insistent.

The girl seemed to think she had a point to prove, and she wasn't letting up until she got Shana to confess she was interested in Adam Kennedy. She wasn't, of course. Okay, she was, but that was as far as it went. In other words, if he asked her out, which he wouldn't, she'd refuse. Well, she might consider it briefly, but the answer would still be no.

Jazmine was suspiciously quiet for several minutes and then gave a soft laugh. "I bet you're hot on him."

"What?" Shana nearly swallowed her tongue. The last thing she needed was Jazmine telling Adam this. "No way," she denied vehemently. She could only pray that wasn't what Jazz had said to Adam in the closet.

One glance told her Jazmine didn't buy her denial. She shouldn't have bothered to lie.

"You're saying that because of your old boyfriend, aren't you?"

"Absolutely not," Shana protested. She stepped hard on the brake at a stop sign she'd almost missed, jerking them both forward. Thank goodness for seat belts. Glaring at her niece, she asked, "Who told you that?"

Jazmine blinked wide eyes at Shana. "I overheard my mom talking to you. I wasn't listening in on your conversation, either, if that's what you're thinking. I tried to find out from Mom, but all she'd tell me was that your heart was broken, and that's why you moved to Seattle."

Shana was too tired to argue and too emotionally drained to be upset with her sister. If Ali had told Jazmine about Brad, then it was because she felt Jazmine needed to know. "I'm completely over Brad. I'm so over him it's hard to remember why I even got involved with him." The words had begun to sound like a worn-out litany.

"Brad," Jazmine said, and seemed satisfied now that she knew his name.

Shana struggled to hide her reaction. Even the mention

of Brad's name irritated her. She might have worked the last twelve hours straight, and on her feet at that, but she had enough energy left to maintain her outrage toward Brad. Still, she would've preferred never to talk about him—or hear about him—ever again.

"You still have a heart, though," Jazmine pressed. "Right?"

"Of course I have a heart." Shana didn't know where this was leading and she didn't care, as long as it didn't end up on the subject of Adam Kennedy.

"That's why you're so hot on my uncle Adam." Darn.

"I am *not* hot on your *uncle* Adam."

"Are too."

"Am not."

"Are too."

"Jazmine!"

Her niece laughed and despite her irritation, Shana smiled. This was not a conversation she wanted to have, but she'd walked right into it and was determined to extricate herself as gracefully as possible. "Don't get me wrong," she said in conciliatory tones. "I think he's a very nice man, but I don't want to get involved with anyone at the moment. Understand?"

Jazmine bit her lower lip, as if she wanted to argue, but apparently changed her mind. "For how long?"

Shana decided to nip this question in the bud. "Forever."

"That long?" Jazmine threw her a crushed look. "You don't want children? That means I'll never have cousins!"

"Okay, months and months, then." At this point Shana was ready to agree to just about anything.

"Months," Jazmine repeated. She seemed to accept that— or at any rate ventured no further argument.

Shana parked in front of her house, grateful to be home. "You know what? I don't want to cook. Do you have any suggestions?"

"I can open a can of chili," Jazmine said. "I'm not very hungry."

Shana wasn't all that hungry, either. "Sounds like a perfectly good dinner to me."

"Let me do it, okay?"

"Thanks, Jazz." Shana had no intention of turning down this generous offer. "Fabulous." Then considering her role as guardian, she felt obliged to ask, "Do you have any homework?"

"A little."

Now came the dilemma. A really good substitute mother would tell Jazmine to forget dinner; Shana would rustle up a decent meal while the kid did her schoolwork. A woman of character would insist on opening that can of chili herself. But not one with tired feet and the start of a throbbing headache, brought on by all this talk about Adam Kennedy.

Once inside the house, Shana left the front door open to create a cooling breeze. She lay back on the sofa and elevated her feet. It was little wonder the Olsens had been ready to sell their restaurant. This was hard work. For part of each day, Shana had her face buried in three-gallon containers of ice cream. Her nose felt like she was suffering from permanent frostbite.

Jazmine immediately went into the kitchen and started shuffling pans, clanking one against the other. "Do you need any help?" Shana felt she had to ask, but the question was halfhearted, to say the least.

"No, thanks."

"This is really very sweet of you."

Jazmine grumbled a reply and Shana realized she'd failed again. A kid like Jazmine, who wore ankle-high tennis shoes to school, didn't take kindly to the word *sweet*. Sooner or later, Shana would need to develop a more appropriate vocabulary. Later, she decided.

A good ten minutes passed and if not for the sounds coming from the kitchen, Shana would be napping by now. Her head rested against the cushion, her feet were propped up and all was well. For the first time since she'd arrived, Jazmine was talking freely with her. She wasn't sure whether she should credit Adam Kennedy with this improvement or not. She'd rather think she was making strides in her relationship with her niece due to her own efforts.

"Uncle Adam says you need a man in your life."

Her peace shattered, and Shana's eyes sprang open. She sat up, swung around and dropped her feet to the floor. "*What* did you just say?"

Jazmine appeared in the doorway between the kitchen and the living room, wearing a chagrined expression. "I…Uncle Adam said you're the kind of woman who needs a man in her life."

That did it. She'd utterly humiliated herself in front of him, and he thought…he *assumed* she was making some kind of play for him. This was the worst possible scenario.

"Shana?" Jazmine whispered. "You look mad."

She wondered if the smoke coming out of her ears was any indication. "That's ludicrous!"

"I'm pretty sure he meant it as a compliment."

Shana doubted it, but gave her niece credit for some fast backtracking.

"He thinks you're beautiful."

He did? Although it shouldn't have mattered, his comment gave Shana pause. "He said that?"

Jazmine hesitated. "Well, not exactly."

Okay, then. "Listen, it's not a good idea for us to talk about your uncle Adam right now." When she saw him next, she'd have plenty to say, though.

"You don't want to talk about him?"

"Nope." The kid was catching on fast.

"You don't want to talk about Brad, either."

Right again. "You could say men aren't my favorite topic at the moment."

"I guess not," Jazmine said pensively. "I won't mention either of them if that's what you want."

"I want." Her serenity gone, Shana gave up the idea of resting and joined Jazmine in the kitchen. Her niece's backpack was propped against the kitchen chair; she seemed to keep it close at all times.

Despite her intentions to the contrary, Shana gave the sexy lieutenant commander plenty of thought. What she had to do was keep her distance. She would be polite and accommodating if he wanted to spend time with Jazmine, but other than that, she'd be cool and remote. Never again would she allow him the opportunity to suggest that she needed a man—least of all him.

Jazmine stirred the chili with her back to Shana. "I probably shouldn't have said anything."

"Don't worry about it." Shana was eager to drop the subject.

"You're not mad, are you?"

"Not anymore," Shana assured her.

"You look mad."

"I'm not," she said.

"Are too."

"Am not."

"Are too."

"Am not."

They both broke out laughing. Obviously Jazz remembered that this childish interchange had amused her earlier, and she wasn't above repeating it.

Shana had to admit it felt good to laugh with her niece; it was almost like having her sister there. Jazmine was a petite version of Ali and after she'd lowered her guard, they got along well.

Shana wondered if she should clarify her position in case

Adam asked Jazmine about her again or made some other ridiculous statement. No, she decided. She'd enlighten him herself.

"You know you're not getting any younger," Jazmine said out of the blue.

Once Shana got over her shock, she had to acknowledge that the kid was ruthless in achieving her goals. She went directly for the jugular. But Shana kept her response light. "After a day like this one, that's certainly true."

On Saturday morning, Jazmine agreed to come down to the ice-cream parlor with her. In fact, Shana had no choice but to bring her. Catherine, her employee, wouldn't be in until that afternoon.

At this point Catherine was only part-time, but with the summer traffic, business was picking up and she'd need a second part-time employee. As the season progressed and the parlor was open later in the evening, she'd add more staff. The Olsens had told her that her biggest expense would be the staff payroll and warned her not to hire more people than she needed. Shana had taken their words to heart, doing as much as she could herself.

"Can I bring my Rollerblades?" Jazmine asked, standing in the doorway of her bedroom.

"Sure." Shana hated the thought of Jazmine hanging around the restaurant all day with nothing to do. Since Lincoln Park was directly across the street, there'd be plenty of paved sidewalks for her to skate. It would be a good opportunity to meet other girls her age, too.

By noon the parlor was crowded. Shana worked the pizza side and Catherine, a grandmotherly woman in her early sixties, dealt with the ice-cream orders. Catherine had been recommended by the Olsens and was great with kids. Shana had already learned a lot from her.

A young red-haired man with two children about three

and five came in and ordered a vegetarian pizza and sodas. While Shana assembled the pizza, she watched the man with his kids, admiring the way he entertained them with inventive games.

Jazmine rolled into the parlor, stopped to take off her skates and before long was deep in conversation with the father and his two kids. Shana couldn't hear what was being said, but she saw the man glance in her direction and nod.

A couple of minutes later, Jazmine joined Shana in the kitchen, which was open to the main part of the restaurant.

"Hi," Shana said, sliding the hot pizza from the oven onto the metal pan. As she sliced it, the scent of the tomato sauce and cheese and oregano wafted toward her.

"He's single."

"Who?" Shana asked distractedly as she set the pizza on the counter. "Do you want to take this out to the guy with the kids?" she asked.

"Can I?" Jazmine beamed at being asked to help out.

Her niece carefully carried the pizza to the table and brought extra napkins. She chatted with the man and his children for a few more minutes, then hurried back to Shana, who was busy preparing additional pizzas. "He asked me to introduce you."

"What?"

Jazmine's eyes widened with impatience. "I was telling you earlier. He's divorced and he wants to meet you."

"Who? The guy over there with the kids?"

"Do you see any other guy in here?"

The restaurant had any number of patrons at the moment, but the young father was the only man—and the only customer looking in her direction. He saluted her with a pizza slice.

Flustered, Shana whirled around and glared at Jazmine. "Exactly what did you say to him?"

"Me? I didn't say anything—well, I did mention that you

broke up with Brad, but that was only because he asked. He said he's been in here before."

Shana didn't remember him.

"I told him that my uncle Adam said you're the kind of woman who needs a man in your life."

Shana's heart stopped. "You didn't!"

"No." Jazmine hooted with laughter. "But I thought it would get a rise out of you."

The kid seemed to think she was being funny, but Shana wasn't laughing.

"Are you interested? Because if you are, let's go say hello to him. If you're not, it's no big deal."

Shana needed to think about this. "Promise me you didn't tell him I'm single."

"I did, and I said you were looking for a husband," Jazmine said gleefully. "You don't mind, do you?"

Shana felt the blood drain out of her face. Slowly turning her head, she saw the father still watching her. She jerked around again and noticed that Jazmine was grinning from ear to ear.

"Gotcha," she said and doubled over laughing.

Shana was glad someone found her embarrassment amusing.

Chapter Seven

Jazmine had her nose pressed against the living room window early on Sunday afternoon, waiting for her *uncle* Adam. He'd phoned the previous Monday, promising to take her out for the day. He'd mentioned the Museum of Glass in Tacoma, where there was a large Dale Chihuly exhibit.

Shana was almost as eager to see the lieutenant commander as her niece was, but for distinctly different reasons. She had a thing or two she wanted to say; he didn't know it yet, but the lieutenant commander was about to get an earful. How *dare* he suggest she needed a man! Every time she thought about it, her irritation grew—until she realized she couldn't keep quiet for even one more day.

At twelve-forty-seven precisely, Jazmine dashed away from the window and announced, "He's here!"

"Good." Shana resisted the urge to race outside and confront him then and there. She'd need to bide her time. She'd waited this long—ten whole days. What was another five minutes?

Jazmine held the screen door open, swinging it wide in welcome. "You aren't late or *anything*," she boasted so eagerly it was endearing.

"Hiya, kiddo," Adam greeted Jazmine and gave her a big hug. "It's good to see you."

"You, too! It didn't seem like Sunday would ever get here."

Shana stepped forward, saying, "Hello, Adam," in cool, level tones.

He grinned boyishly and for an instant Shana faltered. But no, she wasn't about to let him dazzle her with one of his smiles. Not this time. Her defenses were up. As far as she was concerned, he had some serious explaining to do. Still, she had to admit this guy was gorgeous. Well, *gorgeous* might be a slight exaggeration, but with those broad shoulders and the way his T-shirt fit snugly across his chest, she couldn't very well ignore the obvious. His arm was out of the sling now.

"You'd better grab a sweater," Shana suggested and Jazmine instantly flew out of the room, eager to comply so they could leave.

This was the minute Shana had been waiting for. "It's time you and I had a little talk," she said, crossing her arms.

"Sure," he said with another of those easy grins.

Again she faltered, nearly swayed by his smile, but the effect didn't last. "I want you to know I didn't appreciate the comment you made about me being—and I quote—'the kind of woman who needs a man.'"

To his credit, his gaze didn't waver. "Jazmine told you that, did she?"

So it was true. "As a matter of fact, Jazmine has repeated it any number of times."

"I see." He glanced toward the bedroom door; Jazmine hadn't come out yet.

Shana sincerely hoped she'd embarrassed him. He deserved it. "I don't know where you get off making comments like that but I have a few things to say to you."

"Go right ahead." He gestured as though granting her permission to speak. That must be how it was in the military, she thought. These officers seemed to think they could say and do whatever they pleased—*and* they got to boss other people around. Well, Shana wasn't military and she felt no restraint in speaking her mind. And she refused to call this guy by his title. He wasn't *her* commander.

"Are you married, *Mr.* Kennedy?" She already knew the answer and didn't give him an opportunity to respond. "I believe not. Does being single make you feel in any way incomplete?" Again he wasn't allowed to answer. "I thought not. This might come as a shock to you, but I am perfectly content with my life as it is. In other words, I don't need a man and your insinuating that I do is an insult."

"Shana—"

"I'm not finished yet." She held up her hand, cutting him off because she was just getting started. Before he left, she expected a full apology from Adam Kennedy.

"By all means continue," he said, his pose relaxed.

His attitude annoyed her. He acted as though he was indulging her, which Shana found condescending. "Since you're single you must want a woman in your life." She gave him the once-over. "In fact, you look like a man who *needs* a woman."

To her horror, Adam simply laughed.

"I was trying to make a point here," Shana said in as dignified a tone as she could manage.

"I know," he said and made an attempt to stifle his humor.

That only served to irritate her further. "Never mind. I can see my opinion is of little interest to you."

Suddenly they both turned to see Jazmine, who stood rooted in the bedroom doorway, a sweatshirt draped over her arm. "I should've kept my mouth shut, right?" she murmured apologetically. "I'm afraid Aunt Shana might've taken what you said the wrong way."

"So I gathered." He looked down, but Shana saw that the corners of his mouth quivered.

"Shana's right, you know," Jazmine stated for Adam's benefit, as she moved toward them. "You do need some-one special in your life."

Adam's smile disappeared.

Aha! She wondered how he'd feel being on the other side.

"Jazmine took your comments to heart," Shana primly informed him. "She tried to match me up with a divorced father of two."

Adam's gaze shot to Jazmine.

"Well… It didn't work out—but I'd be a good match-maker."

As far as Shana could tell, Jazmine was completely seri-ous. *That* had to stop. She certainly didn't need her niece dragging eligible bachelors into the pizza kitchen every chance she got.

"He might've been interested, too," Jazmine added. "He seemed really nice."

"I don't need anyone's help, thank you very much," Shana insisted.

"Hold on," Adam said, glancing from one to the other. He motioned at Jazmine. "Go back to the beginning be-cause I think I missed something."

"I found out he was single and I told him my aunt was, too, but that was all I did. She wouldn't let me introduce her."

"This is entirely your fault." Shana felt it was important that Adam understand it was his comment that had begun this whole awkward situation.

"You're finished with Brad," Jazmine reminded her. She turned to Adam and added, "He's the guy previously known as the-man-I-used-to-date. Sort of like Prince. That's what Mom said, anyway."

Adam burst out laughing.

"There is a point to this, isn't there?" Shana asked her niece.

Jazmine nodded and threw one fist in the air. "Get out there, Aunt Shana! Live a little."

Adam laughed even more.

"You think this is funny, don't you?" Shana muttered. He wouldn't find it nearly as funny when Jazmine was busy selling his attractions to single women in the museum.

"I'm sorry." But he didn't look it. For her niece's sake, she resisted rolling her eyes.

"I think it's time we cleared up this misunderstanding," he said and gestured toward the sofa. "Why don't we all sit down for a moment?"

Shana didn't take a seat until Adam and Jazmine had already made themselves comfortable on the sofa.

To her chagrin, Adam smiled patiently as if explaining the situation to a child. "I'm afraid Jazmine read more into my comment than I intended," he began. "What I said was that *some* women seem to need a man in their lives. I wasn't talking about you. Although, of course, any man in his right mind would be attracted to you. You're a beautiful woman."

"Oh." It would be convenient if Shana could magically disappear about now, but that was not to be. "I see. Well, in that case, I won't hold you up any longer." She sprang to her feet, eager to get them both out the door before she dissolved into a puddle at his feet. "I—that's a very nice thing to say…" She stared at her watch.

Adam took the hint and stood, and Jazmine rose with him. "Is there any special time you want her back this evening?" he asked.

"No…anytime is fine," she said, then quickly reconsidered. "On second thought, Jazmine has school tomorrow so she shouldn't be out too late."

"I'll have her here by seven."

"Thank you." Shana waited by the door as they left, her heart going a little crazy as she tried to regain her composure.

"Bye, Aunt Shana."

"Bye."

She closed the door. She'd hoped to put the mighty naval officer in his place and all she'd managed to do was amuse him. Depressed, Shana sank into the closest chair and hid her face in her hands—until she realized something. For the first time since Jazmine had arrived, she'd called her Aunt Shana. Twice.

Apparently her status had been sufficiently elevated that the nine-year-old was no longer ashamed to be related to her. That, at least, was progress.

Adam waited until they'd almost reached Tacoma before he mentioned the scene at Shana's. Jazmine had barely said a word from the moment they'd left. Now and then she glanced in his direction, as if she was afraid he was upset, but really he had no one to blame but himself. He did know women who were lost without a relationship, although he didn't think Shana was like that. Intentionally or not, Jazz had misunderstood his remark and used it for her own purposes.

"You really did it this time," he murmured.

"Are you mad?"

"No, but your aunt was."

"I know, but don't you be mad, okay?"

"I shouldn't have said anything. You and I should not have been discussing male-female relationships."

"Did you mean what you said about my aunt being beautiful and all that?"

"Yes." This was only the second time he'd seen Shana; again, he'd come away wanting to know her better. He might have ruined any chance of that, but he hoped not.

When he'd started out from Everett, he'd considered inviting Shana to join them. But it hadn't taken him long to decide that today probably wasn't opportune.

"What I told your aunt is the truth. She is a beautiful woman," he said casually as he headed south on the interstate.

"She likes you."

Adam chuckled.

"No, I'm serious. She's got the hots for you. I can tell."

"I don't think so." Back to reality. Shana might be attracted to him, but she'd never admit that now.

"I know so!"

"Jazmine, listen…"

"Okay, but can I say what I want to first?"

Apparently she was taking lessons from her aunt Shana. "Fine."

"I was thinking about what you said—about not feeling sparks with Mom. But I thought you might with Aunt Shana."

"Jazmine, you're far too interested in matters that are none of your concern. How do you know about this stuff, anyway? MTV?"

She groaned. "Why do adults always say things like that?"

"Because they're true."

"All I want is for you to marry her and be happy."

"Uh…"

"Has the cat got your tongue?" Jazmine teased. "Adults say that, too. No, really, I *am* serious. If you married my aunt Shana, everything would be perfect. She needs a husband and you need a wife."

"I don't need a wife," he argued. "And it's none of—"

"But you'd like to be married one day, wouldn't you?" she broke in.

"Yes," he said reluctantly. He'd had the very same thought just recently, but he'd credited that to feeling sorry for himself after the surgery. Granted, Shana was attractive but he didn't need a nine-year-old playing matchmaker. Although... He smiled involuntarily. Shana appealed to him, and he was more and more inclined to pursue the relationship. On his own schedule and in his own way.

"I can help," Jazmine offered.

"It would be best if you left this between your aunt and me. Agreed?"

After a moment, Jazmine nodded. "Agreed."

"Good, now let's have a wonderful day, all right?"

Jazmine turned a smile of pure joy on him. "All right."

A surprise awaited him when they arrived at the Museum of Glass. The Dale Chihuly exhibit was in the Tacoma Art Museum and Union Station, not in the nearby Museum of Glass. Jazmine and Adam took the guided walking tour of his permanent display and were awestruck by the Bridge of Glass. The five-hundred-foot pedestrian bridge linked the Tacoma waterfront to Pacific Avenue.

Originally Adam had gotten information about Chihuly over the Internet when he was researching a destination for today's outing. Chihuly was known for his massive glass installations, but the man's talent was even more impressive than Adam had realized. Both he and Jazmine loved his vibrant use of color and unique style. Following the walking tour, they stopped at the Museum of Glass. Adam was in for a surprise there, too. The museum was huge: it contained thirteen thousand square feet of open exhibition space. Jazmine was enthralled by the Hot Shop Amphitheater, which was the building's most striking feature. Cone-shaped, it leaned at a seventeen-degree angle, and was ninety feet high and a hundred feet wide. The theater included a glass studio where a team of artists blew and cast glass. Afterward, Adam and Jazmine ate sandwiches in the museum café and visited the gift shop. When

Adam had suggested this, it had seemed like an entertaining thing to do, but he'd quickly become caught up in the excitement and drama of watching the artists work.

By the end of the afternoon, he needed a break, and sat with a cup of coffee while Jazmine leafed through a book he'd bought her.

Before they left, Jazmine bought a postcard of the Dale Chihuly glass flowers displayed on the ceiling of a Las Vegas casino to send her mother.

"Are you ready to go back to your aunt's?" he asked, sipping his coffee.

"I guess," Jazmine said. "But only if you are."

Adam recognized a trap when he saw one. If he appeared too eager, little Jazmine might suspect he wanted to see Shana again. He did, but he sure wasn't going to admit it, especially to her.

Chapter Eight

For Shana, having an entire Sunday to herself was sheer luxury. Catherine was working at the restaurant and this was the first day she'd taken off since she'd purchased the business. Shana intended to take full advantage of this gift of time.

Working as many hours as she did, she'd been putting off a number of tasks and spent two hours doing paperwork. The Olsens had trained her well in every aspect of owning a restaurant, but they'd failed to warn her how much paperwork was involved. Getting everything organized wasn't difficult but it was time-consuming. After working all day and handling the closing in the evening, she was exhausted, and making sense of anything more than the remote control was beyond her.

Once the paperwork was up-to-date, she polished her toenails, and between three loads of wash, she luxuriated in a new mystery she'd been trying to read for weeks. She'd been reading at night in fits and starts, but couldn't manage more than fifteen or twenty minutes at a time. The author was one of her favorites but to Shana's surprise her mind kept wandering away from the page. She supposed it was because she felt guilty about all the things she should be doing.

When she wasn't fretting over that, her thoughts were on Jazmine and Adam. She knew they were going to the Museum of Glass, but that couldn't possibly take all afternoon. Well, maybe it could; she didn't know.

Finally Shana gave up and shut the book. This was Adam Kennedy's fault. Even when he was nowhere in sight, he wouldn't leave her alone.

When she could stand it no longer, Shana logged on to the computer and left her sister a message.

Sent: Sunday, June 12
From: Shana@mindsprung.com
To: Alison.Karas@woodrowwilson.navy.mil
Subject: Adam Kennedy: Friend or Foe?

Dear Ali,

Just checking in to let you know that despite our rocky start, everything's going well with Jazz and me. She's a great kid.

The upcoming week is the last of the school year. I'm thrilled at how quickly Jazmine has adjusted and how fast she's made friends. I guess she's had lots of practice. She's a tremendous help at the ice-cream and pizza parlor and insists on taking pizzas to the customers' tables, which I appreciate.

The other reason I'm writing is that I've got a question about Peter's friend, Adam Kennedy. I must have met him at Peter's funeral, but if so I don't remember. Jazmine seems to think you're romantically interested in him. Are you? You've never mentioned him before—at least not that I can recall. Before you make anything of this inquiry, I want it understood that I find him arrogant and egotistical. Jazmine, however, thinks the guy walks on water. They're off this afternoon to explore some glass museum. I'd be grateful if you'd tell me what you know about him. For instance, has he ever been married? If not, why? I don't want to give you the wrong impression or anything—I do find him arrogant. But he sort of interests me, too. Fill in the blanks for me, would you?

Love,
Shana

At six Shana tossed a salad for dinner. The house seemed terribly quiet, and she turned on the television for company. That wasn't like her. In all her years of living alone, she'd never once felt this lonely. At first she wondered if it was due to the breakup with Brad, but all she felt when she thought about him was regret for all that wasted time—and anger. She was just plain glad he was out of her life. In fact, she rarely thought of him at all and that surprised her.

Jazmine had been with her for only a few weeks, and already Shana couldn't imagine life without her. She missed Jazmine's energy—blaring her music or talking on the phone, or plying Shana with questions about all sorts of things. The difference between the unhappy nine-year-old who'd arrived on her doorstep and the girl she was now—well, it seemed nothing short of astonishing. She'd become extroverted, interested and…interfering.

A little after seven, Jazmine burst into the house. "I'm back!" she shouted.

Before Shana could issue a word of welcome, Jazmine regaled her with details of how they'd spent their day. She talked about the walking tour and chattered excitedly about watching the artists work in the Museum of Glass.

She'd fed the seagulls along the waterfront on Rustin Way and then Adam had taken her for a quick visit to the zoo at Point Defiance Park. Shana could hardly believe the girl could talk so fast and breathe at the same time.

"I guess you had a completely rotten time?" Shana asked, teasing her. Shana realized as she spoke that the lieutenant commander was nowhere in sight. "Where's Adam?"

"We were kind of late and he had to get back." Jazmine's smile widened. "Did you *want* him to come inside?"

"Not really. I just thought he might like to…visit for a few minutes." Actually, after the way she'd torn into him on his arrival, she didn't blame him for avoiding her.

"We should probably have a little talk," Shana said, slipping an arm around Jazmine's shoulders.

Her niece stiffened. "I have a feeling this is the same little talk Uncle Adam and I had, only now it's going to be the Aunt Shana version."

Her interest was instantly piqued. "Really? And what did Adam have to say?"

Jazmine gave a long-suffering sigh. "That it would be a good idea if I left the two of you alone."

"He's right." Shana was grateful Adam had taken it upon himself to explain this. Jazmine would accept it more readily coming from him.

"He also said I'm concerning myself with matters that aren't any of my business."

"Exactly." Obviously Adam had been very forthright during his version of the "little talk."

"I promised him I wouldn't try matching you up with other men."

"I'd appreciate that," Shana said solemnly.

Jazmine sighed again. "I wouldn't like it if you went around talking to boys about me."

That was exactly how Shana had planned to approach the subject herself. "Did Adam make that comparison?"

Her niece nodded. "He said it on the drive back."

"He's smarter than he looks," Shana muttered. Then, because she felt her niece should know this, she added, "A man and a woman can be friends without being romantically involved, Jazmine. It's called a platonic relationship."

The phone rang then, and without waiting for a second ring, Jazmine leaped like a gazelle into the other room. She ripped the receiver off the wall. "Hello," she said urgently. "No, she's here, you have the right number." Jazmine held out the phone. "It's for you."

Shana started to ask who it was, but didn't. Taking the receiver, she raised it to her ear. "This is Shana."

"Shana. I can't tell you how wonderful it is to hear the sound of your voice."

For the first time in her life, Shana's knees felt as if they were about to buckle. It was Brad.

"Hello, Brad," she said evenly, amazed at her ability to respond without emotion. The man had guts; she'd say that for him. "How'd you find me?" she asked coolly.

"It wasn't easy. It's taken me weeks."

She supposed she should be complimented that he'd made the effort, but she wasn't. "I don't mean to be rude, but there was a reason I kept my number unlisted."

"The least you can do is listen to what I have to say," he told her.

"Everything's been said."

"But Shana—"

"There's nothing more to say," she insisted.

"At least give me your address. I can't believe you're living in Washington. Did you get a transfer?"

"That's nothing to do with you."

Jazmine was watching her carefully, eyes wide and quizzical as if she was hoping to memorize each word so she could repeat it.

"I would prefer if you didn't phone me again." Shana was prepared to cut him off, but he stopped her, obviously guessing her intentions.

"Don't hang up," he pleaded. "Please, Shana, just hear me out."

"It won't do any good." She'd gone ramrod-straight, her resistance up. She didn't even find this difficult, although she had to admit she was mildly curious as to why he'd sought her out.

"I don't care. I need to get this off my chest. Just promise me you'll listen."

She didn't want to encourage him with a response.

He continued despite that. "You told me you were leaving Portland, but I didn't believe you. Shana, I miss you. I need you. Nothing is the same without you. I feel so empty. You have no idea how awful it's been for me."

That was their problem in a nutshell. The entire relationship had revolved around Brad Moore and his needs. *He* missed her, *he* needed her. She was convenient, loyal and endlessly patient. Well, no more.

She rolled her eyes and made a circular motion with her hand as though to hurry him along.

Jazmine planted her hand over her mouth to smother her giggles.

"Are you listening?" he asked, finishing up a five-minute soliloquy about how much he missed all their special times. Translation: all the "special" times when she'd been there to see to his comfort. He recounted the little ways she'd indulged him—the meals she'd cooked according to his likes and dislikes, the movies she'd watched because he'd chosen them, the Christmas shopping she'd done for him... Not once did he say any of the things that might have changed her mind, including the fact that he loved her.

So far, everything he'd said reaffirmed her belief that she'd made the right decision. It would always be about

Brad and what he needed from her and how important she was to his comfort. Apparently Sylvia wasn't nearly as accommodating as Shana.

Finally she couldn't take it any longer.

"Are you finished yet?" she asked and yawned rudely to signal her boredom.

Her question was followed by a short silence. "You've changed, Shana."

"Yes," she told him in a curt voice. "Yes, I have."

"I can't believe you don't love me anymore."

Shana noticed he hadn't even bothered to ask about the girl who'd answered the phone.

Brad seemed shocked that she wasn't ready to race back into his arms just because he'd made an effort to find her. A short while ago, she'd been grateful for each little crumb he'd tossed her way. Those days were over. Oh, this felt good. *She* felt good.

"What's happened to my sweet Shana?" he asked. "This isn't like you."

"I woke up," she informed him, "and I didn't respect the woman I'd become. It was time to clean house. Out with the old and in with the new."

The line went silent as he absorbed this. "You're dating someone else, aren't you?"

The temptation to let him believe that was strong, and she might have given in to it, if not for Jazmine. With her niece listening to every word, Shana felt honor-bound to tell the truth.

"It's just like you to think that, but no, I'm not seeing anyone else." She bit back the words to tell him she could if she wanted to. Well, there was that single father who might've been interested—and Adam Kennedy.

His relief was instantaneous. "You'll always love me…."

"No," she said firmly. "I won't. I don't. Not anymore. For your sake and mine, please don't call me again."

He started to argue, but Shana wasn't willing to listen. She should've hung up the phone long before, but some perverse satisfaction had kept her on the line.

As she replaced the receiver, she looked over at Jazmine. Her niece gave a loud triumphant shout. "Way to go, Aunt Shana!"

They exchanged high fives. Shana felt exuberant and then guilty for not experiencing even the slightest disappointment. She was actually grateful Brad had phoned because this conversation had provided complete and final proof that she'd reclaimed her own life.

"Can I tell Uncle Adam about this?" Jazmine asked happily.

"Adam?" Her suspicions immediately rose to the surface. "Whatever for?"

"Because," Jazmine replied as if it should be obvious. "He should know that you really are over Brad. The door's open, isn't it? I mean, you're cured."

Shana liked the analogy. "I am cured, but let's just keep this between us for now, okay?"

Jazmine frowned. "If you say so," she said without enthusiasm.

The kid was certainly eager to get her and Adam together. Presumably she'd abandoned her earlier hopes for Adam and her mother. "I want your promise that you won't talk to Adam about any part of my conversation with Brad."

Muttering under her breath, Jazmine shook her head. Halfway to her room, she turned back. "Uncle Adam wanted me to tell you he'll be by next Saturday. That's all right, isn't it?"

"Of course it is." Not until later did Shana realize how dejected she was at the thought of waiting almost a week before she saw Adam Kennedy again.

Chapter Nine

Ali read Shana's e-mail a second time and smiled. This was exactly what she'd hoped—but didn't dare believe—would happen. Although her sister was skirting the issue, she was interested in Adam; her e-mail confirmed it. Adam had definitely gotten Shana's attention.

It took half an hour for Ali to answer her sister. She worked hard on the wording for fear she'd say too much or not enough. Adam was a lot like Peter in the ways that really mattered. He was loyal, compassionate, with a strong work ethic and an endearing sense of humor. Through the years, Peter had encouraged him to settle down and get married. Personally Ali didn't understand why Adam hadn't. Aside from the important stuff, he was good-looking. As far as she knew he dated, but obviously hadn't found the one woman with whom he wanted to spend the rest of his life. Could Shana be that woman? Far be it from her to suggest such a thing. Much better if a relationship developed without her meddling. From the sounds of it, they were getting all the romantic assistance they needed—or didn't need—from Jazmine.

Once she'd finished her e-mail, Ali prepared for her shift. It'd taken some adjustment, but she'd become accustomed to life aboard the aircraft carrier. Routine helped pass the days, and being able to stay in touch with her daughter through the Internet eased her mind about Jazmine.

The hours went by quickly as she responded to small medical emergencies.

She was almost finished with her shift when Commander Frank Dillon entered the sick bay. His complexion was sickly pale, and his forehead was beaded with sweat. When he saw that Ali was the duty nurse, he attempted a weak smile but she noticed that his jaw was clenched and he was clearly in pain.

Ali remembered him from her first day in the wardroom. Since then, she hadn't seen him at all but thought about him often, reliving those few seconds when he'd reached out to steady her in the passageway. Just seconds—it couldn't have been more than that. She didn't know why she'd read anything into such a minor incident. Still, she'd fantasized about him an embarrassing number of times in the weeks since. No one had to remind her of the professional issues involved in fraternization aboard ship.

"Commander Dillon," Ali said, coming forward to assist him. He held his hand pressed against his side. "What happened?"

"Something's wrong," he muttered. He looked as if he was close to passing out. "I need a doctor."

Ali led him into an examination room, and learned that he'd had a stomachache for the last couple of days. It'd had grown steadily worse and now the pain had become intolerable. She alerted Captain Robert Coleman, the physician on duty, who examined the commander.

Ali suspected it was his appendix, and apparently Dr. Coleman did, too. Following the examination, he ordered X-rays. Ali accompanied Commander Dillon while the X-rays were taken. The commander didn't utter a word, although she knew every touch, no matter how gentle, brought him pain.

One look at the film confirmed her fears. Time was critical; judging by the amount of pain he was suffering, his appendix could rupture any minute. Dr. Coleman scheduled emergency surgery, which he planned to perform immediately.

Ali helped prep the commander, explaining what was happening and why. She hooked up the IV and taped the needle in place. After checking the fluid bag, she glanced down and discovered him watching her. She smiled shyly, unaccustomed to such intent scrutiny.

Frank closed his eyes and drew in a deep breath.

Ali squeezed his hand. "Don't worry, we'll have you back to your command as good as new," she promised.

He was silent until just before he was rolled into the surgical bay. He gripped Ali's hand unexpectedly and with surprising strength. Half rising from the gurney, he said, "It's bad. Listen, if I don't make it...if there are complications..."

"You're going to live to tell about this, Commander," she assured him. She gave his hand another squeeze and urged him back down. Their eyes met and she did her best to let him know that the medical staff would take good care of him and all would be well.

The commander dragged in another deep breath. "I don't mean to sound fatalistic, but I don't have any family. My wife left me years ago—no kids. My brother died a few years back and I've never updated my will."

"I'm sorry about your brother," she told him softly.

His hand clutched hers. "Money to charity. Decide for me. Promise you'll decide for me."

"I will, but, Commander..."

He wasn't listening anymore, she realized. The pain was too intense.

"I'm going into surgery with you," she whispered. "If God decides it's your time, He'll have to argue with me first." Although she was certain he was past hearing anything, she thought she detected a faint smile.

As the surgery progressed, Ali wanted to chastise the commander for waiting so long to seek medical attention. He had risked his life because of—what? Pride? Ignoring the pain hadn't made it go away. An infected appendix was not going to heal itself.

The surgery was routine until they found that, exactly as she'd suspected, the appendix had burst. Extra time and care was needed to ensure that the infection was completely eradicated before it could spread to the entire abdominal area. Peritonitis could be fatal. Having a ruptured appendix wasn't as life-threatening as in years past, but it was serious enough.

After the surgery, Commander Dillon's incision was closed and he was taken into Recovery. Lieutenant Rowland was sent in to replace Ali, whose shift had ended.

"I'll stay with him a bit longer," she told Rowland. Sitting at the commander's bedside, she took his blood pressure every twenty minutes until he woke from the anesthesia several hours later.

He moved his head instinctively toward Ali, who sat by his side.

She smiled and touched his brow. "God didn't put up much of an argument. It seems that neither heaven nor hell was interested in collecting your soul, Commander."

"You sure about that?" he whispered weakly. "I thought this pain meant I was in hell."

"How are you feeling now?"

"Like someone hacked me open with a saw blade."

"I'll give you something for the pain." She stood and reached for his chart to make a notation. "Rest now. Your body's had quite a time of it." That was an understatement, but she felt better knowing he was awake. His vital signs confirmed that he was out of immediate danger.

Ali sat with the commander for another hour and then reluctantly turned her patient over to Rowland.

"Do you know the commander?" the lieutenant asked as she left the recovery area.

"I met him our first day out."

Rowland seemed surprised that she'd stayed with him. It surprised Ali, too. She was busy these days and got as little as four or five hours' sleep a night, but hadn't been able to make herself leave. One thing was certain: this man had her attention. Just as Adam had Shana's…

Frank Dillon was lost in a dark, lonely world. Every so often he heard a soft, feminine voice and it confused him. He couldn't figure out where he was. Then he remembered the pain, the surgery, the nurse—that soft voice was the nurse talking to him. The one who haunted his dreams. He prayed it was her and in the same breath pleaded for God to send her away. Her touch was light, and on the rare occasions when he found the strength to open his eyes, she was standing by his side.

She smelled good. Not of flowers or perfume, but a distinct womanly scent. Clean and subtle and…just nice. It lured him unlike anything else he'd ever experienced. He wasn't a man accustomed to the ways of women. He'd lived his life in the Navy and for the Navy, and he'd learned the hard way that he wasn't meant to be a Navy husband.

He'd married at twenty-five and Laura had left him two years later. That had been nearly twenty years ago. His wife had walked out when she realized no amount of crying, pleading or cajoling would persuade him to resign his commission. She knew before they were married that he'd made the Navy his career, the same as his father and grandfather had. Nothing was more important to Frank than duty and honor. Not his marriage, not Laura, not one damn thing. She hadn't been able to reconcile herself to that and he doubted any woman ever could. Other commitments took second place to military life. He'd accepted that, and dedicated himself to his career. Not once in all those years had he regretted his decision. Until now—and now he would willingly have sold his soul to keep this woman at his side. He needed her, wanted her and he didn't care what it cost him.

Some of his fellow officers had been against letting women serve at sea. Frank hadn't been one of them. Now he wasn't so sure his peers had been wrong. Senior Medical Officer Alison Karas had taken up far more of his thoughts than warranted. He'd decided from their first, chance encounter to stay away from her; he wasn't risking his career for a shipboard romance. Avoiding her was easy enough to accomplish with five thousand sailors aboard the *USS Woodrow Wilson*. It was just his luck that she was the one on duty. Luck or fate? He wasn't sure he'd like the answer.

A cool hand touched his brow, followed by Alison's quiet voice. Unable to make out the words, Frank thought it might have been a prayer. Apparently he was worse off than he'd known, although she seemed to think she had some influence with the Man Upstairs. Her constancy touched him. No one had ever done anything like that before—not for him.

The darkness didn't bother him anymore. He was at peace, even though a vague memory, something about Alison, hovered just out of reach. She was with him. He planned to tell her how much her presence meant to him.

If he lived through this.

The next morning, the *USS Woodrow Wilson* was hit by a raging storm. The massive ship had turned into the typhoon, and there was nothing to do but ride it out. Thankfully, Ali had never been prone to seasickness, but a number of men were sent to sick bay. She had her hands full the first day of the storm, but things had settled down by the second. During a quiet moment, she went in to check on Commander Dillon. He was sitting up in bed, still pale and not in the best of moods.

"What the hell is going on topside?" he demanded the moment he saw her.

"We're in the midst of a typhoon, Commander."

He tossed aside his sheet and seemed ready to climb out of bed. "Get me out of here."

"No." She prevented him from moving farther.

From the way his eyes widened, Ali could tell that it wasn't often anyone stood up to the high and mighty commander. "I'm the navigator and I'm needed topside," he argued, his face reddening.

"This might come as a shock, Commander Dillon, but the Navy stayed afloat without you for more than two hundred years. They'll manage to survive for another day or so. Now stay in bed, otherwise I'll have you restrained."

His blue eyes flared. "You wouldn't."

Although her heart was pounding, Ali didn't dare let her nervousness show. "I don't think that's something you'd like to find out. Your orders are to stay in bed until Captain Coleman says otherwise. Do I make myself clear?"

His gaze challenged hers, but then, apparently reaching a decision, he nodded. Although he wasn't happy about it, he would abide by what he knew was best.

Ali was grateful. Under normal circumstances, the commander wasn't a man to cross; she'd figured that out quickly enough. And if his scowl was any indication, he was on the mend. He'd been in bad shape the first few days, but his improvement was steady. To show him how much she appreciated his cooperation, she patted his arm.

He stiffened as if he found her touch offensive and Ali

quickly backed away. While he was under anesthesia, she'd touched him many times. In an effort to comfort him, she'd stroked his brow and talked to him in soothing tones. She'd frequently taken his pulse and blood pressure and let her hand linger on his arm, hoping he'd sense her encouragement and concern. Perhaps she'd grown too familiar, too personal.

"I apologize," he muttered gruffly.

Embarrassed, Ali retreated an additional step. "No, the fault is mine—I'm sorry." By all rights, she should turn and leave. The clinic was busy. Sailors were waiting. She should get while the getting was good, as her grandmother used to say.

"You were with me in Recovery until I regained consciousness, weren't you?" he whispered.

She nodded, afraid they were taking a dangerous risk by acknowledging this attraction. Not since Peter's death had Ali allowed herself to feel anything for another man. In fact, she'd been certain she never would and now…now she wasn't sure what to think.

"Any particular reason you stayed with me all those hours?" he asked.

Ali didn't know what to tell him. Honesty might be the best policy, but there were times the truth was better avoided. This appeared to be one of those times.

"Your appendix had ruptured, Commander. In such cases, there's a significant chance of complications. It was easier for me just to remain on duty than explain the situation to my shift replacement." Ali used her best professional voice, making it as devoid of emotion as she could.

He seemed to accept her explanation and answered with an abrupt nod.

"Is there anything else I can do for you?" she asked, moving away from his bedside.

Chapter Ten

As promised, Adam Kennedy was at the restaurant by ten on Saturday morning. Shana had anticipated this moment—no, dreaded it—all week. She might've been able to push the lieutenant commander from her mind if it weren't for Jazmine, who found every excuse in the world to bring up his name. They could be discussing the migration habits of Canada geese, and Jazmine would somehow link the topic with her uncle Adam. It didn't matter *what* they discussed, Adam Kennedy became part of the conversation.

Shana didn't resent the fact that her niece called Adam her uncle anymore. It seemed natural for her to do so. What didn't seem natural—or fair—was the way he'd infiltrated her thoughts. And, in all honesty, that wasn't just due to Jazmine.

"Good morning," Adam said as he marched into the restaurant with a crisp military gait that said he was ready for action. He wore black jeans and a casual denim shirt with the sleeves rolled up.

"Hi." Her voice faltered a little. This was one attractive man, a fact she was trying hard to ignore. Nonetheless, her hands trembled as she reached for a paper towel and wiped them clean. "Jazmine brought her Rollerblades." Thankfully it was early enough that the ice-cream parlor didn't have any customers yet.

"I saw. She put on a show for me in the parking lot."

"Oh." Now *that* was an intelligent response and Shana resisted the urge to kick herself. She intensely disliked the way Adam made her feel like an awkward teenager. Until recently, she'd considered herself a competent professional, a woman who could cope with any social situation, and it irked her no end that this man could agitate her like this. "Where are you two headed today?" she asked conversationally, hoping to hide her complete lack of a brain.

Adam sauntered up to the cash register, apparently in no hurry to leave. "I haven't decided yet. I thought I'd get some suggestions from Miss Jazz."

"Good idea." Before she sent him off with Jazmine, perhaps she should enlighten him about her niece's continuing efforts to match up the two of them. "Do you have a few minutes before you go?"

"Sure." He slid onto one of the stools.

Rubbing her palms against her apron, Shana took a moment to clear her thoughts. "I don't know if you've noticed," she began, "but Jazmine seems to be working hard at, uh, getting the two of us together." She paused. "This is in spite of your…little talk."

Adam leaned forward. "I got the hint in our last phone conversation, when she started mentioning your name in practically every sentence."

"She does that to you, too?" Interesting. And, she supposed, predictable. "You're a frequent topic of conversation yourself."

He chuckled. "She's been e-mailing me updates on you."

"Updates on *what?*"

"I haven't paid a lot of attention."

She was unexpectedly miffed by that but decided his indifference was probably for the best.

"By the way, how's Brad?"

Shana nearly bit her tongue in an effort to hide her reaction. "I thought you said you weren't paying attention," she said. "Brad isn't important."

"Really? That's curious because—"

"I have something to discuss," she said, cutting him off before they both got sidetracked by the unpleasant subject of Brad.

"Have at it," Adam said, gesturing toward her.

"First, since we're both aware that Jazmine's busy playing matchmaker, it seems the best defense is to be honest with each other." She half expected an argument.

"I agree."

He seemed utterly relaxed; in contrast, Shana's nerves were as tight as an overwound guitar string.

"Okay," she said, taking a deep breath. "I think you're wonderful with Jazmine and…and mildly attractive." The man already had an overblown ego and she wasn't about to give him any encouragement.

"Really?" He perked up at that.

"Yes," she admitted reluctantly, "and there are probably a few other positive traits I could add."

He checked his watch. "I have time."

She ignored him. "But without going into why I feel a relationship between us wouldn't work—"

"Aren't you being a little hasty?" he asked without allowing her to finish.

"No," she insisted. "Besides, I'm not interested." She wondered if a big red neon light spelling *liar* was flashing over her head. She *was* interested, but she suspected this whole attraction thing was just the result of being on the rebound. She needed to take it slow, ease into another relationship. Letting Adam Kennedy sweep her off her feet was definitely a bad idea.

He stared at her blankly. "Interested in what?"

"You. I don't mean to be blunt or rude, but I felt I should be clear about that."

"No problem." He shrugged, his expression unchanged.

"I didn't mean to offend you."

"You didn't," he assured her and he certainly didn't look put off by her confession.

"It's just that this isn't the right time for me to get involved," she rushed to add, confused now and more than a little embarrassed. She wished she'd thought this through more carefully. "I've only had the business a short while, and all my energy and resources are tied up in it."

"Of course. That makes perfect sense."

"This has nothing to do with you personally." She was only digging herself in deeper now but couldn't seem to stop.

"Shana, it's not a problem. Don't worry, okay? If anything, it's a relief."

"It is?" she blurted out.

"We should keep each other informed," he murmured. "Just like you suggested. Jazmine is a sweet kid, but we both need to be aware of her game plan."

"Exactly." She felt guilty about the things she'd said. "I hope I didn't offend you—sometimes my tongue goes faster than my brain."

"Not at all," he told her patiently.

"Good." It was probably ridiculous to be so worried about a nine-year-old's scheme and even more ridiculous to mention it to Adam. Thankfully he'd taken everything with a sense of humor.

"Uncle Adam!" Jazmine skated into the parlor and at one glance from Shana, sat down and removed her skates. "Are you done yet? Can we leave now?"

"In a minute."

"Great!" Jazmine looked about as happy as Shana could remember seeing her. "School's out for the year." She slipped on her tennis shoes without bothering to tie them.

Shana's cheeks still burned with embarrassment and she was eager to see Adam and Jazmine leave. "You guys have a great time," she mumbled. "Bye."

Adam slid off the stool and with Jazmine at his side, they ambled out. After the door closed, Shana felt oddly depressed, although she couldn't name the precise reason. She didn't want to analyze it, either.

Business was slow for a Saturday, but experience told Shana it would pick up around lunchtime. She had two part-time employees now in addition to Catherine, the retired woman the Olsens had recommended, who was Shana's most valuable employee. She moved easily between the ice-cream section and the pizza parlor, and she was fully capable of taking over if Shana wanted time off, which was reassuring. This was the one buffer Shana felt she needed now that she was Jazmine's guardian.

Around eleven, the young father Jazmine had talked to a few weeks earlier stepped into the restaurant. He was without his kids today. He strolled up to the pizza counter; from there he could see Shana in the kitchen, where she was busy stirring a vat of soup. She'd discovered a brand of concentrated soups that tasted as good as homemade and was pleased with the results.

"Hi," he said casually, leaning against the counter.

"Can I help you?" Shana pretended not to remember him, which was the exact opposite of the way she treated her other customers. She worked hard at remembering people's names and creating a warm and welcoming atmosphere. She knew his, too—Tim—but refused to acknowledge it.

"I was wondering if you'd be interested in dinner and a movie."

His invitation took her completely off guard. "I—I beg your pardon?"

"I...well, actually, I was asking you out on a date." His

voice was a monotone now, as if she'd deflated his ego, and Shana instantly felt bad.

"I'm flattered, but—"

"Your niece mentioned that you're single, and well, so am I and I was wondering, you know, if you'd like to go out sometime."

Shana wasn't sure what to say. She hesitated, and then decided she could only be honest. "Thank you. I'm flattered that you'd ask, but I just don't have time to date right now." She motioned around her. "This is a new venture for me and I…have to be here."

He frowned. "Is there any particular reason you don't want to go out with me?"

A couple of dozen quickly presented themselves but Shana couldn't manage to get out a single one. "You seem very nice, but—"

"It's the kids, isn't it?"

"No, not at all," she hurried to assure him. "It's like I told you—the timing is wrong." That was the excuse she'd used with Adam; it was also the truth. She'd untangled herself from one relationship and wasn't ready to get involved in another.

"You mean I should've waited until you were finished for the day?"

"No…"

He wiped his face. "You'll have to excuse me. I'm new at this. My wife, I mean ex-wife, and I met in high school and well, it just didn't work out. I don't blame her. We were both too young, but Heather's the only woman I've ever dated and—I don't know what the hell I'm doing." He looked completely crestfallen by the time he'd finished.

Shana felt even worse. "Under other circumstances, I'd be happy to—" She stopped, afraid she'd just make matters worse if she continued. "Would you like a cup of coffee?"

He nodded and sat down on the stool. "That would be great, thanks."

"It's Tim, right?"

He smiled dejectedly. "I'm surprised you remember."

He'd be shocked at everything she did recall about the last time he'd been in the ice-cream parlor—even if she preferred not to.

Shana made them each an espresso, double shot. If he didn't need it she did. When she set the tiny cups on the counter, Tim reached for his wallet. Raising her hand, she said, "It's on the house."

"Thanks."

She waved off his gratitude. For reasons she didn't want to examine too closely, she felt guiltier than ever for rejecting him.

"Can you tell me what I did wrong?" he asked after the first tentative sip.

"It isn't you," she said earnestly. "It really is because of the timing. My new business and looking after my niece and everything."

Over the next three hours, she heard the story of Tim's ten-year marriage and every detail of his divorce. The only time he paused was when she was bombarded with questions from customers or staff, or if the capable Catherine needed her assistance.

She also learned practically the entire story of Tim's life. He seemed to need a willing ear and she provided it, between serving ice cream in three dozen different flavors.

"You know, Tim, it seems to me you're still in love with your wife," she commented while he was on his third espresso.

His eyes flared and he adamantly shook his head. "No way."

"Sorry, but that's how I see it."

"You're wrong."

"Could be, but it's obvious you're crazy about your kids."

He had no argument with that. "They're fabulous."

"So—what else can I do for you?" she asked when he showed no sign of leaving anytime within the foreseeable future.

"You could always go to dinner with me," he suggested.

Shana laughed, knowing she'd be in for a repeat of his disagreement with the divorce attorney. She gave him an A for effort, though. "I thought we already went over that."

"Are you sure you mean no?" he asked again.

"If the lady says no, that's what she means," Adam Kennedy said from the doorway leading into the restaurant. He glared at Tim as if he wanted to teach him a lesson. His tone was friendly enough, but his demeanor wasn't. Shana sighed in exasperation. She was all too aware of the interest Catherine and the others were taking in this little scene. Tim was harmless, his self-esteem in shreds following his divorce, and he was counting on Shana to boost his confidence.

"Thank you very much, Adam," she said tightly, fighting the temptation to say a great deal more, "but the lady can answer for herself."

To her surprise Jazmine laughed outright. "Hello, Mr. Gilmore, remember me?"

Tim looked as if he didn't know what to say. He got off the stool. "I guess it's time to go."

"Sounds like a good idea to me," Adam murmured.

"Adam," Shana chastised, but his gaze didn't waver from Tim's face.

As soon as the other man was out the door, Shana whirled on Adam. "That was completely unnecessary and uncalled for," she said, trying to keep her voice down in deference to her staff and customers.

Adam looked away. "Perhaps, but I wanted to be sure he got the message."

"And what exactly is the message?" Shana demanded.

Adam grinned as if the answer should be obvious.

"Hands off," Jazmine supplied. "You're already spoken for."

With her shift over, Ali went to check on Commander Dillon one last time and discovered he was asleep. His face was turned toward her and in slumber his features had relaxed. He looked younger than she'd first assumed.

As she stood there, Ali hesitated, resisting the urge to move closer. She longed to place her hand on his arm, to touch him and feel the warmth of his skin. A chill ran down her spine as she remembered he didn't want her anywhere near him. That had been made abundantly clear during her last visit.

She wished she had someone she could talk to about the way she felt. This wasn't something she could discuss with the other women on board. She could be putting her career in jeopardy. Any hint of a romantic entanglement, and she could be in more trouble than she wanted to consider.

Before she left, Ali logged on to her computer.

Sent: June 20
From: Alison.Karas@woodrowwilson.navy.mil
To: Shana@mindsprung.com
Subject: Hello!

Dear Shana,

Just wanted to see how you're doing this week. I think of you and Jazmine every day. I'm doing well myself. We had an emergency appendectomy this week—Commander Dillon. I might have mentioned him before. Before he went under, he seemed to think he might not make it, and asked if I'd look after his affairs. I told him I would, but thankfully that wasn't necessary. He's recuperating nicely now. I think he's

Ali hesitated, remembering the intense look in Frank's eyes as he confessed he had no family. What a lonely life he must lead. Divorced and his brother dead. It didn't sound as if his parents were still living, either. He'd wanted her to dispose of his earthly goods by giving whatever he had to charity. Ali told herself he didn't have time to ask anyone else; she'd been handy, so he'd reached out to her. Still, she sensed that he trusted her. They were basically strangers but he felt he could speak to her and that she would follow through with whatever he'd requested. Had it been necessary, she would have.

After a moment's hesitation, Shana returned to her e-mail. She deleted the last three words and began a new paragraph.

Jazmine mentioned that Adam was stopping by on Saturday. How did that go? I know you think my daughter's trying to match the two of you up and I agree she has no business doing that. But the truth is, I don't think it's such a bad idea.

Adam is a good man and while you might have a dozen excuses not to recognize what a find he is, look again. This is your big sister talking here. I mean it: take a close look at this guy. Adam is easy on the eyes (nice but not essential), he's intelligent and hardworking and wonderful with kids.

I just hope keeping Jazmine for the next six months will convince you that you want children of your own. I can tell how close the two of you are getting just from the e-mails. It's almost enough to make me jealous!

Your e-mails mean the world to me. Keep them coming.

Love,
Ali

It didn't take long for Ali to get a response. She wasn't sure if it was because of the time difference or if she happened to catch her sister at the computer.

Sent: June 21
From: Shana@mindsprung.com
To: Alison.Karas@woodrowwilson.navy.mil
Subject: Commander, you say?

Dear Ali,

No, you didn't mention anyone named Commander Dillon. What gives? Is he all right? I assume he must be. But the fact that you're saying anything at all tells me you're interested in him. This is a development worth watching. I know, I know, all shipboard romances are strictly taboo. But tell me more!

I'm afraid I made an idiot of myself in front of Adam this morning. Trust me, any romantic interest he might have felt toward me is deader than roadkill. I'm such a fool.

All right, all right, I'll tell you what I did, but you've got to promise not to mention it again. I decided he should be aware of Jazmine's little scheme. That seems only fair, don't you think?

In retrospect, I still feel it needed to be said but maybe I didn't handle it in the best possible way. When I assured him I wasn't interested in him, I came off sounding like...I don't know what. I keep saying it, but this isn't the right time for me to get involved. It really isn't, not with just starting this business.

And guess what? Another guy, who was recently divorced, came in later this afternoon and asked me out. I turned him down using the same excuse and felt terrible. (By the way, it's thanks to the little matchmaker that he knew I was single.)

Oh, and did I mention Brad phoned? Let me tell you that was a short conversation. If I needed confirmation that I did the right thing in breaking up with him, our conversation was it.

Hearing from you is wonderful. Both Jazmine and I miss you terribly. I never realized how much effort went into being a parent. Don't get me wrong, Jazz is one fabulous kid and I'm crazy about her, but I didn't have any idea how much my life would change when she came to live with me.

You're right, Ali, I'm absolutely certain now that I want to be a mother one day. That's a bit intimidating, though. With everything that's happened in the last few months, I've pushed all thoughts of another relationship out of my mind. I still think I need to wait a while. Is that a biological clock I hear ticking? Not to worry, I have plenty of time. Lots of women have children when they're in their mid or even late thirties these days.

Nevertheless, I need a while to clear my head. Adam's attractive, for sure, and I might be interested in Tim if he wasn't so hung up on his ex-wife. (Tim's the divorced father I mentioned earlier.)

Write back soon and tell me more about this commander guy. He sounds like one of those mucky-muck officers. Is that good or bad?

Love ya,
Shana

Ali read the e-mail through twice and discovered she was smiling when she finished. She wasn't going to give up on Shana and Adam just yet.

Chapter Eleven

"It's summer," Jazmine announced the first Monday after the end of school. "Uncle Adam's got three days off. We should all do something special to celebrate."

Shana hated to discourage Jazmine's enthusiasm, but she couldn't leave her restaurant on a whim. "Do something?" she repeated. "Like what?"

That was all the invitation Jazmine needed. She hopped onto the barstool and rested her arms on the counter. "When my dad was stationed in Italy, he took me to Florence right after school was out. We had so much fun, and I saw Michelangelo's David. It's really cool, you know?"

"We have some interesting museums in the area," Shana suggested, but her heart wasn't in it. Given her druthers, of which she had few, she would opt to visit Victoria, British Columbia. She'd heard it was a lovely city and very English in style.

Jazmine sighed and shook her head. "I've been to dozens of museums, but that feels too much like a school outing. This should be *special*."

"What about an amusement park?" Perhaps on Sunday Shana could stuff herself into a swimsuit, make Jazmine promise not to take her picture, and they could head for the local water park.

Again Jazmine was less than excited. "I suppose, but I'm looking for something that's not so…ordinary. Everyone goes to parks. This is a celebration. I survived a new school, made friends and Aunt Shana's still speaking to me." She giggled as she said this, and Shana laughed, too.

"We had a bit of a rough start," Shana acknowledged.

"It took me a while to adjust," Jazmine admitted in turn. "Uncle Adam helped me."

"With what, exactly?" She recalled the backpack advice, and the fact that he'd apparently told her to stop matchmaking—hadn't he?—but she didn't know what else he'd said.

"Never mind." Jazmine slid off the barstool. "That's an idea—I'll call Uncle Adam."

"To do what?" Shana asked, but her question went unanswered as Jazmine hurried toward the phone.

"You should take a day just for the two of you," Catherine suggested, apparently listening in on their conversation. "You've been here nearly every day for weeks."

"New business-owners don't take days off," Shana said. It was true that she'd spent every day at the restaurant, although she'd taken brief breaks and nearly one whole Sunday the week before. She'd felt like a new woman afterward. The thought of one entire twenty-four hour period when she didn't have her hands in pizza dough or her face in a three-gallon container of ice cream sounded heavenly. Getting away was just the respite she needed.

"It isn't for you as much as your niece," Catherine continued. "Kind of a reward for doing so well."

Shana knew she was right. Against the odds, Jazmine had succeeded in adapting to a new school and a new home, and she'd made friends.

A few minutes later, Jazmine set the phone aside and

raced over to Shana. "Uncle Adam suggested visiting Victoria, B.C.," she said breathlessly. "I've never been there and he said it's a wonderful day trip."

"That does sound nice," Shana said wistfully. She was astonished at the way Adam's suggestion reflected her own earlier musings about Victoria. It was almost eerie.

"He wants to talk to you," Jazmine said. She ran to get the portable phone and handed it to Shana.

Shana walked into the back room, nervously tucking a strand of hair behind her ear. She'd moussed it into submission that morning, but whole sections were already attempting a breakout.

"Hello," she said and hoped her voice didn't betray her feelings. She thought about this man far too often and had an intense love-hate relationship with him that he knew nothing about. She was attracted to him and yet she didn't want to be. The fact that he—

"Shana?" Adam said, cutting into her thoughts.

"I'm here," she said primly.

"That's a great idea of Jazmine's. You can come, can't you?"

"To Victoria, you mean? Ah…"

"We'll make it a day trip. I'm off until Thursday. I'll pick you and Jazmine up, then we'll take the Fauntleroy ferry over to the Kitsap Peninsula, drive to Port Angeles and take another ferry across the Strait to Victoria."

"I…I'm—" Shana hesitated when she saw Jazmine staring at her with pleading eyes. She'd folded her hands as if in prayer, and Shana's resolve weakened. "I'll need to check with Catherine before I take a whole day." Shana instantly felt guilty; she'd invested her life savings in this business and she shouldn't be running off for a day of fun. She should be at work.

"Ask her," Adam urged.

Shana turned away from the phone and came face-to-face with Catherine, who had her hands on her hips. "Go. I'll manage just fine. It's only one day, for Pete's sake."

"But…"

"Aunt Shana," Jazmine said pulling on her arm. "Just do it. We'll have a blast."

Shana wasn't nearly as sure. That night, long after Jazmine was in bed and she herself should have been, she e-mailed her sister.

Sent: June 24
From: Shana@mindsprung.com
To: Alison.Karas@woodrowwilson.navy.mil
Subject: Jazmine, Adam Kennedy and me

Dear Alison,

As you probably already know, I'm going off on a day trip to Victoria, British Columbia, with Jazz and Adam. Basically I got talked into it, and I'll give you three guesses whose fault that is. Your daughter could talk circles around Larry King. Mark my words, that kid will have her own talk show one day.

Yes, Adam Kennedy will be there, too. I don't mind having him around anymore. I put up a good fight, let him know I wasn't interested in a relationship and even made a point of telling him about Jazz playing matchmaker. He listened politely and agreed with everything I had to say. The least he could've done was argue—just kidding! Without even trying, he's worn down my defenses. I have to admit I've enjoyed the time I've spent with him. Twice now, after he's visited Jazz, he's stayed for a cup of coffee and we've talked. There hasn't been a hint of romance, although, yes—I'm attracted. I definitely feel we have some chemistry, but I'm too preoccupied (and too scared!) to do anything about it.

Okay, I've bared my soul. It's your turn. What's up with you and this Commander Dillon? I know you, Ali. You wouldn't have mentioned him at all if you didn't care, so I repeat—what's up?

It's almost eleven and I should be in bed. Adam's arriving very early. I offered to drive over to his place, but he said it was no trouble coming to get us.

Write soon. Jazmine and I both look forward to your e-mails.

Love,
Shana

Less than twelve hours later, Shana was on a midmorning ferry that had left Port Angeles for Vancouver Island. An excited Jazmine jogged up and down the outside deck while Adam and Shana drank cups of coffee inside. They were seated on wooden benches, across from each other.

"I can't believe I'm doing this," she muttered. The alarm had rung at four that morning and they were on the road by five.

"Did you see the Olympic Mountains?" Jazmine dashed inside shouting—as if they could possibly have missed them. "I learned in class that some of those mountains have never been climbed or explored."

This was news to Shana, but she wasn't much of an expert on Washington State history or geography.

"Do either of you know about Point Roberts?" Adam

asked when Jazmine threw herself down on the bench, sitting next to Adam and across from Shana.

Both Shana and Jazmine shook their heads. "Never heard of it," Shana said.

"It's a little piece of the United States that is geographically part of Canada."

"What?" Jazmine frowned. "I don't get it."

"The United States and Canada are separated by the 49th parallel at Washington and British Columbia. There's a small point of land that drops below it. That's Point Roberts. Maybe we can go there sometime."

"So it's in Canada but not really?"

"Take a look at a map and you'll see what I mean."

While Jazmine walked over to examine the wall at the other end of the ferry, where a map of Washington was posted, Shana sipped her coffee and smiled at Adam. "She idolizes you, you know."

Adam shifted on the hard bench and crossed his arms. "As it happens, I think the world of her, too."

It was confession time for Shana, although what she had to say was probably no secret to Adam. "I was jealous of that in the beginning."

Adam's gaze held hers. "And now?"

"Now…" She hesitated. "I appreciate the fact that she has you. She needs a strong male figure in her life, especially with her dad gone."

"She's come to love you, too, Shana. And it's all happened in remarkably little time. That says a lot for you, I think. You've been patient with her and you've managed to find just the right approach."

His praise brought a sheen of tears to her eyes. Embarrassed and wanting to hide the effect of his words, Shana quickly blinked them away.

"Listen," Adam said, lowering his voice. "There's something I should probably tell you. There's a rumor floating around that several of us could be transferred to Hawaii. I've wanted to go back for quite a while—ever since I left, really. I just wish the timing was better. I should also tell you it could be soon."

"No," Shana cried, unable to hold back the automatic protest.

Everyone in the immediate vicinity seemed to stop and look in their direction.

Adam leaned forward and reached for her hand. "Dare I hope that response is for you as well as Jazmine?"

Shana ignored the question. "I guess I should congratulate you, then—since this is an assignment you want."

"What about you, Shana?" he pressed. "Will you miss me?"

He wasn't going to drop this as easily as she'd hoped. "Of…course." The lump in her throat was growing as she dealt with the coming disappointment—her own and Jazmine's. This would devastate her niece.

"I'll miss you and Jazmine, too." Adam's eyes held hers, and he brushed his thumb over her hand. "I've enjoyed our visits. Especially those talks over coffee."

As the old expression had it, hope sprang eternal. "It's not a for-sure decision, right? I mean, there's a possibility you won't be going."

"I wouldn't count on it."

"Oh, well," she said, doing her best to seem nonchalant about this unexpected turn of events. He'd probably known for some time and was only now free to mention it. "I guess that answers that." She tried to speak lightly, concealing her sense of loss.

He grinned sheepishly. "I have to admit that Jazmine's matchmaking plans didn't upset me nearly as much as they did you."

Her responding smile felt a little shaky, which was exactly how she felt herself. During the last few weeks, she'd come to like and trust Adam, and just when she was feeling comfortable with him, he made this announcement.

Adam switched seats so that he was sitting next to her. "I probably shouldn't have said anything about Hawaii yet, but I wanted you to know as soon as possible, so we can prepare Jazmine."

"No—you did the right thing." Until she'd learned that he might leave, Shana hadn't realized how much she'd come to rely on Adam. She and Jazmine would be on their own for the next four and a half months, and just then that felt like an eternity.

"Hey, guys," Jazmine said, running toward them. She flopped down on the wooden seat. "I found Point Roberts on the map! It's really cool, isn't it?"

"Really cool," Adam agreed solemnly.

Shana didn't know how a whole day could pass so quickly. Victoria was everything she'd heard and read. Although she'd never been to England, she imagined it must be like this. They explored the harbor, rode a horse-drawn carriage through the downtown area, had high tea at the Empress Hotel and toured some quaint little shops. In one of them, Shana couldn't resist buying a made-in-England teapot covered in delicate little roses, while Adam got each of them a sweatshirt with maple leaves dancing across the front.

"I loved the carriage ride best," Jazmine told them on the ferry ride back to Port Angeles. "I wish we had time to visit Butchart Gardens." She waved a brochure she'd picked up. "The pictures of the flowers are so beautiful. I always wanted a garden...." She leaned her head against Shana and closed her eyes. Within moments she was asleep.

Shana carefully eased the girl off her shoulder and gently laid Jazmine's head down on the seat. Lifting the girl's legs, she set them on the bench, then covered Jazmine with her jacket. Her niece looked angelic, and Shana's heart swelled with love for this child. She felt protective and proud. Jazmine had taught her so many lessons about love.

Adam slid over so Shana could sit with him across from Jazmine. The day had been wonderful but, like Jazmine, she was tired. When Adam placed his arm around her, she gave in to the urge to rest her head against his shoulder. It was an invitation to intimacy, she realized, and she relaxed, comfortable and suddenly happy. "Thank you for such a special day," she whispered as he twined their fingers together.

His hold on her tightened momentarily.

Shana turned her head to look up at him—and that was when it happened. She read the intention in his eyes and knew he wanted to kiss her. At first, she wondered if what she saw was a reflection of her own desire, but instinct told her he felt the same thing. For the briefest of moments, she had a choice—she could either pull away or let him kiss her. Without rational thought, she closed her eyes, lifted her mouth to his and accepted his kiss. As soon as their lips met, Shana knew she'd made the right decision. She felt his kiss all the way to her toes.

His lips glided over hers in a slow, sensual exploration that had her nerves quivering. Luckily she was seated; otherwise she was sure her knees would have given out on her. Then his hands were in her hair, his fingers splayed as he positioned his mouth over hers. When he finally eased away, she needed a moment to regain her composure.

"Wow," Adam whispered.

"You can say that again," Shana said, still caught up in the feelings his touch had aroused.

Adam slowly expelled his breath. "Okay, now what?" His eyes burned into hers, as if seeking answers to questions she had yet to form.

"Now…" Shana hesitated. "Now we know."

"Do you want to play this by ear?"

She pressed her forehead against his chest. "I'm not sure I've had enough piano lessons."

Adam grinned and kissed the top of her head. "Don't worry, I'm in no rush. We'll take this one step at a time."

"First piano lessons, and now we're out on the dance floor. Can't you just hold me for a few minutes and leave it at that?"

"For now."

For now, that was enough. As far as anything else was concerned, she'd have to see what her heart told her.

Chapter Twelve

Ali read her daughter's e-mail a second time and smiled.

Sent: June 26
From: Jazmine@mindsprung.com
To: Alison.Karas@woodrowwilson.navy.mil
Subject: Guess what I saw

Hi Mom,

I had a great day and my favorite things were the carriage (our horse was named Silver) and having tea in a fancy hotel and watching Uncle Adam try to fit his finger in the handle of a little china cup. On the ferry home Uncle Adam and Aunt Shana sat next to each other and I was mostly asleep. They got real quiet and so I peeked and guess what? THEY WERE KISSING. Didn't I tell you they were falling in love? I knew because Uncle Adam comes by almost every day he has off now.

It gets even better. On the drive home, Aunt Shana had her head on his shoulder and then she didn't when I pretended to wake up. They were whispering a lot, too. I tried not to listen, but I couldn't help it. They were talking about Hawaii and I think it might be where they want to spend their honeymoon. Is this cool, or what?

Love ya,
Jazz

Ali leaned back in her desk chair, feeling satisfied and more than a little cheered. Her daughter was full of news about the romance between Adam and Shana, and gladly accepted credit for it. She seemed convinced that Shana and Adam were just days away from an engagement—or maybe an elopement. That certainly wasn't the impression Shana gave her, but she could see real change in her sister's attitude toward Adam.

In their last conversation, before Alison flew out of Seattle, Shana had told her she'd completely sworn off men. Apparently she'd reconsidered. This time, however, Shana had found herself a winner. Adam was as different from Brad as snow was from sun, and Ali hoped her sister realized it.

Her first indication of the possible romance had been the e-mail Shana had sent full of questions about Adam. Several more had followed the original; all had thinly veiled inquiries about him. Shana had become more open and honest, admitting she felt an attraction even if she hadn't decided what to do about it. Despite that, Alison saw the evidence of a growing relationship with every e-mail.

Glancing at her watch, she turned off her computer. It was time to relieve Rowland in medical. As she checked her schedule, her gaze fell on her wedding band and she paused. Should she switch it to her right hand—or remove it entirely? She wanted to pass it on to Jazmine one day. Slipping the ring off her finger, she held it in the palm of her hand, weighing her options. No, she wasn't ready to give it up yet. She placed it on her right hand, instead.

The very fact that she'd questioned wearing her wedding band was a sign. She would always love Peter but her life with him was over. She supposed her uncertainty about the ring had something to do with Commander Dillon, too. She didn't want him to believe she was married, but it might be safest if he did…. Still, moving the ring that represented her love for Peter to her right hand was a compromise.

As far as she could tell, this feeling of hers for Frank Dillon was completely one-sided. If he'd noticed her lately, he hadn't given the tiniest hint. He couldn't. One thing she knew about Commander Dillon was that he lived and breathed for the Navy. He wouldn't go against regulations if his life depended on it, and Alison wouldn't want him to. But it made for an uncomfortable situation as they pretended there was nothing between them. Perhaps there wasn't. She couldn't be sure, but in her heart she felt there was.

Commander Dillon was still recuperating in sick bay. He hated it, longed to get back to work and he was undeniably a pain in the butt. Her colleagues made their feelings known on a daily basis, but Alison simply didn't acknowledge his bad moods. As a result, the cantankerous commander didn't know what to think of her, and that was just fine with Ali.

While others avoided him, she saw as much of him as her busy schedule would allow, which was never longer than a few minutes at a time. Her feelings for him grew more intense with each day.

When she stepped into the infirmary, Lieutenant Rowland handed her his notes. "You're welcome to the beast," he muttered under his breath. "He's been in a hell of a mood all day. Doc says he'll have him out this week, but I don't think that's near soon enough to suit the commander."

That went without saying. When he'd first arrived at the infirmary Frank Dillon had been in agony, which meant his attitude was docile—at least compared to his current frame of mind. After reading Rowland's notations, Alison pulled back the curtain surrounding him. The commander sat up in bed, arms folded across his chest. He scowled when he saw her.

"You've become a rather disagreeable patient, Commander."

"I want out of here," he barked.

"That's no reason to yell. I believe you've made your wishes quite clear."

He narrowed his gaze.

"As it happens, Commander, you aren't the one making the decisions. You can huff and puff all you want, but it isn't going to do you a bit of good." She reached for his wrist and found his pulse elevated. Little wonder, seeing how agitated he was.

"How much longer is this going to take?" he demanded gruffly.

As the lieutenant had reported, their patient was in a foul mood. Having her around hadn't eased his temper, either. "I understand you'll be released this week," she said as she lowered the bed so that he was flat on his back. She needed to examine his incision. By now he knew the procedure as well as she did.

Ali carefully peeled back the bandage to check for any sign of infection. With the tips of her fingers she gently tested the area while the commander stared impatiently at the ceiling.

"This is healing nicely," she assured him.

"Then let me get back to work."

"It isn't my decision."

He sounded as if he was grinding his teeth in frustration. "I can't stand wasting time like this," he growled.

"Can I help in some way?" she asked, thinking she could find him a book or a deck of cards.

"Yes," he shouted, "you can get me out of here!"

"You know I can't do that," she said reasonably. "Only a physician can discharge you."

"I've got to do something before I go stir-crazy." He grimaced with pain as he attempted to sit up.

"Commander, you're not helping matters."

He glared at her as though she was personally responsible for this torture. "Just go. Get out of my sight. I don't want you around anymore, understand?"

She hesitated. "I'm responsible for your care."

"Get someone else."

"Commander," she tried again, but he cut her off.

"Get out!" He pointed at her. "And that's an order."

Alison swallowed down the hurt as she walked out of his cubicle. His words, harsh and vindictive, rang in her ears during the rest of her shift. He didn't want her anywhere near him and he wasn't afraid to say so. Her stomach twisted in a knot, and she felt like a fool for having made assumptions about mutual feelings that obviously didn't exist. Not on his part, anyway.

She didn't blame Frank for wanting to be back on duty, but he'd taken all his resentment and anger out on her. That wasn't fair, and it added to the hurt Alison felt.

Silently she watched as the corpsman delivered his dinner tray. Dillon glanced at her, then turned away, as if he found the sight of her repugnant.

Thirty minutes later, when she walked past, she noticed that he'd barely touched his meal. She considered reminding him that he'd need his strength, but he wouldn't want to hear it. And she wasn't willing to risk another tongue-lashing.

Twice more during the course of her shift, Ali resisted the urge to check on him. Frank had been very explicit about the fact that he didn't want her company.

When she'd finished, she returned to her quarters and curled up on her bed. After her shift she usually wrote Jazmine and her sister, but not tonight. Instead she reviewed the conversation with Frank.

She told herself it was silly to have her feelings hurt by his rudeness, that he didn't mean it, but she couldn't help taking it personally. Earlier she'd always shrugged off his abrasive manner, and she couldn't understand why today was so different. Probably because she'd let her attraction to him get out of hand.

Ali wouldn't be surprised if he was released the next morning, which was just as well. In a little more than four months, she reminded herself, she'd be home with her daughter and soon after that she'd be a civilian. This was an unsettling thought because Ali loved the Navy, but her resignation was necessary. Jazmine needed her, and Alison had given the Navy all she had to give, including her husband.

As she'd suspected, Commander Dillon was released the following morning. Alison hated that his last words to her had been spoken in anger, but she tried to forget it. She wished him good health, but he was out of her life now, and it was unlikely they'd see each other again. Perhaps in another time or place they might have made a relationship work. But not here and not now.

Of more interest was the romance developing between her sister and Adam Kennedy, and as soon as she could, Alison logged on to the computer to check her e-mail. She could count on hearing from Jazmine at least once a day.

To her delight, there was an e-mail from Adam, too, but as she read it, her pleasure quickly evaporated. Adam feared that now his shoulder had healed, he was about to be transferred. He'd told Shana, but didn't have the heart to mention it to Jazmine until he got his papers. Almost in passing, he added how much he'd enjoyed getting to know Shana.

This was dreadful! Jazmine would be devastated if Adam was transferred out of the area, and she wasn't the only one. Shana was going to be just as disappointed.

With a heavy heart she read her daughter's chatty e-mail next.

Sent: June 30
From: Jazmine@mindsprung.com
To: Alison.Karas@woodrowwilson.navy.mil
Subject: Update—sort of

Hi Mom,

Aunt Shana said we could plant a garden! She said we could grow vegetables and flowers. I don't want to plant green beans because then I might have to eat them. Zucchini would be all right, though. Will you give Aunt Shana your recipe for baked zucchini? Tell her to add more cheese than what the recipe calls for, okay? You had a good recipe for green peppers, too, didn't you? I could even eat those raw, but I like them better stuffed.

I think a garden will be lots of fun, don't you? Uncle Adam said he'd help. Isn't that great?

See you soon.

Love,
Jazmine

Alison didn't know where Shana would find time to start a garden. As it was, her sister worked from dawn to dusk, but the plans for this latest project showed her how hard Shana was trying with Jazmine. Somehow, the two of them had managed to talk Adam into helping. How much he could do was questionable, since he couldn't risk damaging his shoulder again, but he seemed a willing participant.

The last e-mail came from onboard ship. Not until she opened it did she see that it was from Commander Dillon. Ali stared at his name for a moment before she read his message. Five words said it all. *Thank you for your excellent care. Commander Frank Dillon.*

"No," she whispered. "Thank *you,* Commander." She had much to be grateful for. Because even if this was as far as it went, Frank had shown her that her heart was still alive.

Sheer weakness had prompted him to send Alison Karas that e-mail, Frank thought as he returned to his stateroom at the end of his shift. Frank was not a weak man, and he was irritated with himself for more reasons than he wanted to count.

He knew he wasn't a good patient. He just couldn't tolerate lying around in bed all day. He wanted to be back on the job, doing what he enjoyed most, contributing his skills where they were needed. If his appendix was going to give out on him, he would've preferred it to happen while they were in port.

The worst part of his ordeal wasn't his ruptured appendix and the subsequent surgery. That he'd come through with only minor difficulties. But he wasn't sure he would survive Lieutenant Commander Karas. After all these years on his own, without female companionship, committed to the Navy, he was finally attracted to a woman. *Strongly* attracted. She invaded his dreams and haunted his waking moments. Every day for damn near a week she'd been at his bedside.

He didn't like it. Just when his mind had started to clear and his system was free of those drugs they'd given him, he saw something he hadn't noticed earlier. *Her wedding ring*. It shook him.

That first time they met, Alison Karas hadn't denied being married and she'd worn a wedding ring—on her left hand. He stared at the computer screen. *Married*. He'd forgotten about it until this week. Then, when he'd remembered—and realized he was fantasizing about a married woman—he'd lost it. Even worse, she'd moved the ring to her right hand. What did *that* say about her?

He'd been impatient to get back to his duties before, but after he saw that wedding band, he was downright desperate to escape the infirmary. *There's no fool like an old fool*, as they said.

His anger had turned on Alison and he wanted her as far away from him as possible. Later he regretted that outburst. She'd done nothing to deserve his tongue-lashing. But he found it difficult to be civil, and all because he'd realized there was no hope of any kind of relationship, let alone a permanent one.

He could accept that, but he wasn't a man who enjoyed temptation and this woman definitely fit that description. Still, he felt compelled to apologize for his rudeness. Seeing her again was out of the question, so he'd decided to send an e-mail. He wrote a dozen versions before he settled on the brief and simple message, then hit Send before he could change his mind.

For better or worse, she had it now, and that was the end of it. He made his way to the first deck and lifting his head he scanned the horizon. All that stretched before him was ocean—a huge blue expanse of emptiness. He saw his life like that and it bothered him.

Until now, it never had.

Chapter Thirteen

Adam was charmed by Jazmine's excitement about their little garden. He'd managed to find someone to turn over a small patch at the back of Shana's rental house. Then Jazmine and her aunt had planted neat rows of red-leaf lettuce, peas, green peppers and three varieties of tomato. Although they'd been warned by the man at the local nursery, they'd purchased a number of zucchini plants, too. Apparently it did exceptionally well in the Seattle area and supplied an abundant crop. Jazmine claimed her mother had fabulous recipes for zucchini. Baked zucchini and zucchini bread and something else.

"Around September if you see anyone buying zucchini in the grocery, you'll know that's a person without a friend," the nursery owner had joked as he hauled their plants out to the vehicle.

Once they were back at the house and the plants were in the freshly tilled soil, Adam watched Jazmine with amusement. Every five minutes, the girl was out in the garden checking on the plants' growth, making sure there were no slugs in the vicinity. God help them if they were. Just to be on the safe side, she carried a salt shaker.

The flower beds—well, they were another story. He'd

lost track of all the seedlings Shana had purchased. Most of them he didn't even recognize. Pink ones and white ones, purple and yellow. They certainly made the yard look colorful. Pretty but… Women and flowers—he never could understand what they found so fascinating. For himself, he thought practical made more sense than pretty, although he hadn't shared that reaction with Shana.

True, he'd had a jade plant once but it died for lack of attention. Shana, predictably, had clusters of house plants—on windowsills and tables—but he couldn't begin to guess what types they were. Knowing Jazmine, he wouldn't have thought she'd be too interested in this kind of thing, either, but apparently he was wrong. The kid loved it as much as Shana did.

"Aunt Shana said she'd be home around eight," Jazmine informed him on Saturday at five. They'd spent a quiet afternoon together. While he watched a Mariners baseball game on television, Jazmine tended the garden. He'd found it relaxing, but he missed being with Shana. He would've stopped at the ice-cream parlor, but he knew that Saturdays, especially in summer, tended to be busy.

Jazmine had patiently watered the rows of newly planted seedlings, being careful not to oversaturate the soil. She'd examined every inch to check for weeds and had ruthlessly yanked up a number of small green plants; Adam suspected they were actually vegetables.

He glanced up from the post-game analysis and saw that Jazmine was standing in front of him. "We should make dinner," she announced. "A real, proper dinner."

"We?" he muttered. In case Jazmine hadn't noticed, he wasn't the domestic type. Besides he had to protect his shoulder. Every meal in the last few weeks had come out of a microwave or in a pizza box.

"We could do it," Jazmine insisted, as if putting together a three-course meal was no trouble at all.

"Really? I wouldn't mind getting takeout. Or maybe Shana could bring home a pizza. Wouldn't that be easier?"

Frowning, Jazmine shook her head. "She has pizza all the time. Besides, home cooking is better for you."

Adam wondered when she'd become such an expert. "You're sure the two of us can do this?"

"Of course."

Ah, the confidence of the young. Still, Adam had his doubts. "You should know I'm kitchen-challenged."

Jazmine giggled. "I cook a lot. I'll do it."

If Jazmine knew her way around the kitchen, then perhaps this wouldn't be so complicated. He could supervise from in front of the TV.

"You'll have to help, though."

He should've known she wouldn't let him off scot-free. "What do you want me to do?"

"The grocery store won't sell me wine, so you'll have to buy that."

His eyebrows shot up. "Wine?"

Jazmine nodded. "And flowers," she said in a tone that brooked no argument.

"Yes, ma'am. Any particular kind?" He resisted mentioning that there was a yard full of flowers outside, although they were mostly quite small.

"I want you to buy roses and we're going to need candles, too. Tall ones."

"You got it." He bit his tongue to keep from reminding her that it wouldn't be dark until ten. "Should I buy red or white wine?" he asked.

Jazmine stared at him blankly.

"Red generally goes with meat and white wine is served with chicken or fish."

"What goes with everything?"

"Champagne is good."

She grinned then, her decision made. "Buy champagne and make it a big bottle, okay?"

"Have you decided what you're cooking?" he asked.

"Of course I have," she told him scornfully.

"And that would be?"

She sighed, as though she was a master chef dealing with obtuse underlings. "I've decided to cook my specialty."

"Which is?"

"A surprise," she said without pause, using her hands to shoo him out the door. He watched her march into the kitchen. From the corner of his eye, Adam saw her pull several cookbooks off the shelf.

After he'd finished his errands, Adam decided to visit the ice-cream parlor, after all. It was just too hard to stay away. As he'd expected, Shana was doing a robust business. Catherine worked on the pizza side with a young assistant, while Shana and another part-time student served ice cream. They had at least a dozen customers waiting their turn. Adam took a seat and when Shana saw him, she blushed, fussed with her hair, then went back to helping her customers. Her self-conscious reaction pleased him. Ten minutes later, she had a chance to take a break.

After washing her hands, she joined him. "Hi," she said, offering him a shy smile.

He hadn't known there was a shy bone in her body until he'd kissed her. That kiss had been a revelation to him. Their feelings weren't simple or uncomplicated, although he hadn't deciphered the full extent of them yet. He did know their kiss had changed them. Changed their relationship.

He'd been attracted to her from the beginning and was sure she'd felt the same way about him. They'd skirted each other for weeks, both denying the attraction, and then all of a sudden, after that day in Victoria, it was there. Undeniable. Unmistakable. He no longer tried to hide his feelings and she didn't, either.

"Where's Jazmine?" she asked. "In the park?"

He shook his head. "At home, cooking dinner. Her specialty, she says. I don't suppose you have any clue what that might be?"

"You left her alone?" Shana's eyes widened with alarm. "In the kitchen with the stove on? Adam, she's only nine! Sometimes that's hard to remember, but she's still just a kid."

"She seemed perfectly fine," he said, suddenly deciding Shana was right. "She's the one who sent me to the store." He slid out of the booth. "I'll get back now."

Shana sighed, then stretched out one hand and stopped him. "It was good to see you," she said in a low voice.

He gave her hand a small squeeze. "You, too. Don't be late for dinner."

"I won't," she promised.

Once again Adam started toward the door, then paused and turned around. "What's her specialty?"

Shana grinned. "It's probably canned chili with grated cheese on top."

He dismissed that. "I think it might be more involved. Whatever it is requires a cookbook."

Shana's grin faded. "In that case, you'd better hurry."

"I'm on my way."

Shana smiled again, and it reminded him—as if he needed reminding—how attracted he was to her. And just when their relationship was beginning to show real promise, he'd be leaving the Seattle area.

She followed him to the front door. "Any word on that transfer?" she asked.

If he didn't know better, he'd think she'd been reading his mind. "Not yet." It wouldn't be long, though. Hawaii was a dream assignment. Who wouldn't want to be stationed there? With its endless miles of white sandy beaches and sunshine, Hawaii had always appealed to him. Yet Seattle, known for its frequent drizzle and gray skies, was of more interest now than the tropical paradise.

"Did you mention anything about the transfer to Jazmine?" she asked.

He shook his head. He couldn't make himself do it.

"Coward," she muttered.

Adam shrugged lightly. "Guilty as charged."

Shana glanced at her watch. "I'll be leaving in about an hour and a half."

"Okay, I'll let Martha Stewart know." Feeling the need to touch her, he reached for her hand. Even with the restaurant full of customers, they entwined their fingers, and it was a long moment before either of them moved. He felt the urge to take her in his arms and she must have felt the same impulse because she swayed toward him before shaking her head and dropping her hand.

"I should get back to work and you need to get back to Jazmine," she said, her voice little more than a whisper.

"Right."

"Bye." Shana gave him a small wave. Adam heard the reluctance in her voice, a reluctance he shared.

Jazmine met him at the front door, took his bags and banned him from the kitchen. "I can't be disturbed," she said grandly.

Adam turned the television on again and sat with one ankle balanced on his knee, aiming the remote. He couldn't find anything he wanted to watch. "Need any help in there?" he called out.

"No, thanks."

Five minutes later he repeated the offer.

This time Jazmine ignored him, but soon afterward, she asked, "Aunt Shana isn't going to be late, is she?"

"She'd phone," Adam said, and hoped she would.

At three minutes after eight, Shana walked into the house. "I'm home," she said unnecessarily.

Adam stood and Jazmine hurried eagerly out of the kitchen. "I hope you're hungry."

"Famished," she said.

As if on cue, Adam's stomach growled.

With a sweeping gesture of her arm, Jazmine invited them into the kitchen. The table was covered with a tablecloth twice the right size. The cloth brushed the floor, and Adam wondered if she'd used a floral printed sheet. The candles were stuck in empty Coke bottles—apparently she hadn't found real candle-holders—and were positioned on either side of the roses, which she'd arranged in a glass bowl. The effect was surprisingly artful. There were place settings, including wine goblets, in front of the three chairs.

"Jazmine!" Shana exclaimed, hugging her niece. "This is absolutely lovely."

The nine-year-old blushed at the praise and wiped her hands on her apron. "Uncle Adam helped."

"Not much," Adam protested.

"We can start now," she said with authority. "Please light the candles and pour the champagne. I'm having soda in my glass."

He bowed slightly. "At your service."

"Everyone, sit down," Jazmine ordered when he'd finished. She gestured toward the table. "I have an appetizer." Following that announcement, she brought out a bowl of dry Cheerios mixed with peanuts, raisins and pretzels.

"Excellent," Shana said, exchanging a look with Adam. They both struggled to maintain their composure.

"This is only the start," Jazmine promised, flitting about the kitchen like a parrot on the loose. "I made all our favorites—macaroni and cheese, Tater Tots and salad. Uncle Adam, there's no tomatoes in your salad and, Aunt Shana, no croutons on yours."

Shana's eyes met Adam's. "She's paying attention."

"I'll say."

"Plus macaroons for dessert," Jazmine added proudly.

"Macaroons?" Adam repeated.

Jazmine removed the bowl of Cheerios. "Yes, *chocolate* macaroons. Those are my favorites, so no complaining."

It was an odd meal, but Adam had no complaints and neither, apparently, did Shana.

"We'll do the dishes," he said when they'd eaten. The champagne had relaxed him and Shana, too, because they lingered over the last glass while Jazmine moved into the living room.

"This really was sweet of her," Shana whispered.

"Very sweet," Adam agreed. What happened next, he blamed on the champagne. Before he could question the wisdom of it, he leaned close to Shana, intending to kiss her. She could've stopped him, but didn't. Instead she shut her eyes and leaned toward him, too. The kiss was every bit as good as their first one. No, it was better, Adam decided. In fact, her kisses could fast become addictive—a risk he'd just have to take. He brought his chair closer to Shana's and she gripped his shirt collar as they kissed again.

She pulled away sometime later and pressed her forehead against his. It took him a moment to find his focus. He savored having her close, enjoyed her scent and the way she felt. Jazmine might see them, but he didn't care as long as Shana didn't—and obviously she didn't.

"You two need help in there?" Jazmine called from the living room.

Like guilty teenagers, Shana and Adam broke apart. "We're fine," Shana answered.

Adam wasn't so sure that was true.

Sent: July 6
From: Jazmine@mindsprung.com

To: Alison.Karas@woodrowwilson.navy.mil
Subject: My plan is working

Dear Mom,

I cooked dinner all by myself! You know what I like best about Uncle Adam? He doesn't treat me like a kid. He spent Saturday afternoon with me because Aunt Shana was at the ice-cream parlor and when I told him I was going to cook dinner, he let me. He even went to the store and left me by myself. I don't need a babysitter anymore.

When he got back, he said Aunt Shana was upset with him for leaving me all alone, but nothing happened. I made macaroni and cheese in the microwave and baked Tater Tots and made a salad. It turned out really good, and guess what?

Uncle Adam and Aunt Shana kissed again, and they didn't even care that I could see them. I pretended I didn't, but I really did. They said they wanted to wash the dishes and it took them more than an hour. Miss you bunches and bunches.

Love,
Jazmine

Chapter Fourteen

If Ali had been at home instead of aboard the *USS Woodrow Wilson,* she would've turned to her favorite comfort food: cookie dough. It was that kind of day. Yes, she knew she shouldn't eat raw eggs. But when she reached this point—of being prepared to scarf down a bowl of unbaked cookies—salmonella seemed the least of her worries. Those ice-cream manufacturers knew what they were doing when they introduced cookie dough as a flavor. That, in her opinion, was the ultimate comfort food.

What had upset Ali, or rather *who,* was none other than Commander Frank Dillon. After managing fairly successfully to keep him out of her thoughts, he was back—not only in her thoughts, but unfortunately, in sick bay.

Earlier in the day he'd returned with a raging fever and an infection. Infection was the biggest risk with a ruptured appendix, and he hadn't been spared this complication. Ali was worried when she saw that his temperature was nearly 103 degrees. Furious, she'd asked why he hadn't come in earlier.

He'd refused to answer, but insisted that all he needed was a shot, and that once she'd given it to him, he could go back to his duties as navigator. When she told him Captain Coleman had ordered antibiotics via IV, he seemed to blame her personally. In his anger and frustration, he'd lashed out at her once again and questioned her competence.

As soon as he was hooked up to the antibiotics, and relatively free of pain, he slept for the remainder of her shift. Before leaving, she'd checked on him, taking his temperature, which had fallen to just over 100 degrees.

She felt both irritated and sad. Irritated that he'd delayed seeking medical attention. And sad because she suspected she might be the reason he'd stayed away. According to his own comments, he wanted nothing to do with her. She couldn't help wondering if that was because of her wedding ring—and yet how could it be? She'd removed it from her left hand.

Anytime he'd so much as glanced in her direction this afternoon, he'd scowled as if he couldn't bear to be in the same room. That was ridiculous. Ali hadn't done anything to deserve this wrath. After all, he was the one who'd sent her an e-mail thanking her for the excellent care. But from the way he regarded her now, anyone might think she'd attempted to amputate his leg while he wasn't looking. She tried not to dwell on the things he'd said to her, either today or during his first hospitalization, but she couldn't help that her feelings were hurt. She'd misread the situation and now he was back and not happy about it, either.

Frank didn't understand or recognize how serious this infection was. With a fever that high, he must've been terribly sick. Damn, he should never have waited this long!

Sent: July 7
From: Alison.Karas@woodrowwilson.navy.mil
To: Shana@mindsprung.com
Subject: It's cookie time!!

Dear Shana,

I'm tired and I want to come home. I sound like a crybaby but I don't care. The day has been long and awful, and if I was home right now I'd have the mixer going, blending sugar and flour and eggs with oatmeal and raisins. Yup, it's one of those days.

How are things with Jazmine? I need some news to cheer me up. Got anything wonderful to tell me? How's Adam? Any news about the transfer?

Love,
Alison

It wasn't long before she received a reply.

Sent: July 9
From: Shana@mindsprung.com
To: Alison.Karas@woodrowwilson.navy.mil
Subject: Fireworks and all

Dear Alison,

My goodness, what's happening? I haven't heard you sound so down in ages. When you start talking about cookie dough, I know there's got to be a man involved. I figure this must have something to do with that commander you mentioned. I thought you said you wouldn't be seeing him again. But apparently you have and it didn't go well. Tell all!

Jazmine is fabulous, but the truth is, I had a miserable day myself. I worked from dawn to dusk, and financially it was my best business day ever, so I should be happy, right? I wasn't. I wanted to be with Jazmine and Adam, who were off at a community fair while I was stuck at the ice-cream parlor.

I can't even begin to tell you how much work is involved in owning a business like this. Catherine was the only employee willing to work this weekend and thankfully, her husband came in to lend a hand. I don't know what I would've done otherwise. I really hated not being with Adam and Jazmine. They must've known it, because they showed up to collect me the minute I closed for the night. I didn't have time to change my clothes or anything. Adam drove to a hilltop where we had a picnic, even though it was almost dark. Adam had bought deli sandwiches and salads. By the time we arrived home, it was after eleven. I'm afraid I was exhausted and not much fun. Sometimes I wonder if buying this business was the wisest choice, but it's too late to think about that now.

Write soon.

Love,
Shana

Alison read her sister's e-mail and tried to translate the message between the lines. Like Alison, Shana was tired. According to Jazmine, she worked long hours, starting early in the morning when she mixed the pizza dough and set it out to rise. She usually stayed until closing, which meant she often wasn't home until after nine. Thankfully her sister had had the wherewithal to hire Catherine, who'd quickly become indispensable. Her other employees, mostly high-school kids, didn't seem all that reliable, but at least she had them.

Adam was spending a lot of time with Jazmine, and Alison knew very well that her daughter wasn't the only draw. He and Shana were definitely getting along, and that thrilled her. But if Adam was transferred to Hawaii, that might be the end of their relationship. Still, Alison couldn't worry about that when she had troubles of her own.

Fortunately, she had Lieutenant Rowland to talk to. He was waiting for her when she reported for duty the next afternoon.

"How's the beast doing?" she asked in a stage whisper. Compared to the commander, their other patients were downright jovial.

Jordan's responding grimace answered her question. "Same. Bad-tempered as ever."

"Oh, great."

Rowland rolled his eyes. "He's certainly got a burr under his saddle—and I think I know why."

Alison did, too. "He hates being sick." No one enjoyed it, but the commander was worse than most. He resented every minute away from his duty station. What he didn't realize was that he wouldn't be released anytime soon. She wasn't going to be the one to tell him, either.

"His problem," Rowland said with an air of superiority, "appears to be you."

"Me?" she protested, flustered that Frank's ranting from the day before had obviously continued.

"He asked me to keep you away from him."

Alison's face burned with mortification. "What did you tell him?" she asked, her voice indignant despite her efforts.

Rowland's smile lacked humor. "That the United States Navy was fortunate to have you, and if he has a problem he should take it up with Captain Coleman."

"Thank you," she said, and swallowed a painful knot of gratitude.

"The mighty commander didn't have anything to say after that."

"Good." Her anger simmering just below the surface, Alison squared her shoulders. "I think it's time I faced the beast on my own."

Rowland's dark eyes flared. "I don't know if I'd advise that."

Alison was past accepting her friend's advice. If Frank Dillon had even a clue what she was thinking, she'd likely be up for court-martial.

Before common sense and what remained of her Navy career could stop her, she tore back the curtain to his cubicle and confronted the commander. Although he appeared to be sleeping, he must have heard her because his eyes fluttered open.

"I understand you requested not to be under my care."

He blinked, and Alison was shocked to see that he refused to look at her. "You heard right."

"That's fine with me, Commander. As far as I'm concerned, you're cantankerous and impatient and rude and…and *more*."

Barely controlled anger showed in the tight set of his mouth. No one with any desire to advance in the Navy spoke to a senior officer the way Alison just had.

"What's the matter, Commander, no comment?" Feet braced apart, she gave him a defiant glare.

"It would be best if you left now," he muttered.

"I don't think so."

He frowned as if he'd rarely been challenged, but Alison was beyond caring.

"You don't like me, Commander, and that's perfectly okay, but I would prefer to keep personalities out of this. I am a professional and I pride myself on my work. Not only have you insulted me but you've—" Angry though she was, she couldn't complete the thought.

His eyes hardened, but he still wouldn't look at her.

Unable to bear another minute in his presence, she turned and walked away, feeling as though there was a huge hole in her stomach.

Chapter Fifteen

Shana was in much better spirits the following weekend. Her business continued to prosper, and she'd hired a new part-time employee, a teenage boy this time, named Charles. Not Charlie, but Charles. Hiring, training and dealing with employees had proved to be her biggest difficulty to date. This was an area where she had little experience and it seemed her lessons were all learned the hard way. She'd had to let the other two go and seemed to feel worse about it than either teenager. Charles was proving himself to be responsible and good-natured, and he and Catherine liked each other, quickly developing a bantering relationship. Shana couldn't even begin to imagine what she'd do without Catherine.

After several weeks of hanging around the ice-cream parlor, Jazmine's entrepreneurial talent suddenly kicked in, and her ideas weren't bad. The kid had real imagination when it came to inventing sundaes and candy treats. She took long strands of red and black licorice and—hands carefully gloved—braided them, decorating each end with colorful ribbons. Then she enclosed the entire creation in cellophane wrap. She hung them everywhere she found space, creating a festive atmosphere. The price was reasonable and the kids who came into the parlor were intrigued by them, so they sold quickly.

Jazmine's creativity had sparked Shana's, and she made up and displayed small bouquets using colorful lollipops and ribbons. The candy business contributed only a small portion to the total revenue but was gaining in popularity.

Working long hours had one advantage, Shana decided; she didn't have time to think about Adam's leaving. She was afraid it would be soon, and if she allowed herself to brood on it, she'd remember how much she enjoyed his company—and how much she was going to miss him.

Adam still hadn't mentioned the possibility of a transfer to Jazmine. Shana didn't feel it was her place to tell Jazz, unless Adam wanted her to, but he agreed the news should come from him. He'd promised he would last weekend, but then for one reason or another, he hadn't. Shana knew it would be hard to tell her and that he wanted to delay it until the transfer was official. She supposed it would be best to say nothing until he was sure. Her heart ached at the thought of Adam moving to Hawaii. Yes, it was a wonderful assignment and one he'd sought out, but Shana wanted him in Seattle, selfish though that was…

At the height of the lunch business, when the restaurant smelled of baking dough and tomato sauce, and it was all Shana could do to keep up with the pizza orders, the phone rang. Catherine bustled over to answer it and her gaze flew to Shana.

"It's for you," she said, holding out the receiver.

Shana finished slicing a sausage pizza still steaming hot from the oven. If it was Adam, she'd call back the minute she had time to breathe. "Who is it?" she asked.

"Adam, I think," Catherine told her.

She realized he might have news; if so, she wanted to know as soon as possible. "Ask him if it's important."

Catherine grabbed the phone and as Shana watched, the older woman nodded at her.

Her stomach tensed with anxiety. Shana could feel it coming even before he told her. Adam had received his transfer papers or whatever the Navy called them. That must be it; otherwise he would've phoned her tonight.

Wiping her hands on her apron, she asked Charles to fill in for her while she answered the phone. "Could you bring this pizza to table ten?"

"Sure."

Shana walked to the other side of the room and took the phone from Catherine. "Adam?"

"I'm sorry to bother you now."

She leaned against the wall, hardly able to breathe.

"Listen," he said, and she could hear the regret in his voice.

She could think of no reason to delay his news, so she said it before he had a chance. "You got the transfer to Hawaii."

"Yes, my orders hit the boards."

"They what?"

"They're official. And I have to fly out almost right away. The officer I'm replacing had an emergency."

There it was, what she'd dreaded most. "I see." Shana closed her eyes. Although she'd known this was coming, she still felt a sense of shock. The tightness in her chest was painful, and she bit her lower lip to keep from protesting aloud.

"I fly out in the morning."

"So soon?" She'd hoped they'd have some time to say their farewells. At least one more chance to talk and decide—not that there was really anything to decide. But it felt wrong for him to go like this, so quickly, without any opportunity for Jazmine or her to adjust.

"I'm sorry," he said.

"I know." She couldn't seem to say more than two words

at a time. "Tonight?" she managed through her painfully dry throat.

Despite her lack of clarity or detail, he understood the question. "Unfortunately, I can't. There's too much to do."

"I know…"

"Is Jazmine there?"

Shana pressed her hand against her forehead. "No, she's at the park skating with her friends."

"You may need to tell her for me."

"No!" Shana's objection was immediate. "You *have* to do it."

"I'll phone if I can, but there are no guarantees. She's a Navy kid. She'll understand."

Until recently Shana hadn't had much to do with the Navy. All at once she found her entire life affected by it, and frankly she was starting to get annoyed.

"I'll be in touch, I promise," Adam assured her. "Leaving you and Jazmine like this isn't what I want, either."

His words didn't lessen the dejection she felt. She remembered, in an immediate and visceral way, the emotions she'd experienced when she saw Brad and Sylvia together, knowing exactly what they were doing. The sensation that she'd lost something vital had refused to go away. With Brad that was the signal she'd needed, because what they'd had wasn't real, not on his part, anyway. With Adam… with Adam all she felt was loss.

"I don't want you to go." She knew it was childish to say that.

"I'll be able to visit. About Jazz—I've got meetings this afternoon, and tonight I have to pack. I'll phone when I can. *If* I can."

Shana knew what he was asking. She sighed wearily. "I'll tell her."

"I'm sorry to put this on you, but if I don't reach her, you'll have to."

"I know."

"I meant what I said," he reiterated. "I'll visit as often as I can."

While Adam might have every intention of flying in to see them, it would be time-consuming and complicated. Shana recalled that the flight between Hawaii and Portland was a good five hours. She'd taken a brief vacation there with friends; it was the longest flight she'd ever taken. Yes, his intentions were good but that was all they were—intentions.

"I've got your e-mail address," he reminded her. "Yours and Jazmine's, and I'll stay in touch."

"You promise?" She hated the fact that she still sounded like a thwarted child, but she couldn't pretend this wasn't hard.

"Yes—I promise."

Shana had no choice but to comfort herself with his word. Doing her best to seem reconciled to what was happening, she straightened. "Have a safe flight, and don't worry about Jazmine. I'll explain everything to her."

"Thank you."

"No…Adam, thank you." Her voice cracked before she finished and she knew she had to get off the phone or she'd embarrass herself further. "I'm sorry, but I really need to get back to work now."

"I understand, but Shana, one last thing—about you and me. We have to talk. Soon, okay?"

She didn't answer. She couldn't. Replacing the receiver, she let her hand linger while she struggled to overcome her disappointment. With Adam stationed in Hawaii, she could forecast their future and she didn't need the aid of a crystal ball. For Jazmine's sake, he'd stay in touch. Later, when Alison returned and Jazmine went back to live with her mother, he and Shana would both make an effort. At least in the beginning. Then their time together would dwindle until they were forced to face the inevitable. It was how long-distance relationships usually ended.

Shana had seen it with friends. Couples would e-mail back and forth, and on special occasions they'd phone, just for the pleasure of hearing each other's voices. Adam could fly on military transports, so there might even be a weekend now and then when he'd be able to visit the mainland, but she suspected those opportunities would be few and far between. They'd both try, but in the end the obstacles would be too much.

Adam had been a brief season in her life. Instead of complaining, she should be grateful. The lieutenant commander had given her back her self-confidence; he'd made her feel beautiful and…cherished. When she'd met him, another relationship was the last thing on her mind. But Adam had proved there were still good men left in this world, and that not every man was like Brad.

"Are you okay?" Catherine asked, joining her. She rested a gentle hand on Shana's shoulder. "Was it bad news?"

"Everything's all right," she said, shaking her head in order to dispel the lethargic feeling that had stolen over her. "Or it will be soon," she amended.

The look Catherine threw her said she wasn't convinced, and of course the older woman's instincts were accurate. Heaviness settled over Shana's heart. She didn't know why her relationships with men always fell apart. In retrospect, though, she realized she'd carried the relationship with Brad. She'd trusted, believed and held on. She refused to do that with Adam. She wanted a relationship of equals or not at all—and she'd grown increasingly sure that this was it. Her future. Good grief, she was reading a lot into a couple of kisses! It was just that everything had felt so right—and now this.

An hour later, just when the pizza sales had started to

diminish, Jazmine returned, her face red and sweaty from her trek around Lincoln Park on her Rollerblades.

"I sold three more of your licorice braids," Shana told her, trying to act normal.

Jazmine shrugged, but Shana could tell she was pleased. Shana had managed to pick up quite a bit of the girl's body language. It wasn't cool to show too much enthusiasm if there was the slightest possibility someone her own age would see it.

As long as Shana remembered that, she was fine. But when she forgot, problems developed. However, if Jazmine and Shana were alone, or if it was Jazz with Shana and Adam, a completely different set of behavioral rules applied.

"Would you like to make up a few more?" Shana asked.

"Maybe."

This meant she'd be happy to, but not if a friend came by and thought she'd willingly agreed to do anything with or for an adult.

"Good."

At closing time, Shana counted out the money from the cash register, while Jazmine sat in a booth curled up with a book. Every now and then, Shana felt the girl's eyes on her. Catherine and Charles were finishing the cleanup in the kitchen.

"Is there anything I should know about?" her niece asked as soon as they were alone. She laid her book on the tabletop, her elbows on either side of it, and stared at Shana.

Jazmine's intuition surprised her. Shana stopped in mid-count and looked up. "Like what?"

Jazmine frowned. "I'm not sure, but I have the feeling you know something I don't. I hate that."

Shana wrapped elastics around the bills of various denominations, setting each stack aside. "I always did, too," she said. After tucking the cash in the deposit bag, she joined her niece, sliding into the booth across from her.

"So there *is* something wrong." Jazmine's eyes seemed to grow darker. "My mom's okay, isn't she?" Her anxiety was unconcealed, and Shana wanted to reassure her as quickly as possible.

"Oh, yes! No worries there."

"Then what's wrong?"

Her sigh of relief touched Shana's heart. "This has to do with your uncle Adam." How times changed. Only recently she'd begrudged Adam the term *uncle*. At first, the word had nearly gotten stuck in her throat, but now it fell easily from her lips.

Shana was going to miss him so much, but at the moment she was furious that he'd left the job of telling Jazmine up to her—even if she'd agreed to it. "What about Uncle Adam?" Jazmine's eyes seemed more frightened by the second. She scrambled out of the booth.

Shana stood, too, and placed her arm around Jazmine's thin shoulders, but her niece shook it off. In her need to comfort the girl, Shana had forgotten the rules.

"Just *tell* me," Jazmine insisted.

Shana decided her niece was right. She'd give Jazmine the news as clearly, honestly and straightforwardly as she could. "The Navy is reassigning him to Hawaii."

Jazmine spent a moment digesting the information. This was followed by a series of quickly fired questions. "When's he flying out? He is flying, isn't he? Does he get leave first? Because he should. What about the garden? He said he'd help and isn't there a whole lot more that needs to be done? Besides, he promised me he'd be here and…and now he's breaking his word." As if she'd said too much she covered her mouth with both hands.

Shana didn't know how to respond, where to start. "He

phoned this afternoon to say his orders, uh, hit the boards and he had to leave first thing in the morning."

Jazmine's eyes flared. "Already?" She sounded shocked, disbelieving.

"I'm afraid so."

"When did he find out?"

"He just got the final word this afternoon."

"But he must've known *something* before now."

Shana nodded.

"He never said a word."

"I know." Shana could kick him for that, especially now that she was the one telling Jazmine.

Jazmine sat down again and glared at Shana suspiciously. "He told you before this afternoon, though, didn't he?"

Shana could probably talk her way out of this, but she didn't want to lie to her niece. "He did, or…well, he mentioned the possibility. But he dreaded telling you, so he put it off. Besides, he wasn't sure it would go through at all and certainly not this soon."

"So he made you tell me." Jazmine's anger was unmistakable, despite the softness of her voice.

Shana nodded. Adam would pay dearly for that, she suspected.

Jazmine considered this information for a couple of minutes, then casually tossed back her hair. Propping her chin on her palm, she sat very still. "How do you feel about this?"

"I'm fine with it." Shana managed to sound almost flippant. "But to be on the safe side, I'm bringing home a container of chocolate-mint ice cream."

Her niece gave her a confused look.

"I'm throwing myself a pity party," Shana explained. "You're invited."

"What are we going to do other than eat ice cream?"

"Watch old movies," Shana decided. The two of them

could snuggle up together in front of the television, wearing their oldest pajamas.

"*Sleepless in Seattle* is one of my mom's favorites," her niece told her. Apparently the kid was familiar with this particular brand of mood therapy. Shana would have to ask Alison about it at the first opportunity. Perhaps tonight, when she e-mailed her sister.

"Do you have any others we could watch?" Jazmine asked. "I've seen *Sleepless* so often I can say all the lines."

"*The Bridges of Madison County,*" she suggested, but sometimes that one made her angry, when what she really wanted was to weep copiously at a fictional character's tragic life. Pure catharsis, in other words.

"Mom said I was too young to see it," Jazmine muttered disgustedly, as though she no longer required parental guidance.

At times it was hard to remember that her niece was only nine. The kid was mature beyond her years. Alison was right about the movie, though. A story featuring infidelity hardly seemed appropriate for a child.

"For her pity parties, Mom likes popcorn best. The more butter the better," she said matter-of-factly. "We had several of them after Dad died. But Mom didn't call them pity parties."

"What did she call them?"

"Tea parties, but we only had them when we were feeling sad."

"Always with buttered popcorn?"

"It goes good with tea," Jazmine said. "I don't think she had a name for them at first. I woke up one night and saw her crying in front of the TV, and she said sad movies always made her cry. Then I asked her why she watched them."

Shana already knew the answer to that. "Because she needed a good cry."

Jazmine nodded again. "That's exactly what Mom said." The girl sighed heavily, then added in a small voice, "I don't want her to be sad."

"Me, neither, but it's part of life, Jazz. It's not good to be *too* sad or for too long, but being sad has its place. For one thing, sadness makes happiness that much more wonderful."

Jazmine looked at her thoughtfully, awareness dawning in her eyes.

"Now, it's been a while since I had an official pity party," Shana said briskly. "One is long overdue." She'd made a couple of weak attempts when she left Brad, but she'd been too angry with him to do it properly. If anything, their breakup had left her feeling strong and decisive. That high hadn't lasted, and she'd found it emotionally difficult to reconcile herself to the end of the relationship—but only for a short time. Thanks to Adam…

She thought that breaking off her engagement—or whatever it was—with Brad did call for a party, but a real party with banners and food, champagne and music and lots of people. She smiled as she considered how far she'd come.

"What's so funny?" Jazmine asked.

Shana instantly sobered. "Remember a few weeks ago, when you said I had issues?"

"Yeah."

"One of those issues was Brad."

Jazmine rolled her eyes. "Tell me about it!"

Shana laughed out loud. "I was just thinking I never really had a pity party over him."

Jazmine cocked her head quizzically. "Do women always throw these parties because of men?"

"Hmm."

Shana had never given the matter much thought. "Yes," she said firmly. "It's always about men."

"That's what I figured." Jazmine shook her head sadly, as if this reasoning was beyond her.

They loaded up with chocolate-mint ice cream, and whipped topping for good measure, and headed out the door. Shana had to make a quick stop at the bank, but they were home before the ice cream had a chance to melt.

Within ten minutes, they were both lying on their backs, dressed in old flannel pajamas, studying the ceiling.

"Remember when Brad phoned you a little while ago?" Jazmine asked.

"Yup." Shana didn't want to dwell on Brad. She wanted to think about Adam and how much they were going to miss him. Brad paled in comparison to Adam Kennedy.

"Why did he call?"

Shana rolled onto her stomach and raised her head. "He realized the error of his ways."

Jazmine rolled over, too. "Are you going to take him back?"

Shana didn't even need to think about it. "No."

Jazmine solemnly agreed. "He had his turn."

Boy, did he!

"Uncle Adam is next in line."

It occurred to Shana to explain that pity parties were usually wakes for relationships. This wake was for Adam and her. Shana was cutting her losses now, doing her best to accept the likely end of their brief romance and move forward.

"What if Brad came to Seattle?" Jazmine asked excitedly, as if that were a distinct possibility. "What would you do then?"

Shana flopped onto her back again. "Nothing."

"Not a thing?"

"Not a single, solitary thing."

"What if he offered you an engagement ring?"

Shana grinned. "First, I'd faint from the shock of it, and then I'd…I'd ask to see his ID. Make sure this was really Brad."

"Would you cry?"

"I doubt it."

"But you'd turn him down, right?"

"Wait a minute." Shana pulled herself into a sitting position. "Is there any particular reason for all these questions about Brad?"

Jazmine sighed loudly. "I wanted to be sure you're really, really over that rat."

"Rat?"

"That's what Mom called him."

Shana smothered a giggle. "Hey, I thought we were throwing this party because of your uncle Adam," she said. It hadn't escaped her notice how cleverly Jazmine had changed the subject.

"We are."

"So, why bring up Brad?"

Her question was met with silence, and then Jazmine ventured, "Remember how you knew Uncle Adam might be stationed in Hawaii and you didn't tell me?"

"Yes, but what's that got to do with—" She hesitated and drew in her breath. "Is there something *you* aren't telling *me?*" she demanded, aware that she was repeating Jazmine's earlier question.

Her niece sighed dramatically. "Promise you won't be mad."

"Jazmine!"

"Okay, okay. Brad phoned again. I answered and I told him you're seeing someone else now."

"You didn't!"

Jazmine giggled. "I did, and you don't want to know what he said about that, either."

Chapter Sixteen

"What do you mean Brad phoned?" Shana demanded. "When? And why?" Not that she cared. Okay, she did, but only a little. He'd talked to her once, a few weeks ago, and she'd been polite and stiff and frankly had never expected to hear from him again. At one time, she'd dreamed about a big wedding with lots of bridesmaids all dressed in lovely pastel dresses of pink and yellow. Her sister and three of her best friends would've looked like a neat row of huge after-dinner mints. At least she'd spared them that.

"He called last week and I answered the phone," Jazmine muttered. "We…talked. For a while."

That sounded ominous. Shana could only imagine what Brad had to say to her niece—and vice versa.

"He told me he wants you back."

"Of course he does," Shana muttered. *That* made sense. Now that she was out of his life, he missed everything she'd done for him.

"When he asked how your social life was these days— that's exactly what he said—I told him about Uncle Adam and he wasn't very happy," Jazmine continued.

"No," Shana agreed. "He probably wasn't." Just like Brad to pump a nine-year-old for information.

"I shouldn't have said anything," Jazmine muttered, "but I wanted Brad to know he lost out on the opportunity of a lifetime."

That was a typically grandiose Jazmine remark, and Shana smiled. Still, it was gratifying to know Brad missed her, even if it was for the wrong reasons. He must've been shocked to learn she'd met someone else.

"I hope you aren't mad."

"No, but…it isn't a good idea to be giving out personal information over the phone."

"I know, but he kept asking me about your social life and if you were seeing anyone, and it felt good to tell him you were and that Uncle Adam is a lieutenant commander in the United States Navy." This was said with a good deal of pride.

Shana bet that caused ol' Brad to sit up and take notice.

"I wish my mom was here," Jazmine confessed suddenly. "I'm worried about her."

Shana wrapped her arm around Jazmine's shoulders and drew her close. "She seems to be in good spirits." Or she had been until recently.

"She sounds happy when she e-mails me," Jazmine said. "But sometimes I wonder if she's telling the truth."

The kid certainly had her mother pegged.

Jazmine leaned against Shana. "This has been good," she said decisively. "It's even better than a tea party. Except we didn't watch a movie or eat our ice cream—but we can do that now. How about…the first Harry Potter movie? I've got the DVD."

"Sure."

"I'm going to miss Uncle Adam," Jazmine told her sadly. "It won't be the same without him."

Shana could only agree.

Jazmine was asleep an hour later. She lay curled up on the sofa with an afghan covering her. Shana turned off the television set and logged on to the computer.

Sent: July 15
From: Shana@mindsprung.com
To: Alison.Karas@woodrowwilson.navy.mil
Subject: My love/hate relationship with men!

Dear Ali,

I hope you realize what a terrific kid you have. Jazmine and I have just spent the last two hours sharing secrets (plus eating ice cream and watching a Harry Potter movie).

Adam got his orders for Hawaii and didn't even have time to say goodbye. Even worse, I got stuck telling Jazmine.

Trust me, I wasn't too happy with him. I would've let him know how I felt about that, but I was in shock. Do transfers always happen this fast in the Navy? Never mind, he already explained that they don't.

Getting back to Jazmine. She took the news about Adam fairly well. I wasn't sure what I expected and I know she's upset, but as Adam said, she's a Navy kid. She did ask if I knew in advance, and I had to confess that I did. Once I admitted I'd been holding out on her, her own heavily guarded secret came out.

Are you ready for this? Our Jazmine had a conversation with Brad! Apparently he phoned and she informed him I was seeing someone else. I wish she hadn't…. Well, to be honest, that's not entirely true. He told Jazmine that he misses me. Interesting, don't you think? Not to worry, I'd never go back to him.

Once we'd both confessed our secrets, we talked about you and discovered we're both concerned. Jazz is afraid you're hiding your feelings from her—and Alison, I have to tell you that your daughter has good instincts. I didn't say anything, but I know you've been down lately. You refuse to answer my questions about Commander Dillon, and my guess is this involves him. I know, I know, you've already said it a dozen times—there's nothing between you. Technically I'm sure that's true, but...there's more to the situation, isn't there?

What you say or don't say to Jazz is up to you, but she sees through you far too easily, so don't try to pull the wool over her eyes. Jazmine would rather deal with the truth than worry about what's troubling you.

Oh, one last thing. The kid has graduated from tea parties to ice cream. You can thank me for that.

Keep in touch.

Love,
Shana

The following evening, when Shana arrived home from work exhausted, cranky and hungry for something other than pizza or canned chili, the phone rang. With unwarranted optimism, she opened the refrigerator and searched for inspiration—something easy and fast that would pass for healthy. Or sort of healthy. The wilted green pepper, leftover Chinese fried rice and half can of clam chowder weren't appealing.

The phone was still ringing and Shana looked around to see where Jazmine had disappeared. Normally she didn't need to worry about answering the phone because her niece leaped on it like a hungry cat on a cornered mouse.

"I'll get it," she called out when she saw that the bathroom door was closed. Grabbing the phone, Shana cradled it against her shoulder and turned to the cupboard in a second attempt to find a supper solution.

"Hello." The cupboard, stacked with canned foods, offered little in the way of ideas.

"Shana."

"Adam?" In her excitement she nearly dropped the phone. She'd hoped she'd hear from him, but hadn't dared believe. He missed her, he said; he'd been thinking about her. Instantly her heart went on alert. She was afraid to put too much weight on a single phone call and yet so pleased it was all she could do not to leap up and down.

"How's my girl?" he asked in a low, sexy voice.

Shana sighed and leaned against the wall. "I'm doing great." Especially now that she'd heard from him.

"I was asking about Jazmine," he teased.

Shana laughed. "She's great, too. I want you to know we had a pity party over you."

"A what?"

"Never mind—it's a girl thing." She felt so buoyant, so happy, she couldn't prevent a giggle from slipping out.

Adam went directly to the reason for his call. "I got an e-mail from Jazmine and it started me thinking."

"You received an e-mail from her already?"

"Actually she sent this before I flew out. Can I ask you something?"

"Sure."

"Jazz said that Brad phoned you recently."

"Jealous?" she asked lightly, dismissing the question because he had no reason for concern. It would be manipulative to play one man against another, and she refused to do it.

"A little," he admitted with obvious reluctance. "I need to know if you're serious about Brad."

"You're phoning me all the way from Hawaii because you're afraid of a little competition?" she asked. "Adam, you should know better than that."

"Competition doesn't frighten me, but I have to know where I stand with you."

"I can't believe you're talking about Brad," she said, letting her bewilderment show in her voice.

Adam held his ground. "According to Jazmine, you have what she calls *issues* and one of those issues is Brad, and I figured—"

"Brad," she interrupted, "is out of my life."

"Apparently no one bothered to tell him that. I know of two times he's contacted you. Are there others?"

Shana was completely dumbfounded now. "You men are all alike," she snapped. "You're so…so territorial. Why are we even having this conversation?" She lifted the hair from her forehead and pressed her hand there as if to contain her outrage—or her growing headache. Unfortunately it didn't work. She could think of only one reason Brad had revealed any new interest, and that was because he believed she'd become involved with another man. He considered Shana "his." Now Adam was doing the very same thing.

"Are you upset with me?" he had the audacity to ask.

"You must be joking." If she had to tell him, then there was something lacking in her communication skills. "Yes, Adam, I am upset. You don't seem to care about *me*. Your big concern is that I might be tempted to go back to Brad."

They both took a moment to let the sparks die down. Shana was afraid to say anything more, afraid the conversation would deteriorate further and they'd reach a point of no return.

The bathroom door opened then and Jazmine stepped out, hair wrapped in a towel.

"Here," Shana said, shoving the telephone receiver toward her. "It's your uncle Adam. Talk to him."

"Shana, we aren't finished yet," she heard him yell.

"Oh, yes, we are," she said loud and clear. She just couldn't resist.

Jazmine tentatively accepted the phone, but the conversation was short. Angry, and uncertain how to cope with her anger, Shana paced across the kitchen floor to the window and stood there, staring out at the garden.

Jazmine turned to her after she'd hung up the phone. "Should I get out the ice cream?"

Shana managed to smile. "You know, that doesn't sound like a bad idea."

Chapter Seventeen

Commander Frank Dillon figured he had to be the biggest jerk alive, but in his own defense, his behavior toward SMO Karas was motivated strictly by self-preservation.

A week after he'd gone back to sick bay, he was released. Unfortunately, it wasn't soon enough. Every second he spent in close proximity to Alison was pure agony. More times than he wanted to admit, he had to remind himself that she was married. Married with a capital *M*. All he had to do was glance at the ring to remember she was off-limits. Granted, she'd switched it to her right hand, but that act of deception actually bothered him more.

He'd fallen for her, and fallen hard. Whenever he saw her, his heart did a free fall—like a paratrooper diving from a plane—until he saw that damned ring. Then he knew it was time to pull the rip cord and put an end to his ridiculous fascination with the woman.

This sort of thing didn't happen. Not to him. He was particularly confused by the fact that although Alison wore a wedding band, she'd sent him some pretty clear signals—signals that said she was interested and available. While he was undeniably tempted, Frank felt sickened by her lack of respect for her husband and her vows. He wanted nothing more to do with her.

Back on the bridge at the end of his shift, Frank knew the crew had been eagerly waiting for the *USS Woodrow Wilson* to make its port call in Guam. Shore leave had been granted.

During his years in the Navy, Frank had sailed all over the world, and his favorite destination was the South Pacific. He'd read many accounts of the action here during World War II, as well as histories of the explorers.

"You headed ashore?" Commander Howden asked, joining Frank on the bridge.

Frank, still feeling the effects of his surgery, had decided against leaving the carrier. There would be ample opportunity on other voyages. "Not this time."

"A few of us are talking about golf and dinner. Why don't you come along?"

"Thanks, I'll give it some thought." Frank wouldn't willingly admit it, but he felt too weak. A round of golf would probably do him in.

Howden started to walk away, then unexpectedly turned back. "I met the senior medical officer the other day—Alison Karas," he said casually.

Frank stiffened at the sound of her name.

"She's a good woman. I knew her husband."

Frank's jaw tightened at his use of the past tense. "Knew?"

Hal nodded. "He was killed a couple of years ago in a training accident. He'd been aboard the *USS Abraham Lincoln*. You heard about it," he said.

"Yes—but I didn't make the connection." Frank spoke quietly.

"No reason you should, I suppose," Howden continued. "I just realized it myself."

Frank felt angry with himself for the false assumptions he'd made. Alison was a widow and all along, all this time, he'd believed she was married and unfaithful. He hated everything he'd been thinking about her, hated the way he'd magnified her supposed transgressions in his mind. He knew why he'd done it—because he was afraid of what might happen.

As soon as possible, Frank went down to sick bay. He needed—no, wanted—to apologize. He couldn't explain his behavior, but he could let Alison know he regretted what he'd said and done. Perhaps the best course of action was to leave things as they were, but he was unwilling to do that.

He found Lieutenant Rowland on duty in sick bay. Not an enviable task when the majority of his shipmates were touring paradise. The lieutenant snapped to attention when Frank came in.

"Can I help you, Commander?"

Frank returned the salute. "At ease. I'm looking for Ali. Do you know where I might find her?"

"Ali?" The young officer couldn't hide his surprise. "I'm sorry, sir, she's gone ashore."

Frank had guessed as much. "Did she happen to mention where she was going?"

"No, sir, but I suspect she's headed toward the Farmer's Market. A few of the other women officers mentioned they were planning to check it out."

"Thank you," Frank said as he spun around. His energy had been waning, but adrenaline pumped through him now as he hurried off the ship. Fortunately, he was familiar with the island and grabbed the first taxi he saw, paying the driver handsomely.

The streets swarmed with sailors, tourists and locals. The carnival-like atmosphere was everywhere. Music played, chickens squawked and locals hawked their wares, eager to separate the sailors from their hard-earned dollars. The market was so crowded it was nearly impassable.

In this mass of humanity, Frank wondered if locating Alison was a lost cause. That didn't discourage him, but he knew his odds weren't good.

What he should do, Frank decided after a fruitless hour, was think like a woman. The problem with that was he didn't *know* how a woman thought. If he did, his marriage might've lasted longer than two years.

Marriage. The word shot through his brain. Even if he located Ali, he wasn't sure exactly what he'd say to her, or how she'd react. He'd apologize, that much he knew. He must've been intolerable the entire time he was in sick bay, and he admired the way she'd confronted him, admired her professionalism. It wasn't easy to admit he'd been a colossal jerk; if for no other reason, Frank owed her an apology. Then, with his conscience clear, he'd walk away and that would be the end of it.

Suddenly he saw her. She was with a group of female officers, examining a bolt of silk. A flower lei was draped around her neck and the sun shone on her gleaming dark hair. Gazing at her, Frank stood stock-still as the human traffic moved around him.

He watched Ali run her palm over the red silk and ask the proprietor one question and then another. Frank couldn't hear the man's response, but apparently she didn't like it because she promptly shook her head and left without further haggling.

She hadn't seen Frank, since she was moving straight toward him. He remained frozen, waiting for her to notice that he was there. The two women with her recognized him first. One of them, another lieutenant commander, tilted her head toward Alison and he saw Alison's eyes swing in his direction. Almost immediately she looked away, an expression of discomfort on her face.

"Lieutenant Commander Karas," he said crisply, stepping up to her. Perhaps she'd think he was on official business. "I need a moment of your time."

She blinked as if gathering her composure.

He scowled at her companions and they quickly took the hint.

"We'll meet up with you later," one friend stated, setting off.

The other lingered a moment, obviously concerned about leaving Ali in the company of the ogre patient. But at Ali's nod, she rejoined the first woman.

"How can I help you, Commander?" Ali asked. Her shoulders were back as if she expected another ugly confrontation.

Frank wasn't good at apologizing. It wasn't something he'd had much practice at. He began to speak, and then paused to clear his throat before he could get out even one short sentence. "I want to apologize for last week."

Her eyes flared briefly, but she didn't respond.

"I have no excuse for my rude and arrogant behavior," he went on, repeating the very words she'd used to describe him. He despised humiliation in any form, but in this instance he deserved it.

"Apology accepted, Commander. No one likes being sick and helpless."

"That's true," he agreed, willing to accept her explanation.

His remark was followed by silence. Frank usually didn't have problems expressing his views, but just then, standing in a crowded market in the middle of a South Pacific island—standing there with Ali—he couldn't think of a single intelligent thing to say.

"I appreciate everything you did to make my stay as comfortable as possible," he muttered.

"You're welcome," she said abruptly. She seemed eager to leave.

Frank didn't blame her.

"Is there anything else?" she prodded when he didn't resume the conversation.

"No," he said without inflection, but he wanted to scream that there *was*. He just didn't know how to say it. Had they been anyplace else, he might have found the courage to let her know he admired her.

Without another word, she turned and walked toward her friends who stood at a booth, ignoring the proprietor and focusing their attention on him and Ali. Both women seemed to have plenty of opinions, because their heads were close together and they talked rapidly. Frank hated being the object of their scrutiny, but there was no help for it. He'd done what he could; now he had to leave things as they were.

"Lieutenant Commander Karas," he called out sharply, stopping her.

Alison glanced over her shoulder.

"I heard—I'm sorry about your husband."

For the briefest of moments, in the second or two it took her to blink, Alison's eyes went liquid with grief. She quickly regained control of her emotions. "Thank you, Commander. Like you, Peter dedicated his life to the Navy."

He nodded and felt properly put in his place.

That said, Ali joined her friends. The three of them left and were swallowed up by the crowd.

If searching for Ali was out of character, what he did next was even more so. He returned to the silk merchant and purchased the entire bolt of fabric Alison had so recently examined. The hell if he knew what to do with fifteen yards of red silk.

Chapter Eighteen

"I'd like to talk to you when you've got a free moment," Catherine said as soon as Shana showed up for work Monday morning.

Dread instantly filled her. It was said bad news came in threes. Adam had left for Hawaii, Brad wanted her back—or so he'd claimed—and now she feared the worst calamity of all. Her most valued employee was about to quit. Shana could deal with just about anything except that.

"N-now is convenient," she managed to stutter. It wasn't, but she'd have an ulcer if she put this off.

Catherine joined her in the kitchen but kept an eye on the ice-cream counter in case a customer came in.

"You aren't going to quit, are you?" Shana asked point-blank. Catherine had quickly become her friend and confidante. "Because if you do, I'm throwing in the towel right now."

Catherine brushed aside her concern with a wave of her hand. "Of course I'm not quitting. I love my job."

Relief washed over her, and Shana reached out to hug the other woman. "I'm so grateful... I don't think I could take much more."

"That's one of the reasons I thought we should talk," Catherine said. "I don't mean to put my nose where it doesn't belong, but like I said when you interviewed me, I worked in the school cafeteria for almost fifteen years. We were a close-knit group and were able to discuss everything with one another."

"I want you to feel free to do the same here," Shana assured her.

A smile relaxed the older woman's features, and Shana could see that she'd been worried. "Okay. I have a couple of ideas I'd like to try out, so we can take ice-cream requests in a more orderly fashion," Catherine said, "but I understand this is your business and I won't take offense if you don't think they'll work."

"Anything you can suggest would be appreciated," Shana told her. "You're my most important asset, and I want you to know that."

"I wrote everything out for you to read at your leisure," Catherine said, handing her an envelope.

Shana tucked it inside her apron pocket. "Please feel free to share any ideas you have with me," she said. "I'm interested in all your suggestions."

Catherine positively beamed at the praise. "Now, I don't want you to get the notion that I'm taking over the shop or being dictatorial," she said.

That notion was laughable. "I'd never have survived the last couple of weekends without you and your husband."

Catherine's eyes brightened at the mention of her husband. "Louis had the time of his life."

They'd been wonderful with the customers and reminded Shana of the Olsens, who'd owned the shop for all those years. Catherine and Louis were so natural with children and treated everyone like family. Shana envied their ability, and knew this kind of friendliness was a big reason her customers returned over and over again. She'd been fortunate to hire Catherine, and Louis was a bonus... and a darling.

"You know who to call if you want another day off." Catherine smiled. "In fact, Louis said if you're ever looking to sell, we'd like the right of first refusal, but I told him you'd just bought the business and it wasn't likely you'd be interested in selling."

"No, but I'll certainly keep that in mind." Shana had invested her entire financial future in this shop. So far, she was meeting payroll and keeping her head above water, but this was her busy season. The Olsens had warned her that the winter months could be a fiscal challenge. Shana hoped to find ways to stay afloat when the weather was dreary. Ice-cream sales would decrease in winter, but she hoped the pizza part of the business would continue to flourish. Thankfully, Lincoln Park was much-used year round.

"Also," Catherine added, sounding hesitant. "I know this isn't any of my concern, but it seems to me you haven't been yourself the last few days."

So it was that obvious.

"Is there a problem?" the other woman asked gently, in the same way Ali might have done had she been there. Trading e-mails was better than nothing but they weren't a substitute for face-to-face communication.

Shana slumped against the wall and automatically shook her head. For three nights straight, she hadn't slept more than a couple of hours. When she did manage to drift off, she dreamed of Adam and then woke tired and depressed.

"Man troubles?" Catherine asked. "You don't need to tell me, not unless you want. But sometimes just talking things out with someone else can help."

Shana nodded, reflecting that the school district had lost a wonderful employee. In Shana's opinion, Catherine was much too young to retire.

"It's just that, well…this is complicated." Shana wasn't

sure how to explain without going into more detail than necessary.

"Does this have to do with Brad or Adam?" Catherine prompted.

Shana's mouth fell open. "How do you know about Brad?" Her eyes narrowed and she answered her own question. It could only be her niece. "Jazmine."

Catherine nodded, folding her hands. She looked about as guilty as a woman can. "Jazmine and I are friends, and the truth of it is, she confided in me because she's worried about you."

"She is, is she?" Shana couldn't wait to ask Jazmine about this.

"Jazmine is a dear girl and she meant well," Catherine said immediately.

"Who else has she told?" Shana demanded. Apparently her heart-to-heart with her niece hadn't been as effective as she'd hoped. Jazmine seemed intent on spreading Shana's problems throughout the entire neighborhood.

"I don't think she's mentioned it to anyone else," Catherine was quick to reassure her. "Certainly not Charles. I can't be positive, of course, but…" Her voice trailed off.

"Of course," Shana echoed. Jazmine was a handful. Spending her days at the park with friends or in the ice-cream parlor with Shana wasn't the ideal situation, but it was the best that could be done for now. Unless Shana looked into some kind of summer camp for her…

"The only reason Jazmine said anything was because I asked her if she knew what was bothering you. So if anyone's to blame, it's me," Catherine insisted, her face reddening. "I apologize, Shana."

"Don't worry about it." But Shana decided she'd still ask Jazmine later.

"Is there anything I can do to help?" Catherine offered. "Like I said, I'm a good listener."

After several sleepless nights, Shana could use some advice. "All right," she agreed with a deep sigh. "My life's a bit of a mess at the moment," she said, then proceeded to tell Catherine about her five-year relationship with Brad and how it had ended. She described how he'd been an important part of her life, and then he was gone; just after that, Jazmine had arrived and on the heels of her niece Adam Kennedy showed up.

Catherine nodded often during the course of their lengthy one-sided discussion.

"Are you in love with Adam?" she asked when Shana had finished.

"Yes. *No.* How can I be?" She paused. "Good grief, I'm the last person who'd know."

"You love Brad, though?" Catherine continued.

"No." This came without the slightest hesitation. "Although I loved him at one time. At least, I believed I did."

"I don't think breaking off a relationship is ever as easy as we want it to be," Catherine said thoughtfully. "We invest our hopes and dreams in a particular relationship, and when that doesn't work out, we sometimes have difficulty admitting it."

"That's true." Shana nodded, remembering the years she'd devoted to Brad with such hope for a future together.

"I wonder if what you really want is for Brad to recognize how much he wronged you."

Shana grinned. That was so true, it was almost painful.

"It gives women a sense of vindication," Catherine pronounced solemnly, "when a man realizes the error of his ways."

Shana nodded again. She wished she'd talked to her friend weeks ago; Catherine saw everything with such clarity and insight.

"Are you tempted to take him back?"

"Not at all…" She let the rest fade.

"You're sure?"

"Yes, but…" The thought had only occurred to her now. "Until I talk to him…" Even as she said the words, Shana knew that a telephone conversation wouldn't be enough. She needed to see Brad, talk to him in person, which she hadn't really done, not after that one dramatic scene when she'd confronted him with what she knew about Sylvia. Then she'd gone to Seattle to think. She'd phoned him, but hadn't spoken to him in person. Shana had never honestly explained her dissatisfaction with the relationship—aside from the Sylvia issue—nor had she made clear that reconciliation was out of the question. Her severing of the relationship wasn't a ploy to get him back. And it wasn't something she'd done on a whim.

Shana looked at Catherine.

"Actually," Catherine said, "I think talking to Brad is a good idea."

"I do, too." Shana removed her apron and carelessly tossed it over the back of a chair. "Can you take over for me?"

"Now?" Catherine asked, seemingly surprised at how quickly Shana was acting.

"Please. I'll take Jazmine to Portland with me."

"I'll need to call Louis, but I'm pretty sure he hasn't got anything planned for the next few days. Let me find out." She walked over to the phone, and after just a minute's discussion, replaced the receiver. "He said he'd be delighted."

"Good." Her decision made, her resolve strong, Shana went outside to collect Jazmine.

"One question," Catherine said, stopping her on her way out the door. "What do you want me to say if Adam phones?"

That wasn't likely to happen, but she certainly didn't want her friend to divulge that she'd gone off to see Brad. "Our last conversation ended kind of badly, so I doubt—"

"You said that earlier," Catherine broke in, "but I bet he'll be phoning soon. He probably regrets how things went as much as you do."

Shana did regret it and although she hadn't said so, Catherine had intuitively known. "Tell him I'm visiting an old friend out of town." It would be the truth, because she planned to call Gwen Jackson as soon as she got home. As she spoke, Shana absently watched a delivery truck pull into the parking space in front of the restaurant.

The bell above the door jangled cheerfully, and Catherine hurried out of the kitchen. Shana followed her, sorry their conversation had been interrupted.

All she saw was a large FedEx box.

"Shana Berrie?" the delivery man asked.

Catherine gestured toward Shana.

"I'm Shana," she responded, trying to remember if she'd recently ordered anything that would come by overnight courier. She couldn't think of a thing.

Jazmine trailed the delivery man inside. "What's that?" she asked excitedly.

"I don't know yet." Shana signed the clipboard and yanked the tab at the end of the box. The sender's name was that of a floral company in… It started with a *W* but a large smudge obscured the rest of the word.

"It's probably from Brad," Jazmine muttered disdainfully. "I told you he wants you back."

"No way," Shana said, shaking her head. Anything he had to send her wouldn't come in a box. She'd been waiting for a small jewelry box from him long enough to guarantee that.

When the carton was open, two orchid leis slid onto the counter. Waikiki—that was it. Hawaii. Well, that was one puzzle solved. Catherine gave an immediate gasp of wonder at their delicate beauty.

"Uncle Adam," Jazmine burst out in a squeal of unrestrained delight.

"Is there a card?" Catherine asked.

Shana searched the inside of the box and found it. *"To my two favorite girls. I miss you. Adam."*

Jazmine draped one of the leis over her shoulders, beaming with joy.

Shana wasn't nearly as pleased. "That was a cowardly thing to do," she declared. Just leave it to a man to let flowers do his talking for him. Well, she'd deal with Adam later, but at the moment she had another man on her mind, and that was Brad Moore.

Chapter Nineteen

Shana felt as if she was on a mission now. What Catherine had said was so true—it was as difficult to let go of the expectations created by a relationship as the relationship itself. She needed to complete the process of disconnecting herself from Brad.

The minute she arrived home, Shana instructed Jazmine to pack an overnight bag.

"Where are we going?" Jazmine asked, catching Shana's enthusiasm. The lei still hung around her neck. Shana wore hers, too. She appreciated Adam's gesture, but not as much as she would have if he'd e-mailed or phoned her first. She didn't *want* to think about him now, and yet it was impossible not to. The orchids wafted a lovely scent, reminding her of Adam and their shared kisses.

"To Portland."

"Portland?" Jazmine moaned. "Why are we going *there?*"

Shana already had her suitcase out of her closet and open on top of her bed. She didn't need much—her pajamas, a set of clothes and clean underwear. Her toiletries and makeup. That was it.

"Aunt Shana…"

She whirled around, almost forgetting Jazmine was in the

room. "I'm sorry. You asked me why we're going to Portland." The girl deserved the truth. "I need to talk to Brad."

"Brad!" Her niece spit out the name as if she had a bug
in her mouth. "Why?" she cried with such a shocked look
that Shana nearly laughed. "You're wearing Uncle Adam's
lei and you want to visit *Brad?*"

"I need to talk to him."

"But why?"

"It's important," was all Shana could tell her.

"You're not going back to him, are you?" Jazmine's eyes
pleaded with hers.

"No. Now pack an overnight bag. I want to head out as
soon as we can." Shana had no intention of being away
from the business for more than twenty-four hours. She'd
already called Gwen and left a message, asking if she could
put them up for the night. If not, they'd get a hotel room—
a reasonably priced one. The trip would be an adventure,
and Shana would make an effort to see that Jazmine had
fun. If there was time, they'd stop at Jensen Beach to shop
and play tourist. Her niece would enjoy that.

Jazmine hesitated in the doorway. "You're sure about
this?"

"Very sure." This was a conversation she should've had
with Brad when she left him.

"Are you still in love with Brad?" Jazmine asked urgently, staring up at her.

"No. I told you that."

Jazmine frowned, apparently not entirely convinced.
"Do you always do stuff like this?"

"You mean act on impulse?" Shana clarified. She didn't
think she did, but she realized she was only beginning to
know herself. Buying the ice-cream parlor had been the
first impulsive thing she'd done in years. Now this. Perhaps it came from a new sense of having control over her
own life.

"Are you packed?" Shana asked, knowing very well that she wasn't.

"Not yet." Her niece dawdled for another few minutes. "I don't think I can leave," she said with a shrug. "My garden needs watering, and Uncle Adam said it's important to give the plants a drink every morning and every night." A smile raised the edges of her mouth. "He said I should sing to them, but nothing too fast or with a strong beat."

Shana smiled, too. "I think they can go without water for a day. You can make it up to them later and give them an extra drink and sing a few lullabies."

Jazmine still hesitated, then finally appeared to reach a decision. She went into her own bedroom.

It seemed to take her niece forever to assemble what she needed. When she reappeared, she was dragging her backpack behind her as if it weighed fifty pounds. "We can go now," she said with an undisguised lack of enthusiasm.

"Good." Shana stood by the car, waiting impatiently. She wondered if Jazmine had transferred the entire contents of her dresser into her backpack, but decided against asking.

"Everything locked up?" Shana had checked the back door and the windows.

Jazmine nodded, climbed into the car while Shana heaved her backpack into the trunk, and fastened her seat belt. Then she sighed heavily.

Shana walked around to the driver's side. "Think of this as an adventure," she said in a breezy voice.

Jazmine's chin drooped to her chest. "Are you going to tell Uncle Adam what you did?"

Involuntarily Shana fingered the lei. "I don't know. Maybe."

"What if Brad gets you to move back to Portland?"

"That won't happen," Shana promised, hiding a smile.

"I just don't understand why it's so important for you to see him again," Jazmine whined. "You said it was over.

You said you didn't want to have anything to do with him again. You said—"

"I know what I said." Shana cut her off, started the car and pulled away from the curb.

Jazmine was quiet for the first few minutes. "Where will we stay the night?" she asked.

"At a friend's place."

"What friend?"

"Gwen. You haven't met her."

"Does she have kids?"

"No," Shana murmured as she merged onto the West Seattle freeway and toward Interstate 5.

"Do I get to come along when you talk to Brad?"

Shana hadn't actually considered that, but the answer wasn't difficult. "Probably not."

Jazmine's shoulders slumped forward. "That's what I figured."

"Jazz, this *isn't* what you think. I'm going to see Brad to tell him something…." Only now were her thoughts catching up with her actions.

"What?" Jazmine asked, looking at her for the first time since she got into the car.

"To tell him I made the right decision when I left Portland."

"You mean you're not *sure?*" Her niece seemed about to burst into tears.

"No. Why are you so worried?"

Jazmine stared out the passenger window as if the concrete freeway interchanges were the most fascinating scenery in the world. "Brad phoned, and I told you and then… then you and Uncle Adam had an argument, and now you're driving to Portland. I'm not stupid, you know. I can connect the dots."

"Well, you're looking at the wrong picture." Shana could understand why Jazmine had reached those conclusions but they weren't correct. "You don't need to be concerned, Jazz. I promise."

"I want you to marry Uncle Adam. Don't you want to?"

"Let me deal with one man at a time, okay?" At the moment Adam was the last person she wanted to think about. "Once I talk to Brad, you and I can discuss your uncle Adam."

"Oh, sure," Jazmine muttered. "You don't have to explain anything to *me*. I'm just a kid," she said sarcastically.

Shana sighed. Jazmine really ought to enroll in a drama class because she clearly had talent. In fact, maybe they could find one when they got back....

"Did you mention this to Mom?" Jazmine asked after a precious few moments of silence.

Shana kept her eyes on the road. "There wasn't time to e-mail her."

"Does your friend have a computer I can use?"

"I'm sure she does."

"I'll let Mom know where we are and what you're doing." Jazmine announced this with a great deal of satisfaction.

"Fine." Shana just bet the nine-year-old would delight in letting her mother know they were in Portland. Smiling, she wondered how Jazmine would embellish the tale.

"What if he isn't there?"

Uh-oh. "You mean Brad?" Not once had Shana stopped to consider that. "I...I don't know." This wasn't a situation in which she'd be comfortable leaving behind her newly printed business card. If Brad learned she'd come by his office, or even his condo, he'd assume the wrong thing.

"He has to be there," she said aloud. "He just has to."

Adam checked his watch and calculated the time in Seattle. Three-thirty. The leis should have arrived by now, according to the delivery schedule. He imagined Shana's surprise and pleasure at opening the box and discovering the leis. The orchids were supposed to pave the way for part two of his reconciliation plan—a phone call.

He wasn't sure how it had happened, but somehow his previous conversation with Shana had gone in completely the wrong direction. He certainly hadn't intended to become embroiled in an argument. He couldn't even figure out what kind of mistake he'd made. Whatever it was, he sincerely hoped she was over it by now.

Adam had talked to one of his friends about Shana's reaction. John, another lieutenant commander, had said his wife always started an argument before he left. Apparently it was common among Navy wives. For whatever reason, women found it easier to send their men off to sea if they were upset with them about something. Adam didn't understand it, but John claimed their disagreement was simply Shana's way of letting him know she was in love with him.

That had taken Adam by surprise. *Shana loved him?* Shana loved him! He chose to believe it because he so badly wanted to. He wasn't much of a romantic, but the thought of Shana waiting for him back in Seattle made him happy in a way he'd never experienced before.

He hurried home to make the call in privacy. When he didn't think he could bear to wait another minute, he reached for the telephone and punched out the number for the ice-cream parlor. Leaning back on his sofa, feet stretched out on the coffee table, he listened to the ringing of the phone.

"Olsen's Ice Cream and Pizza Parlor."

The man's voice shook Adam. "Who's this?"

"Who's this?" the male voice echoed.

Adam dropped his stocking feet to the floor and leaned forward far enough to prop his elbows on his knees. "Is Shana there?"

"No. Who's calling, please?"

"Lieutenant Commander Adam Kennedy."

"Oh, hello." The voice instantly became friendly. "This is Louis, Catherine's husband. I'd better let you talk to her. Hold on."

"Should I call back later?"

"No, no, it's fine. Here's Cath."

A couple of seconds later, Shana's number-one employee was on the line. "Adam, hello." She sounded slightly breathless. "What can I do for you?"

"I actually called to talk to Shana."

She paused a telltale moment. "I'm sorry, but you missed her. Shana took Jazmine on a…short vacation."

Adam's disappointment was keen. "Did the leis arrive?" Those had cost him a pretty penny, and he hoped they weren't sitting in a box wilting before Shana even had a chance to see them.

"Oh, yes, and she was…pleased. Jazmine, too."

"Did she mention where she was going?" Perhaps he should try reaching her on her cell. He'd just assumed she'd be at the restaurant.

"Yes, yes, she did," Catherine said. She seemed distracted; either Adam had phoned at a bad time or she was reluctant to tell him exactly where Shana had gone.

"I'll try her cell," he murmured.

"You could do that, of course," Catherine agreed politely. "But…but she might be out of reach."

"Why? Did they drive into the mountains?"

"Uh, no."

Her hesitation made him suspicious. "The ocean?"

"No, ah—listen, I need to go…. There are customers waiting."

"Catherine," Adam said softly. She was hiding something, and he wanted to know what.

"I'll tell Shana you phoned."

"You said Jazmine's with her?"

"Of course she is," Catherine answered sharply.

"What's going on there?" Adam demanded. "Where's Shana?"

Catherine sighed deeply. "I told her. The minute she said she was leaving, I told Shana you'd phone. Sure enough, here I am, having to tell you."

"Tell me what?"

"Shana's in Portland, visiting a friend. Gwen—a female friend." She spoke with finality, as though she hoped that was the end of his questions.

"Portland?" A chill raced down Adam's arms, one that had nothing to do with the tropical breeze coming through the sliding glass door. "I don't suppose this has anything to do with Brad?"

"You'll have to ask her that." Catherine sighed again. "I refuse to incriminate myself—or her."

Adam snorted. "I see."

Dammit, he did see—and he wasn't enjoying the view.

Chapter Twenty

Shana's stomach tensed with anxiety. What had been a brilliant idea that morning seemed utterly ridiculous now. She waited inside the lobby of Brad's office building, pacing back and forth, trying to put words to the mangled feelings inside her head. She was *not* looking for a reconciliation. But Catherine's insight had made her aware that she'd abandoned her previous life without really settling matters with Brad. There were things that had to be said…except now, all she could think about was Adam.

Thankfully Jazmine was safely ensconced at Gwen's. Her friend was a nurse who worked the night shift; she was up and about when Shana and Jazmine arrived on her front porch. As soon as she heard the reason for Shana's visit, she'd sent her off with a pep talk. Gwen's encouragement had carried Shana all the way to downtown Portland.

However, Shana's resolve had quickly waned when she stepped inside the luxurious lobby. All of a sudden, her tongue felt glued to the roof of her mouth, and when someone casually walked past and greeted her, her returning "good afternoon" came out sounding like "goonoon."

Mortified, Shana hurried into the ladies' room and locked herself inside a stall. She hadn't even bothered to change clothes. Filled with purpose, she'd driven to Portland in shorts and a T-shirt with a smudge of chocolate ice cream on the hem. She was about to have one of the most important conversations of her life, and she resembled someone trying out for clown school.

Sitting on the toilet seat, Shana buried her face in her hands. What was she thinking? She was astonished at her own audacity and horrified at this latest example of impulsive behavior.

Her goal, when she left Seattle in a heated frenzy, had been to make Brad Moore realize what he'd lost—and whose fault that was. She was going to end the relationship properly, definitively, for her own sake, and ultimately for his, too. After coming this far, she refused to turn back. She'd simply buy something appropriate. There was time.

That decision made, Shana walked into an ultra-expensive boutique in the lobby. Either the sales clerk took pity on her or she was afraid Shana was about to shoplift a mannequin, because she immediately shot out from behind the cash register.

"Can I help you?"

"Can you ever." Shana threw herself on the mercy of a complete stranger. "I need an outfit that'll make a man rue the day he—"

"Say no more." The clerk raised her hand. "I have just the dress." She looked Shana up and down. "Size four?"

Maybe ten years ago. "Six," she muttered.

"Four. This dress is expensive enough to be a four."

Shana laughed. She didn't care how much it cost; her ego was at stake.

Once she stood in front of the mirror, Shana barely recognized the woman staring back at her. The knee-length floral dress was simple yet elegant, fanning out at her waist in pleats that emphasized her hips and long legs.

"Wow," she whispered, impressed. She didn't even glance at the price tag. It was better not to know.

The clerk nodded approvingly. "Perfect."

Shana twisted around to take a gander at the back and decided that view was even sexier. She hoped Brad took a good, long look when she walked away.

Not wanting to show up clutching a bag with her shorts and T-shirt inside—that kind of contradicted the classy image—she ditched her old clothes.

The only unfortunate part of the new outfit was the matching shoes. The one pair left was a full size too small for Shana, but the slinky sandals were gorgeous. With a minimum of regret, she purchased them anyway. By the time she walked out of the boutique, her little toe on each shoe had squeezed between the narrow straps and escaped. She'd be fine as long as Brad didn't look at her feet.

Shana was still testing her ability to walk when the elevator opened and Brad Moore entered the lobby. Swallowing her breath, Shana nearly choked when Brad saw her. He stopped abruptly, his shock unmistakable.

"Shana," he cried. He held out his arms to her, surprise replaced by delight. "You look fabulous."

"Yes, I do." Now wasn't the time for modesty, especially in light of what she'd paid for this outfit. She tilted her head to one side and allowed him to kiss her cheek.

"What are you doing here?"

No need to beat around the bush. "I came to see you."

"Great." He didn't bother to hide his enthusiasm. "Shall we have a drink somewhere and talk?"

"That would be fine." She played it cool, refusing to let him see how flustered she was.

Taking her by the elbow, Brad led the way out of the high-rise office tower. Shana struggled to keep up with him, the too-tight shoes pinching her feet unmercifully. Her little toes hung over the edge of the shoes and she prayed no one would notice. Thankfully there was a hotel bar across the street.

Brad led her to a small table, ordered them each a glass of merlot and grinned at her as if she were a delectable dessert.

The cocktail waitress brought their wine and Brad sent a flirtatious glance in her direction.

Once he'd finished paying for their drinks, he smiled at her confidently. "You got my message?"

"You mean the one you weren't willing to say to me yourself?"

He had the good grace to look embarrassed. "I would have if you'd been home. Who is that kid, anyway?"

Shana was surprised Jazmine hadn't enlightened him. "My niece. You remember my sister, Alison, don't you? Jazmine is her daughter."

"I met your sister once, right?" Brad raised both eyebrows. "The kid's got attitude."

He hadn't seen anything yet.

"How've you been?" he asked, but before she could respond he added, "I've missed you."

This was where—according to his script—she was supposed to tell him how lonely she'd been without him and how much she regretted the things she'd said and done.

He waited, and when she didn't immediately offer the desired response, he frowned. "I'm glad you're here. We have a lot to discuss."

"I came because—"

Brad reached for her hand, stopping her. "You don't need to say it. We both made mistakes and we're both sorry. Let's leave it at that."

"You think I made a mistake?"

"That's why you're here, isn't it?"

She took her first sip of wine and let its smoothness flow

over her tongue. "I came because when I walked out on you, I was angry and hurt."

"I know…"

"I don't feel either of those things anymore. I wanted to look you in the eye, see what I used to find so attractive." She sighed. Whatever it was had long vanished. "I really just came, Brad, to clear the air once and for all, and to do it properly."

Brad's expression changed and he stared at her. "You are coming back to Portland, aren't you?"

She loved this city and missed her job. The ice-cream parlor demanded constant attention and supervision. The hours were long and the financial compensation small. As a pharmaceutical salesperson, she'd been able to leave work at the end of the day and not give her job another thought. Having a business of her own was a completely different proposition. The ice-cream and pizza parlor had seemed like an escape from an unhappy situation, but for the first time, she wondered if she'd made the right decision.

"Shana?" Brad asked, breaking into her musings.

"Portland? I don't know," she admitted honestly.

"You love me, don't you?" He asked the question but she could tell he wasn't as sure of himself as he'd been earlier.

Seeing the crack in his confidence weakened her resolve. "That's just it," Shana said. "I loved you so completely and I was so sure you loved me."

"I do love you," Brad insisted. "I know you were upset and you had every right to be. I was a fool, but I swear to you it'll never happen again. I regretted it immediately. I was sick that I lost you because of Sylvia."

Shana didn't trust him enough to believe his promises.

He seemed to be debating how much of the truth to reveal. "We went out two or three times, but that's beside the point. It didn't take me long to realize I'd made the biggest mistake of my life. It's *you* I love, Shana. It's you I want to be with."

The complete absence of the word *marriage* didn't escape her. In other words, they'd resume their relationship exactly where they'd left off. His script again—but not hers.

Brad must have seen the strength and determination in her eyes. "You mean it, don't you?" he asked morosely. "This really is goodbye."

"Yes."

"But you loved me at one time. I can't believe you don't now."

A sad smile formed but she refused to answer him.

His own smile returned. "You do love me. You wouldn't be here now if you didn't still have feelings for me."

Brad's gaze pleaded with her as he clasped her hand in both of his. "You do love me," he said again.

She remained silent, and all at once he seemed to realize she wasn't changing her mind. That was when he said the one thing that, a few months ago, might have swayed her.

"I want to marry you."

Even that didn't elicit a response.

"I'm sincere, Shana. I couldn't be any more serious. You set the date and the time."

Rather than drag this out, she told him the truth. "I met someone else."

Brad frowned. "Is this the guy your niece mentioned?"

"Yes."

"Certainly didn't take you long, did it?" he asked, sitting back. "So the real reason you're here is to rub my face in it."

"No." Until this moment she hadn't planned to say anything about Adam.

"I thought you were in love with *me*. Pretty fickle, aren't you?"

She smiled, knowing she'd asked for that. "I *was* in

love with you, but that's over." She paused. "It's funny, you know."

"I'm not laughing."

She shook her head. "I didn't think it was possible to feel like this about a man on such short acquaintance. Adam's good to me and to my niece.... He's a family friend. That's how we met."

"Bully for you."

"Don't, Brad." She hadn't expected to be this honest with him but it seemed important. She had no intention of being vindictive or mean-spirited. She might not love him anymore, but she didn't begrudge him happiness.

"And what does Adam do?" Brad asked, his words hard and clipped. "Oh, yes, I remember now. He's some big deal in the Navy." He lifted his brows dismissively. "So. Can you tell me exactly why you're here?"

Shana sipped her wine. "I came here this morning, convinced I had to see you. I already told you why. I felt—and still feel—that I had to end this relationship properly."

Brad closed his eyes for a moment. "Okay. Consider it ended."

"Thank you," she said graciously. "I even went so far as to buy this dress at a price so outrageous I'll be making payments for the next six months." She glanced down at her feet and tried to remember what size shoe her sister wore and hoped it was a seven.

"So this outfit was for my benefit?"

Shana nodded. "I wanted you to be sorry you lost me."

His eyes grew gentle. "I was sorry before you got here. I've been sorry for months."

Despite her mood, she smiled. "That's probably the sweetest thing you've ever said to me."

"So you didn't come here to make me feel bad about you and Popeye?"

Shana inhaled softly. She knew exactly why she'd found it necessary to drive to Portland. "No, I didn't," she said softly. "I came to say goodbye."

Chapter Twenty-One

Adam Kennedy wasn't having a good day. In fact, the entire week was down the septic tank, and he blamed Shana Berrie for that. If she was trying to make him jealous, it was damned well working.

"That's what women do to you," his friend John told him. They sat across from each other at Navy Headquarters for the Pacific Fleet. "They mess with your mind and they make irrational demands. Take my wife, for example. Angie got upset with me because there was a cockroach in the house, as if it's my duty as her husband to rid the place of bugs. Can you believe it? She's afraid of a stupid bug, and if I don't deal with it, I might as well not go home tonight."

Barely hearing his friend's rant, Adam scowled. Shana certainly hadn't wasted any time giving up on him. As far as she was concerned, it seemed to be out of sight, out of mind. Well, fine, great, whatever. If she wanted to race back to lover boy, then that was perfectly fine by him.

The hell it was, Adam decided quickly. He hadn't slept well; his appetite was gone and he had a sick feeling that refused to go away. He didn't know how everything had fallen apart so quickly. In his view they'd *had* a promising relationship, with emphasis on the past tense.

The phone rang and Adam left it for John. What he

needed was a bout of hard exercise, but with his shoulder golf was still out of the question and swimming would be just as painful. He could always jog, he supposed, but it wasn't something he enjoyed.

John answered the phone, and Adam watched as his gaze shot across the room. He put the caller on hold. "It's for you. A woman. Says her name is Shana." He gave Adam a significant look, both eyebrows raised.

It took Adam a moment to assimilate that. His pulse accelerated and then immediately slowed. The call was most likely a courtesy to let him know she was going back to lover boy in Portland.

With that in mind, Adam reached for the telephone receiver. He responded in a crisp military tone, keeping his voice devoid of emotion.

"Adam, hello," Shana said, her own voice friendly.

Adam nearly weakened, but he realized she was probably warming him up before she dropped the news. She'd led him on, he mused darkly, and now she was going to make a fool of him.

"I wanted to thank you for the leis. Jazmine and I were thrilled. It was so generous of you."

Adam kept silent, bracing himself.

After an awkward moment, during which he said nothing, Shana said, "I feel badly about the way our last conversation went."

"Forget it," Adam said in the same emotionless tone. He wanted her to think it hardly mattered to him. He should've taken the hint then. Shana was trouble and he'd best get out of this unpredictable relationship. But even as the thought went through his mind, he didn't believe it.

"I blame myself," Shana added, "for picking a fight with you. I was just reacting to your leaving, I guess." She hesitated. "We had so little time, and I knew I was going to miss you so much. Jazmine, too, of course."

John had explained that this was the same reaction he got from his wife, but Adam couldn't really accept that. Why would Shana care whether he was stationed in Hawaii if she was going back to the guy in Portland?

She seemed to realize he wasn't responding. "Are you upset about something?" she asked tentatively.

"Should I be?" He answered her question with one of his own.

"I don't think so." Her voice gained conviction, but gone was the sweet joy he'd heard in her earlier. Now she sounded wary.

"I understand you were out of town," he said, broaching the subject that was foremost on his mind.

His announcement was followed by stark silence. "You know about that?"

"I do. So if you're planning to tell me what I think you are, I'd appreciate if you'd just say it and be done with it."

"Say *what?*"

"You want out," he said flippantly. "So let's just call it quits."

"You're willing to end this without another word?" She seemed shocked—and annoyed.

"I'm not the one who drove down to visit an old lover. You never did say how things went between you and Bernie."

"It's Brad," she corrected. "And you're right, I didn't."

He waited, unwilling to cut off the conversation and at the same time reluctant to continue trading barbs.

"Isn't this all a little silly?" Shana asked.

"When did you decide to go?"

"In the morning. It was a spur-of-the-moment idea. Jazmine and I spent the night with an old friend—an old female friend," she added. "I saw Brad and we talked."

"About what?" He didn't mean to ask and wanted to withdraw the question the moment it left his mouth.

She paused, taking a moment before she answered. "I don't remember if I told you I moved to Seattle in kind of a rush."

"You might've said something like that." He tried to play it cool, but the truth was, he hung on every word.

"So I needed to see Brad."

"I'm sure you did," he muttered, unable to disguise his sarcasm.

His comment generated a lengthy silence. "We had a chance to talk and to say certain things that needed to be said," she finally told him.

She didn't enlighten him as to what those things might be. "So you're back in Seattle?"

"Yes. I have to go now. The only reason I phoned," she said, "is to thank you for the leis. Jazmine and I love them. Now I should get back to work."

Adam had to bite his tongue to keep from pleading with her to stay on the phone a bit longer. He wished they could start the entire conversation over.

"How's Jazmine?" he asked, using the question as a delaying tactic.

"Fabulous…wonderful. Thank you again for the orchids."

And with that, the line was disconnected. He waited a few seconds while the buzz sounded in his ear. Adam replaced the receiver and glared at the phone as he replayed the conversation. He knew he'd made a number of tactical errors, and that was because his ego had gotten in the way.

"So, how'd it go?" John asked conversationally.

"Not good."

"Sorry to hear that. I told you—women mess with your mind. You should've figured that out by now."

John was right; he should have.

The tension in Adam's stomach didn't diminish all day.

At the end of his watch, he returned to his quarters to find the message light on his phone blinking. It was too much to hope that Shana had called him a second time. Holding his breath, he pressed the message button.

Jazmine's voice greeted him. "Uncle Adam, what's with you? You've really blown it now. Call me at the house when you get home. I'll make sure I answer."

Adam reached for the phone. Here he was, conspiring with a nine-year-old. *That* was a sign of desperation.

Chapter Twenty-Two

Ali was quite entertained by the tone of Shana's e-mails in the last week. Her sister was not in a good mood. She'd only brought up Adam's name once, but Ali was well aware that the lieutenant commander was the sole source of Shana's irritation.

Thankfully, Jazmine had been able to fill Ali in. Apparently Adam and Shana had some form of falling-out. Shana had driven to Portland to say a final goodbye to Brad, and Adam was out of sorts about it. From what Jazmine said, they were currently ignoring each other.

Ali didn't usually meddle in other people's romances. She hadn't said anything when Shana was involved with Brad, and she wouldn't interfere now. At least she didn't *think* she would. But those two were perfect together, and it would be a shame if this relationship died because they were too stubborn to admit they were attracted to each other. Although Ali suspected that their feelings had gone way beyond attraction…

Preoccupied, she walked toward the wardroom. She generally ate with the other officers at six every evening, but tonight she was later than usual. Life at sea had grown monotonous, and the days seemed to run into each other without any real break to distinguish one from the next.

When she entered the room, there were a few officers at various tables, but she noticed only one.

Commander Frank Dillon.

Ali hadn't seen or talked to him since they'd met in the Farmer's Market in Guam. Just seeing him again gave her pause. She'd thought about their brief conversation that very afternoon; even now she wasn't sure what to make of it. Her friends, too, were full of questions she hadn't been able to answer. Ali filled her tray and started for a table.

"Good evening, Commander," she said, greeting him.

"Ali." He didn't look any too pleased to see her, if his scowl was any indication.

She sat down several tables away, but facing him. It would be utterly rude to present him with her back. "I do hope you've sufficiently recovered." Ali knew she sounded stilted but couldn't help it. She avoided eye contact by reaching for the salt shaker.

"I have, thank you. And you?"

His question caught her unawares. "I haven't been ill, Commander."

"Yes, of course." He stood as if he couldn't leave fast enough and disappeared with such speed, it made her head swim. Clearly she was the last person he wanted to see. Only this time, Ali didn't take offense.

She'd come to the conclusion that she flustered Commander Dillon, which was a heady sensation. She recalled how gruff and rude he'd been in sick bay and, thanks to their brief conversation on Guam, she finally understood the reason. He'd thought she was married.

The next evening, Alison purposely delayed her meal and arrived at the same time as the night before. Sure enough Frank was there, sitting at the same table, lingering over coffee. He looked up and smiled uncertainly when he saw her.

"Good evening, Commander." She greeted him the

same way she had the previous night. After getting her meal, she chose a seat one table closer.

"Lieutenant Commander." His eyes held hers, and he didn't immediately leap up and run away.

"I have a question for you," she said and again reached for the salt shaker. It was a convenient excuse to avert her gaze. She feared he might read her intense interest in him, which seemed to compound after each meeting.

He straightened. "Fire away."

"Do I frighten you?"

He raised one eyebrow. "Truthfully? You terrify me."

"Any particular reason?"

He expelled his breath. "As a matter of fact, there are several. Most of them would get me court-martialed if I mentioned them."

"I see." She didn't really, but she was definitely curious.

"Does that amuse you?" he asked, his face deadpan.

"Commander, are you flirting with me?"

This question seemed to take him aback, and he frowned. "I can assure you I wouldn't know how. Is that what you think I'm doing?"

She shook her head. "I'm not sure, but I do have another question for you."

"All right. I just hope it isn't as difficult as the first." A hint of a smile touched his eyes.

Alison dipped her fork into the creamy mashed potatoes. "I wonder, do you know anything about a bolt of red silk that was delivered to the ship in my name?"

"Red silk?" He shrugged. "I'm afraid I can't help you there."

"That isn't an answer to my question, Commander."

He glanced at his watch, and as if he'd suddenly realized he was late for an important meeting, abruptly stood. He grabbed his coffee cup and took one last swallow before he excused himself and hurried away.

Alison hadn't known what to think when the silk had appeared in her quarters. She was able to track down the petty officer who delivered it, and learned that the man from the market had brought it to the docks. He'd left instructions that it should be taken directly to her. Alison had badly wanted that silk, but the price was more than she'd been willing to pay.

Just before she drifted off to sleep the night before, she'd remembered haggling with the silk merchant just before she'd run into Frank. He must have purchased it for her. It was the only thing that made sense—and yet it didn't. But judging by the way he'd reacted to her questions this evening, she had to wonder.

The following night when Alison arrived at the wardroom, Frank wasn't there. Her heart sank with disappointment. She really didn't have much of an appetite and ate very little of her meal. She'd almost decided against coffee but it was her habit to end her dinner with a cup.

Just when she was ready to leave, uninterested in the remains of her cooling coffee, Frank rushed in, looking harried.

"Good evening, Commander," Alison said, smiling her welcome. Hiding her pleasure at seeing him had become impossible.

He poured himself a cup of coffee and joined her. This was progress. They'd begun by sitting several tables apart and had drawn closer with each encounter.

He was silent for a few minutes, concentrating on his coffee, methodically adding sugar and cream, then stirring. "You have children?" he asked unexpectedly.

"A nine-year-old daughter."

He nodded.

"Jazmine is living with my sister in Seattle right now."

He nodded again. "Is this the first time you've been apart for so much time?"

"Yes." Then, feeling it was only fair that she be completely honest, Alison said, "This will be my last duty assignment."

"You're leaving the Navy?" He made it sound like an incomprehensible decision.

"My husband loved the Navy the way you do. He couldn't imagine civilian life."

"Can you?" he asked.

"No. But it's something I have to do." The Navy had shaped her life, but now she had to put Jazmine's welfare first. She was proud of how well her daughter had adjusted to a new environment, but a child needed roots and stability. Alison felt obliged to provide that, especially since she'd become, however unwillingly, a single parent.

"Where will you settle?" Frank asked.

"I haven't decided yet. I'm considering Seattle. Jazmine seems to like it there, and it's where my sister lives."

"Is she married?"

"Single," Ali explained. "But she's romantically involved with someone."

Frank stared down into his coffee, cupped between his outstretched hands. "I don't know much about romance." He took a swig of coffee. "I'm pretty much a failure in that department."

"You're divorced, aren't you?" She recalled that he'd told her this.

"A long time now."

Alison studied him as he sipped his coffee. "Given up, have you?"

He raised his head, his gaze burning into hers. "Until recently I had." His shoulders rose as if he was taking in a deep breath. "It's not appropriate to ask now, but I was wondering…I was thinking that in a few months, when you've…resigned your commission, you might consider going to dinner with me. It wouldn't mean anything. I mean, there'd be no obligation on either part, and if you're not ready—"

"Commander," Alison said, breaking into his soliloquy. This was the most he'd ever said to her at one time. "Yes."

"Yes?" He eyed her quizzically.

"I'd be honored to have dinner with you."

He seemed tentative, unbelieving, and Ali smiled.

"More than honored," she added softly and reached for her own coffee. She needed a sip to ease the dryness in her mouth and throat.

"It won't be for several months," he warned.

"I'm well aware of that, Commander."

He sighed and looked away. "Don't take this personally, but it's not a good idea for us to continue meeting here."

Disappointment hit her hard. "Why not?" Their meetings were completely innocent. This was the third night in a row, and not once had they even touched.

"Lieutenant Commander," Frank said, his voice barely above a whisper. "You tempt me and while I'm a disciplined man, I don't think I can hold back my feelings for you indefinitely. Give me a date and a time I can meet you in Seattle and I'll be there."

Alison met his eyes and smiled. "January twenty-seventh. One o'clock in the afternoon. At the bronze pig in Pike Place Market."

She'd chosen the date a bit recklessly, perhaps, but that was Peter's birthday, which made it easy to remember. And she was very sure Peter would approve....

Chapter Twenty-Three

"Aren't you going to call Uncle Adam?" Jazmine was pestering Shana for about the hundredth time that week.

"Why should I?" Shana muttered, scooping ice cream from the bottom of the caramel pecan container and packing what remained into a quart-size one. This was her life these days. For at least two hours every day, she risked frostbite with her face in the freezer.

"You know," she said, righting herself and holding up the ice-cream scoop for emphasis, "when I moved to Seattle, I decided I was finished with men. I didn't need a man in my life then and I don't need one now. I'm better off without them."

Jazmine sat on the other side of the counter, her chin propped in her hands. Shana noticed that she was frowning.

"We don't need boys?"

"We don't," Shana reiterated.

"At all?"

"Well, technically we do, but only for reproductive purposes." This was definitely an area she didn't want to get into with a nine-year-old.

"But aren't they kind of fun to have around?"

She realized she was tainting her niece's mind because of her own negative experiences. That had to stop. Besides, Adam had potential—or he did when he wasn't overtaken by jealousy. The thing was, he had absolutely nothing to be jealous about. It was almost as if he *wanted* to be upset with her. Fine, then, she'd just let him.

"Men have their uses," Shana replied guardedly.

"I thought you liked Uncle Adam."

"I do…I did…I do." While Shana was still annoyed with Adam, she missed him, too. That was the point. She didn't want to think about him, but she couldn't help it—which annoyed her even more.

"You should call him," Jazmine suggested again.

Shana refused to do that. "I phoned last time. It's his turn."

"Oh." Her niece sounded distressed.

"What's wrong?" Shana asked, unsure what had brought the woebegone expression to Jazmine's face.

Jazmine sighed deeply. "I was just hoping you liked Uncle Adam the same way he likes you."

Now Shana was the one frowning. "I do like him. It's just that two people don't always see eye-to-eye." This was difficult enough to explain to an adult, let alone a child. "Sometimes it's best to simply leave things alone."

"It is?" Jazmine squinted as though confused. "Is that how you felt about Brad?"

Shana thought for a moment, then nodded. "Yes, in the beginning. When I first broke up with him."

"But you went to see him again 'cause you didn't like the way it ended, right?"

"Right. I regretted the fact that I'd run off in a fit of righteous indignation. It was over, and I wanted him to know that in a civilized manner."

"You aren't being impulsive now? About not phoning Uncle Adam?"

Coming out from behind the counter, Shana slid onto the stool next to her niece. Sighing expressively, she said, "You're pretty smart for a kid."

Jazmine flashed her a bright smile. "How come?"

"You just are." Her niece had told her what she needed to hear. She'd refused to phone Adam strictly out of pride. Their last conversation had been painful. She'd been light-hearted and hopeful when she called him, but his gruff responses had short-circuited her joy. He hadn't phoned her since and she hadn't phoned him, either. They were behaving like children.

"That's what I don't understand," Jazmine murmured, returning to her original pose, chin cupped in her hands, elbows splayed. "You went to talk to Brad, but you won't go see Uncle Adam."

"He's in Hawaii." It wasn't like he was a three-hour drive down the interstate. "It isn't that easy to get to Hawaii."

"Don't they have ninety-nine-dollar flights there?"

"I doubt it." More than likely it would be five hundred dollars. Shana sat up. Then again, going to see him in Hawaii might help clear up this misunderstanding—resolve this stalemate—and she wanted that. She believed he did, too. One of them had to make the first move and it might as well be her.

Shana was shocked at herself. She was actually considering this. She'd spent all that money on the dress she'd worn to see Brad, and now she was about to spend more. She supposed she could always wear her new dress when—if—she went to see Adam. Why not?

"You could check the computer," Jazmine said confidently. "There are advertisements on TV all the time about airfare deals over the Internet."

"You think I should?"

Jazmine nodded eagerly. "If you find a cheap ticket to Hawaii, you should go."

"I can't close the restaurant."

"You don't need to close it. Catherine ran it when we went to Portland," Jazmine reminded her. "And that was just to see Brad."

She opened her mouth to claim that seeing Brad was different. Well…it was and it wasn't. She'd been willing to make arrangements and a few sacrifices in order to talk to him. And she cared about Adam a hundred times more than she did Brad.

"Remember Tim, the single dad who wanted to go out with you?" Jazmine asked.

"Yes. Why?"

"I saw him in the park. He's back with his wife and he said it was because of you."

"Me?"

"Yup—he said you were the one who told him he was still in love with her. He knew you were right but the hardest part was telling Heather—that's her name. He's really glad he did, though."

"I'm glad, too. But why are you—"

Before Shana could finish the question, Jazmine blurted out her reply. "Because the hardest part is you telling Uncle Adam how you feel—so do it!"

"I will." Shana closed her eyes. She wanted this relationship with Adam to work. All the years she'd been with Brad, friends and co-workers had said he didn't deserve her, and she'd refused to listen. Now the people she loved and respected most were telling her that Adam was a dream come true—and once again she hadn't been listening. But that was about to change.

"It all depends on whether Louis and Catherine can work while we're away," Shana murmured, biting her bottom lip.

"They can," Jazmine said immediately. "They love it here. And if you marry Uncle Adam, they want to buy the business." She leaned close and whispered conspiratorially, "I heard them talking about it."

Now that the idea had taken root, Shana was convinced it was the right thing to do. She knew that if she sat down with Adam for five minutes, they'd get past the false impressions and false pride. She wanted him in her life; it was that simple.

"We're going to Hawaii?" Jazmine asked, her look expectant.

Shana smiled and slowly nodded. Yes, they were going to Hawaii. Adam might think this relationship was over, but she wasn't willing to lose out on her best chance for happiness yet. If everything went as she prayed it would, she just might end up with a Navy husband.

Adam's bad mood hadn't improved in a week. A dozen times, probably more, he'd lifted the receiver to call Shana. This estrangement was his fault. But for reasons he didn't want to examine, he'd been reluctant to phone.

Okay, it was time to own up to the truth. He'd been waiting for her to break down and phone *him*. After more than a week, he might as well accept that it wasn't going to happen.

"You feeling better?" John asked when Adam arrived at the office Friday morning.

"I don't know." He shook his head. "What do you think are my chances of hitching a transport to Seattle this weekend?"

John perked up. "You're going to see her?"

Adam nodded. As best as he could figure, this was the only way he and Shana would ever make any progress. He was ready to take responsibility for his part in this fiasco and admit he'd overreacted. After all, she'd said it was over between her and this Bernie character.

From today, from this moment forward, he chose to believe her. His next task was to tell her he'd been wrong. He didn't like apologizing, but having Shana in his life was worth a few minutes of humiliation.

"This *is* good news," John said, grinning broadly. "Finally."

Adam leaned back in his chair. He'd get to Seattle one way or another, even if it meant paying for a commercial flight.

"Are you going to let her know you're coming?" John asked.

"No."

"So you're going to surprise her?"

"I believe I will," he said, already deep in thought.

He pictured the reunion: Shana would be at the ice-cream parlor with a dozen kids all placing their orders at once. She was great with kids, great with Jazmine, patient and generous.

She'd be scooping ice cream for all those kids, and then she'd look up and there he'd be, standing in the doorway. He'd wear his uniform. Women were said to like a man in uniform, and Adam decided he needed all the help he could get.

He returned to his imagined scenario. Naturally Shana would be astonished to see him; she might even drop the ice-cream scoop. Their eyes would meet, and everything else in the room would fade as she came around the counter and walked into his embrace. Adam's arms suddenly ached with the need to hold her. Until this very minute, he hadn't realized just how badly he wanted Shana in his life. He'd felt the need to link his life with a woman's earlier that summer, and that need had grown stronger, more irresistible, ever since he'd met Shana.

"You really think surprising her is such a great idea?" John asked skeptically.

"Of course it is," Adam said. Why wouldn't it be?

Chapter Twenty-Four

"I am so bummed," Jazmine muttered, sitting in front of the computer after e-mailing her mother.

Shana was disappointed, too, but she tried not to let it show. She'd spent half her day on the Internet, searching for last-minute bargain tickets to Honolulu. Apparently there was no such thing. It didn't matter what she could or would have been willing to pay. There simply weren't any seats available for the next few days. The best rates were for the following week.

"Waiting a week won't be so bad," Shana assured her niece.

"We should let Uncle Adam know we're coming."

That meant Shana would have to pick up the phone and call him, which was something she hadn't managed to do in more than two weeks. Jazmine was right, though. It probably wasn't fair just to land on his doorstep and expect everything to fall neatly into place.

The doorbell rang and Jazmine was out of the computer chair and racing to the front door. Shana walked briskly behind her, uncomfortable with the girl flinging open the door without first checking to see who was there.

Her worries were for nothing. Jazmine stood on the tips of her toes, peering through the tiny peephole. She stared for the longest moment, then her shoulders sagged and she backed away. "It's for you," she said in a disappointed voice.

Shana moved in front of her niece and opened the door. She was in no mood to deal with a salesman or a nuisance call. When she found Adam Kennedy standing on the other side, she was stunned into speechlessness.

"Adam?" His name was a mere wisp of sound. He looked good, no, better than good. *Great.* He was a thousand times more compelling than she remembered, and her heart felt in danger of bursting right then and there. If their disagreement had given him a minute's concern, his face didn't reveal it. He seemed rested and relaxed.

He smiled, and Shana's knees started to shake. It shouldn't be like this, the rational part of her mind inserted. She shouldn't be this happy to see him or this excited. But she was.

"Can I come in?"

"Sure." Jazmine was the one who answered. The nine-year-old slipped around Shana and held open the screen door. Judging by the broad smile on the girl's face, anyone might think she was ushering in Santa Claus.

Shana frowned. "You knew about this?" she asked her niece.

Jazmine shook her head, denying any knowledge. "But I fooled you, didn't I? You didn't guess it was Adam." Then she grinned at the man in question. "We were coming to see you, only we couldn't get a flight for this weekend. We have tickets for next week."

"You were flying to Hawaii to see me?" Adam's eyes probed Shana's.

She nodded, and found the shock of seeing him in the room with her nearly overwhelming. Placing her hand on her chest, she felt her heart hammer against her palm. Even with the evidence standing right in front of her, she had a hard time taking it in.

Reaching for Adam's hand, Jazmine led him into the living room. "You can sit if you want."

Adam chose the sofa.

"You, too, Aunt Shana," Jazmine said, orchestrating events as though she were moving figures on a chessboard. She took Shana's hand next and led her to the overstuffed chair.

"Okay," Jazmine said, standing in the middle of the room between them. "You two need to talk. I can go to my room or I can stay and supervise."

Shana's gaze didn't waver from Adam's. "Your room," she murmured, hardly able to catch her breath.

"Your room," Adam echoed.

"Really?" Jazmine's frustration echoed in her voice.

"Go." Shana pointed down the hall, although her eyes were still on Adam. She was afraid that if she glanced away he might disappear.

Jazmine started to walk in the direction of her bedroom. "I'm leaving my door open, and if I hear any yelling, I'm coming right back. Okay?"

Adam's mouth quivered with the beginnings of a smile. "Okay."

After Jazmine left, there was a moment of awkward silence—and then they both started to speak at once.

"I'm so sorry...."

"I'm an idiot..." Adam held up his hand and gestured for her to go first.

Shana moved to the edge of the cushion, clasping her hands together. "Oh, Adam, I'm so *sorry*. I wanted to call you, I really did. I thought about it so many times."

"I was afraid of losing you."

"That won't happen," she told him. "Don't you know how I feel about you?"

When he didn't reply, she said, "I wasn't planning to fall in love again, but—"

"You love me?" he interrupted.

Shana hadn't meant to declare her feelings so soon, and certainly not like this. The way she'd envisioned the scene, it would be a romantic moment over dinner and champagne, not in the middle of her small rental house, with her niece standing in the bedroom doorway listening to every word.

"She does," Jazmine answered for Shana. "She's been impossible ever since you went to Hawaii."

"Jazmine," Shana warned.

"Sorry," the girl muttered.

"Maybe it'd be best if you closed your door," Adam suggested.

Jazmine stamped her foot and shouted "Okay," but when Shana's gaze shot down the hallway, she noticed that her niece's bedroom door was only halfway shut.

"You were saying?" Adam said and motioned for her to continue.

"I forget where I was."

"I believe you'd just declared your undying love for me. I'd like to hear more."

"I'm sure you would," she said, smiling despite their interruptions, "but I was thinking it would be good to hear how you feel, too."

"You will, I promise," Adam assured her, "but I'd appreciate if you finished your thoughts first. You were saying you hadn't planned to fall in love…"

Shana lowered her eyes. It was difficult to think clearly when she was looking at Adam. The effect he had on her was that powerful. "I think sometimes love finds you when you least expect it. As you might've guessed, my opinion of the opposite sex was somewhere in the basement when I came to Seattle. And then Jazmine arrived. At first I envied the easy relationship you two shared. And my sister couldn't stop singing your praises."

"You weren't in the mood to hear anything positive about a man. Any man."

"Exactly," Shana concurred. "But you were so patient with Jazmine and…you were patient with me, too."

"I was attracted to you from the moment we met."

"Really?"

"You knocked my socks off." They both grinned at that. Then his expression grew serious again. "Having this surgery wasn't a pleasant experience." He pressed his hand gently to his shoulder. "I was in pain, and my life felt empty, and all of a sudden you were on the scene. I felt as soon as we met that I could love you."

"You did?" Her voice lifted with joy.

"And I do love you. I recognized that I had to give you time. Coming out of a long-term relationship, you were bound to need an adjustment period. I understood that. But I don't think you have any idea how badly I wanted to be with you."

"You love me," she repeated, hardly hearing anything else he'd said. "You love me!"

"I know you wanted to marry Bernie—"

"It's Brad, and no…not anymore."

"Good, because I'm hoping you'll marry me."

Jazmine's bedroom door flew open. "Aunt Shana, say yes. I beg of you, say yes!"

"Jazmine!" Shana and Adam shouted simultaneously.

"Okay, okay," the nine-year-old moaned and retreated back inside her bedroom.

Adam hesitated only briefly. "Well, what do you think?"

"You mean about us getting married?" Just saying the words produced an inner happiness that radiated from her heart to every single part of her. "Being your wife would make me the happiest woman alive."

Adam stood and she met him halfway. Seconds later, they were locked in each other's arms and his mouth was on hers. From the way he kissed her, she knew he'd been telling the truth. He loved her! After several deep kisses, Adam raised his head and framed her face with both hands. His eyes bored intently into hers.

"One question, and if my asking offends you, I apologize in advance. I need to know something."

"Anything."

His eyes flickered with uncertainty. "Why was it necessary to talk to Ber—Brad?"

Shana sighed and kissed his jaw. "I wanted to say goodbye to him properly."

"And you intended to see me next week."

She nodded, then caught the lobe of his ear between her teeth and gently bit down on the soft flesh. The shiver that went through him encouraged her to further exploration.

"What were you going to say to me?" he asked, his voice a husky whisper.

"Hmm…" she responded, her thoughts clouded with desire. "Hello, and that I'm crazy in love with you."

"Good answer." Adam directed his mouth back to hers, and soon they were deeply involved in another kiss.

The sound of a throat being cleared broke into Shana's consciousness several seconds later.

"Did you two forget something?" Jazmine asked, hands on her hips. "Like *me?*"

Shana buried her face in Adam's shoulder.

"Howdy, squirt," he managed in a voice Shana barely recognized as his.

"This is all very good, but we have a wedding to plan, you know."

"A wedding?" Shana lifted her head and murmured, "We have plenty of time to work on that."

"I don't think so," Jazmine insisted. "We'll be in Hawaii

next week. We should do it then. Let's get this show on the road!"

"Next week?" Shana looked questioningly at Adam, not sure that arranging a wedding in such a short time was even possible.

"Would you be willing?" he asked, catching Jazmine's enthusiasm.

Shana nodded. "Of course, but only if Ali can be there. I want her at our wedding."

Adam brought her close. "I do, too."

Jazmine applauded loudly. "I know it isn't good manners to say I told you so," she announced with smug satisfaction, "but this time I can't help it."

"We'll let you," Adam said, his arms around Shana. "Because this time you're absolutely right."

Shana leaned against the man who would soon be her husband and sighed with contentment. She'd never known that being wrong could feel so right.

Chapter Twenty-Five

"Mom!" Jazmine slammed into the bathroom of Shana's old house in West Seattle, where Ali was preparing for work. They'd been living there for the last seven weeks, ever since her discharge from the Navy. Her life and that of her sister's had been a whirlwind for the past half year.

Once Shana and Adam had decided on marriage, their wedding had happened fast, but not quite as fast as originally planned. Fortunately—for the convenience of the guests—it had taken place in Seattle, not Hawaii. No sooner had Ali returned to San Diego in December than she boarded a plane to Washington for the wedding. From everything she heard, in phone calls and e-mails, Shana and Adam were blissfully happy and enjoying life in Honolulu.

At the end of her tour, Alison had left the *USS Woodrow Wilson* and within a matter of weeks was released from her commitment to the Navy.

Because Shana had signed a lease on the rental house in Seattle, Ali was able to move there. Jazmine was back in the same school now and doing well. Ali liked Seattle and it was as good a place to settle as any.

The retired couple who'd purchased Shana's ice-cream and pizza parlor had been accommodating and helpful when Ali arrived in Seattle. They loved her daughter and she loved them, too.

"Mom," Jazmine repeated. "Do you remember what today is?"

As if anyone needed to remind her. "Yes, sweetheart, I remember."

"It's Dad's birthday—and it's the day you're meeting Commander Dillon." Apparently her daughter felt it was necessary to tell her, anyway. "What time?" she asked urgently.

"One o'clock in Pike Place Market." Alison had arranged a half day off before she'd been hired at West Seattle Hospital. Her hand shook as she brushed her hair. Frank and Alison talked nearly every day and sent e-mail messages when it wasn't possible to chat on the phone.

Because of Navy regulations, they'd controlled their growing attraction and their intense feelings for each other while they were aboard the carrier. But now that Alison had been officially discharged, they were free to explore those emotions, and to express them. Circumstances had made that challenging; Alison had moved to Seattle and Frank was stationed in San Diego with the *USS Woodrow Wilson*.

"He's going to ask you to marry him."

"Jazmine!" Overnight her daughter had turned into a romance expert. Given the success of her matchmaking efforts with Shana and Adam, the girl was convinced she had an aptitude for this.

"Mom, Commander Dillon would be a fool not to marry you."

Frank and Jazmine routinely chatted via the Internet, too. Maybe her daughter knew something she didn't, but Alison doubted it.

"You're in love with him," Jazmine said with all the confidence of one who had insider information, "and he's crazy about you."

"Jazmine!"

"Yup, that's my name."

Alison put down her brush and inhaled a calming breath. "I'm very fond of Frank…. He's a wonderful man, but we barely know each other."

"I like him," her daughter said.

"I know and I like him, too."

"Like?" Jazmine scoffed and shook her head. "Who are you kidding? I don't understand adults. Every time I tell him he should marry you, Commander Dillon—"

"What?" Alison exploded, outraged that her daughter had this sort of conversation with Frank. Her face burned with mortification; she could only imagine what he must think.

"Don't go ballistic on me, Mom. You know Commander Dillon and I e-mail each other."

"Yes, but…"

"Okay, okay," Jazmine asserted, shaking her head as if she were losing her patience. "Here's the deal. You and Commander Dillon talk, and if you need me to sort anything out for you, just let me know. He's coming to dinner tonight, isn't he?"

"I invited him, but—"

"He'll be here." She kissed Alison on the cheek and added, "I've gotta go or I'll be late for the bus. Have a great day." With that Jazmine headed out of the bathroom. She grabbed her coat and backpack, and adjusted her hood against the January drizzle.

Alison followed her to the door and watched her daughter meet her friends and walk to the bus stop. Jazmine seemed utterly sure that this meeting with Frank would have a fairy-tale ending. Alison wished she shared her daughter's positive attitude. She was nervous and didn't mind admitting it.

In an effort to settle her nerves, Alison reached for the phone to call her sister. Remembering the time difference between the West Coast and Hawaii, she replaced it. Eight Seattle time was far too early to phone Shana and even if she reached her, Alison wouldn't know what to say.

By noon when she left the hospital and drove into downtown Seattle her stomach was in a state of chaos. Jazmine knew her far too well. Alison did love Frank. She had for months, and now they were finally meeting at the time and place they'd arranged last summer. Because she was no longer in the Navy, there were no official barriers between them. As for other kinds of obstacles... She didn't know.

After parking in a waterfront lot, Alison climbed the stairs up to Pike Place Market, coming in the back entrance. They'd agreed to meet at the figure of the bronze pig in front. Her heart pounded hard, but that had little to do with the flight of stairs she'd just climbed. A glance at her watch told her she was fifteen minutes early.

A part of her feared Frank wouldn't show. Shades of that old movie, *An Affair to Remember*.

It had started to rain and the sky was dark gray. This was an ominous sign as far as Alison was concerned. The fishmongers were busily arranging seafood on beds of crushed ice as tourists and shoppers crowded the aisles. With extra time on her hands, Alison could do a bit of shopping. But her nerves were stretched so tight she didn't think she was capable of doing anything more than standing next to the bronze pig.

To her surprise, Frank was already there, looking around anxiously. He seemed uncomfortable and unsure of himself, and almost immediately Ali's unease left her.

"Did you think I wouldn't come?" she asked softly, walking over to meet him.

From experience, Alison knew Frank wasn't a man who smiled often. But when he saw her, his face underwent a transformation and he broke into a wide grin.

Alison wasn't sure who moved first, but in the next moment, she was in his arms. They clung to each other for a long time. It would be completely out of character for him to kiss her in such a public place, and she accepted that.

"Have you had lunch?" he asked, as she reluctantly stepped out of his embrace.

"No, but there's a great chowder bar on the waterfront," she told him. As they held hands, she led him down the same path she'd recently taken from the parking area. She liked the feel of his hand in hers, and the way that simple action connected them.

They ordered fish and chips and ate outside under a large canopy on the wharf, protected from the elements. She felt too tense to be hungry. They talked very little.

"The ferry's coming in," Alison said and by unspoken agreement they walked to the end of the pier to watch it glide toward the dock.

Standing side by side, they gazed out over the choppy water of Puget Sound. After a few minutes, Frank placed an arm around her shoulders. Alison leaned against him, savoring this closeness to the man she loved.

Without warning, he turned her so that she faced him and then he kissed her. His mouth was gentle and she instinctively opened to him. Seconds later his hands were in her hair, bunching it as he slanted his lips over hers and his kiss grew more insistent.

With his arms around her, Frank rested his chin on her head. "I told myself I wouldn't do that," he said in a low voice. "Not here, not like this."

"I think I would've died if you hadn't," she whispered back.

"I'm no bargain, Alison."

"Stop."

"No, I mean it, but God help me, I love you and I know I'll love Jazmine, too."

Alison smiled softly. "She's eager to meet you in person."

His arms relaxed as he brushed his lips against her temple. "I have a week's leave, but then I have to head back to San Diego. It isn't much time to make an important decision, but I'm hoping that by the end of the week you'll know how you feel about me."

Alison didn't need any time; her decision was made.

"I know you loved Peter and that he's Jazmine's father," Frank continued.

"I'll always love Peter," Alison said.

"I want you to. He was your husband and he died serving his country. I respect him and I have no intention of replacing him in your life or Jazmine's."

"Frank, what are you saying?"

He inhaled harshly. "I was hoping, praying actually, that by the end of this week you might know your feelings well enough… What I mean is that I'd like you to be my wife."

"I don't need a week—"

"You do," he told her, "we both do." And he kissed her again with such abandon and joy that when he released her, Alison was convinced she'd rather be in his arms than breathe.

A week later, just before Frank was scheduled to return to San Diego, the three of them planned dinner together. While Alison flitted about the kitchen checking on their meal, Jazmine set the table.

Before they sat down to eat, Frank pulled two small boxes out of his pocket and ceremonially placed them on the table.

Alison was carrying a large green salad and nearly dropped the bowl when she saw the velvet cases.

Frank glanced at her with a mildly guilty look. "If you'd rather wait until after dinner, that's fine, but I know I'd enjoy the meal a lot more if I had your answer first."

"Do I get to choose between two rings?" she asked, wondering why he'd brought two boxes.

"No," he said. "There's a necklace in one of them for Jazmine."

Her daughter came out of the kitchen clutching three bottles of salad dressing. It didn't take her long to assess the situation. "The answer is yes," Jazmine stated matter-of-factly.

"Yes," Alison echoed, nodding vigorously.

Frank opened the first of the two velvet boxes and slipped the small single-pearl necklace around Jazmine's neck and fastened it. "I felt it was important that I make a promise to you, too," he said to Ali's daughter. "I wanted to assure you that I will love you. I plan to be a good stepfather and, most importantly, I vow to always love your mother."

Jazmine blinked back tears and so did Alison. "I'll wear it every day and I swear I'll never lose it." Frank hugged the child.

Then he opened the second box and took out a large solitaire diamond ring. While Alison tried not to weep, he slipped it onto her ring finger. He held her gaze, and in his eyes Alison saw his love and the promise he was making. "I love you," he whispered.

"I love you, too."

The doorbell chimed, and before Jazmine could race toward it, the door opened and Shana hurried into the house, Adam directly behind her. "We aren't too late, are we?" she asked, laughing and excited. "Frank's still here, isn't he?"

"Shana." Alison ran across the room to her sister and they threw their arms around each other.

Frank and Adam shook hands and introduced themselves.

"Actually, your timing's perfect," Alison told Shana, and with tears clouding her eyes, she thrust out her left hand so her sister could examine her engagement ring.

Shana squealed with joy and hugged Alison excitedly, then hugged her brother-in-law to be.

"How did you know?" Alison asked.

"We didn't," Adam answered. "We came because we have some exciting news of our own."

"We're pregnant," Shana burst out.

Now it was Alison's turn to shout with happiness.

"Can I babysit?" Jazmine asked. "I could spend the summers with you in Hawaii and—"

"We'll decide that later," Alison said, cutting her daughter off. "We were about to sit down for dinner. Join us," she insisted.

The two women immediately went into the kitchen. While Alison got out extra silverware, Shana took the dinner and salad plates from the cupboard, along with two extra water glasses. Jazmine promptly delivered them to the table.

Shana paused. "Less than a year ago who would've believed we'd both have Navy husbands?"

"Navy husbands," Alison repeated as her diamond flashed in the light. "It has a nice sound to it, doesn't it?"

"The nicest sound in the world," Shana agreed.

* * * * *